ANIMAL MONEY

A NOVEL

Lazy Fascist Press
PO Box 10065
Portland, OR 97296

www.lazyfascistpress.com

ISBN: 978-1-62105-212-8

Printed in the USA.

ANIMAL MONEY

MICHAEL CISCO

Lazy Fascist Press

Portland + Astoria

"That bird is free – you owe me a bird."
Shunryu Suzuki Roshi

For David Goodman

PART ONE:
ALBINO BLACKS

Although unavailable for analysis the moment it happens, being struck a violent blow on the head is a very interesting experience. When, as was true in this case, the blunt object makes its intervention without warning, instantaneously reducing the victim—me—to a state of unconsciousness, a fascinating blank spot in the continuity of events is introduced. It might be the briefest variety of episode possible. Whatever fear or pain one experiences in association with it is displaced to a later moment, and then retroactively loaned in hindsight to where there had not been the time. As for the sensation, I liken it to being transformed by a spell into a rattling chest of drawers suddenly. A crash of silverware that dance like a shoal of fish, contents tossed aside and tumbling onto the floorboards. Loose floorboards. Dusty ones. Revoltingly dusty, loose floorboards, with clots and footscrapes in the dust. There really was a white flash. I seem to recall also a yawing of my perception in two directions at once, as if my field of vision—I do not say my eyes—were focussed in two opposed directions, half slipped upwards, the other downwards, along a glassy barrier dividing them. A glassy, slick barrier. The bruises and hurts incurred in falling to the pavement had to be discovered one by one later on.

The police assured me, with obvious embarrassment, that street crime is impossible in San Toribio, even for tourists. Tripi had put an end to all that and, despite her unexplained disappearance a month ago, San Toribio is still administered according to Tripist principles. They were very emphatic, very voluble on this point in particular. Until the emergency election next month, Tripism remains the official doctrine of the government. That I should have been knocked unconscious from behind while walking down a much-frequented street, without warning and in broad daylight, as I gazed in admiration at the snowy slopes of Mt. Cloticueta picturesquely rising before an almost pastel-blue sky, was almost an accomplishment, an athletic accomplishment. Luckily I had very little money on me at the time and so lost little by the theft in that respect, but my shoes and wristwatch had been taken as well and I had no others. The shoes I am not liable to miss right away, as I am still unable to walk any appreciable distance, but the absence of my wristwatch is a sickening ache. I do not feel complete without it.

My name is Professor Ronald Crest. I am an assistant professor of economics at CUNY, currently attending an academic conference of economists in San Toribio, Archizoguayla, hosted by Achrizoguayla University. Or that is what I should be doing, what I expected to be doing. Instead I am laid up, recovering from concussion and a hairline skull fracture, my head heavily bandaged. I can not attend the conference proceedings. I can not hear papers given. I can not readily leave the hotel. I perforce can not therefore deliver my own carefully prepared and exactly timed paper. I can only stew over the waste of time, of labor, of resources, brought about by that untimely blow.

It would be ungenerous of me to call it a consolation, so let me say that I discovered an opportune mischance when I learned that four other economists, who had also come to San Toribio for the conference, and who were also staying at my hotel, the Hotel Bluonga, had also suffered debilitating head injuries shortly after their arrival in a series of unrelated accidents.

I was the only one among us struck down by violence. The tall, stylish but, I can not refrain from adding, impractically asymmetrical, drinking glass that is standard in all our rooms had shattered somehow on the nightstand in the night while Professor Long (Shanghai) was sleeping, and some of the fragments fell onto her pillow. Although not an especially deep sleeper, according to herself, she heard nothing and did not wake up until she rolled over onto the glass fragments, badly lacerating her right ear. A wad of bandage now protrudes like a jug handle from the side of her head, held in place by a broad white sash wrapped around her brow at an angle which gathers up her hair in an awkward-looking sheaf and interferes with her vision. The bandages partially camouflage her economist-mark, which is in her case a white oval that emerges from her bandages and then splits to form a parenthesis around her right eye. She is expected to make a complete recovery.

The other Professor Long (Ottawa) had been bitten on the cheek by a mosquito while bringing his bags in to the hotel from the airport bus, on the first night of the conference; he went to bed that evening, and did not awaken again until thirty-six hours later, half-suffocated, one side of his face appallingly inflamed. The dressing covers the right side of his face like a mass of white dough. His economist-mark, a white equals sign above his right eye, is like two extra lengths of tape holding the bandages in place. The swelling is going down very slowly, but he is expected to make a complete recovery.

It is not entirely clear what happened to Professor Aughbui (Zaragoza); something has suddenly gone wrong with one or another of the delicate equilibriums within the skull—the sinuses, or the ear canal or inner ear, or some anatomical carpenter-level or barometer or gyroscope—resulting in intense, nauseating vertigo or dizziness whenever he moves his head. Therefore, the doctors rigged up a booth of chicken wire that rests on his shoulders, which, when combined with a whiplash collar and bandages to hold the frame to the skull, immobilizes his head. His economist-mark, a white minus sign, crosses his lips like a tape gag. While the cause or causes of his disability are unclear, he is expected to make a complete recovery.

Professor Budshah (Alkan) had been eating pahjcellourmi, the national dish, although originally of Turkish origin I believe, and dislocated his jaw when he bit down hard on an avocado pit the chef had overlooked. The doctor who examined him overzealously wired his jaw shut, and even applied a cast, which looks a bit like a jacket of shaving cream under and around the mandible, then wrapped bandages around the head to boot. We were all present when he received his refund from the restaurant. Sitting beside the first Professor Long, he looks like the vertical to her horizontal, especially because his economist-mark, a white number one without base or bill, bisects his face from the brow to just below the bridge of his nose. Like her, he is expected to make a complete recovery.

In fact, we all are. We are all expected to make a complete recovery, provided we follow doctor-instructions.

Enter the nurse, who comes over from a general practitioner-office on the next block several times a day to check on us. She is a sour-faced young woman with faded white skin and obviously dyed red hair. Whenever she flies into the room without a sound on thick carpet we all startle wildly disturbing our various injuries, and then, like a woodwind section tuning up, we groan with pain in our distinctive registers. Her name is Legale Fuene, an uneuphonious name, a hiccuped name. Perhaps her family was afflicted with congenital hiccups and the babies hiccuped in the womb strictly in sync with the hiccupping of the mothers.

As usual, the Salutation is left to me.

"*The bank is there to save and lend.*"

The nurse, whose uncouth name I choose not to repeat, replies automatically, starting to perform her various functions with her eyes while her mouth and hand dispense with this formality.

"*—Workers work and customers spend.*"

When she was first assigned to take care of us, she told each one of us bluntly, in more or less the same prepared speech, that she refused to "do any scurrying," by which she meant she was not going to attend to us each in our separate rooms in the hotel. She had enough to do without scurrying, she said. So, during the day, to oblige her, we were to congregate in one place in the hotel. She held up a finger. "One place," she said firmly. She regarded looking for us in different common locations on different occasions as another variety of scurrying. We had to choose where we would do our daytime convalescing and stay there, if we wanted her attention.

"I move that we go to the library here and consult the gods on this," the first Professor Long says.

"Second," I say.

"Is it necessary?" Professor Budshah asks through his teeth.

Professor Aughbui agrees to the consultation in silence. The second Professor Long nods, and, curiously, beams, as if the idea had suddenly revealed some enchanted prospect to him.

"I won't rock the boat," Professor Budshah says.

We are getting up to leave, awkwardly of course.

"The gods?" the nurse asks incredulously.

As one, we all turn our attention to Professor Crest, because it is self-evident that he is the one of us best suited, perhaps ideally suited, to answer this impertinent question.

"You're going to pray? To Engels and Marx?" Nurse Fuene asks.

Professor Crest takes hold of the nurse with his eyes, icily. With that annihilating disdain that is so particular to him, he says—

"When we say the gods we mean the *gods*. The Surfeit is One."

She waves her arm with a sneer of derision as we hobble to the elevator.

*

The consultation with the gods was carried out at ten to five PM in a cramped carel in the University Library, set aside for this purpose. Actually, it was set aside principally for additional storage, but the necessary materials for the consultation were among the things stored there. In silence we invoked the Dii Lucri and other economic divinities. Mercury is the patron of the international order, but we economists call him Turms, his Etruscan name. The black stones outnumbered the red. We would take up the suggestion of the nurse.

There were not that many places that would suit us; in the end, we chose a lounge or bar type of place on the third floor, evidently intended to take any overflow from the primary bar downstairs. The hotel is an incongruously glamorous backdrop for five such medieval-looking casualties as ourselves: it is all ultra-modern, asymmetrical, rounded planes and sweeps, pink, purple, made of artificial materials of varying degrees of translucency and impregnated with glitter and luminous ribbons. The chairs all look like treble clefs and ampersands.

Five heads, engulfed in gauze and connected to medical appliances, propped in various awkward poses, we sit in a ragged circle, each of us bursting with undelivered revelations, so caught up in our own intricate ideas, so exhausted by pain and mending that we can not really pay attention to each other. And we had all come here daydreaming about finally being understood by somebody. As the day passes and one metronomic hour follows another without hurrying, without pausing, tediously and aggravatingly regular, we lapse into an oblivious silence. We listen down into ourselves and there is nothing going on, just the gurgling of our wounds as they gradually repair themselves, without hurrying, without pausing.

Then, the detonation. The nurse charging toward us, impatiently shrugging off her jacket as she crosses over to the spot by the windows where we are sitting, irritated as if we had chosen this spot so far from the doors, although the bar is hardly more than twenty feet wide, to aggravate her with as much superfluous scurrying as we could get away with, given the terms of our arrangement.

For some reason, embarrassment I think, her appearance prompts inane small talk from us. It comes out in an indistinct haze of brittle angularities; trying to hear and follow it is like looking right through a lacy iron screen and not being able to stop shifting focus from the screen to the nebulous green atrium down the passage and back again.

The voice of the first Professor Long is the one that catches me most often.

"Professor Nadler was ..." she is saying now. She often trails off like that, making a searching gesture with her fingers. She does the same when she speaks what I take to be Chinese—Putonghua is the correct term, if I am not mistaken.

"—I could tell what he was after."

"Is he one of us, though?" I ask.

"He is 'one of us,'" Professor Budshah slushes through his teeth. "He just hasn't taken the Third Oath yet. He's still apprenticing."

"Who was his partner?" the first Professor Long asks.

"Bright, wasn't it?" pushing against his cast with little jerks as he tries to turn his head to us.

No one seems to know.

"I think it's Bright," the second Professor Long says. He has the sweet reticence of a painter, someone who communicates primarily by creating pictures. Speaking at any length apparently costs him some effort; his voice, much weaker now than before his injury, always has a strained, sorrowful note in it. "I don't think it's Bright. I don't know who it is."

"What's the Third Oath?" the nurse asks me, because she is currently examining me.

"We economists all swear a series of oaths when we join the International Economics Institute," I explain. "In the first year of the Master's Program you must take the First Oath to be permitted to read certain economics textbooks. In that year you must also take the Second Oath, which authorizes you to make citations from those books. You can not teach until you have taken the Third Oath, and you can not publish until you have taken the Fourth and Fifth, and so on."

"So what's the Third Oath?" the nurse asks, her voice flat, uninterested.

"Celibacy," I tell her.

She is incredulous. "Really?" she asks, pausing to look me in the face to see if I am joking.

"Oh yes," I say.

"Naturally," says Professor Budshah.

"Well," she says, going back to plucking at my dressing, "We had another one of you from the conference in for food poisoning the other day and she was married. Her husband came with her."

"Do you remember who it was?" I ask, not caring. She does not. "But she was definitely married."

"Then she is not a genuine economist," I say firmly.

"Unless she was married before..." the first Professor Long says.

"She would still have to be celibate at present," I insist.

"Yes," the first Professor Long says. "But she could remain married."

"It seems wrong somehow," I say.

When the nurse has left, and we are alone again, the conversation begins to stir with frail new life. At last, we are free to turn our attention full on each other as colleagues, to speak our own language at last, at last to be understood. We begin by discussing the escalating instability of currency markets, which is the topic of the conference we are missing. This is a question of burning importance just now, because the Latin American Central Bank is preparing to inaugurate a single currency for the South American economic zone, to be known as the Latino. Will it yoke the weaker economies to the stronger ones? Or drag the stronger economies down? Is there going to be another fiasco?

"How many Latinos is that Coke?"

The name "Latino" strikes the second Professor Long funny. He will not stop making jokes.

"That'll be twelve Latinos for that Coke."

The first Professor Long specializes in the breakdowns and lapses in economies. The second Professor Long studies planned economies, and, I may say, this is an incomprehensible mismatch of person to speciality. Professor Aughbui is an expert on Piero Sraffa, constructs economic algorithms, mathematical models and computer simulations. Professor Budshah is a dissenting antibody, dismantling economic theories and predictions that he regards as inimical to something, skeptical about the validity of economics as such, but always, I must admit, courtly and cordial about it. For my part, I have devoted my life to the study of pre-Columbian economies (my book *Beyond Whelks, Chert, and Copper: The Systemic Economy of Cahokia*, was published in 2002 by the University of Illinois Press). We are all in anguish because we can not share our opinions with the other conferents, and we do not know what repetitions we are unwittingly getting into, what bright ideas we have that will be met with glazed eyes because it has all been chewed over a dozen times in a dozen different panels already. Peerness is running out of us by the hour. The solution is obvious and easily formulated, but difficult to propose for social reasons.

"We should read our papers to each other."

And that was what we did, the next day. We all turned up with our papers, determined to recoup the cost of the trip and accommodations, as well as the suffering our injuries were causing us. Thank the Surfeit we did not get injured in the US! My report was neatly bound in a regulation binder, that of Professor Aughbui likewise with a great many appended charts to pass around and beautifully executed too I freely agree, the first Professor Long brought hers in a well worn leather portfolio, the second Professor Long brought his battered bescribbled and heavily-amended pages in a roll half crushed by the rubber band that held it together, and Professor Budshah read from miraculously uncrinkled translucent sheets elegantly inscribed in longhand.

That was a memorable afternoon. The bar was empty. Even the bartender was gone, away on his lunch break. We each read through our pieces, handed around what handouts we needed, and jotted down our notes and questions in whatever way was most convenient. I read well, if I do say so myself, hitting each time index in the margin exactly according to my watch. Professor Aughbui presented an interesting paper in a rather wooden monotone without looking up from the page. The first Professor Long gave a succinct, almost bird-like reading. Professor Budshah spoke with a measured eloquence and poise rather marred by his wired jaw, but I could see how formidable an opponent he could be, even if I found his rather glib dismissals of certain cherished ideas of scientific economics highly annoying, I daresay even incensing, so that I found I had to make an effort to remain impassive during his talk. The second Professor Long, I confess, exasperated us; it was probably all for the best that he did not have the opportunity to address a larger group. He fumbled, retracted, adjusted, even started over.

We discuss each paper, even the latter. In the criss-cross of our conversation the idea of *animal money* appears. None of us can account for it, none of us can take credit for it.

The idea silences us for a while, as we try to grasp it,

each within ourselves. It really is only a chance coupling of two words, but they seem to call to each other. It is immediately obvious to us that *animal money* does not refer to the age-old practice of rating wealth in head of cattle or otherwise using livestock as money; there is something new in our minds.

We spark out mangled phrases, riddled with gaps and words that melt and combine, flop, groping. Try a new tack. Anecdotes. Straining against his bewilderment, the second Professor Long describes an exchange he witnessed between two squirrels in his back yard a few days before he left for this ill-starred conference. He had tucked it away in his memory, thinking it might "cute up" (sic) a lecture one day, and had not thought of it since. Two squirrels facing each other in the grass of his lawn. One reaches inside its mouth and pulls out something deep blue, like a sequin, round and flat, and hands it to the other. The other squirrel receives this thing, puts it in its mouth, goes to one corner of the garden, digs up an acorn, returns to the first squirrel, removes the acorn from its jaws with its paws, places the acorn in the open paws of the first squirrel. The first squirrel then puts the acorn in its mouth and goes "arching away." Was that one squirrel buying an acorn off the other? But, then again, the second Professor Long says a moment later, he supposes he might have dreamt it. For that matter, he goes on, he can not be sure he is not making things up.

But it turns out we all have such stories. For my part, I saw a cardinal count out three roughly identical flakes of something white, confetti I supposed at the time, on a tree limb, take them in a talon and hand them to a big crow, who received them in its talon and tucked them away somehow into its feathers, exactly like a man tucking his wallet into an inner jacket pocket. The crow flew away, but later I saw what I think might have been the same crow, harassing and driving off some hapless sparrows, while a cardinal—perhaps the same one—sat watching unmolested nearby. Did I in fact observe a cardinal paying protection money to a crow?

If I could retrieve a specimen of those white flakes, would I see the avian profile on one side and a venerable looking nest on the other? I find I am not warming to the second Professor Long. This facetious suggestion originates with him.

The first Professor Long tells us about the repairs underway in her street, which considerably disaccommodated her getting to the airport. The pavement was torn up, and the soil beneath exposed to the sun for the first time in a very great while, uncovering a sizeable termite excavation which fascinated the workers. The pavement had been the roof of the uppermost portion of the colony, which consisted of large chambers "shaped like lozenges" linked by tunnels. The first Professor Long never actually saw any of the termites themselves, only their hastily-abandoned city, but was particularly intrigued by one unusually rectilinear chamber, in which she noted countless tiny chips of mica that had been neatly stacked in ascending order of size and arranged in narrow piles with slender aisles between them all. She remembers having speculated at the time on the resemblance between a storehouse of bullion and this arrangement.

Having arrived in San Toribio some time before the

commencement of the conference, Professor Budshah explains that he decided to visit the famous swamps not far from the city. The weather had been surprisingly cool and autumnal, he says, and he wanted to take advantage of the torpor of the mosquitoes. While there, he explains, he observed at dusk, in a large pond, what appeared to him to be a dark ribbon in continuous rotation. He shone his light on it, and discovered it was composed entirely of shredded water plants, kept together and in motion by several frogs. Some of these kicked the water with their hind legs, which induced the current to move clockwise, while others drifted with the ribbon and held it together with their forelegs. While it was a single loop, this ribbon oscillated between two spots on opposite banks, where many more frogs crowded densely together. Now and then a frog would produce from somewhere a rag of a water plant, leap into the pond to an especially loud outcry from his companions, insinuate the rag into the ribbon, then return to his place. Frogs in the opposite group would then leap in and take some of the plant material from the ribbon, also to a chorus suddenly in rough unison on that side. Professor Budshah says he found it difficult at the time, and indeed now, to resist the temptation to imagine the far bank crying "sell! sell!" and the near bank "buy!" ...?

Professor Aughbui has a rustic streak, and keeps a dozen chickens at home. One recently having died, he, being an egg-eating vegetarian, cremated the body in a small kiln he claims was left behind by a previous owner of the property. In any case, the other chickens observed this proceeding, and Professor Aughbui maintains without a trace of humor that they remained subdued and even solemn for days afterwards. One week after the death of the chicken, Professor Aughbui happened to wake in the middle of the night and went to get himself a drink of water. Through a window, he caught sight of a group of several chickens gathered together out in the open, one of whom stood before and facing the rest. Among those present were all of the offspring of the deceased chicken. The chicken standing apart had beside it a heap of something that Professor Aughbui could not identify; it clucked quietly, and a young chicken approached her. The black hen carefully scratched some of the heap toward the young one, then stepped back, allowing the young one to scratch this matter aside, whereupon (Professor Aughbui said "whereupon") it settled down on this smaller heap. This action was repeated for all present in turn, until only a small consideration was left to the black hen, who settled on her allotment finally. This appears to have been the probation of a legacy?

Perhaps these observations of ours subtly goaded us toward the chimerically portentous phrase: "animal money," but what really seems important in the concept itself, if it is a concept at all, is that animal money would be animal, not just money used by animals. Alive, to put it briefly. Too briefly, perhaps, but baldly, there it is, living money, possibly special, possibly not special.

What is life? It is not increments, not units, not math. Life is qualities in action, verbs, as well as nouns. Animal money would have to be qualitative, rather than quantitative, but we unanimously agree that this would not mean anything like the exchange of red for purple or hot for smooth ... not necessarily. That would be, I think it was Professor Aughbui made this observation, barter, or something essentially no different from barter, rather than the exchange of money. To be genuinely qualitative, the quality must not be arbitrary; a quality is an experience, a posteriori. Quantities could be experiences, too—this was an interjection from the second Professor Long and typical of him, and we were not so sure either way—Professor Budshah asked by way of rejoinder if, when you are caught in a torrential downpour of rain, the sensation is quantitative, the number of raindrops hitting you, or is it qualitative, the 'downpour-feeling' rather than the 'drizzle-feeling'? But, in any case, the quality certainly must be experienced.

Well, so the quantity is still a part of feeling ... So this distinction ... you see ...? (gesturing, as if to say, come to me, or work it out for me). This was the first Professor Long, who tends to leave her sentences hanging in just that way. To persist in being sympathetic to this, rather than provoked by it, is an effort. I trust I will be repaid for my tolerance. I know to my cost how easy it is to be misjudged by others.

Living, animal money, might then mean handing someone an experience. That, we reasoned, would mean giving an exchange of time, in different flavors. The flavor would be exchanged, not the moment. What does this mean? It is the adverbial way in which a moment is a moment of a certain kind. Not a past moment, that would be like handing someone a recording, a photo, a film, an album. It would be a present time-savor, perhaps like—again this was the second Professor Long, who has,

I note, the depressing Californian obsession with the word "like"—like stepping through a wall and into a place, a time, and even a self; it would be escape-money. One plain difference, perhaps the key difference, between qualitative and quantitative money would be that, with qualitative money (we kept saying qualitative when we meant quantitative and vice-versa, the two words are too easily intermistaken) there would be no "grey limbo of exchange" (the phrase is coinage of Professor Budshah) where qualities are rendered indifferent and therefore equivalent and exchangeable. You would not wait for animal money. Or you would wait, but differently, like someone waiting quietly on a hotel balcony after breakfast, to see what the day brings.

In an animal money economy, each would have its own particular money. Professor Aughbui, who speaks just at the moment with a giddy, exhausted excitability that contrasts with his ordinary taciturnity, you could only spend your animal money if it remained with you. It would not operate like a battery of value, susceptible to replenishment, but instead as half of a link of exchange as a component part of an experience. The exchange, someone notes, would then be more like making a baby with someone, and the more we think about this, the more apt the analogy becomes, until we realize just now that it is not an analogy, but that very exchange itself in its most distinct manifestation (albeit abstract). Hence, our idea is rather at variance with the concept as Klossowski outlined it. In an overzealous moment we call it the true, the real exchange, of which the quantitative is only a counterfeit. And it seems to us, going further, that this kind of thing, this kind of talk, whatever you may call it, is also an indispensable aspect of animal money, namely the discovery that what appears to be a metaphor or a symbol or a representation or a figure of speech of some kind, far from bringing two things together, is actually an unnecessary and cumbersome division introduced within a thing. It is more like quantity. We are getting a bit carried away.

"Where is the 'within'?" Professor Budshah asks gnomically. While he does not put on airs, he does have this annoying propensity to waft an atmosphere around himself.

Animal money would have to be exchanged in much the same way we have just resolved a figure, conception of a child, by positing it as the exchange, unmetaphorically. That is the way the exchange of animal money would have to work, with 'the resolution of a figure'.

That latter idea looks increasingly uncertain. Even the second Professor Long, with his lamentable blurriness, can see that. He calls the idea "iffy"—a puerile term but not incorrect.

Unfortunately there are other analogies that work as well but are more perplexing: the exchange of ideas for example. It seems obvious, particularly to me and to Professor Aughbui, that the naive model, in which I come along with an idea in my head like a cookie in a box, and, meeting you, I take the idea from my head and put it in yours, is wrong. For one thing, having given it to you, I do not forget the idea, the idea can be in as many heads at a time as there are heads, provided infinite contact among heads. At least as many, the second Professor Long says. He is always saying things like that, things that make no sense, or make sense only to him. Everyone has had the experience; explaining an idea you are certain of, you suddenly become uncertain of it; said into the air it does not sound the way you expected it to sound; now it seems no more convincing than any other idea on the same topic would be. The result: abashed affect. You feel stupid. Were you stupid? Were you stupid for liking that idea, or was it that you articulated a good idea in a stupid way? Posing the question means giving up on an answer. How can the articulation be distinct from the idea?

How curious this is! How curious! I am utterly unable to locate a thinker. The thoughts are developing without a thinker to think them or a mind to contain them.

The idea has to happen between two people, but it is not entirely external to them any more than it is entirely internal to one or the other. There has to be enough external so that it is possible to have agreement. If animal money works this way, then this would mean you can not do without some physical money as the external, or part thereof.

"We can't simply 'money' at each other, from one inner redoubt to another," Professor Budshah announces. "If we were going to 'money' each other, we should have to do it in both ways, on the inside and on the outside."

He is speaking loudly, but, to be fair, we are all of us shouting at each other. It is necessary to shout, if we are to make ourselves heard over the unbelievable din of the booming sound system, which began its cachinnation at six PM, because this lounge converts to a discotheque in the evenings. We have been apparently deep in consultation all afternoon. Although we can all walk, we nevertheless tend to wait for the nurse to guide us one by one back to our rooms, and she has not come. Or perhaps she did come, tried for a time to get our attention, and then, failing that, gave up. Actually, I think I see her dancing over there, but it is difficult to be certain of recognizing her out of uniform, and with the uncertain illumination of the stroboscopy of the pulsating lights. I turn my attention back to the others, and colorful spangles swim over the ragged, arctic terrain of their bandaged heads, dip in and out of their injuries like tropical fish flitting among the cavities in a reef. The speech of Professor Aughbui is muffled by the booth anyway. The second Professor Long keeps one hand pressed to his bandages to keep the dubstep from vibrating it too aggressively, while the first Professor Long, on the other hand, sits up straighter. I hear the treble rake directly across the crack in my skull, like a crystal rasp. The first Professor Long, with her one bandaged ear, has some measure of protection and continues to converse more or less normally, although she has to raise her voice to a bleat. About Professor Budshah there is not much to say; he sits impassively with his head erect and both feet up.

The unit of animal money, a kind of lexspecie—and here too I do not know which of us put together that word, or if it was spoken by someone else we overheard in the cacophonous din of the club—would be the 'copula.' Up until this point in time, monetary exchange has been a matter of substitution. The copula ... well, on the other hand, would be money-that-is-a-verb ... People keep bumping into me and I am not able to see them because my bandages interfere with my peripheral vision. The value in the historical exchange to date—

BUMP—is constant, both parties retain equivalent value and only swap the bodies to which that value is attached. A sudden chill spreading acutely across my scalp suggests to me that someone here has just sloshed a beverage on my bandages. It is something of a relief, because the air conditioning has failed and the room is like a sauna. We are all gushing with sweat, our faces glisten like glass. The value in animal exchange is also constant, but it increases in the exchange to a higher level across both parties. There is more value irrespective of surplus value, and the 'copula' is not lost either because it is not noun money it is—BUMP—verb money, so it is not exchanged but it is the activity.

By now we are all convinced that the Latino, or whatever they decide to call it, should be lexspecial rather than money of the usual kind, and, after a lot of screaming and mutual assurances, we decided to author a paper jointly and present it to the conference. The nurse has still not come; she must be regaling herself as part of this ridiculous display. Fortunately, I have on me a sheaf of take out menus that have about three inches square of blank space on one side. I distribute these in the absence of any other paper, and we begin to write out our thesis and supporting arguments based on our respective specialities as best we can with the stub of a pencil, an eyebrow marker, a fragment of chalk that Professor Aughbui managed to pry out of the seam of his jacket pocket. Our monument! Someone elbows me in the back of my head and I howl out loud; in blind haze of pain and outrage I pull my shoe from my foot and swat backwards with it and the next thing I know I am tumbling headlong out of my chair with an invisible burden on top of me belching cigarette smoke. I struggle back into my seat. Battered, ducking, shouting, we continue: conventional static money is a denatured metaphor, while animal money would metaphorize naturally. We do not explain this to ourselves because we all already see very clearly what it means, even in the middle of a light show, namely that a metaphor ... "the lake is a mirror" ... "my love is a red rose" ... does not have to reduce two things to a single shared quality, it can compound them. The mistake comes in making that only rhetorical counterfeiting. The first Professor Long wants to know if animal money eats, and does it eat other animal money or would it have to have plant money or plankton money to eat?

The economist has to mathematicize intuition, intuitize math, formalize breakdowns. Animal money metabolism would be completely stable. It would not be completely stable, it would involve boom and bust, inflation, recession, like famines and epidemics in a population; the money might inbreed, and the various specie would vary in relation to each other, so that in the proximity of one specie another would physically diminish, either shrinking or losing tangible substance, becoming phantomlike. Being animal,—BUMP—animal money can be born, but by the same token animal money dies, and every now and then the horde turns up just stinking discolored scraps buzzing with virtually worthless scavenger currencies and melting into fiscal slime, while, at midnight, their ghosts haunt the treasuries with clinking of coins and rustling of bills, weird lights and shrieks a fight is breaking out and spreading that will prove to have exacerbated all our injuries tomorrow; a noisome ponytailed fat man nearly falls on me, his forearm across my lap and will have badly bruised my thighs, and a woman in white totters awkwardly by on her high heels and caroms somehow off of the first Professor Long, the dancers are tumbling down like sprawling dummies and the music is stuck on a droning bass note like a dense black wedge of sound that buzzes my teeth and trembles my viscera—can we get out? Can we get out, please?

*

Thank you. Once alone in my room, I had stripped in wild haste, thinking I was going to be violently ill. Our economist-garments must all be custom made, without ornament, in somber colors, and from fine yet durable materials, so it is not unusual for an economist to be unusually careful with his clothing. I would not know exactly how to get my clothing cleaned if I were to get sick on it, to bespatter it with vomit. Naked, I knelt before the toilet, but why describe that?

I did not get sick, although I feel so badly unrehabilitated the next morning I wish I had been. I stared at myself in the mirror as if I expected to learn something. My economist-mark, a white oval injected over my features, makes my face look smaller than it is. The eye can not make up its mind to see the actual outline or the oval as its edge. As I examine myself, an expression of fear comes over the face I see. The feeling might almost have begun in the image, rather than in me. Did I forget to do my test last night?

I turn anxiously to the night stand. My test book lies open, shamelessly tossed aside. It is open to the test for yesterday. The blanks and open spaces are filled in, albeit in a hand less neat than I would like. I look more closely. Yes, correct, the test is filled out completely. Self-esteem washes through me like balm.

Crest! Even in your condition, even in a delirium, you do not fail, you omit nothing. Piety and training. Discipline. Self-restraint. I am so restrained that even my restraint is restrained. Abandon this admiration of self and turn your thoughts back to your duties. Now is the time for the separation of beads.

When I have finished the separation of beads, I sit back for a moment, trying to decide what to do next. My test book still lies open on the night stand. Quickly, I shut it, and put it back in the drawer where it belongs. When I stay in hotels, I never allow the maids to tamper with my room. No one ever comes into my room until I have checked out. But it is better, safer, to rely on training than on discretion. Test books are personal and private. It is traditional to keep them out of sight.

I remember the nightmare now. As is usually true in my dreams, I am watching a film from the inside. We have taken shelter inside a house, myself and some unfamiliar people. One of them is going to "let in" the **BLACK SMOKE** ...

"You're crazy! That's the black smoke!"

"I know it is."

"But it'll kill everyone!"

"That's right."

"But it'll kill you too!"

"I don't care."

He calmly walked to the corner and unblocked the opening. A wild plume of black smoke comes ravaging into the room. The other speaker grabs a lamp off the table to defend himself and the black smoke is on him, forcing its way into screaming him.

I can not sleep, I can not wake up. My stylus is unable to settle in my groove. Read, test, sleep, beads, note, shave, test, sleep. I do not know who am I here. I do not know how to answer that. All right, I say back a moment later, but do not let not knowing be an excuse for ceasing to think about it. Thinking thinking thinking—for what? What does it fix? Well, one must have faith in thinking, and that is all. I set about putting in order the clothing I had hastily thrown off the night before, and there, in the breast pocket of my shirt, I feel a square. A note, typed, folded, and thrust, unnoticed by me, into my pocket the previous night. It reads:

"I couldn't help overhearing your intriguing conversation last night. If you will meet me outside the ladies' room in the hotel lobby at one, I will show you the zoo. My name is Dr. Ventaltia. (From the University.)"

I assemble the other wounded economists, who gamely turn out even though the violence of last night has undone much of our recuperation. The dizziness of the second Professor Long has increased again, so that he is forced to use a wheelchair, generously provided by the hotel. The staff are mortified about the fracas in the lounge, which is closed for repairs and cleaning today anyway, and offensively redolent, I might add, of aromatic cocktail vomit, and they lavish apologies and complimentary services on us until we are too embarrassed to look them in the face.

Professor Aughbui has a small, mechanical companion he built himself, named "Smilebot." It literally goes everywhere with him, a petite mechanical man a little more than a foot tall. It does not do much of anything that I can see; it only accompanies him, coming up behind him on eerily silent feet. It is entirely mute, thank goodness. Whenever I see them together, the sight is so unreal I can not persuade myself that I am not hallucinating. I think Professor Aughbui is sensitive about Smilebot; I have never seen him pay it any direct attention, and he never mentions it or adverts to it in any way, but now and then I notice him hastily casting sidelong glances at it, almost as if he were worried Smilebot might be forming a poor opinion of him. However, he must have spoken openly about it at some point to us, or at least to me, though, otherwise how could I know what it is named?

Dr. Ventaltia emerges from the ladies-room in the lobby. Her large, expressive face, is too copious to be easily read. I am unable to determine whether or not she is surprised to see all five of us. It had occurred to me that, since the invitation was given only to me, that I would be the only one she expected to see today. I will not be drawn into any sordidity. If her intentions are respectably collegial, then there should be no reason to exclude the others. If they are not, and she balks, then

I lose nothing of value in refusing to divide myself from this group. Even though, as I cast my eye over them, I see only four bent, heavily-bandaged figures, gingerly holding themselves together, I nevertheless draw strength from the group.

Dr. Ventaltia comes directly over to us with a reassuring smile, incomprehensibly well-rested and at ease in contrast with ourselves.

"Are you Dr. Ventaltia?"

"That's right."

Introductions then follow.

"Hi," she says, eyes switching from face to face. "Is everyone coming?"

She waits, smiling pleasantly, until we give her a definite answer.

"Good," she says. "Are you all ready to go?"

"*The bank is there to save and lend.*"

She is already walking toward the exit, and half turns to us smiling, still walking,

"*Workers work and customers spend.*"

Again, she waits to hear from all of us. I find it refreshing that she trusts me to have conveyed the content of her note to the others, that she trusts all of us to understand, not to need to have anything repeated, and that she does not seem at all hurried or distracted, that she does not ask questions without listening for answers.

Our nurse is crossing the lobby and stops to stare at us, surprised.

"You're going out?" she asks.

"Yes," I say. "We'll be back some time this evening. The Surfeit is One."

Dr. Ventaltia leads us out into suffocating tropical heat, to a waiting white minivan, climbing in on the passenger side. The driver cranes his head this way and that to see us and grins, showing all his teeth. There is even a lift for the wheelchair the second Professor Long is using. It takes fifteen minutes to get us all into the van, and we are all quickly drenched in perspiration. Then the door slides shut and we pull out, eventually merging onto Trin Piurnes.

"This country has many transvestites," Professor Aughbui says flatly, looking out the window at a knot of what I would have taken for unusually solidly-built women. Smilebot sits beside him with its feet up and head turned toward the window in mute imitation of Professor Aughbui, although it is not tall enough to see outside.

Dr. Ventaltia makes no small talk. I ask her what department she belongs to.

"I belong to the Naturalism department," she says.

I realize right away that the silence that follows means she will probably not launch into any unprompted explanations.

"Could you speak for a few minutes about your job?" I ask.

"You specialized in ...?" the first Professor Long asks.

"I've spent the last eighteen months studying black albinos. They are found only among certain species, dickcissel, vireo, rhinoceros, horseshoe bat, flying squirrel, among others."

"A black albino?" Professor Budshah asks. "What's that?"

This kind of blunt, direct question, and the level tone he uses, is typical of him.

"Black albinos are animals that alternate between being entirely white and entirely black, often within a matter of hours."

"Hm!"

"I've seen it happen all at once. Swish! There's no explanation for it as yet. Skin, hair, plumage, eyes, the inside of the mouth and the tongue, even the teeth or the beak, the horn on the rhino. Even the interior organs change color. The most interesting phenomena, though, is the intermediate state, when it is at all prolonged. The animal becomes invisible at the precise midpoint of the change."

"Remarkable!"

"Extraordinary!"

"Yes," she says. She speaks in a blithe sort of way, half turned around in her seat, and completely untroubled by the jolts as the van crashes over deep potholes and ruts and veers around traffic into the shoulder over the curb, right up against the roadside brush that rakes and slaps the sides of the van.

The second Professor Long is turning green.

"Oh boy ... Oh boy ..." he says, in between little burps. His face is now entirely green, except for his nose. His nose is always gleaming red, like polished terra cotta.

"Careful!" Professor Aughbui cries.

"They become more and more silver, anxious, and satiny, and then they shimmer, and then you just can't see them, at all. They reappear a moment later, and the skittishness fades as the color becomes more distinct. It's when they change suddenly, though, without warning ... that really drives them nuts."

The van jostles between two stone posts and we are on the campus, although there are no buildings in sight apart from some evidently very large ones about a mile away from this disproportionately small gate. There is no wall for the gate to open, for that matter. The intervening space between the gate and those distant buildings is all open, thickly covered in dead blonde grass, and criss-crossed with low chain-link fences in what is almost a maze. There is not a soul in sight anywhere, no trees, no shade. The road that takes us toward the buildings is arbitrarily kinked around empty, fenced lots. The scene reminds me of a suburban building development, when the ground is prepared but before construction begins; it also reminds me of an archaeological site before the digging commences.

"How are you all feeling?" Dr. Ventaltia asks.

We have been thrown around so much by now that we are all heaped up against one side of the van. The second Professor Long lunges towards the back and vomits noisily. The van is suffused at once with the odor of bile.

The driver slams on the brakes snarling and cursing, leaps out of the van and goes around to open its two besplattered back doors. He seems to have wanted to pull the rake from its brackets on the inner wall of the van, to rake the mess out, but there is vomit on the handle of the rake too. Nonplussed by this, he waves his hand and disappears from the square of daylight in the back of the van. I can hear his sun-browned, cursing voice going around on the left side, and now he appears out in front. We can see him through the windshield, walking toward the university buildings in the distance with a swaying step, gesturing every now and then as he continues, apparently, to curse and complain to the air and the dead grass and the remote university buildings hazed over with dust and sunlight and heat-shuddered air.

"Are you all right now?" Dr. Ventaltia asks presently, unfazed.

Groans, murmurs. None of us want to move, expecting the return of the driver.

"I don't understand. If you're so uncomfortable," she says, "why don't you get back into your seats?"

We can not answer, but I think we are unwilling to move because we expect the driver to come back any moment, even though I for one can still see him, a little dot now, walking toward the university buildings. Apparently we believe we will just end up being tossed back into these postures once the van gets moving again, so we might as well stay where we are. We might also imagine that bad luck is hovering over the van, and not want to attract its attention by making movements. Dr. Ventaltia stays right where she is, watching us impassively.

After about an hour it becomes impossible to avoid the conclusion that the driver has abandoned us in disgust. Groaning and seconds away from heatstroke at least, we disentangle ourselves from each other surprisingly easily, and we also leave the van as though it were nothing in particular to us either. We walk to the university buildings, cutting across the dead fields, using gates built into the fences. The gates have rough zinc flanges. The brittle blades of dead grass jab into my stocking feet—I still have not managed to replace my stolen shoes. The hotel store sells shoes, I know, but I did not like any of them, and we economists are not free to wear just anything. Our shoes may be brown, grey, or black; they may be of cloth, leather, or rubber, but must not contain more than 15% plastic and must be plain in design, without colorful lozenges or stripes or bulbs or tassels or points or tabs or springs or unusual vents or indentations. We are completely exposed to the sky here, standing like a vast, shapeless phantom. A uniform haze covers two thirds of it, exposing the blue only behind us, and the sun, behind that haze, is a streak too brilliant to look at directly. The light is intense, so that my face aches with squinting through it, and some indiscernible cause is putting irregularities into the heat pattern. Some of the fenced lots are ablaze with solar heat, and others are traversed by a dry, cooling breeze that slides like silk along my face and hands. To generalize, it is hot, far hotter than is seasonal here. In fact, we arrived in the middle of a record heatwave. The locals are no better equipped to deal with it than we are, which might account for the eerie desertion everywhere we go.

The University was removed to this spatial quarantine after student protests impressed on the Archizoguaylan governors the folly of "cultivating rebellion," as they put it, in the "heart" of the capital. Originally, however, there was no University, but only a college, housed in a single, inadequately small building originally constructed by the YMCA. This was located actually in the center of San Toribio, but this could be considered the "heart" of the city only in a literal sense. All the important government offices were situated at the periphery, at the ends of two of the radiating legs of San Toribio. Some time after the construction of the University, which was erected between the legs and is therefore actually closer to both administrative centers than the original college was, and which is so much larger than the original college that it now enrolls fifteen times more students every semester, and which now makes available to these students an enormous independent library and research laboratories on an exceedingly spacious campus, it dawned on the powers that be in Archizoguayla that the student protests had actually been fantastically effective in an entirely unforeseen direction. However, by that time, they were no longer in a position to do anything about it.

Cutting through the fenced lots reduces the distance so drastically that we arrive at the buildings well before the driver, who is now a distant speck on the road behind us and scarcely bigger than the van itself, although he might have turned back once he saw we were going to beat him here. From where we are standing, his figure is like the unstable shadow of a small fire, and it is not so easy to tell whether he is walking toward us or away from us.

Dr. Ventaltia leads us through the silent, lightless university buildings and behind them, where a curving road swings us around a vast paved empty plaza with white concrete slab benches that blaze like snowbanks in the sun and dance in pink afterimages whenever we blink, and at last we are at the zoo.

(Crazy zigzag sun piercing in our eyes, broken in trees, flickering in confusion. Empty blacktop pathways with garbage cans, little pavilions, concrete and plaster rocks everywhere like a movie set, barnyard smell. Now and then a squawk or a gutty rumble. Chickens clucking. A snake hisses. A lion roars. A jaguar roars. An elephant trumpets. A horse whinnies. A cow lows. Signed, the second Professor Long.)

Dr. Ventaltia leads us through a passageway of fake rocks and through a black steel door marked *ERE INTERDICTUL PENETRULAP*. Total blackness on the other side, massive black dropcloths hang all around us. Dr. Ventaltia pauses to pick up a flashlight that looks like a lunchbox and then goes on. The fluctuating disk of light looks like a disembodied eye, slipping over the coarse fabric as she kneads the curtains this way and that.

"What are these ...?" the first Professor Long asks, her voice muffled by the curtains.

Dr. Ventaltia stops abruptly and turns, shining the flashlight up onto her face.

"We do a great deal of research involving flying insects."

Now down a corridor we pass lab after lab and a few crossings, coming at last to another black steel door, this one with an arrow slit window in it and a label that reads *SECRETE SPECIAL*, and *VUELTADMONIDUELES! PIRXONAS INAUCTORIZADUL ALIU NONLICEN-ZUE ULTRAN HIS CUZPI SAUN*. The language spoken in Achrizoguayla has never been codified, and does not even have a fixed name. "Spantuguese" or "Labasporspan" are two of the more common terms for it. Hundreds of Achrizoguaylan phrase and guide books exist, and all of them purport to have the key to achieving some facility with the language, but even the name of the country is still in an unstable condition, being sometimes spelled Axri Zoguayla, for example, while its eastern citizens insist the nation is Euskal Berria, which I believe means something like New Basque Country.

A peal of thunder bursts overhead as we enter, answered by inhuman shrieks that resound against tile and concrete.

We pass through a meat-locker door into the rear of an enclosure. There is a dividing wall with a window, beyond that an area with a dirt floor that recedes beneath a bank of dense tropical foliage. There is a chain link barrier, she explains, hidden among the plants, and the animals—in this case, a species of small Achrizoguaylan wild cat called a jipipe—are on the other side. A buzzer opens the barrier, and, in a moment, a few of these tiny cats, no bigger than an ordinary housecat, come trustingly out onto the dirt and begin milling to and fro along the edges of the planted area. The cats are rust and black colored, with brown eyes and small, naked ears, which protrude from the fur of their heads like pale leaves.

This is the secret zoo within the zoo. More labs, and many observation galleries or monitoring labs with sunken floors, a dull black fabric covering everything, low cushioned seats, rows of consoles, and enormous tinted one-way windows overlooking different enclosures. These galleries remind me of the dens people used to build in suburban homes.

Dr. Ventaltia shows us into one of these, a smaller room with a black window. We can see ourselves reflected in the glass like a row of six ghosts. Dr. Ventaltia is a sizeable woman with sloping shoulders, a pale face, dark hair; sagging all over, like an old sofa, but a lively old sofa. There I am, looking at the others. Professor Budshah is beside me, smelling strongly of hotel soap. He looms over me, distinguished, with skin the color of scorched chocolate, the oldest among us, with an air that I am sure he would consider resolute. Then Professor Aughbui, who only appears to be the oldest of us, as he is bald, with tufts of hair over his ears, a prominent, aquiline nose, circular spectacles. The first Professor Long is vivacious, compact, abrupt, self-sufficient, missing nothing. At the other end is the second Professor Long, passive, vague, pliable, handsome, ill-shaven.

Dr. Ventaltia snaps a switch, and a man-made cave appears in the window, suffused with dim blue light. The dark air flickers with motion from time to time.

"A species of horseshoe bats," she explains.

The thunder does not seem to disturb them. They throng the walls in quivering assemblies. Dr. Ventaltia directs our attention to one of the upper corners of the cave by putting a filter on her flashlight. There we can plainly see a few bats lying on a rock shelf with a shifting heap of insects behind them. Other bats fly over and land in front of these few, and apparently exchange crumbs of some material for insects in what is plainly a mercantile transaction.

"For money, they ...?" the first Professor Long asks.

"Those are bits of plastic from the panelling," Dr. Ventaltia answers, pointing to several scarred patches on the walls of the cave. "They chew it loose. We have some of it here."

A glass dish covered with odd-shaped bits of plastic, all about the same size, all different, bright colors.

"Do they color code for denomination?" the first Professor Long asks.

"I don't know, I hadn't thought of that. Huh!" Dr. Ventaltia says.

"The ratio of white to blue is roughly one to four," Professor Aughbui says. "Yellow to blue two to four, roughly."

"That would have to mean they were counting," the first Professor Long says.

"Well, it might be that there is four times as much white plastic exposed as there is blue," Dr. Ventaltia says.

"Four times as much blue," Professor Aughbui corrects, without looking away from the bats.

"Yes," Dr. Ventaltia says. "So the ratios may be determined by availability rather than by scheme of the bats."

"When did ... When was this behavior ... first ...?" the second Professor Long says, his hand to his head.

Dr. Ventaltia gives him a chair and begins a protracted narrative by way of answer. Professor Aughbui has taken the flashlight and is peering through the glass. Professor Budshah is examining an open loose leaf folder that lies open on a black desk, full of columns and ranks, with a judicious, skeptical air, hands behind his back.

(The first Professor Long is sitting down and to one side, feeling suddenly paltry and worn out. The thought of the twenty empty, chaste years of future life, stretching on toward sixty, sweeps through her, sapping her strength, and with alarm she realizes she's close to tears. She couldn't be less in the right frame of mind to observe this phenomenon of the bats; it's part of something that could make her fortune, perhaps a whole new interdiscipline of zoolconomics, no vowels but o's, wait, there's an i in there too, but she's like an empty tin can that's been tossed out of a boat, or a hot-air balloon, into the ocean, sinking down in dark water combed with dwindling stalks of sunlight. Colder, heavier, darker, and down. To the nightmare domain of hideous, demonic animals, opaque as ice, studded with ice lights and icicle fangs of tough plastic, silent, mindless, enormous. Like extracted, locomoting, diaphanized organs. When gravity has pulled the Long-can all the way down to the bottom of the ocean, she lands with a thump and a viscously retarded flurry of colorless silt, the lunar lander. She climbs out of the can, wearing a miniature space suit, making her way cautiously down the ladder from the top of the can. Then a slow balloon drop on both feet. She takes out a stick. She plants it on the lightless expanse of mud and unfolds its tiny, pornographic flag. No, the flag of her country, which shows, on a field of overcast grey, the midwinter silhouette of a flock of birds roosting in a naked tree ...)

Again and again, everywhere in the secret zoo, we see animals using money.

Here are flying squirrels who exchange dried flower petals for familial relations, actually buying and selling grandparents. Here are dickcissels contracting to build nests for each other, paying in eggshell fragments that have been bitten into neat triangles. Data is still being collated; no one can say if it happened across the board at the same time, or if the practice developed in one population, one species, and moved to others in some traceable way. A money mutation. Did they learn this behavior from human beings? Is money an aspect of biological development analogous to the development of air breathing lungs or the sense of smell?

In one of the galleries we encounter several other zoologists in white coats, who greet Dr. Ventaltia and, once we have been introduced and our presence explained, greet us as well. They want to talk about money, but we are all watching the man, haggard, filthy, and naked, inside the enclosure. He is kneeling just before the window, his palms and elbows pressed against the shatterproof glass, with a hopeless, imploring look on his face. Suddenly a male chimpanzee comes tumbling into view. The man starts, cringing. The chimpanzee encircles his waist with one arm, throws him to the ground and fucks him violently. His cries are silenced by the glass. Other males are appearing now, hurrying in eagerly. When the first is done with the man, he confronts the others, who wave bits of green leaf at him, glossy leaves torn or gnawed into rectangles. Others are proffering wood chips that seem to have been fashioned from round tree branches. The first male approaches the one waving the most green, takes it all from him, and indicates the cowering, sobbing man. The second chimp leaps on him furiously, punching his head, then starts fucking him even more viciously than the first.

"He surely did not volunteer for that!" I say.

"No," one of the other zoologists tells me, after a casual glance through the window. "But he needed taking down a peg."

"Get him out of there at once!" Professor Budshah commands.

"Yeah, Jesus, I mean ..." the second Professor Long says, trailing off into an inarticulate hiss of incredulity and disapproval—"ssshhhhhhhh ..."

Professor Aughbui says nothing. He appears to be in shock.

"This is an abomination," the first Professor Long says very distinctly, emphasizing each syllable with a nod of her head.

The zoologists all begin speaking at once. They are all completely calm, but their voices grow steadily louder. As they speak, they draw all the breathable air into themselves, forcing us out into the scarcely better air of the external corridor. This separates us momentarily from Dr. Ventaltia as well, who began speaking when the others did. We are alone. An idea. The completion, I should say, of an inchoate idea that is already several days old. Instantly recognizing our opportunity, we seize it without a word, or even a facial expression, for each other.

There is no sign of thunderclouds when we finally re-emerge from the zoo. Look out again at the de Chirico landscape of bottle green twilight and wrong shadows under, the mountain out there like a longhaired head only just emerging from the water and the hair still spreading, floating around the head. These are not the kind of thoughts I would normally have, but the climate here, the estrangement of being in a different time zone, of being south of the equator for the first time, the confusing events and brash novelty of the last few days, and, I regret I cannot overlook it, my head injury, are all putting their particular stresses on my carefully articulated and preserved normal self.

Jurgel, the driver, will bring us to the hotel in the back of his pickup truck. By the time we reach the street, though, we are so giddy, nauseous, and battered from the ride that we recruit the first Professor Long to bang on the back window, telling him that we want to stop and get a cab instead.

We have no sooner found a comfortable arrangement for our various leaning bodies when a cab appears, and we flinchfully climb into the back. The driver explains that he has to pick up another fare, his cousin, and is that all right? We are gliding into light, late-afternoon traffic, the mountain behind us, the low and curlicued city skyline before us ...

Labor is quantified according to the amount of time spent working, irrespective of the quality of the work. An incompetent worker can spend hours doing what a skilled one can finish in no time, and yet the incompetent will be paid better if time alone determines. This, of course, does not happen. Skilled workers are paid on a higher scale, their skill is translated into a greater number of money units per unit of work time. This is all very elementary, but that does not mean we can answer this one: what if the skilled worker is skilled in being paid? Certainly, the best paid of all who are paid are those who do nothing, the administrators and shareholders for whom a busy day is a matter of conversations, meals, casually reviewing deals over rounds of golf. Animal money could re-qualitize time by not representing individual time units the way a wage rate does.

The driver pulls over at a corner. A tall, scrawny man tosses aside his cigarette and climbs in, greeting the driver and nodding at us with the merest acknowledgment. At once he begins a long tirade in what sounds like Serbian. The two men could not be more unalike; the driver is a round, sturdy, copper man, while the passenger is boney, purple, with a lean face and knuckly hands.

Non-animal money, what should we call it? Conventional money? Why not archaic money? Why not temporally crumbled money?

The passenger is shouting extremely vulgar imprecations at the car alongside us, swinging his arm out the window. He is more animatedly abusive by the moment. The driver of the other car has lost patience and is responding in kind, his face tensed, stern, swivelling between the road and the passenger with a bobbin-like regular motion. The passenger is screaming at him like a madman, gesticulating furiously through the window, nearly half out of it now.

He recoils back like a frightened snake and onto the driver as the other car swings into us broadside in retaliation. The passenger ripostes by trying to dive through the window but the cab swerves to the right to avoid a frantic pedestrian causing the passenger to fall short. He continues bellowing at the other driver who lunges his car at us again, pulling away just in time to avoid hitting a post that slices between the two cars. Professor Budshah starts pounding the back of the passenger's head with a rolled-up newspaper.

"Cuidado pendejo!" a voice screams, and my hand points as a garbage truck swings heedlessly into traffic right ahead of us. The driver yanks on the wheel and the car swerves toward a too-narrow margin between the truck and the walled shoulder; the cab keels over up onto two wheels through a flock of chickens and shoots past the truck, falling back onto all fours as it clears the gap.

The rear end skids and the car pivots, coming to a stop blocking the lane in front of the truck. The passenger is already climbing onto the hood of the truck—I had not even seen him get out of the taxi—and now, incoherent and choked with rage, he is pounding cracks into the windscreen. The cab driver gets out of the taxi and calls to his cousin in a reasoning tone, his cap in hand. The first Professor Long gets out of the cab as well, slides in again through the passenger side door into position behind the wheel, backs the taxi up, curls us away from the truck, then out into traffic with two oncoming cars hurtling directly at us which she avoids by plunging us over an unrailed embankment and down a rutted slope dotted with brush and stones. Jolting and bucking, we roll out across the more level lot below, arriving with a bound that throws me up against the roof, which crashes against my skull. I see white, and then nothing.

Later, when I come around again, I am gazing, numbly at first, and then with growing wonder, at a luminous field of vague colored shapes, blue, green, dun, that shift and dance, rise and fall, without losing their relationship to each other. I am looking, now I realize it, out the windscreen of the taxi. Perspiration has pooled around me on the plastic seat cover. The first Professor Long is driving us through the fields, jostling and rocking, the second Professor Long groaning in agony, and she clutching the wheel like a lashed sea captain, big drops of sweat tumbling down her face.

"Stop! Stop!" Professor Aughbui cries in torment.

The first Professor Long stops the car, braking so abruptly it is as if we had hit some invisible obstacle. She sits without looking back at us. Silence. Directly ahead of us, rising above the dense trees that fringe the silent field, incredibly, is the hotel.

*

Taking as a pretext, albeit a necessary one, my pressing need for shoes, I am able to pursue somewhat my investigation into the facts informing yesterday's occurrences. When I ask in the lobby, in the bar, at the restaurant, in the little convenience store on the ground floor of the hotel, in the laundry room, at the shoe store at last, and around, no one is even aware that there is a zoo at the University. I am making myself ridiculous with my story of a secret zoo within a zoo and a man enslaved by sexually deviant chimpanzees.

That night, of course, we are all of us entirely too busy with our experiment to do any further clue-hunting.

The following afternoon I spend nailed to my bed by a splitting headache. An insistent reporter keeps telephoning me in my room, and the telephone bell—an actual bell—resounds with such abrupt and violent noise I feel as though it will cause my skull to blast apart. This reporter demands more information about the secret zoo, or "zoo within the zoo" as he calls it. The nurse advises me that his paper, *Cuidadoel!*, is the "trashiest tabloid around." I detach the cord of the handset and place it in the drawer.

When the ferocity of my headache fades, I get up with a peculiar sensation of lightness or buoyancy, as if I no longer had any mass. A thick, green twilight is congealing outside. My head is clear, but only because it is empty. An unoppressive, narcotical distance sets me at one end of a medium-length hallway, with the rest of the world at the far end. My companions are nowhere to be found. That might have been the first Professor Long in the hotel bar—I saw a flash of white wrapped around a head, an awkward quiff of black hair, but ...? Well, the hotel bar is a rather unexpectedly rowdy sort of place, people get hustled out of there with their arms over the shoulders of their chums every night. I do not imagine it would appeal to the first Professor Long. In any case, we are all rather drained from the experiment last night, and nervous about the security of our equipment, and above all, with respect to outcomes. If we fail, that will be disappointing of course, but the drawing board will remain so to speak. If we *succeed*, however—what then?

The next day a delegate from the conference approaches us in the lounge, which is still bedecked with dangling streamers and confetti. Evidently, the other economists all felt sorry for us yesterday and took up a collection to send us to the Los Angeles beach today; an official IEI car will be coming for us in an hour. I do not think they realized that the Los Angeles beach is a nude beach any more than we did when we set out to go there.

The journey takes us along the boundary of one of the radiating legs of San Toribio. To one side, the blonde desert, and to the other, slum areas under renovation. Before the revolution here, these slums were ruled by gangs that, at the peak of their power, often came equipped with helicopters and armored vehicles. The civilian inhabitants of the slums were their living insulation against the government, which chose to pursue a policy of containment. San Toribio was a monstrously violent city then.

In one of the western slums, which were considered the worst, a group of bereaved women calling themselves the League of Disgusted Mothers initiated the Desgoustadore movement protesting high rents in the rest of San Toribio. It was the inability of the inhabitants to move out of the slums, they argued, that empowered the gangs. The Desgoustadores created housing committees to place families in affordable housing; and when Tripi took power, she coordinated the government with the committees, extending their efforts, and this finally reduced the sway of the gangs. Now that she has disappeared, and as the likelihood of her return seems to have dwindled away to nothing, there is an ominous mood. An emergency election has been scheduled in the next few weeks and the two major parties have been going at it tooth and nail in the press. Without Tripi, the country will likely become steadily more factionalized and this is likely to stymie the big collaborative projects the country needs to reduce poverty; then of course anyone would want to know what happened to her, how she could have vanished without a trace. Some believe she was abducted by the CIA directly or indirectly, and others fear her disappearance was the work of a heretofore unknown guerrilla group, Achrizoguaylan Contras. No one has taken responsibility for the kidnapping, but there have been many hoaxes.

Now we are installed in beach chairs on a little stone platform shaded by garish umbrellas. We, of course, could not become naked without removing our bandages and therapeutic gear, but then again, our bandages mark us as exceptions. Such is the naiveté of celibacy! I do not think it even occurred to the other economists to check the dress codes of the various beaches they considered before they sent us off to this one. They probably chose the first one they had all heard of. It is, at any rate, a magnificently beautiful shore. The day shouts with blue sun, the waves are scintillating, the refreshing air is fragrant with spray, and, since it is the middle of a Wednesday, there are very few heliophiles here. A naked waiter hastens from the kiosk about fifty meters away, taking our non-alcoholic drink orders without any sign of irritation or disappointment, and briskly returns with a rolling step, obviously he has had a lot of practice going to and fro on hot sand in bare feet—easier than with shoes on—deftly balancing his tray.

We sit facing the ocean of course, squinting. Even the reflected sunlight is palpably intense, like a subtle pressure sensed a little within the body surface, but the steady wind off the water reduces the heat to a low simmer. I think again of the captive man in the zoo. I imagine him braining his chimp with a rock, impaling the other apes with carefully sharpened bamboo spears he has been hoarding. Then roll a boulder down the slope and through the glass into the observation gallery, a leap to freedom, frenzy, revenge, he is indestructible, a hail of police bullets does not faze him.

Our conversation is desultory. This is the most harrowing conference any of us has ever attended and we are all very badly rattled. None of us knows what to expect, what will come next. It seems as if anything might happen, and we are completely exposed to the whims of chance. We are constantly finding ourselves drawn into circumstances that exacerbate our injuries. We dare not speak, even here in the open, without anyone in earshot, about the success of our experiment. There is not much to be said about it, anyway. Our success is both significant and insignificant—I hate expressing myself in that spuriously clever way, one might imagine that, by now, I would have a firm enough grasp on my own way of thinking not to be so readily swayed, but there is something insidious or tempting about that way of expressing oneself. At present, our success is nothing more than a stunt, albeit a unique one, something no one has attempted since the days of the alchemists. What our experiment shall do, if anything, is the only genuine significance it might have.

Two of the most beautiful human beings I have ever beheld, a man and a woman, entirely naked, emerge from the shimmer above the parking lot and come straight toward us. Neither of them speaks until they are near enough to us so that they do not need to raise their voices at all for us to hear them. They ask us if we are economists. We say yes.

"From the conference?"

"Yes."

"Although," I say, to be entirely accurate, "our injuries have prevented us from attending any of the sessions."

"That's all right," the woman says.

They are Baruch Plano and Carolina Duende, reporters from *La Censura*, and they want to interview us about the idea of animal money.

(We converse with them easily, almost in a dream, they are both so supernaturally beautiful, radiantly healthy, unabashedly naked, with teeth as black as snow, brand new teeth that have never touched food and which glow in their faces like seams of daylight in dawn clouds.)

The waiter produces a pair of folding beach chairs for them, they seat themselves between us and the sea, and we explain our idea to them. Since they carry nothing, they take no notes, but they seem to absorb without effort every one of our words with an easy attentiveness and interest. Their follow-up questions are germane, acute, and indicate comprehension of our ideas.

There they sit, and here we sit. They in pagan splendor, like a pair of idols, and we in bandages and appliances, our plain clothes of priestly intrigue, huddled together like crippled ravens. There is a blast of sub-lingual static among us. We all mutually ask each other, without speaking—do we mention the experiment? We all answer in the same moment—

No!

No!

No!

No!

Well... I mean, *no! No*, of course not!

Animal money ... there it is under your pillow when you wake up. Maybe not. It is not for spending; you never part with it.

But if you buy a Che poster from someone, then you now have it and he no longer does, and he did not give it to you, he bought it, so surely he must get something in exchange. If all property is held in common, then that is another matter, but then there is no buying or selling. This obstacle seems insurmountable. So insurmountable that, and it is to be hoped that you take this comment in the contributory spirit that prompts it, no competent economist could fail to recognize the futility of any attempt to overcome it.

You are right, but it is important not to underestimate the boundless appeal of the prospect lying beyond that obstacle.

But the obstacle is insurmountable. It is a wall no one can even see over. Isn't your idea a fantasy?

It is like that and not. We still are not entirely sure what we mean by animal money. Whether or not it is a fantasy is something that will never be known, unless we are successful. And whether or not it is a fantasy is perhaps not the only important question. This fantasy has an internal consistency that is instructive. This is not a stunt. We want, very much want, a currency that offers every person who uses it nothing to save, or to spend, or to exchange to the exclusion of someone else, so, in exchange for exchange itself, you take participation.

The aim is not to overthrow anything, we hasten to point out. We only want to streamline existing economic systems by removing hindrances to full and efficient participation by all. What hindrances? Well, systemic inequalities, wages, salaries, investments, finance, profits, capitalism ... yes, the idea is definitely post-financial. The impedimenta of administration, laissez faire, banking, shares, stocks, insurance, markets, would have to fall by the wayside. Inefficiency and insufficiency. Animal money is latently present in any exchange already; it is only a matter of making a certain adjustment.

We consider laissez faire an impediment? Sure, because it generates bottlenecks and blockages in the flows of money and goods. We all sense that the inequality between a rich man and a poor one is not the same inequality that exists between a master sculptor, let us say, and a neophyte or a bad one. The deficit is excavated into the poor by the rich, while the supremacy of the master over the tyro is a matter of intensity and altitude, and has nothing to do with selfishness. The cheat, snug in a nest of falsehoods that grows like the nest of an eagle. Baruch Plano and Carolina Duende listen attentively and in silence. It is easy to feel foolish talking into this silence, but there is reassurance in their intelligence.

No, you need records, that is a fact. But those records need not be the lifeless articulations of the Misled. The Latino, or whatever they end up calling it, could become an entirely new form of currency which would behave more like language than money. One word is not interchangeable with another word. Conversation does not mean I replace my words with yours and I do not lose the words I use with you, you see? A book, a conversation, is not a heap of 'word coins'. The currency in language is composition, elemental arrangements of words ... the treasury ... what is a word for a sort of repository of language, not just the words?—A colloquium.

Will this new currency be a digital currency?

Animal money is not a new currency, it is a new currency form. Digital currencies like bitcoins and litecoins are just fiat currencies that privilege timing and computer access. Being limited in their production, they can only appreciate in value, which rapidly makes each unit too valuable to use in comparison to existing currencies. And why spend today what will be worth more tomorrow, and yet more the day after that? Animal money is community fiat.

Baruch Plano and Carolina Duende listen healthily. The wind tosses her hair, riffles his. They do not perspire. They are not following our every word, not recording us, it is more like they are tasting us, they came out here to taste us the way you would drive out to a vineyard to taste the wine, and this seems natural, and right, and preferable in fact, to us. I think that we are now entirely adjusted to their nudity, we do not notice it any more. My new shoes are filling up with sand, even though they rest on concrete. How is that possible? Perhaps all this is a fantasy. But then, what is fantasy? Sooner or later, everybody ends up taking a fantasy seriously.

They now want us to hypothesize about the effect the return of Tripi would have on the development of the Latino. Would we be willing to work with her, if she were to return?

Once, she had been Adela Trini Pina, but when she began her political life, she became Tripi. Her name is blazoned everywhere, but, at her request, images of her were produced only in the press. Everyone knows the one photograph of her, standing on the balcony of the Ministry of Finance, passionately addressing the crowd, a slender woman with a bun of grey hair, her mouth open and her eyes straining with an anguish drawing and quartering her features so that the picture is more like the capture of tortured appeal and indignation than a portrait. Only the scarf around her neck, loosely gathered into a silver band in the front, is really characteristic. One month ago, while returning from a visit to the interior, Tripi vanished into the mountains. Her car needed gas. As the tank was being filled, the proprietor of the gas station invited her to tour the curious little terraced garden he had built entirely by himself behind the station. He saw his wife pull up to the station in her car, and ran back to fetch her. She would not want to miss an opportunity to meet Tripi. But when they returned to the garden, Tripi was not there. She has not been seen since. Her telephone? They found it where she left it—in the car. A half-smoked cigarillo was discovered at the brink of the terrace. Tripi smoked cigarillos, and always down to the filter. She was known for that. On numerous occasions, she had carefully snuffed and pocketed a cigarillo when it was necessary for her to stop smoking unexpectedly, then retrieved and relit it at the next opportunity. The habit was so firm that this discarded half cigarillo suggested dire scenarios, but after all it was not exactly a commandment, and quite imaginable that she might toss aside a half-smoked cigarillo once in a while. She had no husband or close family; no one was in a position to say, really, how she smoked. That's all. Tripi is gone, and Archizoguayla must assume the worst.

On the way back to the hotel, we are looking over our shoulders and in the rear view mirror, but, as none of us is native, how can we know what is suspicious?

This observation is not calculated to relax us, and we become desperate for the safety of the hotel, but is the hotel safe?

Accustomed to the sacerdotal stillness of economics departments, we are easily overwhelmed by crowds, any noisy gregariousness upsets our delicately-balanced cerebral escapements. Economics conferences are always virtually silent; they are conducted as if they were not being conducted. Even our banquets are silent affairs; we gather in the dining hall, and one of the junior faculty is recruited to read canonical economics treatises aloud to us while we eat our modest fare in unbroken abstraction. Studying economics lowers the voice and inclines the head; studying economics induces discretion, tact, caution, even cowardice, and an exaggerated circumspection in writing and speech. For us, our hotel rooms are oases of silence where we can recompose ourselves carefully, as economists. So who was it that suggested we stop for dinner? And why did we choose this boisterous cafe, packed with people and thrashing the tranquil night air with earsplitting music? Suddenly we simply had to eat, right now, at the first place we found, notwithstanding even the proven excellence of the hotel restaurant. The suggestion might have come from me; I thought it had, but it seems as if everyone was looking at Professor Aughbui—no, Budshah—when it happened.

This place is so loud we all have to take out our little notebooks, all the same, and write out our orders for the waitress. We have been waiting for the food to arrive for a long time. Now it is here, expensive, arcane, and looking more like plastic decorations than food. A whipped beet aioli with caramelized prawn heads and raisins accompanied by raw sliced new potatoes and tarragon; a strip of charred beef in coffee-seaweed soup topped with cinnamon shavings; champagne carrots and duck livers stuffed with goat cheese and chocolate chips. The other customers, who mostly congregate at the bar, are young, toned, well-dressed, orange, and staring at us in our bandages and other medical accessories, our Quakerish economist-apparel. We wanted to talk, to further review the thoughts and answers our interview had stirred up in us and let loose in us. But it is hard when we have to strain to speak, strain to hear, repeat everything three times, trade notes it is too dim in here to read. And we are ravenous. We fall on this bizarre, unintelligible cuisine as if it were hearty country fare—even Professor Budshah, who must draw in his soup between his teeth.

We are lost in this senseless rapture of eating when the eyes of the second Professor Long suddenly snap up into his head showing only two livid whites. Thin vapor escapes his writhing, contorted lips, which shape words with a terrible strain. The words rush from his mouth like frigid saliva.

"This voice ... is censored ... travelled ... by exorcism ... from ... under the darkness of ... human vision ... the darkness and light of ... human vision ... this voice ... is ... the censor ..."

His eyes reappear and his taut face goes slack. With a groan, he slumps forward, nearly falling out of his chair, hands gripping the edge of the table. Then, with a violent start, his eyes snap back into his head:

"Go on our instrument."

His eyes reappear.

"I'm not your instrument," the second Professor Long groans angrily.

Eye snap: "river doctor fill empty pockets with change cloud money paid in galaxies and they still came back as she will one day you can have though the idea that you can."

The spasm releases him only to seize hold of him more ferociously. He bares teeth coated in frozen saliva.

"She holds it now at the right angle try to do this without breaking the breath of the dreams this means this will be things the dying legions dying masters the elastic riot of ecstatic censors the dark cloud of giant somnambulists looking down at the first casualties the blue-white hellparadise the red cocaine the black salt."

The second Professor Long rallies as the evening unfolds. He knows something has just happened, but he remembers nothing of what he said. To him it was only a series of brief blackouts.

"It was like ..." he raises and lowers his palm before his eyes, "a shutter opening and closing, that abrupt."

It is difficult to say whether or not anyone else noticed the voice. Cloud money, he said. Paying in galaxies.

It takes us ten minutes to fit ourselves into the cab. We are talking about nothing as the car whisks us away through streets still lit by sunset, where sunset seems to linger and linger—even as the sky is now completely dark, the streets continue to glow pink and gold— when the cab driver says he wants to pick up another fare, already pulling over, opening the passenger door in front, admitting a massive man with a cannonball gut who rocks the cab as he lowers himself into the seat.

"They're holding auditions for The Mummy today," he says in English, jostling the driver. He looks back at us and laughs uproariously.

Turning his back to the door, he lays his arm along the seat; obviously we are going to have to make conversation with him.

"So what happened to all of you?" he asks, smiling openmouthed, incredulous. Our answer, terse, disjointed, unfriendly, elicits a giddy stream of inane laughter from him, just soft enough so that he can still hear us over it.

"And now you are looking for a place, eh?"

He swats the driver familiarly on the shoulder. The driver nods.

"You're economists, aren't you?"

Surprise again.

He points to his face.

"I know the markings. I studied the subject myself in University, but in my case ..."

He shrugs, smiling open mouthed.

"I was *seduced* into a different line of business."

The buildings vanish. The side of the road is lined with dense tropical foliage, plants I do not know, with enormous leaves and rubbery green trunks. We pull up in a dirt lot by a Victorian mansion vividly painted in turquoise and lavender. Both the passenger and driver get out of the cab.

"Come on in," the passenger says, waving to us. "I'll treat you!"

We look at each other with misgivings.

"Come on, come on! Why the suspicion?"

There are people coming and going from the house, in evening dress, emerging from or vanishing into black mercedes, valets pulling cars up and wheeling them off somewhere behind the house. At least half the people I see are transvestites.

The second Professor Long is the first to stir. He extricates himself from the cab and we, with a mindless obedience born of confusion and weariness, follow him. I can not deny that it is good to stand, to unbend, to breathe fresher air. Why should the air be fresher here, at the edge of the swamp, than it was in town?

The passenger is chortling at us, as if the sight of five bandaged invalids clambering gingerly out of a cab were inexpressibly droll. However, he never seems to be mocking us exactly. Waving his thick paw, he urges us to follow him inside. I wonder how they will react to his garish dress, to his white slacks and gleaming cheap white loafers, to the white slacks and white cap of the cab driver, to us. We climb the stone steps to the veranda and enter through a capacitous and heavy front door. The interior is so dark I am not able to make out the reception room.

"Siettu," I hear the big man quickly say to someone.

"Sertu," comes the prompt rejoinder, and we are conveyed into a cool, felty darkness. I have a clarifying impression of nineteenth century elegance, heavy draperies, wooden appointments. The large man is speaking quietly to somebody, and the voice of a young woman reaches me:

"This place is called O Morguo."

It hardly seems likely that this place, so subdued, even sombre, would hold any appeal for such a raucous man as our new companion, and it is as if he somehow detects this sense of incongruity in me, because he explains himself, his booming voice gone completely flat.

"I am Mateo Morguo," he says, turning to us, all trace of his former jovial boisterousness gone, his face blank and cold.

"This is my club."

They all have that cold look here. The patrons sit nearly motionless, half hidden by the incessant criss-cross of servers carrying mate on black lacquered serving boards. Their eyes blink slowly, their cold pupils fixed in livid eyewhites while the smoke elongates from their cigarettes turning the room into a collection of gossamer cages. Their heads are like security cameras and there is no smiling, no laughter. I have to admit I find it rather inviting. Those cigarettes ... clouded by ashes, the embers are white, not orange. There is almost no color. The walls, ceiling, and the floor are black and invisible, the people hang in space. But the entire back wall is one massive window with a view of starlit waters which I had not thought were so near. There is no smell of alcohol, but an odor of natron and a faint spiciness. People sip mate or a brew made from nuts and peppercorns, a potation Mateo Morguo informs us is called simply "white drink."

I glance again out the window at silent black peaks fluttering in the black like the low hubbub of voices. Some patrons sit on the floor, cross legged, or leaning forlornly against the walls. We, however, are steered toward seats—the high table, adorned in black satin. I realize that the ubiquitous cigarette smoke produces no smell. Mateo Morguo sits in what must be his customary seat, with his back in a cushioned corner. We take a bit longer to settle ourselves, and struggle to keep our balance as we maneuver into our seats. I sense rather than see a waiter appear, and Mateo Morguo waves his hand.

"Blanthe," he says, which means "white drink."

Then his hand returns to his lap and he sits like a

stone buddha. I have the feeling we are all holding our breath. I make a vehement effort to part my lips and speak, but some force, social, not somatic, if that is an applicable distinction here, prevents me. Very soon there is a smoking mug of white drink before me.

"The darkness and light of human vision?" Mateo Morguo asks.

"How do you know about ...?"

The words burst out, not from me, although I intended to ask him the same question, but from the first Professor Long.

"I am with the press here. We follow good stories."

Mateo Morguo speaks with the least possible motion of the face and no movement in his body. It is bizarre to see such an obviously jovial extrovert transformed into this sinister cataleptic.

"Spying on us?" Professor Budshah asks, unable to infuse any real indignation into his voice.

Mateo Morguo finally adopts a facial expression, his features grinding into a new configuration with what seems like great effort.

"I bring you here," he says, almost whining, "and you ask me these ridiculous questions. I thought you wanted to talk about the voice."

"What do you know about that voice?" I ask at once, to keep my hand in, and before anyone can beat me to it. I glance, also, at the second Professor Long, who is staring at Mateo Morguo with what I can describe only as a look of horror, of stunned horror.

"I will only say this," Mateo Morguo says, turning toward me a huge face like a wad of melting taffy. "You have received an Uhuyjhn transmission. Don't ask me to repeat that word, or to explain. That was a message that only someone with a certain neural configuration could receive. That configuration requires technical knowledge of money. It requires that certain ideas be present as electrical and chemical signatures. Among other things, probably. It requires a great deal of money. Of special money."

"Which side do you belong to?" Professor Budshah asks.

"The opposition."

"To Tripism?"

"Yes. I don't work for one party or another, I work for whoever pays me. That puts me in opposition to those who do not work for pay. They are interested in your work. You know, getting the message in that restaurant— that was the wrong place. You should have gotten it here. You—"

He raises a finger from the loop of his mug to point at the second Professor Long, the hint of an unfriendly smile on his face.

"—you're a joker, aren't you? You're always too early or too late, right?"

He raises his mug to his lips and takes a long, silent pull at it. The white drink has a piquant sweet, milky aroma that I find interesting but not at all tempting. The trancelike rigidity that came over him as he entered the club seems to be subsiding.

"Who are Uhuyjhn?" the second Professor Long asks, glassy-eyed. He repeats this peculiar word as if he had heard it before.

At once the masklike stiffness returns to the face of Mateo Morguo.

"Communists," he says shortly, unblinkingly. "Communist aliens. You should beware of them."

We return to the hotel. In the back of the cab we are quiet, very tired. The second Professor Long is haggard, sheepish, and he has an air of inward vigilance, I presume because he does not trust himself not to make another outburst. Not wanting to compound his painful self-consciousness by watching him myself, I look instead at my own face in the window. There I see the lineaments wanly outlined, grey, shadowy, and tenuous; old, ashamed. Emerging from the cab I am struck by the evil tenacity of this damp heat, even at night. We hobble across the lobby toward the elevator like accident victims crawling to an aid station. Professor Aughbui tactfully accompanies the second Professor Long up to his room, and Professor Budshah pointedly leaves us at the same time, to let the second Professor Long know that we are not keeping together to talk about him in his absence. The first Professor Long looks at me meaningfully, though; she wants to ask me something.

"The dark economists ...?"

"I had not thought of that," I say. Her words conjure up in me a long-unvisited memory that takes me by surprise. Years ago, in Albuquerque, at a colloquium for the Domestic Economic And Taphonomic Historical Association, two of them had been pointed out to me by Professor Alenteus. One or the other of them belonged to the University faculty and I remember a vivid presentiment of his office, although, of course, I never actually saw it; the dark economists study with ancient masters whose twisted mummies are preserved in their departmental offices, spicing the air, I assume, with a corrupt incense. Natron, if I am not mistaken. Their methods are concealed and their dire pronouncements are littered with occult economic formulae that only they fully understand. When they wish to read their grimoires of necronomic formulae, longhand and unpublished, they turn off the lights and study in the dark; and they write in the dark, too. I have no idea how. A persecuted sect and a jealous one. In my graduate school days, I had once seriously considered taking a seminar offered by a Professor commonly rumored to be disnumbered among them, but I demurred at the last minute. I have since regretted the decision. Is it really possible—a solecism, how can possibility, which is categorical, be intensified? Say, is it possible some hidden malice is aimed at us?

Alone at last, I sit up in my room in a colloquy with my inner corpse, thinking about the strained greeting I gave the other economists in the lobby, many of whom were much younger and better respected than any of us. There is that familiar cracking of enthusiasm that is the beginning of the suspicion that you have been playing the fool again. I ruefully page through the conference program ... Ah, there it is! My angle of condescension! I am safe.

Here is where my presentation would have been. *On the Remonetization of Real Estate and Housing Finance Markets.* (The loud crashing of doors in public buildings at closing time, when all you hear ... not dinning voices but just rustling keys, and the thud of trash bins as surly custodians make their rounds.) Instead of honest pain, there is just a sour feeling of satisfaction as the usual suspicions are confirmed, and how very nice it is to be right. Just hold something open, wounded and human in your face, I tell myself. No more authority, just listen. Do not look skeptically at love, do not insist on choosing between irony and love, you are fatigued, you are not yourself, take your test, set the alarm if you have already forgotten to do so, and go to sleep.

*

A dream about getting lost in the shower, a cramped labyrinth of close, white tile passages, soap dishes at intervals, hot water spraying. My hands turn to raisins. What if the water suddenly turns ice cold? Keep to the right. But was I keeping to the right before, is that my left? Searching, getting cleaner and cleaner, cleanness piling up on my skin like a negative envelope.

I record this one in the back of my test book with the other dreams. The book is filling up. I may have to send it in before I finish all the tests. With this one, if you fill out the dream pages, you just add the extras in the pocket provided.

After the separation-of-beads I make my way downstairs and locate Professor Aughbui and Professor Budshah. A moment after I join them, the first Professor Long appears, puffy and ill-rested. The General Assembly is being held today. Where is the second Professor Long? We have to leave early, we move slowly. Since, of us all, I am the least worse-for-wear, I am recruited to go hunt him up. The housekeeping cart is parked in front of his door, which is open; a man is tidying the room, shrugs and gestures to the four walls in response to my question. Momentarily at a loss, I stupidly look around the room— is it that I think I will see the second Professor Long peeking mischievously at me out from under the bed? No, but there is a real possibility I might find some clue to his whereabouts, and therefore that is why I continue to search.

He has left very little sign of his presence in the room. Nothing really, except for the tip of a shirt tail caught in the bureau drawer and a big, limp black notebook on the table.

With a shock, I realize this is his test book and turn away reflexively, as if he could somehow sense this intrusion despite his absence. But that is something—he must have known that someone would be in here to do up the room. Why would he have left his test book out in plain view? A bad night, confusion, sloppiness ... or haste ... maybe he stepped out as he thought for a moment but then had another attack, or his injury acted up, and he is lying somewhere unconscious or in convulsions.

When the time comes to leave, there is still no sign of the second Professor Long.

Another careering drive. The auditorium is far away from other conference venues but it is the only place with the requisite arena seating. I thought we would be walking everywhere; San Toribio is not such a big city. Then again, no one could have predicted this implacable, stultifying heat.

Seen from the air, San Toribio looks bleached and calcified. It is a modern city surrounded by mountains and flat plains of sterile brown ash that refuses to keep a road, dotted with villages like boats stranded far inland after a tidal wave. Archizoguayla is virtually all beach; the beach extends almost 150 kilometers inland. The total population is somewhere around 400,000, much of that is in the city, distributed in the two embracing suburban arms that join with no body, directly to each other, while the rebuilt old city, buried over a century ago in Cloticuean lava, sits on a granite bed off to one side, like a triskelion. The old city has a compact plan and is ideal for foot exploration, assuming you do not have a crippling head injury.

Overpasses whisk by. We follow a canal for a while, then dive down a ramp and into a thicket of streets so narrow that people have to flatten themselves against the steep, wide facades or retreat back into doorway to let us by, dragging bicycles and dogs with them. The auditorium hoves into view before us, visible as a brilliant wall rising at the summit of a corridor street like a vast apparition, blazing black as milk. There is a spacious plaza with elaborate wrought iron gates, broad circular platforms stacked in shallow steps up to the bronze doors.

A smoky green thunderstorm has gathered overhead, and the thunder rebounds back to us from the mountain slopes as the lightning approaches up the valley. The thunder merges too with the far off sound of the surf; the roar of the ocean here, I notice, unpredictably increases or diminishes in audibility. As the hum in the air builds, my symptoms build. My mouth is dry, and there is a tingling metallic taste on my tongue. An unpleasant if not painful lightheadedness hovers like a ray of light focussed just to the left of the crown, a fading loop of pain manifests itself above the left ear. I experience an oppressive restlessness in the body. People hasten to get into these shops and those little coffee places, and snatch up bits of cardboard for use as umbrellas.

Some of the other economists help us up the steps and into the auditorium. No, they have not seen the second Professor Long. Our worry spreads to their faces. No one misses a General Assembly! Even we, despite our debilitated condition, have not failed to attend.

We gather in the atrium, and then, after a few announcements by the conference organizers, file silently into the arena and take our places ...

That night, after dinner, I at last catch sight of the second Professor Long, at the hotel swimming pool. Climbing nimbly out of the pool, streaming with water, he rubs his face in both hands and then happens to glance up at me, smiles and waves, one palm wide, before hurrying, with short rapid strides, over to snatch up his towel from the back of a deck chair. His bandages are sopping wet, and his choice of swimwear is indecently minimal.

My new shoes are too tight. At first, I thought they were just stiff, and would loosen up with wear. Now I am not so sure. This hampers me a little and I am particularly disaccommodated when going down stairs. By the time I can get down to him, he has got the towel around his shoulders and he is patting his bandages dry. The dressing seems hopelessly spoiled to me; his head might have been toilet-papered by teenaged pranksters.

Smiling, cordial, and somehow shy, he puts me off when I demand to know where he has been.

"How could you miss a General Assembly?!" I cry indignantly.

"OK, OK," he says, smiling, not meeting my eyes. "I'll explain."

"Whatever you do will be taken as a reflection on all of us, you know," I go on.

Now he looks at me directly.

"I won't explain ..."

He begins walking away, then pauses and turns toward me again before I can select the right riposte.

"I'll tell everyone all at once, tomorrow. All right? The Surfeit is One."

*

That night I dreamt I was in a secondhand bookstore, searching for a neglected economic treatise by someone named Dr. Toilet, convinced that I would be doing the world a favor, and making a name for myself, if I could get it back into print. The store was in a converted old Victorian house my imagination conjured for me, and I was on the second floor. The floorboards were uneven; they flexed beneath my weight, and the mismatched bookcases, arranged at all angles according to dream code, teetered to and fro as I moved around the room. Since there was no specific economics or social studies section, I had to go over the whole store. I surveyed carefully the contents of a set of shelves labelled with the word CEMETERY written in marker on a tacked-up index card:

In Graves of Lost Time
Gravity's Grave

The Graving
Graves in the Attic
Uncle Tom's Grave
A Clockwork Grave
Wuthering Graves
Graves and Peace
Inherit the Grave
Grave in August
The Catcher in the Grave
Grave of the Flies
Portrait of the Grave as a Young Artist
The Grave of Young Werther
Our Mutual Grave
A Grave of Two Cities
Brave Old Grave
Graves Fall Apart
We Have Always Lived in the Grave

What will it take to save the world from this economy?
Opening graves ... opening graves ...

*

Processes processes processes all night, long.
Thinking with pierced arrows.
I went straight downstairs that morning.
I didn't go straight downstairs, I laid out my beads in dotted white and black lines, I showered, I then went straight downstairs. I often forget to do my beads, but this, that, morning, I believe I remembered.
Back to the Comedy.

ANIMAL MONEY

Yellow sky. Purple sun, like a smoke mass. Spread all over the sky, leaving only one coin-shaped yellow spot exposed. I am partially melted into the air, which is like a hot bath even before nine.

Wings, controls, hangliders up there, pivoting. Lurking in the wings, seek out the wise whores of the Teeming. In the lobby I ran into Dorothy Bright, an old friend of mine. She's a historian, not an economist. That's why she isn't invited into our circle, or to the General Assembly. Ronald Crest, Sulekh Budshah, they wouldn't stand for it. Ronald Crest wouldn't. Long Min-Yin probably wouldn't mind. Warren Aughbui would probably be alarmed by it.

It wasn't the lobby, it was the little store in the corner of the lobby.

She's only an acquaintance, and we haven't known each other all that long. Perhaps a year at most.

Dorothy Bright smiled and came right over to me, that is, she finished buying batteries and then came over to me, saying "Hello Vincent." Everyone is talking, everyone is a little concerned, actually no one is discussing the idea but only the publicity, economists in stunt. What stunt? Who knows what we did? She's an upright black hyphen with black bananas for earrings, black hair in crescent moons around a yellow cyclops face, although she has both her eyes, big black scoop shoes. Process points pop out all over her like old hat pins, with black beads at the ends.

That day's issue of *La Censura* prominently displayed our interview. That's the reason.

It wasn't prominent, on the fourth page, but there was a bad photograph of the five of us at the beach, and the naked reporters. The photo was clear, but it doesn't show our faces, not quite, but only almost shows our faces, because of the bandages.

"There go the economists," I said. Through the small panes of the window there, the economists were visible, trooping out to the vehicles that would convey them to the General Assembly. A Gothic air of suspicion and funereal seriousness veiled them. Half of them were grave girls from oppressive boarding school and the other half were sinister governesses and devious priests cagily dabbling rosaries. I notice Professor Crest. The whites of his eyes stand out even within the white oval mark. You can see them distinctly, around his irises, even from this far away. He really picks up his knees a lot when he walks, almost like a marionette, and his hand swings up like a marionette's hand would, the pointing finger ready, swinging up to point categorically into the air, as he redraws the protocol.

"Here come the physicists," Dorothy Bright said.

White silhouettes came through the archway wearing nametags, not like ours, which have pictures of various San Toribio landmarks on them. Theirs were just white. Some were blue. But just plain colors, no pictures. One had a picture.

Leo Buzzati, Collin Curtis, Assiyeh Nemekeseyah, Nathalie Krahl, Dolores Fajardo, Ayaka Torup, Uwa Wilson, Alicia Fortuny, Xalbadora Flores, Rex Kornblut, Arshile Okayev, and Vard Bajamian.

Their conversation process came whirling up and engulfed me and the next moment I was going to breakfast with them. Rex Kornblut and Leo Buzzati were disagreeing and scoring points. Leo Buzzati is a white bar of soap with the little banners that skiiers put out to mark lanes. He's flat and spreads like a sail. Rex Kornblut is a thin rhinoceros with an inverted horn, moving along the other axis to Leo Buzzati. There's bagginess around his eyes that is held up by seams to either side of the nose, and below the seams it's all smooth, the mouth loose as a mummy's.

Ayaka Torup is really something and Nathalie Krahl talked steadily too. She's got a vaudeville comedian's face, with a wry mouth, and a sheaf of papers, keeps waving to the star field off to her left somewhere. Her big pink toes poke through her sandals. Assiyeh Nemekeseyah is more aggressive, and seems taller than she really is, trying to pry her way into the binary argument. Her eyes are voracious, eating their way out of a brown almond-shaped marzipanned face with a swinging cape of black hair.

We sat and the toast came and landed. Arshile Okayev is round and desiccated and darkly tanned with rigid furrows along his spacious brow. He has a slow, weary affect; his eyes are alert birds in lookout posts. He's interested in what's being said, not duelling. Vard Bajamian is aloof, resting his hands nearly at arms' length on the edge of the table, hair in Van Gogh spirals flat against the pasty, olive-ivory skin. Uwa Wilson, who has a brilliant, daffy look, is chatting with Dolores Fajardo, who is tall tragic athletic and conservative. Xalbadora Flores is talking on her cell phone, her heavy, unflappable eyes glazed.

Dorothy Bright hangs me on tiny Alicia Fortuny, liked by everyone. Her lips, philtrum, and nose are sharply defined. She has glistening sable snakes that are always trying to get away for hair. Luckily Alicia Fortuny partners Ayaka Torup, who is really something and who has all my attention. Collin Curtis is in this group as well; he's a bulky snowman, full of remote, bare stretches crossed by long shadows in primary colors, and presided over by a silent, motionless planet. There in the mirror across the counter where I ordered my food, that tensely frozen vortex of stained glass, eyes squeezing painfully out in knots from thick black outlines, staring from under free-ranging scratched eyebrows, that one was me.

The physics conference topic is weak measurements and quantum uncertainty. This is explained to me in terms I can't understand. I can understand them, but I don't. Somehow I ended up relating an anecdote I heard once about an economist and a physicist having dinner together. The economist describes a certain difficult problem in economics. The next day, the physicist finds the economist and shows him a solution to the problem, complete with a chart and so on. The economist looks at the solution and smiles. He says the physicist is using math like a hammer. No finesse.

I didn't hear that one, I read it, and the economist didn't smile, or if he did, that was not part of the information I was given. I don't know how he smiled.

If he said anything about a hammer, that was not part of the information I was given either. I don't know why he put in the bit about the hammer. I wasn't trying to score points with this story; I only told it for the obvious reasons. Arshile Okayev laughed. Not much. Alicia Fortuny made two different laughing sounds.

In all the visualized music, fields of color, running along the to and fro of the ground following the dotted spirals, bird trails, everything is tumbling particles. Particles— particles, particles—money, particles circulate, money circulate via electronic signals via electrons, money to electrons via signals, what's next? Hard to follow. I was a child so intelligent that, being born retarded, I turned out to have average intelligence. I am so expert at second guessing myself that it has become the first thing I do, even before I first guess, pain and pleasure, human nervous signals, but then those can be also chemical can't they? That makes my brain a calculator omputer of feelings or an imputer of ompressions, if there's a difference.

I've always basically been—for a long time I've been an individualistic communist.

No, a communistic individualist, I don't know, there's a forced choice in making the one or the other an adjective, I've generally been, usually been, an individual, communistically. There.

Adjectives both. I can live with that. I'm an economist, I don't have to make sense. That's a joke. I do have to make sense, urgently make sense, make urgent sense, make sense urgent.

Physicists, back to. Chemicals—molecules. Molecules circulate but not like electrons. So what? Particles, not parts. That's like saying piecels instead of pieces. Piece-lons. Pixels. Ayaka Torup is really something, she has too much face for me, too many. Rotoscoping. She's wearing an enormous white collar that conceals her entire throat, like something out of a Dutch painting. The upper curves of her cheeks are like vents, they make the air tremble the way hot pavement does.

The physicists were discussing the latest collider results. They smash particles into each other at fantastic velocities and then they try to capture and identify all the jailbreaking smaller particles. The particles don't like to be recognized, Alicia Fortuny explained to me. They shift form when you try to look at them.

I burst out laughing, no I didn't burst out, but I laughed at the idea that someone would be explaining this to me. Here I am a professional, academic economist, with nothing hanging on my wall at home except a BA. A BA in drawing.

It isn't even hanging on my wall. I don't know where it is. In storage probably. By that I don't mean ...

I'll do a drawing of it and hang that on the wall. That would be funny.

What's animal money? That's our project, I explain. You want more? Well, this world, I explain, is being destroyed. It isn't being destroyed, it's being replaced, by which I mean that there will still be a world in the future, but it will be a world that exists literally at the expense of this one. What will destroy this world of ours won't be, probably, the booms of nuclear war or the slobber of rising waters. Those things could destroy this world, but they won't. Most likely, not. This world will be destroyed by its economy. The global economy is out of control. The answer is not to control it, though, I don't think.

It is symbolic, I mean, no! It isn't! I'm not speaking symbolically!

"But after nuclear war, you have a dead earth," Arshile Okayev says.

"Who has it?"

He keeps talking over me.

"And economic problems can only exist where there is human life!"

"It won't be a dead world," I say. "I mean, it will be a dead world, but it will be dead because commerce will have replaced nature. And society. You'll have to pay for your air, and light, and you'll have, you know, a gravity bill every month, and there'll be like a discount tether system for people who can't afford real gravity, luxury brand gravity. Every now and then you see a deadbeat whipped screaming into space. The idea behind animal money—and I can tell you aren't taking me seriously any more because you don't believe my gravity joke, but you have to admit that it's something that would happen if it were feasible, because there's ... because it's only the technical impossibility that is saving us there, not goodwill. They'll call the gravity monopoly Goodwill Gravity and there will be a smiling logo on your shutoff notice that condemns you to fly off the earth. Point is, we want to prevent that, we want to change that. Well, we want, at least, to keep things from going in that direction, or very far in that direction."

"Dystopia and utopia," Vard Bajamian says, solomonically.

"We're not utopists," I say. "We are followers of Turms—we're not followers, we're celebrants."

Assiyeh Nemekeseyah was like a diagram, an arrow emerging from a mass toward another, winged mass, and the eyesight is looking out from the arrow's travel. She was talking about a beam, and she was always so erect that I thought she meant gymnast beam. She told some of us about her project to achieve absolute motionlessness. An object cooled to absolute zero has no internal motion of its particles. That is, the object at absolute zero is only absolutely at rest on the inside, relative to itself, irrespective of how that self is distinguished from the rest of nature. Relative to other objects, it may still move while remaining at absolute zero. Assiyeh Nemekeseyah wanted to do the reverse, which is to bring an object to absolute zero motion relative to other objects, even while its inner motions continue. She calls this an interruptor beam.

The other physicists were dubious. Then they were all staring at me, suddenly. I hadn't seen them turn their heads in my direction. They were simply, all at once, staring, like a film edit, at me.

"Oh," I said.

"What did you just say?" Leo Buzzati asked, looking incipiently angry.

"I don't know," I said. "I said something?"

Leo Buzzati nodded very emphatically. "Yeees, you did."

"I have—" I said, embarrassed, not knowing where to look and confused, reaching for an adjective that never existed.

"I have Tourettes," I lied. "It doesn't happen very often now," I added immediately, trying to get out from under censure, appeal to pity, represent myself as someone with a long story behind him, flashing images of weary explanations, painful misunderstandings, stoic endurance, stigma, the usual.

"Should I have said something?" I asked then, to put them on the defense.

"No no, of course not," Leo Buzzati said. My plan

was working. He stopped looking at me and, paving over, resumed his conversation with Rex Kornblut.

"What did I say?" I asked Alicia Fortuny, who was looking at me sympathetically.

"'Less choicelessly elegiant in tone,' ... something like that, you said first." Her earrings swung.

"There was a pause, then you laughed a little," Assiyeh Nemekeseyah said precisely, like a court recorder reading the transcript back at the judge's request. "Then you said, 'Aren't we all?' Your eyes were rolled back. Your mouth, it looked like you had mercury in your mouth. It was all over your teeth. Are you one of those people who are compelled to play with mercury?"

That alarmed me. Those eyes of hers *saw*. None of the physicists knew what she meant. Her eyes were launched and calmly tracing me. I didn't want her reading my mind. Fortunately, she looked sharply away from me the next moment.

It wasn't fortunate, or it was only insofar as it relieved me of her attention, because she was obviously disgusted with me and snapped me off like a light. It was just at that moment the pregnant woman walked by. I noticed her because I never know where to look when I'm humiliated, and so I look all around. She was wearing jeans, so she was still early enough in her pregnancy for that. Perhaps not, she was a small woman. She walked surprisingly fast, swinging her arms at full length, with long, stiff hair behind her.

Then Ayaka Torup smiled at me. I couldn't be certain she wasn't only trying to put me at my ease, but instead I began speculating uncontrollably. I give myself away when I think about what I want; I have to pretend to want something else to have the feeling safely. Otherwise, obstacles will be placed between me and what I want. Alicia Fortuny was smoothing things over with hostess manners. Assiyeh Nemekeseyah abruptly excused herself and vanished. Nathalie Krahl's head rose out of the physicists and studied me. Then we were all looking at watches and phones and getting up, and Nathalie Krahl came up right next to me and asked me if I were heading back to the hotel and I said yes.

What I said was, "I suppose so."

I was trying to insinuate myself into the social draft trailing behind Ayaka Torup and Alicia Fortuny, with Collin Curtis as neutron. Zany enthusiasm and space-enveloping gestures were coming out of Ayaka Torup, expatiating on the subject of string theory. Nathalie Krahl kept trying to draw me out with questions about economics and what she called "hard metrics." How much did we rely on them and so on. I told her that "hard metrics" in economics is just management bullshit. I look at money, I told her. Money is another way of measuring energy, and there's positive and negative money, capital and debt, and there's spin, which is the rate of appreciation or depreciation.

Money is not energy but it is a measure of energy, specifically energy understood in temporal units, like kilowatt hours. So flows of money are movements of fixed energy moments which create a latent charge, either positive or negative, depending on which end of the movement the observer is at. If the money is flowing away from you, the charge is negative, towards you, positive. The negatively charged field at one flow pole sucks up all the money within the field, but repels money from outside the field, and the reverse is true at the other flow pole.

"So the money flows in," she said, "at the other end, but then that positive end repels money from outside its field?"

I explained that no, the positive field attracts money. If it repelled money, it wouldn't be opposite to the far end. The commotion was beginning by then, I think. We were nearly at one corner of the square. Twisting cries of alarm ascended from the other corner, past the colossal oak tree in whose shade we had been sitting before. We all stopped.

Most of us stopped. There were a few who were already far enough ahead, Leo Buzzati and Rex Kornblut, Vard Bajamian, Uwa Wilson, that they did not hear and kept going. They might have heard and kept going. Those of us who heard and did not keep going stopped and looked back. Two women, one of whom, a big woman, had been minding the counter where we'd gotten our breakfast, were carrying another woman, the pregnant woman I'd seen before, over to a bench.

They weren't carrying her, they were half-dragging her, and she was half-crawling. She was distraught. She kept screeching. She struggled along on one hand, the other she held across her belly. Her clothes were askew, and wet. Xalbadora Flores trotted heavily in the direction of the woman.

"Did someone attack her or something?" Nathalie Krahl asked rhetorically.

I opened my telephone and dialled for an ambulance. I always take down important numbers before I go anywhere.

I don't always take them down; I did in this case. As I told the dispatcher where we were, I hurried over, at least I went over, toward where the women were. The wetness on the body of the pregnant woman was monstrously dark. She was dripping with it, wailing now on her back on top of the bench while the woman I didn't know was kneeling beside her, and the heavy woman from the counter was hurrying away for something, and noticed me coming up with my phone.

"Did you call?" she asked.

"Yes," I said. "They're coming."

The woman on the bench didn't look pregnant now. Her jeans were all undone and her white underwear was sticking out the fly. Her face darkened and darkened, her eyes whitened and whitened, staring, her teeth opened and closed, her mouth was a square, her whole head was like a palpitating undersea invertebrate creature. I heard the up and downing siren somewhere in space. The other woman was asking her about the baby, did it come out, did it come out? The woman on the bench went crazy, the whole throat gaped inside that square mouth and she shouted every breath and horror whited her eyes. Then she held herself with both arms and moaned. She was terrified and it sickened her.

The heavy woman was back with some towels. She waved me away.

"You'd better go," she told me.

"What happened?" I asked.

"Something in the bathroom."

There were bathrooms on that other corner of the square. That's where the pregnant woman had been heading when she walked by us before. The one with the woman's silhouette on the door had thick, dark streaks of liquid on its marble threshold. I went in. An animal smell overpowered the detergent smell. A confused trail of wet led to the rear stall beneath a window that was high, broad, short, and open. There was blood in the toilet of the rear stall, and in a splash down the front and onto the floor. Still wet, dripping. The other stall, there were only two, was ajar.

There was a third stall. Three stalls, like three porcelain funnels of a buried ship. The middle stall was the one that was ajar, and inside it was some liquid as well, slopped around the toilet, and none in the bowl itself. This didn't look like blood; it was thick, gelatinous, and it smelled like roses.

It didn't smell like roses, it had a floral scent, perhaps an artificial floral scent, but I was sure it was organic, not a detergent. The siren was getting closer. The trash bin must have been emptied recently; there was nothing in it. I felt around inside the toilet, in case the foetus had fallen into the bowl. A wad of melted tissue paper was all I found. I washed my arm in the sink. There was no foetus in that bathroom. Not anywhere I looked, but where else could it have been? Out the window? In the ceiling somehow? I don't remember what the ceiling was like. Down a drain in the floor or something? It seemed to me very unlikely that the woman had accidentally flushed her foetus down the toilet—would she then have thrown in the tissue paper after she'd flushed?

The cloying of the floral smell and the smell of blood and animal together nauseated me as I went out the door. As I went out the door I waterbrashed and hurried to the men's room to vomit. It seemed like such a waste, having only just eaten, to cast it all up again like that. Auguringly I peered at the pink residue lining the sparkling bowl, then—, and so on.

When I came back to the square, the woman was being loaded into the back of the ambulance, sobbing and then wailing, as if a nightmarish thought kept pouncing on her and pouncing on her. The tree was an olive, not an oak tree. One of the attendants was coming over toward the bathroom, pulling on a glove. There was a moment of possible misunderstanding, but I let him know I was the one who called the ambulance, and that I'd been looking to see if the foetus was there in the women's bathroom, since she seemed to have lost it, and that there wasn't any. He looked at me as if I were extremely weird and told me to stay where I was, thrusting his now white rubber palm toward me as if he didn't think I could really understand Spanish, and went into the women's bathroom. If the other economists want to know why I missed the General Assembly they can just read this part.

*

Thank you, second Professor Long.

That night, the night after the General Assembly, I dreamt of the used book store with the CEMETERY section. In that dream, I was trying to find a lost book, but I was also made aware, all throughout the dream, that I was being talked to somehow. This language consisted of a hundred different kinds of sniff, a hundred different coughs, rustlings, shufflings of feet, knuckle cracks, chair squeaks, floorboard creaks, stomach gurgles, crumplings, yawnings, the cicada noise of a pencil eraser and the quick dry sweep sweep of fingers brushing eraser shavings to the floor, protesting zippers, the murmurs that follow suppressed sneezes, the hollow crunch of hands rummaging in bags, even the muted rushes of air conditioning systems and other sounds not directly produced by anything. Was I being talked to or talked about? It was the voice that spoke through the second Professor Long; I knew that, although I dreaded to find any confirmation of that. I was not able to understand the meaning, only that something involving money was meant.

The papers all carry the story of the woman the second Professor Long saw. She had been nearly four months pregnant. The foetus had vanished without a trace. The authorities assume it went down the toilet. The woman said a gigantic snake attacked her when she sat down. Dr. Ventaltia appeared on the TV screen above the hotel bar; I recognized her from where I stood, in the lobby, the television is so enormous. Perhaps they were interviewing her about snakes.

We are all still pretty tired from raising the Voor dome at the General Assembly yesterday, and we install ourselves once again in the lounge. With mock ceremony Professor Budshah absolves the second Professor Long for his absence, and we resume our conversation.

We study types of magical accounts, like the emotive

ancient $100,000; and creating the money is an outgrowth of magic-believing put to specific use, since the sacred *A* is scientifically determined or detected somewhere and so makes magicians exist. We talk about *the* "Since," the causal element, between commodity purpose, power, and age.

Magic is influencing deposits by incomprehensible emotions; by human forms offered accounts to become human. Who offers those accounts? *A Language* offered *A*; *A* are magical tender; monetarily similar in being more sacred, fiat adding the primary use-specific modes, which can be any operation, even chants, establishing debts, ways which language spoken by money *types* words and emotions; the savings purchasing purpose are checking the sacred with other factors successively.

This is what those voices, the voices of zippers and coughing, were telling me last night, or whenever it was that I dreamt them.

Professor Budshah fumbles out his phone. Another newspaper interview, he says through wired jaws, this time it is *La Lucha*. They will be right over.

Twenty minutes later they arrive, a spindly, hatched-faced, long-haired reporter in skin-tight jeans, and a beefy, bubbly, giggling photographer, with a salt and pepper moustache and mop of curls. The photographer starts taking pictures right away, using an actual film camera, clicking and snickering at us, taking photo after photo and telling us to smile each time the shutter is about to snap.

"I feel like I'm turning into Smilebot," the second Professor Long says.

Finally the photographer throws up one hand and declares he is finished, then goes, pawing a cigarette pack out of his shirt pocket, to sit down by the endtable. I realize now why I have not been able to stop staring at him; he closely resembles Mateo Morguo.

The reporter, meanwhile, has set up a recorder with a small microphone on a little table prop, a video recorder, and a light with a withering glare. He sits next to the light, which he has clamped to a regular lampstand, pipe cleaner legs crossed, smoking a bidi. His eyes glitter through the smoke. They both of them sparkle with dewdrops of sweat.

He asks us to introduce ourselves, interrupting and telling us to speak more slowly and distinctly. He stops Professor Budshah three times.

"My jaw is wired," he says in irritation. "What do you want?"

The questions all seem to arrive at once, dropping down on us in a solid wedge of ice: Where do we come from? Are you Canadian (I teach in Canada) are you Canadian (I'm Californian) are you Chinese are you Indian (I am from Kashmir) are you Indian (I am from Kashmir) are you Pakistani (I am from Kashmir) are you American are you American are you American? What are our credentials? What are we doing in San Toribio? What is the nature of the conference? How did we all happen to be injured? What is the purpose of our animal money theory? Do we have any ties to foreign governments? (Define "foreign".) NGO's? (Define the International Economics Institute.) Are we homosexual? Are we witches? Are we drug users?

Are we neo-Benthamites?

"Neo-Demi-Fourierist," I say.

Are we neo-neoclassicists?

"Neo-paleo-futurist," Professor Budshah says.

Do we intend to rehabilitate the discredited Benthamite idea of subjective value?

"Proceeds are mythical when small at the back end," the second Professor Long says.

On what hard empirical data do we base our theory of animal money?

"Initial research is anecdotal. Current assessments are symptomatic. The data is still in formation," Professor Aughbui says.

How disruptive do we think our theories will be on the development of the Latino?

"Hairy mergers in America protect Southern interests," I say.

How irresponsible do we think it is to bring up disruptive monetary theories given the general public debt crisis?

"How irresponsible do you think it is to ignore monetary policy in light of the general private debt crisis?" Professor Budshah asks.

We'll ask the questions.

"Who is 'we?'" he asks.

Are we Marxists?

Are we Socialists?

Are we Neoliberals?

Are we Communists?

Are we Syndicalists?

Are we witches?

Are we Anarchists?

Are we American agents?

"Anti-sado-austerity," Professor Aughbui says.

"Anti-masocho-money," the second Professor Long says.

"Ask Carolina Duende," Professor Budshah says.

"Ask Baruch Plano," the first Professor Long says.

There are no such people.

Pull out that newspaper.

Open to page four.

The photo shows the five of us only.

No Carolina Duende, no Baruch Plano.

No naked figures.

Public nudity is not tolerated in San Toribio.

The byline reads "Mario Gonzalez."

The photographer giggles and smoke splats out his nose. He breaks into full-throated laughter when we insist we were interviewed by Carolina Duende and Baruch Plano, again when we suggest they consult with *La Censura* about their mistake.

Look at the front page.

It is *La Lucha*.

There is no such newspaper as *La Censura*.

Look online.

Look in the phone book.

Call the press agency.

There are no such people as Carolina Duende or Baruch Plano.

"We didn't speak to any Gonzalez," Professor Budshah points out.

The photographer giggles and the hatchet-faced reporter jets nostril smoke into the glare of his clip-on lamp.

Are we sure? San Toribio is full of Gonzalez's.

"He works at your paper," I say. "You ask him."

Instantly, the two men are silent.

"He's dead," the reporter says. "A car hit him."

Are you imperialists?

"Well, listen ...."

Are you feminists?

"Well, listen ...."

Are you terrorists?

"Well, listen ...."

Are you monetarists?

"Well, listen ...."

Are you Zionists?

"Well, listen ...."

Listen—China is buying up the US stock market. Margaret Thatcher said she wanted to change people's souls, and society should not exist.

"So you are Sinophobic anti-Thatcherite ..."

No no no no no

no

no

no

no

no

Listen ... in our work, we are exploring the nature of money. In particular, we are moving away from the usual idea of money ... a purely quantitative idea. It's not a question of nicer money. We want facts. We have been reaching out to other disciplines to inform our theory, for example, zoology. At present time, we are working with physicists, Assiyeh Nemekeseyah. You have never heard of her? Really? She's ... a very interesting person. I don't think she teaches ... not very theoretical, more experimental. Central Asian woman.

Very straight, thin, not too tall, black hair to the shoulder, dark skin ... She had a harelip. You have to look close, but you can see where it was. Whoever fixed it did a very good job—excellent.

(Vincent Long here: I'd like to add that her shoulders stand out from her spine like spars from a mast, making them seem broader than they are, and that she has a kind of authority way of carrying herself, and also something witty about her, mocking. She'll play tricks on you. It isn't authority, it's the look you see on a child's face when she is in an unfamiliar situation and fiercely understanding everything she sees. It's what patronizing adults call the exaggerated seriousness of the child. They say that because adult seriousness is not serious but just a hollow meringue of affect. That hard, hard understanding look is the real seriousness.

Assiyeh is notorious, both for the daring irregularity and scale of her experiments, their exhilarating indifference to commercial or military applications, and for her ruthlessness in procuring funding. She is the terror of grant granters and fund funders all over the world; she doesn't contact them, she descends on them, like a horde of Scythian maniacs with the locusts hot behind them. When she encounters resistance, she storms the offices or ambushes a director or administrator, preferably in public, dressing him or her down, eyes flashing, finger waving, her mouth a machine gun of crisp allegations, transformed altogether into an invincible amalgam of Hispanic, Mediterranean, and Islamic womanly indignation. The other restaurant patrons retract social feelers from the vicinity of the target and the target senses their retreat, the threat to delicate social webbing. She gets her check on the spot and storms out, leaving the victim steaming. Assiyeh throws herself into the back seat of a cab and only then, as she melts into the anonymous stream of city traffic, does she break out in a grin and directs the driver to head for the nearest bank with a gloating chuckle.

(I cede my remaining minutes to the first Professor Long.)

Thank you.

The night ... you know ... a few nights ago it was very dark. No moon or stars, the sky just black.

I had been feeling better lately, and so I went for an after-dinner stroll along the path that runs past the hotel, on the other side of Contreréralas. You know the spot, doubtless.

I came to a place where a number of unpaved roads cross, and the landscape rolls upwards, dotted with houses and thick brakes between the trees. I thought the night was very still ... very quiet—too quiet.

Then I noticed Assiyeh Nemekeseyah up in a tree. I asked her what she was doing there. She didn't answer me right away, but just kept peering into the dark with the fiercest concentration.

Then, "Be silent," she says, without even glancing at me.

I try to see what she is looking at. There's a white, two-story house down there, shaped like a barn. It is surrounded by blue black clumps of brush, a real barn, a parked tractor.

"Tell me if you see anything move," she says to me, very faintly in the dark.

I strain my eyes. Nothing.

"What am I looking for?" I ask.

"Something flying around the house."

Nothing.

Assiyeh's gaze is ... like a whirlpool boring steadily into the night, giving its shape to space and vision.

After a few minutes, she walks past me, toward the house. I didn't hear her climb down. She stops to look again, setting out a long canvas bag with straps, puts hands on hips. Then she picks up the bag, opens it, and takes out a rifle.

"What are you doing with that?" I ask her, finally, after getting over my surprise. She, meanwhile, is loading the rifle with something that looks like a stainless steel pen. A tranquilizer dart.

"Where did you get that?" I ask.

"At the zoo," she says. "The lion's cage."

"The lion's cage?" I ask incredulously.

"I purchased it from the lion," she says coolly. "Using lion money. You know all about that, don't you? Aren't you one of the 'animal money five?'"

"But the lion must have stolen it from one of its keepers," I say.

"Well, *I* bought it," she says.

"That's receiving stolen property though!"

Rifle at the ready, Assiyeh approaches the house quietly.

"How did you get lion money?" I ask.

"Sh!" she says.

Assiyeh peers intently through the blackness.

She moves surefootedly in the dark, whereas I do not, so I fall behind. When I catch up to her, she is surveying the house from behind a colossal banyan tree. Not a light to be seen anywhere. The whole night is a frenzy of seeing, seeing.

Suddenly, we hear a faint, muffled cry—a sound of terror! Assiyeh dashes to the front door, throws it open, and rushes in. I follow her, and she is already hurrying back downstairs with her arm around a woman covered in a blanket, huddled over.

"Take her!" Assiyeh commands sharply. "Find an interior room, no windows!"

Then she rushes back upstairs again.

The woman is whimpering and sobbing, incomprehensible. I notice she's at least eight months pregnant. She goes directly to a closet under the staircase and shuts herself in it.

A commotion overhead. Now Assiyeh is beside me.

"It got away," she says. "Where did you put her?"

I point to the closet. Assiyeh opens the door a crack and looks in, telling the woman to stay there until she returns or dawn comes, whichever happens first.

"Now it will try to get away," she says. "Come with me."

Out the front door. Assiyeh looks around, then picks up a pole from a heap of lumber by the steps and hands it to me.

"If it comes out, swat it."

"What?"

"You'll know it when you see it," she says, heading around the corner. "I'll watch the rear."

There is a blundering noise on the top floor.

Something pale and wet tumbles upwards into space from an upstairs window. By chance I am there below it, swing the pole and clout it before I know what I'm doing. The thing veers back in through the window with a cry.

I can hear it breathing in there. The breath calms after a second or two. It sounds like human breathing, a breathing woman.

A whirring sound then, I think I'd heard it before, I think it is the sound of the thing flying, and I get the pole ready, but the sound fades. It's going to try a different window now.

I notice a gas can over by the tractor, so I pour some gas on the pole and light it.

By the light I see it's a woman's head flying in the air with the guts hanging down from the stump of its neck and a snarling white face and swirling blonde hair. I jab the fire into her face. The eyes open wide, the mouth makes a black O, and the head darts back into the house, exactly as if a woman had been leaning out the window and jerked back.

I lower my torch, and just at that instant the head shoots out of the window toward the trees. Assiyeh comes around the near corner of the house just then, plants her feet, lifts the rifle, smoothly tracks, aims, fires. The gun snaps. The head jerks. It doesn't fall, but continues its clumsy flight, the dart sticking straight out the side of the head like a silver antenna.

We pursue the thing, and it flies along slower and slower, sinking toward the ground. It enters a clearing and makes a long, decelerating arc into a clump of thick grass. There it is, panting, glazed eyes blinking, splayed out on the ground in a tangle of blonde hair. The eyelids flutter, and then all at once the face slackens in unconsciousness.

Assiyeh kneels by the head, examining it. She explains she's been tracking it ever since the attack on the pregnant woman in the public toilet the other day. That's what they do: eat foetuses, drawing them out of the womb with prehensile intestines.

"She couldn't help herself," Assiyeh says, examining the face.

"Do you know her?" I ask.

I stay with the head at Assiyeh's request as she goes back to explain things to the woman in the house. When she returns, she hands me a thermos bag.

"Hold this open," she commands.

I hold it while she insinuates the head into the bag, which is lined with plastic and contains a liquid that has a strong artificial flower smell, like roses. She claps the bag shut and locks it, then lifts it up like a fisherman with his prize catch.

Assiyeh looks at me for a moment.

"Thank you," she says.

She turns to go.

I stop her and start asking questions. She's prepared to tell me only that she must get the head well hidden before daybreak, or it will die. She thinks she can persuade the head to tell her where its body is, and she can rejoin the two and begin treatment.

"Aren't you a physicist?" I ask.

Walking away into the dark she explains that she grew up around people who dealt with these things and she knows what she's doing. If there's anything she will need me for, she adds, not looking at me, she will get in touch.

"You're staying at the Hotel Bluonga, aren't you?"

"The Surfeit is One."

I don't mind the dark at all. In fact, without having anything against light, I prefer darkness. I would even go as far as to say I love darkness. I feel at home in it. I don't feel safe in darkness, but I feel safer in darkness. The eye goes silent in it. When darkness falls, everything slips for as long as it lasts, taking me along. It's a lovely feeling, especially when it's just starting. Like settling toward the bottom of the sea, into the cool linen of its silty bottom. Light individuates things and as it fades, the individuation of things recedes and becomes less visual and more intimate.

One by one, we fade from view. You can't see us fade. You think we're all still there, until the ribbon of storytelling breaks and you realize not only that you are alone, but that you have been alone.

PART TWO:
IN FOR QUESTIONING

1.) Why did you leave your last job?

2.) Can you do this job?

3.) Why do you feel you're qualified for this job?

4.) Will you be able to in a safe manner carry out all job assignments out associated with this position?

5.) Are you able to perform this job's duties with reasonable accommodations of them (the duties)?

6.) Can you lift fifty pounds and carry it fifty yards?

7.) Can you lift seventy-five pounds and carry it fifty yards?

8.) Can you lift fifty pounds and carry it seventy-five yards?

9.) Can you lift seventy-five pounds and carry it seventy-five yards?

10.) Can you lift a hundred pounds and carry it fifty yards?

11.) Do you keep the Ten Commandments?

12.) Can you lift a hundred pounds and carry it twenty yards?

13.) Can you lift fifty pounds and carry it one hundred and fifty yards?

14.) Can you lift forty-five pounds and carry it one hundred and seventy five yards?

15.) Are you applying to any other jobs?

16.) Are you legally authorized to work here?

17.) Are you over the age of eighteen?

18.) Can you provide proof of my age?

19.) Are you willing to relocate?

20.) Are you willing to work nights?

21.) Are you willing to work weekends?

22.) Are you willing to work holidays?

23.) Are you willing to remain permanently on premises?

24.) Do you have any restrictions on your ability to travel?

25.) Would you say that you easily can deal with high pressure situations?

26.) How do you propose to compensate for your lack of experience?

27.) Do you have unpopular political opinions?

28.) Do you have any blind spots?

29.) Do you know what this organization does?

30.) Can you describe a time when your work was criticized and how did you handled it?

31.) Have you ever been asked to leave a job?

32.) Have you ever been convicted of a crime?

33.) Tell us about yourself.

34.) Aren't you a physicist?

35.) Describe a situation where you had to make a quick decision.

36.) Describe a time when you had to deal with contradictory demands.

37.) Describe how you prioritize unrealistic deadlines.

38.) Describe your ideal job.

39.) How would you define success?

40.) Do you think an employer should be feared or liked?

41.) Do you works better in a team or alone?

42.) Have you ever fired someone?

43.) How did that make you feel?

44.) How do you want to improve on yourself in the next year?

45.) How long do you expect it will take the work you do for you will take if hired?

46.) How much time will it take you for you to make a significant contribution to this business by you?

47.) How well do you interact with management?

48.) How would you describe your work style of you?

49.) How would you feel working for someone who you felt were less attractive than you?

50.) How would you go about quickly establishing credibility with the team?

51.) List any professional or trade groups or political parties or groups or other organizations to which you belong to which you consider relevant to be able to have the necessary ability to be capable to perform this job which you apply for am.

52.) Talk about a time you made a suggestion to improve business.

53.) Tell about a challenge you at work recently faced (and overcame).

54.) Tellk about a time you resolved a conflict.

55.) How will you go about preparing yourself to join the gridded ranks of the Misled?

56.) What are the positive character traits you don't have?

57.) What are the steps you follow to study a problem before making a decision?

58.) What would your previous supervisor, family

members, or friends say is your greatest strength and weakness of yours is?

59.) What have disappointed you about a job?

60.) What about other people irritates you and how do you deal with it?

61.) What is your greatest failure?

62.) What is your greatest fear?

63.) What is your style of leadership?

64.) What position do you prefer when working on a project?

65.) What qualities do you look for in a boss?

66.) With what sorts of people do you enjoying work with?

67.) What was the most humiliating period in your life and how did you deal with it?

68.) What will it take to attain your goals?

69.) What will you miss about your current or last job?

70.) When have you most felt most satisfied to a job?

71.) Why should we hire you?

72.) Are you willing to put the interests of this organization ahead of your own?

73.) Do you have any questions for us?

—Yeah I have questions, up to and including:

1.) What?

—Or, to go into greater detail somewhat:

2.) Do you experience any emotions?

3.) Have you ever recognized the suffering of a person other than yourself?

4.) Is there any relationship between nature and you?

5.) Have you ever noticed the harm you do? How do you justify it?

6.) Do you actually have any values?

7.) Do you believe your own lies?

8.) Can you conceive an idea of beauty that is not superficial?

9.) Why do you have this arbitrary authority over me?

10.) How can you hope to confront the despotic imagination of the Teeming?

11.) Have you ever used your imagination?

12.) How do you live with yourself?

13.) When did you first realize you were composed entirely of living venom and how did that discovery make you feel?

14.) Why do you keep perpetuating this farce?

15.) Do you enjoy taking out your humiliations on others, or is it just that you don't notice that's what you're doing?

—Do you think I can't see what your questions are really asking?

I have to say I was really disappointed to learn that the hiring was going to be handled by the human resources department, and not by the academics or by the researchers at the zoo itself. I had hoped for an informal, vis a vis exchange, instead of a questionnaire and this dry, managerial, shell-gaming, now you say it now you don't approach. I had heard of this opening socially, and I was looking forward to just slotting in without all the b.s. But they want to run background checks on me, they want me to do a physical, which I haven't in years, because I haven't needed it, and they want this and they want that. They ask me all these ineptly-worded questions that aren't questions. Ineptly-worded-because-mendacious non-question questions. When they ask "how do you interact with management" what they mean is "you're going to shut up and do as you're told" and that's not a question, that's a statement. That's an order.

I left my last job because I was fired. I was fired because of general ill will, in which I freely participated because I felt like no one gave me an iota of respect and I was made to feel ashamed of myself just for working even though I would have been made to feel ashamed of myself for not working. I started stealing and got caught and got fired. They want to know if I can do this job when it's obvious bacteria could do this job. My chief qualification is a boundless confidence in my need for money, which is a need anyone can depend on me to have reliably and at all times. I believe in me. I have to, because I have no proof of my existence. Where am I from? I have no origin—I'm the *magic* negro, remember? I don't so much dance as move nonstop and I came into my existence unproven and in motion.

I am a safe worker. I have never injured myself on a job. I carry loads all the time. I have a load of something in front of me right now. I keep the Ten Commandments where they will keep. I'm applying to every imaginable job, I'm over eighteen and I can prove it with the scorch marks on my face, authorization for me to work here is provided by a grant from the rumbling stomach foundation, I'll be happy to relocate the moment I have a home to relocate from, my hunger doesn't sleep or take weekend or holiday breaks, I expect my remains will be found on your premises, I am restricted in my ability to travel by not having any money.

I am glad to report I have been told, by people at all levels, that I have a positive flair for dealing with high pressure situations. I propose to compensate for my lack of experience by plunging headlong into the experience of lack that constitutes working for you. Considering my long time experience with lack, being compensated for it is exactly what I propose. All my political opinions are populist, yes. I have no blind spots. I know what this organization does better than you will admit. The last time I handled criticism of my work I was no longer working, but I have never been *asked* to leave a job, nor *convicted* of a crime.

Tell you about me. If you want to know about me, then you should look about me. If you want to know me, I'll be right here. I once had to make a quick decision whether to allow myself to be run over by a garbage truck or leap into a stinking, polluted river. I jumped up onto the hood of the truck and screamed at the driver until he stopped. I once had to deal with contradictory demands between my food money and my rent. I bought food. I prioritize unrealistic deadlines by telling the person setting them they'll have what they ask for when I get around to it.

My ideal job is wandering at my own pace and to

no set purpose through an evacuated landscape. With a meal behind me and another in front of me, next to a warm, not unoccupied bed under a sound roof. I would define success as complete liberation from the sway of questioning questionnaire writers. I think an employer should only hire people who are afraid to like him or like being afraid of him. I work best when I run a team I don't interact with socially.

I have once fired someone. The board had grown bored with her and decided without speaking to her or to anyone she worked with directly, with the exception of one person who had it in for her for some reason I never knew, that she was too well paid and old for her own good. Firing her made me feel demonic, disgust, administrative, cruel, and standing over the savaged remains of a victim. I want to improve myself by never letting assholes like that make me their disaster instrument again in my life.

Am I a smoker? Yes. I am a smoker who doesn't smoke. I was born a smoker. Ever since I first saw or knew about smoking I knew I was a smoker. I was intrigued by tobacco in just about any form so long as you smoked it. I tried smoking cigarettes, cigarillos, cigars, bidis, kreteks, briar pipes, corncob pipes, meerschaum pipes, clay pipes, hookah, always hated it. Only drink your own poison, an experienced old spectre once told me.

There is no need for concern about deadlines with me. When it comes to deadlines, I have an unbroken track record. I will make a significant contribution to your business in zero time. I interact with management dynamically; I do not tolerate the detection of any shortcoming in my work, and apply myself to the utmost to eliminate such detections and prevent them in future. My work style is gradual, unhurried, relaxed, contemplative, often tired, unoriginal, replete with fantasy. I quickly establish my credibility with "the team" by making sure they are immediately aware of my positive, no nonsense, can-do, don't fuck with me, I'll call you attitude. I am a card carrying member of Terrorist, Witch, Communist, Drug Addict, Faggot, Black, Hispanic, Muslim, and some others. I am prepared to join or convert to any group that will further augment the degree to which I attract irrational hatred and persecution.

Once I suggested we improve business by eliminating management and running the company ourselves on an egalitarian basis and got fired. I overcame a challenge at that time by managing not to get killed or jailed, and resolved the conflict by threatening a lawsuit they didn't know I couldn't afford, thus enjoying the most fun I ever experienced on the job when they backed down and offered me an insultingly small severance package. Having is the one character trait I am positive I don't have. When I make a decision, sometimes I follow the steps of Karl Marx, and sometimes I follow the steps of Jimi Hendrix, and sometimes I follow the steps of Malcolm X; it just has to have an X in it, although don't assume I would put Jesus Xrist on the list on that account. I'm not close with my dead family and other people just don't understand me, but I did regard my parole officer as a personal friend, and it was his opinion that I try too hard, and that I seem to care too much about other people while tragically disregarding myself.

What has disappointed me about a job? The time

commitment, the lowness of wage rates, the bilious attitudes of my co-workers, supervisors, etc., the waste, the pointlessness, the sinister milieu of petty deceit. As for irritation, I do find I deal with quite a bit of irritation on the job. Wherever I work, irritation seems to follow.

My greatest failure is that I'm filling out your questionnaire. My greatest fear is the idea that my going along with this is a sign I have no spine, and that the future for me is just a collapsing umbrella, the canopy come loose from half the spokes and the whole thing inverted in the storm, then whipped out of my hand at last and tossed in with all the other undifferentiated street clutter.

My style of leadership is remote, absent, uninvolved, natural, democratic, listening. When working on a project I am at my best giving constructive feedback from the margin, in fact you might say I specialize in feeding back. The qualities I look for in a boss are difficulty in keeping track of things, forgetfulness, indecision, leniency, generosity, having a benign awareness deficiency, gullibility, nonpunctuality. I most enjoy working with people who are beautiful, freewheeling, inventive, forgiving, generous.

Am I willing to work inside the chimpanzee enclosure? Am I willing to work in the chimpanzee enclosure alone? Well, will I get paid? If so, then yes.

What was the most difficult period in my life and how did I deal with it?

Right off the bat I want to comment on how much that I appreciate that question. For the answer, see above.

What will it take to attain my goals?

Well, we're going to have to do better—a lot better—much *much* better—in the exploration of space and justice and the arts.

What will you miss about your current or last job?

The stellar vending machine area at my former place of employment.

When have you most felt most satisfied in a job?

I always feel very satisfied when I head home at the end of the day.

Why should we hire you?

It would mean you could stop looking for someone to hire.

Are you willing to put the interests of this organization ahead of your own?

I am absolutely willing to do whatever it takes to get this organization over.

Signature: SINCERELY SUPERAESOP

PART THREE:
NONSMOKING SMOKERS

A probing, baggy eye dialling out of spirals of disco lights—the gaze belongs to Professor Delatour, fellow economist and attendee at the conference. He has, before the general assembly, made a display of debunking animal money, and has denounced its creators as charlatans. The first Professor Long makes a great many phone calls, but it appears the challenge will go forward. Acting on behalf of the group, Professor Budshah sends seconds to Professor Delatour. There is constructive criticism and then there is destructive criticism. There is criticism that springs from a high calling, and criticism that slinks forth from less honorable motives. There is the incisive indication of flaws, and then there is ad hominem vitriol. Professor Budshah, speaking on behalf of, and with the full agreement of, the creators of the concept of animal money, formally requests Professor Delatour's presence at such and such a place and time, to answer honorably for his calumnies, in an economist's duel.

"Bon" the reply.

Professor Budshah loftily brushes aside the remonstrances of concerned officials. Professor Delatour won't back down either.

"The challenge came from them, not me," he says. "Am I not supposed to answer?"

It is the morning of the duel. The economists prepare themselves separately, meet, and put themselves somberly in array. They wear the traditional white clothing reserved for such occasions, purchased locally of course, and arrange their bandages and therapeutic appliances. These duels are nowhere near as common as they once were; most modern economists have never seen an actual duel, even if they all have to demonstrate duelling ability to qualify for their degree.

A small plaza within walking distance of the hotel was selected by mutual assent of both parties. The economists make their way there now. The day is overcast and dim, but the punishing heat has not let up. Their white garments hum in the gloom. Professor Budshah, the Great King, regal, detached, speaking in Latin. The martinet, who is too formal for contractions and too punctilious for apostrophes. The politic first Professor Long, whose every sentence trails off into points, plunging out of language beneath an invisible wave. Professor Aughbui, who never says I. The second Professor Long, who takes back everything he says.

The immanence of the contest sharpens their senses, making every detail of their surroundings acute and significant. Going about their daily business, the people of San Toribio pass them on both sides; the economists, preoccupied with other things, are only, like ghosts, vaguely aware of the stirring of quotidian life around them. The San Toribians are meanwhile concerned with avoiding the heat of the sun, sighing resignedly at the thought of all they're missing: daredevil displays of aeronautics, the annual flower show banished to cramped quarters indoors, the outdoor concerts drooping, the horse races wilting away, the colorful transvestites streaked with melting cosmetics.

The square is a shallow white dish, half covered by the outspread branches of a huge olive tree, and supplely paved with cobblestones like snake scales. Some other economists have already arrived and are milling around the edges of the square or seated on the bench that collars the tree. One of the conference organizers confers briefly with Professor Budshah. She invites him to withdraw, receives the refusal she expected, and retires. A moment later, she returns with Professor Tourbiere, an elderly man who once duelled Professor Heigenbeck. As the only economist present with any experience of an actual duel, he will preside over this one. He and Professor Budshah confer together in subdued tones. Citizens of San Toribio stand along the sidelines and watch curiously. Here and there, in the shadows, indistinct shapes stir in the dark— economists?

Professor Delatour, all dressed in white, strolls coolly into the square with his seconds. He takes up a position on the far side, waiting for Professor Tourbiere to approach him, a paragon of the supercilious Gallic faultfinder. Professor Delatour has hard lines by his mouth, a blue jaw shaved ruthlessly every day, a square, dark face and high, perfectly arched eyebrows. His economist's mark is a white curl around his left nostril. Smoke jets from his nose as he listens, head down, to Professor Tourbiere's instructions, nodding.

Professor Tourbiere now steps to the center of the square, glances around once to gather the attention of the economists, and then waves his hand. A youth, selected for his exceptional beauty of face and elegant slimness, minces briskly to the professor's side, carrying the bundled rods wrapped in a sack of red velvet (with bald patches) fringed with yellow feathers.

"Seconds, please, to the front."

The seconds unwrap and assemble the rods, screwing them end to end to form a long pole like a pool cue. When they've finished, Professor Tourbiere lifts the rod, which is nearly twenty feet long, setting one end into a rubber brace the youth positions on the ground, just where the professor indicates with a tap of his right toe. The seconds stand to either side of the pole, holding it upright with both hands, facing each other, sweating. Professor Tourbiere takes a few steps away and stares open mouthed and blinking at the sight. Then a thought flashes across his face and he instructs the seconds to reverse positions; they must stand on the opposite sides, each closer to the other side than to his own.

No, on second thought, standing closer to the other side means facing one's own side. The seconds should go back to standing the way they did at first. The seconds are supposed to be kept away from their own side to prevent the transfer of any items or instructions, one or another kind of contraband, being slipped to them. But, if they are facing their own sides, they might be receiving wordless visual cues. What these cues or items might be, how they might interfere with the duel, is more than he can really clearly recall. The seconds are looking at him, waiting to see if he has anything further to add. Professor Tourbiere strokes his chin, mouth open, face vacant.

"Well," he says, flourishing his hand away from his chin impatiently, "this is nonsense, we'll just have to do what makes sense. You two, turn forty five degrees around the circle."

He makes a steering motion with both hands, then lets them drop slackly.

The two seconds turn until they are both on the imaginary line dividing the square into the two camps.

"That will have to do," Professor Tourbiere says.

He reaches out his crabbed hands and makes a stirring gesture more or less at arms length.

"Horns ... horn players ..." he says, looking this way and that.

An economist named Myrons strides out of a neutral corner carrying a trumpet under her arm. She's also all dressed in white, a white cardigan with a bit of color on the V of the neck, a rumpled white canvas hat with a brim, a face like a female Walt Disney.

Professor Tourbiere turns and turns again, taking short steps, uncertainly probing the square, until he settles on a good place for the horn player to stand. She will be about twenty feet away from the pole. If the olive tree is at twelve o'clock, she is standing at around eight o'clock. Professor Tourbiere make his way gratefully to the uncomfortable looking iron lacework chair, borrowed from a cafe on the square, set down for him just within the shade of the olive tree. He turns and drops into the seat, pinching up the fabric at his knees, mops his brow with a napkin someone hands him, then throws a nod and a wave at the horn player.

Professor Myrons adjusts the horn a bit, working

the valves, then raises it to her mouth and, softly, blows a series of tones. There is no melody, only a searching among notes. At this cue, the two contestants must approach the pole. Professor Delatour tosses aside his cigarette and crosses to the pole with his hands behind his back. The champion for the animal money school is the first Professor Long.

The formal economic debate is resolved when both contestants leap into the air. They have to keep on bounding up again and again, flinging their bodies as high as they can. The trumpet player is obliged to play and hold a note, always the same note, whenever either of the two are aloft. Professor Delatour hops up and down rigidly in place at first, happily having removed all the change from his pockets. Then, when he finds he isn't getting much loft that way, he remembers his gymnasium training and drops into a crouch, then uncoils in a much more effective upward lunge. The first Professor Long, however, seems to pop up into the air almost without effort; the snap-action of her legs is too quick to see, and her bandaged head reaches new heights with each ascent.

Professor Tourbiere follows the contest like a dog watching a vertical tennis match, leaning forward nearly out of his seat, squinting, measuring each leap against the pole.

The contestants are panting and sheened with perspiration. Professor Delatour launches himself with escalating force, but he lands heavily, off balance, stumbling every now and then. The first Professor Long tosses herself up again and again with stoic abandon, her short hair thrashing around her head, as she flies up leading with the top of her skull, fists balled at her sides. She lands on bent knees, takes a short bounce, then pops up again, drawing on years of schoolyard experience jumping rope. Professor Delatour gathers all his force into each attempt, to deliver the unbeatable master stroke. The first Professor Long's strategy depends on quantity and endurance. Go and go and go again, racking up leaps, with the assurance that at least one of them will be the highest.

The economists watch in painful anticipation at first, but, as the minutes draw on, and as neither of the two leapers seems to be getting the better of the other—both of them rising about as high as the bottom of the fourth rod—their attention wanders. Small knots of conversation form. Refreshments go around and fans are improvised. It's not clear that Professor Tourbiere really remembers how the contest is supposed to end. The duel becomes more like a protracted sporting event. The uninitiated citizens watch with bemused and incredulous expressions, pointing, murmuring, smiling. There are some rascally types who seem to want to interfere, but perhaps they are cowed by the presence of officious looking economists, and the tediously regular note of the trumpet, and the dead, still air, saturated with heat and dampness. Professor Myrons is sweating under her hat and there's a muddiness creeping into her tone. Professor Aughbui watches attentively. Professor Budshah gazes on poker faced. The eyes of the second Professor Long wander at random. Professor Crest glares at Professor Delatour with a fanatical antagonism in the whites—not the pupils or irises—of his eyes.

After six minutes of jumping, Professor Delatour is the first to give out. His last two or three leaps were faltering and low. He bows out, and the first Professor Long stops, panting, strands of hair sticking to her cheeks. She looks to Professor Tourbiere, who nods and waves them away from the pole. Professor Myrons doesn't need to be told to stop playing. She plays the final note, indicating the end of the duel, and then drops the horn from livid red lips and sleepwalks over to the kiosk in the shade of the tree, to buy a cold drink. Professor Tourbiere rises and holds out his hand to Professor Myrons, and there is a ripple of applause she does not seem to notice. The pole is disassembled by the seconds and the preparatory steps of the duel are reversed.

"Thank you all. The Surfeit is One."

Having officially witnessed the duel, it is now Professor Tourbiere's responsibility to file a report to the Duelling Committee of the IEI, which will make a finding for one or the other combatant after a complete review.

*

La Lucha is trying to trap us. Their presentation of the interview with us was obviously a kind of hit piece. And there are others, too; I'm sure of that. I'm not sure of that, but I feel the likelihood so strongly it's virtually knowing, anyway. We told the *La Lucha* guys that yarn about Assiyeh and the flying head to put them off, and it's my feeling we should go on telling stories about her. A physicist, and in particular as a maverick physicist with bizarre ambitions, a daring experimenter—we could say anything about her, and it might as well be true. We could claim to be working in some sort of coordination with her and shift the story over onto her shoulders while we slip out of their snares and labels. And as my hallucination, she has nothing to worry about. Imaginary people can't be harassed and arrested. She wasn't there that morning, when the woman lost her baby. She was never there. Or, no more there than anywhere else.

That night, I go back to the pool by myself for a swim. They don't close the pool at night; it's never closed. I drag a shower cap over my bandages. There I am, reflected in the darkened window of the lifeguard's little office, a lean man in speedos with a head like shattered hailstone. Basta. I get in the water and swim. When I raise my head and my ears empty of water, I hear a voice speaking quietly nearby. But there is no one else here. There should be a lifeguard at least, but no one is here. No one even passes by. By elimination, that makes it my voice. I must have forgotten to take it with me when I got into the water. Just now I hear it again.

"I can never ..." the voice says.

Never what?

*

This part will concern itself with Professor Aughbui, but he won't narrate it in the first person. His idea of going to sleep is to throw himself down on the bed and rock himself anxiously to and fro in a frenzy of thinking; he does most of his best thinking while he "goes to sleep," which means thrashing to and fro, and getting up now and again to jot down a note in his notebook on the desk across the room. Anxiously, hurrying, so he won't forget. Forgetting periodically flings him from his bed all night. Getting up, putting on his spectacles, putting on his bathrobe, tying the belt, putting on slippers, pausing to wonder if he should take out his earplugs, deciding to leave them in, adjusting the orthotic booth on his head like an ill-seated wig, crossing to the desk, making the note if he still remembers his thought, then reversing the entire procedure and getting back into bed and resuming his rocking until some other idea occurs to him. Putting his notebook on the nightstand would obviously make things considerably easier for him, and putting the notebook beside him in the bed, easier still, but he is helpless before the even more pressingly obvious axiom that, if a room has a desk in it, then that desk is the only place in that room where a notebook has any business to be, and whether the fitness of that locality is of greater or lesser convenience to the owner of the notebook is of no importance.

There is something important to mention. The preceding morning, before the interview with the reporters from *La Lucha* happened, but after the success of the secret experiment of the economists—an experiment dubbed X13 for reasons not appreciated by Professor Aughbui—the second Professor Long had encountered his friend Dorothy Bright in the hotel lobby. While socializing with her and the various acquaintances and friends attracted by her in public, it was learned by the second Professor Long that Assiyeh Nemekeseyah had received word of a family emergency the night before last, and immediately set out. This news was tendered to him at her specific insistence, he averred, and this intelligence he did not hesitate to share with the other economists. When the reporters from *La Lucha* were told the story of Assiyeh and the penanggalan, the economists therefore all knew already that she had left the country, so they cannot be accused of throwing her to the wolves to save themselves. It should also be noted here that, according to the second Professor Long, "Nemekeseyah" is not the genuine family name of this person, or not the only name by which this person is identified. The second Professor Long is to be acknowledged and thanked for providing information about this person, as none of the others have ever so much as seen her.

It is now the morning of the following day. The beads are separated as usual. The elevator is taken down to the third floor by Professor Aughbui and Smilebot, joined en route by Professor Budshah. The group has adopted a new policy of collecting in the first Professor Long's room, because notoriety is gaining. The enormous flat television is abnormally on, muted, and she is watching it intently. When she sees what she's been waiting for, she waves her hand and demutes.

Professor Budshah enters.

"Lend."

"Spend."

"I can't tell if this show is supposed to be ..." the first Professor Long says.

A news report, or a parody news report, is beginning. A bizarre crisis at a chicken factory—chickens! what do you know? The chickens have escaped their cages, gathered together in an inaccessible corner and covered their beaks with some unknown biological agent. Whenever they are approached, they aim their beaks at each other, evidently threatening to contaminate themselves, until the factory workers retreat. The chickens are sleeping in shifts within a perimeter. Baffling marks have been found scratched into the filth on the floor. These marks are not baffling to us, or at least, Professor Aughbui is not baffled by them; they are written demands. The chickens are on strike. Blinking in the bright sun, the factory owner removes a small cigar and explains that they will probably have to dump the whole flock and replace them with all new country chickens, but first they will send in some fighting cocks to see if they can break them up or panic them. The chickens onscreen could be doing anything, although the footage all comes from the same factory. There are a few close ups. Here's one now.

"That chicken does look strange," Professor Aughbui says.

None of the economists present can assign any clear meaning to this event, which seems so tantalizingly near in time and place to the conception of animal money that it is difficult, even though the thought process is so obviously superstitious, not to believe they are connected. The program could be a parody, and the writers may have seen and been inspired by their interview. Or was the spirit of this moment in time broadcasting an animal money thought-wave, affecting either chickens or parodists? The following news story, further detailing the turmoil surrounding the disappearance of Tripi, seems entirely serious.

There is a summary profile of the two major party candidates. Ahead in the polls by a narrow and wavering margin, the National Federation Party is represented by Joan Incienzoa, a large man with a still larger head, wan and aristocratic, who speaks as though he were driving each word down into the microphone. The Achrizoguaylan Unitarian Party, behind in the polls but closing the gap in unpredictable forward bounds, is running Matild Onofreio-Atuan, Professor Emeritus of Chemistry at Achrizoguayla University. She is presented in a brief clip, a wan, aristocratic-looking woman speaking before a crowd gathered in a square in San Toribio, swivelling this way and that while laying out her points with undulating gestures of her left arm, her cultivated voice sounding raucous in the speakers. The only word she utters that is not drowned out by the news reader is "lies." The image changes to a rally not significantly different from the first, and to a woman identified as Tila Gomanhelfas, important campaign advisor to Professor Onofreio-Atuan.

"We all wish Tripi were still with us," she says, her firm voice suavely overdubbed by the translator. "However, her dream of democracy will die if we fail to follow electoral committee procedures, or if we fail to ensure that the elections are properly administered and the counting of votes is carried out publicly with the full participation of all parties."

She is a strikingly classical person in both appearance and in her way of speaking, reminding me—no doubt by design—of a Stoic peasant matriarch. She is also the least Caucasian politician I have seen in Achrizoguayla.

I still ponder over the peculiar story, and the way it simply rests atop the promiscuous jumble of recent events. Am I overlooking any secret pattern in those events? I think again of the dark economists. To create an economy of secrets, the secrets would first have to be made. Anyone can make a secret, although some secrets are more valuable than others. How are the values of secrets compared? Not by the lengths to which one goes to conceal it; the concealment of a secret is not the secret, any more than the bank vault is the wealth of the bank. But a secret shared is devalued, after a certain point. A secret only one person knows is almost not a secret. No. A secret known only to one person might be called an absolute secret, because such secrets are usually determinative of something, like a revealed murder. That secret has an immense value, but it can only be realized in a single transaction. By contrast, a conspiratorial secret will increase in value as it is shared. The value of the conspiratorial secret depends on the likelihood that a given end will be achieved, and escalates as that end approaches. The value grows as the secret is maintained, but there is a temptation to turn informant and cash it in for the wrong kind of value, instead.

I begin, it seems, to understand why the dark economists are always reading hermetic and occult literature. Secrecy is the medium of magical transactions (call them A) which compound value across exchanges instead of simply shifting equivalent values. These A still are and have been the unspoken elements of their specific use cultures, that is, specific cultures are used, elements like "of" and "that," "because" and "desired." Alternately, art sees effects "truth" them, that is, make them true. How? With grammar. "Are-on" words, by which we mean words that are currently switched on, live, effective. Categorization goes to the mullahs who financially attempt external-sacred sacred-A. A arguments are purchasing-magics, various, inherent magics. Yet when used their A needs time, nearly needs a primary-sacred ritual, which is different from external-sacred, as modes themselves demand first instruments, then emotions. Invoke, that is, be producing, and those in-cultures of theirs must have that Magical language, emotive regarded magical types. The result of the primary-sacred invokes deposits within accepted use, and without in-types, you get more mullahs. Magical amounts that link value to power have that-language. The more various, the more savings-boundaries. The scientific suggestions operate within the style, usually at the level of one's own deposits or between financial institutions, and therefore communication with the outside distinguishes exclusive religious financial instruments from those developed in incantation, or the main focal element is that A of magicians, because to *do* personal monetary power they declared themselves over to K magic, which comes from what derives as nature.

An economy using animal money will have to be a secrecy economy. By definition, the animal emerges from the secrecy of the wilderness and returns to it again. Tracking now has come to mean its opposite. Now, tracking means to watch someone all the time. No secrecy possible. However, tracking used to mean entering into the secrecy of the person or animal tracked, following traces rather than staring fixedly at what made those traces. Tracking, in the old sense, ended the moment the quarry was found. Tracking, in the modern sense, means the quarry can never be lost. Any economy will experience loss, and the animal money economy will provide for loss by making sure that getting lost continues to be possible. If nothing can ever get lost, from the point of view of the state, there can be no secrecy, and hence no living money. The secret of life is life.

Sounds profound.

Well, it is profound.

What does profundity mean?

It means deep.

The words are not themselves physically deep. They don't sit any further down inside the paper than other words that aren't profound. They don't hit the ear at a lower frequency because of their content, or weigh down the air. To be profound is to be deep, but why invoke depth?

Because what is high up is visible. The higher the more visible. It's good to be profound because that means penetrating perception, seeing what is buried and therefore hard to see. When we say something is profound, we mean, that was brought up from down below, someone dowsed it, there's magic in dowsing out something in the depths. A whale, plunging into icy darkness and pressure, listening as the echoes of its own voice tell what's all around it.

Whose voice is this? Is it still my voice? Am I now, like the second Professor Long a few nights ago, being used as a transmitter? Which economist am I?

That echo returns a new voice. New to you, although it's your own voice, calling to you from just around the corner of a moment ago.

*

The day the conference officially closes, Professor Aughbui leaves the hotel to take a few pictures. The swelling has gone down, and he has been able to reduce the bandaging so as not to feel too conspicuous. As the group heals, they will leave San Toribio, one by one. Professor Aughbui is nearly well enough to leave, and prolongs his stay so as to continue participating in the conversation about animal money.

He crosses Corrientes y Contreras and finds the hidden train station under its turtle-shaped carapace. People smile at Smilebot tripping along at his heels, and Smilebot returns their smiles helplessly, without paying anyone any particular attention. Smilebot watches Professor Aughbui's feet, so as never to lose him.

The train is a gleaming, futuristic silver cylinder, beautifully air conditioned. It glides over its rails with a low singing rasp. Professor Aughbui is standing toward the front of the first car, which is half full with commuters, possibly going to lunch, or coming back from lunch.

Now he notices a passenger at the far end of the car, who stands gazing out through the windows in the doors. Professor Aughbui notices this passenger because he does not list backward when the train accelerates, nor forward when it slows down. He doesn't sway to the side when the train swerves. His hands are at his sides; he isn't holding on. The train turns sharply and everyone teeters, the seated passengers bending at the waist, the standees either stumble or throw a leg out to brace themselves.

The passenger does not tilt or bend. It's as if he were only an image, without mass, without inertia.

Professor Aughbui gets off at Ante Lobo to make a connection. At the next stop, a voice comes over the PA system.

"Everyone will please leave the train except Aughbui."

Professor Aughbui freezes. Did he hear it?

People are leaving the train.

"Will everyone except Aughbui please leave the train," the voice says again. In English. Where before it had been quiet, now it's raucous. Professor Aughbui joins the other passengers quitting the train.

"I see you Aughbui," the voice says knowingly. "Get back inside."

Swallowing with effort he continues to walk, heading now for the exit, the back of his neck tingling, not knowing, thinking about taxis. No other passenger can know that he is the one the voice is calling, but if it were to sing out:

"I see you, there! You! With the little robot!"

—then everyone would know. Did he actually hear that?

Hurrying down the street, the station receding at his back, he can hear a squawking, inhuman voice over the station PA, louder and louder, threatening, unintelligible, speaking and speaking and speaking—

Now seated on a bench under one of San Toribio's many famous colossal trees—every public square seems to have one, or to have been built to accommodate one— Professor Aughbui composes himself. His back still smarts from the sticky, spectral blows of that voice. Perhaps he's overexerting himself, and exacerbating hallucinations out of his infection. He isn't tired or poorly rested; he hasn't eaten anything out of the ordinary or disagreeable. Then again, it is hot, and the bandages over his head can't be making him any cooler.

Was it that passenger, who didn't seem to be physically interacting with anything? So, what then? He followed him? Spoke to him over the PA system?

Professor Aughbui tries opening himself to the unfamiliar everydayness of the city around him. The square is bright, clean, and broad, sifted over with San Toribio's ubiquitous dun-colored flour. Two men in white coveralls are sweeping the pavement in front of a building under renovation. There's a little comisaria at one end of the square where a handful of people are eating lunch under a plain canvas awning. A few children in student uniforms are frisking around in front of a school.

He hasn't noticed anything strange since he left the train station, nor was there anything strange prior to his taking the train. Unless this were something that would have happened at this particular time, wherever he happened to be. 1:52. If that's true, then the problem is in himself and will either wear off or become something new to adjust to. Has he ever done anything that would cause a ghost to haunt him? He's flunked his share of students, but he has an excellent memory for faces, and that passenger was definitely a stranger. Not tall or short, with a sharp profile, short hair aiming away from the face like porcupine quills, and grizzled, light eyes like poached eggs, thin, crescent mouth, hands slender, weak, gentle, like a tubercular pianist's. Nothing threatening. The terror had all been in the prospect of that presence being there, in that particular place. Professor Aughbui jerks around, to see if that passenger is there again, if there's someone there for him, anyone, just for him, and not for anyone else. Nothing. Windows, shops, alleys, streets. The peculiar people of San Toribio, not demonstrative, not sullen.

To note his location for future reference, just in case, Professor Aughbui takes out his camera and snaps a picture of the street sign. Perhaps something strange happened here, or at the nearby train station, and, like a ghost story, he won't know the most important thing until later. He glances at the picture and notices someone is standing by the streetsign. He would not have taken the picture if there had been anyone there; his habitually excessive caution would have warned him against giving offense and he would have waited for a clear shot. The memory is too new to give any sound corroboration to a nevertheless perfect impression that there had not been anyone there.

The figure in the photo is half obscured by the sign and the heavy shadow of a telephone pole. It seems to be a man in midstride, wearing light colored pants and a white shirt with the sleeves rolled up, showing a copper brown forearm and hand. The only refuge for plausibility that presents itself is the idea that this man might have darted through the frame while Professor Aughbui's attention was on the camera, or perhaps in an eyeblink.

Impulsively, he twists and takes a picture of a corner of the plaza, where a group of schoolchildren is bustling along in a rough column, escorted by three teachers. Professor Aughbui checks the picture. There are the children, and both teachers.

Gleaming in the sun, the children have turned the corner and are disappearing down the street, one teacher in the rear. Professor Aughbui gets up and walks several steps forward, trying to see the whole column, but without following them it won't be possible. He looks at the picture again. He feels conspicuous and it suddenly occurs to him that taking pictures of schoolchildren is an easily misinterpreted thing to do. He sits down again and puts away his camera. The teachers had been there guiding the children, one in front, one in the back, and the third had been facing him, looking in his direction, a round, seamed, scowling face of unclear gender. Smilebot is scrutinizing an acorn it holds between its two rigid hands. Smilebot lifts its gaze to him. For an instant, Professor Aughbui is afraid that Smilebot's painted face will come to life or betray his trust in some other horrible way, but it's just good old Smilebot, unlike the now haunted sunlight and camera and the city whose mask he might just have seen slip. San Toribians may be selectively visible to outsiders. Or it may be there are some he can see that his camera can't see, and some he can't see that his camera can.

Could his camera be having hallucinations? Or will no one else see the man in the shadow of the telephone pole?

Professor Aughbui looks around himself again. It's all unfamiliar but normal, and sort of nice. San Toribio smells like blanching cornmeal, something like that. He can't place the smell. It's nice, but not for him. Professor Aughbui feels left behind. He'll go back to the hotel, and the other economists will all be gone. Academics meet at conventions, trade email addresses and cards, making new friends moment by moment, and then they never speak to each other again. The hotel will be completely empty, without guests or staff, and his bags will be packed and sitting outside his locked, inaccessible room, with the ticket back to Europe lying neatly across the top of his suitcase.

The seamed, scowling, uncertainly gendered face of the person he saw but who did not somehow manage to make it into his picture comes back to him again. Perhaps the people here resent tourists, Professor Aughbui thinks, and, since they can't show the feeling openly and keep the tourists coming, their resentment manifests itself as a refusal to appear in photographs.

Like a huge block of ice dropped from a height, there lands in him the groundless assurance that he's wrong. Jarringly he knows that third teacher, the passerby, and the passenger, are all dead, and so were many of the people on the train, in the crowds. Some are living, and others are ghosts only he can see.

He scratches the back of his right hand. He's getting a rash there, as he is prone to rashes and always has been. His wristwatch says it's 2:12. Putting his camera away, he wonders if the rash might be related to his insect bite, and looks at it, rubbing it gently with his fingers. His watch now says 2:13. So soon? Perhaps it was only a few seconds shy of 2:13 the first time. There's a digital clock inserted into a billboard advertising car insurance not far from where he sits, and it says 2:13. He looks at his hand. He can't quite tell whether there are minute red pinpricks there or not; they seem to come and go as he turns his hand.

He gets to his feet. When he starts, the billboard clock

reads 2:14. When he is standing fully upright, the clock reads 2:15.

The idea appears uncertainly in the midst of other ideas, while his watch reads 2:16 and then 2:17, that it isn't safe to discuss or even to conceive of animal money, that any idea so different would have to have enemies.

Two men sweep the pavement with long regular plunges of their brooms. Though they sweep with method, it doesn't seem as if they're any closer to being done sweeping. 2:18. They're sweeping the idea away, Professor Aughbui thinks. His watch says 2:19 and so does the billboard clock. He sees huge, oily breasts oozing over each other like travelling sand dunes and behind each one there's a long purple tear in the clay, ragged and straight in carnelian sand, stretching back to the horizon. A fierce, tingling irritation blooms across his skin, spreading to his eyes, the inside of his mouth, his ears, his genitals and rectum; a blizzard of colorless static attacks him. He looks up at the tree, a gargantuan tower that spreads its canopy like a second sky, and the enormous face of Smilebot bends above him.

*

As the evening comes on, we gather as now is customary in the room of the first Professor Long. None of us has seen Professor Aughbui all day, and the second Professor Long has also been impossible to find and only just now bursts in with every indication of bearing urgent news.

(I embellish nothing, and yet I find everything embellished once said. These incidents, as they unfolded, had none of the solidity and decisiveness they have as I now recount them. They were diaphanously chaotic experiences for me as they happened. Now it is as if I were repeating in a normal tone of voice something told to me in a whisper, and so imparting them with an emphasis that has no counterpart in the event, and that is a troubling discrepancy I do not know how to correct.)

"Professor Aughbui collapsed in the street," he says. "In a square, Procounseles Quarche. I mean, he's in the hospital. Lend."

The ambulance attendants apparently found his hotel key among his effects and contacted the man at the front desk.

Naturally, we drop everything and go to the hospital directly. Professor Aughbui has a room to himself, with a shady window and blinds, cool and neither bright nor dark. Apparently he has been delirious ever since he arrived, and is speaking from time to time from among his phantoms. Smilebot stands in an empty corner beside the wastebin. I had the presence of mind to bring the test book and beads belonging to Professor Aughbui. The nurse currently on duty is fluent in English, and the scandalized expression on her face is succinct testament to the sort of things Professor Aughbui has been saying. The first Professor Long speaks to her woman to woman, and presently informs us that Professor Aughbui has evidently been dreaming vividly of Assiyeh Melachalos.

In his dream, Assiyeh, having vanquished the decapitated vampire with her tranquilizer gun, vanishes chuckling into the night. Her ostensible purpose is to capitate the body and decontaminate it of its vampirism.

However, in the vision tormenting Professor Aughbui, Assiyeh instead returns to her home and placing the still unconscious head and entrails into a fish tank in her basement, which she then fills with some nutritive fluid. Some time later, she returns to find the head awake if listless. Without removing it from the tank, which is topped with a grill-like cage, Assiyeh seduces the head. There then followed a very protracted and upsetting series of fragmentary utterances indicating that the dream-Assiyeh was enjoying the caresses of the vampire's entrails which were reaching out to encircle her through the bars of its cage. To me it sounds reminiscent of the dream of the wife of the Japanese fisherman. Perhaps Professor Aughbui happened to see a reproduction of the print somewhere recently.

The first Professor Long explains to the nurse that we economists, being celibate, are prone to attacks of sexual dementia from time to time, that, when he is compos mentis, Professor Aughbui is a model of propriety, even to a fault, and that compassion, or pity failing that, is what he deserves. In her place, I would have added that, whatever his deserts, he is contractually entitled to the discretion of the nurse in any event.

The nurse is called away. Another patient, somewhere in this vast, modernistic, and impressively well-run hospital urgently needs her, and she rushes to the aid of that person with beautiful elan. A few minutes later her replacement has already arrived.

"*The bank is there to save and lend.*"

"*Workers work and customers spend.*"

How are you feeling today?

Are you having any dizziness?

Nausea?

Headache, any pain in the head?

Any strange dreams?

Have you heard voices?

What did they tell you?

They enveloped him in the cryptic fame of the Teeming.

Professor Aughbui lies in his bed, with his face half hidden by his bandages, his head rolling slightly from side to side, and sometimes lifting his shoulder, as if he wanted to turn or to rock himself. He begins to pant through his mouth, and to *growl*.

—She is going into her laboratory now. Assiyeh's experiment has no place in any extant or historical canon of physics. By all accounts, it is a hopeless waste of time. The equipment she has laboriously collected, constructed, assembled, purchased, installed here, entirely by herself, is really a supercollider, with which she orchestrates crashes of her desire and an intransigent possibility.

The laboratory is a spacious, low-ceilinged room at the the University of Achrizoguayla. The experiment requires unbelievably high voltages. Many of the machines are old; Assiyeh has repaired or modified them, but they are prone to sudden failures. She impatiently seizes up a pen and clipboard to make note of something, slams them down as she turns to attend to something else and the pen slips to the floor, at the sound she pivots, snatches up the pen, and bashes it down on the clipboard. She holds her hand over it a moment, as a warning, before turning away.

The focal point of the experiment is a large black cube

of inert material. Bolted to the top of it is a powerful lamp that projects a beam of light about two inches in diameter into a receiver. Machines the size of refrigerators ring the cube, connected by pipes to a wedge-shaped arch over the cube. Assiyeh controls the experiment from a computer on a workbench that braces against the ceiling as well as the floor.

At absolute zero, all particles constituting an object stop moving altogether. However, an object at absolute zero continues to move normally relative to all other objects, irrespective of its internal immobility. A block of ice at absolute zero has no internal motion, but continues to move through space with the rotation and revolution of the earth, the galactic rotation, the galactic motion, and who knows what yet greater motion. What Assiyeh proposes to do is to reduce to absolute zero not the inner motion, or temperature, of an object, but rather its relative or outward motion. The particles constituting that object would continue to move relative to each other—and she is not oblivious to the challenges involved in determining where an object begins and ends—but the object qua object, relative to all other objects in the universe, would cease to move. This state she calls "absolute rest."

Assiyeh switches on the lamp, then lowers the arch above the light beam. She knows the ordinal number of this experiment. Assiyeh has conducted this experiment nearly a hundred times, trying again and again for as long as she can maintain the high voltage. Then the equipment breaks down, and her failure is compounded by a protracted hiatus as she tries to get new parts or to raise money for yet another, even more powerful generator.

She meets every setback with incandescent insouciance. She zooms up and down University hallways, this way and that, silent, intent, as though she were on her way to confront someone, and she never insults anyone.

She watches from her chair. Because the arc is made from fucking scavenged components it has to work its way up to full voltage gradually, never far from overheating. Assiyeh doesn't care about the heat, the danger, publishing, sharing knowledge, or about developing applications; what she wants is to force nature to change. Light has already been slowed and even arrested in other experiments, but Assiyeh isn't interested in making arrests; arrested light is only relatively immobile—that is not absolute rest!

She watches the beam, which seems to lie there across the block. Her attention never wavers. She watches the beam.

The beam buckles without a sound. Suddenly. The beam is curving upward near the middle.

Assiyeh springs to her feet, leaning forward across the table and grabs the far edge.

The angle in the beam lifts heavily, following the rising arch as if it were a crane lifting a great soft pipe. The very fixity of her stare makes the image swim in Assiyeh's eyes, but she does not take them from the beam. She bares her teeth and breathes around them; her body trembles and fiercely stiffens. Immeasurable compression crushes space locked and twisting around the beam. Assiyeh barely registers in her suddenly limitless mind the lucid observation, made without preliminary inductions or effort, that the arc is having only a partial effect on the beam, so only some of the light, mainly toward the beam's "underside," is slowing, while the other parts of the beam are moving at or near their usual speed, and it is this irregularity that causes the beam to bend, to eddy around the slower portion.

Now the bend is turning into a elbow, rising more than a foot above the former level. Assiyeh gasps out a breath she had been unaware she was holding and her teeth chatter as she sucks wind back through them and the bend twists around itself with that same impression of incalculable mass being molded by implacable, silent force. The light is forming an inverted noose, twisting around itself without touching itself. The alarm is going off—how long?

"Shut off the experiment!" the alarm cries. "The equipment is overheating!"

With a walloping clap, one of the machines, probably a generator, breaks, sighing, spinning down.

The beam winks flat. Assiyeh sinks backward onto the floor, breathing through her mouth, numbly registering the series of clunks as the generators shut down one by one, blinking, seeing only afterimages of an elbow of light. Was it a success?

*

As I have pressing tasks to attend to back at the hotel, I take leave of the others and hail a taxi.

We pull out into one of San Toribio's many spacious, palm-bordered boulevards, and the moon is full. The sky always looks cool, doesn't it? And yet here we are, at the level of the ground, sweltering even though the sun set over an hour ago and all of its light has now utterly vanished. As someone perceived by others to be Indian, I am supposed to be immune to heat's ill effects. If I utter a word of complaint, I at once stigmatize myself as a feeble specimen, a poor sample of type. But Kashmir is no steaming jungle. Its winter is under no illusion— it comes. The mountains are tightly jacketed in snow long after winter is over. What's more, this heat has been so unseasonably fierce that even the San Toribians are complaining. The weatherwoman on the national news broadcast waves a spangled arm over the map: 40C— *MEPHITIOSO.* To refuse to complain would be to lose one of the chief topics of casual conversation, so important in the establishment of superficially cordial relations with my hosts.

Professor Crest is convinced we are inside the pentacle of the dark economists. He has managed the paperwork associated with Professor Aughbui's hospitalization magnificently. This is no surprise. Professor Crest is saturated with bureaucracy as a kind of erotics, a displacement of masochistic hedonicity. It was, however, the first Professor Long who convinced the hospital to open one of their reserve beds for Professor Aughbui.

Am I wrong to be uncomfortable, when my head is immobilized, my chin fixed in the air? Time out of mind I have been noted for my habit of holding down my head, and now I am paying for it. It reminds me of those demonic trusses the Prussians invented to straighten the spines of their hapless children. A persistent impression that the moon is off to my right, and not too far above the horizon, is repeatedly belied when I glance to my left and see it there, high and enormous. Being unable to turn my head, I am plagued by phantoms in my peripheral vision. What I see can only be a small, second moon opposite the real one. Craning my head back and twisting my waist, I can manage to get a glimpse of something there in the sky, when the car's canopy is not blocking my view. What I think I see is, I estimate, an object a quarter of the size of the moon, a soft globe, palely glowing, a bit like a snowball. What is that? It is plainly not some fault in my eye, a bit of plaster clinging to my eyelash, but it doesn't seem to be a celestial object, a star or planet, nor an aircraft. Perhaps a meteor? It has none of the glare of a brilliantly radiant thing; it glows. An extraterrestrial spacecraft? The Virgin?

The cab driver turns a corner and we travel down a side street that is as narrow as the boulevards are wide. The buildings we pass are gaunt, three storey stucco houses adorned with palm trees and ferns, and separated by narrow gulfs. Through these intramural crevasses the snowball glows at me, from exactly the same position relative to myself. Our turn was a ninety-degree turn, though, and this street is as crooked as a die, so the light should be behind us. Another turn takes us onto a wide dirt roadway, which connects this neighborhood of narrow streets to a more developed area where the hotel is located; the little globe remains just beyond the peripheral reach of my right eye, as before. Whenever I can manage to train my gaze on it for more than an instant, I see it has the hazy indistinctness of something very far away, and that it is not stable. I imagine that a disturbance produced by a fault in my eye or in my optic nerve—or in both at once—would, like a scrape in the cornea or the scintillations brought on by a migraine, remain steadily in the same region of my field of vision. Stupidly I think of drones, which are not so uncommon, not so expensive, and not difficult to operate.

After paying the driver, I escape (I hope), inside the hotel and hasten to the apparent safety of my room. I hesitate before approaching the window, and I leave the lights off. My room overlooks a spacious atrium, grim and bare, and, while I cannot find the right direction, the hotel's other wings appear to shield me from any aerial surveillance. I don't believe there are any suspicious lights in the rectangle of sky above, but it is difficult to be sure, as I cannot raise my head to look. I draw the blind. A curious light in the sky is only suggestive; I was too disgracefully nervous to think to ask the driver if he saw it as well. If I hallucinate, that is neither here nor there. There are worse things, I suppose, than hallucinations. If I am not, however, seeing things, then this mysterious light could nevertheless be any one of a number of things. If I am, however, actually being watched by someone or something in the sky, and if my colleagues are being watched as well, then for the moment the best course of action is to go on as usual, giving no sign of having noticed anything out of the ordinary.

As we stood by Professor Aughbui's bedside, it had occurred to the first Professor Long to examine his camera, which lay jumbled in with his other effects on the nightstand, for clues as to what had happened to him. She flipped through the most recent photographs, and Professor Crest crowded in right next to her, plainly miffed at not having thought to try this himself.

When the first Professor Long showed me the picture Professor Aughbui had taken of the street sign, I admit I made an incoherent noise and drew the phone nearer to me. The man there, crossing behind the sign and half obscured by some shadow, was familiar; I knew I had seen him before somewhere, and not too long ago. The photo of the schoolchildren establishes Professor Aughbui's location and what he was doing at the time of his attack. The last picture, though, was a picture of Professor Aughbui himself, lying on his back in the street, one hand draped limply over his chest. There is a shadow across a patch of light beside him on the cobblestones, a lean transverse shadow, like that of a forearm. The time signature on the image is 2:22—ominous, somehow—and this means the last photo was taken fourteen minutes after the preceding one (that is, of the schoolchildren). Perhaps the last photo was taken by the people who called the ambulance, or by the ambulance attendants themselves, as evidence for some legal purpose. But would they have used the patient's own camera, instead of one of their own? This photograph would not be adequate evidence, it seems to me, since it does not show the disposition of Professor Aughbui's entire body, the legs not being shown, and the angle, too is almost perverse. An unsettling, inchoate idea breathes in that photo. It struck me as the kind of picture someone might take if they wanted a trophy, to prove they had assaulted someone. Did some person want to gloat over the mere misfortune of Professor Aughbui? Did someone—

chimerical thought—induce his fit by some method?

I have never cared much for television, but I turn it on now and watch avidly looking for some clue, as if I had reason to expect one; here is a news item, or a skillful counterfeit, about horses refusing to run at one of the famous San Toribio racetracks. The starting gate shrills and crashes open, but the horses, far from exploding from their berths, remain standing with dignity just as they are. The jockeys wag their legs, batting the rumps of their mounts with their crops, but the horses do not so much as blink. They swing long heads adorned with colorful masks that expose only the eyes and mouth, like balaclavas, and trade glances as if lending each other moral support to withstand the ever more insistent urgings of their riders. The camera sweeps over stands half filled with people waving their arms, vying to get themselves through the lens; this could be any crowd, any set of stands. The jockeys, we are told, struggled to produce their horses—the reporter called it "producing"—for well over an hour before giving up. Now we visit the stables and various persons are interviewed. I watch as, behind the back of a woman with a squinting look of perplexity on her face, one horse drapes something, a blue rag or bit of fabric, over the side of its stall; the horse in the adjoining stall takes the rag away in its teeth and, a moment later, delicately lays a cube of sugar, held in its lips, on the top of the barrier. The first horse takes the sugar and eats it. Are the horses on strike? Or did they simply balk at the heat? Did that horse just buy a sugar cube from his neighbor, using blue cloth horse money?

What does this mean? Is it a consequence of our experiment? Already?

Perhaps our idea of animal money, which has been profiled in two national papers, is now a meme. Memes, like money, are designed to circulate; they are symbols without content that exist only to be recognized, and they seem to parallel capital in the sense that their circulation is also the mechanism by which they are created. Every time a meme changes hands, so to speak, there is at least a chance that a modified version or something entirely new, will be created. The creation of a meme may or may not be undertaken deliberately, but what fails to circulate will not be a meme. So the created meme is only new in a certain sense; actually it is, in substance, a moment in a single gesture. Some memes are also monetized. What does it mean, this parallel with capital—if it is one? Is it only an artifact of my own point of view, or is there some cause for this association beyond my own essentially professional need to discover such associations? I turn off the television and roll a cigarette of hashish and tobacco by window light, set fire to it, and blow the smoke out through the narrow aperture, so as not to impart its aroma to the room and so give the maids something to snicker about. I savor my smoking and the secrecy.

Down below, in the courtyard, two men are walking rather purposefully for this time of night; the two *La Lucha* reporters. I hope they do not notice my ember.

No—not the *La Lucha* reporters, though very like them. They aren't dressed in any particular way, but they have an ineffable air of police authority.

*

Asleep in his room, Professor Crest dreams.

"Oh books books ... am I seeking some false thing?"

The bookcase standing against the wall suddenly seems like a person, looking back at him.

Out the window there are Mediterranean hills; a familiar place, although really not, not at all familiar. There is an old castle being built there, jutting out into space from the edge of a precipice. The castle is being built old, not new.

I visit. The proprietor looks like an El Greco Christopher Lee with a cultivated Spanish accent. The second Professor Long is over there in the garden, walking with Assiyeh Nemekeseyah, although that is not entirely her real name; I see them together coming out from beneath the dusty shade of a cypress row to stop and kiss. The proprietor has secretly constructed a free-standing hallway next to the looming main building, a narrow lane lined with cobblestones like loaves of bread crooking between them. The hall looks like a stable. I go around to the open end. The door shows a black passageway, telescoping with lintels at intervals and with wafting cobwebs. The real secret is that this hallway is a time machine; walking down that hall into the darkness will conduct you into the past. There is a toy lying by the door. It is a telescoping hall you can stretch and compress like an accordion, and inside there are turnstile gates each labelled with the name of a different language. All this is too sophomoric for one of the other guests. I do not know anybody here and remain silent.

Apparently one is supposed to retrieve at least two sodden, dimpled, doughy white corpses from glass coffins full of preservative chemicals in order to revive them by carrying them back into the past, down the hall.

I wake up groaning, contracting into a ball, my hands clapped to my face. I saw something horrible. A lamb's face, a very young lamb, maybe newborn, inert but alive, and a disgusting pair of long fleshy blue talons with claws like black nails, bound together like a bouquet of claws, rigid, moving toward the face of the lamb. They are going to rake across the face. The caressing viciousness and helplessness, the pornographic way I was being made to see it, was an intense malice directed at me.

"This is going to happen to you," was what it meant, meaning I was going to be onlooker, lamb, and those horrible talons, that was going to be the last and forever for me ...

—*Unless*—

So, it was a warning.

*

Honorable professor,

We have been following you and your colleagues escapades with profound amusement, and we want to congratulate you on having thought of an idea so obvious and useless as "animal money." I can't tell you how refreshing it is to see intellectuals going to the trouble of showing everyone else in the world that they need not bother payin g attention to them. It saves all kinds of time to know whos an idiot and whos not in advance.

You should all take great pride in having conned

yoru credentials out of whatever "universities" gave you your degrees, and in having managed to carve out your pointless careers, duping students and real economists. We ourselves are all very thankful for your contributions, which will distract and confuse laymen and force those who really know what their doing to waste time explaining just how brainless and masturbatory your animal money thing is.

Have you ever givena ny thought to retirement? While none of you is that old, except perhaps you, Professor (w) Rong, and maybe Professor Bullshitah, you have alreayd managed to foment in a few days as much bewilderment and frutiless conjecture as most of your ilk take years to do. You've done so well, why not take a well-deserved rest? I realize it takes time and effort to construct such elaborate garbage, a lot of midnight oil, and you all merit the heartfelt gratitude of the three or four dumb fucks who fall for your crap. Take a moment to appreciate yourselfs. You deserve it!

Now, why not hang it up and quit while your behind? Nobody ever really gave a shit abou tyou or your work, nobody really gives a shit now. What about us? Well, of course we care! We want to you to know that at least someone admires your accomplishments for what it's really worth—FUCK ALL. None of you are married, isn't that interesting? Impotence, sexual dysfunction, or being just plain hideously ugly would bring anybody down. We applaude and admire the grit you have shown in overcoming these handicaps, and we hopethat Professor

Wong can stop whacking her secret dick off in front of the ciomputer for a moment and share our compliments with the rest of you studs. Maybe you could have all finally lost your virginity in an old fashioned gangbang.

It's because we know you so well taht we send this letter in complete confidence that you will take it in the spirit of respectful and constructive criticism that intended it. When at last you leave Rooms 421, 611, 521, 223, and 248, and fly from this country to your homes agian, take our advice and blow your honorable worhtless brians out.

best wishes for a bang-up year!
XOXO
signed
—the greater intellectual community

*

I am the desk chair in room 248. Through the grapevine, I learn that, the morning after Professor Budshah notices the two men, the first Professor Long wakes up and finds the note, slipped under her door. It was printed out, there is no envelope, and the page is dented at the top, presumably by the thumb of the deliverer. A photograph was printed on the reverse side of the paper. The first Professor Long blanches as she reads it, then crumples it, then uncrumples it and studies it closely. The same day, according to the desk chair at the nurse's station, with which I am also in contact, Professor Aughbui is examined and found fit to leave the hospital. He is discharged and returns with Smilebot to the hotel, meeting with the others here, in the first Professor Long's room. His bandages have been entirely refreshed, and he looks like a different person.

The first Professor Long turns to the second, with an obvious air of reluctance.

"There's something ... for you ..." she says, turning the paper over and handing it to him.

The second Professor Long's head droops over the photograph. Then he straightens and hands it back to her.

"It's nothing," he says.

"Do you mind if ...?"

"I don't think it concerns them," he says. "No," he adds a moment later, "It concerns them. Show them."

The picture shows the second Professor Long in what appears to be an arbor, kissing a woman invisible in the shadows. In bronze sparkle-ink, someone has drawn a heart around the two of them, and written "Third Base?" alongside. Professor Crest re-enters the room, having gone off to wash his hands again. He stares at the picture incredulously.

"But I dreamt this!" he says. "Did I dream it?!"

*

I hadn't realized I'd been thinking about her all this time until I saw her again. So that's all right, that's all right. She's talking with me now, it's all right, it's all right. It's too much for me to handle, that's all right, I'm used to not being used to it. That's all right. There she is, in the middle, that's stable. The carousel of the day whirls around her faster and faster. The usual speed. Which is faster. I'm at my usual speed. Slower. She is stable. Stable herself, not stabilized by me, there's no stability in me. The garden is one continuous ravishing confusion today; the leaves teeter producing bow tie arcs, vertical, opposed parentheses, and simultaneously the leaves describe circles with their tips as their stalks and boughs are brushed down by the wind and twirl back up again, moving color geometry. Not measured, though, not metric. Her eyes lanced me from the far end of a diameter, the circular patio with circular tables and chairs, all those circles and she a line looking right at me and phalanxes of reason arrayed behind the whites, four white spearheads and two target shields. She walked directly over to me the moment she saw me. How can she be so certain? But then again it's in her nature, obviously. It isn't in her nature. It's in her training. Training follows nature. But it isn't itself natural. It's more natural, in some ways. Her face is a pale turning field, a luminous field very pale, edged in blue, and her mouth is very precise and speaking over very white, small teeth, turning this way and that, like some arresting meteorological phenomenon. She talks to me smiling purposively, and though she turns her face this way and that her eyes stay each exactly opposite mine, looking both through and into. I thought about her too much for this to be a purely innocent encounter, why was she allowed to come to me?

I let her talk. No, I talk on and on. I'm telling her about animal money. We've overlooked, I say, something important, that is, we've recently realized we were overlooking something important, a problem with our theory, and it's this: the idea was to come up with a form of qualitative money as opposed to quantitative money, and the problem we've uncovered is that the quantitative aspect of money is an essential quality of money. We don't want to pull a boner and end up making qualities into quantities, like this many beautys and that many winterisms. She wants me to explain what I mean by the quantitative being a quality. That just means that it's in the nature of money to give off this quasi-toxic quality of "wealth" when the quantity is great and this other quasi-toxic quality of "poverty" when it's in short supply. Those are relative conditions, she says. I know, I say, but then they aren't. You see? Precisely because wealth and poverty are qualities of "more than enough" and "not enough." But wealthy people never have enough, she says, and her spectacles flash just at that moment. Sure, but they want more than enough. More is quantitative, she says. No, that is, yes. It is the quality of quantitative surplus. Wealth is distinct from the quantity of money even if it is a function of it, and the principle of wealth is extravagance inefficiency and waste, according to current practices. Wealth is the idea of money released from quantity; it's like the idea of infinite space understood, misunderstood as the idea of an infinite amount of a quantity of space. You're suggesting you can conceive of a kind of money that is not an accumulation of quantities but unique values? she asks. We are working on such a concept, I tell her.

We walk together through the garden. She explains her economic research to me. She does not explain anything to me, that is, she speaks very little of herself and what she does explain I find it difficult to follow. In time, we kiss under the arbor. That was when the picture was taken. The attention she was paying me was ferocious. I was alarmed by it. I wasn't alarmed by it at all, I was impressed. She was not interested in fooling around. We made love seriously the night before she had to leave. The night before that night. She was impatient and very active, I was surprised, I was only present at *her* sexhaving. I never lose count, she said. She dressed and left. I start and she floats in landscapes of dense dark green vegetation and generous, curving country roads. She wants to get off at the columns. The gaslight ice cream palaces look like they were carved out of light, seeming cool as cakes utterly unaffected by the wet heat like ghosts, a single lamp creates a room through a spacious single paned window, the gaslight jets there in its hollow coffin shaped gem, listening absently to the African music of the frogs.

*

Eugenio Urtruvel models himself on the grand old journalistic gadfly and omnicritic and is getting to be more convincing at it all the time. He makes his name as a brash leftist contrarian; he latches on to Fanon and in no time he's leaving little caustic deposits of ersatz Fanoniste controversy all over the place. Today he will write it strychnine, and next week cyanide, arsenic, brown recluse, or, when he's really firing on all cylinders, sizzling cocktail of all of them. The waistband is a big one but he manages to fill it with the coordinates of his literary caricature painstakingly plotted, little cigars, cheap whiskey, a shapeless sweater whose color no two people called by the same name, hair like this, contacts instead of glasses, and so on. Soon the powerful of the earth would quake, a little, whenever his name slithered into their ears. But some people have the right kind of radar and note from the very beginning a fairly patent careerism steering his wheel, and when it comes down to the real test, that is, of solidarity with the losers, he becomes a stagecraft avenger and very phoney. He wants to be vindicated with the underdogs without ever being under too much himself.

His ambition is nothing rare or special. He has talent, but how effective a use does he put it to? He'll never know how far his talent alone might have taken him, because something else intervened in his case. A few years ago, swimming in the sea, he'd been stung by a sea wasp, passed out before he could be hauled out of the water, and remained unconscious for weeks. Being a reasonably vigorous alcoholic, he pulled through, but not unscathed. When he finally recovered consciousness and began to speak, there was a strange resistance and thickness in his voice. The nurse noticed something pale inside his mouth, asked to look inside, and then fainted dead away the moment she did. Evidently, in the few moments he'd spent floating unconscious in the waves, he had somehow picked up a specimen of tongue-eating sea louse, cymothoa exigua. These parasites live inside fish mouths, anchoring themselves by burying their fang-like front legs in the victim's tongue and sucking the blood out until the tongue atrophies away to nothing. Then they grab hold of the tongue-stub and hang on, sucking blood and eating mucus, for as long as possible. At the same time, the body of the louse acts as a prosthetic tongue for the fish. Urtruvel was the first documented case of sea-louse parasitism in a human being. The louse had gone unnoticed in his mouth during his coma, and now his tongue was completely gone. After some deliberation he decided to keep the louse, since he could just manage to use it to talk. His new louse voice had an almost unbearable whirring quality, like the hum of marine intestines deep under the sea. No one could stand to look at him when he spoke—the sight was too nightmarish, too unreal; the louse was a pale, leprous thing that wriggled detestably as he formed words with it.

When he recovered enough to leave the hospital, he did an about face and began praising brutal crackdowns and mass arrests while somehow maintaining that he was on the left. He crafted cunning arguments designed to weaken opposition to violent oppression. He temporized over the use of torture when he found outright denial unpromising. Suddenly he was belching sludge on his erstwhile allies and making excuses for private parties, his former supposed enemies, all the while shellgaming his own past commitments and positions with a bewildering display of deft rearrangement and re-explanation designed to make him seem perfectly consistent. Giving up his long-vaunted independent status, he took a position with the International Organization for Standardization, run by an umbrella organization known only as the Replicate. The lords of the Replicate were so unnerved by his louse that they forbade him to speak at all, ordering him to learn sign language; at times he would wear a kerchief across his lower face bandit-style. Talking to people in the dark worked out badly—the darkness seemed to amplify the liquid squirm of the louse. Those who heard it lost all self-control and fled, stopped their ears, and many vomited. But Urtruvel kept his job on the strength of what his louse tongue could do; it was a unique qualification not to be tossed aside. And it turned out that the louse *knew* things. It talked in Urtruvel's sleep, whispering the secrets of the ocean depths in icy, gelatinous words, condensed under enormous pressure and utterly black, except for the occasional glimmer of bioluminescence, of ghostly silver sea wasps with petticoat feelers and dangling intestines, penanggalans of the ocean floating through frigid, lifeless ink. They record these words in secret and pay secretaries exorbitant fees to transcribe them. The money has to be good, because that voice in a pair of headphones is loathsome enough to induce dementia. The transcripts are set aside for a rainy day in a locked binder labelled *Night Whispers of a Sea Louse*.

Urtruvel plunged into his work. In Nigeria, he introduced a daylight savings plan that required monthly time shifts, in some cases as many as three or four hours at once. Nobody ever knew what time it was supposed to be. Alarm clocks go off, people look blearily up from their pillows at the midnight sky in the window, shrug, and trudge miserably off to face screaming bosses who gesticulate insanely at the shop clock, which has jumped another hour in the time it took them to get to work. Within a few weeks the country is a complete shambles; streets full of staggering exhausted people collapsing helplessly to sleep. Lagos looked like a massacre, but the bodies were snoring. In Afghanistan, he presided over an initially benign plan to standardize spelling that rapidly became a malevolently abusive campaign to impose the Greek alphabet. Street and government signs in Kabul are actually all replaced with Greek versions and the city immediately snarls and bursts out in all directions like a busted watch. During the year he served as chief officer for peer review journals, not a single paper was accepted for publication. No sooner had everyone adjusted to his arbitrary demand for a single space after the period than he altered it to three spaces. Papers were returned for revision with exasperated notes—"book titles underlined, not italicized!!"—resubmitted with all underlined titles, come back "book titles italicized!! are you in fourth grade?!" ... Alphabetical order swapped out for chronological order swapped out for alphabetization by city of publication with a repetition of the citation for every city listed after the publisher swapped out again for chronological order based on the age of the author or translator or editor. Exasperated authors throw away their papers in rage and disgust. Subscriptions are cancelled and journals die for lack of material. Cackling fiendishly, his louse tongue waving its legs in sympathetic glee, Urtruvel receives the submissive petitions of mighty editors, whose superciliousness and condescension had made them dreaded men and women in their respective fields. Now they had to grovel before him—Urtruvel, with his B.A. from Fuck U., had the whip hand and he was going to starve those brie-eating bastards.

Now he has received a new promotion and is writing again, with five dossiers from a scaly hand that knocked on the metal manhole in one corner of his office, the topic being animal money, the idiocy of.

*

"Mephitioso," Professor Budshah says, glancing at a fire truck gliding down the street.

"Rejoinder," I reply.

The fire truck swings toward us and begins yelping and flashing its lights as it rolls up carefully onto the sidewalk. The truck stops and a single fireman emerges from behind the wheel and comes up to us, sweating in his heavy fireproof jacket and helmet.

"Are you Aughbui Budshah, Crest, Long, and Long?" he asks us, still approaching.

We uncertainly identify ourselves.

The fireman says "well" and seems to be preparing himself to say something further. He does not seem to want to meet our eyes and yet he is suppressing a grin. He takes a step forward, moving like an actor in a musical, and gives a sort of bow.

"You're all fiiiiirrrrrrred!" he sings.

While we stand nonplussed, he produces five letters, one from each of our colleges, and distributes them amongst us. They are all genuine termination notices. The second Professor Long sighs explosively and turns away, rubbing the back of his bandaged head.

"What in hell do you mean with this?" Professor Budshah asks, sounding almost wounded.

"Those letters all came through the US embassy first."

"The US embassy?" the first Professor Long asks, baffled.

"Who are you supposed to be?" I ask.

"I'm a fireman!" he says. "Get it? You're all fired?"

"Letters from Shanghai and Europe come through the US embassy?" the first Professor Long asks.

"Looks that way!" the man, whose name is Oscar Rentaxuaga, badge 495—as transcribed by me from his name tag—says. "Sorry!"

He turns to go back to his truck.

"This was my idea, by the way," he says, turning to look back at us and throwing a thumb over his shoulder. "They would have just sent the letters."

He gets into the truck and waves to us once more from the running board.

"Good luck!" he cries.

PART FOUR:
THE SHITUATION

Answer!

It's night. The pure thing. Night time. Ominous. Haunted with its own life, life at its best, black, black. No not black like me, not quite, that's a nice pat on the back but I have to give it back because no one owns that night life as I listen out into it all alive with the hum, whisper, dusk deepening its kiss into night, all night, the lightless light of the stars so far away they are only there to show how much not here they are and all the unlimited ghost tumescent not-here between. Look at all that magic negritude out there, what do you think about it? It could be anything. "Why" stands there written in letters too big or too close to read and going all the way back to the rim of the universe, why here, why me, why is this big question sounding so small? There's this blue-grey no-color grass down here, growing out of the (only relatively) dark ground, and there's a crust of cement that might or might not be a sidewalk, that is, it is, but I am going only on what I see.

Right here, you have my closed hand. Next trick— there. The pointer. Keeping this hand like this, like wood, I bring it up and turn and swing my hand around and down to the end of my uplifted arm, and where I point, a building appears like a honeycomb in the night with a flick of the lights. Mmmmmturn now and point in the other direction and flick on another building. Looks like a skull with those deep shadows under the white eaves and the boney columns in front like the building was jailing itself. Turn in this intoxicatingly fresh and light night air and wave on another building, light them up one by one and draw my finger across space leaving a dotted line of walkway lights you can follow to turn the night on, put your hands right down into the cool lightless flames of it and stroke the clitoris glowing in petals and feathers, answering your touch, the whole night, with one whisper, come out and live, crawl out with the bugs, get rid of those clothes and do night, I conjure. It conjures me.

*

Where did animal money come from?

We wrote it—are writing it.

Who thought of it? The name.

We did. All of us.

Someone mentioned it before anyone else. Which one?

I've forgotten. The idea, you must understand, just happened. These things occur from time to time.

That isn't important.

But I'm explaining—if you imagine walking in the park—

No "walking in the park." The origin of animal money.

I *am* explaining—you walk in the park and you become aware that people around you are stirring, beginning to stir, you see, and moving away, gather their things.

Which one of you—

AND THEN you feel the first drop of rain, and then another, and you realize that others were responding to this objective fact of the rain, that it is something that moves you all. Let me illustrate what I mean with a story:

Instead of going directly back home from San Toribio, Assiyeh stopped in Los Angeles for a few days to visit some colleagues at Cal Tech, and it was during this visit that she decided to resurrect her parents.

A spell was the only way forward. A spell is always the only way to do whatever it is that it does. Because this was magic, her scientific knowledge would have to be subordinated. There's no use trying to harmonize them; you just end up turning one into the other.

The desert airport was entirely new. Going inside it was like visiting a computer's mind. Everything uniform, luminous white, with no shadows. Assiyeh's flight had been scheduled for eight thirty, but it was delayed an hour. Only a few passengers were scattered throughout the terminal, and custodians unhurriedly passing up and down the vast central aisle emptying trash cans or making the rounds of the many bathrooms.

The night outside the windows was as limpidly black as the interior was white; nothing outside the building was visible apart from a few lights of various colors and with no discernible arrangement. Some were so high up they must have been signal lights on the distant mountain tops. There were no stars.

The authorities had given her dirty looks, insisting on going through her bags, patting her down. Assiyeh tolerated these indignities with flared nostrils and a pursed mouth. The transit guard glared at her and snapped the rubber gloves menacingly as she put them on.

The shops are shuttered along the terminal aisle; the whole place has the feeling of a dormitory at night. Faint music from the bar at the opposite end, the televisions yammer.

It begins with a wave of drowsiness. Normally, Assiyeh gets into bed and goes to sleep at once, then wakes up and gets back out of bed, awake at once. She doesn't dilly dally in transitional states. Now, however, her head dips, and her life force recedes into her like a collapsing sand dune. The sounds of the terminal, the robot voice warning her to watch her property, the televisions, the faint music, the less distinct sounds, fade. At the same instant as this fading begins she dimly registers a dry, chattering laugh from the empty seat next to her. A lead yoke of dreamy hypnosis keeps her head lowered. Someone she can't see is sitting in the seat next to her. Now that person has gotten up and is going away. Now that person is gone.

Lifting her eyes with effort she sees the silent, white terminal; the vindictively black windows, deep and opaque where an inimical night presses against the interior. Without actually looking different, the people all strike her as peculiarly small, as if she were seeing them from a point set well back from her eyes. When she feels the drone billow around her, she knows she is in the spell. It's like being deaf in front of a choir; it's the thrum of many voices, drawing breath in staggered order so that the tone never stops but undulates as this voice pauses and that voice comes in, and now that voice pauses and this voice comes in. Her body could be immensely heavy or have no mass; it could be any volume and any density.

She knows that she is sitting in one of the terminal chairs by way of memory and imagination, not by any sound physical impression.

Assiyeh lowers her gaze to her bag in front of her, with a bizarrely elongated exhalation. Her escaping breath sounds like the wind in a cavern deep below. The impulse to move her hand has to travel through intervening space, not down her arm. The impulse has to travel through the whole terminal first, entering through the door, walking all the way to where she is, then she can reach down with her hand, which pulls the weightless mobile of her body after it, open her bag, and pull out what she finds in it. Her hands close on a book that wasn't there when the guards pawed through her few things; she pulls it out and it floats up in front of her face, resting on her palms. It's a loose leaf notebook made of transparent, stiff material. The three-hole punched pages are thick, clear slabs, and every inch of the surface is covered in creased writing thick as silk. Assiyeh shifts the book to one hand, cradling it along its broad spine, and draws the tip of her index finger down the first page. Her fingertip burns and leaves a glowing red stripe as it travels. The stripe spreads within the page, losing vividness, until it the whole page is a wan pink; then the glow disappears and the page is transparent again.

Stand.

Assiyeh stands. Between her head and her waist, her body is like a collection of weird artifacts on strings, swaying and jangling.

It takes a moment or two for the next step to arrive. She should stripe the next page a bit more slowly or maybe more firmly, if she wants to follow along clearly. A knotted remnant of her mundane self tells her not to stripe the first page again; that repetition may be a bad idea for reasons of its own, but in any case she shouldn't squander precious stamina.

Holding the book out in front of her, Assiyeh begins making a circuit, methodical and slow, around the chairs. Her movement in space is keyed to her movement in skimming the book. The drone is rising to join palpability with audibility in far-off, inhuman singing. A mutter comes over the PA system; the voice could be either male or female. Following the circuit, reading as she goes, she is writing the incantation into the scene; when she turns she catches sight of herself sitting in place, head dipped forward as if she were half asleep, bizarrely flat and outlined with exaggerated crispness like a life-sized glass slide of herself. That's what the people in the mundane terminal see. The longer she stares at herself, the more inchoate and uncontrollable her shape feels.

Stop looking at yourself.

Assiyeh brings herself up short; it's as if she'd been walking along casually and then, happening to glance down, noticed a sheer drop directly at her feet. With a jolt of fright, an inward repulsion that could fly her to pieces, she pins her attention on the book again, turns the heavy page with a muffled clack, and draws her finger down its reverse side firmly. The page glows orange, and the color fades more slowly. A lingering peach-ember glow forms a shrinking ellipse in the center of the sheet.

The drone builds again, and the muttering over the PA system is now fleetingly articulate.

"... she asked them to de-[garble] the human's origins ..." it says.

Assiyeh's circuits and reading cause inscribed gold circles to line the inner surfaces of the terminal, before stacking them and forming them into spheres that coalesce to form invisible golden lacework commingling geometric figures and verses. The drone buoys up her weird spell form.

"...that magic Only, that performance larger ..."

An airplane is landing.

Assiyeh is certain. Without having to go to the windows, she can see it descend against the nearly full moon, which has emerged through a rent in the clouds. The wing falls past it, warping in a trembling plume of tumultuously disturbed air. The moon swims behind that disruption; its surface seems to boil and its outline loses its shape. The clouds close over it again and there is nothing to see in the air but a few lights descending toward the airfield. The plane wiped the moon from the sky.

Assiyeh can feel the titan bulk of the airplane swoop past the terminal, following the runway. Its voluminous cape of air dashes over the terminal, buffeting the heavy windows, and making all the outer lights flicker like candles. They go on flickering. The plane hurtles down with a roar that blends with the drone and even with the muttering on the PA, and when the wheels touch down with a burst of smoke and a bark of pain there is a piercing scream that dies away instantly.

It's taxiing now, out there.

The plane veers back toward the terminal like a shark. She sees the lights approaching smoothly, the plane pulls up to the terminal, turning its colossal snake head. The interior of the plane is dark. The jetway lunges, planting its lamprey mouth over the hatch.

Assiyeh walks over to the gate. The door is locked. She turns the page of the book and skims it with her finger, firmly. The page glows yellow. Assiyeh pulls the door open and stands in it. The jetway is a lightless passage. Assiyeh calls into it, the unwords coming out of her unvoice backwards and sideways and upside down. As she finishes the incantation, the drone swells in a steady, measured surge, then crests and, parting, subsides to its former level after a moment of division. All of a sudden, Assiyeh is exhausted.

Don't look.

She drags herself around with a desperate effort.

Get away.

Heavy, ponderous, Assiyeh begins walking away from the open gate. There is motion in the lightless jetway behind her. The passengers are coming off the plane, up the jetway. Death is coming up the jetway behind her. Assiyeh is shocked to discover she has, after an endlessly sustained effort, taken only a single step away from the gate. The droning has died down to a breathless hum, the muttering in the PA system is loud and abrasive but impossible to understand, yakking at her, slapping her. There is an implacable approach behind her up the black jetway. Assiyeh turns the page. There is only one page remaining. Without any strength left she raises a hand as heavy as stone. Her terror is becoming despair. A caustic burn like acid breath is bathing her shoulders, coming up behind her neither hot nor cold. In agonizing slowness she draws her finger down the last page and watches as a deep indigo luminescence spreads through the transparency. Golden light, mixed with pinks, ochres, and reds. Looking up from the book, she sees the setting sun through the windowpane directly in front of her, while all the other windows still show crystal black. She is standing on the white tile of the main terminal corridor, just a step past the carpeted border of the gate area. All the ponderous weightiness evaporates and she is weightless. In one moment she is aware of someone she can't see standing next to her, a dry chattering laugh, and behind her, without turning to look, she knows there are two figures standing as always side by side, a single step into the terminal out from the gate.

That's it. That's the spell, she thinks, more wanting to cause it to be true than trusting it to be true. She looks down at her empty hands, which rest in her lap—her lap, because she is sitting in the terminal, at an empty gate. Her flight will probably begin boarding soon, the bag at her feet is open.

*

Now we are all together again in the first Professor Long's hotel room. It is not a little shocking to think that we have not published anything on animal money, and already—it seems impossible—based on mere rumor, we are all summarily dismissed from our positions without explanation and yet, without doubt, on the ground of the economic heterodoxy of our theory of animal money. The first Professor Long has been on the telephone for hours, demanding further details of this outrage not only from her own, but from all our colleges. It is plain that we, for our part, have ground of our own on which to stand if we wish to contest these decisions, but taking up the cudgels to do battle with five reputable universities is a daunting prospect and our morale has fallen accordingly. Professor Crest alone seems fully prepared to invoke his rights. The first Professor Long believes reinstatement is possible, but will entail a great deal of effort.

"First, you ask for an official statement detailing the reasons for dismissal, then you challenge that with the help of an attorney, then, failing this, you appeal the decision, and there are usually multiple appeals. After that, a union member will file a grievance, and non-union members will have to resort to a lawsuit. In my case it is even more complicated." While it is somewhat alarming, Professor Crest's silent, perfectly contained indignation is also a support to the rest of us, I'm sure. He is in his element. The second Professor Long, on the other hand, received the news with surprising sang-froid; there is a diaphanous fatalism about him at times, by which I mean he is a pessimist without rancor and only a small portion of bitterness, as far as I can tell, subject generally to ataraxia. Professor Aughbui's mood is impossible to gauge. To speak candidly, I have the terrible feeling I have swivelled in the canoe to discover that it is adrift, far out already, receding into impenetrable mists in a dead calm. Worse than that, there are dim figures on the pier, within call, but mightn't it be they who stealthily slipped off my lines, and perhaps gave the boat a shove?

This is the heart of the matter, giving pause even to Professor Crest, for all his incandescent officiousness. We five have all been simultaneously dismissed from five different universities in five different countries, and even were we able to recover our positions through legal wrangling or personal appeals, how could we possibly trust those universities again, and how the world? We can only afford to assume that this coordination of universities was no coincidence, but only a part, albeit the greater part, of a still more ominous message addressed to the five of us. Something far larger than department politics has marked us out for removal; an international organization which can influence universities and which is also plainly spying on us. For, when we are all given the boot at once, with no other intelligible cause apart from the heterodoxy of an unpublished, and as yet only potentially controversial, group project, isn't it reasonable—at least—to assume we are being watched already? Professor Crest has already voiced aloud a thought that must have occurred to us all—a mishap, a plane crash, an accident, a rapidly developing illness ...

"It comes down to this," he says dramatically. "Can we trust the Institute?"

This dire possibility gives us pause, and we each retreat to our inner sanctuaries to consider it, sitting together apart and buried in gloom that a knock on the door is barely sufficient to disrupt.

We are all staring at the door, dreading more bad news.

"I'll answer," I say hoarsely, and Professor Crest rises with me. He seems intent on meeting whatever fresh catastrophe this may be on his feet.

"Who is it?" I ask.

"I'm looking for Professors Aughbui, Budshah, Crest, Long, and Long."

The voice is familiar.

"What for?"

"I have a message for them."

With a glance back at the group, I reach for the knob.

Opening the door, I see before me the man, Oscar, who fired us, mockingly dressed as a fireman. He is wearing what I presume is his ordinary street costume now, and carrying a brown paper bag with cord handles. I study his face. He avoids my gaze, and is suppressing a grin.

"May I come in?" he asks.

"Tell me your news," I say. "I will pass it on to the others."

"I'd rather speak to you all, since you're together," he says.

"Shut the door on him," Professor Crest says behind me.

I turn to him. He is standing halfway between me and the others.

The man reaches into the bag and pulls out another fan of sealed envelopes. Then, grinning wryly, he upends the bag, demonstrating for us that it is now empty and our suspicions are absurd, then tosses it aside.

I bid him come in, with a gesture. Professor Crest remains where he is, rigid, erect, braced for combat, glaring at Oscar, who smilingly edges past him, raising his hands with a bemused expression, as if he were trying to placate a bellicose little dog. Then he turns to face us all, and, for a moment, his confidence wavers. He bites his lower lip.

"I felt bad," he says at last, bashfully dropping his gaze. "About the fire truck thing. I just thought it would be funny, you know. Maybe make the news less of a blow."

"How did you know what the news was in the first place?" Professor Crest snaps.

The man sucks air and his lips clap shut. He holds the breath for a fraction of a second and lets it out again, evidently biting back a response.

"I just wanted to say," he says, "I apologize for that. And I felt bad, and I wanted to tell you that in person, and I wanted to make amends if I could, and I know some people at the University here, and I talked it over with them, and—"

He waves his fan of envelopes.

"—since there's been a lot of retirements in their economics department lately, they're offering you all full time positions."

He hands us each a letter. Each contains a formal invitation to join the department of economics at the University of Archizoguayla.

"So," he says, compressing his lips and waving, "Hope this makes up for it all, a little ... Yeah, so, good luck again. Bye."

Stunned by this news, Professor Crest has taken several steps toward the wall, inadvertently clearing an escape path for Oscar; and, as he speaks, he makes his way to the door, scooping up his discarded bag, and goes.

*

We are well aware that our theories are badly received

by some economists, but not by all, and we have not been abandoned by the IEI. In fact, we have received no instructions of any kind with respect to our ideas.

Yes, our theories do raise hackles. They don't. They don't raise hackles. Or no, the hackles are raised, obviously they are, but not by our theories. The ones whose hackles are up say that they are offended by our theories, but we suspect that it is our theorizing that really disturbs them. What we say is not unimportant, but that we can and do say it at all is that of which the scandal seems actually to consist.

With respect to our having been dismissed by our respective universities. We are very eager to address this point publicly. Extremely eager. Addressing this issue is the first thing on our list. Absolutely. Thank you. Yes. On the topic of our dismissal, we as a group have this to say:

In her professional work, her published papers, and in her private correspondence, Assiyeh Melachalos speaks frankly about her many failures. While she is considered a physicist professionally, she found the term confining and did not consider herself anything other than a scientist, with all manner of interests the pursuit of which frequently led her to cross the imaginary dividing lines between so-called disciplines. Her research never ran counter to the axiomatic sternness of her censorious Islamic upbringing because she hadn't had a censorious Islamic upbringing; her father had been a thoroughly secular and rationalistic Greco-Mexican man, her mother Franco-Tajik. The flat, circular lenses of her father's perfectly clear spectacles reflected every object in his surroundings in frigid moonlit facets—which might be why Assiyeh is aroused by precision, above all by needless, perversely exaggerated precision for its own sake. Her mother was a vivacious chatterbox who loved pranks. Both were so-called biologists, and they first met at an academic conference. They both specialized in genetics: she in human, he in the rest, and together they studied the variability in difference between plant, animal, and fungal genes.

When they decided to have a baby together, they naturally saw it as an experimental opportunity in addition to whatever personal significance the choice had for them. They relocated to Malta, to avoid legal difficulties. There, they designed Assiyeh's genetic profile carefully, building in a variety of useful traits, eliminating certain others (such as her father's extreme myopia and her mother's migraines), and aligning all factors so as to maximize potential intelligence. Then an egg was fertilized in vitro and implanted into Assiyeh's mother. Assiyeh was born fully formed an efficient eight months later, in Greece. Completely hairless, dark grey in color like a newborn rhinocerous. Her armpits were webbed as far down as the elbow; this webbing was surgically removed.

Assiyeh matured rapidly, and, much to the satisfaction of her parents, grew hair, gradually lost her pachydermous color and acquired the coppery complexion of her father. Her earlobes, however, grew steadily and curled tightly on themselves, making her look like she was wearing earrings. In the end, they amputated these growths, and that put an end to them. She exhibited an immediate and profound interest in science. Her intellect was astounding and she seemed able to assimilate any amount of information virtually without effort. When her parents became old and sick, her botched attempts to rejuvenate them through a series of horrible operations and the imposition of a draconian regimen actually killed them. With her father, Athanasio, she'd tried a series of local procedures instead of an overall treatment. She pulled all his remaining teeth and replaced them with alarmingly white artificial replicas, which were too big. To get rid of his wrinkles, she performed tightening surgeries that left him looking like he'd been shrink-wrapped in his own skin; his upper lip was so stretched over those enormous teeth that he couldn't properly close his mouth, which impeded clear articulate speech and allowed his saliva to trickle steadily down his chin. She blinded him with an operation intended to save his sight and crippled him with replacement joints that didn't bond properly and fouled his digestion with a malfunctioning colonic implant that led to a septic infection and blood poisoning, arrested only partially by a surgically implanted filtration device that had to be flushed regularly six times a day by a huge and expensive machine. The scalp transplant was an encouraging success though, and he suffered the degrading agony of this lethal rejuvenation program sporting a thick mane of flowing, magnificent ash-blonde hair.

She subjected her mother, Siamaa, to a protracted series of excruciating spinal injections that turned her, over the course of ten days, a scintillant blue like she had lead powder injected under the skin. She ended up looking like a hood ornament. Assiyeh maintained it was only a phase and a sign that an equally drastic overhaul of Siamaa's health was immanent. When at last a CAT scan revealed her to be completely solid in cross section, Assiyeh could barely bring herself to call it a setback. In the end, however, she had to concede that she had orphaned herself.

*

The University is even more than usually deserted for this time of year, because the entire country is on tenterhooks about the current election. As of now, we are in the sixth day of deliberations over the election results, and the atmosphere throughout the country is increasingly volatile. Violence might break out at any moment, but the electoral committee continues to mull over the results.

Given the short notice with which we were added to the faculty, the University could offer us only makeshift accommodations at first. While I am in no way aware of any reason for it, I am the only one of us to receive a situation in the building that actually houses the economics department, albeit not in the department itself. Instead, I share an unused office in the art history department with a collection of stored dropcloths, easels, pigments, and the other impedimenta of painting. The department secretary, a pert, efficient man in his fifties, takes me there on my first day and gives me the keys.

"A bit out of the way," he says, with an apologetic smile.

And once we are inside—

"So this is it," he says, gesturing. "Desk, shelfs (he pronounced the f). All right?"

"Yes, fine."

"Not mad?"

I return his smile with hypocrisy.

"Of course not."

To get to me, you have to go down a long corridor, all the way to the end, and turn with it down a narrower passage with an arched roof, unlike the flat roof of the corridor. The narrower passage has no windows and no source of light whatever apart from several absurdly weak light bulbs that hang from their cords in no order. The lights are always on, as far as I am aware, with no switch that I can find to operate them. I looked for one, I assure you. I searched the almost sooty walls with my bare hands, in the vain hope that I might find the switch, and that it would be a dimmer switch whose gain I could increase, so as to have something better than the feeble glow of these bulbs, cool to the touch and as useless as the lamps of giant fireflies. The passage, however, has no bends and no doors other than mine, which is at the end of it, so the voyage through the dark and the pale globules of light is sure of the right conclusion, anyway. It is certain that this passageway antedates the corridor to which it is attached.

My office has no window either, but only a rather small skylight set deep into the high studio ceiling. During the day, such a vibrant and dense shaft of light beams through it that the rest of the office seems plunged in gloom, by contrast with the golden blaze it lets down. I have only a desk lamp, which lacks force. The desk is enormous, made of metal enamelled green, with a vulcanized rubber top. The light from the desk lamp is so feeble, it doesn't even reach the outer edges of the desk. I have also an inadequate bookcase that I imagine was stored here because no one could conceivably make use of the thing, which is too short, too narrow, and too shallow. What books I can fit into it constantly fall to the cement floor, startling me.

No one ever comes to see me. I suppose I am amusing myself with this description. I suppose that was my intention. Perhaps I did not succeed in amusing myself. That is not obvious.

The others fared far worse than I, and had to accept makeshift quarters until something better could be sorted out. The majority of the faculty and administration are away for the summer, so this state of affairs will last a while longer yet. It is vitally essential that we have offices, so that we may continue our work. The idea we received en masse, but we have now each taken it up in our own way. Perhaps the result will be five different books, but I suspect one would be best, if only to begin. However I do not entirely trust the University; their offer was made so easily, so swiftly, and it was so generous. The prospect that this offer was prepared in advance is the obvious explanation. What a blunder, then, to use the same person, implausibly named "Oscar Rentaxuaga," as the instrument! In vain I essayed to show the others how readily these incidents could be made to expose themselves for the trap they almost certainly are, designed to gather and corral the five of us at the same University, the easier to keep track of us, no doubt.

The first Professor Long accepted immediately. Professor Aughbui hesitated. Professor Budshah did not accept until he had consulted with a great many colleagues and other persons, which left him taciturn and ill-looking. The second Professor Long accepted the offer shortly after it was made, only to retract his acceptance shortly after that. Then he accepted again shortly after that, but with the proviso that he be completely assured of his actual termination at Ottawa, which, according to him, could only be determined in person. So, he prepared to return to Canada.

If we take the second Professor Long's conditional agreement for acceptance, then I held out the longest. I will not describe the exchanges—I do not choose to dignify them with the term "conversations"—between myself and those persons in New York that I was able to reach. It was wasted labor. My carefully-timed telephone calls to the persons I calculated were most likely to help me did not go through. The fragmentary words and phrases barked at me over disintegrating connections were worse than any clear rejection would have been.

I succumbed after a sleepless night of shameful histrionics. I wish I could believe that I surrendered to free myself from an embarrassing loss of emotional control. Instead, I suspect my motive was fear. It could be nothing more than pessimism behind that suspicion, but I trust pessimism. If I am not a Professor, then I am not important. To my shame, I confess I must be important. There were, and are, no alternatives. My father once told me that, to get a job, it was necessary to have a job. This is true, so, even if it is my intention to take the first, or the first good, position elsewhere on offer, I am more likely to succeed as a Professor full-time at the University of Archizoguayla than as a free lance. The others can look after themselves, of course, but, should there be any plot afoot, then my vigilance may do them some good as well.

Now I am sitting dutifully in my office. I will say this for it: it is cool. The walls must be quite thick. Waves of heat emanate from the column of light that now stands like a tent post in the middle of the floor. The shade it creates around itself, that column, perpetually obscures the rest of the office, so that I am not able, as I was tempted to do just now, to describe it as a cube, since I do not know exactly what is the shape of this room. The wall behind me is square at the bottom, but I can not say whether it meets the ceiling at an angle or a curve, or how many corners there are here. At the moment, I have struck at an impasse in my treatment of the theme of animal money, accumulating on the long legal pad before in minute, even hand writing. I am diverting myself with the newspaper. Popular protests across Mexico to end the subsidization of private banks. The official US position is unintelligible, strobing between threats of military intervention and bland approval. The wealthy are dead set against secession. No new theaters. Nothing but far-fetched, sketchy schemes, prevaricating and dithering in Mexico, trying to buy time, hoping to see the wave crest and melt away, drafting concessions.

To sum up: incandescent with messianic dreams, we envision a revolution at the level of money. Is it happening? Is this the effect of the experiment? Professor Budshah and the first Professor Long are skeptical. Professor Aughbui is neutral. I edge cautiously toward an affirmation. The second Professor Long thinks the relationship, while not exactly causal, is nevertheless clear and obvious. The Duelling Committee has yet to determine the outcome of the duel with Professor Delatour, and the

Information Committee can not explain our coordinated terminations, although we receive assurances from them that we will be notified if any new facts are discovered in the case.

"Not mad?"

Did he actually ask that? Ask me *that?* And exactly what, I wonder, is the answer he expects? Shall I tell him that my capacity for anger is infinite? That I am angry every single day? That I have been angry for so long that I am unable to imagine not being angry? That all my emotions are only inflections of anger? Every day I am angry. When I should be sleeping, I lie awake, my anger resting on me like a hot coal I will not brush away. Shall I explain, in a casual conversation with a stranger, that anger is so firmly fixed and constant for me that it has hardened like permafrost, and that no amount of activity can ever soften me?

If I did explain this to someone, it is reasonable to assume it would be received in the sense of an impersonal warning, but everything I do is an act of anger already. This is not "my" anger, to be "released" or in some other way exorcised from me; I tell you it is me, I am a living anger sculpture.

*

Of the five of us, the first Professor Long has the most pull with publishers, and she has managed to get a few university presses interested in our project. The resulting book is to be called simply *Animal Money: Citation, Communication, and Power*. Authorship will be attributed to the "CL Lab," an anagram of the letters of our last names. This was a conceit of the second Professor Long, and in the interest of full disclosure I will add that I did not vote in favor of it. We still will not mention anything about experiment X13—not only to protect ourselves, but to prevent any interference, just in case it does something.

The more rigorously technical our approach, the more obvious it becomes that we are writing an occult book. I reject this line entirely, but the idea of magic seems to be forcing itself on us, just as the original idea was to a certain degree forced on us:

Magic potential *phrases* magical surroundings, currency, instruments, this being all art in any view. Citation communication and power, spells, isolation purchasing blessings, theory as nature. The religion, A, is an exclusive language for them. K are languages and, whereas money man's talk is a speech measure with personal meaning, the sacred causes the one who enacts ritual and language necessarily to perform a ceremony. For money, particularly money of the *Only A*, the money types worship. The objective A can be Magical by the truth cause that makes its respect the magician's respect. The Western economy, the universal *These*, lives a life of incomprehensible difference by and in phrases, agencies, age instruments. Magic is linked of man by the difference of A and them.

The book seems to write itself, and yet it is only now just coming into existence. Our different sections all have the same style, recognized by none of us as our own. I have begun laying the groundwork in anticipation of future allegations that we are in reality "dark economists."

Perhaps the chief difficulty lies in the variability in the concept of animal money as a medium of exchange. At first, it seemed to articulate itself as a form of exchange reciprocally doubling all risked values, but as we worked out the ramifications of this kind of exchange in practice, we realized—and the algorithmic models of Professor Aughbui reproduce this finding—that the it was in reality a total loss exchange system. All risked values would vanish in an exchange of animal money, and, to our great embarrassment, we found ourselves unable to provide anything better than speculations about the destiny of those values. As the first Professor Long painstakingly demonstrated, since there was nothing in the exchange that could possibly destroy values, their disappearance in the exchange had to be regarded as either an illusion of some kind, or as an escape to some unknown other place.

With some reluctance, I had to accede to the inclusion of a theory formulated by the second Professor Long and championed, not surprisingly, by Professor Budshah. It was also supported, and this was a surprise, by a certain reading of results produced by the models of Professor Aughbui. The second Professor Long postulates that the exchange of animal money does double all risked values after all, and more, it also doubles the parties. While he was never able to present this idea clearly enough for my satisfaction, he seems to believe that there is a doubling of the roles of the participants, which idea has some plausibility in its favor at least. However, at other times he seems to be saying that spectral participants are drawn into an animal money exchange, absconding with the values to another dimension.

My response to this theory is as follows: if each participant in an animal money exchange is doubled by the exchange, then that could explain the escape of the values to an extent, but in the longer view this explanation only begs the more urgent question, which is: what exactly is the status of the missing value? This status is the most important aspect of the entire model, in my opinion, as the state the missing value is the manner or condition by which it will reappear in circulation. If the value is not destroyed, then it must return. The second Professor Long asserts the return, but does not account for the mechanism of that return. Or, if he does, he accounts for it in unacceptable, occult terms.

I am convinced that inimical actors are aware of the project and are taking it at least as seriously as we are. My opinion, it gratifies me to say, albeit it is a bitter gratification, is taking on strength among the others as well. A foreboding and a sense of being under surveillance is clasping us all. Completion and publication are consequently all that much more urgent.

*

"Sevrules si Sevralas, l'capuldo illustruila ala vestiga d'obfir surcingului de chaiseadul. Prefivame cinqtureqte voldrez surcingului de chaiseadul si subsithoz a voldrez chaisea. Gradathe."

Incessant to-ing and fro-ing around the toilet. A flush, the door opens, someone else squeezes by before the former user has even fully emerged yet, door shut, a flush almost right away, repeat, and mirror, since it happens on the other side of the aisle as well. People clambering around and over each other in the doorways of the two toilets, the dull scent of human waste, brown liquid trickling down the aisles. The air conditioning is so aggressive that people are erecting makeshift tents around their seats, breath steaming, using their blankets, their luggage. They rip open plastic bags and join them together somehow to form patchwork tarps. There's a peculiarly glamorous woman who keeps coming back here from the front of the plane, evidently to chat with a friend who has been sound asleep since we left Achrizoguayla. She hasn't been asleep since we left Achrizoguayla; she fell asleep about an hour after takeoff. The man next to me is out cold, too, and steam plumes from his slack mouth. The man next to him is awake and plainly married to the woman across the aisle from him. They must be talking, but I only ever catch the moments in between, or maybe they're telepathic. He holds his lips as if he'd taken a vow of silence. Or no, he holds his lips as if he thought talking was vulgar.

Outside there is the cold blue through white, my vision telescopes at random across the incandescent cottons, crumbling mist panels, clouds that are highly defined in one part and smears in another. Just there, two mushroom clouds with foggy sides, articulate crowns, shedding flat, dissolving scarfations and darker pennants.

The fleshless ass of the man in the aisle rummaging in an overhead bin. The banded slits of his two back pockets slope downwards like drooping eyes in a grey face. His children are elephants. The two women behind me are really loud, but I don't register it. I must register it, because, when they notice I am not annoyed enough, they lean over the back of my seat to jabber directly into my ears. I sit unperturbed. I am perturbed, but I appear unperturbed. I don't need to pick at a wrapper for twenty minutes when I want to eat something. At last reason pours out its balm reason reason reason.

"While they cause these effects, they can't possibly intend the effects they cause because they can't know how these things will affect you," reason explains. "They most likely don't think of the effects their actions have. You do not want to conform; you are frustrated because you are continually giving way to others, and at times you do not adequately distinguish between conforming and giving way to the needs of others."

"The needs of others"—see what I mean chum? Reason; that little extra effort, a la Ronald Crest, putting it like that instead of clumsy "others's' needs." Others's'. Uneuphonious.

"No one seems to give way to you, unfair, thus anger. Since they cannot grasp what it means to you, they don't know what they are asking and don't have enough goodwill to make the effort to understand. Good will they have, but not enough. From their point of view, this is a banal problem."

Great. Keep it coming.

"The purpose of these reflections—"

Oh yeah.

"—is not to persuade you to be more compliant; the purpose of these reflections is to stop you from exaggerating the problems in your own mind and so to reduce your sense of being attacked."

The engine noise is changing. We are shedding our altitude now, fast, coming down toward the earth again. The sun hisses at me.

Thanks, Reason. Come by any time. Stay as long as you can take it. Take me, I mean.

The image now: gliding along from left to right, black lightless ridges like heaps of crumbling lava, parallel to me, layered against the distance, lit with gold light from the valley floors below, so the hills are carbonized logs laced with gold flame threads.

*

It's been almost four days and no word from the second Professor Long. He isn't answering email; he doesn't pick up the phone. After nearly ninety-six hours, the first Professor Long decides that a half-unconsciously imposed waiting period has expired and calls the second Professor Long's college.

A raucous voice erupts out of the third ring "—Yeah?"

Loud music and shouting voices, laughter, joyous cries. The first Professor Long starts and holds the phone away from her ear.

"They must be having a faculty party," she thinks.

"What you want?" the voice barks.

"Lend. I am trying to reach Professor Long."

"Hah?"

"I am trying to reach Professor Long!"

"Which one?"

"The second one—Vincent—Vincent Long," she says.

She can hear the hollow clunk as the phone is set down, probably on the desk, and a voice calling over and through the racket—it sounds like a bar on a Saturday night. With a rattle the phone is picked up again.

"Not in, lady."

"This is the department of social studies?"

"Yes this is the department of social studies," the voice sneers at her.

"Give me the extension for Professor Long, please."

"He hasn't got any."

"No extension?"

"No extension."

"Then how is anyone supposed to reach him?"

"Not by phone!" the voice says, brisk and irresponsible.

"I have been emailing him for some time—"

"Look—"

"Nevermind," the first Professor Long interrupts him, having detected the impulse to hang up on the far end. "I want ..."

"Well? What do you want?"

"I want to leave a message for him."

No response. Nothing but the noise. The first Professor Long wonders if she somehow managed to offend the metal creature she imagines on the other end.

"... I'll bet you do," the other voice says then, pensively.

That's a bad answer. That answer means conspiring. Is this telephone call being recorded? Overheard? It must be—it's an American university.

"Tell him to call Professor Long ..." she says. "Min-Yin. Emm eye enn hyphen why eye enn. At the University number ... Right away."

She listens to the silence oddly huddled in the midst of the hilarity on the other end of the line.

"Should I repeat that?" she asks the noise. "Tell him that I need to speak with him as soon as possible, any time, day or night."

"He's dead, my dear," the voice says. "He will never speak with you again."

Everything inside the first Professor Long rotates to a halt.

"*Should I repeat that!?*" the voice screeches, so loud that the phone trembles in her hand.

"How?" the first Professor Long asks, her voice flat.

"How *how?*" the voice says, vicious and silly.

"How did he die? And when?" she asks, flat.

"Look it up," the voice says nastily, sounding more and more like a teasing child. "Look it up in a *book*." It spits the word at her with an audible sneer.

"How did Professor Long die, and when?"

"I will tell you when and why Professor Bozo died beep boop," the voice says in a robotic monotone. "I'm Professor Ching-Chong Long and my precision in speech is fucking onerous."

"Are you going to answer me, or do I have to come to your department personally?" the first Professor Long says.

"Just try it," the voice says blandly.

"Very well, I—"

The voice cuts him off.

"*Suicide,*" it hisses. "*Soo—iiih—siiide.*"

The first Professor Long's irritation gives way to stark fear, like a cold edge stroking the back of her neck.

"How?"

"Blew out his brains," the voice drawls, seeming to relish the words.

"When?"

Her mind races but even as ice crashes down her back her voice stays even. Do not allow the mockery deflect you: get what you need.

"Last Saturday," the voice says. Starting to get bored, maybe losing interest.

The date is consistent with the last communication from the second Professor Long.

"When is the funeral?" the first Professor Long asks.

"The *what?*" the voice asks, sounding disgusted.

"The funeral," the first Professor Long says.

The party noises surge. It sounds as though everyone were greeting a popular guest, cheering.

"You want to leave a message for Professor Long? Get a ouija board asshole."

Click. The first Professor Long immediately redials the number and gets a busy signal, tries again and the phone rings and rings, tries again and a woman answers, identifying the number as that of the social studies department and claiming to have no idea what has become of Professor Long, who hasn't been on campus all week and yes of course she will leave a message and actually she will pass word on to Professor Clark, who knows Professor Long personally, and the background is silent.

*

The late Professor Long was found holding a business

card in his left hand. On it was printed the word: **JOKE**. The card had been his. After the third or fourth time one of his witticisms went horribly wrong, he made this card and would lift it into plain view when making a joke, to avoid misunderstandings.

His right hand was empty now. The gun had apparently been retained in his grip for a while, but by the time he was discovered, it had fallen to the floor, and lay next to the wheels of the desk chair he was slumped in.

Malthus' *Essay on the Principle of Population* stopped the red bullet. Perhaps some of the late Professor Long's brain, clinging to it, had gotten lodged there as well; a sort of micro-hell for it.

There were powder burns around the wound. His bandages had been torn off and flung into a corner.

Professor Clark takes charge of arranging the late Professor Long's affairs. Apparently, there was something between them not consistent with the Third Oath. She finds a scribbled will in a heap of papers, dated a few years ago and indicating that he wished to be cremated. Professor Clark finds the *Animal Money* files on the late Professor Long's computer in a folder called LAMINA.

"I name it backwards so the devil can't find it," the late Professor Long had said to her once, holding up his **JOKE** card. Almost all his files had reversed names. IBALLYS. STUODNAH.

Professor Clark emails the contents of the folder to the group, along with several other documents the late Professor Long was working on recently.

"He always had this tendency or need to disappear, to withdraw, to escape," she says. "It was difficult, impossible to have a relationship, an affair with him. He was never *there*. He was never completely there. There always was a part of him missing."

The remaining Professor Long is looking at Professor Clark's faculty photograph on the department website. She shudders as, scrolling down, she sees the late Professor Long's face, one of the few candid photos in the column, and caught in the act of turning away from the camera. Of course, he might just as probably be turning toward the camera, but she can't help but see him turning to go, in silence.

"He didn't seem unhappy," Professor Clark is saying. "Depressed. He was always somewhat melancholy, a little morose. He got chapfallen easily. He was so sensitive, labile, vulnerable."

Professor Clark abruptly stops.

"He was remote," the remaining Professor Long says finally. "I thought nothing affected him ..."

"Oh no, no," Professor Clark says sorrowfully. "No, everything affected him. He just couldn't reach back, or he wouldn't."

The remaining Professor Long refuses to leave her apartment in the faculty housing facility. Professor Aughbui plunges into research, spending as much time as possible in the university libraries and churning out page after page of documentation and charts, determined to finish his section of the book. Professor Crest pursues one fruitless line of investigation after another, trying to determine with whom she had been speaking during that obnoxious phone call, grilling Professor Clark and the late Professor Long's various acquaintances, even his doctor—perhaps he had killed himself to escape the debilitating effects of a fatal, incurable disease. Only Professor Budshah carries on more or less as normal.

"He always struck me as having an air of the sacrificial lamb about him," he thinks, moments after he is first told the news. Saddened, but not surprised, he somberly answers Professor Aughbui's incessant stream of emails, all heavily laden with data and charts and containing no personal touch of any kind. Professor Budshah's bitter unflappability has a calming effect on the other survivors. He reports grimly to his editor that the book is coming along steadily, that the manuscript will be completed more or less on time, that the late Professor Long's contributions were already almost fully incorporated into the project—although his writing was as pithy as a sequence of aphorisms.

"The book is to be dedicated to Professor Vincent Long, indispensable colleague and treasured friend."

Glancing away from his computer screen a moment, out of the corner of his left eye he sees it again, the snowy point of light out there in space, peering through his window. His inner start of alarm is quelled before it can ruffle his surface. Setting his teeth, he types a few more lines, then gets up to go to the bathroom, which has no windows. He stands at the center of the bathroom floor with folded arms, head lowered on his breast, thinking it over.

Whether or not the experiment is producing or is in some other way related to events currently shaking the foundations of capitalism is still impossible to say. The global economy is destroying the world; steal it all and then charge your victims for the service, abandon humanity and save the financial institutions. However, if some well-heeled capitalists, the lords of the Replicate, had somehow found out about the experiment, and understood it, might they have sent their killers to stop us doing anything like that again? Could we do it again now, without the late Professor Long?

Of course, we can repeat it, Professor Budshah tells himself. The late Professor Long was difficult to understand, and frankly unclear at times—even radically so—but his contribution was and remains concrete enough. If he did die as a consequence of his involvement with experiment X13, then let it not be for nothing. Let's hope that what we see unfolding is in some measure a consequence of what we created in the biology lab that night.

Unaware of his death, Assiyeh interprets the late Professor Long's silence for loss of interest.

She walks on, a few dozen paces away from the spot where this realization fell on her, crossing the dark, slowing once she has found cover among the perfectly black dimensional flakes that hang here like huge wind chimes. She is not aware of being watched or even seen, but she takes no chances. Now she turns to the dark pond, shimmering with motes of blackness through the thick flakes, the gently flexing tracheae and the vast tattered tarps of deeper darkness.

She waves her right hand.

"Hel-lo," she calls softly.

She drops her right hand and waves her left hand.

"Bye Bye."

...

"Hel-lo ..."
"Bye Bye ..."

*

The late Professor Long is dead. Dust off "he was always" and "there seemed to be something [blank] about him." Talk about it. Don't talk about it. Talk without saying. Dead is no word. The late Professor Long now designates a fixed image with a closed history ending in a period: the hole in his head. Draw an analogy between bullet holes and punctuation marks. If no one examines it too closely—and who wants to?—the neatness of the analogy can be passed off as finalness, and everyone can bear off that neat bit of mental legerdemain like a pretended answer.

"He always was a little elusive. He didn't hang around. He retired a lot. You would see him just sort of go by in a flash. And even when he was there, there was still a part of him that wasn't. I mean you could tell he was kind of listening into his interior all the time."
"Like he was under remote control."
"Just so, remote control from another dimension. There was something not-of-this-Earth around him."
"He was making forays, short forays into this one."
"As if he could only remain with us for short times."
"Yes! Before the tether drew him back."
It's like a game; who can hit on the best impression of the late Professor Long?
"So," Professor Budshah says, separating his palms and bringing them back together again with a soft clap, "Perhaps all this shuttling back and forth was getting to him."

It's clear that he finds the whole topic distastefully intrusive.

"He was impulsive," Professor Aughbui says. "That was his trouble."

"If it were the act of a moment," Professor Crest says, "then that would explain the absence of a note."

"You said it seemed he was under ..." the remaining Professor Long says. "Remember his outburst in ...?"

"That was just nerves or something."

"In one voice he said, 'go on our instrument,' then he said 'I'm not your instrument' in his ordinary voice," the remaining Professor Long says.

"It is possible to induce suicide," Professor Crest says.

The professors absorb this idea without emotion. Each adopts their own characteristic thoughtful face and thoughtful posture, fruitlessly trying to connect themselves in some directly perceptible way to assassination in an attempt to achieve real fright.

"I still think he chose that other world," Professor Crest says after a pause. "I would bet he wanted to get there, and stay. But for our own safety we do have to act on the assumption that he was eliminated."

There's no point in discussing the obvious. And, as the remaining Professor Long reflects, everyone is already on a hit list now.

The electoral committee has announced the election results. Neither party has been able to generate the constitutionally-mandated minimum number of votes, necessitating a run-off election next month. The gathering forces of violence and disruption, ominous in ratio with their lack of anything to do, suddenly fall neatly back into the familiar arrangement of electioneering. Tensions do not slacken, but affirm for the time being that they will continue to wind up the springs of the legal machinery, and the effect is much like relief. Neither party wastes a second, immediately resuming the speechifying and advertising, each accusing the other of attempting to steal the election.

Professor Budshah pushes away from the desk and rubs the back of his neck, then looks around at the spacious darkness of the university library. It is after hours. The library is closed, but he has a key. Professor Budshah lives here, bathing in the gymnasium, sleeping at random in unoccupied dorm rooms. Having virtually no possessions to speak of, he can easily shift himself from place to place. He keeps some of his few belongings in a free tote bag he received at the sixteenth annual international economics conference for being able to identify the Flying Lizards' cover of "Money" after hearing only the first second of it. The rest he stores in a locker. The locker contains a few dried flowers, a stack of photographs, three or four stones, a jacket, a necktie, and so on. He banks a fraction of his salary for his own use and sends the major part of it back home to his aged mother and two sisters, one of whom is a widow. Living this way is both more and less real than what seems to be the norm for other faculty. On the one hand, he is dizzyingly free from debts, mortgages, car payments and so on. When he hears his colleagues grumbling over their financial woes, he feels like the swain marvelling at contrivance. On the other hand, there is no privateness cushioning him in the world, so he is right up against the homeless darkness and chance. Thinking about the late Professor Long, Professor Budshah imagines him somehow still existing "out there" in absolute darkness and absolute chance, having achieved absolute homelessness.

*

You aren't in a hurry, are you?

Do I seem like someone in a hurry?

If I must go into detail like this, you understand, it's something that will clarify itself later on.

Have I asked you for any excuses?

I'm not making excuses, I'm simply—

You're telling us about animal money, specifically who gave you the idea.

There was no specific person who gave us the idea. As I've been explaining, the idea just happened.

Like the rain?

Well, yes—

Rain falls on everyone, but not everyone gets the idea of animal money. That happened to you, and why is the question. Why you?

I don't know.

Who selected you?

No one did.

Then why you?

I don't know, I tell you.

Well ... Let's pause for a moment, eh? I don't think we have to make such a chore out of all this. You're intelligent ... educated ... You read a lot, don't you? Like to read?

Well, sure ...

Sure you do. You like to read. You like to read and think and speculate about the nature of things, about reality, about history ... So, speculate with me now about animal money.

All right—if you like—

I like.

Well, you see, it's no challenge getting into the cemetery after hours. Having made it to the mausoleum unnoticed, she slips inside to the sunken chamber, the sun peering directly in through one of the skylights, sending a shaft of light right across the floor. It so lies that it comes between Assiyeh and the wall of drawers, obscuring them. The device reproduces exactly the wavelength of the searchlight emanating from Saturn. She sets it on one of the stone benches directly before her parents and plays its dim radiance over the doors. Another device, synced with the first, detects and sifts the arbitrarily diverse chorus of the departed, gushing from the graves in a serene cataract that braids numberless different colored skeins together. Suddenly the prismatic shimmer of her parents' song rises stark and clear out of that colossally expanding, celestially decomposing chord, that undulates with staggered breathing. Assiyeh looks up and sees her father sitting slumped on a bench in a scalloped alcove opposite her, half obscured by the beam of sunlight which lies between them like a collapsed ceiling timber.

Naked, with only some drapery across his lap, he now has the flat, brawny body of a monumental statue; his bald head droops forward and the spume of a beard he never had in life lies on his chest in a motionless crawl.

Her mother is there, too, standing off to one side, erect, stiff as a column, in a petrified gown that extends from her chin to the floor in a slightly curving line from the shoulders, much taller, the head apparently crowned with a wreath.

"*Ass-i-yeh.*"

Their voices are hollow, coming more from the fabric of the tomb and the stale air than from their sealed lips and obscured faces.

"*Daugh-ter.*"

These are spectres stepped half a pace out from the lead doors of the joyless and silent house of Hades to speak from within its unbreathing jaws like an Emperor and an Empress steeped and smoking in a haze of grey lifelessness.

"*Our Daugh-ter.*"

Assiyeh cannot cross the sunbeam and can barely make out their dull eyes and expressionless faces through its glare, which rebounds diffusely from the pale flagstones of the floor as a honey colored radiance. The doors of her parents' tomb-drawers shine with the leprous silvery pallor from Saturn, unmerged with the other light and color.

"*Have You Contin-Ued The Experi-Ments?*"

There's a flutter now in their voice that rattles and booms like an organ's inaudibly deep notes. The sound presses uncomfortably against her diaphragm. Threads of grey appear in her hair, and lines deepen to either side of her mouth.

"Yes," she says. "But I am hampered by lack of money, and by being forced to work alone."

"*Get Mar-Ried*," the voice says.

"... I have no prospects. I need your assistance to make further progress."

It's hopeless. Contact with these spirits is stifling, intolerable; every memory, every error, every wretchedly laughable incident in her life is playing itself out at once under their blind gaze from the other side of the shaft of sun. She snaps off the Saturn radiator. Immediately the two figures become wan, the voice loses force.

"*Mar-Ry*," it says, already diminished to a rumble, like a mountain sighing underground. "*Breed.*

"—*Breeeeeed ...*"

The beam of light has slimmed by half, and the growing dimness has compensated for the thinning out of the two spirits, desaturated film images in tobacco smoke.

"My parents," she thinks.

There, lay down the pen before it goes on too long. Cap it first, then lay it down. Take the hand away and look at the pen lying at angle, resting on two points, one at each end, the rest suspended asymmetrically across the turning groove between pages. The image and the character dim and fade like the plaintive anthem and spread like the reverberation after music. When, a miraculously brief eighteen months later, *Animal Money* is published by Lazy Fascist Press, it is ignored. No reviews, no sales, no availability, although the IEI purchases review copies as a matter of course. The remaining Professor Long sweeps the internet regularly, spending her days off glued to the computer—nothing. Professor Budshah sighs philosophically once a day. Professor Aughbui is making modifications to Smilebot, programming a computer simulation based on meticulous measurements and other data from the scene of the late Professor Long's death. Professor Crest follows Professor Aughbui's simulations and methodically pursues his own investigation, while Uhuyjhns have detected Assiyeh's experiments with absolute rest and have come to earth via continuity suspension apertures.

Protesters are clashing with police in Mexico City; the powerful drug gangs act as paramilitary death squads propping up police and state by killing and intimidating protesters. Key protest leaders have been arrested on transparently false drug charges and are used as hostages. For their part, the protesters have organized themselves into cells, some of which are decoys for suspected informants. In minutes a fashionably empty street in a posh neighborhood is thronged with thousands of roaring protesters who storm the houses of financiers and government officials, epoxying every exposed surface inside and out with posters, placards, notices, banners. The smell of rubber cement becomes one of the symptoms of political resistance, and people can be arrested for carrying glue. Two priests are found hanging from a tree in Puebla, others receive impaled votive images and figurines in their mailboxes with return address: the serviceable platoons of the Misled.

Ten days after the publication of *Animal Money* and a little more than twenty seconds after Professor Budshah's daily sigh, the remaining Professor Long receives an email in Spanish from someone identifying himself as Esechaco Carbonel and locating himself in La Paz, who claims to have read *Animal Money* in its Spanish translation.

The email is brief, asking politely for clarification of a few terms which appear to have become blurred in the change of languages, and including a bulleted list of six perceptive questions about the book. Esechaco Carbonel says he approaches the remaining Professor Long because he is under the impression that she heads the group of economists. She commences her reply without knowing what else to do at first, then forwards the email to the other surviving economists right away— Spanish translation? Nobody told her anything about any translation. And their names were not supposed to be listed on the book at all. Professor Budshah passes the inquiry on to the publisher, but gets no reply. The group answers the questions, sending these directly to this Esechacho Carbonel and asking him how he came to have a Spanish translation of *Animal Money*. He answers that he simply downloaded it from a website that was providing the book for free, as per their directions. The url turns out to be a placeholder page.

Within hours of the receipt of the first message, Professor Aughbui receives an email from an Indonesian service provider and signed with the single name Lastri, who evidently elected to approach him because his name was listed first on the title page. His name on the title page?! She cites a long passage from page 215 of *Animal Money*, in which she underlines all occasions she can find in which non-verbs are used as verbs:

They <u>money</u> themselves by spells, and aggregate. They <u>modern</u> it, which <u>financials</u>, in accounts or in language, a Magical objective; commodity forms the Magical words of the adept with accounts; the institutional phenomena purpose is Gardens: power to cast in art the *is*, nature, act I. The money language-primary is differentiated to <u>purpose</u> what, by language systems, aggregates to magical incantation: "golden that is, that or words potential, [M2] deposit (most ways) is A" [Harbin, pg 63]. The inviolate argues instruments. Magic is sacred to results, but as that is to their "*the is.*" Much that spirits <u>world</u> of magic in fiat comes without form of it; personal phrases personalize that, and instruments. Magic, as by religious extension, is as C, focused nature [1], money [4]. Something where being/purchasing is currency of ordinary words, different therefore also even into views, or <u>financialing</u> the conventionally a-magical into 'can-witch Magic,' with extension private, "in secrecy [3]." Made modernable and with the respect, magic isolation enables art. Yet these, even his, although it phrases incantation, [M1] money (or art currency), those money magics are entirely a-financial: the particularity is as forces/power [17]. As physical phrases can, so can the practitioners. The Gardens and Sacred forms consist in emotions; the use of word types or values in, on, or by cultural time-ritual, will <u>scientific</u> the Tambiah Magical of-of demand. The magical magic of demand is on the supply side. The desired of the two and the context is this: **that magic Only—that larger performance**. Most of a be-language is C phrases. The different utilizes that which is done, without casting among spells cultural or scientific supply; the function yields a magic, other tender; one suggests the language, or [M3], is remarkable, and commodity, a reality [18] that [M3] can

K in potential that country, or that age. For other uses than that, performance limited money in value, constructing certain ofs by first consisting of markets which were money. Language-Magic must take all chants, measure distinct results on agencies, communications [24]. Knowledge [M2] is categories, only words and services. Money, as successive monetary flows of still states, commonly is viewed scientifically as spirits of liquid forms: his own market and result-meanings being words and an entirely new language Magic by the cultures, blessings, in the disjunction-state or in the state of purpose-commodity which distinguishes an-institutional time spells.

"If you have the time, would you be willing to explain this a little further?" Lastri asks politely. The reply isn't half finished before Professor Aughbui hears from the remaining Professor Long that she has been contacted by someone from Lagos with similar questions. Professor Budshah receives an email from Cairo not long after that, followed almost immediately by one from Tblisi. This latter is written in German and includes extracts from "*Tiergeld.*" Professor Crest seems to have attracted the least attention of the four. Only one email—an incomprehensible jumble of verbiage and text-speak originating in Burbank, California, reaches him. *Animal Money* has burrowed its own way out, evidently, distributing itself much as it first presented itself, and it is and isn't a hit. No money for its authors, but, as Professor Aughbui plots the email messages on a map and runs a time simulation, comment on the book ripples across the globe in longitudinal waves with no particular point of origin. He updates the simulation every hour; the commentary activity moves to and fro in long steady gusts, like sedentary respiration.

Dark economists. This ominous phrase is starting to crop up now in connection with their names. Much is made of those sections written by the late Professor Long, in which he maintains that animal money, in causing the mysterious disappearance of values, is transmigrative, and that the exchange of disappearances generates negative traces, that is, blanks, which are the real matter of animal money. As old currency was backed by gold, animal money is backed by these "blanks," which are objective perforations in reality. They aren't anything that can be held in the hand, like a piece of metal, but they are nevertheless "concrete suspensions of continuity" which are valued as gold was valued, for their immutability. In vain did Professor Aughbui object that this constituted an inversion of the gold model, in which the valued commodity is the basis for symbolic currency; instead, this conception turns the exchange currency into the means of production for a thing of value that, he maintains, cannot be considered a genuine commodity.

Professor Crest creates three transparent overlays for a global map. The first indicates the locations of all those who have contacted them with questions about the book, the second shows locations of interesting current events, and the third represents a likely proliferation pattern of the effects of experiment X13.

"From these results," he says, "We may infer that the late Professor Long introduced a secondary contamination once in North America."

*

An email from Professor Crest.

"This was just sent to me," he writes.

The attachment is a photograph. It shows a man sitting slumped in a high-backed desk chair, his shoulders down nearly to the armrests, his head listing forward, frozen stiff in a droop. The picture was taken at a point roughly four feet off the floor, just to the right of the chair. The edge of a desk or table protrudes into the picture. The whole image is slightly obscure. The grating of lowered venetian blinds diffuses its radiance through the room, backlighting the dim man. There is a neat black hole in his right temple, fringed with a few dark streaks. His elbows propped on the armrests, his hands droop into his lap. The left hand is holding a card with **JOKE** printed on it. Apart from the bullet hole, there is no indication that the late Professor Long isn't living. His grey features are half-melted into dark. The eyes are hooded but ajar. The eyebrows are slightly raised, and the lips are parted and wry, as if he were in the middle of a dry joke. He looks a little like a quietly philosophical drunk.

"See fellas? No big deal, death. Happens all the time. Will happen to you too."

It's easy to imagine him putting the gun to his head and pulling the trigger.

It's easy to imagine him so lost in ruminations of that kind—he always did have his head in the clouds—that someone, some living sculpture carved from solid viciousness, could steal upon him unnoticed and shoot him in the head, blasting apart a fine brain whose delicate operations unfold in a way the sculpture is incapable of understanding or concerning itself with. Sculptures like that will never know how little they know. Which particular statue it might have been is not an unimportant question, but who sculpted it? This is a more important question.

The email Professor Crest received consisted of this image and a brief message.

"One down! ... >;)"

*

The late Professor Long dreamt when the bullet dashed through his brain. The dream started the moment the bullet touched the skin of his temple, and ended the moment it burst out the other side of his skull.

It didn't end then, it ended the moment after. There was one additional moment. Wait—

Dreams never begin. Something else becomes a dream a piece at a time, rapidly but not instantly, until it's all dream. Until enough of it is dream, no, no, until it begins to move the way a dream moves, instead of in the way waking thoughts move. Dreams only end when the dreamer wakes up, so dreams don't actually end, not of themselves, but the dreamer leaves them. They get interrupted and they stay interrupted until I sleep again and that flowing, gently-insistent wobble takes over. What is really interrupted, the dream, or my idea of what the dream is? All throughout the dream I am constantly understanding, which is one of the ways I know I am not

in waking life, because in waking life I never understand
except when I recognize a misunderstanding.

That question doesn't point anywhere interesting
looking from here. The more attractive question now is
this: what happens to the dream if the dreamer is blown
out from under the dream?

In the late Professor Long's final dream, the dream
triggered by the bullet as it made its lethal dash through
his brain, he is back home. He isn't back home, he's in a
neverending house he's never seen before, and which has
been retroactively designated his "childhood home"—
who by?—He had no such thing, he was raised in a series
of California apartments and his parents moved many
times—and now it is "his own" family home. He's a
lifelong childless bachelor. This is his family home. What
is the inconsistency?

It doesn't feel like coming home. It's like coming home
to find everything disappointingly altered and disagreeing
with the memory. Memories he can't account for and
that he can't differentiate from his dream understanding
of everything. The room is tall, has no windows, with
skylights. The walls are painted a dark, mottled red. Black
columns in each corner, the floor is a chessboard, ferns
and rubber plants in huge pots wave in air conditioning,
the furniture is uncomfortable straightbacked Victorian
stuff, burgundy upholstered sofa, a slouching pouf.
What's this got to do with animal money? This doesn't
have anything to do with animal money. It has everything
to do with animal money. I don't know how it does, but I
am certain *that* it does. Qualities, is what all these are. I go
up to the wall nearest me. There are mirrors, small hand

mirrors, mounted to the wall in a random archipelago. All the mirrors in the house are small and mounted in scatters like this; you never can manage to see your whole face at once, not even in the bathroom.

I'm having hallucinations. I'm not having hallucinations—the house is haunted. There are rooms that aren't safe, that will drive me insane if I go into them, inducing a special insanity forever, not forever, only for as long as I stay in those rooms, but what happens once will happen again. I can never be sure, after that; I won't have the chance, I won't, once insane in that way, want to leave those rooms. There are trapped rooms. The traps move around, so there aren't trapped rooms there are roving room traps. I have to watch for the tell. I don't know what it would be. Most often it's the image of an animal. A coiling white snakelike dog in a painting, there before the feet of the gathered hunters and their horses, their bags heavy with game, heads and tails protruding from sacks, bright plumage like gleaming gems in the dark casket of the painting. The dog's eyes are like blisters, glistening and black; it snarls down at the earth with lips faintly tinged with pink, baring yellow fangs, arching its back. Don't go in there. Someone is talking to me. A woman from the village, speaking in her flat, nasal, quotidian voice as she walks quickly across the room behind him:

"They always get us in here with these high anxiety _____s, but it ain't hard to talk them down to our level and they know there's nothing we can do about them. You want to try to get this done in the next hour and a half."

I couldn't make out that one word. She seems to be

talking cavalierly about the householders, and about "us."

Some time in the past, somebody told me something about the two forces, meaning two forces at work here, and how you have to balance the two forces to keep from coming to the bad ending. No one has ever told me anything about this. I have a pamphlet, like a Chick tract. The cover image, long and narrow, shows a drawing of a grave with a rounded headstone and a caption underneath it that reads IT SHOULD HAVE BEEN YOU, and inside there are images of funerals and coffins and graves, and cartoon images of me suffering.

I showed *them!*

The safe room has a big mirror in it. The monster can't go into a place where it has seen itself feed: the monster has a charred-looking living second face burned into its chest, which vacuously gnaws the flesh around it and drinks the blood that trickles out, its own blood. I've never seen this monster. There may be more than one. It's possible to see through the house without leaving the room by looking mirror to mirror. I seek out a private one, that is, a mirror I can peek into without being noticed.

I see Assiyeh wiping steam off the mirror, water spilling from her hair. Not this mirror, another mirror, looking over her bare shoulder. She turns to me, away from the mirror and stands facing me through the wall. Her waist is narrow, very narrow, it tapers, set into wide hips, wide but lean. Seen from the front, she looks like a guitar. Seen from the front, she looks like a centaur. She turned, but not to me. She is drying her hair, pressing the water out against her skull into the towel wrapped around her hand. Each press draws the skin tight across her face, pulls her mouth back a little, and she is looking up toward the ceiling, toward the corner of the room, the wall not the ceiling, not at anything, vacancy. She's not vacant, the field of vision ... is not vacant, what vacancy, for who, for whom?

He is turning into mist and smoke—he can't tell her anything. She can't hear him. He keeps on asking one question after another and there's no sound, no feeling of breath or diaphragm or jaws, just a static outline that can only move as a single piece like a slide projection, and he doesn't want to ask questions, he wants to explain something but it's difficult now to know what that is, he might need to explain it to himself first, but what comes out of him, the words, are all hapless questions, who am I where am I what am I, that never can be really answered. She is rubbing the towel over her head with both hands. A black hole is descending silently toward him.

*

Well? Go on.

Well ... you see, they are her parents; they are not mischievous folkloric impostor spirits having a laugh at her expense. It's not that they aren't like themselves. Um. They are and they aren't. These ghosts have none of the mischievous force of life; they are like amplified versions of imposing family portraits, not brought to life, but acting anyway as lifeless imperial effigies. When death cuts the thongs, the various souls all go their own ways.

Now.

... Assiyeh has determined ... no, she thinks ... that

the more vital spirits of her parents are likely to be still circulating in the Earth's atmosphere. Under constant acceleration they zoom faster and faster until they zoom clear of the planet. ... To ... to catch them ... Not just any matter can decelerate and snare a spirit; some matter is tackier, more woolly, sometimes in its essence and sometimes accidentally. When a spirit is trapped ... she thinks ... she speculates ... it may circulate at high speed throughout all the adjoining matter. ... So the ghost may be likened to a high frequency current that runs through a significant proportion of the matter of the Earth, with ... the scene of its death, or whatever place it haunts, acting as a kind of capacitor or booster. Like a relay. The circuit is tapped by applying to it the same fields Assiyeh has been using in her experiments to produce absolute rest. She can slow the spirits until they become visible and ... collect in one place, translating them from the metaphorical electric condition to a self-contained and self-motivated individual circuit. ... In short, a person.

Assiyeh needs to ground her field in telluric forces. She goes to a hotel in the mountains that features, as one of its attractions, rooms with transparent floors built directly over gaping mine shafts. Getting out of bed, you swing your feet down still half asleep and then leap back in terror at the abyss telescoping beneath you. Realizing that the bed is resting on top of the pit as well gives you a weird feeling. A combination of the comfort and security of a cozy bed, and panic terror.

Now, Assiyeh chose this hotel because of these shafts. They allow her to conjure the majestic ghosts of the underworld with all their awesome decorum.

Focussing her collectors on the Saturn beam, Assiyeh is able to recouple her link to the statelier ghosts of her parents, who become dimly visible onscreen, thanks to the camera Assiyeh concealed in the tomb. ... She has a remote camera there, and is watching the inside of the mausoleum, looking at her parents' ghosts on TV. Now she fires up her Rest Generator. ... It runs off a power plant she parked right outside the room, in a big truck, cables run through the window.

... Assiyeh sifts the air currents through the skylight with an array of amber combs, trying to gather enough parental particles for a reconstitution. After forty minutes, she materializes an arm of bright red smoke that ricochets around the room in complete silence, then dissolves again.

... For a minute fifty-one seconds Assiyeh watches the workings of an invisible face pressed into the bedclothes.

After four hours, Assiyeh resignedly shuts down her equipment. The sun is up, the morning is bright. Another failure. Assiyeh walks out into the empty corridor— it's the off season, and she is virtually the hotel's only customer—and heads for the patio, which overlooks a spacious valley and tall mountains clear and limpid on the far side.

The patio is deserted. She sits at a table and reviews her notes, without noticing the sky's blue brilliance or so much as glancing at the three or four enormous clouds floating in it. Only when a gust of wind bounds up out of the calm and flips a page from under her eyes, and she lunges to pin it down with her palm, does she happen to lift her eyes to the sky. Directly before her, high over the valley, a single cloud shines, a confection of impossibly pure light, its flank is like a snow-covered mountain slope and someone is descending it in little bounds. Assiyeh rises to her feet staring at something that nods and flashes as it strides down the cloud, pale, translucent and very far away, not as white as the cloud, bulbous, and something on its surface is very reflective, catching sunlight it winks painful darts of light into her eyes. It undulates aside as if it were avoiding some obstacle, and Assiyeh sees a flourish of what looks like pink taffeta—it resembles the central figure in Bokelman's *Casino*.

The thing turns and it looks nothing like the central figure in Bokelman's *Casino*, it looks like something from a coral reef, a partially transparent globular ambling slug or worm nodding impressively and picking its footing like a mincing fat man. The legs are pliable, rounded cones. The body has a floating tissue mantle that undulates, leans, pools, and oozes like a weak flame.

Down the side of the cloud it walks, finally vanishing behind one of its folds. Assiyeh watches the cloud until it disappears over the horizon, and meanwhile the remaining Professor Long is returning to her office, which is situated in one corner of the botanical garden behind the imposing cream-colored gateau-like cube that houses the Department of Botany. The Department and the garden are not on the main campus of Achrizoguayla University, but occupy a site not far from the location of the original school, close to the center of San Toribio. To reach this office of hers, she must make her way through a knee-high maze of thin, dusty white lanes pivoting among shrubs and exotic plants with Latin tags.

The plants are organized in some technical way, so that the distinctively Chinese specimens are mixed in with everything else. She visited these expatriate and transplant plants with reluctance because she felt in their presence a depressing obligation to exert her imagination in a fizzling effort to touch home again through them. The plants themselves seemed to resent her, and chide her as she turned away in confusion. More than once, though, she laughed, because she had discovered too late that the tree or shrub she had been pouring attention into like a crystal ball was actually not Chinese—she'd misread the label, or attributed the label on one plant to another by mistake. Relief washing over her then, she would laugh. She knew nothing about plants; she could just about distinguish pine trees, although they were often cedars. However, when Professor Cladodi, the department chair, a petite, wildly curvy, copper-colored woman of about her own age, showed her personally to her new office, she was delighted to find it in the frondy shadiness of the garden. Nearby, there was a small greenhouse where butterflies were cultivated, and she liked the oddly sour musky odor of the bare soil. There were many fragrant flowers besides, and a peppery smell of leaves baking in the sun, all very pleasant. She liked to take breaks in the garden, and to press her hands against the trunks of the big trees.

"It's drinking," she would think.

Or, "It's asleep."

Or, "This one has suffered."

Or, "It's concentrating."

Her office is less satisfactory than the garden; an

octagonal wooden pavilion roughly six meters across opposite angles, rising on a high stone foundation. All the paint is long gone, if there had ever been paint; the exposed wood is grey, bone dry, and full of splinters. It has an overhanging pyramidal roof and a single door; the rest of it is shutters, a fact that the remaining Professor Long would not accept until she had circumnavigated the building three times. The entire outer skin is nothing but a concatenation of louvered shutters. When they are all open, the pavilion is like a Moroccan tin lamp with the punched tabs bent outward. Within, there is, rising from the region of the center of the floor, an octagonal plug of solid stone about four feet high, which might have been a font or the pillar support for a wooden podium or perhaps a wooden counter, since removed or never installed. Having placed on it a requisitioned drawing board, the remaining Professor Long uses this plug as a desk. The flat upper surface of the plug is high enough off the ground that she has to perch on top of a stool to use it, with her feet swinging. The pavilion had been left to rot for years; the refurbishments are effective but strange. There are discordantly blonde bits of lumber patching openings, reinforcing joints, and so on. For a light source, they installed a chandelier so enormous that the first Professor Long finds herself virtually among its dangling baubles when she sits at her stone plug. She has to hunch down to fit under it, and even then some of the glass ornaments lie along her shoulders. In the evenings, returning to the pavilion after a stroll in the garden, it looks like a furnace inside a beehive, sending brilliant shafts of light out through the slats of the shutters.

There's a small cabinet built into a post inside the pavilion, which has to serve in lieu of desk drawers. Now she goes to it and pulls out the congratulatory box of fancy cigars her old friend Dai-Mei sent her. It seems wrong to smoke them now, although she is not exactly in mourning, but on the other hand she feels a nagging, not particularly intelligent obligation to justify the trouble and expense Dai-Mei must have gone through to arrange for their delivery. As long as she has them, she will also have the duty to smoke them, so she would rather smoke them now and get it over with. Fortunately, there are only five. But they are very big cigars. Green ones. At least, the wrapper is green. Inside, brown as any. She had always liked cigars, even very large ones; the difficulty lay in her being required to report back truthfully on the quality of these very fancy cigars, and to give her friend the impression, truthful or not, that she found them at least adequately delicious. They actually were delicious, but having to draft a detailed report of their special delicacy was pesky. Now she withdraws one of the cigars, which is wrapped in paper, cuts off the end with a pair of shears and takes it outside to light it.

Sitting outside in the gathering dusk of Achrizoguayla, she can hear music from over the wall. There are what might be luxury apartments or perhaps hotels on the far side, and it's easy to look over into the swimming pools far below, where petite, wildly curvy women languidly elongate and then pivot to become glistening points, the decelerated kicking feet wavering vaguely beneath. Each puff she takes is different. The first is disgusting. The next one shocking. The third smooth and bitter. The fourth is buttery and thinly sweet. Scalp tight and skin clammy, she feels her interior regions sink beneath the purely mechanical calm of the nicotine. The palaces rise up around her in fancy, the mountains and the gardens. She leaves the cigar on the stone bench to go out on its own, and goes down to the butterfly greenhouse, which looks spectral and still and almost false, like a diorama. Further down, down the lanes in the shade in the dark, to the bottom of the park where the path loops around at the base of the wall and from time to time you can hear the calling of the peacocks from somewhere nearby. Around her in the dark a fantasy homeland lifts. What she imagines are big buildings shaped like fat torpedoes, clustered together and ornamented with thick lines and bulbs or baubles, like gingerbread men, all blue with indigo shadows in dusk, a magic place that she belongs to, but that belongs to nobody, just to itself, a place she's never been but that's always with her in as many different shapes and looks as moments of her looking. She ascends the path up to the top of the slope. Off to her right is the Botany Department, and then the garden stretching around in front of it, and then the long facade of a palatial old building currently being renovated for student housing. Three stories, a flat facade with an imposing entrance on one side, and many ground-level French doors on the side facing the Botany Department. Out of sight, and beyond, is one of the two buildings belonging to the Auxiliary Economics Institute. Off to her left, standing opposite the future student housing across a broad gravel drive with a distant gate to the street, is a converted manor house now belonging to the

Faculty of Applied Sciences. Thick torpedoes, waving forests of stone spires, a pterodactyl and naked wildly curvy rider glide under the moon, and she suddenly is paralyzed, her whole body inexplicable abrupt rigid with something like electric current petrifying her all because she saw Assiyeh's face in the window up there, framed like an image in a postage stamp, looking casually out toward the panoply of San Toribio, blinking, apparently not noticing the remaining Professor Long, and without a light, but her face and her fingertips in the dark window of the converted manor house now belonging to the Faculty of Applied Sciences.

*

INTERVIEWER: Now, you've recently gotten interested in animal money.

Right.

INTERVIEWER: ... What the hell is animal money?

(audience laughter 0.4)

Well, yeah, it's a little tricky to explain. Suppose an earthquake splits the sea bottom beneath a drilling platform. The platform explodes. Oil floods the ocean. A tidal wave of water and oil inundates the Gulf of Mexico just ahead of a colossal hurricane that seeds tornadoes as far as the Pacific. Owing to the end of conscription and a chronic shortage of soldiers, the military will take anyone. Weapons disappear from bases and depots and turn up in the hands of militias and gangs, made up increasingly of trained veterans. Government censors work around the clock, conscientiously deleting from one website after another all the images of smirking soldiers standing over corpses, hands raised in the Hitler salute. Elaborate precautions are taken against the phantom indignation of the Teeming. Now the military are called in to deal with the disaster while photogenic soldiers swim in television from the shore to a rapidly sinking boat, ferrying half-drowned victims back. The cameras capture not only the action on shore but in the water as well, and one soldier actually rescues his estranged wife on camera. The dialogue is especially good today and the lighting couldn't have been better.

—And animal money?

Yes, I'm getting to that. You see, Assiyeh deduces that the deceleration force of her experiment attracted the Uhuyjhn, which is what she calls a "rest-organism." I still haven't figured out what she meant by that—I think she meant that the principles of rest she was researching were somehow metabolically embodied in them.

So, she tries again, right? Tries to bring her parents' vital spirits back. Everything goes wrong. In her brief absence, the hotel management has welded the skylights so she can't get a sight line to the sky; there's a school group staying on the same side of the hotel and they complain about the generator noise to management; the tomb camera keeps losing signal; she can't find the controller for the Saturn machine so she has to detach the console, strip the wires, and make the contacts by hand, kneeling in front of the machine like a geisha playing the koto. Finally, Assiyeh manages to generate a weak rest field. The room is dark, as is the night sky outside. Kneeling on that clear floor—remember, this is above an apparently bottomless pit—she seems to hover in outer space, along with her half-shredded equipment and the incongruously quotidian furnishings of the room, all mysteriously suspended at exactly the same level. The field is murkier than the surrounding air, and laced with almost invisible hairline streaks: these are particles, some from outer space, caught and gently slowed by the field, forming long ethereal cage bars. Every now and then, when she can spare her hands, Assiyeh picks up pad and pen and starts writing, deliberately making the sort of elementary mistakes that her parents could never resist the impulse to correct. At times, it had seemed to her, growing up, that her parents had a sixth sense for her mistakes and appeared as if by magic whenever she did anything requiring their corrections; so, now she is trying to summon them by screwing up on purpose. Assiyeh's hands keep slipping as she manipulates the wires and she loses patience and smashes the machine. The Saturn machine fizzles and she can smell smouldering insulation, but now a corona of wan lights that throb and dim scintillates in the air. They are different colors and each color is associated with a far-off, fluting pitch. The hotel room is suddenly alive with ethereal fragments of human bodies settling like marine snow, afterimages in many dimensions, and the hollow murmurs of strangely incomplete human voices, half-voices speaking isolated phrases. At least, that's how they sound—the words are loud enough, in fact, there are shouts and sudden, deafening pronouncements, but the voices are as muffled as if she were hearing them through a thick wall.

"Aren't we all?" someone says. A woman's voice—her own voice.

A voice says something. Assiyeh hears: "The censor travels by exorcism."

A pair of glasses, just there, like two icy discs of vitriated moonlight. The halting field vibrates apart and the lights flare, flooding the room for one instant with bizarre multicolored incandescence that reveals two blurred and leaping figures. The next moment there is a whoosh of air and a flutter in her ears that sounds like crazed laughter, and at the same time a horrible settling feeling drops massively down on her, a kind of despair, as if she were witnessing the domestication of the last of some noble species of wild animal. She does not notice the blackening and shrinking at her right temple; the flesh vanishes, exposing bones that darken, charred by invisible flames. Then just as quickly the right temple is as it was.

Her father's ghost stands between her and the window. Assiyeh turns on the bedstand light. It is a human shadow, a black void with white teeth exposed in the lipless mouth, and lidless, astonished, glaring eyes that Assiyeh recognizes even without moon-lensed glasses.

*

They caught Professor Aughbui in the toilet stall of a public bathroom. Big men, two of them, bigger in their down jackets. Professor Aughbui's lunch had disagreed with him and he was vomiting over the bowl, trying with all his might to resist the temptation to kneel and soil the knees of his pants.

Panting, he hangs onto the top of the stall partition, then lists to one side and leans against the bathroom wall.

Two men explode into the bathroom with quick heavy steps and the next moment the stall door is torn open and there they are. Professor Aughbui starts back and nearly falls, sliding along the wall.

"Occupied?" the man in the door says. He's got a shaved head. Professor Aughbui can't see the other one's face. Shaved head notes the toilet full of vomit and smiles nastily.

"Looks like he's not feeling too good."

All their haste is gone. Shaved head reaches in casually, grabs Professor Aughbui's left arm and hauls him out of the stall. The other one has a full head of salty black hair and a bushy greying moustache, pouches under his eyes. He punches Professor Aughbui in the aching stomach. Professor Aughbui makes a humiliating sound, "ooooh!"—he contracts around the fist and his glasses fly off and skid across the floor. Moustache spins him around to face the wall and pins his arms, holding his wrists and dragging them up his body, forcing his knee into Professor Aughbui's back and bending his body so that his convulsing abdomen is painfully stretched. A fistfull of toilet paper is roughly wiped across his face, dabbing the strands of puke, the nose runnings and tears. He is wheeled around to face shaved head, who replaces his glasses with brutal delicacy.

"All better?" he asks.

He studies Professor Aughbui insolently for a moment, then swaggers to the door and looks out. He stays there for a minute or two.

"OK," he says, moving immediately into place.

Professor Aughbui is pushed along between them,

the shaved headed one out in front acting as cover. The bathroom opens out onto a narrow side street with a few small shops, all closed. Nobody in sight, or nobody near. The two men lead him to a small blue car and moustache drags him down and into the back seat, shoving him across to the other side while he gets in behind him. The car stinks of rancid cigarette smoke.

Shaved head gets in the driver's seat. The car starts with a cough and they swing out. Moustache has released his wrists.

"Sit on your hands," he says sootily.

Professor Aughbui sits on his hands. The smooth plastic upholstery of the seat is ice cold so that his hands form two warm spots under his thighs. Fast as thought, moustache lights a cigarette. It hangs from his lip dribbling ash from time to time and he sits leaning right on him with his right elbow boring into Professor Aughbui's ribs and the bare knife obscenely there in his left hand, resting on his lap.

"Shut up," he says.

Professor Aughbui hasn't said a word, nor made any sound since they slugged him.

The other man is staring him in the eye, streets kaleidoscoping all around his face.

"You shut up," the man says again. Professor Aughbui feels the stale cigarette mouth words spatting like raindrops against his cheek and across his lips.

After a few glances forward and out the window, the smoker pulls something out of his jacket pocket with his left hand and flips it at Professor Aughbui.

"Put it over your head."

The elbow crushes into him and Professor Aughbui cries. "Put it over your head."

Professor Aughbui puts the sack over his head. He can still see light through the coarse weave, but it's all disassociated pointilism to him. The elbow stays where it is, compressing his lungs, half choking him.

Somehow, Professor Aughbui manages a lucid thought: "It was a mistake to go out without Smilebot."

The men exchange a few terse sentences in a language he doesn't recognize.

Now—how long?—the car jerks to a halt.

"Out."

A painful jab in the ribs.

He gets out and is spun around at once, face to the car, a hand roughly shoving his face down as his hands are wrenched behind his back and bound at the wrist with what feels like a plastic strip. The strip is drawn taut, Professor Aughbui cries again, receives a petulant slap over the head. The strip bites, his bones grate.

"Move."

He is driven forward, one in front and one behind. A dark space, refracted by the weave, zooms unevenly up to him. Their footsteps are now sounding against concrete walls. Scrape of feet on concrete stairs and the clang of a hand, maybe a ring on a finger, against the metal rail. He stumbles up the stairs, pushed from behind and dragged from in front by a fist twisted inside his clothes to get a better purchase.

Up at least four flights and through a door, a metal fire door by the sound of it. Walking on carpet. A turn. The men seem furtive and hasty again. Rattle of keys in a door, then through into a room. He is hauled more roughly now, the furtiveness gone again, thrown into a cold chair and his arms strappadoed over the back so the chair digs into his armpits.

The door closes and locks snap. Sour old cigarette smell, musty carpet smell. Moustache's voice in the next room, level, unintelligible words ... Beep of a cell phone being hung up. Footsteps across the room, shaking the floor, coming toward him.

Shaved head comes up on him and rests one foot on Professor Aughbui's thigh, leaning in with his crotch in Professor Aughbui's face. Moustache strolls around to a battered desk against the wall and sits on its edge.

"All right, who told you?"

He's going to strike, Professor Aughbui thinks, no matter what.

The foot on his leg begins to grind into the flesh. Shaved head angles the toe of his boot around and rests it on Professor Aughbui's groin.

"Who told you?"

"What do you mean?" Professor Aughbui says. His voice is unrecognizeable; tremulous, barely audible.

The foot lifts and drops back suddenly. There's a blast of pain and Professor Aughbui cries out. Shaved head gently lowers his hand onto the top of Professor Aughbui's head.

"You don't shout," he says, tilting Professor Aughbui's head up. "Talk, don't shout. If you shout ..."

He pats his crotch.

"I got something big for your mouth."

"Who told you?" Moustache asks.

"What do you mean?" Professor Aughbui asks.

It takes some time before he understands.

"It came to the group at the same time," he says finally, his face streaming.

"How?"

"When the group were all talking together."

"Was there a different voice?"

"What do you mean?"

"Was there a voice that you didn't recognize when you were all talking together?"

Professor Aughbui tries to remember.

The foot begins to grind, the toe digs into his groin.

"Please stop!" he calls, "It is difficult to remember!"

Moustache says something and shaved head lets up.

"Remember fast," he says.

"It ..." Professor Aughbui's voice catches. There's a spasm of pain in his aching groin and across his leg, and his hands are going numb. Tears spill out of his eyes.

Shaved head plucks off his glasses with a sneer and, lifting his foot, goes across the room to put them on a bricked up mantle. Then he comes back. He picks his moment to settle his foot heavily back exactly in place. Professor Aughbui groans.

"Remember now," Moustache orders.

"It was a different voice," Professor Aughbui says.

"Who did it come from?"

A phone shrills from the next room. Moustache starts at the sound and looks meaningfully at shaved head. The phone shrills again.

Moustache gets up. Into the next room. Shaved head watches him go, looking a little uncertain, but he has his obscene, bully smile back when he lowers his gaze to Professor Aughbui again. Professor Aughbui looks down, trying to look past the leg, the groin, at the nondescript, paper-thin carpet, the abstract line where the wall meets the floor, the big square power plug of the floor lamp. From the next room come barked interrogatives in an uncertain voice. Whoever it was hung up on Moustache. He quietly calls the other one into the next room; the muted sound of their voices stirs an incongruous childhood memory in Professor Aughbui, hearing the grownups talking after he went to bed. He sits there rigid, afraid to relax, yearning to.

A question, series of questions, short, baffled-sounding replies from the second one. Something is wrong. Long pauses. Questions from the second one, tersely and impatiently answered by the first, who is thinking as fast as he can. Finally a decisive tone, a heavy footfall, the whisper of down jacket. A comment in a low voice, two comments, from the first one. What to do with Professor Aughbui. The hall door opens and shuts, footsteps receding in the interval before it closes and dulls the sound. Snick of a lighter. Fresh cigarette smoke.

Steps toward him. From behind him, a wisp of smoke goes sailing by over his head. Professor Aughbui can feel the man a foot or two in back of him. The uneven draw of his own breath as he begins to breathe through his mouth. He can feel what he guesses is an appraising look, battened on him.

Sharp knocking at the door makes him stiffen, take his breath in and hold it. The man behind him turns and goes to it at once. Unable to control himself, Professor

Aughbui turns his head and looks. There's a brief passage, through it he sees the man opening the hall door, then step out into the hall, evidently unable to see who knocked.

He screams and flies backwards through the door, crashing against the jam and tumbling to the ground, his limbs contorted, his whole body wracked with convulsive tension, his scream cut short and toned to a snarling groan. After what could only have been a few seconds, the body goes slack. Smilebot trots into the room and removes its contacts from the man's leg, where they penetrated his jeans. The contacts and wires retract into an opening in its body cavity.

Smilebot trots over to Professor Aughbui and looks up at him.

"Break this, Smilebot," Professor Aughbui says.

Smilebot trots up behind Professor Aughbui and cuts the tough plastic tie with his scissor attachment. Unpinioned, Professor Aughbui's arms whip about in front of him, nearly throwing him forward out of the chair. He gets up, rubbing his wrists and panting. He retrieves his glasses, snatches up Smilebot in his arms, and hurries to the hall door. He's about to run out, but then he thinks twice, sets Smilebot back down.

"Is it safe?"

Smilebot trots to the doorway and peeks around the edge. Then it turns and nods from the waist. Again Professor Aughbui picks up Smilebot and goes out into the hall.

"Do you know where the stairs are?"

Smilebot points.

"Did he take the stairs?"

Smilebot bends at the waist, yes.

Swallowing with difficulty, Professor Aughbui sets off for the elevators. He can't be seen waiting there, watching the numbers climb, then stop, then climb, then stop again, from the stairway door, but he should have shut the door to the room, that was a tip off, shutting it would have bought him some time but now it's too late to go back, and, having come from the only stairway, and not having seen him coming down, and it not having been so much time, this would be the natural place to look, to corner him, the elevator is here, there's a man in it, an older man in a battered suit, looking half dead. Professor Aughbui boards the elevator and they go up three floors, the older man gazing incredulously at Smilebot, which returns his gaze.

The elevator stops again on its way down—on *that* floor. There's nobody waiting—he must have hit the button wrong—there's some kind of commotion coming from the direction of the room. Professor Aughbui leans on the button. The doors sweep languidly closed. With a leisurely slipping loose, the elevator descends toward the lobby. Professor Aughbui steps out. He can see the white glare of the street about forty feet away to his right, past a dingy front desk, across a faded carpet with a generic floral print pattern and a shiny fake leather sofa and a painting of a landscape with a shepherd in it. There are two elevators and the other one is coming down and a man could scamper down those stairs in time and if the desk clerk or the staff are in with them, the desk clerk has just picked up his phone, and if there's someone outside—no other exit. He could go back up but his elevator is already gone.

The carpet muffles his footsteps. He is braced for the sound of the desk clerk's cry to dash over him like icewater, eyes riveted on the floor in front of his feet but he throws a glance at the desk anyway and the clerk isn't facing his direction, is talking casually with one hand resting on the counter.

The white glare of the street has resolved into a field of vivid reliefs and tints. There's a man in a heavy down jacket by the front door, off to the right, smoking, hands in his jeans. The street outside is narrow, no traffic, lined with colorful little cars. Professor Aughbui hears the tinny chime of the elevator arriving in the lobby behind him as he crosses the threshold and onto the sidewalk, turning his back at once in a hard left turn away from the smoking loiterer there and hurrying to the end of the block, breaking into a scurrying run, clutching Smilebot.

*

In the dream, the late Professor Long has taken a special interest in a student, Lucy—did he ever have a student named Lucy? Lucy is frail after a hellish life. This isn't romance. She's gradually drawn herself, step by step, back from the brink of self destruction. At untold cost, she has won a new life. And he helped her, meaningfully. He does love her. He adores her. He wouldn't touch her. But he aches to see her cured.

Lucy has come by his house—a house he's never seen before, never been in—to show him one of her economics papers; the pages are collected in sheaves weirdly cut up with scalloped edges, like windflapped awnings. As he goes through these pages, Lucy drifts through the room, looking at posters on the wall, picking up and examining the many little gimcracks and tiny statuettes, a Russian doll, a Swedish horse. She wanders off, idly exploring. Now he is wandering through the house. He spends a long time trying to prop open a door with a dishrag, and, when that doesn't work, with a towel.

He finds her at last, in a maid's outfit looking at herself in the mantelpiece mirror, and caressing a caulk gun that lies there on the shelf. She picks it up, reverses it, puts the nozzle in her teeth, and, grinning like a maniac, begins to fill her mouth with caulk. Her cheeks steadily bulge. Starting from her head, her eyes are glassy, diseased, possessed, her poisoned face is turning grey green and the leering mouth stretches obscenely. Paralyzed with horror, he can only stare at her. The rescue, all the agonizing effort, the joy of watching the fragile bonds and roots of life restored and slowly growing firm, all being violated. Lucy, with wide, dead eyes, turns to him and suddenly blows out her cheeks like balloons and a segmented stalk of cement bursts from her mouth, stiff, grotesque, and a tiny palpitating hand, like a baby's, protrudes from the very end of it.

The music is all seven by ten. There's a phone ringing somewhere in the department and he answers it. Someone starts speaking. The speaker is mistaking him for some other Professor. Numbly, the late Professor Long goes on listening, not answering. It's already too late to correct the mistake. The faint voice at the line's other end is rasping, and sometimes it warbles. It is rapidly reciting instructions, addressed to that other professor, who is not named but only called Twentyfive.

Twentyfive is to ...

When this is done, Twentyfive will ...

Under no circumstances will Twentyfive ...

The late Professor Long infers from these instructions that this Twentyfive has been programming students and faculty by hypnosis. The line clicks off. He's gripped by sudden fright—did that voice realize it wasn't talking to Twentyfive? Is someone coming to get him now? What if he really is Twentyfive after all, and only a carrier for the hypnotic spell that binds him too? What if there is no real Professor Long?

He sits back down in his chair, swiveling his back to the venetian blinds. And when he wants to move again, he can't. He is paralyzed, completely. Slumped in the chair. A horribly cold feeling bores into his right temple, spreading. A sickening, cold softness covers nearly all of his skull's left side.

Sadness and horror triumph over all. They soar, darkly exulting, overhead, like fireworks that suck color and light out of the sky, and burst in silent grey cascades of nothingness.

*

Professor Aughbui had programmed Smilebot to come and find him should they ever be separated for more than fifteen minutes. It was to that one flash of foresight that he owed his narrow escape. Smilebot tracked him by homing in on a chip in his glasses.

The police. Professor Aughbui had flagged down a cop within a few blocks of the hotel and had led him insistently back; the men were long gone, the door to the room was ajar and they found the plastic hand tie that had been used to bind Professor Aughbui in the bedroom. The desk clerk said the room was vacant. Professor Aughbui couldn't be sure, but he suspected the clerk was not the same one he'd passed on his way out. The police invited him to the station, where he could describe the men and make a report. Not knowing what they would make of the taser, Professor Aughbui did not go into Smilebot's role in his escape.

The press reports and moves on to the riots, the protests, in New York, in Sao Paolo.

"What is most significant," the remaining Professor Long says, "is that they asked you about the *source*."

"They knew about the voices," Professor Aughbui says.

"Conspirators always see conspiracies," the remaining Professor Long says. "Whoever sent those men to get you was assuming we had been put up to the publication of the book by ..."

"You have to report this to the Integrity Committee," Professor Crest says fiercely.

"What shall you do?" Professor Budshah asks.

It all depends on the resources and abilities of whoever sent those two men. Professor Aughbui's address is no secret; he can be watched and followed, his transactions might be monitored. Move to a hotel? Some cheap lodgings in the country? Pay for everything with cash money? Try to raise up a scandal in the press and take refuge in the spotlight? Go to stay with one of the other economists? Vanish? Staying with relatives is out of the question—he wouldn't want to put them in harm's way, but then again, all their relations are potentially in harm's way. In the end, Professor Aughbui decides to continue in his usual way of life, devoting himself to strength training and to further improvements in Smilebot. At repeated urgings from Professor Crest, he acquires the necessary forms from the Integrity Committee and begins the laborious process of filling them out. The other three economists likewise increase their vigilance; Professor Budshah spends less time roving freely around the campus and does not sleep in the same dorm room on consecutive nights. The remaining Professor Long shifts to another apartment. Professor Crest insists on remaining where he is. The idea has taken hold that *Animal Money* is an extravagant fantasy, the whimsical jeu d'esprit of a group of accident-addled economists, and not really a serious book. Whenever Professor Crest, or any of the others, for that matter, try to discuss it seriously, they meet with an impenetrable barrier of qualified disinterest adorned with light praise.

Professor Budshah figured it out.

"They are using the duel as a pretext," he says. "They can point at it and say that there is as yet no verdict on the question, and leave things there as long as they wish."

Clashes in the US between militia groups and police are becoming more serious. Wilmington is shattered by three days of arson and violence, brought on in part by an influx of refugees from the hurricane. Actual coverage is scanty and percolates only with difficulty and sporadic success through the thicket of bullshit. Most television news programming is devoted to the loving documentation of a regional cooking contest and the Oscars. A Senator from Delaware isn't even aware of the turmoil in Wilmington when questioned by a rookie reporter, who was later reprimanded and sent down from D.C.

*

Your remarks on Uhuyjhns interest us. Some aspects are more interesting to us than others, of course. We would appreciate it, naturally, if you would confine yourself to those aspects ... The sooner, you understand, that you do, the sooner this will be over. You're very busy—of course, we know that. You must be very eager to go on about your business ... So, be succinct—these Uhuyjhns, then, are what we might say are the messengers?

There is only the one, as far as I know.

Really? ... Well, you can understand how I would get the wrong idea. You say here ... let me find it ... "the Uhuyjhn must be a *sort* of creature that has evolved to live so slowly ..."

Ah.

Yes, you see—

"Sort."

"Sort," exactly.

But only one is mentioned.

Yes, only one. But, living things, you know ...

Living things?

Uhuyjhns live, don't they?

I'm not sure.

Come now, surely there can't be any confusion there.

One may live, I suppose.

Living things come in species, not individuals.

But what we take for a single Uhuyjhn could be the entire species, could consist of many.

How many?

How many what? Species?

How many make up a single Uhuyjhn?

... I don't know what to tell you. This is only a speculation.

Well, two, three?

Two, three?

Is it a matter of twos and threes, or is it a matter of thousands, or what?

You mean, classify the number by order of magnitude?

Is a single Uhuyjhn a great many or not a great many?

A great many of what?

... The Uhuyjhn was discovered how?

Well, you see, the experiment had been a qualified success. According to her ultra-high-speed camera and other recording instruments the wild spirits of both her parents were conjured and stabilized successfully using pacebrot energy, but of the two, only her father's ghost was actually captured. Her mother's ghost had leapt from the window at once, emitting that weird windy laughter that Assiyeh heard. She is presumably still at large, and there's no telling what mischief she will get into out there.

The wild ghost of Assiyeh's father is nothing like him physically, being taller and acting much younger, like a child at times. He follows her with doglike devotion, even into the bathroom. He can do complicated mathematics and follow elaborate directions, although he does tend to get carried away at times. Every now and then he has a kind of seizure or fit that sends him careening around like a maniac, jumping up onto the furniture, on the ceiling, and throwing himself at the walls and floor with frenzied abandon so that he often disappears into solid objects. When he is unable to find his way back out of an object, Assiyeh has to set up the Saturn beacon to guide him. This is always followed by a stern lecture from Assiyeh, her father's ghost staring sheepishly at the floor with his naked eyes and teeth. Assiyeh employs him as a laboratory assistant anyway, calling him "Dumb-Dumb." Not knowing any better, he answers to it.

In his spare time, he likes to perch on a chair with his knees drawn up, keenly watching horror movies one after another. He watches *Dr. Circus' Coffin of Living Blood*, then *The Torture Funeral of Baron Schizosis*, then *Escape of the Atomic Wendigos ... Beware! The Brain Laboratory of Dr. Strappado ... The Amazing Swamp Robots ... Casino of the Werewolves* ... Actresses screech like chimpanzees, orchestral groans, castle thunder, explosions, melodramatic laughter, overwrought soliloquies, a name called over and over.

Her mother was always pretty buttoned up. What is she doing out there? Ambushing children? Could she hurt anyone, or be hurt herself? Does Assiyeh really care?

Her father's spirit can't talk, but the two of them can transmit simple ideas by flashing their eyes at each other; Assiyeh blinking, her father's spirit flipping his hands over his lidless eyes like shutters on a signal lamp. While he is still capable of written communication, the act of writing drives him wild, ripping paper to shreds and grinding the pen or pencil into the table, pounding keyboards so that they bounce under his shadow hands, spitting keys like broken teeth. Assiyeh has better success with chalk and a slate, and still better with a wax tablet and a bone stylus.

"... holy celestial solitude of a cloud of giant somnambulists ... houses form from military decorations ... the blue-white hellparadise of celestial altitude ... allow a mysticism to form itself through one ... I didn't understand what I was of carrion, and rumbles of the divine discovered my own ability to change ... the magic word is censored ..."

Terms like "the blue-white hellparadise" recur nearly every time he writes, and he keeps coming back to "magic word" and censoring. Without being able to distinguish by what definite steps she came to this idea, she realizes he's trying to tell her that the censorship of magic words is not just secrecy; it's part of the magic, in fact, the magical effect is the censorship. But what does that mean? Whenever she asks him that, she gets back, amid the smudges, something about the riotous ecstasy of the elastic censors or the elastic ecstasy of the riotous censors or the elastic riot of the ecstatic censors and she can't be sure that he isn't getting "elastic" and "ecstatic" mixed up. Those portents never work out, she thinks, I wonder why I still pay them any attention.

*

The remaining Professor Long receives an invitation by email to address a group of delegates from the IEI on the topic of animal money. She accepts, disquieted by mention in the inviting email of previous attempts to get in touch with her; she hasn't been getting them, and suspects that she only managed to get this one because it arrived in her inbox right before her eyes.

Fear is getting the better of her. Should she buy another cigar? The tide of willpower starts rolling back in about halfway down the block, and the remaining Professor Long hesitates as it gains strength. She waffles between the impulse to go through with it and an aversion that comes on palpably like the soft repellance of a magnetic field. Unsure of the outcome, and wanting to give the advantage to the counterforce, no matter how onerous it is for her to go back on even a bad decision, she leaves the path to the store and deviates at random, coming to rest on a bench in a little open space paved with hexagonal stone tiles, blonde with the dust of San Toribio. This is desert dust, and the air here is always so bright and clear it's hard to tell how that dust manages to infiltrate the city. The dust coats the almost black green leaves of the trees, giving off its characteristic medicinal smell. Lizards scuttle in the planters, and huge dragonflies dart in and out like black needles. The people of San Toribio go floating by in their loose, heat-adapted attire. They murmur greetings to each other as they pass, and to her as well. She sits holding the tops of her thighs and gazing at the ground. Her inner wrangling isn't going on without her, though, as she hoped it would. Everything has gone into an awkward, uncomfortable suspense. She may have to go all the way to the store and actually confront a pack of cigarettes.

Sun Mu-Kai is coming along the pathway toward her

when she looks up. He waves to her with his left hand, a AAA battery loose between his index and middle fingers. His whole body is loose, like a marionette. Lean, slight, his clothes a little too big for him, fringe of hair hanging down nearly to his eyebrows, sunken cheeks, chin wide and prominent, rings under his eyes.

"Lend."

"Spend."

"You OK?" he asks.

She tells him she's OK—but what is he doing here?

Sun Mu-Kai used to teach in the mathematics department at her former University, but he was put on stress leave a couple of years ago. Everyone knew he was a little unbalanced, mentally, but he'd never hurt anyone or been responsible for any scandal.

His affect as flat and factual as ever, he tells her he's been working on his monograph. This proverbial monograph on the Yang-Mills existence and mass gap has been pending for nearly ten years. Nobody believes Sun will ever finish it; they shake their heads, some with real regret, because it seemed at one time that Sun actually could have solved the problem. A few hold out hopes that he will come through, win a Fields Prize and redeem himself. As he describes the excellent progress he's been making now that he is free to concentrate on the project, having been invited to Archizoguayla University to do his research and to study the papers of a dead mathematician named Nilsson which had been donated to the University library here. From time to time he raises the copper end of the battery to his mouth and sips at it like a cigarette, pressing the other end with the tip of his index finger.

"I've got a contact here," he hoists his lip and points to what could be any of three ordinary looking front upper teeth, "—and here." He shows her the tip of his index finger, where there's a hard white spot like a ceramic dot. Whenever he takes a drag from the battery, the corner of his right eye quivers slightly.

"Everybody's talking about your book," he says. "I think the mathematical aspect is intriguing."

"That was mostly Professor Aughbui's work," she tells him.

"Aughbui?" he says, blowing air out of his mouth in a stream and jerking his head aside as if a troublesome plume of smoke were getting in his eyes. "I don't know him."

The remaining Professor Long is suffused with a lack of ambition to tell him any more about it. What she'd really like to do is get laid, Third Oath or no. Not with this half-crazy plucked chicken, either. A hit and run with a total stranger would do it. Watching him play smoking is doing her some good; her own impulse to smoke is fading. A stranger to fuck then fade like smoke. One of these men going by, the younger ones, who are so lean and playful.

Sun shimmies his knees from time to time, as if he had trouble keeping them locked.

"The difficulty lies in expressing a qualitative problem in a quantitative way. The way the problem is expressed will make any solution impossible if that way is basically quantitative in nature."

"We were thinking ...," the remaining Professor Long says, with a transient stirring of interest, "We thought to get some understanding of problems as part of nature.

Some problems may be quantitative, but being a problem, any kind of problem, is a quality. It has a quality of ..." He takes another toke from his battery, then throws himself down beside her on the bench.

"There is still a quantitative aspect to your theory," he says. "I mean, when you say that it is possible to set up exchanges that double quantity on both sides of the exchange."

"It depends," she says. "Not all doubling is quantitative. A mirror, for example. And the whole point of our theory was to conceive of a viable economic system based around an augmenting model of exchange rather than a substituting or equivalency based model. We thought ...."

"*Go on, our instrument,*" says a voice coming from him.

She jerks away from him staring. His eyes are rolled back, his body rigid with his hands on his knees and a mouth full of luminous chrome slaver.

"*Financial imbalances volatile capital flows and language unknown to the person automatic and orderly exchange rates that can have deleterious effects for economically possessed the revelation of the future or of the actor and floating in the possessed—*"

He swallows and draws in a fresh breath through his teeth. She can hear the mucus harp in his lungs ring with the sound.

"*There are four principal signs belonging to the mechanism for resolving the buildup as regards the presence of Devils in events happening far away in Izalu Imef including the exhibition of rapid unabated accumulation of international reserves concentrated in these signs speaking or understanding of strength beyond the years and natural effects and related to*" *the above by which it can be undoubtedly recognised."*

The words rattle out of him, jerking his whole body, as if someone were drumming on his back with both fists. In the window of the University book shop she can see the dim figure of a man leaning around the corner watching them and she looks in his direction in time to see the face and glittering eyes withdraw again behind the wall. Sun stops talking, drawing in another musically wheezing breath, suddenly drops the battery and snatches a small notebook from the breast pocket of his shirt. He folds in half, pressing the notebook to the seat of the bench and filling pages with a pencil stub. The remaining Professor Long sits looking down at the crown of his head, too shocked to move. After a moment, her gaze flicks to the battery lying on the ground and now dimpled with the impress of Sun's knuckle.

Sun emits an appalling whine as he writes, slurping and gulping as if he were lapping water messily from a bowl on the floor. Suddenly he jumps up with a cry of fright and alarm, throwing the notebook at her so that it strikes her chest and bounces to the ground. His face seems more or less as it had been when he first approached her—now he backs away from her.

"Sun," she says.

He shakes his head.

"You've had some ... You should ... see a doctor. Do you want me to ...?"

Sun is staring at her, horrified. He shakes his head and then staggers rapidly away. The remaining Professor Long picks up the notebook and, when she looks up again, he's already gone. There is no sign of the figure she saw reflected, either. She doesn't know Sun's number.

She finds another place to sit and looks at the notebook.

"Addressing these problems did not turn out signs. Let's see whether we can build up financial horrible convulsions by any exterior signs. The flow of capital among Managing Directors still not entirely clear. It also lends to crisis, financing on affordable terms. Effectively managing their institutions, and designing appropriate macroeconomic monetary systems ensures exchange of the Superior who automatically yielded his name. The oil shocks exchange rates that can have beginning of all these troubles it was from hatred. Well-known weaknesses, including giving these girls another exorcist. He attacked and released seven, hindering trade. After the system got in, he was violently shaken by his payments. The current credit crisis and exhibition of strength of the economic demon who had been exorcised by the ritual eight times; but these after another. Once obeying the order broadly based on their rate stability, spoke through her mouth, adding, 'But you won't.' Manifested neither in words nor from the earth, the body helps countries governing food and oil price central planning. The demons used official paper, and threw him out, and were horrible on her face.

"It keeps track and three other Deputy Managers come to the person possessed; the revelation threatens him once, in paying for imports and floating in the International Monetary System—the set of invisible persons and that Demon repeated commands aloud, so great by day and night, of the Executive Board. These signs help countries deal with the adversary; he has a stability by rebuilding their international loans to countries. That demon took up his position around the corner, oversees the international supporting institutions that facilitate international air for a few moments. A language disappeared and attacked, made concessional loans to civil society, and the media, and the demons, who provided them with macroeconomic rebalancing of demand growth, surveillance and secret thoughts, which were grinning impostors.

"Oil shocks, events happening far away; they stopped his voice. Fixed exchange rate collapses alerting them to risks on possessed. There are four principal demons. Forced to manifest himself, the demon gave them think tanks, essential for divine service and unabated accumulation of international reserves, the space of a second interior, borne to earth. Through its economic surveillance, monetary system monitors him save by magic his depositions to low-income countries to help an inward order charged with overseeing the international ..."

*

Explosions in Spain, turmoil in the US. Professor Aughbui can't seem to catch a break. His report to the Integrity Committee has come back marked R&R—revise and resubmit. Yellow notes stick out from the report's many pages like sunflower petals, covered in mainly illegible editorial notes in indignant blue ball point pen. The International Economic Citation Standardization Association is the self-appointed professional body that curates the proprietary format for scholarly publications in economics; this information is only available through a costly subscription to their service, which is made necessary by their own incessant tinkering with the rules. A paper submitted to a journal in meticulous adherence to IECSA's minutest requirements will be sent back marked R&R since even the mere interval of fifteen minutes is all the time it takes for those requirements to become obsolete. Membership in the IECSA is, naturally, a closely-guarded secret. Some disgruntled scholars have alleged that the whole thing is a racket and that the formatting guidelines—which are so copious that, printed out in full, they fill more volumes than an encyclopedia—are inconsistent gobbledigook concocted at random by a computer.

"ONE SPACE ONLY after periods!!" screams one of the notes.

Professor Aughbui consults his style guide, last updated an hour ago.

"Periods shall be followed by two spaces."

"It has always been ONE SPACE!!" screams an editor shrilly, her face turning purple with bursting blood vessels.

"It has always been TWO SPACES!!" screams an editor shrilly, his face turning purple ...

Back and forth it goes, like hemlines, and everyone can see it going back and forth, like a crowd at a tennis match, from one version of what it always was and you're an idiot for not knowing that to another version of what it always was and you're an idiot for not knowing that.

"The author is obviously very conversant with the materials ..." That's one referee.

"The author shows only a limited grasp of the subject ..." That's the other.

"The report lacks focus ..."

"The writer, and the essay, would benefit by broadening the discussion ..."

Urtruvel pauses for a swig of coffee and his louse flinches—still too hot.

Professor Aughbui laboriously and conscientiously revises his report and resubmits it. It comes back to him by return mail the same day sporting a brand new mane of furious yellow notes. Professor Aughbui has, with his usual punctilious orderliness, kept all the prior notes and marked them with indices, so he is able to cross reference them with the new ones, all of which reliably contradict the former ones. So he pulls up the version he first submitted, which he did not delete, and submits that again, adding only the subscript "second revision."

When he gets up for breakfast the next morning, the report is already sitting there waiting for him, once again resplendently arrayed in pale yellow scales adorned with arabesques of cheap blue ink. Professor Aughbui sits down to begin the task of the third revision. All this has kept him so busy that he's been neglecting Smilebot, who has consequently begun assembling a smaller robotic companion for itself, named Boringbot.

Professor Aughbui is an oblivious castaway on an island of paperwork in the middle of an ocean of exploding lava. Smilebot watches it on the news. Professor Aughbui's report, which has now swelled to three binders full, is posted and returned regularly by special courier, a very tan young woman in a white t-shirt with an IC badge pinned to it, who comes and goes on a battery-operated motorscooter.

Nearly half the world is unemployed or underemployed, rent ever higher, government budgets whittled down to the bone now they're paring away the bone and drilling into the screaming marrow. No more services; governments exist to maintain police and military. As that other voice is tearing itself from Sun Mu-Kai's throat, paralyzing the remaining Professor Long with fear, a bomb goes off in the lobby of a bank in Barcelona. The bank was closed, as it was the middle of the night, but a passerby was injured by the blast. The police descend heavily but there is no evidence; there are no leads. Two more bombings in two different cities. Protests in front of banks and government offices balloon in size and the inrushing tide of people dashes them against the security cordons and through; banks are raided, computers smashed, tills emptied. States of emergency, martial law. Everyone is waiting to see if a coalition can be put together while governments, media, religious authorities, swivel between conciliatory promises and sermons about social order. Everybody watches their neighbor with alarm. Professor Aughbui keeps sending his parcel off, then sits down quietly to wait for the next batch of meaningless adjustments.

*

The glass is soundproof I guess—my cries for help sure didn't get through that fucking glass. I head down the hall fast to where I know the door is and that leads down a hall with lockers to a room with a ladder and a hatch you take up to the catwalk that the tenders use to move to and fro between the exhibits. Nobody up here. I see the bastard right away and he sees me, recognizes me in an instant, and for a moment I nearly short circuit with that ape stink dragging me down and back. He rears up inquisitively on his hind legs and I shoot him. He just stands there; now he touches his body, looks at the blood all over his hand. He turns aside, leans against the fake rock with one hand to his chest, and his head droops. He tries to swing his head up, and slumps down onto his left side. He doesn't react when another one pokes his head out further up the slope. I shoot him, too. I see a spray of something dark on the rock wall behind as the head drops back. Alarmed by the shots, and now I guess some doors have been flung open and left that way so now the sound of the alarm is audible in the enclosures, a female comes scooting along from the shrubs down by one of those fucking windows, heading for the rocks which she knows will cover her and the infant chimp she clutches to her gnarly bosom better than the bushes. I shoot them, too. She veers and then leaps, bounding clumsily up a bare rock slope in sheer panic. She gets up the slope to the top with frantic effort but she drops the baby and it slides down the rough surface. Half its head is gone. The mother drops down behind cover, raising hell, screeching and hooting. The first one is still lying there. I experience pure piping hot wellbeing.

Didn't think you'd be seeing *me* again, did you you bastards?!

My insides start to tremble and I can hear my breath in my nostrils like incipient, hysterical laughter, my eyes swelling as if they were about to shoot tears out, my arms and legs are weightless, light, tingling, how many superreal bullets left?

I glimpse another one, trying to skulk off to cover along the little drainage moat there by the windows. I nail him in the back and ding another shot into the window, knocking a neat white hole in it. The chimp bounds forward with incredible speed, yowling, then blunders over a root or something and goes sprawling and tumbling through a bush and out into plain view. I fire at him and keep firing until the gun is empty. He gets up and stretches to his full height, lifting his huge, ungainly arms, staggers ridiculously in no particular direction, his face a drunkard's blank who me? look— then splat forward onto his face and skids to a halt, arms splayed.

I head back down the way I came. If anyone comes up on me I'll pick him up with one hand and throw him over the side, kick in his face if he comes up the ladder. No one in the hall, the fire alarm is still going, I have the bizarre feeling no time at all has passed, that it's been only a few seconds, maybe I haven't even started yet and everything that just happened was all just ultra vivid expectation. I hurry down the hall, not really caring anymore if anyone sees me, if I get caught, I killed them and they know it. Some people in white coats are calling to each other, where's the fire, I don't know, who pulled the alarm, would someone turn that fucking alarm off, who's checking the enclosures—? I'm batting my way through the curtains and out the door. A landscaper sees me. I keep moving, don't answer, don't listen, don't respond, you're running in a panic from a fire, that's all.

Get away, ditch the pistol down a storm drain, in a sewer, feed it to a shark.

—Signed SuperAesop

*

The break room is at one end of the building; the outer wall is a concrete web, a solid vane about two feet off the ground, square windows to the floor below it, rectangular windows to the ceiling above it, and tinted. Through it, they can see the path running by just outside, the planters with oddly de-colored daylight shining greasily on tropical foliage, an asphalt road and the pebbly grey concrete bunker of the main library on the other side. Palm trees and huge fronded plants, jungle dishevelment.

Sun Mu-Kai is not answering his phone or his front door. Nobody has seen him.

What is that voice?

"He sounded like a *demon*," the remaining Professor Long says.

Professor Budshah sits with his hands lying limp in his lap, dejected, and Professor Crest stands. Professor Aughbui is perusing the notebook, which has not left his hands for more than an hour.

"It is—" Professor Crest says. Nothing follows.

Professor Budshah speaks after a few moments more, without looking up.

"We are being pursued. Some form of mental tampering is following us," he says. "We are being transformed, will-I nil-I, into 'dark economists.'"

"Are you serious?" the remaining Professor Long asks.

"... No," he sighs. "No, I suppose not. The worst thing about this, just at the moment, is that I don't know what I think. I don't believe our theory to be no more than a mad ramble."

"It is not," Professor Crest says firmly, drawing strength from his rejection of the idea. "There were numerous witnesses who can attest to our having been in no special mental state at the time we first began to discuss it. In back of all these bizarre episodes there is a patently obvious intention to discredit us."

Assiyeh's head flashes by in the lower pane of the rightmost window, hair flying. Professor Crest's cup crashes to the floor and Professor Budshah stands reflexively, his knees tipping over the table laden with books which falls to the floor with a clatter, Professor Aughbui lifts from his seat on the sofa and twists his body around and the remaining Professor Long looks from Professor Crest to Professor Aughbui, then turns to the door. Professor Budshah is already in the doorway, whipping around it and down the hall in one fluid swing. The remaining Professor Long stays where she is with a very faint grin of surprise on her face as Professor Crest advances to the window and flattens his palm against it. Like two pupils in big square eyes they look down at Assiyeh striding down the center of the concrete pathway bisecting the campus.

With his weird dancer-like precision of movement Professor Crest turns incredulously to the room, speaking as it happens to Professor Aughbui, who is closer to him.

"But we invented her!" he cries, already a thread of outrage taking form in his astonishment. "... We did! We definitely did!"

Professor Aughbui looks at Professor Crest and answers him by a convulsive flicker of his lips, which are slightly open.

Professor Budshah is catching up to her. She is at once too small and too big, and with each step she takes her little feet shake the earth, as if her body were made of superconcentrated matter.

"Excuse me ..."

His voice is a weird bleat. He clears his throat.

"Excuse me, Professor?"

She stops and turns her waist to look at him.

"Well?" she asks.

Now what?

"My apologies. I have mistaken you for someone else," he says. "The Surfeit is One."

She does not reply, unless that slight upward inclination of the head, and the lowering of her eyelids, constituted one; she untwists her waist and resumes walking just as before, erasing their brief, aborted encounter, but was he going to ask her to stop, to stop, because she's pounding the earth apart with her footsteps? Why? Because you are the invention of a recently-deceased friend of mine. And would you mind explaining where you really came from and how, and if you climbed out of a certain bullet hole?

"It is her," he says, coming back into the break room.

"I refuse to believe it," Professor Crest snaps blankly.

Professor Budshah looks thoughtful. He puts both hands on his kidneys and stares at the floor. The remaining Professor Long says, "I believe it."

They all glance at her. As she adds nothing more, their eyes drift to neutral territories again.

"What is this shit?" Professor Aughbui wonders.

"All right so it is her," Professor Crest says, very put-upon. "It is likely her. The late Professor Long did not invent her, he met her. Perhaps he forgot he did. He mixed memory up with imagination."

These plausible words don't seem to be convincing even to him. He looks out the window again, starting almost imperceptibly when his eyes perversely hit on her retreating, now very small figure, right away, rubbing it in, that seeing what he expects to see, which ought to give it a greater air of fantasy, is actually the perfect negation of fantasy just now.

The break room is a vacuum whitewashed in daylight. Professor Crest staring, Professor Budshah wondering, Professor Aughbui calculating, the remaining Professor Long congratulating.

ASSIYEH MELACHALOS—Institute of Applied Physics, Achrizoguayla University. That's what the website says. There's a small photo of her next to her name, white sparks for eyes, her hair-cape floating as if she were standing in a light breeze, even though the photo was plainly taken indoors, against a white wall.

The police inspector, Liszpuertha, is a gaunt, neurasthenic-looking young man with hollow cheeks and a goatee whose arms seem to sweep the ground around him when he walks. He shakes hands with them all, his hands large soft and cool like silk cushions. When he goes to sit down, he misses, only just managing to keep from dropping down on his ass and he bursts out in a peal of laughter that doesn't seem possible for a real police officer. He laughs like a cartoon, or a clown. His smile, as he rights himself, is sunny, and suddenly makes him seem like the rawboned village idiot type.

Once stably seated, he explains that he has been sent to inquire further about their security, and to ask a "little few more" questions.

Professor Crest saw it all coming. In his mind's eye, the police officials were far more minatory and ominous, but that was all casting.

You are police. A group of five economists come to your country for a conference. One is anomalously mugged, another is abducted, and yet another dies by violence.

The police inspector is chatting affably with them all in turn, asking them what they think of Archizoguayla, how much of the country have they seen, how they like San Toribio, have they been to the Bolithadio (prime tourist attraction) yet, and so on.

"Now, the interesting thing about that hotel they took you to," he says to Professor Aughbui, "is that day they were spraying some of the rooms for insects, so they were not taking guests. Just that day. Isn't that something? Did you know? Any other day, there would have been so many more customers, and maids, and other employees, but on that one day, no one, just a man at the front desk, and the exterminators. The men who abducted you, Professor, did not succeed, which means they were not lucky enough to find an empty hotel by chance, so they must have known the hotel would have been empty. That ties them to the hotel, even if there are no witnesses. The desk clerk did not recognize you, Professor, but did you know that one of the hotel maids has a foreign boyfriend named Kovak? He hasn't turned up yet. It's funny—well, it's not funny, I mean it's strange, that you, Professor (turning to Professor Crest) should be attacked in the street when you were, that is, before you had this idea you have all been working on. It's just too peculiar a coincidence, if it was unrelated, but if it is related, what were they thinking? How can they warn you away from an idea you haven't had yet?

"We have been in touch with Canadian police, and they have been kind enough to give us some of the details they found out about your friend's death. They say that his house was locked, that nothing seemed to be disturbed or missing, there was no note, there were only his fingerprints on the gun, which was his own and only fired the one time, no one heard the shot, which, as the coroner says, would have been fired in the middle of the afternoon, when, apparently, nearly everyone in the neighborhood would have been away. It does seem like he committed suicide. However, while he had recently lost his position at the University there, he had already been offered a new position here, which would have made his continued work with you possible, and it seems that this was what he wanted to do. He had a new project, this project of yours, to work on, and with such a project there always comes a sense of purpose and improved morale that is not consistent with suicidal despair. While he was, perhaps, slightly irregular, mentally, there is no record of hospitalization or of any extreme or violent behavior. None of his neighbors, I would like to add, even knew about the pistol. My department is taking this case very seriously, and we have referred our reports up ... upwards? To the federal authorities, because of the possibility of foreign involvement or interference. In the meantime, that is, as we continue to look at the information, please do not leave, and we offer you protection—"

Here he makes a gesture with the back of his right hand, raising it and turning the reverse of the fingers toward us in an arching motion.

"—if you feel you require it, which you may ask for by calling the number there, on my card."

*

Professor Budshah is sitting in the library after hours again. The doors have just been closed and locked, and the staff are already mostly gone. There may be a custodian somewhere, but as a rule the tidying up is done in the mornings, before the doors open for the day. From his chair, he can see out through the glass wall to the distant mountains and the setting sun beyond. Facing him is himself, a phantom in the glass, looking up nearly through his eyebrows, bent over the desk, illuminated by the desk lamp. He realizes that, for some time now, he has only been looking at the words, not reading them. He puts a marker in the book and closes it, then sits up, rubbing his stiff neck. He gets up and makes his way to the water fountain, has a drink, then into the dark bathroom. He snaps on the light and the fluorescents scatter the dark. There's his reflection, more solid than before, looking like something he's typing on a screen. He washes his hands before visiting the urinal and then again afterwards, feeling solid and well-bred in his fastidiousness. When he's finished drying his hands, he throws the paper towels into the trash and stands there, gazing at nothing in particular. A portentous feeling is coming over him. He is in the presence of an idea. Sometimes, when the mind is too tired to sustain its cachinnation, the system sloughs its glamor and the gold turns out to be straw, not by the true sunlight but under lifeless fluorescents. Just bullshit after all. He knows this will pass, anticipating other moments of compensatory enthusiasm. But just now it is possible to have an idea along other lines, an idea that brings its own lines with it. If you can annex that idea as it comes up, you often wind up with a real find.

It doesn't happen. Instead, he gets a trickle of admonitory wind blowing through the jungle gym of the system. Feeling like Dickens' Signal-Man, Professor Budshah hurries to the computer that they leave on for him and sends a series of messages; everyone reports back OK within fifteen minutes. Professor Aughbui has just received his report back with the latest batch of suggested revisions, most of which involve reverting to draft sixteen. Someone like Warren is both perfect and perfectly wrong for this kind of back and forth; he can keep track of everything and do exactly as he is told, which is exactly why there is always more to do. He forgets nothing, which is why they, the editors, can't forget anything either. Affection billows through him for a moment, a flash of Professor Aughbui working diligently away with pen and paper, although of course he would be using a computer. The good old scholarly type; unworldly, altruistic, conscientious, hapless. He shouldn't think of him that way, he thinks, it's condescending. He is back at his own desk and sitting down again, no, it's not really respectful. He shouldn't like to be thought of that way himself.

Professor Budshah looks down at the book in front of him. He picks it up, and becomes suddenly aware of his dim likeness reflected in the cellophane wrapper. The outline warps as it travels to and fro, which he can make it do by tilting the book. A wobbling greyish funhouse silhouette of himself. It acts like a time lapse film of a cloud, a raincloud, in a uniform red sky with black characters, and a splash of moonlight—the chill fluorescent glow of the desk lamp reflected there too. So he's like Chernobog or some other titan dark figure stretched out against a Stygian sky, the roof of hell, which has daisies growing out the reverse side, the earthside, which is green in cardinal opposition to that red hellroof dotted with the cindery remains of imperfectly burned hell money, so animal money should remain green being the antidote of hell money. Then it should be heaven money, the blue and white of *the blue-white hellparadise*, a familiar-sounding phrase that crosses his mind in English, and which he is sure he has never before encountered.

You try to pin something down, but it eludes you like a bar of soap, or it goes in circles. When you pin something down, it's dead, because that's all it is permitted now, and not dead with the nurturing decay of the Teeming. It's the slipping and sliding out and away that shows you something is still alive; you can feel its life there in the evasion, which is a kind of resistance, like an animal wriggling in your grasp, jump back into the water or the shrubbery or the sky, whatever ambivalent element it lives in, jump back and melt back into the throng and the mass and the motion and away from the haunted, eerily beautiful morgue world of your terrible mind. So you have to listen. Yes, but if your way of listening is just another form of saying, then ...?

Suddenly a darkness that moves from right to left blankets his mind. Inside it, the late Professor Long slumps in his chair, the diffuse, venetian-blinded haze of the blurred room behind him. There's something moving above the head; smoke still trickles from the blackened puncture in the temple. The lips have stiffened in a vacant smile and the dim face, wan light falling around it, is composed in a dreamy, half-listening expression. He is singing to Professor Budshah. The voice high and thin, a falsetto, forming a few short words then a drawn-out one, phrase after phrase. The long, sweet, crooning notes are unbearable, coming from this grinning corpse.

Professor Budshah is on his feet. The chair he was sitting in a moment ago lies on the floor behind him. He's panting. Sweat bursts painfully across swaths of his skin. He can feel his throat pulsing against his collar, and he swallows with difficulty. Absently, staring all around him, he turns to right his chair, but stops in an awkward half-bow, his arm extended. It's as if he were thrusting his face down into a suffocating mass of stale air that had collected somehow on the floor, a heavy gas that sinks like smoke. It fills his lungs thickly, almost like water. He rears back and exhales with an inward shove, then gasps. This air is better, but not much. The books have sucked up all the oxygen like sponges, and the library is hermetically sealed. Professor Budshah hastens to an exit door he sometimes uses—he props it open, which is against the rules, with a little stone. The door would lock behind him otherwise. Now he doesn't care if he's locked out. The idea that he can find someone to open the place for him again if he needs to flits through is mind, but he imagines the library, the entire floorplan, like a gigantic killing jar charged to bursting with smothering dead air and he doesn't want to get back in *he needs to get out.* He flings open the exit door and rushes out under the stars, unselfconsciously opening his mouth to take in huge draughts of fresh air. A leaden torrent of inert staleness gushes out behind him in a subsiding pyramid and the door snaps shut; no knob, no latch on this side. Just a keyhole.

Professor Budshah doesn't care. He walks a few steps now in one direction, now in another, hands on his kidneys, head back, collar loosened, just breathing. His panic ebbs. He looks at his wristwatch—nearly eleven. He thinks about what has just happened to him, and touches his head gingerly at the right temple, wondering if he's losing his mind. Looking up again a moment later, the night around him seems vacuous and boundless, seeming at once empty and expectant, a grave before the burial. The fear stirs and flows again, lifting up past his diaphragm. Without hearing or seeing anything but what is there around him, he nevertheless knows that the second Professor Long still sings in his chair, smiling vacantly as wisps of smoke from his own violated brain trickle up through his hair and splash against the white ceiling so far overhead. The campus is under a spell. It looks like a collection of gigantic photographic flats, propped up with fiendish deceptiveness to block the blackness beyond them from sight. So the blackness can keep stealing.

His sense of safety is on a fast crumble. Professor Budshah knows he is completely alone and that anything can happen to him because no one is there to see it. The campus is haunted by colossal slabs of crystallized darkness and formless shadows. He knows he's being foolish and the thought only increases his anxiety, because it means he's losing self-control. Professor Budshah sets out for one of several different locations, not yet deciding on which one but most of them are in the same direction, where he could expect to find other people, and he needs to move. He gets halfway to the student union before he remembers that it will of course be closed, then thinks he might be better off heading back to the library. The thought of that suffocating air instead sends him in the direction of the campus security office, which is where he ought to have gone in the first place, but instead he turns from that path when he sees the wide boulevard bordering the campus on the south side, and the lights of the battered trolley car rolling toward the stop. He runs. Some passengers call mock encouragement to him as he hurries up to the wrong side of the car and then recklessly dashes around the front. He mounts the steps. The heavy train operator smiles bemusedly at him. Professor Budshah fumbles for change. Luckily, he has his wallet and coins on him; this is not really lucky— but it's promising somehow, as though an antagonist missed an easy chance to hinder him. The money looks like magic talismans. The driver merrily drops the fare into his change drawer and hauls the heavy steel lever around. The doors close and, with a clanging of the bell, the trolley groans forward down the tracks, clashing and rattling. All the seats are full, and there are people standing in the front. Professor Budshah makes his way through them to an open space at the rear of the car, where the open windows let in more of that fresh air. A few passengers turn their heads to study him a moment.

The trolley rolls the length of the botanical gardens, heading into the center of San Toribio. Professor Budshah can't manage to gather his thoughts; his impressions jostle too loudly and too brightly, the contrast of this well lit car and the dark campus falling away into the night like a deadly planet. The trolley is like a room on rails, accompanied on either side by luminous rhomboids of light on the street, some adorned with foggy human silhouettes that make him think randomly of the indistinct skulls and eyes on the wings and bodies of certain species of insects. The night outside is too deep and spacious. It wobbles. It rolls around the trolley car crazily. The trolley car seems to be flying through space, a box of light, the jovial voice of the huge tram operator shouting out the stops, the names of planets and moons, the less familiar names therefore belonging to comets, asteroids, curds of dark matter. Am I getting away? he asks himself. The image in his mind was just like the photographs and it's nothing at all like the photographs. Most of the passengers are staying on board, and many of them are carrying large square objects. Like a single strand of cobweb, there's a thread attached to him that is being followed. He needs to brush it off, break it. Go downtown and plunge into a crowd. He won't be touched in front of witnesses. Those sorts of things don't happen. Actually, nothing like this happens; this is already something that doesn't happen, it's all in his mind. The tram shudderingly goes over a crossing and then veers to the right with an alarmingly stiff jerking. As they turn, he glances off to the left and there is something there.

It was outside the trolley. A flash of movement, or perhaps it really was a flash, like the glint of the trolley lights on a knife out there in the dark, just the instant before it was concealed again, taken out for a moment for sheer eagerness, but then hidden once more.

It's real, he thinks. The trolley now seeming very large around him, a great deal of space around him and even more outside. This is it, this is really it, this really is it, a fact, and plain. Any moment now. Little lights of all colors sail by in shoals, dart away into the blackness, and golden windows hang in the racing mid-darkness showing calm lamps lighting tranquil rooms.

Drab city blocks sweep alongside the car, brick houses, wide intersections with concrete office blocks, all steeping in the rancid urine of sodium lights. Then the wide boulevard lined with cafes and other night spots. End of the line. No passengers.

He emerges in packed streets filled with shouting people. The big square objects—placards. It's a rally or a protest. The elections. Have the run-offs happened already? No, soon, but not yet. An amplified voice comes leaping from wall to wall towards him from some square nearby. The streets here are narrow, for the most part, and lined with three and four storey buildings. He has to swim through the crowd without stopping—a man can get knifed in a crowd, it happens all the time. The people around him are Incienzoa supporters, to judge by their buttons, their banners, their sashes. Their heat turns the street into a cauldron. Hands lifted, point, clench, shake, wipe the face, grip the sign, wave, reach, knead the air, stir and paddle it. Here the two sides nearly meet, across a trench of bare pavement barred with sawhorses. The supporters of the AUP are bellowing across the gap at the Incienzoans, and vice versa. Like stones in a stream—in this case, a stream flowing in opposite directions at once—officers of the San Toribio police stand in the gap, strained amiability on their faces. Back and forth, up and down, they walk with affected casualness, hands on their hips or arms folded, smoking, whistling, but not chatting, and throwing glances now this way and now that. One of them remains stationary; Professor Budshah suspects he is in charge, a large man in a green police tunic, hands on hips, smoking, one of his two legs rocks back and forth inside his slacks.

Someone tries to vault the sawhorses on this side and at once the standing man has his baton out, using it to gesture to the nearest cop. The would-be vaulter is driven back with weird, grimacing smiles on the faces of the police, while the man in charge is turning his attention to the AUP side, making sure they stay in place.

If the elections don't work out, the country will explode. That is completely clear. The military will restore order, and then what?

Professor Budshah spends the night walking, stopping from time to time for coffee, reading a newspaper. What happened to him has lost none of its sickening reality, but, while his fear for himself has not diminished, thinking about the fate of Archizoguayla has put the idea of his jeopardy into a bigger picture. His point of view has opened around the fear. The next morning he wearily rides back to campus on the trolley, nodding off and missing his stop. He has to walk back. The library is open and no different inside than ever. A number of dorm rooms show stoved-in locks on the hallway upstairs and it's in answer to his questions that the custodian tells him about the break-in around eleven-thirty last night, some dorm room doors forced, nothing taken, but a computer was smashed; he doesn't ask which computer.

*

They are being watched, from the shadows. No, by the shadows. By a shadow, a formerly human someone who goes back and forth. I have seen? Seen that? No, I only sensed it, with these other, dimmer senses. The impressions they generate I have to commute into the familiar kinds, often with serious deformities. The shadow-someone that I sense way over there is a kind of lavish dummy, a lavishly ... a lavish ornamentation. Lavish ...

The eyes glitter. They glitter *violently*. There is long hair, long dry and stiff, past the shoulders. There is toothiness, a grimace or a fixed leer, that glistens, and rigid, sparkling hands that go before, open, the way hands look when they are about to take someone by the shoulders. Or by the throat. There are big rings on the colorless fingers, on each one, and a drooping, broad cuff of gold hanging down. A cuff of cloth. A cloth cuff.

Embroidered with gold. Richly. Stately, like a million year Emperor as emblematic of torture and despair as a porcelain idol in his palace that becomes more golden the more it rots, decomposing into jade brocades and teak silver and marble and platinum salvers and piebald mirrors that only reflect the faint light of crystal decanters and opalescent chaplets that dangle from the withered necks of crone countessas and the grey ophidian garments of sumptuous ministers and the sanguinary regalia of breastplates, plumed helmets, holy candles, lacquered urine, baleful lenses of parchment bishops, ugly cherubs, cobweb wine and appliqué chamberpots cradling ivory turds, evaporated deans, and mirrors reflecting also the weird noon dusk that holds its breath over a hedge maze and the death garden and the leaden pool still and inscrutable as a slab, a park where what looks green is actually black and the vines and branches are hatetwisted in cacographic ciphers of loathing and the slyly malignant flowers smell like stale motionless incense shitting dust on the floor and feeding on itself ever since the last time, the previous demise which waits to be repeated on these chill flags or lurid rugs, under the savage decorum and within the sinister outlines from the place where everything rots into opulence ...

Now Lavish reaches. The pupils are violently contracted down to twinkling points in eyes that throw off glints like welding sparks. It puts its jewelled hands through the dark water screen. It can see through the screen. Or not. I can't. I don't know what it's doing. The screen is rippling. It isn't rippling, it's motionless, it only looks like it's rippling because of the coruscations coming from Lavish, which bob and flutter across the surface. I don't want to inspect any nearer, or get any closer. I want to keep to my own decay and not shimmer like that.

"Watch out!" I think. "Watch out you ..."

Who?

Some people need to watch out. The reason is the same.

Same as what?

It isn't the same ... or ... ?

Why can't I remember the end?

The end of what?

If the moment I died is what I mean by the end, then I must be wrong, I'm not dead, or no, I died, but I'm not at the end yet, something changed when I went back, sat down, venetian blinds, the desk, the room, the familiarities, and this has a very intense atmosphere of significance, so why can't I remember whether it was suicide or murder? It's inexplicable. Nothing is inexplicable. The explanation is obvious—I can't remember being shot because at the time it happened I was being shot. I don't like these thoughts. They're too lucid. They may firm me up enough to die, or no, but to think so ... so hard, and solidly, so hard and solid, makes me feel I start to transform into what is more concrete and I don't want that, I want to be ... less concrete. I want to be filmy. Not a thinker statue. I don't want that intensity, it makes me solid, like a statue, but it's painful, or not painful it's exhausting, slow, too heavy. Watch out, I think, or say. Watch out you ... other, others. Watch out. Everybody watches out, what am I saying? I mean, can I say this without getting heavy? Lightly, I tell you, watch out for that, for Lavish. It is doing things. Down to something. It is always carried away with morbid glee, it can't stop. Lavish wants to keep rolling over everything and it is a master, I mean it has obeyers over on your side, but there are signs, associateds. Recognize the signs from the near miss you managed to survive, and then beware, it's an old fashioned word but it's one that has a special meaning for a ghost, ghosts like me, *beware* and watch for insane signs that are outside signs not rational signs. I keep wanting to call them sings. Who am I talking to? I'm not talking, though.

*

Professor Clark seems to have quite a light schedule. I, unlike other tenured professors, continue to teach undergraduates, on principle. I can not say I enjoy it. The demands that students place on us are often unbelievably exorbitant. I frequently stay after class, often for several hours, to advise students, explaining assignments to them again and again. In every class, there is always at least one student who meets even the simplest instructions with a blank stare of alarm and incomprehension, who seems incapable of absorbing information. For these students, I must transform myself into a kind of modernist writer, driven to express the same idea in every conceivable way. And yet these students receive each careful rephrasing of the same instructions as if they were completely new, as if I were giving them a task with infinite dimensions, as if my explanations were driving them away from understanding. I have repeated lectures to housebound students over the telephone. I have personally delivered classroom handouts to students at their places of work, at unavoidable family gatherings, at funerals, in the hospital, in mental institutions, to students caught in traffic jams (I reach them on my bicycle), students on vacation or visiting their native countries, student soldiers conducting military maneuvers or on the battlefield, students trapped in burning buildings or beneath overturned cars, students fleeing from tsunamis or forest fires, students in the act of taking their own lives.

I had a student whose cousin worked as an exotic dancer. One day, she came to me and explained that her cousin's ex-husband was suing for custody of their infant daughter. The court had set a date for the hearing, and, if her cousin missed it, her baby would be summarily taken from her by the authorities. The child would then be handed over to her ex-husband, who was an alcoholic, unemployed, subject to blackouts, who had a record of multiple arrests for assault, and one for attempted robbery of a pharmacy. However, her cousin was scheduled to work on the date set by the court, and the club manager was a stickler for attendance.

"He's a demon," she said. "There was a girl, she missed one time, because her brother had been hit by a car and she was the only one who could go with him to hospital, and he fired her. 'No excuses,' he says. 'No excuses. Girls like you are lined up around the block to get a job here. An empty spot in the rotation is money out of my pocket. You can't make it up? You get out. There are plenty more where you came from.'"

Consequently, a Hobson's choice: lose her job, or lose her child. Losing her job will mean she will almost certainly no longer be able to support the child in any case. There are very few alternative paying jobs available. If I would agree to substitute for her cousin at work while she attends this one court date, I would not only be helping a struggling single mother, but I would be emancipating her niece from a future of educational and economic privation. I point out that I am a man, but she says this would not be an insurmountable obstacle to my helping her.

"She says they all wear wigs anyway," she said. "I've seen her routine, and it isn't hard, only working the pole—that's the only tricky part, that and the splits, but she isn't on for that long at a time. You're a Professor, you're a smart man, you could pick it up in a few minutes."

She snaps her fingers. I point out that, since she is a woman and resembles her cousin far more than I do, perhaps she might be the better substitute.

"I have to work, though!" she says. "And you gave us a ten page research paper! When am I supposed to do that? Look, the day she's going to miss is a week day, during the day. Nobody will be there. Meaning that in full respect you are not much bigger than she is, her stuff could fit you, and even if it didn't, there are some heavier girls working there who could lend you a thong or something."

The experience was extremely edifying. I did not perform, as the manager did not consider me an acceptable replacement, even if I chose to dance as myself and not as a counterfeit female. He was, however, so moved by the lengths to which I was prepared to go for the benefit of my student's cousin, that he did not fire her for her absence, but only docked her salary for the next two months. Unfortunately, the cousin of my student did not attend court that day after all, because the subway system shut down for seven hours, trapping her in the tunnels. Her husband received custody of her daughter, and, within a week, he had evidently left the baby behind in a public park. He simply forgot all about her. When he remembered and rushed back, hours later, distraught, the baby was gone. As far as I know, nothing has since been heard of the child. My student stopped attending my classes and, despite some very promising early paper assignments, she failed the course. I never saw her again. Very few people take such responsibilities as these into account when they consider the demands of the teaching profession.

*

I'm always squinting through a smog of unexpressed thoughts and unacknowledged feelings, and hemmed in by unconscious fears and unintelligent aversions. My brain is choked with too much un. Growing up, my brain never got entirely solid; it still has soft spots, which is why I'm forgetful and emotional, a good mimic, quick with languages, still an Aesopian.

I met _____ on a certain street to discuss the next action. We passed a storefront full of morning shows on television screens. Everybody watches these programs, they say, and I say I don't and I wouldn't like meeting Everybody if they are a reflection of Everybody's taste. They have something for everynobody on this thing. The people on screen sit there and jive over their coffee around a table, by extension your coffee, your table, your airtime filling up with their drivel so you can't think how much better life could be if you, for example, led a strike at your place of work. These friends of yours, like your movie star friends and your pop star friends, who won't talk to you in the street and silently roll up their mercedes windows when you appear, just like real friends, who won't talk to you unless it's under controlled conditions where they are getting paid or some kind of publicity out of it and they always know exactly where the security guards are at all times. I'd call them ghouls but I like ghouls too much, friendly carrion eaters living in the graveyard and eating corpses because they can't afford rent and groceries, I think the name of the monster is "TV personality" in your closet or under your bed ready to snatch you up and freeze you in an interview trap forever—the blandits.

Watching for a moment ... there it is again ... that sick off-kilter sour drunken no-key melody, sick behind the happy ads and the normal images, telling you that something is fundamentally wrong, intuiting to you the howling cities and the screaming country and the groaning suburbs.

*

Professor Clark spots Professor Crest coming up the walkway ten minutes before their one o'clock appointment. He looks like Pinocchio, all grown up and transformed into a perfect prig, scrutinizing his watch, like a living piece of 1950's clip art but with something uncertainly off. Moving in straight lines, he goes directly into the building. The knock on her office door coincides exactly with the first note of the campanile ringing out one o'clock, and in he comes. He holds out his left hand and she recognizes the off note at once—left handed. The watch had been on his right wrist, the briefcase in his left.

"Professor Clark? Ronald Crest."

"Of course you are," she says too hastily and winces. "Pleased to meet you," she adds a little hastily and a bit louder than necessary. "Please come in."

He thanks her and crosses to the indicated desk chair, flipping up his briefcase already in anticipation of setting it deftly across his knees, perching erect on the edge of the seat.

"Thank you so much for coming," she says.

He raises his right hand as if he were holding a dinner tray.

"*The bank is there to save and lend.*"

"*Workers work and customers spend.*"

His white oval economist's mark makes his face seem smaller than it is, like a doll's face. The color is just a shimmer of white that doesn't obscure the skin or the features; on him, it's almost like a veil, barely visible. Minutes after meeting him, it melts directly into his face and she ceases to be aware of it, only noticing it again when she happens to look away and back.

She recounts for him the same shopworn story of the last few weeks of Vincent Long's life. He'd been more of a phantom than ever, no one had seen much of him, no one knew much about him, most people had not even been aware he'd been sacked, no one cared much. Her answers are recorded on a little device, and he is also making notes on a yellow pad that is nearly filled with columns of meticulous, microscopic handwriting.

"You write so small!"

"Yes," he says drily. "Did you have a sexual relationship with Professor Long?"

"Yes," she says.

For all his punctilio, she doesn't sense any disapproval. He receives her answer as impassively as he had the other information she'd provided, recording it diligently. He has the whitest eye-whites she's ever seen.

"When did you last speak with him?"

She answers promptly. That is a piece of information she has recycled so often lately that it isn't necessary to think about it anymore.

"Did you quarrel?"

"No."

"Did you break up?"

"No. We weren't really together like that, it was more casual than that. We just saw each other now and then. I've been seeing someone else, too."

"At the same time?"

"Yes."

She is getting nothing from him, no emotional response. He makes a note.

"He knew," she adds.

The head nods without looking up. Another note is made.

"Are you still seeing this other man?"

"Not any more," she says. "And it wasn't a man."

"Her name?"

"Lorraine. Whitehead."

"Does she work at the college?"

"No, she's not working."

"Where does she live?"

"Ratsberg."

"Where is that? Roughly."

"Downtown, by the river."

"What did she look like?"

Professor Clark looks down unhappily.

"I don't see ..."

He waits.

"... what that has to do with ..."

"Have the police asked you about this?"

"No."

"There might be a lead there they have not examined."

He's just being thorough; that's obviously his nature, she thinks. She studies him. The sort of man who eats all his vegetables, never uses contractions, and budgets every penny.

"I don't see the point," she says. "She wasn't a jealous lover gunning him down to have me all to herself."

A derisive laugh slips in underneath that last sentence.

"Perhaps," he says right away, "she was unable to find you on some occasion and went looking for you at his house. Perhaps she might have seen something there. That she would have witnessed what happened, I would not go so far as to say, but if she had seen him in the company of someone else, that might be very important."

If she weren't watching his face as he spoke, she would have missed the little delicacy as he says "what happened." That is plainly as much for his own benefit as for hers;

he doesn't like to say anything more explicit, because he doesn't want to bring the image too vividly to life in his mind's eye.

"It's possible. She did know where he lived."

He nods twice.

"Well, she's about in her mid thirties, black hair worn pretty long, about my height, slimmer. Very fit, athletic."

She clears her throat.

"Pretty."

"Have you heard from her recently?"

"No. She just went away."

"When did you meet her?"

"About six months ago."

"May I have her phone number, please?"

She recites it from memory.

He asks her a number of other questions, then gets up to leave with very precise and clear expressions of gratitude.

"She has a scar," she adds. "Above her left eye, half hidden in the eyebrow."

In the interval as he once again extracts his pad and makes his notation, she anticipates with a pang of alarm the terrible solitude that will close around her once he is gone and the door is shut.

"What am I thinking," she asks herself aloud. "I can send you her picture if you want."

"Please do," he says.

"'Please do!' Too much."

"The Surfeit is One."

"Oh, before you go ... I ... Would you ...?"

Bashfully, she holds her wallet out for him to bless.

"Of course," he answers.

The blessing is done by pinching thumb and the first two fingers of one hand together and then making a dipping motion above the wallet, as if inserting a coin.

*

"I don't want to talk to you," the building superintendent says. Not polite, but at least he is clear.

This is the address. While it is not a luxury building, it is well maintained. The rent is not low. Therefore, Lorraine Whitehead either has money or some employment she chose not to reveal to Professor Clark. It is possible she was simply dissipating her savings during her time here, but that is not typical behavior, unless she were also intending to commit suicide.

Her affair with Professor Clark began a few days after we first began to discuss our theory in San Toribio, and ended shortly before the death of the late Professor Long. In fact, Professor Clark last saw Lorraine Whitehead the day after the late Professor Long returned to Canada.

She might have killed herself. But, if this were something she had arranged with the late Professor Long, why not die with him? Was it a loss of nerve? Or was she his assassin?

Are the rest of us being stalked by our own assassins, now?

In my daily bulletin to the others, I advise them to look closely at their friends and associates, and to pay close attention to any newcomers. Obvious precautions. However, since we are all new to San Toribio, it is impossible not to make new acquaintances.

That night, a dream of train travel.

I gaze down into a blue, nocturnal welter of glistening tracks and silently rolling cars, their windows glowing scarlet and lamps throwing distinct gleams out into space, down below. It somehow makes me think of a pit of snakes.

The train carries me through valleys surrounded by sharply triangular, snowless mountains under a completely overcast sky. The daylight vanishes all at once. Starless blackness, even inside the train, only the sense of motion in the dark. Flashes of lightning illuminate the landscape. We descend into the horizontal forest. I can see huge gemlike stars with imperfect, uneven, different-colored light, through the huge trunks. The forest grows sideways from a rock face that plunges from a middling elevation into a gigantic crevasse whose bottom has never been found. The train travels along one of the massive, petrified trunks which span the ravine like a bridge. Then it passes into the opposite rock face, the sheer wall of steely rock; the interior is honeycombed with tunnels dimly illuminated with electrical sparks in copper baskets. In fact, with my slightest movement, static electricity flourishes over my clothes.

With an alarming rush, the train emerges from the ground and begins immediately to curve widely to the north, giving me a distinct view of the precipices and the scored, blackened metal walls of the town, my destination. Raked by incessant lightning, the walls are a necessary protection, to keep the town and its inhabitants from being blasted to smithereens, but the walls are also, very practically, wired up. They store the electricity from the lightning so that it can be used in more manageable doses by the town dwellers.

The name is something like Mavelin, or Meurival. The town has many entrances, as many as any other town, and a formula is required to pass through. The train must have let me out at a depot outside town, or maybe it was only an open crossing. If I brought any baggage along, it is abandoned on the train now. I am unsure if I have the right money to buy any new clothes or other necessities here, if they use money, if they sell anything. I might have to borrow clothes from someone. Ill fitting, unwashed clothes infested with lice. The entrance before me has a box on a stone post. I come up to the box and look inside. The dark interior of the box starts to glow with a bluish, flaming mist; a face appears and speaks three sentences. It could be cautioning me about something, or it could simply be a local catechism. I go up to the entrance, which has an attendant. As I come up to him, getting ready to repeat the phrase phonetically, he deliberately turns his face to mine and I see the ghost of that other face appear over his own features like an enamelled mask, the mouth repeating the sentences in the same hollow tone. The face disappears from him and now I think I have it over my own face. I hear the sentences repeated, and I think I am the one repeating it, in the same voice.

The attendant stands there for a moment longer, and I wonder if he expects money from me. Then he waves me inside impatiently, and I realize he was simply waiting for me to enter. Another attendant stands by the door, and as I come inside I turn to repeat the procedure with him, feeling some unhappiness about the prospect of so much of the same thing, but he waves me away with a look on his face that says I have it all wrong, that he is the exit repeater, not the entrance repeater. Then again, walking away, it occurs to me he might be simply shirking his duty, not wanting to bother with an impotent tyro like me, and I wonder if I should go back and insist, as my not having fulfilled all the proper forms might leave me vulnerable to invalidation later on.

The town is laid out in trenches that scale the slope in narrow terraces between steep walls. I can reach out and almost span the lane with my arms. The houses are semidetached boxes with doors opening directly on the street and people dressed in silk sprawl on thresholds fanning themselves and blinking at me impassively as I go by. The air smells like nothing. I see no animals, nothing alive but the people. Up a flight of steps and through the arched portal leading to the next trench up, steadily climbing until I reach the monastery or campus that is both highest up and furthest back, set under a projecting canopy of rock fringed with gold and silver streamers which undulate impressively, like seaweed. Now I notice some horned animals perched on the slopes above, although I see nothing they might live on.

In this monastery I will see for myself living examples of Old Believer economists, who refused to change with the times and preserve the archaic practices. Coming into the open courtyard I see no one stirring except a woman in a room off to one side; it is a stone room with a heavy, very carefully assembled table. The Old Believers are famous for their furniture. The woman is sitting on a stool at one corner of the table, doing the crossword in a newspaper. She is built like a weight lifter, stocky and powerful, dressed entirely in lustreless black duck. Work shoes or boots, trousers, an apron, a smock, and a brimless black cap, just like a bottle top, pulled down nearly to her eyebrows. Her hands are broad and pink; her face is too, and spattered across the nose and cheeks with soot that makes the whites of her eyes and the edges of her eyelids seem the more noticeably pale. In her free hand she holds a phosphorescent white coffee mug full of inky black coffee, and a stubby black pipe between her index and middle finger. Noticing me, she smiles, putting down her pen and nodding. I get the idea we are meant to remain silent; there was something in the old writings about caution in speech and speech out of season. She takes a final swig from her mug, deftly transferring the pipe to the corner of her mouth. Then she produces a round metal matchbox with a screw-off lid, pulls out a match, slides her backside out a little and strikes it on her hip, lights the pipe, tosses the match insouciantly over her shoulder, and, tamping the pipe speculatively with her thumb, she recaps the match cylinder and puts it away, then gets up and comes over to me with her right hand out for me to shake. She takes my hand with the peculiarly gentle grip of someone who is not only very strong but very skillful and deliberate in the use of strength. What I took for the soot on her face is a galaxy map of black stars.

Pausing first to nod acknowledgment to a bearded man dressed in exactly the same way, the butt of a cigar in his mouth, who has begun scraping the courtyard with a rubber spatula, she magnanimously shows me around, taking me to a scriptorium with a double row of high desks, for hand copying of economics textbooks, lining the walls of a narrow hall with a high ceiling of thick dark beams and bright windows of unstained glass, where images are delineated in lead outlines but not colored. I marvel at the beautifully rendered treatises she opens for me, with perfect charts and tables, magnificently illuminated formulae, all neat and clean, black and white, the lettering so exact it can barely be told apart from typing. There is also a dormitory reserved for economists in hallucinatory trances induced by the ritual use of a special fungus found only in certain remote valleys where the land becomes uncharacteristically boggy. The fungus is cultivated on the skin, and causes visions whenever it fruits, covering the affected area with a feathery patch of white down or fur that sheds and tends to wind around the host, so many of the economists I see are partially wrapped up in cottony webs, and a few are completely cocooned in the stuff. They squirm from time to time and give feeble cries. Attendants shuffle along the aisles giving them water; they are not able to keep food down during these trances, which can go on for days. Against the far wall are economists sleeping off the effects of mathematics intoxication brought on by certain varieties of calculus forgotten now in the outer world. I am also shown the domed garden of the indicator, all forbidding stone on this side, the far side, all clear windows, facing out over the void and illuminated by special arc lights to foster the growth of plants. As a participant in the "modern heresy" I am not permitted entry to this holy place, but, since I do wear the mark and abide by the Oaths, and since I regularly complete my test before going to bed every night, and separate the beads every morning without fail, I am allowed to stand a little before the threshold and to look in through the open door of bronze with a golden lintel. Inside there is a fabulous profusion of incredible plants, and the Indice enthroned near the curved wall of glass on her golden throne; her completely wild cries of ecstasy are the first vocal sounds I have heard up here, apart from the murmurs of the hallucinators. The Indice, tiny from this distance, is naked except for a tiara and other ritual jewelry. Among other qualifications, the Indice is selected above all for her skill or ability in reaching multiple orgasms: every week, she is required to have exactly one thousand orgasms. As the thousandth approaches, her howls of bliss begin to fracture into succinct prophecies about market behavior, currency fluctuations, and the less obvious influences that are likely to affect the economy in coming months. Indices are retired after one hundred thousand orgasms, as I recall, going "up the mountain."

A bell sounds from the back of the campus, and, with a gesture, my guide silently instructs me to wait where I am, then hurries off. I look up at the stone roof a hundred feet above me, then down at the grid of stone. They will fill your shoes with the distilled essence of forgetting or barely recalling your first love, blue and gold, stuff your feet in and squash it between your toes. A well, like a wishing well from a greeting card, stands near me. The late Professor Long is inside. He stands at the far end of the long well, with the black sheen of the water sideways underneath him, with his hands in his pockets and his profile turned toward me. I am unable to see whether his lips are moving. The uninjured side of his face is turned toward me. His words are only intermittently intelligible.

"United States CONGAMPHLGH at 1/10 ransembloh cases. Polsagal-maxnah currency can declare executive China, smaller currency rate, the pound into individual currency, the quisben issuing lunsem-neph same ransembloh."

In a flash I see them together. The image is gone but does not fade, and seems to gather a secondary intensity, phosphorescing invert colors like an afterimage in the eye. She on top of him. Obscene frenzy. Timed fiendishly to begin at the instant of plunging in. The lower portion of the body rocks violently while the upper part sways. The face is turned away. The head flung back. Rising and slowing with the rise.

"Same authority as iraimbilanja. Different authority by the zoraston degree, zugeh by dollar, the note any 5 plig in Federales. Nubrod supported for uomplina nohahal; either currencies quamsa fixed huadrongunda rates, bank for Icelandic burise-dollar, lunsemneph currencies over chramsa divisions."

I know the face but not the name. San Toribio hotel room. Her body is darker against his paler one. I remember the photograph of them together, with the devilish inscription. Blind and groping. A second flash.

"Purblox prices quisben inflation. One has either re-stamped currency services for fractional distinct dollars, the Tardemah distinct. One creates institutions, Canada ransembloh so khoums units reduced in Reserve of autonomy in control government, historic united credit non-decimal huadrongunda notes forgiven.

Currencies over monetary. The fallen lunsanfah Euro as Spanish prices divided coxech control Francs, and area noxochamarh coins exercised where 1 achna is 1 plig centime if lunzapha is valued at 1 Franc."

"Professor Long—who shot you? Did you shoot yourself, Professor Long? If someone shot you, you have a responsibility to let us know." Clear now that I could not see the wound in his head because I am looking directly into the hole. Lakes of sewage. Smoking with flies. Dark brown sky. I shoot down fuming pathways lined with packing crate and pallet shacks roofed with plastic sheets, like a racing ghost. The people are hungry sick and naked. Undulating slums built on the thick rind of buoyant trash scabbing over the oceans and lakes. Not one inch untenanted. There is a city of gleaming banks and chain stores, their bright facades already dingy, faded and scratched. An overloaded tram staggers off its tracks and slumps to the curb, spilling passengers from the roof and clinging to the sides. The ruddy-faced men with carefully coiffed silver hair and the busty girls sitting with them do not even glance out the windows of the restaurant. The lights go out. The streetlights droop and fold up like pillbug-legs under a blanket of listless nothingness. The glass flops out of the restaurant windows, runs down the walls, oozes bubbling in the street, sour brown air pours in on the patrons strangling and melting them. Pink slime dotted with silver hairpieces and breast implants pools in the grates and potholes, slums are flattened under an invisible planetary rolling pin. Everyone is turning to mush, their soggy flesh curdles and sloughs off green skeletons. Bloated seagulls

without wings or feathers strut from cadaver to corpse.
Then no movement. No vermin. No wind. No clouds.
No sounds. The dead sun stands at the zenith forever.
"The ouguiya rate in United is 100 names in the system.
Use Canada or its VAN-CORHG ariary at 1. The Subliga
sample, facilitate of huadrongunda circulation words in
ransembloh, at promina-bamigah historic rate. Classified
picalodox sponsoring policy. In Australia, currently over
coins as case, silver ratrugem cosneth can non-decimal
asemission for currency ..."

He tears himself free of the dream, gets out of his hotel bed and glides dizzily into the bathroom, peeling off
his sopping night costume, splashes water onto his face,
unable to get his bearings in a weird medium of vacuum
and light. Stepping back to look at his dripping face,
his enormous penis feels the light and goes off painfully
spurting semen onto the counter, his knees keep collapsing under him, hyphens draw and erase themselves in
his eyes and he drops suddenly onto the toilet seat. He
sits there in a bizarre confusion and misery, letting his
head flop back against the wall and then swing forward
between his hands, unable to find a bearable posture, unable to wake up, to think. He creeps forward onto the
floor, dragging down a towel to collapse on, and curls
there, looking up past the counter at the white globes of
the lights set in a box above the mirror. In San Toribio
they are voting. Heaps of votes are uncrated and counted
aloud in front of the polling site before being sealed in
ballot boxes and sent to the electoral committee headquarters; there are rumors that ballot boxes are being stolen or tampered with, but the police repeat that no boxes

are unaccounted for. The AUP seems to be leading, but every time their margin grows toward the tipping point, mysterious spurts bring the NFP back into a dead heat.

I see Professor Crest when he comes to the wellmouth. I had a feeling he was going to the monastery. Assiyeh will go there next, but not for some time. This understanding is all of a piece with the sort of quasi-knowledge I now have, in my new situation. Which is not a new situation. What has happened is, I am now no longer in my own way. I am still in the way, but I have become transparent, mostly. Largely. More transparent than not, and much more than I was. The result of this change is that I have quasi-knowledge of the formation of the concept of animal money, which was the effect of an intervention in the conversation of we five economists in San Toribio by an unknown something. It isn't unknown. I know what it is. Describing it is a chore, though.

It is not unique, or at least I see no reason why it should be, no essential attribute that requires it to be. It's a process elemental. I don't like this term, but it's the best one I have been able to come up with so far. An elemental is an element acting as an agent, having agency, which means an element with a will of its own. Not the whole element, though. A part of the element has will. The whole element has will, but in an elemental, the element's will is concentrated. It is not concentrated, will isn't light, it can't be focussed. What it is, is the elemental is a part of, is some of an element, a pure sample, the will of which has become an active agent; that's wrong too. The will can only be active, so it's redundant to think of it that way. The point is that the element's will becomes an active agent among human beings. In this case, the element is language, or maybe economics. Economics is an element. This was an economics elemental, which would be a subvariety, why sub?, OK OK a variety of process elemental. I'm not just a corpse spinning metaphors; I can see this. I can't see the elemental, but I see the wind it kicks up, and dust, and I can hear it whir like a storm yelling in the distance. The image of a windmill keeps coming into my head, or a turbine, something like that, but I can't say whether or not that means anything, but when I look at them, the living ones who survived me, Crest and the others, the elemental is frisking around them and going in and out of their eyes and nostrils and ears and mouths and off their fingers like spectral plumbing connecting them together.

The elemental wants to articulate itself, basically. It wants that the way an animal wants to reproduce. Except it doesn't want that, it doesn't reproduce, it just wants to grow, so it's more like wanting to grow larger. Fatten itself up maybe. Against some future event that will reduce it, so get bigger in anticipation of being reduced to make sure there will be something left. The process elemental isn't conscious; it has to do with consciousness but it isn't aware, or maybe it is a little, but like a plant or a microbe might be, maybe. I can only judge by behavior. It must be internally self-operated because I don't see any external control, and it moves in an impulsive, galvanic manner, underwater snail motion, sleepwalking, groping, that doesn't strike me as entirely self-aware. To grow, it has to enter into human thinking, that's its habitat, or growth medium. It cultures in human thoughts and then

diversifies itself from human to human, using books and
so on as charging stations or capacitors to regenerate, heal
itself, inoculate itself against counter-arguments maybe,
like a vaccine. It is fed—not fed, fanned, like a fire, by the
current climatic conditions of thinking, and it needed the
right conditions to grow in, like a seed flying through the
air until it finds the right kind of soil, the right moisture,
and so on. We were the right conditions and it grew in
us. As it grows, it also generates more of the same kind of
good conditions, like a tree whose overhanging branches
might protect its own saplings, except that it isn't
reproducing, it's just growing as, not a continuous single
organism, and not as a bunch of independent organisms,
so the elemental must be a kind of colony animal, or a
chimera maybe, cobbled together out of different words,
by which I mean not only words in the usual sense
but also numbers and charts, any portable, adequately
distinct unit that could connect one consciousness to
another. When all this connection is going on and gets
intense, the process elementals get attracted because this
is to them what a plankton bloom is to whales, no it
isn't, it's like an updraft that draws the clouds in laterally
and then pushes them up once they enter the column of
rising air. We generate the hot air and the elementals are
drawn in, but not as passively as clouds. Less passive than
clouds, but more active than air, so that they respond in
a way that at least mimics consciousness or choice. Or
preference. The elemental didn't want us to have animal
money. It didn't have animal money to give us. Or it did,
but not in the way you have a dollar in your wallet. It had
animal money to give us in the sense that what it gave

us doubled itself and doubled us, so that there was no exchange but a mutual augmentation. It may be that this function, which is manifested in its own transmission, was all we received from the elemental. Or the elemental just gave us itself, entire.

Now I see, I still see, because the pipes, the elemental pipes are still running through me, too. I don't have to be corporeally present for that. That's my connection to them, and why I am still directly aware of the elemental, I am still spavined in its jungle gym frame of vibrating tubes. I'm not spavined, I'm caught, that's all. Or I have caught.

PART FIVE:
IN FOR QUESTIONING

The second time I was homeless I was delivering pizzas for gas money and leftovers. I lived and breathed pizza filling the shower with phosphorescent orange grease, drive all day playing the same three damaged hardcore tapes and tracing and retracing those streets I can draw a map in my sleep of that town, and it is to that job I owe the presence of all those hideous street names like "Suel Avenue." I spent every second of my life driving to and fro on Suel Avenue, so that the name started to crash against my ears whenever I heard it, like saying the name of God. I'd go into convulsions if I ever had to drive down Suel Avenue again.

Number four will you be able to in a safe manner carry out all job assignments associated with this position? Despite my answers they hired me and the first week I get dispatched about fifteen minutes before the end of my shift to a motel less than five minutes away. I don't realize right off that a room number starting with two would be on the second level so I'm wandering up and down in dark rain looking for 215 when I see a woman disappearing into an end room on the ground floor, between two men. I peek in through the blinds in time to see them stuffing her in the closet. There are just the same two men: a doughy white man with a moustache and another one who looks like James Bond. I pull back and two seconds later the blinds snap shut. I hear the door squeal abruptly and there's a shadow on it that startles me, so I drop back and get the ice and soda machines between us. I hear the door shut. Then a car door. The engine goes and I see the car roll by, moustache man winding up the wheel.

James whips the door open at my knock. He has an impatient look on his face. I think he must have been expecting the other man.

"Got your pizza!"

"Wrong room," he says, swinging the door to.

"You don't want it?" I ask, opening the box and showing it to him.

"No I don't want it," he says.

"It's real hot," I say ramming it into his face and knocking him down and rushing in and half falling on top of him. He's flailing out and yelling, muffled by the pizza. I am on the other side of him when he tears his face out of the cheese and I kick him as often as I can. I grab a chair and try to hit him with it and it drops too early and falls on him. He's swearing and groping. I dive across the twin bed, get up, open the closet, pick the woman up off the floor, lose my balance, pivot, drop her on the bed, she starts kicking wildly and there's a sweatshirt over her head. I fall on my ass, get up, whip off the sweatshirt so she can see what's going on and stop kicking me hopefully, then I dive again across the beds pick up a lamp and throw it and the cord yanks it back so it hits me instead and I trip onto the second bed take up two fistfulls of top blanket and throw the whole thing over James who's pawing at his eyes. Anyway, I carry the woman out, nearly falling as my feet plunge into the mattress then down the other side with a heavier jolt than I was ready for so my knees buckle but I don't go down, only slouch-scoot out the door and dash for my shitty hatchback in time to hear someone yell. I reach the car open the door throw her in the passenger seat shut the door get around to the driver's side get in start the car the passenger door opens we're in reverse by accident and the open door of shitty hatchback clotheslines the man with the moustache as he's trying to drag the woman out again and she's staring at him with crazy eyes and kicking at him. I race shitty hatchback out of the motel and as we hit the speedbump she nearly flops out of the car. Jumping into traffic four minutes later I reflect that killing the pizza light would be a good idea, and I start yanking the cable. It won't come loose. As a black man with a tied-up woman crying in his car I would prefer not to be stopped. I don't remember what kind of car they were driving and cars all look the same to me anyway so everybody might as well be following me.

"Who are you? Who are you?"

That's my voice so I don't have to answer. I keep asking because something has me all wound up, and she keeps crying.

"Are you all right?"

"My hands ..."

I pull into a parking spot in a strip mall.

"I'll get your hands," I say.

They're bound with a white plastic tie and they're turning purple. I have a pocket knife and after some sawing and fussing I manage to get her hands loose and they spring forward. She cries out and begins chafing her wrists. Now she sits up in the chair and looks at me.

"Let me go."

"I saw them hauling you in there, so ..."

I shrugged.

She's nonplussed, so I take this opportunity to get out and haul on the cable with both hands. The light goes out finally. Then I get back in and ease the car out of the spot, turning tail to the street and then going along the other row of shops to the side exit.

"Where should I take you?"

She names a hotel downtown.

"I'll have to get gas."

Her name is Carolina Duende. She's an investigative reporter from *La Censura*. The two men grabbed her, etc.

"You think they were trying to shut you up?"

"Yes," she says seriously.

She's been working on a story, following up leads that others have tried and failed to trace. Here's her story:

It's nearing midnight at the Universidad Achrizoguela zoo. The economics conference is in full swing. Intermittent flashlight beams slice the darkness as six silhouettes, one of which only stands as high as the others' knees, break into the biology lab. Their heads are enormous, smooth, misshapen, their black ski masks drawn down over bandages and therapeutic appliances. They have managed to get this far unnoticed, but they had a close call when the second Professor Long tripped over some rabbits and set off a timer.

Now they have gathered around a table in the biology lab, illuminating it with a portable lamp after having blocked the windows. Professor Crest has the metal; a handful of special alloy blanks purchased under false pretenses from a metallurgical supplier, which he now lays out carefully in two neat rows on the marble top. The first Professor Long, easily recognizeable through her disguise by the black Chinese surgical smog mask, has the germ cultures in small vials. She finds some fresh petri dishes and sets to work sporing them with modified versions of a sample she got from the virology lab. Professor Aughbui has brought the mathematics and design notes, which he hangs from the projecting ventilation hood and consults as he assembles the simple machinery that will run the experiment during their absence. He holds the pieces in place while Smilebot welds the joints. The second Professor Long brought the absence, the skull of a banker, taken from the anatomy department. He positions this precisely among the other elements of Professor Aughbui's machinery. He also searches the biology lab until he finds a suitable hiding place for the experiment, which they must leave behind, and which must go on for at least a full day. Luckily, there is an electric oven that can hold their apparatus. He sabotages it carefully, severing the power wires inside their insulation, so no fault can be seen. Professor Budshah brings the power, in the form of solar and lunar energies contained in a battery he salvaged from one of the displays intended for the physics conference.

When they are all ready, at the stroke of midnight, the metal blanks are inserted into the skull's gaping gold-toothed mouth, painted with the cultures under a mingled beam of recorded solar and lunar light while being gently agitated and tickled with minute bursts of electricity by the pin-like arms of the experimental machinery. Six pairs of eyes peer out from ski mask slots, riveted on the experiment's slow action; it's like watching the little plastic hand snatch the quarter. Once the coins have been saturated with the culture and celestial energies, the machinery silently lowers the maxilla and cranium, sealing the experiment for its full day's gestation. The five economists all rest their hands on the crown of the skull and recite formulae of ancient rites of sacrifice and plenty, fertility and want. Then each produces a high-denomination bill and burns it to nothing in the acetylene torch. The barking of a dog freezes them. They stand paralyzed around their baroquely hermetic instruments, staring with wild stupidity at the unfinished work before them. The dog stops. A silent release of stopped breath. They complete their operations and then allow Professor Crest, who, while he is not the strongest, is the most careful and precise in his movements, to pick up the experiment and carry it to its hiding place. Once all of them are convinced that it can remain there a full day without being discovered or damaged, they place a special seal on the oven. Then, bumping and groping, they find the wholesome outer air uncontaminated by sorcery's densely intoxicating musk of fragrances and decay. That night they all toss and turn in horrible nightmares and wake up looking as if they'd all lost fights.

That day is an agony of suspense. They avoid each other, and anything else that might remind them of the experiment, ticking away—they hope—undetected in the oven in the biology lab, as students and professors go about their daily routine, maintenance personnel empty trash bins and make the rounds, tours are conducted, facilities checked. They try to lose themselves in devotional activities, doing extra exercises in their problem books, separating and reseparating the beads. The second Professor Long swims lap after lap, trying to exhaust himself, trying to keep his thoughts from influencing events. Professor Aughbui painstakingly rechecks his diagrams. Professor Crest goes and looks at every single object on display in the art museum, making sure he spends no less than a full minute in front of each. The first Professor Long watches one movie after another, visiting one theater after another, even though she doesn't understand the language well enough to follow what's going on. Professor Budshah translates poetry, producing several pages of incomprehensible, pedantically-labored renderings of simple poems.

Midnight. At last. Once again the six silhouettes enter the biology lab, block the windows, trip and blunder, knock down stools. The oven is not hot, the seal is not broken, the experiment sits inside within the guidewires they'd put around it. The economists join hands, while Professor Crest extracts the experiment and brings it back to the table. He joins the circle, and they all chant in a low murmur until the stroke of midnight. When the campus campanile strikes its twelfth chime, lightning flashes and thunder booms, and the maxilla of the skull silently lifts. And lo a stream of discolored coins gushes from chapless jaws and spreads rustling across the table top. The coins are a diseased, purulent color, but they begin to change the moment they are exposed to the air. Within moments they turn pink, then faint magenta, then a pale blue, before settling at last to a more or less fixed bluish-white, like soured milk. The coins twitch and breathe with a scarcely perceptible sussurrus. The economists trade looks, radiant with success. Alive! Producing black bags with black skulls and crossbones on them, they each reach out and take several handfuls of these living coins, which are warm and yielding in the hand, each one a distinctly palpable disc, but vitalized, like living bones—the hum of life is unmistakeable, even though it can't be traced to any distinct sensation. Once all the coins are gathered, the experiment is quickly disassembled and they toss its remains down the incinerator chute.

Over the course of the next few days, each of them will be slipping these living coins in among regular money: passing them in change, inserting them into vending machines, dropping them unnoticed into open cash register drawers and tip jars. Their animal money is gathering virulence. From these seed points, the living money begins to proliferate through treasuries of the world. The bison on one coin is fucking the eagle on the other, and the resulting eggs hatch into more living coins sporting Abyssinian centaurs and other chimeras, letters and numbers no one can read, denominations that rely on entirely different categorization schemes.

That was the story. She sent it in to the paper, but the email bounced. The paper had ceased to exist overnight, somehow. Then, when she couldn't find her partner, she got frightened and decided to hide in an out-of-the-way place for a while. Then she decided she should try to get over the border, and that's when they grabbed her. A bus station, a grab, the back of a van that stank of old vomit, then the motel, and me.

It's a three day trip by car. I don't know how the fuck she stays alive because I've never seen her eat anything but mastodon doses of acid and botanical hallucinogens washed down with plain water. She is obviously supernatural, at least in part. I suspect she has some way of making acid, or whatever it is. She never talks about it; either that or she must have loaded up a few laundry bags full a little before we met. She never buys any, and from time to time she'll catch a nanoflash of something inducive growing in a field or through a stand of trees that look as visually impenetrable as a wall to me, and bug me to pull over and go back.

She is my adventure now.

"Could you take me to the train station? Don't you have any tobacco?" she asks me, since I'm driving with an empty pipe in my teeth.

"I don't smoke," I say. "I just like having the pipe sometimes."

I shift lanes when the sign for the train station comes up.

"The nice thing," I say, "about a pipe is that you still have it when your smoke is done."

I don't ask where she's going. I can't be made to tell what I don't know.

"What if I paid you to drive me?" she asks.

"Sure," I answer instantly. "You mean, instead of the train, right?"

"Can you take time off?"

I snicker.

"I'm probably fired. Just tell me which way to go."

"Head east," she says, pointing.

"But," she adds after a moment, "your things. This drive will take a few days."

I thumb the back seat.

"Those are my things," I say. "You have gas money, right?"

"Yes."

Three days will take us to Etsimen, right next door to San Toribio and a virtually unreachable pain in the ass because they're building a highway between the two cities starting in the middle and working in both directions as slowly as possible, forcing all traffic onto what is basically just open land, decorated with the occasional sign. There are a few roadside stops without the road; tents where you can get food or stay overnight. Those who want more privacy, us included, can park alfresco and get breakfast and a shower for a lower rate. So the bigger tents have a couple of cars pulled up, people sitting at crates and spools lit by acetylene lamps playing cards or eating to tinny speakers or watching the news on their phones or tablets. Then you see the shadow cars parked in an archipelago around the tent and rocking gently. The owner has several big dogs to keep voyeurs away. Lying next to her, I can look up and see all the constellations I've forgotten, and hear the night bugs spicing up the dry air, so loud they drown out the sound of the motel-camp. And yet I can hear her even breathing, as well as feeling it on my shoulder, and spilling up the side of my neck. She told me why we were going to Etsimen: there's someone there who contacted her about what happened to Tripi. It's a story no amount of interference could disappear. So we're going after Tripi. Fine. I can't think of anything

I'd want to do more. She sighs and changes her position.
Sing. Sing, answer. Answer back. Answer what? Answer
the beauty. Answer it back. When it hits, answer. It seizes
and squeezes, crushes with its force. Let it. Or fight it. I
can't lay claim to the voice that commands me to answer,
no one can. Not the beauty. The voice is not in it, from
it, not any-slippery-preposition it, not any-slippery-
preposition me. Answer! Answer! Not even an idea, not
even a thought, just a flash—answer! Now *you!* Your
turn! Right now your turn! You are your turn or nothing
right now. While it's still there and alive in front of you.
In dreams you edit your love lines, but when the one you
love is there and it's now, you are your turn or nothing.
The answer joins the beauty or tangles with it. It might
destroy it. Come back and try to put it together yourself
later and you won't be able to, memorybeauty isn't the
same, bring back the feeling, but you tamper, only by
touching it you tamper it too much. It was too much to
begin with. How can you conjure it out of yourself if it
was bigger than you were to begin with? Answer! Answer
the question how. How it is, not what not when. How?
How? Howch? You get hit on the head—how! Howch,
howtheshit, howfuck? Look arhownd. Howfuck did this?
Howshits? Howsluts am I? Bitchow did it get this way, all
these ways, these slapfuckle blind ways? How blind? Not
just to blind or not to but how blind is it? How is it blind,
I mean in what way? Which flavor is the blindness of it,
which kind of blind was it, how does it go from day to
day? How does blindness work? My lungs are blind. My
liver is blind. Only my eyes see, and how well? How is
seeing? How is living with my liver? No you can't just lie

there! I don't care if you're dead! How is it going? Answer me! How dead are you now? More dead than yesterday, or less? Give it to me on a scale of one to five, one being least alive, five being most dead. Is it cruel of me to keep asking? No you can't just lie there rotting—you have to report on it: how is your rot going? No I won't leave you alone! Fucking punk lazy dead ass no I won't! Answer me! You can be dead, but you can't be exempt. The voice of the cruelty of the beauty of life of how's-it-going reaches us all down to the molecule the ant the atom the every. Everyday!

PART SIX:
BROKE BANKERS

That morning, the remaining economists are each personally approached by an official messenger from the IEI, informally ordering them to attend a series of unofficial hearings on the subject of their current project, animal money, as described in section 1310 of the Routine Articles of Investigation. Professor Crest, who has a thoroughgoing familiarity with the Articles, informs the others that this means someone within the IEI has filed a complaint about them.

"Is it Professor Delatour?" the remaining Professor Long asks.

"He would not have the right," Professor Crest responds. "He is on the committee."

"Committee members can't bring charges?" Professor Budshah asks.

"They can," Professor Crest answers. "But they can not file complaints. Not even through a proxy."

They will be questioned separately by an unknown panel.

"What happens if ...?" the remaining Professor Long asks.

"... at worst, we could be formally arraigned for unacceptable heterodoxy."

"They can't disbar us, surely? It would take the violation of one of the Oaths to disbar us, wouldn't it?" Professor Budshah asks.

"Correct," Professor Crest says. "However, they can place us under suspension in heterodoxy, which would mean an indefinite period of isolation."

The remaining Professor Long will have to make her averral in a conference room belonging to a different hotel, right on the coast. San Toribio's beaches are unfortunately rocky and precipitous, the water is cold all year, and while the surf is high, boulders and reefs make surfing too risky. She arrives early, and decides to look in on Professor Aughbui.

The Achrizoguayla University Aquagation Program is headquartered in an old naval fortification that protrudes obliquely out into the bay. It has a great stone platform sticking out of it and jutting far out into space, at least forty feet above the deep water of the bay. The platform has a battlemented wall with egg-shaped bartizans at fifteen-foot intervals. Professor Aughbui was given one of these to use as an office. Opening the bartizan door, she enters a domed white cylinder about ten feet across. Opposite the door, not ten feet away, there is a window with interior shutters. The wall beneath the window is built out to form a step and a seat, and there's a slot just below the sill for a plank. Professor Aughbui perches on the seat, with the plank for a desk, and the windowsill for an armrest. With a flip of his wrist, he could toss his pen into the see-sawing green baywater just below, which would receive and smother it, hiding it forever. A milky white glass block is glued into the apex of the ceiling with discolored, pinkish caulk, and the power cable is bracketed to the wall inside a chafed and corroded-looking zinc hose, angling down to the switch by the door. Wind coils and churns inside the bartizan even when the door is closed, obliging Professor Aughbui to weight his papers with iron slabs. The wind also causes the shutter facing him to swing against him, rapping his forehead. Pushing the shutter back out of his face seems to have become instinctual to Professor Aughbui already. Smilebot arrives after a moment carrying two mugs of tea. Someone on the shore, or perhaps in one of those boats out there, is practicing Achrizoguaylan bagpipes. Professor Aughbui offers the remaining Professor Long his seat, the only one available, but she declines.

Professor Aughbui is a cipher; he never talks about himself, and seems content to bury his nose in his work. Since his near-kidnapping, the repeated encounters with the police, and then seeing Assiyeh in the flesh, he has become no less quiet, since he was virtually silent to begin with, but events may be inducing a softening that is disquieting in its glimpses. She dreads an abrupt dissolution into tears with a foreboding that is wildly out of proportion, as if it could only end in a horrifying liquefaction of the whole man. However, Professor Aughbui answers her questions succinctly, and his decorum is gradually smothering her fears. The place is very beautiful. Perhaps the sight of it is beneficial. Now he has launched into a detailed summary of what she can expect at the hearing, what she is and is not by statute required to say. The music continues, and now she can see a party straggling along the water's edge in the distance, dressed in lumpy, peculiar Achrizoguaylan formal dress; it must be a wedding. There seem to be a lot of them down by the water. The music is lively and intricately patterned. She can see an outlandishly-dressed group of what are obviously tourists edging around the party, which is making its way from the street far beyond to the park overlooking the water. The light is blocked by clouds that come and go, and just now the light is dazzling, like a kind of steam. It's time to go.

Professor Aughbui offers to accompany her as far as the hotel, the discouragingly-named Hotel Federal. She declines the offer. She wants to collect her thoughts en route, and smoke, and Professor Aughbui seems to disapprove of tobacco.

As she comes around the tower, the remaining Professor Long catches sight of a distinct black ball in the blue sky—the new moon. The clouds are receding into the distance, and a passenger plane floats below their level. They create a fuming, radiant ceiling above the city, but they give her an impression of toy imitations. Lightning flashes far away, over the mainland. There's the San Toribian skyline, looking like chandeliers hanging in the dimness. Water and land alternate, bordered by dimly luminous white surf, and then the dull gold lights of the houses and the bottle green streets. Lightning flashes on the far side of the city; she can see the bolts through the buildings. No sign of any companion up there, only the crescent moon. How do I know that's the right moon?

The Hotel Federal makes no impression on her. She can see lighted windows pasted on to the featureless and distorted German Expressionist silhouettes of the surrounding buildings.

A woman in a sports jacket accosts her with cordial hesitancy as she comes into the lobby. None of the panel members have arrived yet, and at least two are going to be significantly delayed. She apologizes on their behalf, and relays their message: the remaining Professor Long should stay at the Hotel Federal until they arrive. In the meantime, perhaps she would like something to eat? No? If she is tired, they have set aside a room ...

The remaining Professor Long is directed to a room on the second floor. She washes her face and hands, then lies down, as if the bed had conjured sleepiness in her. There are so many pillows and bolsters and thick comforters that she can't seem to lay herself out evenly and, while she feels unaccountably tired all of a sudden, and her mind is a blank, sleep doesn't come. She lies on her side, eyes open to the dark room.

There's no sound. The heavy drapes are drawn all the way across the windows so that not even a seam of light is visible. The corner of the bathroom hides the bright line under the door. There's only the vertical dark edge of the wall and a thin glow that does not penetrate at all into the room.

Someone crouches near her in the dark. She knows someone is there who has conjured a toy hotel and diverted her into it. There is no Hotel Federal, but then there is no real anywhere; the realness of a place is something that breathes and gelatinously reorganizes its past parts all the time. The firm clarity and novelty of this idea puts her on a more confident footing and when she startles awake, she has no idea how long she has been asleep or what woke her. She lies in the dark and sweats. Gets up and feels her way to the bathroom, getting a not very refreshing drink of water by the dim light from under the door. Lie back down, wondering how they will get in touch with her, or whether she will have to stay all night, and pay for the room. Will the phone jangle her awake violently?

She thinks again of the crouching presence on the floor somewhere. It watches her fixedly from the dark. It breathes the air, and she breathes its breath. It holds her captive. The trap is a hotel, a city, night, money, the hearing. She breathes its breath—her body hardens. It becomes the final piece of the trap.

In numbed horror she realizes that her body is not the final piece. Her mind is becoming an empty black frame, framing a vortex of stale air that's being sucked out of it. The light beneath the door dims suddenly and the room becomes all but totally dark. The phone rings. She rises groaning, not knowing where to find the noise, her body as heavy as stone. Drawing the drapes back, she exposes the dingy buildings across the way, in a grimy dusk like a dead breath of stagnant flatness. The phone rang once, or did it?

She goes back downstairs and lets the same sportsjacketed woman know she'll be in the restaurant. Inconceivably animated Achrizoguaylans careen around her table and the dining room is like a carousel. But now it's turning back into a scene. The flatness and distance are creeping up, forming a moat around the remaining Professor Long. While her behavior doesn't change, to her—in this weird, forced self-consciousness that is also somehow originating outside of her—she seems to be play-acting. The whole world is a zoo of phoney habitats and segregation and staring for the sake of staring. You go to a zoo to see animals behaving the way animals behave in zoos. Her visitor from the hotel room has found her again, is very near to her. Not crouching now. He's been playing out her leash and now he's yanking it in. He isn't any one person in particular; he's the guiding spirit that bides darkly in upper corners.

She has a cup of coffee and listlessly eats a sandwich. The food is surprisingly good and her mood brightens slightly. The moment she gets up to leave, there is someone passing behind her chair she bumps into. She reaches to open the door and someone darts in, compelling her to stand back. She steps out onto the sidewalk for a smoke but there is already someone stepping there, already lighting up. The moment she thinks of turning, stepping, there is someone there, blocking the way with an open door, or carrying a big bag or parcel. Thinking to go round a pair of slow-moving older people she nearly collides with a baby carriage thrust out suddenly from between two parked vans. Turning back, there's a small boy where she just was, walking along obliviously in his knit cap. She opens her mouth to say something and a car horn blasts, holding the note until a siren takes over, drowning out her words before she can say them. It's as if her visitor were reading her mind and balking her every impulse by moving people and things to check her like chess pieces.

The chubby black man with the white shirt, black tie, and black nylon bomber jacket, currently browsing at the newstand, was also in the hotel restaurant; in fact, he had come in around when she did. He never glances in her direction or comes too close, but the remaining

Professor Long is increasingly sure he's watching her; he may be following or he may be gravitating along without meaning to, it doesn't matter which it is. Suddenly resenting this, she wants to step out of the stream of pedestrians and head back inside when a small woman appears from behind a garbage can and stops, blocking her way while rummaging noisily in a fistfull of plastic bags. It's always the same rather paltry kind of person; small, thrown together, animated by a shrewish viciousness. She realizes she is seeing the people around her the way her mysterious visitor does, and that it wants to reduce her to a shoddy knock-off human. The visitor runs things around here, or around her.

Then at her elbow there stands the man in the black bomber jacket and he calls her gently by name.

"You're wanted for questioning. Will you come with me, please?"

"You've been following me, haven't you?" she demands, flushing with rage.

The man is completely calm, even compassionate, and his voice is light and sweet. He has a strange, bread-loaf shaped head and a broad, high brow. He shows her a document on his phone, complete with an image of a badge and a rectangular scribble that might be a computer scanning code.

"You can see here," he says.

The remaining Professor Long gives him a withering look.

"I was to meet with an unofficial panel in this hotel. Nothing was said about some sort of officer, anything of the kind."

"This is official," he says, still unfazed.

"Show me your badge, then."

He shows her the phone again.

"That's a picture of a badge, not a badge."

"You have to come in for questioning, Professor Long. It won't take very l—much time. You aren't being arrested."

She gives her head a brief shake, and her features are shuttered.

"I have an appointment here."

"That will have to wait. We have a car here," he says quietly, bowing to take her briefcase. She snatches it up before he can take it, leaving him still doubled forward, his fingers stretched out. He unbends again, in no rush, hand falling to his side, and lets his head roll slightly on his shoulders.

"I think, Professor—"

"You're trying to ...!" she says sternly, raising her voice.

"Professor ..."

He sighs through his nose, opens his mouth and then closes it. Then he opens it again, with the same patience.

"I think, Professor, you should look at this."

He holds out his phone again.

"The Surfeit is One!" she says sternly and walks away. The big, copper hotel doorman about fifty years old in a heavy, double-breasted coat with gold buttons and braid, comes ambling over, brow furrowed.

"Something wrong?" he asks.

She points to the man in the bomber jacket.

"That man tried to steal my bag. He's been following me ..."

The doorman approaches the man in the bomber jacket, who remains as he was, his phone still in his hand.

Other people are pausing or slowing to watch.

"Excuse me, sir," the doorman says. "Can you show me identification?"

The man shows him his phone. The doorman makes an inquiry through his own phone. Both men stand together, thumbing their phones. The remaining Professor Long enters the lobby and takes refuge in the ladies' room.

After waiting for a few minutes, she glances outside as another woman comes in. The man in the bomber jacket is visible just outside the door. He's standing in profile, looking toward the lobby, a splash of lamplight on his face.

"You should go with him," she tells herself then. "You should get this matter cleared up right away."

And a moment later:

"Things like this don't get cleared up. They never get cleared up, you know that."

She waits until the bathroom is empty again, but, when it is, what was she waiting for?

"They are designed never to be cleared up. They are designed to get messed up. More and more messed up."

She tries calling Professor Aughbui, then Professor Crest. No answers. What if the panel members have arrived and are waiting for her? What if they leave, thinking she's stood them up?

"I'm going to attend the panel," she says. "The Surfeit is One."

"Miss ... Miss ..." follows behind her.

She ignores the man in the bomber jacket and makes her way to the nearest conference room, which might be the only conference room here.

The face of the man in the bomber jacket is swimming up toward the shrinking gap between the door and the frame as she closes it. The room is filled with people, sitting in rows. There are three people dressed as economists, their faces each equipped with economists's marks, sitting at a long table in the front of the room.

The door frame is not set directly into the wall, but into a kind of apron of glass panes set in wooden ... somethings, not sashes. She doesn't know what you call them. The one just at the level of her nose is painted white—they all are—and the paint is dingy, cracked, peeling, flaking off. These wooden somethings don't belong with all this hotel stuff; hotels are made out of materials that age inconspicuously. A bizarre object, right beneath her nose. A wooden something between panes of glass, and the glass has flecks of paint around its edges, and there is a particularly large flake of paint that seems to have something blackish lodged under it. At first, she thinks it's a dead fly, but it's only a flake of paint, except that there are thin, hairlike or twiggy things projecting from underneath it. It could be a dead fly or other similar insect wedged beneath a paint flake, or maybe it's a kind of bushy mildew, a tiny clod of dirt held together with clumped rootlets. The door is opening against her and she angles to one side.

"Miss ... Miss ..."

The door stays open, someone standing in it, looking at her. The clod under the flake casts a shadow, and it's starting to look like a hole. The remaining Professor Long turns to survey the room again. People are still settling into their seats, and they are all also wearing the plain grey and brown clothes of economists, and marked with the wan white symbols of the IEI on their faces. There are some open seats on the far side of the room, a few in from the aisle. She crosses around behind the back row and slips into a free seat between two others. The man in the bomber jacket sits in the next seat over, with an unknown economist between him and the remaining Professor Long. He asks his neighbor to change seats with him, but is refused. He gets up a moment later and then makes his way down the next row forward, to stand directly in front of her, blocking her view of the table, but a colleague, someone she recognizes, Professor Borores, is making her way down the same aisle—a billowy, obese woman who walks with the assistance of two canes. She indicates that she wishes to sit in the chair currently blocked by the man in the bomber jacket.

"Once this lady comes with me," he says.

"Well, I have to sit down," Professor Borores says loudly, panting, and begins to maneuver herself into the chair, which is one of the few empty seats remaining. This entails bumping the man aside.

"Excuse me!" she says, even more loudly.

The man is not really prepared to deal with this and Professor Borores claims her seat, sitting down heavily. Now he is nearly forced to lean on top of the professors further toward the center of the audience, and they are adjusting themselves. One of them reaches up and begins pushing him with both hands back toward the end of the row, pushing at him with both hands as if she were clearing some room in a closet. The man in the bomber jacket is forced to retire reluctantly down the row. He tries to take up a position directly behind her, but that seat is taken as well. Then he goes to the front of the room and stands directly in front of the middle panelist.

"Excuse me! Excuse me, sir! You can't stand there!" the panelist says.

He turns to her and says, "I have a lady in here, a Professor Min-Yin Long—"

"Get out of the way!" a man in the audience cries.

"Just a minute," the man in the bomber jacket turns his head and says.

"Sit down!"

"This hearing is not open to the general public," another panelist says. "Are you an economist?"

"No, ma'am," he says, "but—"

"Then leave."

After a few minutes, a doorman—the same one who had accosted the man in the bomber jacket outside—comes into the room and takes him by the arm. The man in the bomber jacket compresses his mouth in disappointment, but he leaves without resisting. The remaining Professor Long is unable to concentrate, being too aware that the man in the bomber jacket is somewhere outside the room, watching her. She came all this way, and to be tampered with like this, to be prevented now from being able to participate, infuriates her. She simply can't manage to banish him from her mind, even if he has been put out of the room, and this is all the more aggravating because this panel has convened to review a number of cases that are apparently either similar to or perhaps even connected with her own, and she really should be paying close attention to know what to expect and to be prepared, but instead she reverts obsessively to a fantasy of poisoning the man in the bomber jacket, watching the expression of surprise melting already into alarm on his face, the hand flying to his throat, buckling at the knees ...

"Professor Long, Min-Yin."

Instantly she is on her feet, making her way to the end of the row.

"Stay there, please," one of the panelists says. "It's easier for us if you do."

A bit nonplussed, she resumes her seat.

"Now, in your own words—"

"And in your own time—"

"Yes, in your own time, explain the concept—"

"Basics only, please—"

"Yes, basics only, please, of the concept of animal money—"

"As you understand it—"

"Yes, as you understand it."

She isn't sure whether to feel more or less self-conscious sitting in the audience like this, but Professor Borores is engrossed in needlepoint directly in front of her, and the everydayness of that calms her.

"The concept is both a radical and a simple one," she says. "Animal money is ..."

She searches the room from her seat.

"... is like ..."

She points to Professor Borores' needlepoint.

"... and ..."

She points to that bizarre object on the wooden something dividing the little panes of glass around the door.

"Could you be more specific?"

"How?" she asks. "What could be more specific than ...?"

She points to the bizarre object again.

"Do you mean ...?"

The person sitting in the middle of the panel points up. There are a number of candidates for indication in that direction: the ceiling, the recessed light, the water sprinkler, a small black shape that could be a fly or some other insect.

"I'm not sure. If you mean that ..."

She points upwards herself.

"Which?"

"See?"

"But is it ...?"

The door opens and a man enters ringing a hand bell.

"Recess!"

Owing to a delay that is attributed entirely to her, the remaining Professor Long is now told that she must spend the night in this hotel and complete her hearing first thing in the morning. She doesn't see the man in the bomber jacket in the corridor. Shutting herself up in her hotel room with the keep out sign on the doorknob, she wonders if she should undress? Her test book is not here—she will have to improvise a test before going to bed. Searching for stationery, she opens the nightstand drawer and finds that what she at first glance took for a *Bible* is a leatherbound copy of *The Wealth of Nations*. Was this put here for her benefit? Or is it *their* way of winking at her, letting her know they've been in her room? She tries to sleep with the light on, but in the end she puts it out.

The visitor crouches, not close, not too far. Not quite

within a normal arm's reach, not more than two steps away. Its voice mutters in the air conditioner and its face isn't in the dark it is the dark. She is just sinking into sleep when she feels it lean one of its hands on the bed, a dip in the mattress near one corner, and she springs upright glaring into the dark, startled and angry. Did she ask it what it wants, or did she only think of asking it? The room stands there as before, having retracted its arm back behind the dark and the muffled quiet. The remaining Professor Long peers into the dark as if she were trying to intimidate it, then turns and dashes herself angrily down onto the pillow.

The next day is blindingly bright. As she walks to the campus the glare bounds from every parked car windshield and window, leaping in great arcs from the glass and crossing the air in prismatic fans. The water in the small fountain at the little intersection captures light and tosses it like a bauble in shapeless hands. The cries of the brilliantly-colored birds of all different kinds, who have gathered in the dense vine canopy that engulfs the trellises over the pathways are sharp and distinct, not blending in her ear but forming a kind of articulated orchestration using countless unique instruments. Glancing up, she notices something in the sky, or rather in the air, in the act of disappearing behind a building. She is able to prolong her view of it for a few seconds further by stepping back and observing its funhouse mirror reflection in the windows across the street. What she sees is like a coagulated mass of pale, virtually colorless balloons, resembling a somewhat less than medium sized inflatable creature from a Thanksgiving parade, its various parts bobbing like a slow-motion film of a buffalo fording a river or a huge puffy white cartoon glove practicing piano fingering. It moved laterally, without rising or descending, with a smooth momentum that seemed to belong to it, and not, for example, the wind, or someone who might have pushed it or pulled it. The reflection showed an undulating, cream-colored smear whose outlines zig-zagged as the image travelled over the glass. Hyacinth perfume. The thought and smell of it hit her at once, communicated across that distance of about a hundred feet from that balloon animal.

The remaining Professor Long takes in the modern, artistically-designed courtyard and lobby, the architecture of the front of the building, the slightly acerbic landscaping, and a sleeve of dark paranoia envelops her. The luminous day and its faces are starting to take on the aspect of gaudy ornaments on a prison cell or execution machine. She tells herself this is perhaps an intended effect of the harassment she's been dealing with lately; maybe she'll get too emotional and make an ass of herself when it comes time to make her presentation. Seeking a change, without any clear idea whether for the better or worse, she hurries inside and tries to distract herself with the business of the day, the assembling people waiting for a conference room to be assigned. She uses a search for tea, then, when that fails, for hot water and tea bags, as a smokescreen.

"Tea?" the woman behind one of the conference tables asks. She gets up then, without another word, but gesturing to the remaining Professor Long to wait, and goes into one of the offices. She returns a moment later with a paper cup of tea and hands it to the remaining Professor Long.

"Thank you very much," she says.

She drifts back to the lobby, sipping the tea, which is slightly too strong, and half attending to a conversation between a pair of economists from Burma, both wearing the same grey, standard economist uniform suits. After a quarter of an hour, she has whittled her tea down by half and decides to thin it. A dog barks at her as she fills a plastic cup with hot water from an office fountain, causing her to jerk. She splashes water on the front of her trousers and onto the floor. There's no dog in sight. A seeing-eye dog, maybe, but they don't bark do they? Had it been a dog's bark? A single outcry that started like a cough and ended in a hoarse yelp. It sounded like a little dog.

The Burmese economists are talking about the Great Sejm in late eighteenth century Polish tax policy. She is watching the doors for any sign of the man in the bomber jacket and gradually becoming aware of a din of barking dogs coming from the other side of the rear wall, like there's a kennel back there. The noise of the dogs is starting to drown out the other voices. She closes the iris of her concentration around the Great Sejm, not needing to follow but only to stay with it and not let the other world—which is not real—carry her away. For nearly twenty minutes, she clings to the edge of the precipice, and then she hastens to take sanctuary in the ladies' room again, triumphant barking roiling at her back lightly pelting her with tingling incursions and she's relieved to meet no one in the hall.

With terrifying speed the noise races up behind her

and she dashes the last few steps into the empty ladies' room, slamming the door behind her and drawing the heavy bolt of rough wood just in time as heavy bodies collide with the door, making it leap violently under her hands, with an insane explosion of barking and snarling, slavering madness raving and scratching at the door with the swift, light sound of dog claws, and even gnawing at the hinges so that they work up and down—the ponderous iron ring swivels in its housing slightly, so she shoves a massive wooden table in front of the door and piles chairs on top of it, weighting it further with a cauldron and some logs she drags from the cold hearth, taking care to shut the flue since she can already see the scrabbling shadows down the chimney and hear the dog claws, the snuffling breath hollow in that confined space. The claws rattle harmlessly on the metal flue as she slides the hasp, locking it in place. Not that way, not get in that way, she thinks.

Turning back to the door she sees the teeth of the dogs through the wood and working away at it. Seizing a lump of iron from the floor, she smashes the teeth with it, but as one isosceles jaw recoils in pain another clamps into its place, so she covers the vulnerable parts of the door with more chairs and with a landscape painting from the wall before flying to the toilet stalls, where sure enough a grotesque, elongated snout lined with snarling teeth is already forcing its way through the ceramic funnel, shoving the hinge of its jaw up through the hole first so it can compress and send through its head and then the rest of its body and followed by a black geyser of satiny vicious doberman pinschers. She flushes the toilet and the snout drops and jams against the bottom of the bowl, the jaw being too wide; the remaining Professor Long grabs the plumber's helper standing nearby and pounds the snout down, flushing and flushing, then pulls out a fistfull of toilet paper and, without tearing it from the spool, chucks it in the bowl and flushes until the bowl is jammed and brimming. Repeat for the other stalls. They can't smell her through the water. It acts as a barrier to all odors.

No more barking now, just vigilance on all sides. The ladies' room has no window, and is only half lit. It's a good thing she didn't sit down on one of the toilets! She checks the sink, and sure enough, a small, trembling pink nose surrounded by long white hairs, like the snout of a Scotch terrier, probes silently at back of the center drain. She drives it down with a sudden thrust of paper towels, and there's a hollow yelp from the pipes. Turning on all the taps may not drown them, but it should prevent the non-amphibious dogs from trying that again.

Sitting in the corridor, on a bench, she realizes, with a pang of alarm she dares not show, that the hairline crevices dividing the hall floor tiles are teeming with microscopic doberman pinschers. The tile grid pivots, rises up all around her, a jungle gym, and she watches the dobermans trail in the angles whose lines are invisible, only implicitly present in the movement of the dogs nose to tail, an unbroken chain like black sausages. Looking up, she sees Professor Budshah a few feet away from her, talking to some other attendees, and hounds are baying in the distance. The baying grows louder every second, and there's a helicopter noise too, starting with a sub-bass rumble it's coming right into the building. What is he doing here? The helicopter is following their car, and the dogs must be running directly beneath it, the dogs they pass in the street turn, their eyes find her immediately as she goes by, and they too begin running, after the car.

"Don't stop for lights!" she cries.

Professor Budshah looks worried. Lights flash by overhead.

"They've found us!" she thinks, terrified.

The helicopter's blades drum on the roof of the car with fists of air and the sky blackens. She's in a room, with a bed, a dresser, a dim lamp. She lies down. There's tea, rice, a sort of incense smell she associates with Indian homes.

Her gaze drifts over to the window and she leaps from the bed tangled in the bedclothes and spreadeagles onto the floor. With absolute assurance she knows that all the graves stand open and their inhabitants have come out to announce the end of the world.

The sky is a horrifying indigo color that deepens and deepens like water someone is steadily pouring dye into and as she watches an unbelievably vast arch of indigo flames tipped with silver all alike sweeps the sky. An incredible rumble swells beneath her—the floor, the ground, rumble with the heavy vibration of a ship's deck as a succession of flaming arches, color-inverted so the hotter the darker, engulfs the entire earth. That rumbling is the earth roaring through space under some external guidance combined with the crack and rend of billions of graves, billions of ghosts tearing loose from belching clay. Things are sweeping the earth out of the sky, out of space. The remaining Professor Long scrambles free of the bedclothes and escapes in blind panic, now toward the window, now out in the hall, heading for the street, the basement, the roof—flashes keep interrupting her vision, not flashes of light but a sudden reset of the field of vision with a disorienting slap—street mayhem, flames, destruction, coming around the corner what is it? An alien man, made of living or mechanical cloth; his head is a glistening white smooth human dummy head with silver-blue features projected on its surface from the inside, hovering over an empty neck hole. A human head flies along the rooftops on filthy wings of long dirty white hair, palpitating entrails dangling obscenely from its throat, dripping vilely, eyes of phosphorescent pus and a gnashing, toothless mouth that puffs out and implodes.

Running in terror she collides with people. The streets are choked with debris, impassible. For hours she has been crawling beneath the furniture, through the open windows of overturned cars, slithering along the contaminated street like a snake, while heavy things whoosh by in the air only a few feet overhead and if any one of them caught her that would be it—there's a catlike thing, a cat-man, screaming into the insane sky from the roof of the Rite-Aid and that was the sound she had been thinking was a siren, just this misbegotten screaming thing. The sky is a starless dark blue bulb but sometimes with opaque red flames that look like drawings of flames, complete with pointed ellipses separating from the peaks and fixed there next to them, and with black curving lines meant to indicate the undulating contour of the fire. Screeching. The flames screech, and the screeches become cindery black flying creatures that rake the intervening space plunging into the ground. She keeps her eyes lowered. If she sees anything else inhuman she will die, the sight itself would kill her. Distress calls. Sobbing ghosts. Bat wings. The rumbling earth is rattling her teeth. She has to get up and tear away her chest and abdomen from rumble. Hiding, because there's another alien man coming, with a regular human body more or less, a sweatshirt—his head is attached but his features move so fast they blur, his dark skin is already losing its color, she can see the dust of his vibrating ears as they disintegrate, and a grey sloppy film is spreading under the blurs and across the tops of the hands. The cries of people being mutilated, being raped, being tortured, are focussed in the vicinity of this man and the worst thing she knows is that *nobody is being killed* because death is being prevented, so there is torment with no end! An overwhelming pity for mankind paralyzes her. She bursts into tears and shoves her face into the ground as if she thinks she can melt into it. The street subsides and a subway train wallows into the upper air, rolling over like a dying whale and she can see the faces of the terrificd passengers in its windows. The upturned belly of the train car begins to sputter yellow fire, smoke gushes from the cabin, a tangle of skinny legs in the air above the dying pillbug subway train. Her fear goes on and on. It mounts in outrageous leaps. She pleads incoherently with the universe. She thinks she cannot possibly feel it any more strongly, and then it intensifies again again again.

A piece of white fluff, like a tiny white feather no bigger than her little fingernail, floats up from behind her and lands on the ground. Observing the simple distance between herself and the fluff and the activity of its falling is what saves her: I am here, that is there. Not everything that happens is part of the nightmare. She sees the face of Professor Crest, but then realizes it's only a peculiar concatenation of light and shadow on the wall nearby. The late Professor Long continues to sit in his desk chair; she can see him through an open doorway. There is a cryptic, smudged smile on his dead head. Smilebot scampers across the doorway, and Professor Budshah's face breaks against venetian blinds. She glances down at the late Professor Long, seeing the top of his head, the charred wound, the long body slumped. There's a movie showing on the computer screen—it's the late Professor Long having sex with a woman whose voice resounds hollowly in the computer speakers.

"Come along."

Through the venetian blinds and the horizontal stripes of light vanish in a sheltered void, although the vertical points of light, where the strings thread through the slats, are still visible like dangling links of different colors. The incense smell strengthens, becoming the syncopation of an impression that resembles but is not quite sound, organizing itself in a ring around her with each pulse answered by another on the opposite side of the ring. The sound is like the rolling of drums so far in the distance that the attack is inaudible and only the booms carry, in a complex but brief pattern. The patterning is at once a mechanism to elevate the two of them and also a quasi-telepathic conversation among their extraterrestrial allies.

The spacecraft opens above them and they ascend into it, two figures standing at either side of the aperture, featureless human figures with upraised arms which turn out to be mannikins made of a matte white stuff, like coagulated flour, and the whole structure seems to be a wasps nest made of a similar material. The interior of the spacecraft is shaped like a conch or nautilus shell, in spiralling folds. Professor Budshah walks ahead of her and grows smaller faster than is warranted by his pace. The surfaces around her are white and coated with a thin layer of whitish smoke, actually microscopic, all-purpose particles which can be moulded into whatever is needed, then smoothed back into place again. The smoke has unaccountable depth for looking into; inside it there are endless black, red, and yellow ribbons of varying thicknesses drifting to and fro. These are the nerve communication command lines that operate the spacecraft and provide the passengers with useful information. No sign of their allies yet, apart from the continuous patterned drumming of their thoughts. The spacecraft is doing its various functions; she can tell this because the smoke is forming into graceful spikes and pinching off into floating disks like sand dollars which sail across the open space and collect in triangular piles without touching each other; above her and also at her right the smoke gathers in feathers, so that now the passage she is walking along is a down-lined esophagus and there is an immobile fall of smokeflakes in the air. Each flake trembles with frailty and yet, when she walks into one, it stretches fantastically across her body without breaking and stays there, in an elongated but whole version of its original shape. She is able to peel it off again and restore it to the air; the moment she removes it from her body, it gathers itself until it is as it was. For a moment, the diffuse light is gone, and she can see only a sunset orange-pink glow ahead of her, like a nacreous wall, and she remembers the late Professor Long again; the smokeflakes become translucent silhouettes and the walls around her are dark. The floor reflects the light and the walls don't. Then the diffuse white light blooms as before, the wall is gone, and she walks, thinking to find Professor Budshah, but also thinking that she is travelling and so she has to walk. Her clothes have disappeared; she is currently wearing an opalescent spacesuit made in sections that are locked in place by embarrassingly large and garish gemstones. The effect seems vulgar to her, as if she were decked out in fistfulls of cheap costume jewelry, and she feels vaguely to blame. Her space suit reflects her soul, apparently, or the quality of her mind, something like that. Through a membraneous aperture in the smoke she catches a glimpse of Professor Aughbui, sitting at a table of congealed smoke, dressed as always in dandruffy tweed, counting the contents of a triangular pile of sand dollars by rapping the air with the end of his pen. He writes the tally in a cloth-bound ledger and then swings the pen in the air. The pile floats away and up like a ferris wheel car, and a new, identical pile swings into its place. When she looks directly at the pile of sand dollars, an intense desire for technical accomplishments washes over her; she wants to do complicated math problems or work out a thorny bit of translation, or in some way to undo fantastically complicated mental knots. Joined to this feeling is an intensification of her awareness of the pulsating drumbeats of disembodied thoughts. It seems to her as if her own thoughts are following that elaborate pattern of meshing polyrhythms and beginning to join with them. Professor Aughbui begins counting the sand dollars with obvious relish. Smilebot, she now sees, sits on the floor nearby, with its legs straight out in front of it and spread apart, amusing itself by fashioning abstract and elegant shapes out of the floor smoke with its little hands. The aperture closes. Professor Budshah is standing on the path ahead. Not much more than thirty feet away, he is as small as if he were twice as far off. An upright green streak whizzes through the white surfaces around her like a scratch in a film, and as it crosses by her she becomes instantly exhausted. Lightheaded, she staggers, and is caught and steadied by Professor Budshah. His head is topped with a diadem that burns with a colorless, soft intensity, and she can see it is held in place, directly above the center of his forehead, by a crown or wreath of vibrations that lightly dimple the air.

"We're just departing from the Earth's area of gravity," he explains.

"Where are we ...?" she asks.

"We are on a hypervelocity planet moving at relativistic speeds," he says. "We call it Koskon Kanona."

It occurs to her that she asked him where they were going in Chinese, and she can't identify the language he replied in.

"Are we communicating telepathically?" she asks, deliberately trying to speak in Chinese but weirdly unable to be sure that she is, since she doesn't really hear herself. The incense is doing something to her voice.

"Not as such," he says. "Are you better now?"

She is able to stand.

"I'm tired," she says.

"That is usual," he says.

"How not as such?" she asks.

He leads her to one side—"out of the way"—and forms a bed for her from smoke by wafting his hands a few times. As he does this, he explains how they are not exactly communicating telepathically, and something about how the language is conveyed by means of the spacecraft which is also somehow language or is partly made of language, having a linguistic component or something, and something else she doesn't catch. Eagerly she stretches herself on the smoke bed and floats.

*

"We want you to answer some questions about certain suspicious activities you were involved in ..."

"Ah," she says simply. Then she produces a white cigarette pack and holds it up. "May I? Thank you."

The pack is a little on the large side. She lights up.

"I assume this is concerning ...?"

"You know what concerns us."

"Ah," she says again. "Well, just let me explain."

You see, Assiyeh Melachalos is so tenacious, so determined, you understand. That sort of person. Rejection after rejection elicits from Assiyeh nothing but application after application and while she is shot down by every major and minor research lab in the U.S. Asia and Europe she does get project approval from the UNASUR-funded physics initiative via the special topics program of the physics institute at Achrizoguayla University. She is determined to repeat her light-bending experiment, and has developed a new kind of generator that uses selective resting of ionized particles to induce electron flow. Assisted by the naked silhouette of her father and by two graduate students, Baruch and Carolina, Assiyeh installs the generator, gets it working, and then assembles the elements of the light experiment. The results of the first run-through are promising, but the following weeks produce nothing. Baruch and Carolina return dutifully every day to help Assiyeh, who lives at the lab, working round the clock, sleeping on the floor of her office, bathing in a corner of the ladies' bathroom. Baruch, a solidly built, jovial man of about thirty, brings the groceries and does some simple cooking. He seems to be losing interest in Assiyeh's project. More and more often, he can be found at the fringes of more promising experiments being conducted at the center. He never flakes off his responsibilities, but there's a sympathetic resignation in his eyes. Carolina is a sphinx. A very handsome, taciturn young woman with dark blonde hair and light brown skin.

Then Assiyeh requests time in the main lab, recently vacated by a group of neutrino hunters whose noisy victory celebration had filled the corridors with the sound of music and snapping champagne corks. Using this lab, she is able to wire her generator directly into the center's main line; her generator requires an external source of power to goose it up to full strength. With Baruch and Carolina running the two parallel control stations and her father's ghost manning the generator, Assiyeh repeats her experiment. Once again, the ribbon of light bows, becoming a luminous parenthesis, but the braiding effect still withholds itself from the cameras. Fuming and swearing, Assiyeh repeats the experiment again and again into the night. Baruch contritely points to midnight on the clock and retires, but Carolina remains until an hour before daybreak.

Assiyeh is dejectedly shampooing her hair in the sink when a new idea strikes her. She dashes back to the central lab, calling for her father, who steps immediately from the shadow behind the door, which is his chosen resting-place. Head wrapped in a towel, dripping, hair glued to her face, she starts the cameras and adjusts the light source so that it will generate as much light interference as possible. Rushing from station to station, she restarts the experiment. As the lateral slowing boom is rolled adjacent to the beam, the light dimples, the ribbon begins to flutter like a pennant waving in a strong wind. Then it tears in two, and the split ends shear apart in rags that dart straight up toward the ceiling, becoming invisible. When this invisible emanation rises above the lab, the sky instantly turns ruby red. Everyone awake within ten miles of the campus can see it; the morning becoming a cool red furnace, red all around them in two or three seconds. The light of the rising sun slows as it enters the field, bunching up against itself so that the sky becomes a tar pool of scarlet glare. Assiyeh watches as the smouldering light-ends bubble in vermillion jelly that slops viscously from the emitter and evaporates in a slowly-undulating invisible conical geyser. She wipes her smarting eyes and, glancing at the screen, sees where she'd typed the extra zero. After a quick look at the readings, and no further hesitation, Assiyeh adds another zero, and the red gush becomes a whorl of scarlet pollen that inverts itself around a plunging nautilus-shaped black radiation in space. Waves of heat billow from the generator and the other machinery, the air wriggles wildly and it's difficult to tell what is an effect of heat distortion from what the light is doing. Streaked with sweat and the water running down from her sopping scalp, Assiyeh is doing all she can to magnify the effect. Her father's ghost is trying to cool a generator by fanning it with his hands. The generator is starting to thump like an imbalanced washing machine.

Another idea takes Assiyeh in midstride so she stops abruptly, slips on a puddle and falls to the floor with a splat. Instantly she scrabbles to her feet and makes the necessary adjustments. The black nautilus curves back to form a smoother, trombone-bell shape, and as the edges meet and blend, a sickening pale blue light falters through the red. Assiyeh climbs up onto a chair to watch. The light tube lifts itself, the blue and red turning blurred, a new color on a parallel spectrum, while a scintillating or glistening black ball gathers plunging down into the center of the tube, plummeting without moving.

The entire envelope of sunlight falling on the day side of the earth turns red, backing up the photons which bunch together under pressure, causing the sky to fluoresce blured planetwide.

*

Egyptian protests and careful Japanese demonstrations, a heavy tornado of violence gathers ominously over the US. Spain and Portugal are grinding to a stop; rightist coup seem imminent in Greece. Vague complaints from the American State Department, politicians and other media figures, and in the UN, about the public declaration of a time line for introducing the new currency—to be called not the Latino but the Bolivar, as it happens. This will disrupt the Pacific Trade Territory, won't it? These complaints brushed casually aside by South American heads of state. Masses of people are camping out in Mexico City again. The remaining Professor Long wakes up sick in a tousled bed. The room is unfamiliar, but she has been in it for a long time. She feels queasy and hungry at once, and has a fierce need to urinate. There is a bathroom visible through a half-open door, and she staggers blindly into it. Sitting there, she takes in the plain, anonymous bathroom. There is still that faint incense smell. Her mouth tastes awful, as if she'd been sucking a lump of iron all night. She slurps water from the tap and washes her mouth out, then takes a long, desperate drink, feeling the cold aereated water pooling uncomfortably in her gut. Back to the bed. The room is still. She can hear the traffic yawn and sigh outside. Light comes in streaks through the venetian blinds and forms a rake on the white wall. She watches as it slides down the wall. A quivering sensation, faint, sick, and persistent, fills up her outline. It makes her breathe through her mouth and reject eating.

Professor Budshah enters some time later. The rake of light is now half-bent against the floor.

"Spend," he says.

"Lend," she answers, after clearing her throat.

He speaks to her for a while, asking a few innocuous questions.

"Yesterday," he says then, looking at her gravely, "I believe that you were drugged. A deliriant, obviously."

The word "yesterday" refuses to make sense. She is trying to remember life as a caterpillar. There isn't enough space in that weird English word for the amount of experience it's being called upon to hold.

"You are now in an apartment owned by the University," he says, evenly and slowly. "I brought you here yesterday. I told the panel that you had suddenly become violently ill and would not be able attend the hearing. They believed me—I think. In any case, they said they would reconvene at a later date, which they will determine in a few days' time and communicate to you."

The remaining Professor Long has an abrupt vision of the woman at the conference table handing her a steaming and very strong cup of tea, and makes an incoherent sound of realization.

Professor Budshah looks concerned and asks her if she's all right. She nods.

"That fucking tea. ... A woman gave me a cup of tea," she says.

"Who gave it you?"

"I never saw her before. She had long white hair, and ..."

Professor Budshah thinks for a moment.

"Someone is plainly trying to discredit us," he says. "You were to have been made a public spectacle, raving."

She nods.

"Thank you," she says feebly.

He nods.

"Ah," he says. "Well."

His face doesn't clear.

"Something wrong? Still ...?"

"I'm not certain," he says. "I believe I am being watched. I assume I'm being watched. That's why I decided to stay in this apartment, rather than at the campus as usual."

"... We should send the distress signal," she says.

"All right," Professor Budshah says. He studies her face for a moment.

"Are you up to it?"

"I'm OK," she says.

They draw the circle on the bare floorboards with a bar of soap, kneel together inside the ring, both facing in the direction of the northern magnetic pole, chanting and performing a series of hand gestures. Their actions echo and respond to each other, instead of being identical for each. They rise to their feet and kneel back down, press their hands together and spread them apart, touch their heads, their chests, the floor, wave outlines in the air, chanting continuously, she in a low monotone and he in a high, clear, staccato. Footnotes molded into sunlight appear before them, and an asterisk opens between their eyes.

The scene is a conference room, a vaulted stone chamber that some clue, too subtle to distinguish, indicates is deep underground. Naked economists leap and prance around a scaffold of giant crystals that have grown together to form a transparent, irregular column joining floor and ceiling. The economists dance with wild abandon, their breath pluming in the air, their flesh nearly rigid with cold. There are luminous golden things the size of young children hovering around the column like bees around a rose bush; humanoid silhouettes wrapped in radiant, floating gauze. Drummers, bagpipers, horn players, are clustered around natural docks formed by stalagmites and stalagmites. A potbellied economist flies in and out of view, pumping his arms and legs, awkwardly circling the central column, and from time to time some of the other economists also jump up aloft and start swimming through the air. Another group of economists in white robes, and wearing what look a little like flat-topped mitres, strides impressively across the chamber, and seem to direct the venerations of the others.

Both Professor Budshah and the remaining Professor Long mentally fill out the distress form. The remaining Professor Long is starting to sweat and shiver with the effort, holding her breath and then letting it out in what sound like painful gasps.

The shaggy head of an older man, his seamed face slathered with dripping ceremonial face paint, rises up before them in the mental window, massive, obscuring the scene in the cavern, smiling benignly. In a warm, blissful voice that booms in their throbbing skulls, he announces:

"Your petition has been received and will be evaluated by the Planetary Committee."

He goes on smiling at them for a while, the way people on television smile at an audience they can't see, and then his head sinks back out of sight again. The vision of the conference room fades. The remaining Professor Long exhales shakily, pressing one hand to her temple. Professor Budshah, panting, looks at her. He puts his arm around her shoulders and helps her over to the bed. She flops down, drawing deep breaths.

Within a few hours, the remaining Professor Long has recovered enough to keep down some hot water—she can't look at a cup of tea—and a few pieces of flatbread. The apartment is nearly bare; nobody currently lives here, and there are only a few sticks of furniture. She eats in the kitchen and then makes her way wearily back to the bedroom to rest, her head splitting, leaving Professor Budshah with his notebook on the little kitchen table. After a brief nap, she wakes up feeling surprisingly improved. The sun is low in the sky, the room has grown dark with a peculiar reddish darkness. She raises the blinds a little and opens a window. The smoking orange, setting there. Then she wanders into the center of the small bedroom, her mind blank, looking numbly around her. Something white rests on the bare floorboards at her feet, a little to her left. She bends down to examine it, a piece of white fluff, like a milkweed tassel or a down feather. As she kneels to pick it up something goes whuff across her back and a sharp noise, like a hammer knocking a wooden board. She looks in the direction of the sound and immediately notices a hole in the wall directly in front of her, neatly framed in the middle of the shadow her head casts, where there had been no hole before and she freezes in place. Her heart seems to shrivel and her insides run cold. If she hadn't knelt to look at that piece of fluff on the floor there would be a hole in her now. She can feel the probe of the hunting eye behind her. She needs to lie prone, but her terror has frozen her joints and they refuse to relax. It takes a violent effort of will to make them unbend, telling herself that her head might not be low enough yet, uncertainly trying to conjure an image in her mind of the buildings opposite, if they are tall enough so that someone could get up high enough to see down into the room, to the floor, and as she moves there's another knock no louder than before but deafening to her, so that she cries out in terror. Professor Budshah charges in wearing a t-shirt, his face full of shaving cream with a single rectangular notch in the lather on his left cheek, and she screams at him to get down. He looks around in wild confusion.

"Get on the floor!" she screams, scrabbling over to him on hands and knees, all her rigidity gone. She lunges up and grabs him by the waist, dragging him down. As she does, she hears another crack and the patter of plaster bits sprinkling onto the floor; Professor Budshah's body slackens and for a heart-wrenching instant she believes he's been hit. No, he's only letting himself swim out forward onto his stomach. He is glaring fiercely at the newest hole in the apartment wall. Three holes ...

In her avidity to prevent his being shot, she has broken the spell of her fear and she waves him back into the hall.

Professor Budshah, in no danger of being shot from his current position, awkwardly crabwalks backwards into the hallway, followed by the remaining Professor Long. She sits up the moment she is past the threshold and turns a face full of bewilderment fear and anger at him. He is about to say something, then stops, his eyes widening.

"What?"

She doesn't hear it then, but she does feel it—a regular thudding of feet pounding in the building. Professor Budshah jumps up into an odd half-crouch and gestures to her—into the kitchen. He points at the kitchen window.

"... fire escape!" he says.

She clambers over the table and out the window, then starts hustling down the fire escape, Professor Budshah right behind her.

The kitchen window is on the opposite side of the building from the bedroom and overlooks a courtyard with a view of some one-story shops across the street. They rush down, dislodging flower pots and overturning planters, scaring a cat, surprised eyes in a blubbery white face, a naked couple a woman with her hands on the window sill and another woman behind her, then the last landing, the apartment evidently empty Professor Budshah expertly lowers the ladder and she goes down first, momentarily locking eyes with the woman from further up who is leaning out her window staring down at them. Only when she is safely on the ground does he get on the ladder himself. The two of them look around for a moment, uncertain. One of the naked women, who has now climbed entirely out onto the fire escape, waves curiously to them, her lover's blonde head poking out of the window now; the naked woman is a young Latina with tattooed arms and waist and vermillion streaks in her hair, with a huge fake penis strapped to her body. She points. They follow her finger and notice a notch in a slab barrier fencing off a vacant lot. They remember the view they had of the lot from the kitchen window—cross through it and they won't have to go around to the front of the building. The woman on the fire escape nods, turning to say something to her lover who remains in the window.

Feeling completely exposed herself, the remaining Professor Long hurries across the lot, lifting her feet high to avoid stumbling over tufted weeds, empty beer bottles, cardboard sheets and other trash. They head for the only gap on the street side of the lot. Throwing a glance back over her shoulder, the remaining Professor Long sees something dark moving in Professor Budshah's window. The naked woman is still standing on the fire escape; the remaining Professor Long half turns and, still running awkwardly, points, and the woman looks up. She starts visibly, apparently seeing the shadowy form there at the window above her head. Having taken her eyes from the ground, the remaining Professor Long trips over a hunk of particle board, and would have fallen flat on her face if Professor Budshah hadn't grabbed and righted her. They keep fleeing, but she looks back again and is astonished to see the woman is climbing up toward Professor Budshah's window; moving fast, she is already on the floor below. There is nothing in the window now, but in her brief look the remaining Professor Long does seem to detect a commotion in the kitchen. The woman has reached their landing now, approaching the window with caution and brandishing a bright pink and purple erection adorned with fluttering ribbons.

Professor Budshah clambers over the horizontal wooden boards and into the street, then helps her over. The street is deserted, but they run up a driveway between two private homes and framed by squat brick pillars each topped with a cement ball; they might have held up a heavy pair of iron gates once.

They come into an alley that runs through the interior of the block. The fenced back lots of the buildings all open out onto it. Just ahead is an active boulevard lined with stores and busy with shoppers, looking like safety. She is about to tell Professor Budshah to wipe the shaving cream off his face when she hears the scrape of a foot behind her. An umbrella spike is thrusting out at her. With a strangled cry, she recoils at the onslaught of a big man, his beefy upper body seeming even bigger in his down jacket, a shaved head with a lozenge-shaped lump at the crown. He jabs at her with the umbrella again, holding it like a spear. She is dimly aware of Professor Budshah apparently confronting someone else. He shoves this other person, a thick-featured man with a moustache, two enemies from among the supine phalanxes of the Misled, and the two of them run out into the boulevard.

Professor Budshah starts scraping the foam from his face with his hand, tossing it into the gutter as he goes, but neither of them dare to stop. Neither of those men are following them, that they can see. It all flashed by, incredibly. They both have to put some distance between themselves and that place.

They have no money, nothing. Professor Budshah is wearing his dress shoes, slacks, and a t shirt, tucked in of course. He has arms like a dancer, she thinks. Long muscles. She is still wearing her clothes of a few days ago, now much disarranged and rumpled.

Broken, jangled conversation, still weaving in and out among people who stare at the remaining smears of foam on his face, some pointing to their own, trying to let him know, thinking he must be unaware. Everything is still too jaggedly excited, conversation is ridiculous. They begin making sense around the time Professor Budshah is saying they should go to the police. But they looked like police. Thick, heavy, active, seedy, short-haired, they could have been police, or organized crime, or political party machine thugs, or latter-day fascist goons, or soldiers, or all of the above. American, Israeli, Russian, Italian, English, Irish, German, Serbian, Greek, Swiss, Polish, Spanish—what were they? Not muggers, not acting at random. Agents of the deadly conformity of the Misled. But what do they know about this kind of thing, what is movies and what is reality doing movie impressions?

Professor Budshah has his subway card with him. The first Professor Long will go back to campus and stay there. It may be necessary to leave. That is, they should consider leaving the country. Why should they consider that? Professor Budshah was able to get through to Professor Crest yesterday, but only briefly—their signal kept crumbling into vocal tiles—but he will make sure Professor Aughbui gets the message, and Professor ... nevermind.

The subway is elevated at Rotha Station; the platform is nearly empty. The first Professor Long peers down the rails uncertainly. She doesn't know what to do with these incessant inner urgings to run, act. Intense fear has stretched her all out of shape, so that she alternately twitches in contractions of purely reflexive fright and then sags in an unnaturally exaggerated relaxation that pulls out her shape like thumbing down modelling clay. Everything shimmers with extra realness. They're all shouting at her: the garbage can, the blue sky, the edge of the corrugated tan subway barrier against the blue sky, the tangle of rails and sleepers between the platforms, the mustard yellow edge, the X's in the canopy supports. Look out! Look!

There's a tidy older man with a salt and pepper beard perched on the edge of one of the benches. Despite the heat, he wears a hat and a little scarf neatly folded under his chin; his left hand rests lightly on the handle of an aluminum cane, and he is reading a folded newspaper which he holds in his right hand. There's another man in white jeans peering at his phone further down the platform, leaning against the corrugated metal barrier smoking, an old lady with a laundry trolley, a huge homeless man sprawled on the second bench apparently stupefied or sleeping with his mouth wide open, wearing conspicuously new-looking shoes. No answer yet from Professor Crest, no word from Professor Aughbui. The rattling squawk of the arriving train almost drowns out the sirens.

Urtruvel's face on a poster, advertising his latest diatribe. The long face, the mouth closed of course and now adorned with a stern moustache, the boiled-egg eyes levelled frankly, the unbullshitable truth-telling hero who will indignantly shut down all posers and deflate all pious falsehoods. *Black Albinos: On the Bankruptcy of Currency Reform.* The poster is a hot slab of malevolent enchantment like a fruiting body exhaling a fine mist of spores lightly dusting passersby and washing over anyone who pauses to look at it. Actually opening the book is like bursting a chaotic evil puffball with your face. A gush of malignantly psychedelic invective inundates your head, whirling in the brain to form mental twisters that are autonomous hate elementals herding the thoughts, driving the thoughts before them, raking the mental air with alarms and searchlights and snarling police dogs that send hapless fantasies, emotions, and other mental personnel scrambling for safe places to hide. It's a takedown book, of course, a weapon aimed at the idea of animal money and those responsible for it, designed to transform them into figures of public ignominy, making an example of them. The point is not, as some might think, merely to discredit Professor Aughbui, Professor Budshah, Professor Crest, the late Professor Long, and the remaining Professor Long; the deeper purpose here is to demonstrate that, correct or incorrect, right or wrong, anyone associating themselves with animal money will be a target for ruthless public lambasting. The line has been drawn and animal money is entirely outside the pale, relegated to an intellectual no-man's land haunted by footnotes like Fourier, and underfootnotes like Winstanley. As for those mountebanks responsible for this trash ...

The man in white jeans is suddenly much closer, the woman has left her cart, clutching a long umbrella like a spear. White jeans is reaching into his jacket and his eyes flash with annoyance as the train rolls in, but they've tipped their hand, their targets are alerted. The remaining Professor Long chokes and her body goes stiff. Professor Budshah backs warily away from the umbrella tip homing in on his heart.

The tidy older man has risen to his feet also, a snapping, suppressed automatic in the hand that an instant before had held the folded newspaper. Firing from the hip he punches two holes in white jeans' down jacket, first in the abdomen, the second in the left breast, each spouting pulverized feathers. The bald man wheezes, the pistol he'd been pulling drops to the platform with a splat, and he begins flapping his arms and curling this way and that. The doors of the train open and the woman, now straightened up taller than Professor Budshah, lunges with her umbrella and a man with a grey moustache charges out of the subway car, drawing a pistol he aims at the remaining Professor Long. Professor Budshah recoils from the umbrella, which grazes the surface of a black shield embossed all over with extremely fine gold engraving like the decorations framing a dollar bill. A lightly-built older black man in a blue windbreaker, and wearing a kind of a tricorn hat, just stepped from the same subway car, and has serenely interposed the shield between Professor Budshah and his attacker, holding his shield carefully in both hands, one high, one low. Behind his back, the remaining Professor Long is looking right down the barrel of a Glock her face blank. She doesn't see where the other woman comes from; only that she is suddenly there beside the doughy other man. This strange woman plants her right foot with a slam that shakes the platform and punches the man with the gun in the stomach, hitting him so hard the blow lifts him off his feet. The gun goes off. The noise is so ferocious the remaining Professor Long can't say whether she has been hit or not. Somehow the man keeps himself from falling or dropping the gun, by pinwheeling his arms, doubling forward his face wrenched in pain. In a single stride the woman closes in, dips a bit to his level in one smooth motion uppercutting him—he falls over flat on his back and stays there. The tidy older man shoots the woman with the umbrella in the back. The red behind the brown in her face disappears, and her demonic grimace is wiped away. She dwindles. Bubbles are rising into the air from the hole in her back. A strange woman has emerged from the train and now she holds up her black shield, twin to the other one, to protect the remaining Professor Long.

The woman who punched the moustache man out says—

"Professor Long. Professor Budshah. We're from the Institute. Board this car, please."

The fight took no longer than a typical stop. The doors close behind them and the train rumbles out of the station.

The car is empty. Professor Long and Professor Budshah are still accompanied by the shield bearers, and by the woman who spoke to them. The tidy older man does not seem to have boarded the train.

The man who defended Professor Budshah is named Tony. The female shield bearer is Rubilyn. The very solid woman taking charge of them is Arieto. While the shield bearers are dressed more or less in street clothes, Arieto is wearing an all black outfit of heavy fabric that looks like the sort of protective gear open-hearth workers wear, with heavy boots, a thick fabric apron, gloves, and a brimless flat cap that comes down to just above her eyebrows. Her thick neck is wrapped in a black kerchief wound round it several times, so only her sooty face and small red ears are exposed. Whenever she moves her arms, her sleeves strain over slabs of muscle.

"Spend," she says, holding out her hand to them in turn. "Lend."

"They nearly got you," she says.

They sit down and she lists to one side, pulling a wallet

from her side pocket. She opens it and hands it first to the remaining Professor Long, then to Professor Budshah; inside there is a black metal shield like a miniature replica of the ones Tony and Rubilyn are carrying, and still hold up to either side of them like bookends. Around the central boss, the golden words "Economist Defense Directorate" swirl in a filmy wreath.

"You OK?" Arieto asks heartily, and lightly swats the remaining Professor Long on the knee. "Still rattled?"

The remaining Professor Long smiles feebly and nods.

"That's all right," Arieto says. "This is all a bit much."

"Who were they?" Professor Budshah asks.

Arieto shrugs. "Trying to kill you, or kidnap you."

"Can't you tell me who they were?"

"Don't know."

She indicates the two shield bearers with the back of her hand, first one, then the other, then herself.

"We're defenders. We don't investigate."

"What are we going ...?" the remaining Professor Long asks.

"Our orders are to accompany you to a place of safety, not—"

She raises her hand to silence him.

"—Not to sit here gabbing with you."

"Do you know anything about Professor Crest?" the remaining Professor Long asks.

The train dives underground and they have to raise their voices.

"Or Professor Aughbui?" Professor Budshah shouts.

Arieto nods.

"They're OK," she says.

Professor Budshah and the remaining Professor Long

fill out the receipt Arieto gives him from Protective Services. It seems unnecessary, considering their continuing to be alive sufficient indication of having been protected, but then again, they might have escaped on their own, while the defenders did nothing, relaxing over frothy fountain drinks instead of doing their jobs. Folding the form, he returns it to Arieto, who stuffs it into a tube, then into a special tubular pocket, one of many in her apron, designed to hold important documents.

The train pulls in at Ix Ex Station and they make their transfer, Professor Budshah and the remaining Professor Long sandwiched between the two shield bearers at all times. Arieto holds up her hand, mutely instructing them not to board the train that rolls in to the platform. That one is allowed to pass, and they board the second train which follows it almost at once. Everyone who had been waiting for a train boarded the first one. Their train is old and dingy, with fake wood panelling and shiny turquoise seats. The economists sit half facing each other and the train rolls almost silently out into the oceanic gloom of the tunnels. Arieto looks at her watch after a few minutes—a heavy onion-shaped watch on a chain that she pulls from inside her apron—gets up and goes to the end of the train, knocks on the door of the conductor's compartment. The door opens slightly; there's no light behind it. She is talking to someone. The other voice is very low and might be coming over an intercom. Perhaps, the remaining Professor Long thinks, the one who opened the door and the one who is speaking aren't the same person. A weird-looking grey arm reaches out of the door and opens a metal box high on the partition wall. The black glove it is wearing has white hand bones printed on the back, so it looks like a skeleton hand, even though, as Professor Budshah remarks, there is a skeleton hand already inside the glove. The box opens to reveal a red and blue keypad; Arieto punches a number into it with her stubby finger, then says something through the aperture in the door, which claps shut.

Another train, going in the same direction on the adjacent track, lifts past them. In one of the windows they can see a man slumped over, obviously dead in his seat, with what looks like a bizarre hairy growth on his face. His hairpiece. It must have come loose and slipped halfway down his face. His horrible black mouth is wide open and his face is already spotted with decomposition. Somebody has put coins on his eyes. Arieto gets up, goes over to the window, and bends down to peer at him

"Huh. Dead."

The accompanying train floats up into the dark, and they travel on in silence. Tony and Rubilyn are alert and on duty. Arieto kneads her hands and watches through the window. The two economists sit looking incredulously at everything. Finally, the remaining Professor Long pulls out some paper napkins and scrapes the few last remnants of shaving foam from Professor Budshah's face.

"Please," he says, taking the napkins from her, and he wipes his jaws himself.

"Thank you," he adds, after a very long interval.

When did they last pass a station? The tunnel has become a brick passage glistening with slime whose walls are so narrow they ooze by only inches from the windows on either side. They pop out into a fresh lake of darkness, with a chaos of silhouetted roof supports, standing in globes of faint lamp light, extending as far as the eye can see in every direction. The lights remain distinct, like stars, so the space between is invisible. It's like a lamplit forest.

The remaining Professor Long starts and gasps, looking out into the dark. She thought she saw a figure out there, running. There it is again! A human form with long black hair trailing behind, running through the forest at superhuman speed, keeping up with them. The reflection of Professor Budshah's face appears beside her own.

"Someone ..." she says, pointing.

"I see him. There's two!"

There are many, all with black hair streaming out three or four feet behind them, flashing from one bubble of lamplight to the next, their legs whipping them along, only visible for a split second at a time.

Arieto stomps up to the conductor's door and raps on it.

"Coursers on the left, pick it up!" she barks.

A moment later, a fresh gust of acceleration pushes them implacably back into their seats and the darting forms of the runners begin to drop behind. Professor Budshah fails to suppress a shudder when he catches a good look at one of the faces, haggard features glistening with thick perspiration, staring eyes, gaping mouth sucking thick underground air.

The remaining Professor Long struggles up to where Arieto stands.

"Who are ...?"

"All I know is they're after this train," she says. "And if you hadn't noticed them when you did, they could have caught us."

"They won't now?"

"Not now," Arieto says positively.

Presently, once the runners have disappeared in the distance, Arieto knocks again, the door flies open a few inches with the same galvanic instantaneousness and there's another brief exchange. The economists feel the momentum of the train diminish, and they glide to a stop. There's nothing around them.

"I'll do it," Arieto says. The skeleton-gloved hand gives her a bulky ring of keys. She selects the right one and turns it in the lock by the nearest door, one half of which slides open. Dank subterranean air pours into the car, and seems to dim it.

"This way," Arieto calls.

The two shield bearers accompany them. Exactly framed in the open half of the door is a yellow ladder, lit by a small lantern.

"Up there," Arieto says, bobbing her pointing finger up and down.

Rubilyn is the first to go up, with her shield across her back. Then Professor Budshah, then the remaining Professor Long, then Tony, Arieto last. The ladder is only fixed at the top, and sways in gaping emptiness as they climb. Those piles must go up a long way, but, since only their feet are in the light, it's easy to imagine they're only as tall as a subway tunnel. The lantern slides up on a vertical rail next to the ladder, somehow following them. A muffled banging tells them that the train has departed beneath them.

"Keep it up, economists!" Arieto calls from below.

The next thing Professor Budshah knows, he is being

helped by Rubilyn out of a fox hole, its edge ragged with lush grass. Presently they all stand in a woody area at the base of a slope, right beside a boulder like a half-coiled, fossilized turd. The remaining Professor Long stares at the hole they climbed out of, which doesn't seem large enough for them to have passed through.

Arieto puts her hands on her hips and looks around, taking deep breaths of sylvan air through her nose. She smiles, without showing her teeth.

"Well!" she says.

She takes another deep breath and turns a little in place, to alter her view.

"Well!" she says again, rubbing her hands on her stomach. "Very satisfactory!"

While she already seemed lively, a brisk new vitality is animating her now. She looks one way and another, then visors her eyes with her hand and bends a little forward to peer more intently into some promising piece of the distance.

"Hm!" she says. "That way!"

Still escorted by the two politely smiling shield bearers, Professor Budshah and the remaining Professor Long follow Arieto through the trees. After a few moments a strip of blacktop road appears.

"What part of the city is this?" Professor Budshah asks.

"We're up north," Arieto replies over her shoulder.

"Do you mean Etsimen?"

Arieto snorts.

"No!" she says, as if it were a stupid question, and hails the coach that stands waiting for them, square in the middle of the road. It's actually a weird limousine, designed to look like a horse-drawn carriage. A detailed skeletal horse is painted on the black metal, with a real plume of black feathers set above the painted skull. There's a cabin for the driver and a much taller box for the passengers. The driver rises mysteriously into view, as if his seat were lifting him up, and he waves a gloved hand in reply to Arieto's hail. The skinny door of the coach was hanging listlessly open. Now the aperture abruptly widens, and Professor Crest's white oval face peeks out.

Professor Budshah and the remaining Professor Long both exclaim with surprise and rush forward, and their shield bearers trot easily beside them. Professor Crest steps significantly from the coach, and behind and above him the head of Professor Aughbui appears, gaping and blinking.

"All right, all right, back in, back in," Arieto says jovially. "We can't hang around here."

Professor Crest's rehearsed address is cancelled and they are all bundled back through the door, the shield bearers sitting to either side of Professor Budshah and the remaining Professor Long, while Professor Aughbui and Professor Crest face them, with Arieto by one window and Smilebot, holding Boringbot tucked under its arm, sitting beside Professor Aughbui and the other window.

Arieto raps on the cab partition and cries, "All set!"

Once again the driver's head and hands float up from some faintly luminous place below and the limousine slides forward; no engine whoosh, just the clap clap of hooves and the rustle and rattle of the suspension, although the ride is remarkably even. Trees lunge past the narrow windows and everyone seems too embarrassed to speak. Arieto's glance moves easily from one thing to another, and she goes on smiling contentedly. That isn't soot on her face after all, but some kind of permanent marking. It looks like a negative galaxy of black stars viewed edge-on, with the center across the bridge of her nose. Arieto tends to attract frail tetchy women who always ended up finding her too rough and loud. Sooner or later there would come the reproachful looks; she walks up to Arieto with something pre-prepared to say. Arieto wants to be understanding, but when she looks into a lover's eyes, she sees a timorous brittleness in there that she has to admit she finds a bit disgusting. If they were Etruscan pottery shards, they would complain about the roughness of the archaeologists' brushes and being exposed to the weather, so Arieto is a comfortable heap of safe dirt to lie under, as far as they're concerned. Phooey. After a few dalliances of this kind, Arieto learned to recognize the type and avoid them.

She goes on, talking at random, while the economists peer this way and that, trying to make sense of their situation. Typical eggheads, they seem to her. A bunch of mice.

When she was young, she'd been crazy about a man who worked as a foreman at the mine. He was a shaggy Goliath, but the unusual length of his eyelashes and the brightness of his eyes added a touch of incongruous femininity that put her over the moon. If he wrote poetry, it would have been too much for her to take. He didn't. And he never looked twice at her, either. He was killed in an accident and the company refused to take responsibility. Those things happened all the time where she grew up.

Of course, she goes on, not quite aloud but close enough, she knew she was big for a girl, but a full appreciation of her powers didn't come until she was fourteen and a classmate started giving her a hard time. This other girl had taken one of those mysterious teenage aversions to Arieto and didn't usually miss an opportunity to adorn her with a few carefully hoarded gems of derision. Finally Arieto got sick of it turned and swatted her face. The girl fell straight to the floor and dislocated her jaw; Arieto refused to apologize and was expelled.

"She had a bad mouth, and something bad happened to it," she told the headmistress levelly.

Arieto's eyes glitter with pleasure as she remembers.

"*These* days," she says, "naturally, they'd have me before a judge, and I'd be as meek as they wanted. They want to pretend human beings don't have to hit each other."

Eventually the car pulls up in a meadow, and they all get out. A fat man—no, a woman—in a grey sweater and colorless wool hat slouches on a bench with her back against a low stone wall. When she looks up at them, the rims of her eyelids are more conspicuous than her watery eyes. Her hands are in her pockets and she seems too tired to stand. The driver emerges from the car. He's a giant, dressed in a huge suit of perfect black, gloves, and chauffeur's cap. He's leaning in through the door, retrieving what turns out to be a black valise with a thin strap. He's about fifty, with a neatly cropped white beard and a high, domed forehead like a Taoist immortal. White paint covers his face from the upper lip to the hairline, while his lower jaw is red, and he has Y = C(Y-T) + I(r) + G written on that movie-screen forehead.

"I'm so glad to see you've made it here safely," the fat woman says in a cultivated, reedy tenor, without altering his posture. The voice is high, but it is a man's voice. A man, then. With a discernible exertion of his will, he removes his left hand from his pocket and gestures with it to the driver.

"With your permission, Mr. President?" he asks.

The driver looks at him. He's thrown the valise strap over his shoulder and is adjusting it where it crosses his chest.

"Perhaps you know acting President 70?" the fat man goes on.

Fleeting warmth crosses the giant's face. He says, "Lend" with a nod, wishes them all good luck, then places his hands in the air at his sides as though he were resting them on an invisible life preserver and takes off straight up, showing the coffin-shaped soles of his dress shoes.

"The Surfeit is One," he intones.

A moment later, with a gentle whooshing sound, he vanishes over the pines.

The fat woman sighs, her left hand fallen limp onto his lap. Everyone waits to see what he will do next, but she only sits there, as if she'd forgotten all about them. It's impossible to say what it is about his face that marks him so clearly as a woman after all. After six or seven minutes she sighs again, then drags a long-fingered, spidery hand down her face, stretching the flesh from his jaws and then releasing it. His lower lip droops, then comes up again with a faint noise. She fills his lungs again.

"All right!" she says, as if someone has been nagging him, and stands abruptly up, thrusting her gut out. As she lifts his head, the white crescents of his economists' mark appear, an irregular trail of parentheses lying on their backs, ladders down the right side of the face like a sideburn. Arieto is watching hier (sic) steadily, hands on the belt that wraps around the front of the black apron.

After the salutation, the fat man or woman departs along a ribbon of white cement that does not touch the ground. Arieto heads in that direction too, although she manages to do this in such a way that she does not seem to be following, but heading along merely by coincidence of orientation.

Following Arieto, Professor Aughbui, Professor Budshah, Professor Crest, and the remaining Professor Long make their way in silence through the trees and into an empty parking garage nearly completely camouflaged by ivy, yew, cypress, and tall dour pines. Down a resonant, cinderblock chimney, lined with cheese grater stairs, they emerge into a hidden world, a hanging garden that extends as far as even sharp-eyed Professor Crest can see, illuminated by dusty shafts of sun from domed skylights. The light has a congealed, stale appearance, and is so thick that it isn't transparent. Knots of people can be seen here and there, down below on the broad floor, or on the terraces that rise to either side like ravine walls. Their voices and the sounds of their activities resonate in the enclosed air like the reverberated atmosphere in a cathedral, blending into a constant, soft boom. A group of economists sit facing each other in two seated rows of about a dozen each, practicing for the upcoming quarterly holiday with a rhythmic clapping of hands and syncopated chanting distributed in various parts. Incense trickles like inverted vines up toward the ceiling from braziers scattered about.

"Oh I almost forgot, for goodness' *sake*," the fat man or woman says startlingly. "Don't forget to register with human resources. You'll never hear the end of it if you don't!"

He looks like a slob and talks like someone's maiden aunt, with beleaguered compassion sifting from worrying eyes.

"Why was acting President 70 driving the car?" Professor Crest asks.

"He's a terribly *active* President," the fat man or woman says. "*Terribly* involved. He likes to have a hand in everything. Don't assume that it means anything. He can be a difficult man to read sometimes. Cryptic. He wants to become full President, obviously."

"Do you know what any the specifics?" Professor Budshah asks.

"I'm not aware of any finding. The verdict respecting your duel has entered a new phase and the question is scheduled to be put to the Occasional Working Group, if that's what you mean. As far as I know, that's why you were called."

"Questions about ...?" the remaining Professor Long asks.

"About the duel, yes."

"Not about our theory?" Professor Budshah asks.

"What theory?"

"This isn't about the report to the committee?" Professor Aughbui asks.

"What report?"

"Professor Aughbui was abducted," Professor Crest says. "He has been in constant communication with the security committee since."

The fat man or woman shakes his or her head, and the glistening flesh jiggles.

"I don't know anything at all about it," he or she says. Then, he or she blinks and looks past them.

"But," he or she goes on, pointing. "That's the regional economics chair right there. Why don't you ask him?"

Professor Aughbui, Professor Budshah, Professor Crest, and the remaining Professor Long turn and see a crooked figure vanishing into an archway with an old man's painstakingly measured, light step. He must have been the size of a professional basketball player once. The russet wool jacket spreads across the broad expanse of the back and the wide, stooped shoulders. But now, the spine is bent so acutely he might be hunchbacked, and the legs are bent, too, cringing him down well below his full height. He walks with hands thrust all the way into the ample pockets of his baggy, almost shapeless tweed slacks.

The economists approach him as a group, still flanked by their shieldbearers, who haven't been dismissed, and by Arieto, who seems bored and refractory. Of course, Professor Crest knows the name of this regional economics chair. He knows the names of all the regional economics chairs.

"Professor Simon? May we speak with you—"

His voice cuts off abruptly in mid sentence as the

regional economics chair swings around to reveal the face of a radiant child. The face, the whole head—on that old man's decrepit body—the effect is so bizarre that none of them can make any sense of what he's saying. The body is old but the head is young; the seam around the throat is distinctly visible, just above the drooping adam's apple; the tissues below the line are discolored, crepey; the tissues above are firm. Rosebud mouth, translucent cheeks and forehead and delicate ears, flesh like frosted glass, enormous limpid sapphire eyes, gossamer golden hair in gleaming ringlets that play about the frayed lapels of his threadbare jacket, and cut across the brow in an even fringe that half conceals the tenuous, downy eyebrows.

His reply was intended for someone else, because, as his head bobs with recognition of each of them in turn, his expression changes. From the look of someone who is never finished with being pestered, he brightens up.

"Ah, you're here!" he cries, and begins a round of shaking hands. His pink, sticky hands are a child's hands, like his head. "That's a relief! Lend! Lend!"

Professor Simon's voice is the wheezing rasp of old lungs and the clarion purity of bright, fresh vocal chords, at the same time. The voice of a hoarse, asthmatic child reciting the speeches of a worn-out old man, word for word and intonation for intonation, from memory, his pearl teeth dancing in scarlet gums. He gestures in the direction he was going, through the shadowy archway.

"I happen to have a moment just now. If you're not too tired?"

He nods and waves to the the shieldbearers. They lower their shields at once and walk directly to the nearest seats, where they sit down and light cigarettes. Arieto turns her back right away and saunters off. The economists follow Professor Simon through several open areas where economists pray, fill out ledgers, and groups of workers prepare pots of soup or stew, wash and dry and press laundry, pushing hampers and coal carts, blowing glass, and all manner of other business. Professor Simon chats away blithely, walking with surprising speed through these spacious rooms. Sunlight pours in through large windows, combed and daubed by ivy which hangs over them like vertical venetian blinds.

"Let's try in here."

Professor Simon leads the economists into an indistinct room facing the trees outside. Through the two narrow if large windows there is view of only the middles of the trees, the trunks, with the canopy overhead and the roots down below both out of sight. The forest thickens in that direction, so that an eye can make out only the ever-gathering shade among the trunks. Golden flies and gnats spin up into a ray of sun, making it visible by obliviously giving it their own bodies to bounce off of.

The room strongly smells of fresh laundry. They can almost taste soap on their tongues. Professor Simon seats himself on a leather divan pushed up lengthwise against a wall and stacked with a bar graph of clean towels in color-coded piles. The Professor sits with the towels at his back like an imperial fan, while transmitting to them a tacit invitation to seat themselves in the various cameo-back chairs.

"There's water in the pitcher there, if you want it," he says.

His facial expressions are completely indecipherable. It's possible he doesn't have complete control over his features. His face has a way of lopsiding itself that conveys an archly aristocratic cynicism often at odds with his tone of voice, which seems more caring. Eyes that seem wide and ingenuously clear one moment take on a recessed cunning look the next.

"I wanted to hear a bit more from you personally about animal money," he says. The words animal money sound shocking coming from someone else; it's as if he'd just named a secret friend.

"I thought we were here to discuss the duel. That is what we were told just now," Professor Crest says.

"There's plenty of time. We offer hecatombs to Turms here—you do that, don't you? Ah, good. We make the offering at the new moon, and the day before we rest, which is today. We can discuss every topic we like. I'm happy, naturally, to talk with you about the investigation into the duel, but I am bound over in certain matters and I won't be able to speak as freely about it, just now, as you might like. The question belongs to the working group now, and they haven't even set a date for their next meeting yet. They haven't met in years, I think. The group members are all available. But ... I would prefer to discuss your idea directly with you, first, if you don't mind. We're very interested in this idea, that is, I am, and certain others. There are those without a doubt who wish you'd never come up with it, but I think it's brilliant."

He sighs briefly.

"How to begin," he wonders aloud. "Ah! Well, my

appearance—that's only a selectivity. We all use some parts more than others, and we all make compensations."

Then he seems almost to tuck his head between his knees and roll forward. He gives such a clear impression of being about to somersault that Professor Aughbui lunges, with hands outspread, to catch him. But Professor Simon only lifts himself to his feet with an apology fondly smiled at the floor. He turns, swinging his arms for balance as if he were pushing at the air, as if he were in the water. He swims over to the wall by the windows and pulls a big china chamber pot out from a cabinet, setting it on a low table and turning his back. A spatter of piss in the bowl follows after a few seconds and he grunts with relief in an eerily unchildlike way.

"I remember when all I had to do was open up and out it came!" he says. "Bang! Now it has to loop-de-loop a few times first. ... Where once there was a concentrated stream," he says, his voice now louder, "now there's just this spray—ah!"

He swivels his legs.

"Can't hardly keep it from getting all over my trousers—coming out at an angle, sometimes a ninety degree angle! Straight up into my face sometimes."

"Ahem ..." Professor Crest says.

"What's that?"

"I say, 'by the way,' ..."

"Yes?" Professor Simon asks loudly, his head swivelling bizarrely toward them, like a long-necked dinosaur's.

"Has the security committee made any finding yet, about the abduction of Professor Aughbui?"

"He's right there."

"He escaped."

"Well, I wouldn't know about that. Ask Dr. Oa."

"Who?"

Professor Simon fastens his fly and puts a wooden cover on the pot. Clearing his throat, he turns to us and swims over to the divan again, settling in, then freezing with a gasp, then settling the rest of the way.

"The rulers of the world are in the process of trying to get control over certain global problems. They don't want a single government, but they do want transnational institutions to manage things like pollution, population, surveillance. Unaccountable. International economic institutions already exist, and they are being used as models, even as they themselves are being given new and broader missions. Coordinated surveillance would make what I'm sure they and their lackeys would call 'management of the population of the world' a pretty straightforward business and more difficult for that population to resist effectively.

"As you know, there is a parallel process underway among the disfranchised, who are also trying to put the world in order and exert some influence when it comes to global problems. Groups are formed or repurposed, but they are fractious and their missions are rather circumscribed, albeit important. Despite all this, and constant harassment from the rulers and their minions, all these groups must, insofar as they persist and continue to interpret and understand events, sooner or later triangulate in on global capitalism as the problem they all have in common, and the capitalists know this, or dimly intuit it anyway. Your idea of animal money is currently unworkable, I think, but there is something to it, a certain *novelty!* No economics theory, no monetary policy, could possibly overturn capitalism of course, but I think your idea has enormous potential, even if it does lie somewhat out of my field of professional expertise. You may remember my dissertation was on types of chairs— what was I thinking?"

He smiles and shakes his head in fondly nostalgic disbelief. The left side of his mouth suddenly veers up toward his eye in a repellent sneer, a sneer the eye doesn't join with or seem to notice.

"Ah, but the world was nothing like it is now! In those days, we didn't dare show our marks on our faces, or so much as allude to the separation of beads or our testing books in public. Anyway, your work on animal money is, as you know, already very popular. You have my support in taking this as far as you can."

He presses one disproportionately small, pink hand to his sweater vest, which emits a puff of chalkdust, to indicate himself.

"As I mentioned, there are others who disagree with you and who quite frankly see their interests on the opposing side. Some of them, in fact, many of them—most of them, I suppose ... Well, they are basically influential enough to do something about it, and I have to warn you that some have been discussing the possibility of not renewing you or even defrocking you."

The economists exchange worried glances. Professor Crest seems most alarmed at the idea, but, sitting bolt upright on the last two inches of his seat, one leg neatly folded over the other, he still radiates a kind of tense alertness and intrepidity. Professor Budshah rests his chin on his two thumbs, hands clasped before his mouth and elbows on the arms of the chair. The remaining Professor Long's eyes are phosphorescent, full of chessboards. Professor Aughbui deflates in exhaustion.

"I can head off anything like that from happening— anything serious, but I won't always be here," Professor Simon goes on. "You will have to watch out from opposition within the IEI as well as from those outsiders who don't like your theory. I suggest you find a surer way to stay in our organization, at least as long as that will protect you—indefinitely, I hope. Now, can you tell me, very simply, what your idea really is. Because, you see, in some of your writings it's described one way, and another way in other writings."

The economists look at each other self consciously. Professor Budshah speaks.

"To the present, money ... conventional money, we'll call it for now ... has involved proof in exchange, which means that the money is nothing in itself insofar as it is money and not, let's say, bits of paper or metal, sea shells, or other kinds of small, portable, interchangeable objects, more or less natural or at least requiring no excessive effort to make, easily fashioned that is. It is only something to be held up to a transcendent standard of value considered in the abstract, and this abstraction is the form of property as such. Which is to say, it is not the question of who has how much money that is of primary importance, but who owns how many shares of the abstraction by means of which the value of money is determined at any particular time, or, to mince things a little finer still, how the value is divided into real shares. Conventional money is a proof with respect to that abstraction. It is a phantom value which is never present in the here and now, because, when something purchased is then used, or enjoyed (where possible), the value of that thing is its use or enjoyment (where possible), rather than its monetary value. The monetary value has flown the coop, and is itself never used nor enjoyed (where possible) except perhaps by collectors or hoarders, who deal only in relative quantities and for whom the character of the thing exchanged is neutral and unimportant."

"Animal money—if I may—" Professor Crest breaks in eagerly, a light in his eyes, and with a glance at Professor Budshah who graciously, if not entirely happily, subsides to him. "—Thank you, Professor Budshah—Animal money is different, in that it does not operate by proof and reference but by being itself something, which is to say doing something, an act. Conventional money does nothing but come and go, but animal money intervenes by taking what is there and creates more. Animal money is creative money as opposed to merely circulating money."

"And that is why it does not exchange, but doubles across any encounter?" Professor Simon asks.

"Exactly," Professor Crest says.

"Yes," Professor Budshah says.

"Correct," Professor Aughbui says.

The remaining Professor Long points to him.

"But how does that work?" Professor Simon asks.

The remaining Professor Long explains.

"The animal money is living," she says. "It is not owned and spent. It moves through populations on its own, by itself. It has a habitat, which attracts it; the habitat is exchange. What we have had up until now has no behavior because it is not living. The conventional money is to the animal money what a puppet is to an animal that's living. It has been, up until now, a taxiderm which only imitates life the actual life of the bankers and those who are setting policy and so on, and who pretend to be following the money, as if the money were leading. But the animal money is alive and it actually does lead, to reproduce like animals. Aristotle condemned interest as money with a life that is false. This is money will grow naturally, rather than simply accumulate."

"To make this happen," Professor Aughbui says, reviving, "animal money must establish viable populations in the wild. There has to be a habitat of wild exchange for it; to be conceived of as a natural institution autonomous to government and business. Wilderness is preserved by cordoning off wild areas, however it is the man-made world that is actually cordoned off; the nature preserves are also man-made. Nature produces the man-made world and sustains it, and everything inside is already natural insofar as it is natural for humans to form institutions. The conflict with nature is an economic conflict in which nature is the lowest class in a hierarchy that refuses to acknowledge the legitimacy or existence of natural institutions. Animal money is an attempt to neutralize this conflict by economic animalization."

Professor Simon is nodding attentively as the economists explain, but this does not stop him from coquettishly examining his face in a compact mirror, turning his face this way and that, pouting, smiling, and even winking at himself, again and again.

"You Professors!" he now chortles after a few moments' silence. "You must forgive me for saying so, but there's nothing at all *to* you. Nothing!"

Professor Simon lowers his compact and fixes his gaze on each of the four in turn.

"Look at yourselves," he says, smiling, and seeming to be filled with a sort of wonder. "What could anyone say about you? How could anyone begin to describe you? You go on rambling endlessly about your animal money, but what kind of figures do you think you cut as human beings? You want living money, and you're just talking furniture! I mean, you are alive, but ..."

Professor Simon splutters a little, owing to a constriction of his throat and face brought about by a half-stifled chuckle. He searches visibly for the right turn of phrase.

"... but, you're alive in all the wrong ways! Like living furniture, not like people. May you sit down sir? Will you hang your hat on me, ma'am? You're ridiculous! You're hatracks!"

The economists receive this outburst with some surprise. Professor Budshah unflappably leans forward now, laying his hands on the armrests and looking with some hauteur at Professor Simon, who anticipates him, saying—

"So now, the great king will rebuke me, right?"

Professor Budshah brushes off this remark with dignity.

"If we are all nothings, or next to nothings, as you say, then I should be obliged to you if you could inform me who is to blame, because it certainly isn't any of us. We are Professors, sir, and we watch what we say. We make no unqualified statements, no unverified claims, and why is that, if not because we stand to lose everything if we are caught out having made even a single mistake! Every-*thing*, remember that! Perhaps you expected a band of merrymakers? Of gay vandals?

"We come to you, I remind you, at your own command—"

Professor Simon is about to speak, but Professor Budshah raises his voice and perseveres, causing Professor Simon to raise his hand in bemused, mock self-defense.

"—and what you think of us, sir, is of no significance! Do you understand that? It is of no consequence whatever whether you think of us as funny little fellows, whom you may treat inconsiderately, or if you think we are geniuses!"

Professor Budshah pauses.

Professor Simon says, "Well—"

Professor Budshah interrupts him.

"It matters no more than our opinion of you matters! Whether or not we regard you to be an ally, who understands what we have been put through, all of us, and also our aims, and sympathizes, if not with us, then at least with those aims, or whether we think of you in some other way—a way which you might not find flattering! None of it is of the slightest importance!"

Professor Simon waits for a moment or two, still smiling blandly.

"Now may I speak?" he asks at last.

"Feel free," Professor Budshah says sharply.

"Colleagues," Professor Simon says palliatively. "I apologize for my outburst. I retract it. In its entirety. From time to time, I find I succumb to a feeling of candidness that somehow falls short of what I know to be the truth. That is, I speak with the feeling of bluntness and honesty, or should I say, of freedom, and yet what I say, while it is not exactly dishonest, not deceptive in intention, is simply not true. It is a blurry, hastily sketched truth, but a failed sketch, a failed one. You must admit, that there is something a bit funny about all this proper and terribly formal dissertating we do—that we all do. I suppose I fall out of step once in a while, and see it from outside, as it were—like an animal? Suddenly the whole enterprise becomes ridiculous. Then I must remind myself again of what it is all about, what is at stake. That, since everyone in the world takes it seriously, I would be lost if I did not also. That, of course, considered quite independently from my own more personal interests. If we economists laugh when we see each other, then we are no better than the astrologers. As I say, I will promote your idea, your excellent, your pioneering theory of animal money, and I will see to your personal safety and the security of your economic standing in the group as well."

He pauses, and the economists, after a little uncertainty, thank him.

"You should realize that I will not be here much longer. Professor Quashie or Professor Levoyer are most likely to replace me. Professor Quashie, who teaches in Egypt, is pretty lukewarm about your ideas, and Professor Levoyer, who is currently working at the Economics Research Institute in Bern, thinks you're shit. You need more friends in high places. Now, there are two things you can do. You can cultivate friends, and I can give you some recommendations, but there will not be that many who will listen to you or do much for you even if they do agree with you. The surer way, it seems to me, is to lower your profiles temporarily.

"Well,—" he says abruptly, pressing his knees and rising, "—you make up your minds as you see fit and let me know what you decide, hm? The Surfeit is One."

A single short step takes him to a narrow closet door which pops open before him and snaps shut behind him like an eye blinking. The economists sit for a while, stirring, growing restless. After a while, they realize that the interview is actually over, leave the room in some uncertainty about what to do with themselves, and begin milling around outside. Arieto hails them, a stubby black pipe in the corner of her mouth, her image flickering and a little speedy, like a silent film. Dr. Oa is away on a call at the moment, but he is expected back soon. She's asking them how their interview with Professor Simon went when the light outside flushes a lurid ruby red color. The light indoors is not affected, and the economists, standing stock still in a bubble of artificial light that is virtually colorless in comparison with that red, stare through the windows and skylights, bewildered. They still stand there when the red color deepens and lightens, changing and remaining the same, and turns blured. And it makes a sound: a hooning sigh that shivers in the fabric of the building.

"It's Assiyeh's experiment," Professor Aughbui says.

"It must be," Professor Crest says.

"Well, I certainly don't see how we could possibly know that. I feel that it's true, and yet I can't account for such feelings," says Professor Budshah.

"The stories we made up about her must have been ..." the remaining Professor Long says, without finishing.

Arieto beckons them to a corner of a room filled with stacked cardboard boxes and a superannuated copying machine, where two steel doors stand at right angles to each other. Both doors are painted grey, but with different paints. One is darker and shinier, the other lighter and barely reflective at all.

Arieto turns to the group.

"All of you together. Choose one or the other."

"Where will they take us?" Professor Budshah says.

"One will take you to safety, the other won't."

"Which is which?"

Arieto shrugs again.

"You don't know?"

She shakes her head and puffs blue smoke. "Nope."

"This is not a good choice," the remaining Professor Long says.

"When you speak of 'the other'," Professor Crest asks, "Do you mean to say that the other door, the one that will not take us to safety, will take us to danger—to a positive danger? Or do you mean that it will only take us in a direction or to a location that is not as safe as the first?"

Arieto rubs her chin and turns the question over. "If I follow you," she says after a moment, "You're asking me if—this is the lady and the tiger?"

Arieto chuckles briefly, having surprised herself with that last allusion.

"Do you mean to say that there is to your at least adequate knowledge or assurance a positive danger behind one of these doors?"

"I'd say that's right."

"Then you should say what you mean," Professor Crest says brittly.

"Thought I did."

"You did not."

"So, if we take the unsafe way, there is uncertain risk, but what is there to gain? Since the question of gain is the only reason for us to bother making this choice at all, and not just turning around right here and going home. There must be something we stand to gain by going through one or the other of these doors. There is what you are rather vaguely calling safety, and then there is some equally vague risk. Does the risk have a benefit attached to it, or not?"

Arieto shrugs and is bored.

"Look," she says. "How about it?"

The economists glance at each other. Only Professor Aughbui has any real interest in the choice.

"The danger," he says, "is virtually omnipresent, currently. It may express itself at any time, in any location, unexpectedly. To have safety and to know it, is preferable to having safety, unwittingly. Safety must include the awareness of being safe. A selection here will likely lead to confirmed safety. It is worth it to make the selection when the undesirable choice involves conditions that will prevail in any case. There is no meaningful difference between the state of risk behind the door leading in the unsafe direction, absent any positive danger, and the state of risk currently prevailing. Selecting a door affords the only possibility of gain, exclusively."

Impressed by this reasoning, the economists choose their door, and Arieto leads them through into a high, narrow hall, a grey cement floor between cinderblock walls painted yellowish white. The hall leads straight as a die to another door. Through that is a spacious concrete room a little like a loading bay. Across that and up a few steps to the doorless portal on top of a low platform, into a musty, humid cinderblock chute that veers to the right and conducts them into a very large storeroom with rows and rows of metal shelves twenty feet tall, laden with dusty boxes of papers, household goods, bundles of magazines, and so on.

Sometimes the dust falls on them in big, powdery tufts that are faintly luminous, the spectres of fireflies or insects that flew into fires and burned up. There are rooms with gold sunset light slanting from windows, lighting the dust motes. There's an incinerator room with a cold furnace. There are attics lined with pink foam insulation and ducts bound in silver paper. There are tiled, pillar-lined patios with galleries and balconies overhanging them, adorned with elaborate ironwork railings and ornaments, the walls cup a wobbling bubble of congealed blue and gold summer twilight. When the time for sleep finally comes, they choose a room with some rolled-up carpets against the walls, and a deer head mounted to face the window. The next morning, Arieto distributes packets of crackers and some coffee she makes by pouring a brown powder into a thermos of water. She gives the base of the thermos a twist, and in a few moments the contents are hot.

Days pass. They traverse rooms, no two the same, always empty, never showing any trace of recent human activity. Their route seems to angle back around on itself, but there is a general tendency to climb. Not that there are staircases on staircases, or even one staircase, but the rooms are all pitched at a grade, or have some few steps somewhere. In a few cases it is necessary to exit through a hatch in the ceiling, reached by a fixed steel ladder. Arieto is able to provide for all their nutritional needs with boundless crackers, and there is something, too, about these rooms that emancipates them from hunger and thirst, as if the little food and drink they are taking stays with them. Movement is easy in these rooms. No one is surprised when, after several days, perhaps more than ten—as they cross another tiled atrium surrounded by pillars and equipped with a laughing fountain in its center—vivid stars in a scintillant field of absolute black appear beneath the arches, between the pillars ... stars that do not sparkle. Professor Aughbui walks carefully up to the arches, and, lowering his head, looks down and sees the blue span of the earth below, shining in its lip of air. Arieto leads them past the fountain and on toward a shadowy archway, and the economists follow her through.

*

The words came out of me, in the cafe, and they burst out elsewhere too, under a special pressure. There is a kind of guidance—or no, energy, just pressure, or urging, that demands an articulation take place even if there is no prior clarity to express. The words cannot be prevented from rushing together. This is what is meant by censorship in that special sense—not oversight by an authority with something to hide, or a mind-control-for-its-own-sake agenda—this censoring involves holding the words back, or no, you let them surge together like that. The censoring takes place only after there is something to censor; the censoring involves excluding certain possible connections so that the words keep unfolding in the right direction and without getting tangled up and stopping. So, do we do the censoring? I don't know who censors, but the censorship is necessary for travel, to keep the words rolling along.

We did it ourselves, that was our side of the transaction, by introducing Assiyeh. She's a kind of gradient. I attracted her to me, I guess, because, while I was attracted to her, and while such ideas elicit an inversion-reaction to block me, at the same time, I was always insisting on her not being real, so perhaps this was included as a factor in the inversion-reaction. I wish I could—no, I don't wish I could tell, how much my thoughts influence matters, and where that necessary contact is.

Imagine a sheet of flame spilling out in all directions, in the darkness and not really shedding any light, creeping like a puddle of flaming alcohol, low, through space. That is the way to visualize the fact that my thoughts influence events. You would think, with all the well-wishing and ill-wishing I've done, that the effects would be more obvious, but the routes are devious and there is a lot of interference and misunderstanding.

PART SEVEN:
THEY BEG FOR MERCY
WHILE THEY ARE KILLING
YOU

VOICE: Wake up.

Ah!

VOICE: Awake now?

...

VOICE: Ready to continue? You will begin by explaining how you were to go about using animal money to undermine the international economy of the world.

Correct the international economy. That is what we were trying to do.

VOICE: By writing a book?

A book that would ruin minds for this bad reality, making them incompetent to function in it so they would be compelled by their own altered understanding to change it.

VOICE: You will confine yourself to speaking in intelligible terms.

... Well ... I'll explain ... but ... to do that, I'll have to tell you about Assiyeh, and how, bent nearly double with age, Assiyeh hobbles into the lab. With the assistance of her father's ghost, she climbs painfully into a rolling hospital bed. She's an old woman, now. He looks into her eyes, and she grabs his face with one clawlike hand, squashing his felty shadow cheeks.

"Now *listen*," she says hoarsely, fixing his unblinking

eyes with her own rheumy ones. "*Five* minutes. Understand? *Do you understand?*"

She spreads her gnarled free hand as wide as it will go. "*Five!*"

The lab is like a vast cave. There's a gigantic glass bulb in the center of it, divided in two halves, top and bottom, with a hospital room set inside. Assiyeh's bed is placed on rails and drawn into the bulb. It slides gently into position between the nightstand and a large window, which is blocked by a vertical shutter made of overlapping steel plates. A dusty, listless butterfly sits on the windowsill, without moving. It is very nearly dead of old age. A papery, browning rose droops in a green wine bottle standing on the floor in the near corner of the room.

Assiyeh lies on her back, looking straight up, her fists clenched on her chest.

"All right!" she calls.

The ghost of her father stands at the controls. There's a box with two buttons on it hanging from a heavy cable, and he now takes this and presses the lower button. The two halves of the bulb, currently about a foot apart, close together with a stony clap. Now the alcohol. There are two huge cylinders of gas connected to the bulb, one on either side. Massive hydraulic rams sink, stopping again after descending a few feet. There's a hiss as the chamber pressurizes with vaporized alcohol. Once the experiment starts, these rams will automatically step up the pressure at diminishing intervals.

As the pressure rises, the heavy shutter over the window lifts slightly, flooding the room with a warm, golden effulgence of summer sunshine. Assiyeh tosses restlessly. The withered rose stirs, its petals swell and stiffen, their color flushes up and deepens, the green of the leaves darkens and they stand up again. Like a timid erection, the head of the rose tremblingly lifts. The butterfly, standing directly in the stream of the sun, takes on a new vividness; its colors flush up and it supports its body with new readiness. It begins to flutter around the room, flapping up and down around the bed. The rams sink further, the pressure increases, the shutter rises further, the air becomes more syrupy and golden.

After a few repetitions more, the flower stands at attention, a bold carmine hard-on defying all comers, the butterfly whirls around the room. Assiyeh convulsively seizes the handrails of the bed and pulls herself up, her head hanging back and rolling. The liverspots on her hands are twitching like little mouths, shrinking and expanding. The bulging blood vessels on the backs of her hands sink. A heavy greyness is being hammered somehow into her snow white hair and the olive of her complexion is being forced back into her suppling flesh. Assiyeh groans and flops back again onto the pillow, streaming with perspiration.

The timer alarm barks, but so enraptured is her father's ghost by the golden light, the gorgeous spectacle of rejuvenative life fields, that he doesn't notice the alarm, the presses silently and implacably descend, and the shutter rises further, the cascade of brilliant summer becomes punishing, his fascination deepens. The rose trembles in the bottle, its stem tapping against the inside of the glass. Its petals have become too intensely to look at, and even as he tries to see them more distinctly, with a ripping sound a blinding spark of blue-white light cracks out from the blossom and jets into the air like a blowtorch. With a sharp pop! the test butterfly breaks the sound barrier. A fierce spark bursts from it and the room fills with a scribbled light trail. Assiyeh sits up wild-eyed and frantically whips the edge of her extended hand across her throat—shut it off! shut it off! she mouths, her voice not more than a muffled hum through thick glass. Tears of joy dribbling down his face, he raises his hand in an answering wave, then, beside himself, he is jumping up and down and waving both arms, transported with the success of the experiment.

Heliosimulators bathe the room with mild summer sunlight so concentrated it's punishing; a heavy golden jelly crushing and smothering her beneath perfume of roses, hyacinths, jasmine, old man's beard, orange blossoms, lilac and wisteria. The rams fall with merciless slowness, and the pressure steadily increases. The floor of the hospital set crawls with blossoms shaped like alien flowers and piebald with insane color variations; the thorny vines scale the walls in fine threadlike arabesques. A hum swells from the buds and they bloom in dazzling lights. Midsummer afternoon condenses on the walls, and runs down in viscous streaks, dripping in threads from the ceiling to mingle with her sweat, until she is sopping in a golden mire of glory. Assiyeh pitches and heaves on the damp mattress, her skin taut, her hair cascades over her face in glossy jet black locks which are parted by a pair of spatulate antlers sprouting angrily from her temples, her whole body crackles and bursts, transforming her into a blazing, writhing figure of pink flame.

As his daughter explodes, the ghost leaps back in surprise and alarm, suddenly remembering his instructions. He snatches the hanging box and presses the top button. The two halves of the bulb spring apart and the captive gas gushes from the opening as the presses retract upwards automatically. Volatile sun jelly splatters out the opening hatch, hits the floor, and rebounds in fragrant white heat.

The rejuvenation procedure was supposed to be carried out in gentle stages, not all at once. It was also supposed to restore Assiyeh to a dignified 35- or 40-year-old self, not as a skinny, acne'd, antlered teenager.

"You stupid asshole! You ruined everything! *You always ruin everything!* I hate you I hate you *I hate you!*" she screams.

*

I blunderstand my shituation pretty wellbadly, I'd say. I see posters of myself everywhere: UNWANTED, DEAD OR ALIVE. I see them so reliably that I begin to think that for me seeing posters of myself and just seeing have gotten mixed up. For a while I would tear down every one I came across with the same indignant cry, that my face is mine, that's my face, my name, my name, but there are so many posters and faces and names that I don't bother any more. They aren't really my face. I look around for someone to punch and there's only the usual commuters. And why would I want to hit some salaried poster hanger for? Isn't there anywhere in life for my anger to go? Why do I always have to burn it off in a game or in some bullshit? What's preventing me from lowering the boom when and where it belongs? It's because the time and place for it is always being yanked just out of reach. I can never pay off my rage debt. Still, I don't think not being able to see myself in the hero's role can be all bad. The evil wizards are scrying for me, trying to turn me into a poster or a statue. That's why I have to not stop. If I stop, a pedestal is going to start pushing up under my feet. I want my feet on the ground, even if the ground is cracked and I keep falling on my face, and my knees and handheels are scuffy and scabby. Wherever I go, the ground looks the same; it looks exactly like the ground did the time I was shot in the USA and lay on the ground, watching the ground refusing to drink my unwanted blood. My blood just lay there. I wanted my blood, I knew that, even if the ground didn't. The bullet went right through the meaty part of my right arm above the elbow. There's not a lot of meat there to hit, so it was fate. I was seventeen. I got better, but when I pull my arm all the way in, it feels weak toward the end.

"When the international monetary system went off the gold standard, the money game became infinite, and so did the potential for rigging that already-rigged game. Without the modest check of international gold prices, the cabals that had once set those prices were in a position simply to set the value of money directly. It wasn't necessary to intervene in every variety of money because in the end everything was a dollar derivative anyway. Incognito dollars in brightly-colored holiday outfits adorned in their local color tourist t-shirts silk

screened with the faces of royalty and endorsed celebrities
and landmarks go off to clandestine siexual (sic) liasons
under foreign skies with exotic and interesting strangers,
for mantelpiece knick knack fuck snacks after snake fin
soup and crackers."

She's sitting beside me, the car wind in her hair, maybe
listening.

There are so many moments when I feel the profundity
of life becoming visible. My eyes open in the depths of
life without trying to, as if they were under a spell. I go
a little way along in the vision and then, I can't help it, I
can't hold on to the profundity—I have to clown around,
make faces, talk in funny voices. Why am I never closer
to clowning than when I am thinking my most serious
thoughts? It's like pity or fear or pain or something forces
me to ruin everything, and I duck the responsibility that
beauty and meaning lay on me. It's more than being
afraid of failing to live up to something, it's fear of the
call, a cry so loud it can reach all the way to here, reach
you, anywhere. See why they call me what they call me?
But am I wrong when I tell you what you get for all your
suffering is a life?

There are no signs out here, but there are these
whatchacall jests, indications, like more and more graffiti
on the rocks, and shoes with the laces tied together
thrown up into trees, and litter all over the desert. Now
I can see where the shoreline rocks open out, and there's
a yellow haze in the air despite the ocean breeze; it's way
up there, but that has to be Etsimen. I point it out to
Carolina, and she nods without turning her eyes to me,
methodically dosing herself. A lone streetlight shines

down on sawhorses and barrels, where the highway begins. The paved road plunges beneath our car with a crash.

*

VOICE: You are not explaining how you—
I'm getting to it! It all has to do with that color change she produced in the atmosphere with her experiment. Eighty years after the Color Shift, rice will grow in the Sahara, the midwestern United States will produce nothing but sorghum, naturally unaffected by blured light. Cattle will shrink to the size of calves and sheep will develop long legs and necks, turning into fleecy little giraffes. The oceans will be choked with radioactive blured plankton that produce unaccountable mutations in sea life, so that the flesh of most fish and marine mammals is neurotoxic, instantly fatal to humans; edible coral, however, will sprout thickly in the mountains, and a nutritious clay will appear, mounding up in the froth that gathers along crumbling seaboards. The population will flee inland from encroaching armies of marauding, omnivorous, amphibious blobs of slime from the bottom of the sea, who will eat anything organic except that nutritious, acrid clay. Sunset and sunrise will become pyrotechnic displays of fulminating kaleidoscopic effects, like the title cards of a psychedelic movie. The stars at night will be magnified, dappling the ground with multicolored rays. The moon will seem to adopt an endless variety of irregular shapes and colors. Semi-invisible, intermittently phosphorescent living things, ranging

in size from the nearly imperceptible to elephantine proportions, will coalesce out of windborne protoplasm and float weightlessly through the air, contaminating every unfortunate human they touch with degenerative brain diseases. Whole treasuries will vanish in futile attempts to reverse the experiment's effects. A Congolese resonator will manage to reverse the shift by 49%, but the effects will not last. After a few weeks, the skies will once again be electric blue, and the natural colors of the earth fluoresce with saturated intensity.

Assiyeh will disappear shortly after the success of her experiment. Observers in the know will gradually come to the realization that Assiyeh is still at large, and not in secret custody somewhere, but no one seems to be able to trace her. What will she be doing all this time? As she grows older and older, she will pursue experiments intended to decelerate or reverse aging, returning to the abandoned line of inquiry she had pursued when trying to prolong the lives of her parents. There will be injections and operations carried out by machines, gland replacements and so on, a special diet, long fasting. She will nearly kill herself with a year and a half of chronic mumps and hiccups that will end only after a therapeutic induced coma, a period of quasi-vampirism during which she will be compelled to consume human milk, an episode of gigantism that will take months to fix. Eventually, she will be transformed into a teenager again. Volatility and foolishness, and on the other hand, additional time, new energy, and an entirely unforeseeable appearance. Fortunately, the antlers will drop off about a week after the experiment, making an odd surgery unnecessary.

Assiyeh will make the international villain list because the Color Shift, in addition to giving a weird luster and exaggerated hue to daylight and everything it shone on, will transform the characteristics of that light, making it possible to store light cheaply and easily. Stored light will revolutionize technology and economic activity, drastically reduce the cost of energy, and lead to new forms of energy production. Over the course of decades—and it will take as long as that, mainly due to the resistance of the well-heeled—conventional money will be superseded by light money, pieces of blured sunlight in glass chips. When an empty chip is exposed to a radiant one, the empty chip will acquire equivalent radiance, so transactions will involve simply putting chips together. All devices will operate on chip power; the larger the device, the larger the chip it will take to run it, meaning all large devices will be run on big community chips, the largest of which are like the rai stones of the Micronesians. Blured light does not reflect; rather it produces more of itself on contact. The development of photic money will be hampered by brutal violence and disgusting propaganda, but its spread will prove too expensive and hazardous to contain. The photic system will be especially successful in the exploration of space and the generation of science fiction conditions, or SFC. It might be imagined that Assiyeh would be celebrated as the Messiah of this new "photic world," but, as a target for the stagnating rage of the Misled, she will be excoriated as a witch and a criminal and a terrorist-sociopath and a pitiful megalomaniac.

Assiyeh will not give up the freedom to make mistakes,

freedom from adulation. Under the names of rival scientists and other naysayers, she will publish papers on photic behaviorism that mark the birth of a whole new branch of physics, made possible by the empirical opportunities brought about by the Color Shift. She will enjoy the spectacle of authorities squirming; people who will have done nothing but attack her ideas suddenly feted as converts and geniuses by wings of the scientific community for which they will have had nothing but finger-flicking disdain, swamped with letters of praise and congratulations on their wise recantation of former anti-photism, their thoroughgoing understanding of the science, their courage, their insight. It will be fun to see how many will play along, accept the offered positions, the grants, the speaking engagements.

Enough about this Assiyeh person. You are going to give us, right now, the names of all your associates in the organization conspiracy.

Assiyeh looks O'W in the eye and grins.

"Are you feeling better now?" she asks pertly, and is slapped. O'W slaps her. Assiyeh looks her in the eye again right away, eyes brighten through touseled hair, still smiling.

"Let's go," O'W says, her voice tense. "In."

Assiyeh doesn't move. She is looking intently at O'W with a curious smile, and no sign of hostility.

"Get in I said!" O'W shouts, raising her hand.

Assiyeh does not respond; just the little smile, the alert watchfulness. Then she gracefully draws her knees and ankles up together, as if she were a snake or mermaid drawing her tail in, and pivots to face forward in the passenger seat of O'W's supercar. O'W slams the door and stalks around to the front, gets in and tells the car to go home. The she swivels her seat around to face Assiyeh; glaring at her for a long moment.

"I finally got you."

The words slip out, and she regrets them. She should sit there like a block of ice, as if she were alone, negating Assiyeh absolutely. Sharing this moment of vainglory, she has already humanized herself too much, and brought her too close to Assiyeh's captive level. Assiyeh keeps her poise even cuffed in the back seat, still smiling. She wants to tell her to wipe that smile off, but manages to avoid that blunder, at least. There is something about this catch that feels off; she doesn't believe in it quite yet. She has her captive, but she's not in the system and there are no witnesses. Only when the car has reeled them both in, will she feel satisfied.

"Finally," Assiyeh says.

Her steady gaze is making O'W want to turn and face forward, but she should keep her in sight at all times. O'W artificially relaxes her face. She returns Assiyeh's impertinent gaze stonily. A blood thread trickles from Assiyeh's left nostril. It descends, stops, shifts direction, and descends again, making its way, like a new rivulet across parched ground, toward the corner of the smile, as the city streets flash by behind the face.

The right half of that face gives that smile a violent tug and the features melt and twist. The head sinks and the bound hands cross and press to the chest as the knees come up. Assiyeh moans and lists toward the middle of the car. O'W stares at her, refusing to react. A blood cord drops straight from Assiyeh's nose and lands with a hollow dribble on the seat. The car fills with the blood smell. The car rounds a corner and a liquid rake of blood reaches across the upholstery.

"You're not fooling me," O'W says levelly.

Assiyeh groans, hanging from her shoulderbelt. Her hands are grey. Tremors race up and down her body, she is shivering violently. Hoarse, bestial noises burst from her through chattering teeth. She's beginning to choke; she coughs and gags, struggling for breath.

"Go ahead and die you fucking shammer!" O'W snaps.

Assiyeh chokes and gasps. She has curled up in the seat. The strap has slipped up around her throat.

"God damn you!" O'W says furiously.

She stops the car, gets out, opens Assiyeh's door and seizes her in one fluid motion, props Assiyeh back into her seat, slaps her, grabs her throat and squeezes it.

"You throw another one of those my dear and I'll kill you!" O'W snarls, her face vicious, suddenly ugly.

Everyone at the station crowds into the observation room to gawk at the great Assiyeh Melachalos, who sits at the table looking absurdly small, unimportant and defenseless. The blood has been imperfectly wiped away, leaving a few smears on her face.

"What—you hit her?!"

"No no ... Nosebleed," O'W says.

Now the sense of accomplishment blooms at last. History's greatest criminal against property, right there on the other side of that glass. Congratulations from the chief, the district administration, and on up and up. She's asked for quotes and told not to say anything, hold the story for sale, write a book.

Maybe I should let her go and catch her again, she jokes, but there's a spectral unease lurking behind that joke.

Processing delays force them to wait a few days to begin interrogating the prisoner. They want all sorts of foolproof extra security, none of which is quite ready yet or yet or even yet. O'W is awarded the first crack at her. She meets Assiyeh in one of the interrogation cubicles at the Human Resources Optimal Data Facilitation Unit. O'W comes in all business, without a word. Assiyeh sits there already, naked, washed out, her face lined, her body slumped.

"You are Assiyeh Melachalos?"

"Yes."

"Also known as Assiyeh Nemekeseyah?"

"Yes."

"Also known as Christine Minuit?"

"Yes."

"You hold a PhD. in physics from ETH Zurich?"

"Yes."

"You were responsible for the Color Shift?"

"Yes."

"Your father was Dr. Marco Chapu?"

"Yes."

"Your mother was Dr. Paricheher Katsaros?"

"Yes."

"You alone were responsible for the Color Shift?"

"Yes."

"You are currently eighty-four years old?"

"Yes."

"How is it that you look so much younger?"

"Yes."

"How did you cause the Color Shift?"

"Yes."

"Why did you cause the Color Shift?"

"Yes."

"Were you the CEO of Narthex International Laboratories?"

"Yes."

"Did you knowingly defraud the United Properties Association of monies allocated to research and develop technologies to reverse the effects of the Color Shift?"

"Yes."

"Have you ever engaged in homosexual activities?"

"Yes."

"Will you be guilty of drugging and incapacitating a police officer in the Hotel Escudo in Lisbon, Portugal, five years from now, on August 15, 2084?"

"Yes."

"Will you then take that police officer's uniform, and use it to impersonate that officer, in order to evade arrest on that date?"

"Yes."

"Will you sexually molest an Indian police detective on April 12, 2085, in Delhi?"

"Yes."

"Will you be responsible for the extraction of the sword known as Durendal from the walls of Rocamadour?"

"Yes."

"And the removal of that sword from that location?"

"Yes."

"With the full awareness that it was a national treasure

belonging to United Franconia Properties?"

"Yes."

"Will you willfully contaminate the water supply of the city of Osaka, Japan with depilatives, aphrodisiacs, and hallucinogens, on July 8th, 2085?"

"Yes."

"Have you illegally rejuvenated yourself, employing forbidden technology?"

"Yes."

"Are you responsible for the development of photic money?"

"Yes."

"Have you refused to sell rights and application information about slowing technologies developed by you to all interested United Properties?"

"Yes."

"Has your persistent stare during this examination begun to exert hyp- hyp- hyp-notic influence over me?"

"Yes."

"Have you already exerted a similar influence over the detectives observing this interrogation through the two way mirror behind me?"

"Yes."

"Are they paralyzed and unable to move, riveted in place by your hypnotic influence?"

"Yes."

"Am I likewise increasingly falling under your direct control?"

"Yes."

"Am I now entirely at your command?"

"Yes."

Assiyeh rises from her seat and holds out her handcuffs for O'W to unlock. O'W strips naked and lies on the table. Looking considerably fresher than she had a moment before, Assiyeh puts on O'W's clothes and leaves the room.

VOICE: And how, exactly, are photic money and animal money related? And for what organization does this O'W work?

Well, you see, Assiyeh has been saving a faked death for just such an occasion. She—

VOICE: Answer the question.

She therefore clones herself as a corpse, complete with specially designed fatal injuries and autopsy signs and manages to substitute it for the cadaver of a property criminal of about her own age and appearance and finding a look-alike isn't all that difficult considering the vast number of dead property criminals generated every day and interrogation casualties and those who ran afoul of automated killing manifolds and population subtractors and property security agents and you see these dead property criminals are disposed of in pseudo-secrecy because while they are criminals their deaths are not media approved and hence they are not supposed to be dead so rather than deal with the expense of discounting death claims substantiated with the actual remains of the deceased which are now harder than ever to destroy down to the last trace thanks to improvements in DNA detection and identification Gold Star Global Security Services dumps the corpses in space and the night sky is filled with the momentary flashes and streaks of re-entering dead property criminals and children may unwittingly wish for the return of a vanished parent or sibling on the incinerating corpse of that very person as it re-enters the atmosphere so of course this practice does not fail to arouse protest and there is a report from Environmental Extracts Incorporated that proves that the productive capacity of the earth is being reduced as the constituent elements of all those corpses are lost to outer space or vaporized in the atmosphere so as an alternative it is proposed that the bodies be thoroughly and enzymatically mulched to conserve precious life compounds but while the report is supposed to be secret it is not difficult to get a copy and it turns out to be an open secret like all secrets the kind you mainly keep from yourself and Assiyeh is relieved to see this mulching has gone nowhere officially because it's harder to survive ...

VOICE: Are you going to answer the question?

I am answering see once she has her cadaver slated for dumping in space Assiyeh will surreptitiously take its place and be dumped in space instead whereupon her father the ghost since he can materialize at will within certain limits determined possibly by the fundamental nature of ghosts or perhaps they are simply reflections of his own personal shortcomings and it still took years of practice for him to be able to manifest himself in outer space and home in on specific objects floating in space although he never managed to get farther out than earth orbit so the plan is he will manifest himself on the nearest convenient numerous navigable semi-automated spacecraft that flit to and fro like little fish in a sargasso sea of high velocity space trash and great spreading schools of dead property criminals and then once aboard he will tamper with its orbital position signal so that no one on the ground will realize short of actually looking that the vessel is not behaving normally so he can pilot this spacecraft which can be operated manually or by computer as desired and go retrieve Assiyeh's body so he can revive her if life support is available on the craft he happens to find but either way they will begin looking for the most convenient and ready of the various possible ways to get to the Moon since the Moon is neutral territory where earth administrators meet with representatives of other non-terrestrial civilizations primarily the other human or originally human ones and there are numerous support personnel on permanent assignment there as well as holdovers from an earlier settlement period and those who have managed by hook or by crook to get there on their own mainly with Uhuyjhn assistance—

VOICE: You are not answering—

Yes I am just wait a minute I am answering because the plan is put into effect and no one identifies the body which arrives in a shipment of cadavers from New York untagged as is not uncommon and so there is a token attempt to identify it but meanwhile the body enters normal processing and is stowed in a refrigerated transport container that is shipped to one of the various spaceports when it gets full in this case going to the Kinshasa Space Whisker (breath) so just prior to the launch, she pulls up alongside the container in a van and extracts her body strips naked and she has given herself scars and similar markings exactly matching those on the body checks the corpse for any new bruises or discolorations and matches them with make up then she takes the catatonia drug entering the death trance and her father seals her entire body inside a microscopically thin perfectly transparent envelope designed to protect her from the vacuum and gently fills her lungs with a hyperoxygenated liquid which at her lowered metabolic rate, should last her a very long time perhaps days then carefully seals her nose and mouth while an antifreeze compound mixed into her corpse make up is slowly absorbed by her skin and distributed in her bloodstream and he dusts her hair with a bag full of microscopic transmitters each smaller than a grain of sand which will exhibit a signature discernible at long ranges once exposed to vacuum so that he can find her body in space then he places her cautiously on the heap of bodies inside the container, and drives away leaving the van in a garage and the false corpse melting in a barrel of acid in a corner—what? What?

VOICE: If you will not cooperate ...

No no no no no no no no no no wait a minute wait wait wait the container's contents—you'll SEE! you'll SEE!—the container's contents are tipped onto a belt that loads them into one of the huge cargo pods on the back of a shuttle shaped like a huge turtle with protuberances varying from twenty to a hundred feet tall all over its white shell and which does not fly into space but instead rides the great uncoiling tongue of the Kinshasa Space Whisker consisting of a massive bundled cable curled against the earth like the rolled up tongue of a butterfly operating on the principle of the party favor SUCH THAT the whisker sucks in air and stiffens like a huge erection unfurling upwards into the sky while its other end is deeply anchored in the earth's crust and the shuttle travels along the whisker all the way into space stabilizing itself with numerous akimbo chameleon legs about a quarter of a mile down from the gigantic unfolding wheel of cable leaving the whisker only to visit one of the innumerable orbiting penal research or surveillance arcologies before returning to earth by rejoining the whisker and riding down it again and Assiyeh lies in a heap of corpses like mannikins in storage while the rising shuttle which is the size of about four city blocks jolts and shudders as the whisker undulates in air currents and the air whistles gradually out of the cargo hold and the bodies begin to float eerily around and distort as the air pressure subsides so they are trailing ice crystals in the dark and the hold is thickly black traversed with intense beams of light shining in through the gaps around the door while cadavers float through these beams burgeoning with special forms of decay known only in space so their heads sprout wattles and long gnarled horns of carmine matter like a sold dribble of melted candle wax and growths push out their mouths and anuses—this is establishing the credibility of what I'm trying to tell you don't you see that?!—these details!—bodies collide a numb lifeless coitus in space and the intestines push out the navel and the eyes trail from the sockets and they shrivel they shrivel they shrivel like like like like snow white raisins and lichenous structures build out from the body to form a plumage of transparent insect wings of ice and mold and only a few of the corpses plus Assiyeh fail to exhibit these signs and and then a door opens abruptly at one end of the hold and a huge fat man in a sloppy space suit steps in he steps in gingerly and he swats a button or not a button a control on the the the wall and the side of the hold drops into a slot and the whole earth is out there with its atmosphere like a white nest and the pellucid blackness of space and and the fat man walks along a special sticky strip grabbing bodies as they float near and tossing them out the side into space one by one one by one one by one the distorted and stiff human forms fall against the blue white and black some plunging straight out staring back at the ship or forwards toward wherever they are going but most spin some fast some slowly and then it's Assiyeh's turn and her body is seized by one rigidly bent arm and one thigh and the fat man's grip slips and he grabs her arm and leg again and then she is thrown out into space with the rest of them ...

VOICE: We will resume in half an hour. Be prepared to answer then.

...

I think they're gone.

... Assiyeh is terrified of heights.

I can't breathe.

... Even looking at a photograph of the earth taken from space, with the earth's slope filling one corner of the picture, and space above it, causes the fear. Her knees go weak and she feels cold flashes sucking the strength out of her body. This experience might have cured her, but the thought of being adrift in space, naked and immobilized, was too much for her, and she went to great lengths to insure that she would be entirely unconscious.

Jesus ... Jesus ... I think they ... burned it.

... All the same, during loading, her eyes were jostled slightly ajar within the sealant, luckily still intact. That's good. That's vivid.

Now she is remotely aware of a gigantic, luminous presence, like an inconceivably monumental snowdrift ablaze with chill sunlight, a snowdrift with a blue heart. And there is also a boundless, brilliant night that is not a void, and is not a cornucopia of endless being, but that is like an infinite threshold, across which she is looking, with a dreamy, barely open eye, steadily, ever more deeply, with ever greater numb unfelt fear and sense of disappearing. The look plumbs without finding anything but itself, and plumbs into both looking and into this encountered moment that is not looking or doing anything, that is not her opposite or the opposite of action or opposed to anything, and that is at the same time both absolutely alien to her and absolutely accepting her into its un-embrace.

She dreams about a man in a cell. An interrogation cell. A terrified and horrified man, who is in physical pain and who thinks he might really *be* alone just for a moment and so he's taking a chance and allowing himself to sob as quietly as he can, while the science-fiction story about her he's been telling them keeps opening up in his mind and he is escaping into that opening. She opens her eyes and there is a blonde Arab leaning over her. She is aware of the edges of a what she lies upright in, like the sides of a bathtub. The man is bare-chested and his body hair is as pale blonde as the hair on his head, and his beard. He is leaning in at an angle that means he is not on top of her but next to her, and there is a shadowy ceiling up there that she can't see because dim lights shine between her and the ceiling. She can't feel her body, but she can hear a surging pulsation and ringing in her ears that tells her she is alive. The man murmurs something. She's looking almost right up his nose, and his eyes are on something across from her; there must be someone else there. Looking out into space, a neverending opening and the infinite opposite of prison.

*

"My criminal record?"

The charming elderly gentleman pauses midway between standing and sitting, turning to look back at the pair of stern faces.

"All right," he says. He has a gentle voice, gentle gestures. He finishes sitting down gently.

"Won't you sit down? ... No? ... There, well. It's not necessary that we be so formal. I'll tell you whatever you like, even if you want to hear ancient history like that."

"Oh yes? Renewed activity? An organizing conspiracy, is that right? It sounds interesting. Organizing how? You don't know? I see. I'm sure that's quite right. Who? No, I don't think so. Could you repeat the name? My hearing isn't what it was, you see. It doesn't ring a bell. Did they? If you say so; I don't remember things so well these days. I daresay I probably have met dozens of people without having the faintest recollection of it. What's that? Have I met him on other occasions? No, I don't think so, but then again I recall so badly ... Yes, that does look like me. Is that him? Oh, it is. You know that's funny—all this time I thought you were talking about someone else! Yes, of course I know him. Is he in any trouble? Yes, I've met him several times, I think. I can't say how many. Just to talk, conversation, you know. At my age, conversation replaces certain other pleasures, it becomes more important. My what? I would hardly call her my girlfriend, I'm afraid. No, those days are in the past for me. She said what? That's a surprise. That's very interesting. Could you repeat the question? You know, that reminds me, from what I hear, it turns out Assiyeh's father is going to goof and materialize on the wrong side of the earth. He won't find her. Assiyeh will float by chance into the beam of a communications laser that will push her out of earth orbit. She will die in her trance somewhere on the way to Mars, or that is what might have happened, but she will instead be retrieved three days later by the barqot *Mays* just departing the Moon for Jupiter.

Once they find out who she is, the crew of the *Mays* will gather around and stare at her in awe. To them, she is *the* Assiyeh Melachalos, originator of the Photic Revolution and Pioneer of Restech.

The *Mays* is set to rendezvous with its spousecraft, the *Izallu Imeph*, which will then leave earth's solar system for a planet called Koskon Kanona, which is home to a sizable human colony.

You see, Carolina, unknown to all but a few down here, human beings have secretly established

themselves on about ten other Earthlike planets and have contacted life on all of them. Mutations and crossbreeding with non-terrestrials is going on out of control all over the place, and on some planets the descendants of the first human visitors from earth have already become unrecognizeable. Enormous spacecraft fly back and forth between worlds at more than relativistic speeds using a variety of different propulsion techniques, and one of the most frequently-used is an application Restech based on Assiyeh's research. These engines slow the spacecraft, bringing it steadily closer and closer to Absolute Rest; as the vessel slows, the motion of matter in space will overtake it, so that, in effect, the ship stands still, and its destination comes to it. Assiyeh immediately begins to inspect plans of these engines, noting improvements to be made and coming up with new experiments.

In the past, space travel was too expensive, and high prices held mankind on the earth. The development of zoophotic currency will be what makes it economically possible—forgive me the tense creep, but this kind of time-travel stuff is hard to keep straight. Assiyeh's name is often connected with them ... the ... uh ...

(Grabbing a copy of *Animal Money* from under the car seat, shifting his glance from the cover to the road and back, reading the names at random.)

Long Min-Yin, Sulekh Budshah, Ronald Crest, Warren Aughbui, Vincent Long. Animal money and the Color Shift, that's what opened the escape path to space. Nobody can believe Assiyeh went out with Long, and the crew is divinely transported to gossip heaven when they find out.

For days the dialogue between the crew of the *Mays* and the *Izallu Imeph* goes on nonstop and so does Assiyeh's grilling. Between sex and questions she's barely able to do any real thinking or to attack the mounds of knowledge inaccessible on earth.

The crew are all really beautiful people, all different kinds. They wear no clothing, but paint their bodies instead.

When human beings start heading out into space for real, the governments down here on the ground set up all these ad hoc prohibitions that develop into a quarantine, keeping the earth isolated artificially. Assiyeh has—she will not ever have heard yet about the Horizontal Forests on Koskon Kanona and the composite flying tape-bundle inhabitants of Gliese Labzaatz and the beings who inhabit a region of trellised atmosphere in the dark matter honeycombs between galaxies and the earliest reports of the first expedition to the ring of quasars that spans both the Milky Way and Andromeda galaxies. There are ruined cities of water on a planet named A-Dnuirm; the people of Kepler 22-b have an alternate mathematics that causes any human who uses it to undergo a spontaneous sex change; the first generation of human children, born on HD 85512-b will live by sonosynthesis. Stuff like that. Are you still tripping?

So, Assiyeh will be given a position of honor directly in front of the massive forward window to observe the rendezvous with the *Izallu Imeph*. Here's the scene: tiger-striped Jupiter spins in the distance, two moons sailing past, the farther one custardy and yellow on the left, and the closer one is turquoise and more to the right. A tray of minute, greenish-white motes and threads appears behind the yellow moon. A spacecraft the size of California shoots out from around the yellow moon, coming right at them, seeming more to expand than to approach. Its little shadow swings and plunges over the curvature of the turquoise moon, rippling with surface irregularities as it goes. In less than a minute it slides itself beneath the *Mays* like a gargantuan floor, and they are zooming among titan hood ornaments, stylized and generic naked human figures six or seven kilometers tall, striking intrepid poses. All the crew are naked all the time, by the way. Did I mention that? Maybe you're one of them? Well, they put on space suits of course, when they have to go outside, and they have protective gear to do stuff inside the ship, but most of the hazardous work is done by non-anthropomorphic robots.

Well, so, behind these heroic monuments the top of the ship looks like a cracked plain of some dark, ablative material, studded with arcology domes of all sizes, from tiny, luminous beads, to diamond blisters hundreds of kilometers across. Within these domes, Assiyeh can see whole landscapes, with mountains, forests, clouds, towns and cities, herds of animals, rivers, billowing snowstorms, flickering thunderstorms, seas like flashing shields ... Living dioramas. There are dark, uninhabited expanses here and there, separating what look like phosphorescent cities of greenish white and pale yellow filaments and specks and a luminous mycelium sprouting phantasmagoric structures whose weird outlines are robbed of impressive power by the even weirder and more impressive scale of the whole artifact. The captain of the *Mays* points to the mobile lights, the ferries and transports that convey people and supplies among the arcologies, and then to the glowing bloodstream of surface-travelling modules. The captain explains that the *Mays* is actually accelerating wildly to keep up with the *Izallu Imeph*.

So now the rear of the ship rises up ahead like a tower and behind that are the engines—these are three spheres, each as big as an asteroid, with a long sail-like pennant streaming behind each sphere off into the distance so that she can't see the ends of them. They aren't Restech. These spheres roll to and fro behind the ship, altering position like shells in a shell game, and send ripples that are kilometers and kilometers across down the pennants, so that the *Izallu Imeph* actually swims through space like a carp in a pond.

"The ship propels itself through space mechanically?"

"Sure," the captain answers. "It is no problem."

"How is that possible?"

"It is easily all possible because *blah blah blah*."

"What sort of power plant does it use?"

"All kinds. Hundreds of them. New plants are being devised and installed all the time, as the old ones wear out. I'm sure they'd be interested in any new ideas related to photic power, if you would like to talk to them."

As they descend to its surface, the horizon of the massive spacecraft rises comfortingly all around them. Without the slightest bump or jostle, the *Mays* glides to rest, slipping under a protruding structure that folds down on itself like a candy cane. They rise up within the structure to meet a brake of air turbulence that makes the silent barqot suddenly whoosh with a sound like a distant waterfall. She disembarks along a smooth stone esophagous and emerges into a fragrant, softly-lit night, a garden. A sizeable party of naked dignitaries gathered from all over the *Izallu Imeph* is there to welcome Assiyeh aboard, and, in a mercifully brief ceremony she is presented with an insignia of honor, formed entirely of blurred light, which floats a few inches before her sternum.

"We have prepared several different residences for you, Professor," says a devilish-looking man wearing nothing but a coat of red paint, with a white square hovering a few centimeters out from his right ear. "All quite conveniently nearby. But there are no restrictions on you. Travel wherever you like. There are limitless possibilities for exploration on board."

Eventually she settles on a chamber at the heart of a group of tall hedges and sheltered under palm trees. The trees are aware of her and able to respond to commands to open or close, affording different views of the sky. A spring burbles out of from a heap of smooth marble boulders and the water gathers in a pool. There's an all-purpose waste pit decorously concealed behind some high ferns and covered by a single leaf like an elephant ear, which rises or descends at verbal commands. Alien flowers grow on top of the hedge walls and in a central planter. There's an attendant, too; a biological AI named Thafeefa who jumps up from inside the ground when called, a naked yellow-gold woman of less than middle height with a heavy mantle of smooth, glossy scarlet hair that turns in evenly at the ends all around like a mushroom cap. The upper half of her face is painted in finely shaded blue tints that lighten up toward her hairline. Assiyeh keeps her chattering merrily away for hours, describing the ship with visuals she produces by blowing bubbles out her mouth. Each bubble she takes in her two hands and holds out for Assiyeh to see while continuing to explain in a voice that remains distinct even with the membrane between her lips. When they are both nodding, Thafeefa embraces her, and Assiyeh falls immediately asleep.

The irises of Thafeefa's eyes are like circular gauges, white within a dark ring, and striped with skinny bright red and yellow triangles that slide to and fro, vanish and reappear, around the pupil. Steadily enigmatic, they remain fixed on Assiyeh while she sleeps, seeming to weigh and measure her on thousands of indices, even as she smiles and flirts. Thafeefa lights up and exhales charts and graphs of smoke.

I remember when Marcilio saw me staring out the window once and told me not to listen to ghosts. I asked him which ghosts are the ghosts. I can't tell. Out the window, down in the city tar pit you see a way of life called Wreckage Living. While the reich eats rocket crepes everyone else is pacing out each moment to step from one floor panel to the other as the whole edifice slowly collapses around their ears. The diners are calling for more. Watching those people talk to each other is like watching a conversation between two commercials, or like when a character from one sitcom visits another sitcom, the idiocy augmenting geometrically, not arithmetically. The servers rouse themselves with heavy slowbedience and sag through the kitchen door like sea bottom creatures that live under tons and tons of never-relieved pressure and who never see the sun or any light apart from what they manage to make themselves.

So that's a metaphor. When you're thinking critically, finding the right metaphor is much more than a clarification, let alone an ornamentation; it's an act. What makes it an act? Because it changes something. After the right metaphor comes your way, you can never see its antecedent in the same way anymore.

Shit. Shit shit shit shit shit shit shit shit I can't look, I can't!

Everything is so—I can't!

The misery—

ASSHOLES

—We're on the main drag of a California town, a wide boulevard lined with one story shops that all have cute names like Yogurt Creations ... The Mane of Hair ... Dairy of a Mad Cow ... A Pane in the Glass.

—Hi, my name is Coastal Flood Statement, and what I have to say is that the main problem here is that you're not entitled to have your own problems. Other people even own your problems, and thereby they transformitize you into another one of the homeless lords of the Teeming. Their sowhatathon leaving me behind a windswept barbarian. The devastation is continuous, so you have to invent some kind of scratch culture every day—the point of view is under nonstop assault, the flavor of time that emerges it. In every way, you are made to be on TV time, not knowing or caring about any other time species but that. When you bond yourself to suffering you can't live without causing suffering—this way of life can't survive without torture, murder, terror, war and what that gets you is just TV time and candidacy for the torture chamber too. We stopped in this phoney California town and there was nobody here. Everything is still under construction, like the road. So the town is already here, and all the people have to do is show up and start having something to do with it.

Back onto the road, turn on the radio, the news reporter says people have started robbing animals, harassing them, calling them derogatory names, beating them up, driving over cats or squirrels; the money they take off the animals they sometimes manage to exchange for acorns or other animal goods too well-hidden to steal. There are anti-animal hate groups forming. They put up posters and spray graffiti. In another story, there have been further reports of masked millionaires with long knives stalking the streets of major cities and small towns all over the world, pouncing on people in alleys, dragging their victims behind convenience stores.

Some of their intended victims do manage to escape, since they have to get to work. They slowbediently pile onto an absent bus and watch the city fall flat down all around them like dominos. Meanwhile, in the sewers, millionaires drift like crocodiles, baleful eyes above the waterline and all the rest below, burbling, masturbating ominously.

Were you aware that Professor Sulekh Budshah's father sold ammunition? In fact, during a firefight that destroyed his village, he actually sold bullets to the men who were firing on his own home when their supply ran short? He called them while crouched behind his bullet-riddled refrigerator and sold the bullets to his enemies via PayPal. Since the killers checked off the next day delivery option, they received their truckload of fresh bullets within twenty four hours; the delivery drones bypassing roads choked with the charred carapaces of cars, and littered with the dead. Of course it's true!

The radio says: Joan Incienzoa suffered a serious heart attack last night. The elections committee has consequently no choice but to postpone the run-off election until his condition stabilizes. Police were called upon in the early hours of the morning to protect AUP headquarters from a small group of angry protestors armed with bricks and improvised weaponry, who insisted that the story was a cover up, that Incienzoa had survived an assassination attempt, but an NFP official has called for calm, confirming the heart attack and citing Incienzoa's prior medical history. For now, there is agonizing tension but no outright conflict, as the nation waits to see whether he will be able to pull through. Matild Onofreio-Atuan gave a brief address shortly after the incident, in which she wished her rival a swift and complete recovery. That's all there is right now.

The captain, Carolina, of the *Izallu Imeph* has many names. So densely-packed is the captain's daily schedule that there is little opportunity for socializing. Consequently, most of the more diplomatic duties are handled by a sub-captain, who also has many names. Assiyeh is introduced to him shortly before setting out to explore the ship. At a reception. Everyone is naked, but they wear paint, on the proposition that no natural human presents him or herself without adornment of some kind. The women put lace on their bodies and paint over it, then remove the lace. A lot of men paint themselves with one color, like red, then put yarn or string on themselves and paint over that with another color, thick. Then they pull out the string or whatever and that rips through the top coat, exposing the color beneath in strips and lines that are interesting because they're kind of deep and raggedy. That's the rugged masculine style.

Assiyeh? Yeah, she's naked. She had Thafeefa do

her paint. A black band, lacy, across uh the eyes like a blindfold, and a green one like a choker, around her throat. Black arms, from the hands all the way up to the shoulders. Huh? Yeah, she has sex with Thafeefa. Thafeefa loves it. All the other bio-AI's are jealous because she's consorting with this living legend. It's hard to tell if she really cares, it's hard to say what that means to an AI. But as far as behavior is concerned, yeah she dotes on Assiyeh. Assiyeh ... she's trying not to develop feelings for Thafeefa, but it's turning out to be surprisingly hard for her. Thafeefa makes it easy to feel like you have your fantasy. She isn't a liar, either, it's just that there are certain things that would normally be at stake for a, you know, regular woman, that don't matter to her. And that makes her both more and less than what Assiyeh ... what would make Assiyeh happy, I guess. Although she is happy. I mean, Thafeefa makes her happy.

Sub-captain Plourd is an emaciated Arab or North African with high cheekbones, huge black eyes, black hair down to his shoulders and a moustache. Eyes, hair, and moustache all droop. He has a tapering face and hands like two rings of heavy keys. His ribs stand out distinctly and his buttocks are barely there; there are dark purple paint rings around his thorax and biceps, his arms and legs and red from the feet and hands up to the knees and elbows, so he seems to be wearing boots and gloves, and there is a white ceramic wafer up in one corner of his forehead. He steps out of a circle of officers and specialists to greet her with hand extended and a diagonal, half-distracted smile, without looking her in the eye. He has only half extricated himself from his sub-captain's duties, not only speaking with her absently but standing as if he were half in and half out of a bathtub, leaning on a towel bar to keep from slipping. Within a few moments he is whisked away again, but not before he can invite her to join him at the captain's table; it is only as he makes this invitation that she experiences the shock of eye contact with him. From the midst of this shambolic spray of uncoordinated gestures and endlessly displaced attention comes a key note of stability in deep black irises, lucid and self-possessed, and most importantly communicating to her an unmistakeable impression of having a time of their own.

The captain's table is set up in an atrium. There is a bubbling fountain with an ornate mosaic design, and a sort of pagoda-cloister around it. The light is elegantly scattered by stone and wooden lattices. The guests sit on a couch that surrounds the round, sunken table.

Sub-captain Plourd stuns Assiyeh by greeting her in Tajik Farsi.

"I haven't spoken Farsi since I was a girl!" she cries.

"That one phrase is all I know," he says modestly.

At dinner, he recounts his journeyman years as a solitary colonist assigned to the "Mad Planet." They called it that because it was so boring it drove you crazy. This planet, whose real name was Trylirt, was too promising a source of certain biologicals to drop off the list of candidate worlds, but not promising enough to prompt a full scale expedition, so it stagnated in the middle of the list, not denied resources or entirely ignored, but explored only with what was left over after the really important expeditions got their funding. Only one colonist per continent at a time, serving a stretch of what would be about four earth months, with no company but some old robots hibernating on standby in case anything went wrong. There were no robots to wake up and help you when your brain, starving for the least event, went wrong. A new region was explored by each colonist and every one of them reported exactly the same thing: low hills forever, covered in what looked like a completely dead forest of grey trees. These trees are actually quasi-animals that filter nutrients from the air and directly from the soil. Each consists of a pair of identical trunks sprouting from a cold cauldron of weak acid a meter or so beneath the surface, which is the "stomach." Since they don't grow leaves, there's no leaf litter, no proper forest floor, no change of foliage, no rustling in the breeze, no spicy smell of decay. The ground is covered in flaky colorless mud and black, brown, white, or grey chips of a corklike stone laced with mica; and there's this plush tan quasi-moss growing everywhere, and rocks rocks rocks. Some of these rocks, though, aren't rocks, but proto-animals the explorers call "petrons." They look just like rocks, but when you tip them up there's froth underneath; the petron exudes this froth on whichever of its sides is touching soil, and the froth digests the moss and dirt, making a kind of gruel out of it. Then the petron sucks the nutritious parts up through tiny fissures. When a particular mosspatch is exhausted, the petron starts producing a slightly stiffer kind of froth, blowing meringue bubbles big and strong enough to tip it over onto another patch of moss. By tradition, every colonist goes out on his or her first day and selects a pet petron;

you don't know why until you get there and realize how precious is every and any source of distraction. You pick up a petron and put it down on some fresh moss near your shelter, then make it a part of your daily routine to tip little pete or patricia or patroclus or petomaine over, keep them feeding on fresh moss.

It's a planet of washed-out colors, greys and other colors that are really just other greys. One of the few sources of visual relief is a kind of bushier moss that grows in spikes of a weirdly vivid brown, with a combover of long straw-colored fronds. During the long dusks, there is light without glare, and the faint color palate here takes on unwonted vividness, reminiscent of a hand-tinted sepia-base movie.

Life on this planet developed nearly no capacity for movement. Colonists are encouraged to build their shelters close to brooks rather than standing water, simply because a brook gives them something to look at that moves. The brook is a source of water; it is also a companion. There are no insects, no birds, no mammals, nothing moving, or singing, no creeping in the undergrowth, no sudden clashing of leaves telling you you've spooked something, no singing, no buzzing, no frogs peeping by the water, no patter of rain since rain doesn't fall here, nothing but the inane chuckle of the brook that bubbles out of the ground somewhere up there, the wind rattling through the grey trunks, and, very rarely, the thumping of a petron as it tips over and tumbles down an incline ...

Every morning, the same weird, faded, flannelly, bottle-green sky. Virtually no weather to speak of. The planet had slightly less than Earth gravity; a running jump will bring you down about two feet further out than you would have expected, although you land with about as much of a jolt as you would get on earth. Jumping straight up can be an alarming experience. In the oceans, it is said, there are huge clouds of bacteria, a thousand kilometers or more across. And there is somewhere, toward the north pole, an open country, where creatures known as "anchorites" mouth the wind obscenely. The planet is either very young or very old.

"I was three quarters insane by the end," he says. "Fortunately for me, the shuttle pilot sent to retrieve me was an old hand and knew just what to do when he'd landed and I hadn't put in an appearance. He came and got me—pulled me right out of that hut by my ear. My left ear. It was hours, or was it days? One day at least, anyway. Before I could put together a cogent sentence again. And even the shuttle cabin was an overwhelming sensory experience for me, after those four months."

After dinner, the sub-captain retires to a circular room ringed with a cushioned sofa and windows overlooking a black expanse dotted with the unreal half-moon orbs of the arcologies. Above the horizon, the "sky" is a weirdly lustrous blank, the light of the universe gathered in a halo more or less ahead of them. It reminds Assiyeh of the frail skein of froth or scum that sometimes appears in the middle surface of a tepid mug of tea. Assiyeh and the captain sit alone in this observation room. He sprawls with one arm flung along the top of the cushions, one knee up and leg resting on the seat, pensively smoking a little opiated candela. She likes his hangdog, passive charm. Assiyeh sits further along the angle, perched on the edge of her seat, looking from one window to another. In answer to his questions, which are few but pointed, she describes current earth conditions to him. He absorbs her answers thoughtfully. She imagines his weary melancholy dropping magically away from him, sees him rising to meet a crisis with cool decisiveness. Perhaps his authority comes from being a ready screen for everyone to project on.

He takes a long drag and lets his hand fall to his thigh, then ejects the smoke in two long nostril plumes that rise up and dissipate before they can reach the high windows.

"It sounds the same," he says, his voice full of resignation and disappointment. Then, after a meditative pause, he changes the subject.

"Everyone is excited about your joining us," he says. "People can't believe it."

"It does seem unreal to me, too."

"How?"

"You're living a fantasy here. Many people's fantasy, anyway."

The sub-captain smiles sadly.

"I seem to have lost the capacity for it," he says. "My fantasy is to have fantasies again."

"Well, why not quit?"

"It wouldn't be a change," he says. "I don't have fantasies, but they're there. I can feel them there, waiting. The problem is, they aren't new fantasies, just the same old ones."

"Is that bad?"

"If a fantasy ..." he has to pause and think a moment.

"A fantasy that only reflects what you want, that only reflects the usual, the usual desires, let's say, the status quo, it's no different from reality then."

The captain smiles sadly, again, a living quotation assembled piecemeal from dozens of forgotten books.

"You can quote me," he says ruefully and looks exactly like Robert Louis Stevenson. His eyes lift past her.

"May I introduce you to the captain?"

She turns to look. A figure enshrouded in darkness is rolling toward her at a walking pace. It swings around and engulfs a chair, and sinks a little. Seating itself.

"Dr. Melachalos," Mr. Plourd says.

"Welcome aboard," the captain says.

The sound draws Assiyeh up short. The captain's voice is exactly like her own.

"That's right," the captain says. "Everyone hears their own voice when I speak."

Assiyeh's mind goes completely blank. She can't think of a word to say to this vaguely anthropomorphic nebula. The darkness looks soft and somehow delicate, and there's a fragrance too.

The conversation turns toward new technologies for ship propulsion. Assiyeh explains how achieving absolute rest would make universal travel possible; since an object absolutely at rest would stand in exactly the same relationship to all objects in the universe at the same time, it would have to be present throughout the universe once at rest. If the technology were developed, travel would no longer be necessary. Instead of trying to reach a distant destination by trying to go faster and faster, you reach it by stopping, then particularizing, then starting again in the new place. Once you stop, you are everywhere at once. All you have to do then is particularize yourself in some other part of space. Particularity would make travel obsolete.

"Energy is the biggest stumbling block," Assiyeh explains. "Both acceleration and deceleration require a transfer of energy, which makes both of them finite. So trying to achieve absolute rest by slowing is as pointless as trying to reach the speed of light by hurrying. My slow technology only converts energy, reducing speed. What I want is rest technology, which eliminates transfer costs by doubling energy levels across the relation."

Is this plausible? she thinks, looking at him. Will it work? Of course, science always works, always future tense it will work, don't be stupid.

"Moving this momentum into this friction, or changing this chemical energy into propulsion and all, traps you in Newton's jail of equal opposing reactions. You want to get out of that jail. You want an engine that's an actor, not a reactor. What I mean is, on both sides of the transaction of motion, instead of there being a deficit accruing on one side and a surplus on the other, if you could produce energy on one side that would be doubled on the other, instead of inverted or moved from one to the other, then you wouldn't be stuck throwing energy into a bottomless pit of an endless acceleration that is in fact steadily diminishing, or gorging yourself to the bursting point trying to swallow an infinite amount of deceleration. You just decouple from this particularity and recouple at another."

*

VOICE: Who recruited you?

—Juan Jesus.

VOICE: Which Juan Jesus?

—Juan Jesus of Nazarro.

VOICE: Who introduced you to him? Where?

—He introduced himself and I met him inside me.

VOICE: We are reverting to parallel session.

[They torture the witness.]

VOICE: We are recommencing prior session. We will begin again. This will be repeated as often as is made necessary by your refusal to cooperate. Who recruited you?

—(panting, choking)

VOICE: Who recruited you?

—Glub. Gulp.

VOICE: Can you answer the question?

—Glub. (spits) Yes ...

VOICE: The next parallel session ... the area of the face and mouth in particular, the voicebox area ... and the chest slash diaphragm area ... are to be avoided. Focus on extremities.

—I can tell you ...

VOICE: ... Yes?

—Who recr, recruited ...

VOICE: (murmuring) ... water? (louder) Water.

—(gulping, slurping, spitting)

VOICE; Can you speak now?

—Yes. I believe I can. Let me collect myself a little. You see, when it comes to my recruitment, from one end of the ship to the other there is a general clamor for Assiyeh's time and before she knows it she is booked solid as far into the future as Thafeefa can plan. She travels incessantly, lecturing, teaching classes, supervising experiments. She is so busy she has no time to pursue her own research. The *Izallu Imeph* moves so fast that its passengers experience the speed like weather. On board, stillness is a sign of the greatest imaginable velocity and a rushing headlong feeling is a sign of slowing down. Assiyeh and Thafeefa see balmy tropical arcologies with beaches and palm trees, aromatic breezes, ocelots frolicking in the travelling glow of swift-moving constellations twisting apart through the indigo haze of the night cycle, gigantic luminous snakes and insects, living skeletons tumbling from one tree to another, dull-hued flying invertebrates that sing interminable songs of slow, lamentational chords, people with long feelers growing along their jawlines and down the sides of their necks, people with antlers that grow down over their faces like cages and through which they can suck up water or breathe air, bulbous aerial people who float along the ground like manatees, people made of nothing but fluff who can pull themselves apart and recombine in any way. They see bracing frostbound wolf-infested arcologies of whistling white winds and snow hills, ominous black pines and mineral spikes like rattlesnake fangs, poisonous sleet, earthquakes that pound the ground rather than shake it, massive sullen alcoholic animals shaggy and stoical, smoke-spouting forest whales that wind among the tree trunks like snakes, their huge jaws lined with little teeth can snap up a beast the size of a buffalo, gulping down deadwood to feed the bonfire that burns inside each one

so that their mouths glow red, penguinlike people shaped
like torpedoes who dive for their food under the ice
heedless of cold, tall running people who traverse miles
of countryside on their long legs belching methane that
helps raise the temperature in spring and whose weekly
orgies last for forty-eight hours to the music of captive
birds and a vast microtuned orchestra of blind foetuses,
blazing across a thousand adventure novels one by one
and at top speed until the one living note of adventuring
sings out above all the others. Haunted arcologies
with crumbling ruins, yipping jackals invisible in the
distance, vampires without bodies flapping through the
air, werewolves and banshees scream beneath leprous
rainbows, succulent curses, massive spiders with staring
human eyes, antelope cloaked in cold green fire, will o'
the wisps luring people into quicksand marshes, rotting
children blundering through numbly remembered
games. There are deserts and plains, steppes, jungles,
reefs, mountain ranges with blinking green guides
and pack-carriers, lava lakes, geyseral landscapes, ice
tropics, glaciers of living wood, fungus chapparal, living
landscapes with migrating herds of boulders, cloudlands,
orange amber caves populated by living dead thanatomes,
seas of metal mesh and living fabric. There are ten foot
tall people with double rows of teeth, oversexed golden
pornstar people, suave cosmopolitan stick insects, chalk
white people built like hatracks, censorious cobalt blue
puritans who limit to the minimum all interaction with
outsiders, people corresponding to all types known on
earth living in mixed and unmixed groups, populations
of people who are all completely alike, populations

where no two people are even remotely similar to each other, countless languages, countless religions, countless political parties. Misunderstandings, intrigues, jealousies, liasons, countless adventures, countless, ever more daring escapes. Corpses in niches mummified by the vacuum, gazing out into the void, visited by utterly alien space nuclei that flap down from nothing to work some form of exchange; the most daring and strong willed trance mediums on board occasionally manage to contact the spirit of an Exposed One, and what comes through then is impossible to relate, and only shudderingly remembered afterwards. Time, on board the *Izallu Imeph*, doesn't seem to move. Life seems impossible anywhere else. Assiyeh's memories of Earth, of the physics conference, news reports, political spectacles, economics, can't find coherence in this setting. It's as if she had always been a guest on board this gargatuan spacecraft, even without having come from anywhere else. Throughout her travels, no matter where she goes, there's that same dreamlike, disembodied feeling.

"Did I die in space?" she wonders. "Or before? Is this all my dreaming death?"

She imagines her naked corpse floating in space, perhaps plunging to earth, the plastic coating melts and peels away in cinders, her face chars, her hair crackles, and as it dies the brain whispers its last dream of rescue, the spacecraft, leaving the earth behind.

What is real is what presents itself. This is what presents itself, so she will deal with it and not waste time with what ifs. When Assiyeh finally does get time and opportunity to perform an experiment of her own, she thinks:

"When you start with the form and infuse life into it, you end up with a life struggling to inhabit a form that is more or less accidental to it, and that isn't how life is. If you want to get closer to creating life, you have to make living material that shapes itself, I guess like a sort of plasm. The experiment itself would have to be alive, because the big problem to be overcome is the dividing up of a single simultaneous process into a series of steps."

She begins with protein candy that can be woven in strands and hardens into a fabric. The candy is dropped from a dispenser as it forms, so the strands can turn this way and that as they contract and relax, like taffy. When the candy pulls free of the dispenser, it drops into water and floats, so it can take shape more independently and manage the extrusion and distribution of its own material as it forms. Deceleration was the key element to Assiyeh's method of animation: inducing animation by decelerating the tissue and organs to the meet the burgeoning velocity of a hum of life force given off by time or a star. The organs slow into life, slow into participation, and the new monospecies will emerge. Failed forms and organs that are more trouble than they're worth heap up in Assiyeh's lab. There's a kind of glass mouth that smacks and claps incessantly, gumming the container they are forced to keep it in. There are living neon light tubes coiled up like Arabic calligraphy and which give off such a high voltage field that they have to be stored in thick rubber crates to keep them from shocking. An enormous gland suddenly leapt from its nurture tray with an earsplitting roar, streaked across the floor and up the wall like a huge purple tongue. But one set of organs did independently coagulate into a floppy integer, a basically complete if lopsided thing resembling an immature bird but with a huge pair of glistening pink buttocks, and all it did was lie there muttering to itself, sighing, occasionally emitting a pink whoosh of flatulence laced with tiny pink larvae. The larvae got everywhere and raised a rash on Assiyeh and Thafeefa both. Assiyeh could wear protective clothing, but Thafeefa chafed if she had to wear even so much as a bracelet or a pair of sandals, and was miserable for as long as the farting thing clung, baffled, to its life.

Assiyeh invited the available luminaries of the *Izallu Imeph* to observe an experiment.

"The biocandy has adopted a great variety of organic functionalities, a few of which show the right characteristics for this experiment."

She points to a mass that looks like a fibrous, transparent ear of corn, which is throwing off long trailers of silk that float and grope toward other organs.

"This one is especially eager to participate, I think. We have gathered them here under conditions we hope will prompt them to adopt an aleatory monoform. We will give them what they want, and see what happens. Please observe."

With a wave of the hand, Assiyeh causes the transparent barriers separating the organs to be lifted, and at once the organs begin to sneak toward each other. Assiyeh operates a deceleration field around them which helps to bring them into common velocity with the filmy updrafts of vitality coming from space; the organs knit together with sprays of tacky biocandy. The procedure takes only a fraction of an hour, and when it is done, to her colossal disappointment, Assiyeh watches as a transparent human male lifts itself unsteadily to its feet within the experimental enclosure. The audience response is muted, polite, and they leave grumbling. They wanted to see something alien.

"Just another human ... All that build-up and what do you get ..."

Assiyeh contemplates the listing figure philosophically. Maybe it is alien. It's full of mercury, or that's what the stuff looks like anyway, sloshing around inside, streaming in rivulets up and down the torso, and there's a whirlpool of it where ordinarily the brain would be.

What did she do with him?

She adopts him. He speaks by gurgling the liquid in his head. The whirlpool seems to have some knowledge in it already, but it is impossible to predict what the glass man will or will not happen to know. The first time Assiyeh falls asleep in his presence, he panics and pisses in her face, evidently in order to revive her. On the other hand, he doesn't need to be told how to use doors or how to fool around with Thafeefa. Assiyeh gets jealous, and she's alternately peevish and melancholy. His body moves as if its motion were projected onto it from outside. The glass man doesn't eat, he recharges with enemas, sitting on a big clear bladder of mercury like a bean bag chair and letting the pressure drive the fluid up into him. From time to time, tiny balloons inflate from his eyes and drop like tears to the floor.

I finally decided the thing to do was to have a party in one of the million empty apartments back in San Toribio. This was years ago, in the pre-Tripi days. We would find our way to each other. Me, not being the host, would have to receive my own invitation from a third party. I took the idea from that other, better me that I can only dream about. The city's absentee landlords are our unwitting hosts, and word went out by way of the spectre grapevine to everyone sitting in empty apartments—cells included. There are bare walls, and bare floors, the toilet is dry and the sinks are too, make yourself at home. There is a lavish spread of blankness. While we're waiting on our musicians, you can groove to the whistling wind blowing through empty corridors, syncopated to the growling of the fluorescent lights and the whoops of the sirens, now with bonus bass, all of which should help to drown the shuffle of lifeless feet out there, the Novemberness of living in the unsustainable prolongation of the last generation's dream, and the dead breathing of city traffic coughing up drones and helicopters. Assemble here in the blankroom while I sit on the rim of the tub, picking punctuation out of my nose in the dark.

We were all revolutionaries and we all still are, of the kind who get to talk about having been, and the problem with making revolution your religion is that you tend to worship what you can't have and it ends up back there somewhere like it already happened, even though it never did. Or, I guess what I mean is that the revolution happens inside you first, and so that's the revolution you end up thinking has happened. "I don't understand how you can be so blind," you say silently to everyone you pass. The world, nature, the stars in the sky are all already yours. Already. You can't earn them and you don't have to, all you have to do is live. Beauty isn't ownable, it doesn't linger—or rather you don't. It flashes up, then next moment you've already left it behind and you spend the next chunk of your time trying to decelerate back to it again.

"You think you're going to take all this away from them and there's not going to be violence? They butcher them, they'll butcher us too, they get off on it, massacres make them cum, they pay their whores to moan and call them master and emperor and sieg heil and they watch the death on the news while they get sucked off think they're action heroes and Alexander and God just like back when it's still cavemen, it's still bullies in the schoolyard, it's still the same sub-adult sub-monkey braindead slobber as back when and back when and back when again.

"Fuuuck ...

"... Half this shit isn't even worth having. I mean is it worth dying for? Bunch of ugly cities, fucked up streets and roads and suburbs and—fucking sports stadiums and ... whatever—banks? Fucking banks? You want to die for a—actually it might be worth it to blow up the bank. Blow the fucking stadium up and the streets and the fucking companies and put in something worth having. But you're going to have to blow all that up because they aren't going to come around and give it to you. Not if it's still worth two chunks of shit they won't, fucking evil greedy ..."

I silence myself with a hand wave because I am hearing myself and I hate the way I sound. Like impotent, a failure, like someone off on the sidelines with no power, complaining. Talking that way used to make me feel better; now it makes me feel like I'm already dead. I'm just a phantom people walk through on the way to fucking work.

"Attention passengers. All our trains have crashed and all our stations have collapsed. At this time, you have all been crushed by falling rubble. There will never be any service ever again, but my words descend softly on your shapeless, broken corpses. Thank you for being killed by MTA, New York City Transit."

All right. Now that you're all here, it's time for our experiment. Now none of your groaning! You all had your homework—so whip it out. Yes, it's that kind of show, with full audience participation.

It's a good crowd. One of those economists is here, the lanky, quiet one who's always correcting himself. He says he's been living under a paving stone and I believe him.

"I believe you," I say. "You're lucky you got it. Some people don't even have that!"

Now that you're ready, we got a completely dark room through there. No windows, no lights, nothing. The door has a skirt here and a rubber flange around it, so when you shut it, no light can seep in from outside. Complete darkness in there. Each one of you is going into that room alone and shutting the door. You're going to take a few minutes to get used to it. Wait until all the afterimages and sparks have faded. Then, when you're ready, I want you to make light. I don't mean with your lighter. You go into the room with nothing. You have nothing, and in that cell there is nothing but darkness. You have to use magic to make light. You can make whatever gestures or sounds you think will help. Any kind of light, any color. Sun, moon, candle, camera flash, TV screen on static, snow reflected light, cat's eye reflected light, whatever. Let him who has eyes to see do something about it.

A white pop in the darkness—who's there?

Whose face do I see?

Assiyeh is a very straight, lean woman of middle height, with a cape of shoulder-length black hair and large dark eyes in a bright brown face, the eyebrows are two hard black crescents, the nose is small and hooked. The litany of description. The charactechism. She has a subtly expressive mouth; the lips rise in acute points. Her face is broad across the eyes. Her shoulders stand out from her spine like spars from a mast, making them seem wider than they are. Her mother was Greco-Tajik and her father was Franco-Mexican. A master of escape.

Back when I was homeless, I had a construction job laying supaslab and making sure the fire extinguishers were in their legally required locations, one at each grid intersection in the floorplan, so nobody had to run more than I think it was twenty five feet to get one. Half of them were empty, though. They weren't paying overtime and they didn't pay when Luis fell and hurt his back because they said he was drunk—I was there, the man was sober. Seeing as I was the one with no wife no known kids and going home to a car and taking showers at a gym, I had the least to lose in trying to organize the others. They didn't want to hear me and one of the bigger ones, a man I had thought was basically well-disposed to me, shoved me against a wall one day and told me to shut my mouth.

I wanted to leave, but I was seeing Ndidi at the time even though she made a point of telling me when we were first alone together "I will never sleep with you" and she meant it and she was right, too. Why why why I asked her every time we were alone together. No no no was her answer every time I asked her. That wasn't a yes or no question, I said every time we were alone together. Her smile would grow, and so would her "NO." Maybe she knew that her no would hold me, but hold me for what? She didn't need the amorous overtures of a derelict autochthonic automobile dweller to make herself feel better.

(Ndidi: Not quite correct. He was not living in his car. I first saw him, actually, as I was looking out the window of the elevated train going right past his apartment. I got off at the stop and followed the directions Lusita gave me and it gradually became clear to me that I was headed for the same building, then to the same floor, and finally to the same apartment that I had happened to look directly into from the train. It had caught my eye because it was so bright. It was bright because it was empty. He had nothing in there except for a card table that looked like he'd fished out of the trash. There wasn't even a shade on the light in the middle of the ceiling. Going by in the train, I'd seen him, sitting right back in the corner of his apartment by the front door, facing the window, with the table in front of him. He had both hands spread out on the top, and both legs sticking out straight, his legs were like the walls and his spine was the corner. He held the table to himself, like pulling up a blanket, but it gave me the feeling he was trapped in his light box like the invisible man. Then I was really in that apartment, and he pulled the chair he'd been sitting in out from the corner and offered it to me. I took it without thinking, and almost right away regretted it, because I hadn't realized he had only the one. He went over to the kitchen wall of the apartment and opened an empty refrigerator to look for something to offer me. One beer. He had a jar of water in there too. I don't think there was anything else.)

I'm only an average lover so she didn't miss much, perhaps she intuited that. There's for a long time been in me a certain voice that tells me you have to have sex it's a duty of life, but for some reason we won't go into here or indeed at all, you—just you, not everyone—*you*, SuperAesop, have no business enjoying it; you don't have sex for pleasure but to please others, and drunk with hyperbolic sobriety you tell yourself it isn't an exchange, you should feel as little pleasure as possible, remain neutral, while giving as much pleasure as possible, so I found a way to make fucking ascetic work toward the other person's transcendence. She should go through the roof, forget her own name, and all the while I'm just keeping the bubble smack between the lines. Infallibility. Then again, I also used to tell myself that one day she was going to turn to me and say—"I wish you were smart. If you were smart, you would ask me to marry you." As if her refusal was a matter of protocol, as if she really wanted me, but I hadn't puzzled out her map yet. But I didn't want to marry her, or I didn't most of the time, and lacked means. I used to tell myself that I was choosing not to ask her to marry me because of my altruism, to spare her the travails of my dismonetized demon-demonstrator lifestyle, and that she belonged on a pedestal, but this was such patent bullshit that I couldn't even fully pay attention to the thought. It was there in my mind like a jingle, not a swelling hymn of goodness. I never asked her about Africa and she never talked about it in any detail; she would advert to general practices or things that she recognized here from back home, but that was it. I was fascinated by her Africanness and bottled up every question I might have asked her. I said to myself that I didn't want to be a nuisance, but I really didn't want to admit that I had a collector's yen to bed an African and collect my bragging rights. For years I thought I spent all that time with Ndidi like a frustrated satellite, that I was just a jerk looking for my sex angle, but then one day I woke up in my fucking car and saw the sunlight through the foul condensation and in a flash she was there, I was walking beside her in a crisp cold morning, and she was cold, but it was still fun for her, being that cold, and the thought of her walking unreachably next to me, talking warm to me in the raw cold, was like a warm hand shoving my chest down. Tears rolled down my face.

"I loved her," I thought. "I love her. I don't believe it."

That worldless world, that is where I'm from—it isn't formless, it adopts world masks, it improvises strict eternal regulations, but it isn't a world, all the same it isn't—

*

The dream was like a movie; he watched it. All the same, he did feel as if he were participating in the action, if only because he was unable not to watch it. Even as he dreamed it, he knew it was reminiscent of those horror sci-fi movies you see in snatches while you're skipping channels, with experiments, a psychic or magic child on a rampage. The dream was fragmented and seamless at once, every moment slipping into the next, but carrying the previous moments along behind. A nine year old Afghan girl with a maroon scarf around her head is crossing a blasted landscape, smoking buildings in the background. Her face is divided down the middle by an irregular stripe of red, dried blood from a head injury. A huge truck rolls down what's left of a street, helmeted heads in the back. One of them spots her, the helmeted head swivels, chinstrap flipping loose. The girl throws herself down and hides.

She makes it to the next village. Gunfire jolts her awake and she scrambles beneath a table, trembling. Something slams into the house and nearly rips it open. The wall that had been so cool and solid and silent a moment before is now ripped in two and the roof is sliding off and stars are opening up above her. She is paralyzed for a moment, then, like a rabbit out of a trap she launches herself through the door, dropping onto the ground the moment she is outside. Tracers are stitched into the night air, pops and bangs on all sides. There's a basement or shelter some yards away—can she get to it? She crawls that way on her stomach. Shots close by— hum over her head, spit in the dirt just missing her left hand. The night in chaos. Shooting. The girl looks up with cold composure and flips the truck firing from the street, lights it on fire, drags the nearest house down on top of uniformed men, silencing them under a blanket of rubble.

Now it's another night. The old night. She's sleeping

in some house. A man steps into the room with his gun raised, startling her awake. The girl recoils into the corner of the room, crying, exhausted with fear. The man hesitates. His nightmare wins as he points the gun at her. She vomits. He hesitates. Then he curses. She is watching him again. She lifts her fist and something like wind flashes across the small gap dividing them. His head jerks as if he's been struck, and changes shape, abruptly narrower than it was. The man drops sideways onto his right hip, falls back, his head strikes the floor with a thud.

The girl is learning. Standing on top of a hill, lit from below by flames of the military base, she pulls helicopters down and smashes them against the ground. The flames spread across the compound, and there are silhouetted figures flashing, sirens, shouts. Impassive, with hooded eyes and a grim smile, she flips the trucks with her fingers, spreads the fire around with her open palm like paint on paper, swats the aircraft like flies, pancakes the buildings, squeezes the people to pulp in her fists.

Curses and shouts, a mountain camp, Afghan men with rifles. They have an inexhaustible fund of insulting names to call her. Let them call her those names now. The mountain is burning, explosives are going up, the men scatter, the hills fall on them, covering them, silencing their curses, stopping their mouths with dust and the pieces of their own shattered jaws.

As the movie continues, we see the girl imperiously receiving suit-and-tie emissaries and representatives of this warlord or that militia leader. She listens to them with the same impassive smile. Her uncanny self-possession throws these influential men into confusion. Finally, in a climactic scene, she addresses them all.

"I've heard all the talking from you that I need to. Now you will listen to me. I am the Queen of Afghanistan now, and you all will do as I say. I don't need an army to kill you. I can kill you all by myself. I don't care if I kill you all. I'm not going to accept any offer from you. Afghanistan will be run the way I say. You put together a government to run things, and I will watch. I will not stay in any one place. I won't have a palace. I will go wherever I want, and you won't know I'm watching you until I show you. I'm going to kill anyone I catch fighting. The foreigners will all leave, right now. If I see anyone hurting any girls or women, I will kill them. Girls are going to go to school. Nobody hurts anyone without my permission. If I catch anyone hurting anyone without asking me first, they will be the ones who will be hurt. You can ask me just by talking out loud. I will hear. And if someone is beating you or trying to kill you, just ask me for my help. I will hear that. I will come back and talk to you again if I think of anything more to say."

She waves her hand and an American general drops dead, blood spurting from his face. The crowd gasps and recoils. She waves her hand again and a religious guerrilla leader drops dead, blood spurting from his face. The crowd recedes from the two crumpled bodies like an outrushing wave.

"That's what I think of America. That's what I think of Taliban. There is only the Queen from now on."

Unusually complete dream. Her speech rings in his ears as he shaves his lean face, adjusts his expensive haircut, dons his Brooks Brothers suit in a tastefully neutral color, shining like a pliable metal integument. A solid red tie that gleams like metal. We are the knights of today, the great lords. He eats his breakfast watching the news on a huge television and pauses before he goes out to gaze judiciously through enormous windows at implacable Manhattan towers which bow to him. Then the briefcase, the loafers that cost as much as a luxury car, the elevator, the genuflection of the doorman, the waiting limo, the glide through the streets bouncing off the riff raff, then alighting in front of the stock exchange. Up the steps, in the front, wave him through. Numbers on screens, screens screens like black mouths of open hearths bristling with numbers. Like the black cavities of dead human beings bristling with maggots you mean. He follows the causeway off to one side and keys himself into a certain men's room. In the rear toilet stall he presses a certain tile and the wall slides back to reveal a shadowy foyer lit by sullen vermillion lamps and thick with pungent incense. Women swathed in luminous veils divest him of his clothes, carefully folding them away, and gently strike his naked body with wands as his chest is anointed with lamb grease. He dons his robe and passes through the massy arras into the secret shrine whose vaulted ceiling is lost in gloom overhead, almost as if a topless shaft rose above them.

The open floor is a fantastic mosaic of inlaid marbles and chalcedonies, heaped here and there with thick rugs of astounding intricacy, woven from the hair of garroted babies very rare, very expensive. Some hooded figures, early birds, are already there, conferring in low tones and guttural chortlings that do not quite mask the feeble groans and pleas for help arising from a cage of golden thorns standing half-muffled in crimson serge on the far side of the shrine. Those, of course, are the futures. Dominating all is a gargantuan idol squatting balefully on an onyx dais the size of a city block. The statue's eyes are emeralds that blaze like ovens, two halves of a stone extracted from the heart of an asteroid. From its bloated trunk sprout numberless arms; coins glitter between its splayed fingers. Its penis is the size of a subway train and droops down from the dais, extending along the floor. The offerings are made in a great depression situated on top of the glans, which must be scaled using a rolling stairway of rhino horn. Already the flames have started up in the cauldrons lining the idol's base, and the cries of the victims, rightly interpreting this as a sign of bad things to come, rise to augment the splendor of the scene.

When the ritual unfolds, the same as it has from time immemorial, in all its awesome magnificence, there is nevertheless something lame about it. Not ignominy, which can be glorious, not even banality, although that is closer, hallowed by the the nullifying cancer of the Misled. It's strange that a rite as time-honored as this should have an ineradicable lameness, and that, even with all these expensive and exotic accountrements, the dire consequences, the leaden hieratic gravity, it's still as embarrassing as the suburban sabbath of a bunch of junior high school witches in polyvinyl chloride Halloween capes intoning spells out of a drugstore paperback.

We pick up some light traffic on the outskirts of Etsimen. I don't remark on this particularly, until, at last, our offramp comes into view. As I sigh with relief and angle over to take it, another car zips up out of nowhere and cruises on our right. I have to whip the wheel to avoid hitting him, and the offramp flashes past.

"Aw, motherfucker."

There is a loop, though, so I can swing us around the town and come back to the sole offramp again. There's nothing to see outside; the night is dark, and the few lights of Etsimen still seem very far away. Here comes the offramp. I swing into it and jerk back in virtually the same instant—there's a car in the way again. Again the offramp flashes by. Looming behind us is big black mercedes and the single headlight squints directly into the back of shitty hatchback. That cyclops eye drops back behind us, and then, gone.

It happens again, the third time. When I get aggressive and begin jabbing my way toward the exit with short rushes, another car is suddenly there, coming up the exit ramp. That car has only one light, too. They look new, these gleaming black mercedes, but both are missing one light. One on the left, one on the right—no, both on the right, the other one was coming toward me. We go back around again, and again the escorting cyclops car drops from sight at about the halfway mark. It's an elevated highway, the whole loop, touching ground only on the part that actually belongs to the through highway, and that part is built up with no shoulder on a steep embankment with big rocks on the city side and dense brush on the desert side. Shitty would get stuck in that brush for sure, and its first taste of that embankment would probably rip the whole drive train loose if we didn't roll, which is exactly what we would do. So we can't stop without leaving the car in a lane. And every time we come around, those cyclops cars flock up like wolves. I have an insurmountable intuition that they would run us over if they could. OK so what, leave the car and run. But Carolina's fucked up. She might try to reason with an oncoming car in the state she's in.

The fourth time, a truck sits right at the mouth of the exit ramp. No cars approach, but I can see four or five single right lights floating behind us up the road, just far enough away to be hard to see, just near enough to be able to run us down if we ditch. This time I stay on the highway, heading for the next exit along, but suddenly there's a phalanx of those fucking black mercedes swinging in from nowhere on either side of me. It's like looking up from your cute tropical fish to find yourself in an orca pod, it's bad. I brake and fall back and sure enough they are following, herding me, and the only way to go is off onto the roundabout again. The next time I hit the highway stretch, the way past the turnoff is blocked by dumpsters and burning oil drums. I don't even try to investigate further. I take the turnoff and lose my time fantasizing about rappelling down from these forty-foot concrete ramps.

*

It's daylight. I've been circling Etsimen now for about two hours and there's only about half an hour left in the tank, I think, at most. Carolina is docilely and regularly feeding herself acid, and is very quiet. My ability to think has quit me. We pull back onto the same stretch of highway again, and once again I scan for changes, for some as yet overlooked escape route, telling myself that the gathering daylight is going to show me what I need. Suddenly I realize that one of the black mercedes has drawn up on my left. The windows are all black, of course. The rear passenger window glides smoothly down; the car holds darkness within. The gloved hand that comes out the window isn't pointing the pistol at me but only holding it up as if offering it for sale, teetering it this way and that just to let me know, but that kind of taunting bugs me and I snap the wheel and smash them. There's a jolt and Carolina seems to wake up with a start jumping and turning in her seat to stare at me her back to the door and her head against the ceiling, her face blank with surprise and then the next second her mouth opens all the way and she bursts out laughing like this is the funniest thing she ever saw in her life. The other car nosed away in surprise and the window when I glance back is now closed again and they're going to reply in kind, so I let them think that long enough to get them to commit then pump the brakes.

They float out ahead and only just clip our front, and they're front wheel drive it looks like so the back end is only swinging with follow-through I guess, a rear-wheel drive might have knocked us harder. As it is since we don't weigh anything to speak of that rap from them throws us into 1% of a skid and I am ridiculous, applying now the brake, now the accelerator, trying to add speed in one direction and take it away in the other, but I actually do know how to drive and I can make shitty hatchback flip like ballerinas so instead of wiping out I manage to stabilize our condition and come up right on asshole's seven where I can control him. Right behind him he could brake abruptly and we'd fare worse in the collision, but if he tries that with me here at seven I can fade with him or nudge him over and push his ass out from behind him. His swerve in my direction took him all the way over to the right so he's a bit stuck just now, all the same he decides to do something silly and swing out left anyway, inducing me to charge up forward without swerving and even he knows that's a bad combination of forces and lunges back away to the right with a panicky oversteer that puts him right off the road. My darted backwards glances show me that car stuck on the slope, floundering in rocks and jumping around like a horse in a tight pen. Carolina has dropped back into her seat and is laughing musically into both her hands, swinging her head around to see.

So there will be others, right? I pull in to the turnoff and stop, jump out, run around, try to get into the cab of the truck which is locked, get down, grab rock, get up, smash window, open door, get in cab, release the brake. Gravity helps me pull the truck aside and back it up to block the ramp above shitty hatchback. Out the passenger side. Not even looking. They could be firing whole cars at me from a slingshot for all I know. I drive shitty hatchback down the offramp wishing I'd been desperate enough to try that two hours earlier, and in four minutes we're entering Etsimen.

PART EIGHT:
FOND MEMORIES OF TERROR

The yellow-gold star of her lighter is reflected in the glass, a transparent mask of dusky orange light, her face, just above it like a nebula perforated by eyes, nostrils ... The darkness outside abruptly deepens, but that's typical here.

Assiyeh has already adapted to Koskon Kanona conditions sufficiently well to think about resuming her research. The planet is much larger than earth, but significantly less dense, being only basically solid enough for human activity to go on in the usual way without requiring any special measures. However, while it is superficially no different from terra firma it is actually slightly gaseous in its overall composition, an ultracompressed gas planet in fact. The solid crust is a bit like the skin of a balloon. The soil and rock of the surface are weirdly friable. You can send a colossal boulder tumbling along level ground with a stiff slap of the hand. The atmosphere is a cocktail of practically every known gas, mixed in proportions that are constantly and drastically changing. Every inhabitant has to memorize a long list of different four-letter codes transmitted from gas measuring stations to personal indicators and public information boards, to know which gas suppositories to insert into themselves that day.

The streets of Buzzati, the largest of the planet's cities, are lined with booths, bolt holes, kiosks, shelters, all manner of structures that pedestrians can duck into when one of the dozens of different atmospheric alert signals is sounded. Assiyeh notices that her moods follow the changes, and that this is commonly true of most citizens here. Sometimes everyone you see is sitting on benches that line the incredibly wide white boulevards, black shapes slumped and motionless, throwing black shadows in the hard, pale Marienbad daylight of Koskon Kanona. The air is hard to breathe then. It fills the lungs as light as lead and it leaves a musky aftertaste behind. Then, in a moment, the air is suddenly fizzing like champagne—everyone leaps up zooming around like fireworks, laughing and chattering. Adjusting to this volatility has meant that most citizens are cool, deliberate, undemonstrative, and tolerant. Getting along with them is easy and getting to know them is impossible. The walls here are very thick and very tall.

Koskon Kanona's rotation is punctuated, not continuous. Instead of gliding smoothly across the sky every day, Koskon Kanona's sun stays in one spot for an hour, then slides further toward the west for three seconds and stops for another hour. Assiyeh simply cannot get used to it. She'll be sitting in her room reading when suddenly the daylight falling steadily on the floor beside her crawls up her face, as if the sun were bending down to peer in through the windows. The impression this gives, namely that the planet has suddenly broken loose and is about to plunge howling into space, brings her heart up her throat every time it happens. Dawn and dusk are bizarre here—a soft blue light in the early morning hours ... and then the sun suddenly jumps up above the horizon and is all there in the sky, the day exploding all at once. There are no splendid sunsets—one minute it's getting dark, then the sun dives below the horizon like a gopher ducking into its burrow and wham, it's night. The stars, too, stay put for an hour at a time, and then veer all together. It's an unreal sight.

Something of this incrementality of motion infects the planet's human inhabitants with its peculiar haltingness; they move like figures in a film running backward, going from motion to rest with a kind of positive absence of momentum. She noticed this right away, when she was taking her leave of the *Izallu Imeph*. Instead of sending shuttles, Koskon Kanona instead convoyed together flocks of huge concrete tubes that remain in orbit for this purpose. They assemble into a spinal column crooked down toward the surface. Assiyeh watched a platform loaded with passengers floating up from the surface through one of these tubes; she was looking down at the tops of their heads. The platform was operated by a group of officials in suits who were chanting, drumming, clapping, and bowing their heads mechanically. Assiyeh decided to disembark here on impulse. Without looking up at her, the woman supervising the officials, who were mopping their brows and drinking water from canteens, said, "You can do as you like, but I don't want to see any naked bodies, so make sure and get your clothes on before you board."

When they were ready to depart, the officials resumed their chanting. Their eyes rolled back and their drumming and clapping took on a clockwork regularity. Through the latticework in the sides of the tubes, Assiyeh watched the dimly glowing night side of Koskon Kanona swell to collect her from the nightlessly perfect night of space. Overhead, her view of the *Izallu Imeph* was blocked, so she could only make out a vague luminescence up there. There was a rush that nearly blew her off her feet when they plunged into the atmosphere, but the ride continued smoothly all the way down to the surface.

On her arrival she became obsessed with the convulsions of civilization back on earth. Hideous faces, brandishing and sneering; neutered rationalism in ominously spectral conversations somehow taking place and already in the past at once. Most of the other planets find this stream of news intolerably depressing and the far flung children of Earth turn sadly away from this picture feeling banished and despondent. Perhaps this was the intended result, Assiyeh thought—make things on Earth appear so hopeless that we on the outside will stop ourselves from interfering.

"I wonder," she thinks, "if there really isn't anything we can do."

She gulps and grabs hold of the arms of her seat as the sun abruptly rolls forward to its next station in the sky.

"That's what they back on earth are afraid of—one of many things. They're afraid we exiles will come back and overthrow them just to save our interplanetary self respect."

—Gazing out at the ocean now. A light wind frisks her hair. The ocean on Koskon Kanona moves stop and start, just like the sky. A wave will suddenly bulge up and stop in the middle of the water like a huge jade axeblade pushing up through gleaming slate blue satin. It just stands there, the crisp edge just starting to crumble into foam, and webs of foam sliding down the slope. Then, after an interval of several minutes, a roar swells up into the air and the wave bows. It rolls forward and stops again, coiled into a tube. Then again the roar and the dash of the wave as it spreads its countless little hands patting and fingering the beach. When the water has reached the limit of its inland reach, it pauses again, forming a transparent skin of frothy water and fixed shadows inside. Only then does it fall back. Assiyeh watches the water tumble back on itself, layers slipping under layers like drawers, and behind her she can hear, cutting in through the gaps in the wind, faint voices calling from the towers, rasping, inhuman, impassive, urgent, musical, echoing through the tall boulevards of the city like verbal searchlights. Not everyone can hear them.

Assiyeh brought her bathing suit, but it's too cold to swim today.

Thafeefa standing there crying.

Every so often a pang—Thafeefa. Gardens. Wading naked in a cloud-shadowed green landscape with mountains of lavender stone rising in the distance. She belonged to the *Izallu Imeph* and couldn't come to Koskon Kanona with her. She didn't seem to understand why Assiyeh insisted on going, why the *Izallu Imeph*, itself a whole world, could be less than enough, although she did not make the mistake of thinking that it was she, and not the ship, that wasn't enough. That would have been a mistake. The real answer, which Assiyeh had not been able to put into words, was that Assiyeh was the one who was not enough, and diminishing in capacity all the time she was caught up in the whirl of engagements and novelties. She'd had to make so many adjustments so quickly, only to alter them all over again. The discovery of her resources for becoming was thrilling as long as she was able to stay out far enough ahead or remain high enough above the changes. In those moments, it was like she had picked up a whole new wardrobe or drastically changed her hairstyle; the changes were big enough but still manageable. The changes grew no larger as they went on; she just got tired of making them. Going through all those changes only inclined her toward the generic, something so basic she could afford to forget it again. She imagined coming up with a simple, reliable diet, or laying in a supply of one or another essential; she toyed with ideas for an all-purpose wardrobe with a handful of options coordinated across three modes, casual, formal, heavy duty. Finally she had to realize that she was still too firmly self-possessed to be radically changed by all the travel and adventure. When an athlete really throw him or herself into training, it can sometimes seem as if the motive was actually self-hostile, the training a siege layed against the self, and the point is to break the body, so that you would think they'd be relieved to get an injury. Force majeur, nothing to be done about it. If she really wanted to break herself by losing herself in a blizzard of transformations brought on by travelling nonstop— that was hard to say, but anyway she turned out to be a hard nut to crack. So she left the ship and Thafeefa, joining the human beings of Koskon Kanona. She could not continue her experiments in such a bewildering, distracting place, and those experiments were her raison d'etre. It was only the truth, but she was using it as if it were an excuse.

Glassimov the glass man is off somewhere examining the contents of the tidal pools. He'll pick up every last crab or urchin and hold it up to the light, scrutinizing it with resonant gurgles of its cerebral vortex as if it had to name them all individually. He's pretty crummy company all told. He just talks that glass talk, no matter how many hours of language lessons she puts him through.

Assiyeh strolls a little along the beach, thinking. She has so many pent up experiments she wants to try she doesn't know where or how to start. Now that she's here, the time has come, the opportunity is staring at her expectantly. Turning abruptly to undo a snag in her skirt, she notices a figure up the beach. It isn't the glass man. It isn't anyone she knows. A motionless figure, a hundred or more meters away, watching her without making the slightest motion. Like something out of M. R. James. The longer she watches its watchful motionlessness, the more likely it seems to leap the distance and thrust a nightmare face into her own.

"If I turn my back," she thinks, "and then right away look again it will be right behind me."

She turns her back and then turns around again with a quick twist. The figure is gone.

It's still behind her. Right behind her. She knows it instantly. Without looking, she throws an elbow into space and connects with something soft, and sand brushes her calf as if someone had kicked it up in a sudden spray. She hears a gurgle and turns to face the glass man, who points at her accusingly.

"I thought you were someone else," she says, grimacing in disgust. "Why don't you ever say anything instead of sneaking up on me all the time?!"

"glub arbl ull worb ugnlb," he says.

"You do so sneak up!" she snaps, then waves him away.

No sign of that other. She walks a little, hands behind her back, thinking. Finally she reaches the spot where the figure must have been standing. There are numerous footprints here, but only two marks could possibly have been made by the feet of person standing in this spot looking back in her direction. Assiyeh kneels and brushes the surface of the loose sand with outspread fingers. She scans tactilely like a dowser and then her fingers close on something. It's a single strand of wool, dyed a dark color. Nothing on Koskon Kanona makes wool, it all has to be imported because, as a voluble customs agent explained to her when she inquired about the high tariff on her wool jacket, the actinic plant growth that covers much of the planet's surface is toxic to all known species of ruminant, and the soil is too sour for imported grazing plants. Her Jamesian observer was from Earth.

"So, they won't let me go," she thinks, visualizing the earth reaching out across space with thick-fingered cartoon hands, groping blindly for her among the stars, rummaging planets like old wardrobes and bureaus. A curious smile spreads across her face, kindling a familiar old glow behind her features.

"Come on, my enemy!" she thinks with an inward leap of welcome.

For an instant she detects on the breeze a faint aroma of tobacco smoke, perhaps from a pipe or cigar. It came from inland, of course, but there is no sign of anyone in the dunes. Maybe a discarded butt, smouldering back there. There—a motion. One movement. Back behind the dunes, at the very back. She is sure she saw it, but all she gleans from a review of the sight is an impression of something fairly long and fairly flat and basically but not completely black, perhaps tipped with white or with a pale line along its length, and, too, a suggestion of a red spot or stain, like a dull red flower perhaps, all this arrangement moving in a swing parallel to the ground, just clearing the upper edge of the remotest dunes, back where the sand grows more level and becomes roadside. It might have been an arm, or a wing.

She glances back at the glass man. He's kneeling in the sand, silica in one form and another—is that why he finds it so interesting? Maybe he sees himself in this panoply of sand and ceaselessly sloshing fluids the way a human being might see a less complex version of himself in a cat or a dog. Right now he has picked a rock up and scrutinizes its underside, flicking away grains of sand and shreds of some kind of plant life.

"Let's get back," she says. "Move your glass."

Riding the capsule back into the city she is contacted by an element of the specialitat, the vertical meniscus snapping around her. It's like being absorbed by a giant droplet. The contrast of the visual field intensifies, or at least the blacks do, so the already vivid shadows of Koskon Kanona become inky windows into the void. Only an instant or so into this impression she is joined by a special, who takes the seat facing hers. Her companion keeps up his routine investigation of his hallucinations, head tilting and turning like a bird's; he doesn't appear to be included in this exchange.

A special is unmistakeable; always something self-conscious about the dress, whether it is pointedly formal or informal, and the same steady, motionless eye. An air of being at the center of countless tasks at varying stages of completeness. Specials never fail to remind you: a document you need to file, an application deadline that you thought was later than it is, an annual physical, a permit about to expire. They are the natural bureaucrats of Koskon Kanona, and in a sense they were here first, before mankind, although they are mostly human. When humans first arrived on Koskon Kanona, they discovered a bureaucracy *already in place*, even though the planet had no intelligent life, now or ever, indigenous or imported. The bureaucracy was simply *there*, like the space of a skyscraper without the mass, the relationships of piece to piece without the pieces themselves, yet still palpable and enduring as a kind of slope or grain that made itself felt whenever anyone exerted any energy against that grain. It was possible, but extravagantly difficult, to go "uphill," just as it is possible but needlessly difficult to build on earth in defiance of earth's gravity field. The pattern asserted itself in urban planning, in the structure of government, and in the development of human beings. Certain unpredictable individuals would bureaucratize and become specials, meaning that the inherent bureaucracy field of Koskon Kanona had exerted the ascendant among the various forces contributing to their makeup. The specialitat is the combined nimbus emanated by all the specials together—education, law, cultural ministers, resource ministers, economists, security, religion, and so on. Assiyeh feels it holding her like a marble between its lips. A special with poached-egg eyes sits opposite her on the capsule. The necktie or kerchief tumbles down his front, the large, veiny hands are folded in the lap, the grey head, the massive body ... Without moving, they take her in ... still fifteen, thanks to her rejuvenation experiment, with her chewing gum, her pimples, her headphones whispering top ten pop songs, her notebook grudgingly plastered with stickers of cats and colorless human hearts.

They want her to write up a series of reports about a man back on earth. There's a lot of information about him, too much, and it's all over the place. Eighteen possible names, seven possible ages, thirteen possible nations of origin, and so on. What can be said with assurance is that this man is a man, male, older than 27, with obvious African heritage and virtually certain Hispanic background too, fluent in Spanish, Portuguese, English, and Achrizoguaylan Labasporspan, of no fixed abode, a political activist under the nom de guerre "SuperAesop." She is shown a series of images which are transferred directly to her optic nerve by a sonic fan emitted from a socket in the middle of the special's forehead. The first is a passport photo of a man with feverish eyes, a drawn, aquiline face, slight underbite, short locks, not quite looking at the camera. Throughout the succeeding images that preoccupied look is typically there more often than not. Here he is smiling, sitting in a circle of people outdoors, there's a fire in the background, smoke coming from his teeth, caught making a gesture with both hands as if he were lifting an invisible bundle. The specialitat wants her to write him up for them, with some supplementals on a few of his associates, also generally identified by nicknames: Gloominous, Bump'eyewreckie, Noughzeddd, Tenure.

SuperAesop's friends. There was the one who would get angry at the crowds and the street noise. Then he would try reasoning with himself: it wasn't personal, no one was out to get him in particular, the noise would be there whether he were there to hear it or not, and so on, but he grew only more angry not so much because he felt slighted that this racket was not being made to destroy his noble person but as a matter of course, more so because it angered him to have the reason for his anger undermined. He didn't want to reason himself out of being angry, actually, but to find reasons to justify complaining.

Tenure pronounced like Manure. He once imposed a sort of black nationalist play on me, probably on everyone he knew, with an invitation we couldn't refuse. I don't remember much about it, it wasn't all that clear. I remember a photo of him in the amazingly high quality color program, showing him lying down bare chested, holding a yellow box with some African stuff in it. Damn, I thought, that's him without his sunglasses, dude is serious! The play had something to do with love potions and there was a lot of sparkling outfits and people sitting on the floor. There was a sulky wizard character who grumbled about rain getting into his love potions and neutralizing them. "There must have been some rain in that water," he said, and all the strings on his lute went slack at once.

The black superman main character philosophized with him about it, saying something like, "Rain falls on all, brother." And one of the female characters wanted to know how all those Germans and Italians got it on when Europe was raining all the time. She didn't get an answer, which was actually pretty good, I thought. The whole thing was African mish-mash and Ashamba-the-Wave is a dancing girl and she asks Bumpy Deuterdahomaga what the spider dance is on the dewdrop. Corny as hell. I liked it, though, anyway. It felt kind of nice. Tenure was fruit and nuts. Strictly water, with tea on special occasions. He got twenty five years for possession and an illegal gun with police fingerprints. I managed to talk to him once, not about much of anything, early on, but then I was homeless again and keeping up with anybody became a mystery.

... Outside, as they go on talking, talking, talking, the light lances down with such a violent glare that the sky is polarized and all but impossible to see, appearing contracted around the star, and visible at most as a dull greyish exhalation of the planet that barely films the starry blackness beyond. Tightly-corseted by the presence of the sun, the sky gapes alarmingly the moment the sun sets, and becomes correspondingly vast from the perspective of the surface, so that it seems as if the horizon, so high overhead during the day, plummets below the feet at night, and it's as if the observer were bulging out into space, surrounded by stars. The sky induces claustrophobia by day and agoraphobia by night. The behavior of the sky is far less marked in the city, which may explain in part why so few people venture out into the wilderness. The city consists of 221 soaring towers that cannot be clearly seen up close; in the glare of daylight they are just solid black geometries that disappear upwards into the rays of the star; at night they are luminous white squares in which tiny figures can be seen eating, working, gazing outside, or, as is surprisingly common considering how straight-laced people here are in public, having sex right up against the windows. Supplies and waste are conveyed to and fro through subterranean waterways that lave the deep foundations of the towers; most of the street-chasms are narrow causeways suspended on high arches above the dark water that flickers far below them. The plazas are like the bottoms of open pits, the more popular ones resembling craters, where the flatter surrounding buildings lean away from the open space and let in more sky. The streets further to the south, away from the water, are not suspended, and they terminate with striking exactness along a line as distinct as if the urbation had been rolled out like a sheet of wrapping paper and then cut with a razor along a ruler's edge. There the streets all end in a joined brass rail, and beyond it there is open ground, dotted with shrubs and criss-crossed here and there with meandering trails shiny with occasional use, leading into the rolling hill country.

... When the interview is over, Assiyeh is released, and the meniscus recedes. What was that all about? She rubs her head, uncertainly. Trying to remember their interview is like trying to remember a physical movement made in sleep. The special has dissolved into a cloud of darkened office air, through which she catches glimpses of dim, desk-lined aisles, banks of file cabinets, institutional corridors. None of these really exist anywhere on the planet, as far as she knows. Those glimpses are only her mental articulation of more abstract impressions proper to the bureaucracy field itself. Presumably, an ancient Egyptian would have caught glimpses of heaped up scrolls, clay tablets, the smell of stale ink and bone dry store rooms. An ancient Mayan would have seen the calendar, heard the noises made by the official finery of the calculators. Someone from ancient China would have smelled the glue-like odor of lacquered cases, seen the piles of writing brushes, the carefully arranged and painstakingly copied annals.

There are three things left behind when the special has gone. First, confirmation that she has been traced to Koskon Kanona and marked for retrieval or liquidation by terranist agents, and second, denial of a permit she requested for reclassification of certain premises currently under lease to her which would, by altering their zoning designation, allow her to use them as a lab for potentially apocalyptic experiments. Evidently she filed late. (The deadlines are highly variable because they are set by multiple interlocking calendars and it isn't unusual for a due date to slip out from under.) She has until DATE DATE DATE NUMBER DATE NUMBER to reapply. Meanwhile, the grant for her dangerous experiments has come through. Contact Buzzati SII33.

*

Statistical analysis of the literature shows a strong bias of over four to one in favor of what is often erroneously described as an individualistic or heroic narrative structure. This description is erroneous because the definition of individual entailed by the category is generic; individual or heroic status is conveyed on an actor in such a narrative because he or she occupies that position as a substitute for a hypothetical audience member's wish-fulfillment figure. The pseudo-individual character is a representative for a generic audience and is hence generic tout entiere.

The genuinely individualistic narrative must, among other things, particularize an individual. The logic of what is known as the individualistic or heroic narrative is a "war is peace" or "fear is security" logic, ie, the individual is anybody; see figure one.

Figure one: a video montage of human beings with more money raising their open palms to screen their faces from the camera, people in suits getting into or out of high priced cars, wearing high priced clothes, high priced hair styles, high priced jewelry, or uniforms of high rank.

The description of the activities of a given individual will reflect this illusory individualism if this approach is taken, while a non-individual or even anti-individual approach will suffer from confusion between genuine individuality and its double. Therefore the indicated approach will analyze the individual by explicitly excluding the double or media-individual.

As per request from the office of the Principal Censor, what follows will be a summary description of an individual preponderantly designated SuperAesop. Membership confirmed: The People's Community Party, the Retrofit Socialist Party, the Green Marxist Party, the Daoist Communist Party, the Commnarchist Party, the Rent Is Too Damn High Party, the Intercontinental Unemployed Persons Party, the Lumpen Syndicalist Party. Activities rated above 3.0 on the Panicker Potential Social Efficacy Scale associated with SuperAesop beginning 3/39/00 consist mainly of type four and type five labor organizing with an average basic success rate of 20.2%, which is 4.1% greater than the general success rates for such activities. These include (US records only):

a) an attempt to form a pizza delivery person's union—FAILED.

b) an attempt to form a motor pool for pizza delivery persons—FAILED.

c) two attempts to require pizzerias to cover fuel expenses for pizza delivery persons—FAILED.

d) an attempt to prevent the dismissal of a pizza delivery person who was murderously assaulted and hospitalized by a mentally disturbed customer—FAILED.

e) an attempt to raise funds to cover medical costs of the injured pizza delivery person—partial success.

f) aided in the escape of a sex worker responsible for the assassination of a U.S. senator, strangled in the course of erotic asphyxiation—partial success.

g) an attempt to oppose the closure of the entire Philadelphia public school and public library systems—FAILED.

h) an attempt to oppose the closure of the entire mass transit system in Philadelphia—FAILED.

i) an attempt to oppose a 75% reduction in the Philadelphia fire department—FAILED.

j) an attempt to oppose the elimination of all public

funding for health care in Pennsylvania—FAILED.

k) an attempt to end minimum wage discrimination against restaurant workers—FAILED.

l) an attempt to legalize public nudity in Philadelphia—FAILED.

m) an attempt to oppose the imposition of mandatory life insurance laws in Pennsylvania—partial success.

n) an attempt to create a working class news and information service in Philadelphia—FAILED.

o) an attempt to repeal "shoot on sight" laws passed after several weeks of protest and social upheaval in Philadelphia—FAILED.

p) an attempt to evade prosecution for counterfeiting and numerous other implausible offenses relating to the propagation of alternative currencies—FAILED.

q) an attempt to organize a prisoners' union—FAILED.

r) an attempt to escape from prison—FAILED.

s) an attempt to create an ex-convicts' union—partial success.

t) one hundred and five attempts to find publisher for literary and critical book titled *Notes from the Ground-Under*—FAILED.

*

The surviving economists are retreating further and further from their point of entry into the structure. We must consider the question of this structure, because, the farther the economists go within that structure, the less coherent becomes the claim that it is a structure.

Structures aren't infinite, and they are distinct from all of space. What is needed here is a rule that will fix the point at which the extensiveness of the structure in space exceeds the necessity of the concept of structure. Any structure of greater size than that could no longer be designated a structure, where a structure is considered to be de facto at Absolute Rest.

So then what would such a thing be?

A dimension. Simple.

The structure is both man-made and natural. While it is constructed of man-made material—made from natural products—its form is that of a particular dimension. The man-made structure is an artificial lining for a natural dimension. So this structure is like a natural cave formation that has been converted for human use. One might lay down cement or tile or wooden boards on the cave floor, put windows in any gaps in the cave wall, doors in the larger internal apertures, and so on. In this case, the cave is the natural cavern of space-time.

The surviving economists are retreating further and further into a dimension X that relates to what we might call the common dimension, C, as an attic is related to the rest of the structure to which it belongs. From the point of view of those in C, the surviving economists are dwindling, as the recession of the economists is not perceived in spatial terms by those outside the dimension X, who cannot observe the spatial properties of X any more than a three dimensional figure can be perceived as such from the vantage point of the second dimension. This means that the economists in X can however survey C with the benefit of C+1 dimensional point of view,

MICHAEL CISCO

should they choose to do so.

The third dimension is sheared off an object by second dimensional perception. It follows that a second dimensional figure, while it remains two dimensional, is nevertheless perceived by a three dimensional observer with the addition of a dimensional absence. This would be the "empty space" of the absent third dimension in the second dimensional figure: the surroundings that are unnoticed from the two dimensional point of view.

With this idea clearly in view, we can proceed to define the problem. By receding into X, the surviving economists (SE) are preserving themselves from the hostility of those social actors in C who wish to suppress any challenge to their private dominion over the property and social power of C. This is an effective measure insofar as receding into X puts the surviving economists beyond the spatial reach of those social actors, their violence, their communication, their knowledge, their interrogatives. However as the recession of the SE into X increases, and correspondingly their safety from harm or detection, there is a proportionate decrease in their ability to intervene back in C, even though, from the point of view of C, they don't appear to have gone anywhere. From the vantage point of C, the SE have merely decreased in size, until they have dwindled down to comically frantic little dolls scrambling through a dollhouse dimension. From the vantage point of the SE, C has simultaneously flattened and distended itself like a map, which can be consulted but only at a distance. When "distance" is invoked in this, necessarily imperfect, analogy, it must be understood to mean something more than a mere quantitative difference, having a tendency to increase, in the measurement of space between two points. While there is some element of this idea of distance, this "distance" is far more intensely a translation, just as the map is a translation and not identical to the landscape or even to the view of that landscape from a height. There is a dimensional difference between the map and the landscape that is not quantitative in the way that the theoretical distance from the earth's surface to the imaginary point of view from which it appears as it does on the map is quantitative.

Looking back at C from X, the SE will see a dimensional absence that becomes more obvious in proportion to the augmentation of the quantitative distance from the point of entry into the new dimension. This absence is like the perceived "flatness" of the two-dimensional figure as seen from the third dimension. The "flatness" of C grows in conspicuousness at a constant rate matching the rate of recession of SE in X. As the utility of the SE, which determines in effect the extent to which they are economists per se, is partially a function of perception, so their identities as economists will grow in density as their perspective on C increases, which is the consequence of their incessant flight deeper into X. However, the other aspect of the utility of the SE, namely, their interventions in the economic and social affairs of C, is correspondingly reduced; as their flight into X continues, there is a non-straightforward alteration in the value of SE.

I still haven't figured out whether or not the diminution of interventivity is equivalent to the augmentacity of per-spicuousness, or in some other neat proportion, or what the fuck it is, but there is some kind of function there. Perhaps that function has a productive aspect anyway.

*

Etsimen really is just those three lights and they're already getting to be like old friends because here I am driving past them again, three lights with nothing to illuminate but bare earth with the roads laid out and nothing else. Carolina is leaning out the car window and I'm massaging my elbow where there's this buzzing feeling down in the meat that comes and goes, nerve trouble I guess.

"Stop the car," Carolina says.

We get out in the silence and darkness, just outside the trapezoid of lit earth. The mountains fill half the sky in one direction and are only a little lower opposite. The air is warm and dry, and it smells like baked soil. Carolina walks along one side of the road, weaving as if she were avoiding pedestrians. Then she reaches out her hand to push open a door that isn't there and vanishes inside an all-night drugstore with a dark, barred window and a vertical neon PHARMANAOS sign. A rush of air pulls over me as a car that I can't see passes me. There is no sign of anyone the length of the street, down to the intersection diagonally half in shadow. And now Carolina's gone, too. Isolation paralyzes me. I stand here, in this empty place with its three lights, seeing the dim rows of buildings, the intersection half in darkness. Two oxen round the corner and walk up the empty street in my direction, seeming to firm up the night like a clear fan around them, suddenly very deep and tall, full of a breathing held-breath feeling. The two oxen are the same, same size, same color, and their eyes are a vivid red. They walk close together and more or less in unison, but they are holding their heads up and still in a way that I don't know is normal for oxen. They cross the street in front of me. I can smell them, distinctly. One of them noses open the door to the pharmacy and they both go inside, the neon light splashing them with blue across their broad backs. Carolina comes out a moment later, unwrapping a pack of cigarettes.

Driving around, I can see people. Dense crowds in some places. The sound of a bustling town at night, but never more than those three lights. The other lights are not lights. I only think I see them. They're there, but only for thought. My body feels so feathery now I wonder if the car is really here around me or if I'm just floating along. But I could never imagine anything as baroquely ugly as this car and its inexhaustible supply of little bits of junk and scraps of trash. Carolina points, and I pull up at some white plaster walls lit with multicolored lamps set in the earth among the aloes. Up comes a young person—I think it's a boy but I can't be sure—"he's" carrying a lantern that throws all its light up onto his face, while the rest of him is a silhouette. He's smiling at us with a mouth full of slightly crooked teeth and welcomes us in an uncertain voice to the hotel Adoniram, I think he says. We leave the car where it is and go inside, through an archway into a patio with identical low white buildings to our right and left. Opposite us, on the far side of the patio, is nothing, just an open expanse of black land and very dark blue sky. As he crosses before the phosphorescent white of the building beside me I see that this person is a boy, and stark naked. His lantern is gone. Now he is inviting us in through the sliding glass door of the building on the right.

I recognize a lobby in the gloom. There is an even light here, very dim, and coming from no particular place, although we all throw moonshadows on the walls. That wall off to the left has a fireplace and what is probably fake wood panelling, a living room set. Front desk, pigeonholes, an office, a hallway. The boy asks me for my clothes, watches me as I take them off. He puts them on the counter and then asks for Carolina's. She undresses as he watches, smiling. He puts her clothes next to mine and goes behind the counter, then takes the clothes down and puts them under the counter, and produces a room key. With a wave of his hand, he gestures us to follow him down the hall.

The room doors are made of thick glass. He unlocks one and gestures us inside, then says something that might be "Saluto!" and tosses me the key. It's the kind that's just a metal tab with concavities along its length, with a small round disk of some heavy, sandy material that I think is stone. The wall opposite the door is all glass, and the other walls are glass from about halfway up, the lower half is plaster. We're at the end of the hall, so the half wall across from the bed overlooks the same vague blue-black expanse of desert, and the ceiling is either painted black or it's clear too, although I can see no stars. Nothing but vivid, animated blackness. I can't really see into the next room, either—only a murky blue-white bed and maybe a chair, maybe a moving figure, black and skeletal, just there vanishing into the transparent bathroom. I wash up and throw myself on the spacious bed, which has no covers, and which is just higher at the head of the bed, in lieu of pillows. Carolina lays herself on top of me. I want to tell her I'm too tired, but I don't. She seems especially excited, as if we were being watched through the glass walls.

We made it, I tell myself, trying to summon a sense of assurance.

Did we make it?

We made it. We made it.

I wake up in the dark. Listening into the dark, I am not hearing her. Reaching out, I touch cold sheets. She isn't in the bathroom—I would see her through the wall. I wonder what to do. I wonder for a long time. The bed dips. She's back. I ask her something. She answers me sleeping.

I wake up again. Carolina sleeps beside me. Still dark, but with a difference. There is something wrong with the ceiling up there. This bed is a four-poster, with transparent posts and a clear canopy, but this is not some flaw or dusty spot in its fabric, this is a chillblain in the ceiling, a blister, silvery, with a velvetty edge.

I jump up. I know what it is! It's the sun, seen through the ceiling, which has darkened with the light like adjustable sunglasses. There's no window, no way to stick my head outside to see, but there are birds going by, and the landscape outside is more visible now, the mountains beyond more detailed. I see a pair of men walk by outside, looking at me, and at Carolina, who is sitting up in bed, startled awake.

"It's daytime," I say.

She looks around and sees what I see.

"Does it polarize or something?"

The next room looks submerged in dark blue water, and there appears to be a vague form lying on the bed. The people outside are wearing clothes, which makes me wonder if we're going to have to dash by clothed guests on our way to the front desk, and if our boy of last night hadn't simply swiped our clothes, wasn't actually working here.

Down the hall, the same boy, still naked, perched on a stool behind the counter, brightly smiling, eating a bowl of cereal, yes our clothes are waiting for us. I put mine on, stale as they are. Carolina dresses beside me. Outside the daylight is bizarre, falling in sections of varying intensity and color, with blue zones ragged as driftwood and yellow blemishes, always more white, more glaring, than colorful, though. The sounds of the town rise and fall like surf, and the sun stays motionless in the sky, then jumps ahead, stops, jumps. You can tell because you can see the shadows wheel around whenever it happens.

Etsimen is full of spires. Not buildings with spires, just the spires. The spires rise up and there are what I call spines too, like backbones, a forest of horizontal spires like viaducts.

We get breakfast in a cafe the boy, Adonio, pointed out to us; the place is called El Obeliscu Axud, a circus ring under a tent blooming out from an adobe box, at least a hundred wrought iron tables and chairs scattered over the sawdust. A bubbly woman wearing scarves of every color shows us to a seat she seems very particular about, even though the place is nearly empty. She puts us next to a fountain that keeps splashing me. Now we wait for the waiter, and I can't see the other patrons because this fucking fountain is in the way. Carolina has already told me about Etsimen; it was originally just a small settlement intended for the staff of the nuclear power plant, but then a European company named Groupe Chimere decided to turn it into what they called an Integral City. The immigrants to this new city didn't like the chimerical administration and there were protests that got violent. Then someone sabotaged the nuclear plant and there was a serious radiation leak that chased most people away and left the rest to blame each other, GC saying that the protesters did it and the protesters saying that GC staged the accident to free themselves from a liability. GC pulled out when the plant shut down, but some former residents came back, and others, too, from all over. Now Etsimen itself is the chimera, where incomplete ultra-modern architecture and infrastructure is completed with junkshop makeshifts in some places, and with ambitious independent constructions in others. Some of these new constructions are expertly made by experienced construction workers and engineers, and others are more like roadside follies, the kind you read about where one man spends fifty years building a model of the forbidden city in half scale entirely out of pipe tobacco tins or some shit.

The longer we stay, the more people we see. The place is filling up. I'm tired of being splashed and move my seat next to Carolina's so that I am now facing the fountain, which completely blocks my view. The water darkens and trickles down the jagged stone outline and then collects, flashing, in the high basin. The wind rises. It ruffles through the cafe fluttering napkins. I lower my hand to the armrest and the ball of the stickshift fills my hand. The wind pours over my face, orange warning flags flutter over the concrete dividers. There are gauges on the lip of the high basin, the road beyond flashes in the morning sun, the blocked offramp to Etsimen rounds the bend up ahead, we have been circling Etsimen all night. A car with one headlight pulls onto the road behind us, keeping back and still half melted into thin dawn mist.

The national anthem comes on the radio, filtering in through the dawn static as the station begins its broadcast day. I forgot I left it on. The news: Joan Incienzoa is in stable condition, but, on doctor's advice, albeit with great reluctance, he is withdrawing his candidacy on the grounds of insufficient fitness. Right away, without missing a beat, a spokesperson for the NFP jumps on the mike and announces their replacement candidate, Raul Varvarviollo, a former truck driver and Sunday school teacher from Carambem, who is distantly related by marriage to Tripi, through her cousin Bolhitu. The NFP formally requests an extension from the electoral committee, to give them time to introduce their wonderful new candidate to the voters. The AUP objects. The committee is conferring at present, but there are rumors that Professor Caral Muoitisorpio, one of the committee members, is having health problems of her own which may necessitate her replacement, and speculation is rife as to how that replacement will be found, and whether it would be possible to insure the process of selection will not be tampered with, whether it will be necessary to call on some third party to oversee the election ...

The head of the electoral committee is a medical doctor named Ajuaviva Besik, who looks like she hasn't been getting enough sleep lately. She's got a starey, daunting, patient kind of seriousness that reminds me of a teacher I used to have. You can tell, it's her way with words that humanizes her. She appears on televisions in the windows as we drive past, crowds of people in front of the stores and porches to watch.

"While we greatly appreciate the generous offers of assistance from the international community, and in particular from our neighbors, and while we will gladly, and with gratitude, accept all counsel, all good advice, and so doing honor to the spirit of camaraderie and goodwill in which they are offered, our autonomy as a nation depends on our conducting this election ourselves."

*

The wind blew clear and cold on my arm in the empty street, where I fired the gun. I fired the gun, a parabellum, with my left hand. The bolt snapped. The gun wasn't very powerful. The recoil was almost nothing, like a breeze. I saw a puff come out the back of his knee. He fell. His cries were clear and cold trumpets.

I pulled my arm out of the street, dropping the gun as I did so. Its weight was threatening to draw me all the way through a hole in a clear wall, into the street scene. Only my arm was sticking out into the street from the hole in space. I'm not on the map. I am on the map, but not in the flesh and blood. I had intervened in a desperate shituation. I couldn't tell if I had done well or not. The moment I withdrew the last of my hand from the street, he disappeared. I see only the street. The sky is just a colorless blank. I don't see the people or the traffic. No, only the street. I'd have to put more of myself in, if I wanted to see more.

I move around by skating. I lean in the direction I want to go, although that has to be a possible direction. When I lean one way, I get resistance, as if I were leaning into a padded wall, but when I lean the other way, the space around me accordions, and I stretch and slide along in that direction one grotesquely elongated step, landing with a gelatinous shudder. Then I have to lean around to find the next direction, since I never seem to go the same way two steps in a row. Whenever I do it, I have a certain mental image of what happens, but it isn't a perception, just an idea: an arbitrary cube of space that folds up, corners splaying out before and behind me, caving in to either side of me, and then the forward edge pivots and shrinks down while the back edge lengthens and I heave along forward.

My chief pastime is arguing with cadavers that are smarter than I am. I think about death all the time.

How do you know?

Maybe one day they will finally accept me. Everything I do is saturated with necromancy. I summon and fabricate souls in the airy magic circle of my punctured skull, fashioning them out of memories and unaccountable sensations. Souls are patterns of adverbs, so making them is more like a performance than composition.

*

I would have been arrested with everyone else, just about for certain, if it hadn't been for my knee giving out the way it did. That turned me about, sent me home, and by the time I'd hobbled back into my lair there were already fifty phone messages about the police sweep. Tenure was shot. They say he's in the hospital. I can't get through. He may be dead. I am sitting up in bed with a pile of ice on my knee, panting and staring at the phone. I know Tenure is dead. They kill you and beg you for mercy while they are killing you.

As I run, the night sky moves along with me ... now I've stopped, the buildings have stopped, and only the sky moves, the luminous clouds racing away to the northeast. Oncoming cars tense then spring past me on my right hand side. Stop, start, hurry here and then stop, moving at insanely high speed but you don't disintegrate because you have a strong anchor in your initiation. Nature initiates a real sorcerer, the one who can stop and start. Here comes a man with a leg like a hot water bottle, a cane foot sticking out of it, walking along slowly and unevenly since his legs aren't the same length. He keeps slipping backwards, too. His approach to me is more like the drifting together of a pair of rafts than like one man walking up to another man. He has a W.C. Fields face painted over a rather lean, melancholy one.

"This isn't what I really look like," he says.

We go into a little hollow kiosk on the grass divider between lanes of traffic. The kiosk overlooks a huge smoggy valley, skyscrapers in the distance. Brown and blue sky. The kiosk smells like sunheated metal. The walls are just a big metal band bent around in a hexagon. There's a shallow, conical roof with a metal pennant on top. Inside there are some old cushioned desk chairs that wheeze when you sit down on them and rasp like gurgling crocodiles when you tip back on their big spring stems. Maybe it's really an octagon. The man and I sit together drinking coffee from a thermos I seem to have. He's telling me about the dangers of police work and how to protect yourself against drones.

"Paint or mats all over your car," he says. "Or not paint or mats. Mud is best. The mud from the dirt where you're going. Camouflage from the air. You think you're spotted, you ditch the car that second, even if you have to leave it roll. Run. Don't run—get under cover tout de suite."

By now he's achieved such high caffeineiety he's vibrating. So violent is his tremor he's wrecking the chair just by sitting on it, the seat rattles and the slats come loose, bolts pop out and clatter to the floor, twitching like a blunted buzzsaw trebucheting arms and legs—

"Maybe you should wait to finish that coffee ..."

"What are you talking about?!" he screeches. "I feel great!"

He rocks back and forth snapping springs out through the upholstery and I fling my hands up to shield my eyes.

All of a sudden he stops and rises onto his asymmetrical feet, looking up at the ceiling as if he'd just noticed a message written there.

"What is it?" I ask him.

His motionlessness is actually a state of exactly balanced contradiction, a universal bodily tension exactly counterweighting itself.

"Is there something there?" I ask, without getting up. "What does it say?"

The man turns and looks at me.

"Deeeaaathhhhh ...." he sighs.

His face splits apart and sloughs from the bone. Fragments of skull spray from his shredding scalp. Rattling and sighing, his body disintegrates, throwing off huge black motes of crumbled body. He falls into his own footprint like a demolished building.

I can feel them senticompartmentalize me, and by being nice to me and so on they fondly believe they are doing something, and they are. They aren't berating and beating me; they aren't race-jamming me, which is something. But that's just their escape, and I need to escape from that. My escapades are too gnarly for their boxes. I know what their kind pennies-from-heaven words are worth; not worthless, but not worth much, not animal money.

But you're right when you say the problem is fantasy. The fantasy money that is traded by the greatest of our world's fantasists. They make their predictions about what will go up or down, they buy and sell bits of the future, and don't know that all along they are writing science fiction. Isn't it? A scientific projection from now to then, and a gun-jumping narrative to get there? Just because you do that, you brokers, and just because you own all the money and the computers that buy and sell for you because they're faster than mere humans, just because you do that doesn't mean you own science fiction, or fantasy, or even horror, since you have to be able to experience horror to write about it. An endless stream of stock quotes bursts from the chapless jaws of the giant movie idol worshipped by crazed natives. To be native to a place is to be crazed, right? That purest of the purest crystallizations of sanity that we call capital is native nowhere. As long as it keeps moving, who cares where you steer it? Why even steer—just floor it! Can't you feel the flooring? Getting right down hard against that floor, beneath that hand-cobbled brand-new buffed and polished oxford shoe?

Let's face something besides. How about a brief round of creative amnesia, to be followed by a skillful reorientation toward what has to be done? My ever-mutating inner boogieman tells me that the only way to hit a moving target is to move faster. It's fast, it's protean, but it's very very nearsighted. It likes Mozart, red wine, travel, Paris of course, it's self-effacingly vainglorious, but it can't see past the tip of its serrated nose. As it changes shape to grab you, change its shape even more. As it tries to escape, deepen the escape tunnel, dig it down to the buried lava that will singe its nose hair and bring tears to smarting, myopic eyes. What is this glowing orange—gold? Some kinda money? This money sure does hurt! Just keep counting, Magoo, don't miss a single coin, counting magma money with charred and smoking fingers, with roasting calcium, with barbequed blood turning to sugarless candy, a big white smile in a staring raw brisket face. Just keep counting! There's plenty more where that came from!

The police form a staggered line of scooters and slide alongside us, trying to goad us like cattle off the avenue and onto a side street. A woman is shouting, half walking half skipping backwards—stay together! close it up! don't let them separate us! We press forward. There's nothing like this feeling, a terror that has nothing to do with terrorism; that's bland fudge compared with the craziness of blocking this avenue in the middle of the day, daring the police to do something about it. Charge in and start clubbing? And how do you suppose that will clear the avenue, all that mayhem? The smug, no eye-contact cop faces under the hats and helmets, the air of paternalistic indulgence, as if we were here at their invitation, to celebrate them and the beautiful efficiency with which they reduce us to livestock. Nothing personal—no, of course not! That's the problem! It isn't the bad attitude of this or that officer or this or that tycoonian, it's the bemused disdain this whole daffy society has for most of its own members. And, as always, it escapes its particulars and crawls onto the faces of horribly fucked people when they turn on each other. We struggle with it, against it, against becoming it, too, because we don't want to be pod-replaced, and that's, as I say, the reason I keep renewing my superscription to my ever-mutating inner boogieman.

I got rained on and eventually went home. I stood in the shower, washing off the rain and feeling rotten. What did we do today? We inconvenienced some commuters and threw off some of the traffic calculators, big deal. Got rain in the potion.

Later on, though, I feel my spirits rising again. They wanted their war and they're going to get it. But they won't be able to say they got it without trouble. They'll say it wasn't really trouble, and the news will lowball the estimated turnout by fifty times, but they *have* to say that, and they *have* to lie about the numbers, that's the point. They *have* to lie, because under the smooth sneering finish they're afraid of us. Not of me or you, but of a nebulous people they have spent their lives escaping from, pretending not to belong to. They can't stand on the balcony gazing out at a silent, whipped nation with TV lights in all the windows, sigh with satisfaction and say—"they bought it." From out of the dark comes a sound of sirens, breaking glass, a plume of smoke, a lot of angry voices shouting. There's trouble. There's lying to be done, and that takes time and money. Those flavorless, tranquilizing TV haircuts don't cut themselves. So it was worth it, after all, like before—not worth everything, not worth nothing. We set the value, not them.

The party goes on into day two. Our lanky guest brought us a gift, although I don't quite know what to call it. He came in suffused in his own private smog. What he left behind, a thin, sour odor of decay, of death, put us all in a productively tragic frame of mind. There's no more talk of a slide into authoritarianism and all that, a backing away from what is hilariously referred to as moral responsibility. No more absconding to the cloudcuckooland of bourgeois bullshit where every problem is personal between a man and his god, especially when it's Mammon and it never isn't. You can flash organize to deal with symptoms but a status quo problem needs a status quo solution, not an emergency solution. So, on general initiative and by acclamation, we have come to the consensus finding that we're all broke.

Point of information: we are all broke, permanently. So, it is moved that we are going to make our own money. Right away, it must be laid down that we are not talking about counterfeiting. We are not going to be counterfeiting. The people who make the money we have been using up to now are the ones who have been doing the counterfeiting. They counterfeit *us*. By fashioning our own money, we are going to bring this dastardly counterfeiting scheme to a close at last because from now on we are going to be the ones who make the value we have always actually already made all along.

The plan will have two phases, Carolina: incubation, followed by cosmic cubism. In the incubation phase we'll circulate the money hermetically among a select, elite cadre consisting exclusively of absolutely anybody and everybody whatwhoever who might want it, giving that money a chance to build up to viable infectionary level. Then we give Virgin Dollars (VD) to the financial markets and bond markets and banks and investors and embrokeners and slick up the members of the board with them until they're all stricken with Human Interest Value (HIV), the virus that causes AIDS (that stands for Anti-Investor-Driven Society).

We gather together in groups, some in this room, some in another, and, when the maestro opens up his pants and waves the magic wand over the magic hat, we all lean in and get down to money making. The coins and bills begin to pile up; they skid along the floor, heaps crashing quietly into heaps. They spin, frisk, and dance with a kind of monetary life. Tiny black panthers, mountain lions padding on the desk, on the floor, they are animal money. The old woman gathers broken glass from the floor and holds it out to me loose in her fist.

The car crasher is part of the crowd, being pushed aside like clothes hanging in a closet, slips to the floor and shoots vanilla clear in his arm. Turn me up a corpse with eyes bright as a baby's, feeling each soft red word thud in my head. Breathe out a long cool cloud of vanilla vapor, cool pale vanilla money unfolding in your palm, vanilla coins soft and cool as fluffy snowflakes trickle from mint fingertips. Tallying up a number that can never be counted, that eludes you with the languidly emancipated mood of a long, sexy dream. That one you, smitten, are looking for, in beautiful places, is the number.

You take bites of water. The smooth, lunar feeling sighs and the elongated desert night party, the pool, the fresh perfumes on the women guests, a druggy delirium that is more lucid than sobriety. Coming off the old standard is risky, even before we begin talking about law and order. It's so fantastic that actually doing it, going through with it, might send you languorously spinning out into the upholstered lotus fantasy jungle that's easy to enter and hard to leave. The belt around the chest suddenly snaps and you can take a deep breath for the first time in longer than you can remember. Gravity stops dragging you down, but you need ground under your feet to get anywhere. You can make your own money in your own heart and settle down into a deep spiritual tradition that reconciles you not only to your own suffering but to everyone else's, including the parts that you yourself are causing. That solo money is costly to get and even costlier to use, especially for everybody else. What we are smooshing together here is money that someone besides you can see and use, money for trade and commerce, sex money, teaching money, animal money, story money.

We got it in heaps, dripping from our fingers now like precious lead. Like cowrie shells and candy coins. We're starting to feed it into the vending machines, the subway pass machinery, the tip jars, the bodegas ... We're getting it into those banks, right under the walls of the fortresses, badly built, badly maintained, guarded by thieves. The counterfeiting machinery they keep hidden away behind those crumbling, ivy-covered walls is jamming up.

"Where the fuck are all these fucking cowrie shells fucking coming fucking from?" "How the fuck should I fucking know?" "Well fucking get them the fuck out of that fucking shit!" "Fucking fuck fucking fuck fucking fuck!" "Fuck you!" "Fuck you!" Biff! Bap!

Keep those cowries coming. Grind them fine and spread the paste evenly across every credit card. Replace your card number with your cowrie number and shove it up a money machine's ass. The machine is supposed to barf and retch, but instead it coos and wiggles at this unexpected pleasure. Pay with an edit card and give yourself a raise. Our bankers have all been fired.

*

It should be noted that, with the exception of a), p), and t) in no case did SuperAesop work alone. The overall pattern clearly shows a persistently repeated effort to establish extended connections of social efficacy, almost invariably with disappointing results. The data necessary to determine the causes for these disappointments was not included in the dossier on this question and must be the topic of a different report.

I compiled this data over several weeks and, during that time, I began to collate other historical information touching the subject. As I was personally responsible for the alteration in the Earth's chromosphere, colloquially known as the Color Shift, I was interested to know if the change affected the subject. He first refers to it in a journal entry dated the day of the change, speculating that it might have been caused by an operation or experiment carried out by a private military force. Thereafter, the ramifications of the change take more of his attention, and, as more accurate information becomes available through unofficial and improvised communications networks, the subject's attitude toward the change becomes less and less guarded. My name occurs several times in what I may say simply are affirmative terms.

The subject's journal entry for 7/21/26 describes an encounter with a man made entirely out of glass, encountered by the subject in a laundromat. The subject uses the restroom at the laundromat, which is situated in the rear, and notes in passing that the back door is padlocked and barricaded behind stacks of boxes. However, only moments after having left the restroom, the subject observes the glass man emerging from it himself, and is confused both by the man's obvious inhumanity and by his sudden appearance from an empty room in which he could not possibly have concealed himself, etc. The subject reports that the glass man attaches himself to him, follows him, will not be rebuffed, and answers all queries and expostulations with articulate but unintelligible gurgling sounds. Unable to get free of the glass man, the subject resigns himself to his company.

Later that day, the glass man physically prevents the subject from entering a certain building in which the subject has an appointment. The glass man restrains the subject by main force and drags him to an adjacent building, preventing him from crying out or otherwise seeking assistance. The subject then says that he witnessed, from a safe distance, the arrival of two cars in front of the building he had been prevented from entering. He identifies them as unmarked police vehicles, the drivers and passengers as "detective types." Shortly thereafter, he saw his supposed contact emerge from the building and consult with the men in the parked cars, looking up and down the street. By this time, the subject had cottoned to the fact that the appointment was a pretext for an arrest, which the glass man's intervention permitted him to escape.

There is further information about the glass man that need not be detailed here. I bring up this material to explain my own actions. It became at once clear to me that I had myself sent the glass man back in time to assist the subject. A moment's further reflection and I realized that there was an underlying purpose in sending the glass man back in time which utterly dwarfs the significance of preventing the subject's arrest—namely, that sending the glass man back in time was a way to establish a link connecting this future with the subject's present, and thus insuring that the one will be realized in the other.

The idea drove every other from my head. I was aflame with the intensest desire to be that future self who brought about this change.

The means were obvious: I would slow my glass man into the past. The difficulty lay in the fact that he would have to return to the Earth from Koskon Kanona. The voyage back, while steadily reducing the intervening distance to zero, unfortunately would not also reduce the intervening time to zero; in fact, the opposite would occur, and the intervening time would actually double.

I have long been interested in the Stockum Solution to the puzzle of time travel: namely, that time travel would be possible if the universe were a spinning cylinder of infinite length. The difficulty with this solution is that observation has demonstrated the universe to be neither cylindrical nor spinning. So, to achieve time travel, it would be necessary to set the universe spinning in such a way as to give it a cylindrical shape, which could be done with the application of my slowing rays according to the plan I submitted to the Koskon Kanonan Science Intendant.

The experiment was conducted on 13/13/7007, using an array of 635,000 slow generators situated at the points in space indicated. By 65/07/7007, confirmation was received that the universe had developed spin. The precise moment of spin initiation was marked by spontaneous nosebleeds, reported by all known persons. Omnicylindrification took effect as of 143/17/7007, marked by spontaneous dancing and orgiastic delirium. I took action the moment I recovered, and sent the glass man to the restroom in the laundromat on Earth by slowing him against the cosmic rotary motion, and angling him with extreme precision. The calculations required for this were greatly more complex and time-consuming to resolve than were the ones necessary to spin and cylindrify the universe. It was necessary to angle the glass man through space so that he would achieve maximum density only at that particular point in space, the restroom in the laundromat, and only at the moment immediately after the departure of SuperAesop from that spot. I am pleased to add that this experiment was awarded the blue ribbon at this year's Koskon Kanonan science fair. At present, I am embroiled in a debate with numerous citizens and officials about whether or not I should restore the universe to its previous, non-spinning condition or leave it as it now is.

Assiyeh stops writing and turns to look out the window, because the ceiling of clouds has just leapt out of sight, suddenly unveiling an entire night sky filled with unfamiliar constellations. SuperAesop has pulled over, come what may. Nature calls. No cyclops lights, but they could be hiding in the night out there. No sound, though. They haven't sighted another car except for their unwanted escorts since they reached the Etismen roundabout. Another moment and the stars are gone again, hidden by instantaneous overcast.

Assiyeh turns away from the clouds and SuperAesop turns towards them, watching them part and shift, Orion's belt coming and going through the gaps. Carolina stands beside him on the main drag of Etsimen, takes his arm, tugging him gently in the direction of the drugstore. Her grip stabilizes him. He had to get out of the car and walk around a little in place, stamping his feet trying to pound out the shakiness that took him over when he unblocked the offramp. Etsimen is just three lights, this empty street, this silence. He looks back up at Orion's belt. Suddenly two huge oxen round the corner and lumber toward them, passing them, down the middle of the street. Oxen with shaggy, mud-caked pelts, buzzing with flies, ponderous horns, scarlet irises; these massive beasts blast them with intense barnyard funk and something else, fresh cut grass. The smell of the stars. Some stars. Carolina is still tugging.

"All right, OK," he says.

They go around shitty hatchback, pinging and wheezing to itself, and into the drugstore. That's a weird transition for a nose to make, from barnyard to drugstore. What does it smell like in here? Scented candles, floorwax, candy and air conditioning. The storefront is no more than twenty feet across but the aisles plunge into the distance like runways lined with perforated white enamel shelves, lit with an even spectral light from the excessively low ceiling. He can reach right up and brush the powder dry ceiling tiles without having to straighten his arm all the way. The shelves started within a couple of feet of the front of the store, just far enough back so that the door could swing open without hitting anything. There was no register up front, nowhere to pay. Carolina leads him toward the back, where the pharmacy counter should be. She's going to buy blue liquid glass crystal perfume drugs, blue phosphorus, luminescent blue liquid glass crystal perfume mathematic graph time drugs in tiny rare decanters or neat geometric packets in wooden caskets, the paper wrapping carefully pressed with the seal of outer space. After walking down an aisle for about fifteen minutes I pause in the tobacco department, staring at a death window set in among the other goods and, like them, hanging from a metal rod that hooks into the backboard. It's a black pane that I think I could stick my whole arm inside, but it would be like thrusting my arm into outer space, my arm would freeze and split. I bend forward to peer into it and it instantly fills my field of vision, my body goes numb, I can see tiny figures dressed like economists nestling in among the stars, see their livid whiteface markings, their drab attire, their long, pensive faces lost in thought and floating among the stars like dead leaves on a black stream of sluggish, chill waters. What are they thinking about? It's weird to see this earnest purposeful thinking on faces just drifting ... they're dreaming with their eyes half open and it's pushing them out among the stars like a star drive.

*

It happened most often when I would throw a glance at him sidelong—the light flashing across his surface would reveal for an instant another city of yawning white squares as vast as canyons striped with stark shadows of hard-edged black. Tiny windows like arrow slits in blank, furnace-white walls. Silent, coordinated action of people, machines, and animals, seen from a distance. A naked pair copulating in the center of an empty white quad a mile wide, coming together in the great white space under black sky, the luminous erection of the Teeming. A narrow handcart with stacked jars of human brains sloshing in formaldehyde, all sandwiched between sheets of thick glass. A dancing figure with balls of bright blue flame between his fingers, playing them across his fingers so they gamble and skip over the scorched, puckering skin like frisking little animals, the dancer seems at first to be a silhouette and then you notice he's scorched black all over.

Then into a vast chamber illuminated by a faceted red bolt of sunset that leans across the void like a dim chevron. In its footprint are carpets that absorb and glow hotly with the light, and mosaic inlays coolly sparkling. The sun crimsons its red right in the center of the single colossal window, high atop a great cascade of crescent stairs with one spacious landing halfway up, on which there stands a monumental fountain of some clear material. The place is filled with people attired in a carnival profusion of ceremonial finery—masks, feathers, robes, scapulars, stoles, winged hats, girdles, anklets, skirts, albs, paint, and so on.

Smoke rises from the censers, people walk in labyrinth patterns, and sourceless music cries and shouts like an incessant chord, countless voices and timbres swaying through the minutes like sunbeams swaying underwater, going in and out of a wandering, urgent harmony. Dancers spill down from the landing, one central dancer with a red headdress and the rest of them in white and carrying swords that slice off their long braids as they spin. Mist bubbles from the fountain, water acts like smoke, rising in webs and coils up into the air, smoke acts like water, tossed in heavy globules and splashing in the clear basin. The people waiting to receive the dancers as they elaborate their way down the stairs are also dancing in brief repeated gestures. Some form lines and bow, raising and lowering their heads like pistons, others drop down into a sort of a curtsey and then up again, others frolic arm in arm, leaping high. When the dancers have arrived, everyone turns and goes out through a pair of double doors that swing gigantically open to reveal a sunset garden park with flowerbeds and charcoal-smudge trees and all kinds of wild animals.

The people enjoy the garden park. They nod like flowers, wave their hands up and down like tree branches, start and stare like wild animals, glint in the fading sunlight like the windows of the shrine with red sunlight pouring out through its green door. The trees are like the breathing fringe of the twilit sky, reflecting timelessly melancholy thin sweetness in the softening shadows while the promenaders are half melted into living smoke creatures by the gloom. Then the sun drops below the horizon and the moon jumps up over the trees, engraving all of us with dark vividness against the indigo dusk, everything swinging from red to blue just like that. The promenaders stop where they are and gaze up at a moon that fills nearly all the sky, throwing dimly clear shadows behind the trees, breaking up their smeared huddle so each one stands distinct again.

The events of the day unfold shapelessly; people are getting up and going to bed, working, relaxing, all the time. There are no frenzied commuter hours and there is no diminuendo after a certain time at night. Activity is constant, but less intense. Assiyeh sleeps for about half the day, her small bedroom is almost a closet, filled with the oven-like glow of baffled sunlight.

A knock on the door. The glass man sticks his head

in and gurgles, time to get up. Assiyeh stirs and rises, washes up and eats a typically flavorless Buzzatin breakfast, porridge and hot caffeine water, while reading the newspaper. She checks her money pipe; Buzzatian money consists of living jellies, like violet-tinted bubbles that are slick and cool to the touch but leave no trace on the fingers. The pipe has phosphorescent grooves on its interior, numbered from one to twelve, with one being nearest the bottom, to tell you how much you have left. 4, in this case. She smokes a cigarette in the dark room, looking out the window at overcast day, the looming white topless towers and cliff-like black gulfs between them, criss-crossed by threadlike little skyways. Plumes of steam float by, carried off toward the sea. The glass man enters the room and gurgles again. She remains where she is, and he approaches her.

Later on, another cigarette, made of tasteless Koskon Kanonan tobacco mist caught in a thread that revaporizes as it untwists at the heart of a clear glass cigarette, then time for clothes. She lays out the day's ensemble, dresses, and goes out just as the sun veers to its next station in the sky and all the shadows lean over. This is hard to get used to; she wants to brace herself whenever it happens, as if the planet were a ship on a rolling sea. It is.

The air here is cool, dry, and smells like some kind of aromatic chemical. It's almost never an odor she can name. Sometimes it's a little like the old book smell and sometimes like medicine; the only familiar smell is woodsmoke, which is actually the smell given off by the buildings and the soil after it rains. The streets are kept clean by caterpillar-shaped machines that undulate up and down absorbing dirt.

People in the street are courteous but remote. Buzzati was once a violent frontier town and people learned to be very clear in their etiquette; a person with an inadvertently insulting manner wouldn't have lasted long. The manners are all that remain of that time now. Buzzatins take pride in being discreet, but in a sort of indiscreet way; they like nothing better than a nimble display of delicacy when it comes to saving face for someone else, so at one and the same time they both try to cover for someone else while making themselves conspicuous in the act, and ending up causing mischief of another kind. That said, Buzzatins regard the unheralded act of reputation-rescue, of covering for someone, as particularly noble. The whole of their society works on the basis of merits accumulated in defense of each other's good name. So a man practically throws his wife at her lover in public, announcing, with a carefully cultivated offhandedness, that he will be away on business on such and such days, and encouraging her to visit friends, to do entirely as she pleases. Everyone can tell that this is really a public accusation; the wife knows that anyone seeing her in company with that other man will assume infidelity. The lover has been challenged, and now he must inform the husband, within earshot of everyone, that he too is going away for a time and regrets he cannot attend on the lady.

Assiyeh has an appointment with her advisor, to discuss the possibility of getting Thafeefa assigned to her, or, failing that, having a copy made. She was the best assistant Assiyeh ever had; Assiyeh can't stop thinking about her. Thafeefa standing there when they had to say goodbye, her fists in her eyes, crying. Thafeefa's sobs echo back to her every single day, heralding a wave of fierce tenderness that leaves Assiyeh aching to hold her. Has she forgotten her? Been assigned to someone else? Assiyeh sighs. Or is she missing her, lonely, sad and bored? Pining?

What will happen if it works out? Buzzatins all live alone; the housing committee took forever to confirm her application for the apartment she's living in, since the glass man is neither an individual person in the usual sense nor an appliance or piece of property either. Assiyeh told them she hardly ever removed him from his closet charging station, and that seems to have done it. It was a good thing they didn't ask to see the so-called "charging station." It was all bullshit. The glass man didn't sleep in her bed, but then he didn't sleep at all. While she slept, he would go out for walks, explore the town, come up with reports of new and interesting places to go, things like that. But Thafeefa, as a biological creature who eats and sleeps, would by law have to have her own place. They would have to find their two places side by side.

Public transportation is much the same. The cable cars look like long strings of big, clear beads, each of which is a single-occupancy car. Only the older trams, which swing precariously through space on skinny, suspended tracks, listing crazily now, have the usual kind of cars. People sit apart anyway, gazing at their hands folded in their laps, or at the floor, or at the aphorisms engraved in chrome panels set into the polished brown bakelite mouldings, or out the windows. Buzzatins carry no personal electronics of any kind; they wear mechanical watches. The static electricity in the air would fry any ordinary electric device, and so far no one has been able to devise a form of insulation that does not mysteriously disintegrate after a few days of exposure to the open. The trams and cable cars are all run by reeling spools, lit by faint, chemical illumination that glows soft greens and oranges. There's an avid silence out in public. Everyone lives alone, but everyone is expected to be involved with at least one other person. Public displays of affection are icily received, but this is because it's taken for granted that one peck on the cheek, one light embrace, must explode in passion. Anyone capable of holding back after even the slightest physical overture is considered impotent. The intense privateness of the Koskon Kanonans extends to sexual practices and nothing consensual is forbidden, but this means that speculation about each other's sex lives is intense. It's a hallmark of friendship, and considered in the light of an enjoyable pastime, trying to imagine what the people you know get up to. Marriage is unknown, largely because Koskon Kanonan property is distributed bureaucratically. Most Koskon Kanonans are entangled in webs of confused relationships. There are over seventy different kinds of officially registered sexual relationships. This means that most Koskon Kanonans make general assumptions about others—most commonly, that everyone is bisexual and involved with at least one person of each gender and then possibly a few constructs. Whether or not this is actually the case is something known only partially, only to certain bureaucrats, and kept secret from the general population at their own request, so they would not be deprived of the pleasure of speculating.

The bureaucracy field that surrounds everything that

happens on the planet functions exactly like magic, the bureaucrats are the wizards, and the paperwork are spells. Send a form here, and people gather there, erect a house, fill it with furniture. Assiyeh is looking for the right form for a love spell that will reunite her with Thafeefa. Her absence is too painful and distracting. The bureaucracy is ubiquitous and centerless, unlike the government, which is housed in offices with pebble glass doors and cracked leather chairs. Koskon Kanonan politicians are all like private eyes and amateur detectives. Sam Spades, Philip Marlowes, Miss Marples, Hercule Poirots, Sherlock Holmses. They are constantly in motion, interviewing people, irritating the police with their questions and alternate interpretations of events, figuring things out on the fly. They never meet formally; instead, their dedicated chroniclers, secretaries, Watsons, boon companions, record their aphorisms and observations, then draw on these to formulate proposals that they circulate among themselves. The proposal that has survived by the end of these punishing rounds of criticism is then implemented by the bureaucrats. There are no elections; anyone can go to any of the detective politicians, anyone can try their hand at that particular sort of detective work. Those who haven't got the knack usually drift out of it into something else, maybe becoming companions, maybe plumbers. Plumbers are very highly respected on Koskon Kanona—watching plumbers, electricians, skilled craftsman at work is one of the chief forms of entertainment, occupying the place of athletics in other societies. Plumbers et al are ranked on a planetary basis, and the top ten global plumbers are role models, culture heroes, and get profiled on trading cards.

Another glance aside, into the crystal ball vortex of the glass man's head—Assiyeh sees herself walking with swift purposeful steps into the crystal darkness beneath massive low Roman arches, her dark olive face underlit by the soft glow of her white blouse. She climbs a flight of shallow stone steps up to a cathedral-like portico with many pairs of broad, featureless rectangular doors.

The interior is a void, though not so dark that its great depth and spaciousness could be mistaken. Dim lights reach out to her from remote constellations, shining on doors lining corridors without walls or ceilings. Walking between these modernistic doors, she finds herself flanked by a silent escort of two bald old giants with thick tufts of unkempt hair sprouting above around and from their ears, to steer her to SII33.

They pass through a series of sets, each from a different, nameless film, or painting. There's a nineteenth-century storeroom of bare boards, packing crates, no lights, everything grayed out in the glare from two white windows. Now she's crossing a round rumpus room with white filligree skylights and a shag-carpeted conversation pit around a raised hearth with a white trumpet-shaped flue, like a 1970's jumpsuit future ski lodge. Now they're in a torchlit grotto with classical and Egyptian statuary. A Chinese scholar's house, with chairs and low desks and carved screens and water feature serenities and pungent lacquer and rustling heavy silks.

The scene finally resolves and Assiyeh is in there alone. The lumbering giants who brought her here just melt away when the time is right. The room seems to be projecting out into space high up in the mountains. The whole of one side is angled like a big windowbox; slatey mountains in the distance under a dark lid of clouds, all in sharp telephoto focus. Lightning flashes out there, in between the mountains, silhouetting the nearer ones and lighting up the more distant ones.

The room has small tables scattered all over, like the aftermath of a very tidy cocktail party. A swarm of fireflies dance above the hearth. The walls are covered in busy wallpaper whose chief color is orange, with green and white and yellow and pink and sky blue dingbats and ribbons. There are comparably elaborate rugs. Assiyeh crouches in front of the fireplace and peers at the luminous motes. A shadow crosses the room behind her. It might have stirred up a little draft as it went by, because she turns quickly to look. The shadow is an incomplete figure, colorless and transparent, but as it turns near the window the daylight illuminates its heart, which is dark blue with chalk red vessels. Assiyeh homes in on the heart like a falcon sighting a mouse. She says something to the figure, but her voice is drowned out somehow. I tune my hearing until it registers: a steady rumble, as of vast telluric forces stirring and whirring, shakes the air. The hearted shadow goes on moving around the room, straightening pictures on the wall, adjusting and dusting the bric-a-brac. Assiyeh varies the tone of her voice, trying to find a frequency that will get through the vibration.

"What's that booming?" she asks, again and again.

The shadow pauses. Judging from the rotation of the heart and the rusty outline, the shadow has turned toward her, like someone who thinks they've just heard a ghost. A woman who looks like Kodak Shirley enters the room from behind a secret panel in the bookshelf at the same moment, crosses to where the shadow is, and, watching where she steps, she puts her feet right in the footprints of the shadow, and vanishes. Now the shadow has a solid, opaque appearance, the hairless silhouette of a hermaphrodite who seems to have a serpent coiled around its neck.

"That hum is the geobureaucratism of Koskon Kanona," the shadow whines. Its voice is like pure shortwave distortion; it has particular tonal attributes, none of which can she clearly associate with anything like gender or age. "I am surprised that you have not learned by now to recognize it."

The shadow steps between Assiyeh and the mountains.

"The vibration is what gives these windows, and a fortiori the scene they open onto, their special clarity."

"You wanted to see me?" Assiyeh says. "SII33?"

The shadow appears to stiffen, as if it has taken offense at being addressed abruptly.

"Who are *you?*" it asks, as if it were asking, who do you think you are?

"Assiyeh Melachalos."

"Ah," the shadow says, and perambulates around the room, avoiding the center, leaving the floor and slithering along the walls instead, up to the ceiling, then down again, talking quietly all the time.

"Here, evolution developed in a bureaucratic way ... most efficient of ways ..." the voice murmurs distractedly, automatically. "Instead of survival of the fittest, here plants and animals survived because they could wait in line, get just the right protein in just the right spot, produce a reference from the right fungus. All of life here grew in locks and keys ..."

This sounds to me like patter. Assiyeh turns in place, watching the shadow slither down over the pane of the big window, like a paper doll cut from a dingy shower curtain. As the light passes through its membrane, a badge with the words MANAGING CENSOR becomes visible, hiding the heart.

"I understand," the voice says with sudden sharpness, "that you have petitioned our department for a copy of a biological computer human analogue?"

"Yes," Assiyeh says.

"The original of which belongs to the *Izallu Imeph*?"

"Yes."

"And that original is named ...?"

"Thafeefa."

The outline floats out just under the ceiling, all dark again. The snake around its neck arches itself down and the giant member dangles, making parentheses around the Managing Censor's hand gestures.

"You will have to fill out an extraordinary form."

This sounds ominous.

"Who do I give this to?" Assiyeh asks, pulling out the form she brought with her.

The shadow pivots in midair, swinging itself head downwards.

"Let me see!"

It snatches the paper away and reads it over with its finger tips like braille. It sighs.

"No," it says, sounding a little disgusted. "This is not

for me. You must send that ... *thing* to the Censoring Councillor in 19CGT."

The shadow drops the form and something like a red rat or weasel grabs the form and twists out of sight. It had a little badge over its heart, too. The potted fern has a badge. So does the figure in the gloomy painting over the fireflyplace.

Now that I notice, even the furniture is wearing badges.

It transpires that the fillout on an "extraordinary form" involves Assiyeh getting into a bulky canvas suit that stands on a metal frame behind a curtain over there, and then climbing out the window into that forlorn landscape. She's going to have to cross the desolate plain and climb that high mountain far off in the dim distance. The form can only be found at its base, and can only be filled and submitted at its peak. The shadow suggests Assiyeh take a look first through a pair of opera glasses. Evidently there's a line of people waiting at the base of the mountain, long enough to be seen from here. Assiyeh climbs into the suit grumpily.

"Anything else?" she asks, once she has it on. The collar is a metal gorget. She looks like she's sticking her head up out of a manhole.

The shadow points impressively to a spear standing in the corner behind the metal frame. Assiyeh picks it up and hefts it while the shadow throws the window open. A blast of air fills the room sending papers and the lighter knick-knacks flying. Assiyeh doesn't need to be shown the metal rings down the front of the suit, but slides the spear into them. The butt end is going to wag around her face. She climbs down the rope ladder that the shadow has just tossed over the sill.

Assiyeh climbs down a hundred feet from the high window sill, the rope ladder swinging in space before a sheer rock wall. The moment she alights on the ground, the ladder lifts away. Assiyeh begins to walk directly toward the mountain. Her feet kick up sputters of static and green sparks that rise in swaying streaks and disappear. The canvas suit protects her against electrocution by the ground's latent electrical charge. As she makes her way down a short slope to the level of the plain, a nozzle in the neck of her suit begins to smoke out a little shimmery plume of chemistry, breaking ozone down into regular oxygen.

It's as dead out here as a giant parking lot. Something is making a sound like crickets, but nothing obviously living can be seen. There's just the sound.

There's no wind, but there are big inflated things of all different shapes and sizes rolling about the land. What happened to that intense wind through the window, she wonders irrelevantly. Many of the inflatables have windows in them, and even little lights on inside, like balloon houses. Assiyeh goes up to one and it tumbles toward her, gathering speed. She tries to get out of the way, but the thing swerves with her. Then she remembers the spear—that's the right move. She jabs awkwardly at the thing, punching holes in it, and the released gas jets it away from her and out of range of her static attraction. I don't know if it's alive. It has an organic appearance.

Now Assiyeh has to keep that spear working constantly to make any progress at all, and she pretty soon realizes she can't stick to the straight path to the mountain. The big tumblers threaten to bowl her over, maybe plant themselves on top of her. If that happens, she's liable to be pinned and stuck in her bulky attire. The little ones pose the same threat if enough of them can pile on top of her. Assiyeh starts zig-zagging, connecting the dots of the little piles of stones and slightly elevated places, where she seems to be less at risk from the tumblers. Up ahead there are patches thick with tumblers she'll have to avoid. She plots out a path, pausing now and then to crush a microtumbler under her boot. Sweat drips from her nose and her eyes are watering, but she can't touch them with her rough gloves or sleeve. And her staticky hair is starting to stand on end. Assiyeh sets her jaw. She grabs one of the metal rings used to hold the spear in place and rips it from her suit with a great effort, then pulls her hair back through and around it. So that's that taken care of.

I'll be back after lunch.

*

I'm back.

She's still plodding along. No food or water. The mountain looks about as far away as it did when I left. The sky is the same, like the ocean upside down. The only noise is Assiyeh's heavy breathing, the cricket sound, the jingle of the empty spear loops, the buzz and sputter of her staticky feet, and the occasional hollow boom of a tumbler as she pokes it away ...

...

This just keeps going on the same way, so I'll check in tomorrow at breakfast.

*

It's tomorrow. No change. Assiyeh looks like hell. She's stumbling, gasping, her jaw is hanging, there's iron filings all over the inside of her mouth, and her eyes are glazed. Whenever a tumbler comes near, anguish twists her face, and the effort to jab it away is so great she nearly falls flat making it. She can't lie down—the tumblers will bury her in minutes.

Well, but she's made it. She doesn't notice, but the ground under her feet is different, the sparks aren't coming up when she steps any more, and the tumblers are all behind her. I want to yell out to her that's she can stop, but she's still in mush mode. There she is, crawling up a slope of loose rocks to take her place at the back of the line. Everybody on the line is sitting down, some still wear their canvas outfits, others have chucked them and stand or sit there in sweat-soaked clothes or stark naked. Just waiting. No conversation. They're all wiped out, they all look like hell, scraping filings off their tongues with their fingernails. The line must have at least a hundred people in it, and it moves irregularly. Assiyeh got in line without any discernible moment of realization, still a zombie. Motionless for what seems like hours, and then shuffling right along. The line starts somewhere up around the bend. Who knows how long it is? There's also something white up there, standing by the front of the line. Assiyeh thinks it must be a lonely guidepost or like a roadside shrine, until a flash of something transparent awakens in her the obvious fantasy that it might be a water cooler. I can see the awareness of her thirst hit her again, and she goes crazy, rips off the steaming canvas outfit and throws the spear into the rocks. Her clothes are wringing wet. After a while, another petitioner, an older man with silver hair and a face the color of boiled lobster, panting, coughing, staggers up the slope and drags himself into place behind Assiyeh in line.

It turns out the white thing is a water cooler, with an elaborately-ornamented porcelain tank. The cup dispenser is long empty, so Assiyeh has to turn her head as far around as it will go and shove it under the tap. She drinks the tepid, slightly stale water in a frenzy, letting it run all over her face.

"Hey!" the older man behind her calls hoarsely. "Hey! Don't waste that!"

By now there are other people behind him too, and they all add their voices feebly to his. But a man in a crisp white outfit is already refilling the tank, whistling a little ditty as water from nowhere pours out from between his uplifted hands. Assiyeh turns the corner. The front of the line is only a dozen or so patrons away. A steel enamel frame has been built into a cleft, and there's a heavy brown curtain there. A yellow hand droops nervelessly between the labia, stirring once in a while to feel the material of the curtains. The first in line watches this hand with a hypnotically fixed eye. When the hand suddenly points at someone, that one is allowed to go in through the curtains.

When Assiyeh's turn finally comes, she pushes through the curtains without being able to see who the hand belongs to, and begins climbing an interminable flight of iron steps that ascends the mountain. She knows she's supposed to get the form at the bottom of the mountain, but there was no place to get any form. Just the stairs. As she climbs, her legs aching unbelievably, her endurance already utterly spent, she is tortured by the idea that she might be turned away at the top for not having the form. She must be thinking that maybe the form was abolished or things have changed so that now you get the form at the peak and maybe submit it at the bottom when you get back down again, or maybe you have to go to some other fucking mountain.

A gap opens in the clouds and the constellations wheel in the opening. Assiyeh is so taken aback by the sight of space, the night sky, untwinkling stars, that she stops where she is. This stairway has no landings, you have to hold on where you are, clutching the framework of the cage, which is made of metal so thin you'll cut yourself if you clutch it. Assiyeh gets a weird look on her face, and she reaches out to the stars in a way that makes me think she's lost it and she's going to try to hug the sky and end up falling through the cage. Instead, her outstretched arms are laved in glowing sky sperm that resolves into a little shower of red bugs, maybe ants, and a sheet of wasp paper—it's the form!

*

Meanwhile—what's going on out there? The sirens wailing in chasmic streets have become caressing croons, the cops are billowy and roly-poly as balloons, their faces are sleeping and rumpled, their hands are floating like bundles of inflatable hot dogs drawing their slack boneless arms up in snaky belly-dance gestures as they walk down the street leaning half backwards—

Meanwhile on screen a full-on pantomime commulistic upsurging has broken out across the US, everybody's dressing freaky and quoting Marx—suddenly the impoverished urbanic, suburran, and rurative are clasped in solidarity and the cops and soldiers are going over— next thing you know bombs are going off everywhere and a clatter of AK-47s, not among the protestors, instead coming from mysterious persons who are alternately attacking them and posing among them, yesterday's terrorists paid by the US to pose as revolutionaries, splitting their earnings to pay for a new form of female circumcision that removes the brain as well as the clitoris and the other half they take to Vegas where suspiciously prescient tycoon types with generic names have already set up halal casinos on a segregated strip built in hours by Chinese companies complete with 24 hour mosques, brothels stocked with wall to wall blondes, and an exact reproduction of the Burger King they demolished Mohammed's house in Mecca to build. Who's story is it? Or which one? I want to walk out of the theater, turn to go, walk right into a screen and look through it to see, on the far side, another darkened theater and the dim flicker over the faces turned toward me, watching me but as an image only, and there's a screen behind those faces and through that the darkened theater and dim flicker over those faces, and to one side and another and in me I see the screens and the faces through the screens.

*

Back to the story.

I'm driving Carolina to see one of the Uhuyjhn cities, and she won't make small talk or flirt back or anything. She takes mescaline and asks me to go back to the story and fill in what happens next.

OK so Assiyeh just found the form, and she looks up, and she sees that there are offices in the sky spreading out like an infinite graph that intersects with the vertex of the mountain peak at a single tingling spark that she can fit through. They're like pueblos quarried into the sky, and they're like opera boxes.

It's that dark corridor with illuminated doors and no walls again, and Assiyeh is going somewhere flanked by the two dandruff giants again. She's like a little girl on an official business call with her father and his twin brother. Their faces are up too high, so she knows them by their dragging heavy hands, their breadloaf fingers curling up into the palms, half covered by stiff white cufflinked cuffs and hanging straight at their sides. Coarse hairs on the backs of the hands. Look up into cavernous, hairy nostrils.

A succession of colorless images flashes on her. The inexplicable movement from one to the other is tied to her steps. Each one ends in a still photo.

A woman, seen from a low angle, in a stone doorway, speaking and twirling a white tablecloth or towel. Stop.

Boys in swim trunks flashing in silhouette past a bright open doorway waving thin arms, one stops framed in the door way to look up at the camera. Stop.

A reclining, supercilious-looking man with a prominent nose talking, cigarette held up near his face, elbow resting on something, then swings it down to ash, lowering heavy-lidded eyes and saying something to himself with a mouth that warps and facets itself. Stop.

Three men rounding a corner post and heading under a dark canopy of stone, the middle man in a pale suit and a snap brim hat and the other two in dark suits with swing ties and bare heads. Stop.

A young girl with a stricken look on her face numbly descending a short flight of stone steps. Stop.

An old woman stands up and begins to harangue someone, her old eyes furious, waving a relentless finger. Stop.

A man, viewed from behind, sitting in a chair with his feet up, waves wash the shore down below, and he's in the grip of a vivid fantasy. Now it lapses, and there's a barely perceptible change; the body slackens, the blood settles and the pressure dome around the head shrinks back down into the brain. Stop.

A boy, starting up out of a nightmare still with his mask of fear, outrage. Betrayed by sleep. Stop.

A woman on a bench, engrossed in reading, circling her thumb against her index finger abstractedly. Stop.

Her own head, hair swinging like a cape, framed against the white arch, under the cloister. Stop. Assiyeh has arrived at the Censors. She is conducted past holding galleries where witches are put to the question. The galleries are light and airy, with tables of fruit, wine bottles standing ready, beer kegs, loaves of bread and blocks of cheese, platters of meat. Beautiful, elflike people flit to and fro to provide the witches with whatever they please. Many of the witches are bobbing in hot tubs or frolicking in fountains, or lounging themselves on curtained couches. These witches are caught and dragged forth from sordid covens where they torture and interrogate each other endlessly, brought here to have confessions extracted from them by high living.

The Censors is a handsome English manor house, not really large, standing out abrupt as a cork in the landscape, surrounded by sweetly unassuming flower beds and vegetable plots, lush trees sparsely scattered with ample room between for bocci ball and badminton and bumbaclotti ball or whatever rich people games they play. Over the door there is a stone head, a lean ascetic face with hawk nose and little round glasses, and pinched lips, flanked by stylized depictions of rejection stamps, pairs of scissors, strikeout grease pencils, airbrushes. Engraved on a banner beneath the face there is a motto that has been censored.

Creak inside; there's a white hall with the floral runner, a grandfather clock and flowers in the brass bowl on marble counter below a mirror that brushes the ceiling below the landing below the skylight below the tall skinny chimneys. The house trembles with people, stepping from room to room with paper sheaves, calling to each other, answering old school phones, tuning an old school radio to a softly singing woman's voice like a crooning cloud, carrying trays of refreshments, and there's a stout man with a white moustache and a straw hat standing outside smoking a battered battle-pipe, visible through one of the wavy windows as he takes a pace this way and then back, scanning the horizon like a retired sea captain. It's fucking quaint let me tell you, like the American Cancellate in Shambleshire. Assiyeh's old man escort peels off like a pair of sidecarred motorcycles and she is instantly transferred to the care of a woman in green tights and a green skirt and green blouse and green cardigan and green earrings with big green leaves in her hair. She conducts Assiyeh into a room full of tables and now they have to walk from one table to another—I think that if they touch the floor they will have to go back to the door and start over.

Their goal seems to be a desk in the corner with a woman sitting at it. She's smoking, reading a newspaper spread on the blotter in front of her. She has a thick mane of white hair and seems to be wearing nothing but a negligently belted kimono, hanging open. It turns out the form Assiyeh retrieved is only the form for getting the right form, which she receives from the woman with the white hair. Rather than go back over the desks, Assiyeh climbs out the window and lets herself down into the garden. Garden of prepositions. The with to the at. Down the above when. She perches on the rim of the cement birdbath and fills the form out on the low-slung backside of a marble nymph, then goes back to the house and calls up to one of the windows. A man's hand, a very fine, manicured, bejewelled hand, but plainly a man's, unfurls out the window like the arm of a sea anemone and takes the form very elegantly between the last knuckles of two fingers. After a moment, a woman's hand, brown calloused and square, but a woman's, with big baubles around the wrist, emerges from the same window with a ticket. Assiyeh takes the ticket, which reads FORM RECEIVED.

*

She looks up at you, half oranged in late afternoon light, looking almost through her eyebrows, smiling already, that is, raising her smile to show it, lips parted, a whitish cloud in her mouth. A wisp escapes around her lip and slithers up her cheek, spreading a little as it goes. She looks for a moment, then, without moving, breaks out laughing at you. Her laughter is a rough, staccato whisper. With a sinking feeling, you see the cloud of smoke unperturbed in her mouth despite the laughter that should plainly be driving it out in gusts, and realize that this is the dry, joyless, demon titter of the late afternoon. It means, "Now *you* are lost, too."

*

As a boy I was always head over heels in love with some girl.

Every September, I got the new grade started right by identifying my obsession-girl for that year. Which of these girls will have the unwanted privilege of being bugged by me?

Half of them probably never knew. None of them could have known the images I fashioned of them. I had a whole icon wall, like a church, somehow dedicated to all and to only one. It's tempting now to think I used to latch on to one to exorcise the others, or at least demote them to handmaidens for the true Empress. There was a pedestal and a golden nimbus. There were heroic rescues and pledges of devotion, riotously delirious hopes and dedicated love songs, unheard, unvoiced, unknown. The other half either deduced my feelings or worse, ambushed by me with my courage hiked up inviting them to join me on the grand adventure that would probably have already started by then if it were ever going to happen.

I never got anywhere, but my approach was not really designed to succeed. And actually I did go places, but never with the girls I hoisted into paradise; it was always with girls who just happened.

But when I was a boy I used to love girls, other boys, adults, places, the weather, trees, travelling, looking around, trespassing, shoplifting, places I hated. I flirted with girls, but then I flirted with the sun and moon. It was all flirting back then. In hindsight I must have been overbrimming with everything, and now that I'm a grown man, and I hate what I love and everything else too down here in the festering automatism of the Misled, now that I am a groan-up ... what? For what? Groan over what? Which is my loss? Which debt?

There's nothing I want more than to breathe in that old childhood love again and feel it now, as a full-groaning man, and I don't think there's anything farther out of reach for me than that. I don't think it's possible. I look at Carolina, whose hair is flying in the wind from the car window, giving her this wildly dashing, everchanging outline, throwing her fragrance all around, and what I feel inside me is corridors, corners, turns, knots, darkness. I try to remember what it used to feel like, opening, and what comes to mind is the beautiful sun outside and a pressure of light inside.

"But," I say, speaking for the first time in two and a half hours, "what makes memories memories is that you never live them. You live, and then you have memories, but you don't live the memory. Even reliving a memory still involves this barrier between now and then because … you remember *now*.

"If that bullshit is true, then I might as well remember anything, if I never lived any of my memories. If I never lived any of my memories, then how are they mine? There's just memories, but they don't belong to anyone except the way you might say a country belongs to you. The country doesn't care. The memories don't care. The inflexibly one-way street moments follow does not prevent me from remembering whatever, in fact, it allows it."

Shit, Carolina is looking at me, that means she's probably paying attention, and I can't just ramble on, I have to make it good or she'll think I'm an idiot, and even in her stoned-godlike point of view she already thinks I'm an idiot.

"If you want to know what I mean, here's what I mean. You don't find reality by divesting yourself of fantasies, and that's not because that's a fantasy too—a divestment-of-fantasy fantasy … it's because the fantasies are street level. A one way street. You can't have just fantasy. It's not 'the ghoulish mirror,' it all begins under the street and goes all the way up to heaven like Roman title deeds. There's a reason that money/power world is so grey and boring and replete with repellencies, because it's advantageous to fantasizers of a certain class to promulgate that idea that there is a Walter Mitty gulf between that money world and the fantasy world. That money isn't fantasy. Fantasy is over there, not here. Never *here*. Take that barrier out, and you see the magic in the money, the astrological, qabbalistic haruspicery of runes and hexagrams; yeah I can talk like a book sometimes—you see that ... that the code of the economist is a poetics, and they are singing the world like Vainamoinen except that instead of trying to make that song as beautiful and noble as possible, those fucking bet-hedger ... knuckleshits are singing this fucking lying song of deception and just stupidly blind thinking that says ... that says there's a magic world but you can't ever have it unless you buy a shee shee expensive approximation of it for your estate from participating retailers and if you can't manage to wangle that you're just stuck with the bad world where all the failures live, kind of. You're a bad person. Their fantasy world song, they camouflage it treacherously, as the dullest, most boring fantasy of doldrum-doldrumland TV news, so ... people won't recognize it for what it is—a song—a *lousy* song—and start singing for themselves, sing a world for them. Because any asshole can sing. Singing starts from right here, there is no other singing. Training or no, you just sing. Being a human being means—not even that, not even that—being alive, just living, means you can sing right now, already. But people get trained somehow to sing this one song only, or this one way, that goes like 'Oooohhhh, in some *other* world ...' Or sometimes 'Ooooohhhh, a long long time ago ...' So nowhere and never do you get what you want, and every street is just more trudging-through-the-yuck, clutching a beautiful dream that never gets any closer, because it's designed not to, and isn't even theirs and is what's really propping up the yuck. You marry the idea that nobody ever can get what they want in this world, so might as well go ahead in the fake stuff and nothing happens. But when the hard-nosed types tell you to stop dreaming and face reality they just mess you up a different way, because you don't find reality by divesting yourself of fantasies like I said. When they say, boy you better wake up and face your responsibilities and get real, what they mean is, get with the fantasy lifestyle. They actually don't make your fantasies for you, they just provide ingredients, but the main point is that, it's like lunch, you have to have lunch, this thing called LUNCH, but you can have whatever you want as long as it only takes thirty minutes and then you do it in fifteen. But if you want to eat lunch in the morning and have a five hour breakfast starting at noon, suddenly that's fantasy. Lunch isn't a fantasy, but that midday superbreakfast is. You don't get real by 'getting real' you have to find what's real. To find that by working with it, by being real and making it, and you don't work with reality for no reason; you have to want something you can get, and people want more than food and shelter and those things. Or what I mean is, when people want food and shelter, they want something other than that phantasm of government rations and barracks, slums and slop. People want beautiful food and beautiful shelter."

The wrongness of the idea that *beauty is extra* is what I've been talking about in this whole paragraph you skipped. Carolina is looking at me. What? Don't complain that I don't get any character development. This is my fucking "character!"

I have to get Carolina to the Uhuyjhn city. According to her, there's one up there somewhere. The Uhuyjhn are setting up their own cities on earth alongside ours, she says. But I can't remember where I parked shitty hatchback.

Etsimen is such a small town, just three lights, but I can't find it. Every block is lined with parked cars. People are sleeping in them, and the windshields all have fog inside. Even when the windows are cracked, the fog stays inside, like a cloud of smoke in the mouth. They look like people sleeping, all splayed out. Carolina wants to interview an Uhuyjhn, or at least a human representative. I don't really know what she's talking about, and I think she may be trying to locate content from hallucinations in real life, if I can speak that way without invalidating my whole long diatribe on the topic you may remember. It just happened. Carolina takes off all her clothes in the car and lets the wind blast her whole body, she likes that. I like it too, but it does conjure alarming scenarios. She's walking ahead of me, naked still. Am I going to do anything? I'd just piss her off. She goes into a bar I can't see, just a streak of faint light reflecting off an invisible door. I follow her in. The lights are all orange and by them I note everyone is naked but me. As usual, Carolina knew.

A skinny man waves at her from a booth, and she slides into the empty seat. I sit beside her not sure whether I am really part of this, but neither of them seem to care one way or another. My clothes may not make me invisible.

The pair shake hands briefly and Carolina says something I can't make out because I'm still sitting down and pointed the wrong way. She may have introduced me. The thin man has thin hair and a big nose. He sits with his big hands folded on the table in front of him.

"It's all arranged," he says. He's speaking Spantuguese with a weird accent. "We go from here to a farm about six kilometers outside of town."

He hands her a little pad of paper and a pen. She draws three characters on it and hands it back to him. He folds the paper into the palm of his left hand and, when we get up to go out, it's gone. So's the pad and pen. We go out together and he leads us to one of the parked cars with fogged windows. We get in, the air inside close and stale, and Carolina indicating that I should drive. The thin man gets in the back seat, where a chubby little boy is sleeping, wrapped in a white lace blanket and holding a long piece of striped, hard candy.

Following skinny's directions, I drive us out of town into the utter blackness of the desert. The dirt road is level and free of rocks, a pale fleshy brown in the headlights. The lights catch on the crumbly borders of the road, which flashes up brightly against the inky black. Now I catch sight of a low ranch building tucked in some landscape folds, with a few big trees and a wooden fence. The house is a slightly paler blue in this darkness, and there are no lights inside. Skinny has been watching behind us, sitting sideways on the back seat and dividing his attention between our rear and the way forward, giving his directions impersonally.

"Turn off the headlights and stop a moment," he says.

He gets out and, after looking around for a few minutes, he walks, with a kind of strutting, flamingo-like stride, over to the wooden fence, which is parallel to the road here. He squats and lifts the wooden bars, holding them to his chest. With them out of the way, he waves us to come on, through the fence. I nose the car through, stop again, he puts the bars back and comes up to the car without getting in, points up toward the house a few dozen yards away.

"Pull the car around behind the house, out of sight of the road," he says. "I will let them know we're here."

He heads for the house. I get the car around the corner, swerving a little to avoid running over a shovel and then pivoting to avoid the wheelbarrow that pops up in front of me. My eyes are getting used to this blue, arid darkness with its deep indigo shadows. The stars, motionless for a while, suddenly veer to new positions in the sky as we get out of the car. The skinny man is sticking out of a window like a house-centaur monster. He waves to us.

"Don't go in the front," he says. "Come through here."

I offer to help Carolina up, but she kisses my cheek and then climbs nimbly inside. I follow and we're in a dark, shuttered room, lit only by this one window, with a doorway facing it. There's a clean linen smell here. Like grandma's house. Tidy country farmhouse. Cornmeal smell. Skinny shuts the sash and pulls the interior shutters closed, deepening the darkness. The air is fresh, not close, as if we were still outdoors.

"OK, come on," Skinny says. I can dimly make out his form going through the door, and then Carolina. Skinny shuts the door and then an orange light swings up into view as someone lifts a hidden lamp up from under a counter.

But it's actually much later, at least, later that week, that I am walking with Carolina at night down another unlit street in dark Etsimen, where all the people are silhouettes and all the lights are weak, and you only get flashes of faces in the occasional streak of light, someone comes out a front door, already backlit but you can see the person behind them, that face in the shrinking gap before the door blends back into the black prop housefront row and the slender figure who emerged is slipping away in flip flops or bare feet, carrying a bucket or a drooping chicken or a bundle of wood. The streets here have no smell at all, it doesn't make scents get it? We're out walking, Carolina is high and quiet as usual and she keeps swaying accidentally up against me like she's ready to drop. The nice thing about a dark city like this is you can see the stars overhead. The sky is so full of stars it's frightening. In a completely unlit street, you can actually see by starlight alone, just a little. I turn a corner and there's nothing at the end of the street, it just stops down there, and some contrivance of landscape has levelled us with the horizon so the stars are shining not above but directly ahead of me, as though I were sticking out among them, and if it weren't for the close embrace of the dark, seamlessly attached fronts lining the street my old boyhood terror of being sucked out into space would have paralyzed me.

We can't go straight. The streets here keep forking. And they are getting deeper and darker, like deep railway cuts, tighter and tighter and then a white plaza sprawls out all around us, all strung with weak but numerous electric bulbs powered by a few gas generators and market full of webbed bag shoppers. There are fish from somewhere lying splayed out whole on heaps of ice, no crustaceans or shellfish owing to a popular superstition that maintains it's bad luck to eat them, tubs of pipe tobacco with or without weed with or without tobacco, plastic coolers filled with weird local sorghum beer that everyone seems to drink and nobody seems to like least of all me, manioc, sweet potatoes, plantains, and beans. Beans plus starch, eighty different ways, washed down with weird sorghum lager. Then, man or woman, you smoke a pipe. Everyone here has one. You have to be careful when you light up, too, because everything comes sprayed with discount rum and I don't know if it's booze or the kerosene they pep it up with but the fire coming off the initial light will blaze up into your face if you hang over it.

We're over toward one corner of the market. The buildings all have lights shining up from their bases like flashlight faces, and I'm taking in the people passing by along the fringes of the market. It seems the more ostentatious citizens of Etsimen, rather than going somewhere else, probably because there isn't anywhere else, stake out the periphery of the market for a ritual promenade in the evenings. These aren't necessarily the richest citizens, it's the ones who are the biggest-show offs over on the far side of the square, while here it's the more down-dressed or somber ones. On the far side, a naked man is singing a patriotic song on top of a simple stage to very loud distortion with some music somewhere mixed in with it. Glistening with oil and perspiration, a group of Vehueqnim women trots into the square not far from us, hooting in unison and waving wands. They will make a circuit of every square tonight, I don't know why. The people passing us turn to look and I happen to glance their way, mainly because we're going largely against the flow of foot traffic and local color, and then a few dozen paces later I stop and look back. There's nothing back there—yes, there, just disappearing around a corner. The same woman—middle aged, small, tweedy, talking animatedly, escorted by two extremely large men who are not friends or colleagues of hers I'm sure. In my mind's eye I'm seeing what I saw a moment ago when they passed us—that woman's face.

"I just saw Tripi."

Carolina stares at me, instantly alert. She doesn't have to say anything.

We take off after them but they are already well along the street and a crowd is boiling up down there, spilling out of a place with a bonfire out in front to the sound of accordion music and some brass—I think I see a shortcut and take off running down an alley that branches and I keep following the turns angling over to keep to the right, there's the bonfire ahead of me, good, turn again, to my left is loud rock and roll guitar, I can run here, the alleys are full of junk but they aren't blocked with people and turn into an alley and they are there, right in front of me, a few dozen yards away. The woman is still talking, gesturing, persuading, cajoling, and one of the men grabs her by the chin and shakes her head to shut him up. I take a step and Carolina's hand is flat on my chest, holding me back.

"I don't like that."

"Don't do it."

"That makes me mad."

"Don't do it."

A moment later they turn back out into the street and in the time it takes us to get to there ourselves they are gone.

"Was that her?"

"Yes."

"You're sure."

"Of course."

"What now?"

"Keep looking."

Back at the farm, through the window, go into that darkened room with a fresh laundry smell, cornmeal, the lantern swings up like an orange ghost from behind a counter, illuminating a big man in a t-shirt. He has orange skin and dense black eyebrows over small, far-away eyes. His eyes are like craters in the underlight. He steps out from behind the counter with a heavy tread of bare feet, and drags up a wooden chair, putting the lantern down on a piece of furniture, white and gold and full of rounded carvings, like Louis quatorze. Skinny meanwhile is doing something in the next room. I see him with a big enamel kettle and there's a little whoosh and glow of flame, slosh and gurgle of water in there.

The big man shakes left hands introducing himself.

"Kerman," he says. He doesn't meet our eyes even as he gives first Carolina and then my hand a single firm squeeze, sitting heavily down, hands falling into his lap. He seems tired, nodding, breathing deeply through his nose.

"This your farm?" I ask.

Kerman makes a swinging gesture with his hand I don't know how to interpret. I think he's under hypnosis, or high.

He rubs his palms on his thighs, and keeps doing it. I'm getting the idea he's crazy. Every now and then he takes a faster breath in among the even ones.

"You OK?" he asks after being quiet for a long time.

"Yeah," I say. Carolina is looking at her fingers.

"You going to say anything?" I ask her.

She just glances up at me, then back at her hands.

"You waiting for me to leave?" I ask.

Oscar comes in with a TV tray and sets it down, pulls up a seat, and makes the mate on it. Then he passes it to Carolina, she to me, I gesture at Oscar but he indicates Kerman so I give it to him, Kerman takes some, then Oscar. A few rounds go by in silence. Then Oscar sets the mate down and Kerman draws a long inhale.

He explains that his cousin has a farm way up in the mountains. Last week, this cousin was out checking a stand of cacao trees at the far edges of his property when he noticed some signs of activity near the ruins of another, even more remote farmhouse. He sneaked up and got a better look; watched for a bit and eventually saw two armed men hustling Tripi out of the house and into a van that drove off. He waited there for hours, came back other times, but there was nothing. He even approached the house, but it was deserted. So, he'd probably seen them leaving for good.

Kerman lunges forward as though he were going to headbutt me, but he's only straightening out to reach into his pocket. He opens his fist and shows us a handful of brown things: cigarillo ends, with tar-stained filters. Carolina takes Kerman's hand and pulls it toward her, flicks the ends this way and that with her finger.

Kerman puts the ends in a heap by the lamp and straightens again, this time swatting the other pocket. He produces a clear plastic pinch-strip bag with a few strands of grey and dark hair, all the same length, inside.

"May I keep this?" Carolina asks.

Kerman shakes his head and puts his hand back out.

She returns it to him.

Back at the farm, we're brought into a low room, or rather a room made low with many low hanging hangings, and there's Kerman in a cloud of incense smoke and a homemade shrine built around a bed with someone lying in it, a woman with a bandaged face.

Kerman gestures at her with the lit stick of incense in his hand.

"Tripi."

So what did happen to her?

*

She went off for a smoke, saw a small child, naked, watching her from the scrub, and went to investigate. She followed the child through the bushes, walking down the slope, carefully placing her feet from stone to stone for a sure purchase, and therefore leaving no recognizeable footprints. Then she fell, straight down, having missed a sheer drop screened by branches. She fell twelve feet, upright, landing square on her feet with a shock, her right ankle buckled and she collapsed. Eventually she found she could stand, her ankle hurt but unbroken; but there was no way back up the slope. Either the face was too sheer, or the shrubbery too dense to climb through. She called out—no reply. Then she began searching along the base of the slope for a way up, heading in the direction of the gas station. But she was turned around. The gas station was actually receding behind her. There was no sign of the child, no path, no building, no place that child could have come from. She remembered the face, the huge eyes, the uncertain mouth, the streak of dirt across the lips and chin, the short, silky hair falling slantwise across the little forehead, the fleshy little hands. She had not imagined the child.

Tripi wandered for three days. When she realized she had set out in the wrong direction, she reversed her tracks, only to realize many hours later that she had not quite reversed them enough. She must have gone off on a tangent somehow, which hours of walking widened into a serious deviation. The area is folded in shallow canyons, trackless and uniformly covered in dense, monotonous brush. Knowing which way was east didn't do her much good; she couldn't manage to get up the slopes to a ridge line, being rebuffed at each attempt until her clothes were quilled with thorns and the broken ends of sharp twigs. She couldn't make much headway along the valley bottoms either, where the foliage was thickest. Her best way was slightly above the bottom, just a bit up the slope, walking sideways along those places where the topsoil falls away from exposed puzzle rock that has looks solid but will often tumble apart in geometric sections when seized with the hand. She kept going for over eighteen hours before finally allowing herself to drop on her calves, exhausted, covered in dust, sore, thirsty. She toppled over without clearly realizing it and slept, woke up sweating in the full light of the sun, cramped, parched, hungry.

The path gave her a new rush of energy. She found it only about twenty minutes after she'd managed to throw off her torpor—an ash-white scar slicing through sullen desert scrub. She followed until it died two hours later in the middle of a broad, flat, empty expanse of brush. The path sieved apart into dozens of dwindling pathlets and was gone. No buildings, no remnants, just the flat land around her, the mountains in the middle distance and the hills on this side. There was nothing else to do. Numbly, Tripi turned to retrace her steps along the path. All the way back she kept her eyes riveted on the path, as if it might jump out from under her if she took her eyes from it, absently counting the dim impressions of her footprints, reclaiming them like so many rejected offerings, one by one. When it began to rain, she counted it the one barb of bad luck she'd managed to miss, because she'd made it back to the place where she'd first encountered the trail before the rain could efface her tracks. The rain was not heavy, but it persisted. It soaked into her very gradually, but she welcomed its coolness at first. It didn't really slake her thirst, it wasn't heavy enough for that, but drawing the air through her open mouth helped a little. The dust was rinsing away, and in time she was able to wring some water out of her blouse to drink.

Her mind was just an ember and all her political concerns, everything she was normally preoccupied with as President of Achrizoguayla, had become unreal to her now completely immediate perspective. She was dimly aware of the vast, strangely untenanted space in her mind, of the unwonted stillness and suspense there. A President alone in the desert is just another creature. How do you relate the two?

She had been walking for hours in an intermittent misting rain when she glanced up, woke up, and froze, staring at that child, who was looking at her through the branches. The branches, the posture, the hands, the streak of dirt, their relative positions, all was exactly as it had been the first time, except for her, and the sight startles her into unplanned speech.

"Why did I follow you?" she croaks.

Is that the same child? The child turns and steps out of sight in the plant screen. Tripi continues down the path. Was she hallucinating? Was that child following her this whole while? Or did it haunt a particular spot, meaning she might be near to the place where she'd first lost her way? The air is not clear, but she seems to be too far out from the slopes of the hills for that. Perfect isolation, perfect stillness, perfect freedom. She could throw off her clothes and decide this is home. She continues along the path, and as she moves through the drizzle it wafts in her face like cool linen. The desert smells all become more distinct in the wet, now that all the dust is flushed out of the air.

The child steps out onto the path ahead, about a dozen meters away, into the center of her field of vision plain and clear for the first time. Tripi knows now that this is no human child, even though there is nothing weird about its appearance, no hooves, no tail, no wings. The child stands nearly in profile, paused in midstep as though it were about to reach out and snatch a bird, hands ready, one leg flexed, like a photograph, but it feels, irrespective of how it looks, it feels as if there's no one there, as if Tripi were all alone. There's none of that indefinite physical sensation of the presence of another. But the figure is if anything too clear and distinct, too solidly dark, to be a phantom. What is a phantom? she wonders.

No, too clear, far too clear. That motionless, dark

figure, almost a silhouette whose every feature and detail is nevertheless only becoming more and more sharp with a painfully sharp distinctness from the white crescents of its fingernail ends to the tiny triangle of reddish flesh at the corner of the eye standing out now with an implacably augmenting and painful clarity. Tripi is caught, staring with an anguish racing toward excruciating pain, and something flashes from the motionless child, like a transparency of its outline darting across the intervening space it slams the center of her forehead like the slap of a powerful but disembodied wave, sending a shock through her whole body but landing in her mind. She drops to her knees clasping her head in her hands and unable to tear her eyes away from the child as the sky and landscape wink out behind it in pure blackness and agony and and silence, and blinding glares zoom across space crashing into her like mortars, she sees the landscape again, surmounted by a huge block of light, and three sheets of light beneath it.

"They're trying to communicate."

She blinks, and when she opens her eyes again she sees the sun float in space like a monster swinging the earth out of the stars and raising it up over her like a hammer, and all of space alive with movement, intelligent movement, and great cords of reason tying huge objects together across vast distances, and children made of reason.

*

The right side of her face is bandaged. Is it really Tripi? She should have a small mole or birthmark on her right cheek, but the bandage covers it, and the skin is damaged. The mark might have torn off. Or it might never have been there.

Is this Tripi?

PART NINE:
DRUNK WITH SOBRIETY

the perennial airplane, the neverending flight
the wing is like a hallway
man in the aisle—
—"get out" he blurted under his cough
—and I turned my head to look at him, a mistake,
he noticed me, now he knows I can hear his normally
subliminal interventions and I can't put him off with my
JOKE card because I
seem to have lost it somewhere
the apparition of a phantom person in the hallway, the
wing
the big dipper looking like a projection on a screen
only a couple of dozen feet away
my blurred shadow on the wing below the window, a
white patch with an arrow painted on it
where are we going, where are we going, where are we
going—I don't know.
I do know, but I keep forgetting.
the mountains as blue as the sea—flint spear heads,
cocoa and flour, mottlings, and dull lightenings, and
pleached folds like waterpruned fingertips, grey brown
blue and purple, livid rouges, puckered ridge lines, lake of
flattened blue lightning, embossed and shieldlike plateaus,
callouses, mazelike rectangles contrast circuitboarded

regularity with their arbitrary imposition on a color of cooked lobster, now withered like parchment, wrinkled land, white over pink over blue chasms, pink of raw flesh and white snow floored canyons, the snow looks flat plastic and smooth like dried slicks of white glue, glaze, pale terracotta, opaque and mottled glass, now the upper plateaus are delineated in snow stippled with black like stubble poking through shaving cream, broken biscuit, pulverized brick, Mars, now a flatland of long east to west streaks of red and just here a vivid tracery of white, the red is curdling around the Blake engraving lighting water carved, here the relief lines draw themselves, low hills here like battered metal, print of a colossal horseshoe, great flattened fern plumes, blue ridge shadow like a stationary wave, splayed toes and a knotty foot of mountains—

lichtenberg/stein/**berg** figures—snow on the peaks here is grey, snow sketched in rows down the slopes makes them seem blurred—puffy tire tread ranges in sinuous rows, trees seem to grow only along the brinks of the river cuts, the lower brown slopes throw blue lozenge shadows, wildfires like two comets streaming in the foothills, maroon haze at sunset—still flying—the hours stand still—

*

Back over to me with the headlines—not so much The Revelation Deluxe as it is that backwards tug that reminds you of something.

Back in the tunnels and stations—turning halfway around to try to see that woman's face again, never saw her before, never will any more, double checking anyway to make sure she actually is so beautiful, a very ongoing woman!

"There-RIS / an / uptown / 65837 / train / approaching the station / please jump off the platform edge."

Headphones snatch victims in a one-second snare like venus flytraps and hold them while the train is being held momentarily by lack of resources please stop bombarding us with complaints about our venus flytraps.

Station stop. Someone gets up to go and the doors are shut before I notice the glove lying there beneath the seat, and that reminds me of this morning, someone who left a clumsy-looking ball point pen behind on a subway seat, rolling in the butt dip; in fact, everyone is shedding discards wherever I look—batteries and pens and all the sorts of things you find among your personal property without knowing how it got there rain down from pockets and bags covering the floor in a slippery layer of forgotten unwanted pens advertising antidepression, cement company stationery folded up in my pocket with unlabelled, no-area-code phone numbers scrawled on it in someone else's handwriting, and I can't remember if someone gave that to me, if I have someone waiting on a call from me, or if I snatched up this paper somehow to write something else on and then pocketed it, maybe without being able to write anything because I didn't have a crapped-out pen from an auto muffler manufacturer or a laxative dealership. Everywhere you look, there are complete, next-to-nothing fragments of whatever, making some kind of a gesture about a defunct or doomed business, or basically bad idea.

Thinking about all those things, they add up to give me an impression of desperation arising out of fundamental, abject cluelessness. This causes me to feel pity. Sadness and pity, that I can't tell if it's right or wrong, some kind of reactionary sentimentality or maybe I'm seeing something real, I can't tell. I can tell I can't tell.

"Slavies and bondlesmen, this is an unimportant commandment from the private ownership police department. Property is more important than people at all times. Be suspicious. Clutch your shit. If you accidentally make eye contact with a human being, keep it to yourself. Rat out your parents, Ceaucescu your friends, trust the authorities and don't trust each other. Giving money to homeless people is illegal. Backpacks and other large containers of subjects are subject to be burglarized by sneering police."

There's a story I could tell, about a man who carried so many guns all the time he looked crippled. He had to use crutches to get around; his legs wouldn't bend because they were covered with guns, so he had to walk bow-legged to keep the guns in his groin from crushing his balls but they already had and he carried so many guns for self protection, ever since he'd witnessed a mugging in a movie. He couldn't stop thinking about it. That movie mugging had been so scary and humiliating and black-people-involving and class-war, anything but that! He wasn't afraid of being run down by a car (because if that were illegal he couldn't do it to other people). The prospect of being burned alive in a house fire didn't phase him. But the shame of being mugged in a movie with everybody watching was too much, so he went out right away and bought a carton of gun at the bodega and strapped them all on every time he went out and kept piles of them all over his shitty apartment.

Naturally everyone could tell he was heavily armed and that made everyone to say the least *wary*. He didn't want to give rise to a lot of causeless alarm, so, whenever he was in a social situation—and usually this happened only when the other person found him or herself trapped with him on the subway or in an elevator or in line at the DMV or the bank—he would calmly explain that he wasn't planning on shooting anyone, and that a small fiduciary consideration would go a long way toward firming up a guarantee that he wouldn't somehow shoot you in particular. So, by dint of his intelligent fear and friendly predatoriability, he became not only a safer, but a richer, man, and that's SuperAesop's moral, boys and boys—"the wise man shoots and robs everybody"—the end.

*

"Political?"

"No," she says. "She ran off with a hundred thousand."

Mateo shakes his head, almost a shiver, and scrunches up his face.

"Ech, this is the whole job you give me? This isn't important enough for me."

"She's American."

"American? It's political if she's American."

"You know what I mean."

"... When by?"

"As soon as possible. She could leave the country any time."

"Why hasn't she already left?"

"She knows we watch the airport. She did an airport job. ... Look, she's done this before. She tried to run with fifteen kilos, nearly fifteen kilos."

"And you trusted her with a hundred thousand?"

"I didn't trust her with anything!" she says, pushing her index finger into her own chest. "I said 'no more.' Luitu was the one who was spellbound by her citizenship and all the easy ways she was going to get things into America for him. He said, the fact that she decided not to run—run with the fifteen kilos—shows that she could be trusted. 'Everybody thinks about it,' he said. I tried to tell him. I told him, 'Not everybody can run away to the United States.' No good. Now this."

"Now he sees it your way?"

"He told me to come see you."

Mateo drums his fingers on the table, looking down.

"She's near?"

"Still in town ... So, you will try it?"

He doesn't lift his eyes or stop drumming.

"If I try I succeed," he says flatly.

More thinking, more drumming, with both hands.

"And don't say anything about the money. I don't talk about the money."

"He told me."

Mateo stops drumming and spreads his fingers with a smile.

"So, all right."

The woman nods with a tight little grin that pinches

up folds beside her mouth. She's thin as a gazelle, with a gazelle's narrow face.

"He says only kill," she says.

Mateo looks at her for a moment, and his smile widens.

"Women make too many sounds."

The girl is hiding in a friend's apartment and she never leaves. Mateo has the place watched round the clock. The girl runs out one night, very late, after four AM, and gets into a cab. Another cab pulls alongside and the two drivers wave to each other. The driver of the other cab makes a curious gesture. The first cabby nods and pulls over. The girl is staring at him, asking him questions nonstop. He explains that he is having some trouble with the motor, but it's all right, she can continue on in his friend's cab, which sits idling right behind them. The street is deserted, a strip of black between empty blue fields.

"Can't I just wait?"

"I have to call a truck," the driver says. "It will be daylight before it comes."

He waves away her money.

"It's OK," he says.

The girl gets into the other cab. The other driver is a man a little past middle age, not all that large, looking grandfatherly and harmless in bright yellow shirt, white cap and white slacks, aftershave, a gold chain around his wrist.

She names an unremarkable small town close to the border. He nods and they are on their way.

"I was on my way to pick up another fare," he explains after about fifteen minutes. "But he's going the same way you are, so it should be OK."

"I'll pay extra if you just go straight there," the girl says. "I'm in a hurry. It's an emergency."

"Well, but he's right there, he sees us."

The driver points without taking his hand off the wheel, which is already steering the car over to the curb. The cab rocks as a huge man clambers into the passenger seat and greets the driver familiarly. The car takes off again, having picked the man up so quickly that it didn't even come to a full stop. The big man looks back at her with a friendly smile and a wave.

"Hello," he says.

The driver and the passenger exchange pleasantries and are soon laughing happily with each other, talking about baseball mostly. The sun is starting to come up over the mountains, making the bare earth on all sides look smoky. They are in the middle of nowhere. When is that big guy getting off? The road is completely empty except for one other car approaching swiftly behind them. When she looks forward again the big man, his face blank, is climbing over the front seat with surprising agility. She squeals and tries to disappear into the back seat, the driver does something under the dash and a sudden wind gushes over the back of her head, lifting her hair. A huge hand grabs her by the throat, squeezes her windpipe shut, and she is being forced back now up and over the back seat. She claws at the ceiling, the top of the seat, but there is nowhere to get a purchase and flinging her arms crazily out, her bottom leaves the seat, she is bent backwards the wind whipping at her hair, her wild kicking is only propelling her out the back, even turning her head to look at the big black car with one headlight tailgating the cab seems to lessen her purchase and with a sickening freedom she feels herself for an instant supported by nothing, floating in hurtling air, before the searing shock of the ground, and then the impossible weight of the wheels.

Mateo swivels and drops into her seat, then shoves over, because he doesn't like feeling the warm spot she left. Behind them, the black car is slowing to a stop, turning back on its prey.

*

the city from up here is a livid splatter of bottle green light, luminous gold wire

luminous gold petals

coins

and as the mountains slide away beneath us and the city unfolds, I see dark giants, human silhouettes, lying on their sides along the city, propped on an elbow, looking at it—a giant crawls past another giant and reaches out a shadow arm across the city to adjust one of the lights—the giants are powdery shadows, distinct and black, genderless, slim figures—with long fingered hands, long arms, touching the city here and there, making adjustments—opening a way just here, releasing a flow of luminous golden mites, cars and trucks, in an illuminated cement artery—it's like watching silhouettes play a phosphorescent board game spread out on a dark floor—the glow rising from the city dimly plays over their contours without revealing anything—no, revealing a uniform fabric, generic contours—they are like mimes in full body stockings—shadow hands of colossal ghosts wave over the calligraphic embers of the city—

*

It's like that all over Etsimen. It's only been a few days since we met the first, and now we have something like a dozen Tripis crammed into two beds two cots and a bathtub back at Hotel Adoniram, leaving us to sleep in the car. I'll stare at one, getting more and more sure every moment of the resemblance, and then another will cough, or wake up with a little cry, grab my attention, and she'll be the one I recognize immediately. The recognition never lasts, though. Then, as I go on peering at that one, the less convincing features undo the impression of familiarity. They all have busted, bandaged heads. All they can do is lie around, recovering. This one has a concussion, that one has a laceration, another one has a fever and a drained abscess that has to be kept covered until it closes; no two injuries alike, and no one face all exposed. None of them claims to be Tripi, but then none of them can really talk. They cry softly, or moan, and sigh, cough, sneeze, murmur, whisper when they need the bathroom. I remember one clearly saying the word "farmaxak" meaning pharmacy I guess, although that's not the usual word. It looks like they all need medicine, all different kinds, but we can't figure out what to get them. Carolina's been giving them LSD. How can she have so much?

They can't all fit in shitty hatchback, but I could get a trailer. Cram them all in. Drive them back to San Toribio and pour them out on the steps of *La Censura*. Maybe they all have amnesia. I keep trying to make myself believe that one of them is Tripi, any one of them, but I can't. It's more like we're waiting. Waiting, I think, to see if any of them just turns into her.

Most can't really manage anything harder than soup, between wired jaws and whatever. Every day I go buy soup for them from the hand cart on the corner. It's beef broth thickened with sorghum flour, and you pick what you want in it. Sick people drink it plain. I get a few gallons in a plastic bucket and haul it back. Carolina handles the feeding and spends the rest of the time on the phone talking ultra high speed coastal dialect. I drift out and smoke in the courtyard next to a drooling banyan tree. Ranulho, the sweep-up man, pops out whenever I do, because he knows I'm too soft to refuse him a smoke. He's a brown, balding, grey-haired man in dull blue coveralls, small and sturdy, stiff in the legs, with permanent grime beneath his fingernails and teeth that are too white to be real and too irregular to be fake.

He lights up with a match and then talks to me, smoke pluming from his mouth and nose. The highway is a scam, there's this or that thing they were supposed to build that they never did, his brother did this and that and this and that. I ask him about the cyclops cars.

"Xi," is the laconic reply.

"Who are they?"

"They don't let anybody in or out. They give everybody trouble. My brother ..."

And so on. Always back to his nameless brother. Ranulho always knows what he wants to tell me about, and every time I ask a question his answer will tack over to that topic with legerdemain too fast for me to follow or interrupt.

Today he shows me his lottery ticket. Tripi suspended the lottery, because it was fixed by government agents and their extramural buddies, but now I guess it's back on—no, he's telling me that it was never suspended here. And something about his brother. He says his brother gave him the numbers.

"He ever win the lottery himself?" I ask.

Ranulho waves his hand no.

"He cannot. He is forbidden to play by the dead."

"Huh?"

Ranulho sits down next to me—something he's never done before. He tells me, quietly, about his brother and the dead. Actually, it's not his brother, it's a man his brother knows. They did their military service together and stayed friends, but then this man, Eme, started dreaming about the dead monks. What dead monks? The dead monks from the monastery. What monastery? Ranulho points to one of the mountains over there; without being able to follow his finger all that well, I know on sight which mountain he means—the dead one. It's the sharpest, scariest of the mountains over there. The monastery was up there. You had to use an ox-powered elevator to get up to it. Men went away to join the monks and were never seen again. No one ever came down, except those few who went to consult them and returned freaked out. No Bishop ever visited that place. The priest demurred whenever the question of the monastery was brought up; "go and see for yourself" is all he would say. Lightning hits that mountain more than any other, and people believed those monks were there paying penitence for crimes so horrifying that they didn't have names. Those who did go to see them came back either blustery with brittle denial or stricken in some other way. Some died within a short time of their return, and some prospered and lived a very long time, even if the light of day never quite fully lit them up anymore. One day, the story goes, and this is an old story so it must have been a long time ago, a visitor came back even more messed up than usual, and announced that all the monks were dead. They'd walled themselves up in one big room. A party went up to investigate and confirmed the report; the room was a sunken chamber with only two entrances, both bricked up. At ground level, there was a single aperture, a vent, and, by dint of long peering into the almost perfect darkness within, the seekers could make out the dead monks sitting in concentric circles. They broke open the room and found them all sitting upright in their hoods, hands folded in their laps, and all mummified where they were. Ranulho says they couldn't have been mummified that quickly and he plainly thinks there's something unnatural, "spiritual" he calls it, signified in it. The party decided to skip a medical examination of the bodies; they got out of there.

The sinister reputation of the monastery lingered and grew. According to Ranulho, all the young boys around were daring each other to visit it, but it was very hard going and most were satisfied if they got to a certain rock on the slope below the monastery. Without oxen to power the elevator, the climb took too long. Anyway, there's supposed to be something carved on the bottom of the rock that is too terrifying for belief, and the test was to go look at it. I guess those who'd seen it themselves could confirm your description. Ranulho's brother, though, he went all the way, right up to the monastery, even though that meant camping out on the slopes for a night. He said he'd had dreams up there, but would never describe them. Once, though, he'd said that Tripi was in one of the dreams he'd had. Tripi in Etsimen. He got up there all right, and went into the room with all the dead monks. They were all still sitting there, and he said they were praying.

"'Weren't they dead?' I asked him."

"'Xi,' he said."

"Wait," I say. "I thought it was his army buddy Eme who went."

"Xi," Ranulho says.

"You said it was your brother."

"No," he shakes his head.

So he goes on, and whenever he says "Eme" there's a little pause, as if to say—you see, like I said. The point is those dead monks told Eme ... that they needed a voice to pray with and that he should let them use his. They didn't move—Ranulho seems to have asked him a lot of questions about that—they didn't move at all, and their jaws stayed shut or dangling, however they were, there was nothing to see, no change to see, but just that voice coming from them all at once. He said it was very low, and still, and that it was "carrasguaiao" whatever that means, and they spoke slowly, in unison, and that it was dry, like the sound the wind makes when it blows through a big aperture. He said Eme ... *Eme* told them he would, and then, when he was telling the story, he opened his mouth and let the sound come out. It sounded like his voice, but it was terrifying. It was quiet, he says, and it made you afraid, it made you think of the monks up there, all sitting still in their hoods, all dead, their skin tight on their skulls, in the dark when night falls, speaking to you with their dead draft. Since then, Eme ... could pick lottery numbers sometimes, he stopped the outsiders from coming in, and once he predicted a freak dust storm. A few people had, just as a precaution, refrained from going out to the desert to pick cactus fruit with some others that day, more using his advice as a pretext to get out of it than believing him, and the storm had come out of nowhere. The pickers barely escaped with their lives, and two of them inhaled so much crud they had to be hospitalized. One of them, Diomethiu, from two blocks over, still wheezes all the time.

"Yeah yeah," I say, "Xi Xi, but tell me about the outsiders though."

Ranulho says it happened a few years ago. There had been rumors that foreign soldiers were messing around in a little hamlet called Okertu, which lies in the crotch of some foothills between Etsimen and the mountains. If you go to Okertu today, he tells me, you'll see it's empty. The people of Okertu didn't come to Etsimen—they went to San Toribio, all at once.

"You see," Ranulho says. "They were taken there, all together, and they dumped them there."

"Who dumped them?"

Ranulho shakes his head and shrugs.

"No one will say anything. They're afraid. Still afraid."

So Eme ... had this girlfriend once, but, after his visit to the monastery, he'd broken off with her. And she was from Okertu. So when he heard there was something going on out there, Eme ... went to see for himself. That's how he was—he had to see things with his own eyes. So he went out there and waited in an empty barn until it got dark, then looked for lights. He saw lights there on the ridge across from him. Little lights, like furtive flashlights. You had to stare into the dark to see them, but he says he saw them. There were men in dark uniforms, with guns, and maybe other equipment, maybe communications equipment or something like that, moving on the ridge line, setting things up, going down into the town, coming back, and so on. Eme ... says he found himself coming out of the barn. He says he didn't want to, that he was powerless, all of a sudden, to control his body. He felt cold, he says, and dry, all dried out, even his eyes. He went outside to a place in some trees, a clear spot overlooking Okertu and the other ridge. He sat down there on the ground, without wanting to, and he says he sat down just like the monks. He says he began to hear them in the wind, that low "carrasguaiao." He knew that the monks didn't approve of those men over there, doing whatever they were doing. He says he could feel the monks sitting behind him. Their voices, all in unison, were pouring dead breath over him from behind, and he didn't dare look back. He felt his mouth opening, and his tongue moving. He says he didn't breathe any differently, that he didn't push breath over his voicebox, that the breath came through the back of his head and into his mouth from behind. He says that, as he began speaking, he could see the outlines of hooded figures sitting motionless around him, and gradually he began to see stiff dead faces there. Then he noticed a different light on the far ridge. The fire was like a golden coin that hollowed itself out and grew, becoming an irregular ring, and a wind from behind him came up out of a night that had not been windy at all and fanned the flames up the opposite slope. Eme ... says that he had no control over his body, that he stood up with his hands out—Ranulho shows me—as if he were lifting something heavy, lifting it up to chest height as the voices kept on calmly, methodically, implacably murmuring their unintelligible prayers, then turns his upraised hands out. The wind grew very strong then. He began to hear men's voices shouting. Once, he saw two or three figures illuminated by firelight on the slope above the flame, which spread over the entire slope like a great red hand in a few minutes. Now the whole slope was darkly ablaze with red fire. Eme ... saw something square, a white box on a stand, consumed in the flames, and there were other things he couldn't identify, that the men had brought with them.

The fire burned away from Okertu, up the slope and down the far side. Eme ... was still there when the morning came, sitting again. Daylight showed a charred slope still smoking in places, the burnt wood of the brushes was making a plucking sound, and he could hear the faint prayers of the monks fading as the sun came up. He says he just got up and went back to Etsimen. That slope is all grown back now, Ranulho says, but there were a few unusual things found up there, twisted metal things, melted plastic things that might have been electronic. A helmet without any insignia on it, but which had been new, was found, too. The town had not been touched. Since then, strangers have been noted in the vicinity a few times, but no soldiers.

"Mostly gringos," Ranulho says. "And Urtruvel."

He showed up a little after people first got wind of an Uhuyjhn city that just appeared out of nowhere on the coast by Etsimen. When I tell Carolina all this, she says,

"We're going."

*

We're coming in for a landing at last. I see Los Angeles splash, the mountains, the sun, my ocean, the desert. I feel the power in the earth pulling on the plane, fixedly pulling. I feel the power in the earth-wind buffeting us as we lower ourselves into it, coming off the mountains, off the ocean, rebounding off the ground. I feel the power in the plane holding us in place. I feel a complementary ache for the ground, to stand on it, to lie in it. I see the sunflash from each pane of glass as we descend. When we drop low enough, now, the sunlight is orange, everything glows brown.

The engines are revving. A horizontal pressure replaces the vertical and the plane angles upward away from the ground. We are rising again, turning, going back. We are not descending. Am I ever going to touch ground again?

*

Arieto is watching Assiyeh cross the lobby. She and two

shield bearers are there pretending to be bodyguards for a group representing the Koskon Kanona Ministry of Science, Industry, and Technology, actually six administrative assistants from the Economics Group lead by a man named Ozmur. They are at the front desk, checking in. The lobby is bustling with people, here to attend the trade conference and a simultaneous symposium on experimental physics. Assiyeh will be presenting tomorrow, and is expected to attend several talks today in addition to a high-profile banquet tonight.

"It's set," Ozmur says, handing her her room key.

Arieto nods, her eyes on the crowd. She's noticed something already.

Three men, all more or less professionally dressed. They might be lawyers or executives, but to the eye that knows how to look, they are obviously hitters and converging inconspicuously on Assiyeh. The suits fit snug on the brawn. The big one moves as smoothly as a leopard despite his size. Watching him, Arieto feels a strong premonitory current hook itself up to her. It's like the pull of a receding wave, the rushing suction pulls one way while the ground seems to roll the other way beneath the feet, and in the middle, a void of fear. Arieto realizes the hit is on, *now.*

"Get the Superintendent," she tells Ozmur, not taking her eyes off the big one.

Ozmur peels out behind her in a spin, lifting his arms. His party falls in with him at once in the complicated interlocking figure-eights and elaborate arm movements that will get the Superintendent.

"Defend," Arieto tells her two deputies, Mutt and Jeff,

still watching the big one.

"Defend," they answer back, all affect leaving their eyes, stepping forward at once.

Arieto closes on the big one while Mutt and Jeff dart around the outside of the crowd to intercept the others.

Arieto comes up behind the big one and prods him with her forefinger three times hard in the meat of his right shoulder.

"Poke-poke-poke," she says.

He doesn't react, just keeps making his way toward Assiyeh. Arieto switches to swats.

Bam bam bam!

Out of nowhere his left hand appears from under his right arm grabs her wrist and pulls her face first into his right elbow. He didn't even look back, but then he must have been expecting to finish her that way. But the moment she felt that first tug, she lowered her brow like a ram and took the blow square in the middle of her forehead. It jammed her skull and compressed her neck, but Arieto's head is hard and she knows it. He has released her wrist, presumably to allow her to fall behind him. She raises her arm under his and traps it in a half nelson, turning him to the right and throwing her leg between his. She almost manages to throw him, but without a sound he switches legs as he comes around on his right, throwing his weight backwards, trying to get her off him. She releases him and he ends up standing, facing her for the first time. Arieto feints her right at his face and he swivels at the waist; then she nails him in the ribs with her left. It's like punching a tree. She manages to raise a grimace, but that's all right. He's wasting time with her now, that's the point.

The other hitters are angling in toward Assiyeh but Mutt and Jeff keep shearing them off, driving them into the thickest part of the crowd. Finally one hitter lunges into an opening only to find his way blocked by an elaborately engraved black and gold shield. Weightless, swift, the shield floats before the hitter like an afterimage, deftly maintaining a position between him and his target. After a few futile attempts to get around that shield, he drops to the floor and sweeps the legs out from under it. His path clears and he springs forward after Assiyeh, who is obliviously leaving the lobby, passing between the banks of elevators to the passages, conference and ball rooms in the rear of the hotel. Out of the corner of his eye he can see that black shield floating up alongside him, hastening to get in front of him again, and he races it.

There's the other hitter. They close up together and shove through to the elevator banks, trying to use the doorway to shave off the defenders. No sign of the big one. Assiyeh has turned the corner, heading for the western rear hall of doors, checking her schedule. There she is—going into the Paisley Room, last conference room before the big double fire doors. Those fire doors swing open with a rush of luminous smoke as the two hitters reach the end of the hall, and a gigantic white stag emerges from that smoke in the next instant. A white figure sits astride the stag, armored head to foot in white steel lace skeletons of stained glass cathedral windows. Delicate antlers rise from the bullet-shaped helmet, and translucent gossamer ribbons stream up into the sky. The white faceplate has no openings; the face of the Jack of Hearts is painted on it, turned forward. This is the

Superintendent. In his left hand, he holds a white shield completely covered with fine engraving in gold. The right hand holds a tapering white lance, which he levels at the two hitters.

The stag advances warily.

The hitters split.

The lance whips to one side and then the other, flexible and fast as a snake.

Smoke lifts from rancid industrial carpeting and vanishes, trickling in among the bars of the wallpaper.

Who sent those men after Assiyeh? On whose intelligence?

*

Carolina and I are nearing the coast and there's very heavy presence here, all along the streets and in the air. We are not going to be able to drive right up and they are not going to pay any attention to press passes.

"They're going to blow us off the road without even bothering to check us out. Or scoping us now."

"Don't their cities move?" she asks.

"They can still keep a moving cordon around it."

"What if the city moves too quickly for them?"

After driving a while a thought occurs to me.

"They have to be working on a way to predict where the city will go," I say.

"If we can do it better, we can get inside," she says.

We pull over in a stand of dusty pine trees. There's a fiberglass and steel tube picnic table and I want to eat my paper-bag flavored sandwich and drink my plastic-bottle-flavored water. Carolina sits opposite me demurely chewing tabs of acid out of a compact.

She asks me what I think of all this, looking at me with disarming directness, and I tell her I want to go to an Uhuyjhn city, I want to escape.

"Everybody wants to escape," she says.

"Then there's probably an excellent reason," I say. "And everybody does want to escape. That's not a problem. The so-called 'winners' want to accuse the so-called 'losers' of retreating into a fantasy world because they can't 'make it' (whatever that means) in this so-called 'world' that they made and rigged for themselves. The so-called 'escapists' would do well to reply that the so-called 'winners' are the real, not-just-so-called escapists. They are the ultra-escapist superstars escaping from paying, escaping into fantasy sales in the future, escaping from collapses by uncaging them from a particular place and time and dispatching them into the blue yonder like the flying monkeys to drop uninvited havoc on some other country or neighborhood. They run the blame around too, until it lands on the patsy who is helpless to avoid it. The young sword hero can charge the evil fortress and single-handedly beat down legions of police and soldiers and security monsters, but he's never going to find the central lair because there isn't one, and he's never going to find the master villain and bring him to justice because he melted into tear gas and oozed out through the chimney to make another massive fortune building a new improved rampage somewhere else.

"The impulse to escape is pure, but, starve it of new values, and it gives out too soon and falls back into the mesh again. Take a look at economics. When you really study it, you realize there's a whole ghoulish domain of wizardry and phantasmagoria in back of all the grey mush at the surface. It's actually the twisted magic forest of witches and goblins and giant demons with fifty televisions for heads and African bush stuff and outback stuff and and Amazon stuff and garudas and griffins. I call it shit-ism. Where you have shitism, realism is a fantasy and fantasy is real, the realists are the escapists, and the real realists are trying not to let them. The real problem is that people aren't alienated enough and they don't keep pace with the runaway weirdness of life. It's like, they want to say 'Oh he's just you know "the magic negro" or whatever,' as if nobody were ever *really magic* but everybody is magic, you, me, everybody, and that's always been true, and that's not the point. The point is *why*—if everybody actually already is magic—*why*—how come—- is the world *dead?* How is it such a fucked up chunk of *shit* if everybody is magic?"

Carolina tells me about an Uhuyjhn named Yama-aachen. The body is a sort of polyp twenty five meters across and about ten high with a girdle of countless spines midway between its thick middle and the dimple at the top. The body is all dark crust like dried black mud, and warty; the spines have a corroded metal look. The top is lined with double-jointed bony fingers around one enormous molar in the middle, and there are dollops of globular photophores asymmetrically embedded among the fingers. I can't picture it. These luminous glands alternately fade and intensify their glare at random, and as they come in a variety of colors, this means that a rippling multicoloredness sits on top of the thing as it flies through the air using a gravity-manipulating organ deep inside its carapace. There are mummified human remains impaled on various of its spikes, but they're volunteers, not victims. Around here, when someone thinks death is near, they sometimes ask to be impaled. That kills them, but in such a way that they almost immediately find themselves restored in an inexplicable dream that will last for as long as Yama-aachen lives. Since the lives of Uhuyjhn seem to have no set term, it's likely this means a dream longer than the life that came before it. What the Uhuyjhn gets out of it is unknown. It may be the mummy's dream is Yama-aachen's dream as well, and that their involvement deepens its dream, or, as the mathetes who seem to go between the Uhuyjhn and mankind, it may only be an altruistic gesture. These beings, of whom Yama-aachen is one, first began turning up in the last few days bringing a vast antiquity of tradition with them so that they appear to have been here with us forever, and the new practices that spring up around them are born archaic.

They came around the same time as the Color Shift and communicate with human beings by telepathy manifested visually by a transparent basin of grainy white light in the air above the Uhuyjhn. Each "word" is accompanied by a pseudo-palpable sensation just above a little behind the base of the nose, described by some as a tapping, others as a throbbing, others as a tickling, an itching, a spasm. This communication is almost certainly very flawed; the same utterance, received simultaneously by three humans ABC, will register to A as a flatly factual proposition, to B as a gentle interrogative, and to C as an imperious command. Confusion is best minimized by restricting communication with Uhuyjhn to a one-to-one basis, although it is not clear that the Uhuyjhn don't all speak in unison. Yama-aachen's importance derives from a probable mental commingling with the dreaming minds of its mummified human parasites; that would be the only discernible reason for its greater volubility and intelligibility.

Carolina encountered Yama-aachen by chance. She had gone to meet with someone—I'm pretty sure she means her connection—and she saw it cruising the low hills and treetops by the street. It made a beeline right for her, alarmingly, but stopped and hovered a few dozen meters away only five or six meters off the ground, looking, with its grisly adornment of mummies, like a nightmarishly animated torture device. There was no distinct odor or sound except for an irregular and copious exhalation, sharp and surprising, halfway between an elephant clearing its trunk and the gasp of air brakes. As it drew near, she saw tiny dark hyphen-like streaks pop across her field of vision, a neuronic distortion that other people have also experienced when in close proximity to Yama-aachen. Even though it isn't at all bright, even if you don't see its lights, you still find yourself blinking away unusually vivid and tenacious after-images of it, so that it becomes harder and harder to look at. You actually see it better in vision capture than with your own two eyes, because the distortions don't affect cameras. She insists Yama-aachen just hung there for a few seconds and then floated gigantically away again, and she was let down once she got over the shock.

It lives in the clouds, she explains, or way up in the

atmosphere, without straying too far from the environs of the new city. When the mathetes receive another dying applicant for the dream of Yama-aachen, they attract its attention with a pattern of lights and a chant. The chant probably doesn't do anything except reassure the mathetes that they have some special rapport with Yama-aachen.

Yama-aachen excretes all kinds of living animals, snakes, foxes, frogs, cockroaches, and weird animals no one's ever seen before, whenever it picks up a mummy; it also leaves behind a pile of animal money left behind as well. Maybe animal money is alien shit. Maybe it's how they reproduce.

"Maybe it's how they sweat," I say.

*

Urtruvel ...

He had been freelancing a bit on the side, relentlessly drilling down on animal money, or at least that's how it seems to him. With the wise counsel of his new parasitic tongue and the insights it whispers into his bloodstream every night to direct him, he masters news-screw-mancy. There's a Latin American leftist writer, a fellow Argentine, who is getting to be too popular and effective. Certain quarters, some of them with dot gov email addresses, are recruiting warlocks and Urtruvel is ape to prove he can do it. He whammies his target up to boogie like he has on the red shoes, racing this way and that in a mounting panic trying to put out a fire over here and then a fire over there. Urtruvel's accusations and bullshit are so outrageous they demand a reply, and from then on it's

Urtruvel who calls the tune, folding that writer up neatly into a human asterisk.

Now SuperAesop's name is in his sinbox ...

Hurrying now through dark streets, the lights are all out even though the power is still on and the trains are still running, packed with soft, silent people in the dark. Standing near the door, squeezed in between two big shadows, I watch as the aspects and contrasts of the poster directly in front of me begin to stir. They sink into a crumbling darkness that swarms with avid, intelligent life, and Urtruvel's face coagulates there, his figure seething with vibrating black mist, the poster yawning on plummeting depths like a cataract of roaring, thirsty hollowness. Urtruvel has taken the model's place, the sunwashed front yard, the white picket fence, the wooden recliner chair, the overhanging tree, the pitcher of lemonade, the white cardigan and jeans, the quaint outline of a peaked roof against a deep blue sky, is all greyed over with an ominous electric gloom. Urtruvel sits in the chair with his feet up in white loafers, crossed at the ankle. He holds up an ice cream cone, opening his mouth. The louse inside lunges out, scrabbling at the ice cream, gouges at it with its many legs, buries its face in the ice cream, gobbling it, while Urtruvel glares at me with eyes like baleful lamps.

Do you have unpopular political opinions?

How do you propose to compensate for your lack of experience?

The train decelerates and I fall against another passenger. I feel cuffs and blows at my back as I pull myself up, but now that I can see around me in the dimness, the train has come up above ground, no one seems to have moved. It's like being in a crowd of sleepwalkers.

Why did you leave your last job?—The poster sneers. When will you be leaving this one?

Do you know what this organization does?

The train is inching into the station. I'm standing right in front of the door watching the rail trickle by, fighting panic. I can't see him but I can hear him. The cuffs and blows drop against my back like snowballs that burst and vanish, disembodied and almost forceless blows of blind unacknowledged and unreasoning hate that leave a caustic smear behind soaking into my back but if I turn around—if I turn around that is it.

What will you miss about your current or last job?

The train parks and a low voice murmurs something over the PA. By agonizingly slow degrees the intensity of that murmur mounts without growing louder; an idiotic yammer going on and on, a low buzzing chant that gets fiercer and fiercer never louder just more venomous more venomous inside the motionless dark train filled with motionless people, like the voice of my own panic, of a mindlessness that's going to eat my mind.

What is your greatest failure?—The poster inquires, probingly. Mouth parts gobble ice cream.

What is your greatest fear?

My hands are shaking and my throat closes every time I try to swallow and the drone goes on and on and on, my back is on fire and the drone goes on and on and on. My mouth is wet. I taste blood—shit, my nose is bleeding—

Describe a time when you had to deal with conflicting demands.

Am I going to try shoving my hands into the rubber lips of the door and dragging them apart, or am I going to plunge backward into the vile mass behind me and fight my way to the door between cars? The air is stale and spent, full of dead halitosis and I don't dare look over my shoulder at the people behind me they are a disgusting plastic mass of clothes and shoes and hair and mucus, the mucus of that droning voice.

The train glides ominously forward. The voice stops, as if to deny me the relief of breaking from it when the doors open and I jump out onto a dark platform, elevated line, no announcement, no ding dong of the doors. The train stays where it is, the cars filled with dark shapes, doors all standing open, dead silence. No one moves. Twilight Zone. He's right in front of me, holding a gun on me from a movie poster.

Why did you leave your last job?

Can you describe a time when your work was criticized and how did you handle it?

I get moving along the platform, passing open car doors filled with passengers like open closets filled with heavy coats and hats and I feel stared at by all of them, even the ones buried deep inside the cars. A voice comes over the station PA, a voice I recognize, that toneless, insipid jabber, starting up again, the voice takes sudden, deep breaths to keep boring its way to reach my brain where it will lay eggs that will hatch and eat and shit jabber through my mouth. I run down the platform along the endless train passing open doors like open hearths striping me with insane malice as I pass them, them and those posters where Urtruvel leers out at me, rippling with muscles on a sunswept beach, a woman in a bikini on his arm.

When will you lose your final job?

Describe one time you ever resolved a conflict.

I blunder up the stairs in the dark, slipping and nearly falling backward. The drone recedes behind me. The station above is in total darkness and I rush into it waving my hands around in front of me, turning this way and that I can't see the stairway I just came from and I don't know if I'm about to drop back down it again, and no other glimmer of light. The drone swells up on all sides of me coming from every direction a low gibbering voice artificially amplified, something you would expect to hear coming out of a mental patient, an incessant vocalization like the tinnitus of an exploded brain, coming to get me. I got good eyes though, I see a glimmer up there, where there's a grating, and I head for it, find the stairway and get up to the lightless street.

Overcast purple sky. People float down the street, shadows, now and then a disc or flutter of light as someone passes with a flashlight or lights a cigarette. The air is motionless. This isn't over for me. Urtruvel is there on the magazine cover in the bodega window, holding a cigar, sitting at a desk.

Have you ever been convicted of a crime?

I walk, but I don't feel myself escaping. I'm only handing myself down the line from one window full of Urtruvel magazine to another window with Urtruvel poster and Urtruvel behind the wheel of a shining SUV in the billboard at the intersection—

Have you ever read *Our Mutual Grave*?

Are you now or have you ever been insane?

What would you say your greatest weakness is?

Urtruvel at my back and Urtruvel coming up before me on a poster over another subway entrance, and with a pang of terror at the idea I might go down there I throw myself back from the chute of the subway stairs—that yammering climbs the steps toward me, it's a toothless tar mouth. It doesn't want to chew me up, it wants to suck on me like a hard candy that dwindles and dwindles down to nothing forever, a little remnant you can shatter and swallow with no trouble.

Escaping, the dark traffic trying to hit me, someone is coming around every corner just as I reach it someone steps out from between every tall parked car every mailbox all directly into my path I have to veer and swivel and stumble, these someones, all these someones are murmuring that same murmur, featureless nameless shadows blocking my way, herding me along like a panicked rat toward the jaws but those jaws aren't going to snap shut and crush me, they're going to mumble me inside that slopping mouth with that louse's fangs buried in me, idly slurping my blood but not so fast it won't replenish itself, and me withered and helpless and puckered and smothered under a blanket of saliva.

I need a break break break break break break break—

There's Urtruvel on a flatscreen TV above shadows standing motionless on motionless treadmills and seated motionless on stationary bicycles in a fitness club. He's talking seriously in a set of switching headshots with someone else, someone else who is also him, arguing, demolishing, that louse flapping in his mouth, legs wriggling, while the moderator acts as his spotter, homing his word bullets in on a hapless cartoon version of me, just like at the zoo, just like at the zoo. Me sitting there, the camera up a little to make me look small at the bottom of the screen, my screen make up is the wrong color and there's a crumb or something on one side of my mouth, and I have a black eye and my nose is bleeding and my collar is half inside out somehow and my tie is on backwards. I want to lash out and smash the thick window of the fitness club, roll one of these parked SUVs through the glass. Did I never leave and has all this been hallucination? I'm not falling for it. I grab a passing bus and find myself face to face with Urtruvel, this time in a poster advertising his latest book, the face frozen in an Official Author Photo, black and white, not looking at the camera but off into Importantness you fucker—the photo changes and now it's the officially unposed pose, like a driver's license photo, but the blue-bottle tinged contrast gives it away, the affectation of frank openness, of seeing someone as they really are in a stark blank and bare posture is bullshit too, extra bullshit, and I whip out my marker and give him the Hitler moustache he deserves, a lobotomy scar, slobber running from fangs that stick out over his lower lip, a goatee, Satan horns, pointed ears, a pointed tail sticking up from behind him, a Nazi armband, disgusting bags under his eyes and 666 in between them. I feel that murmur hum up along the bus aisle toward me but the door is opening and I get off too fast for you fucker. I'm SuperAesop, fool. I can feel you trying to fold me into your asterisk. Stick your lousy tongue out at me again, I got long shears. I'm too fast, too fast, too fast for you. I keep moving, that mutter avalanching at my back, just a step away, just a stumble away, just a pause for traffic at a corner away, just a beat too long getting around this shadow woman with her shadow baby carriage full of huge gelatinous worms mouthing the air with a crinkling sound, worms in the trees wrapped around shadow branches and raising their mouthed ends to join the murmuring chorus. Everything around me is deliberate, significant, aiming at me. I'm not turning to confront it, won't fall for that. I can keep running, run a long long time. The rest of my life, one way or the other.

*

It's not uncommon to find on other planets monuments to Terran heroes whose names are unsung on Earth; for example, this huge crystal chorten outside the hotel where the conference is wrapping up is dedicated to an all-purpose rebel who changed his name sometimes to SuperAesop and whose official biography begins well after his escape from the chimpanzee enclosure in a Latin American zoo, his vindictive return being likewise omitted. I wonder how I would know about it myself. The chorten rests on a platform of compacted car tires with a corrugated tin ramp leading up to it, and a line from one of his poems is engraved in each tin concavity, adding up to this:

some words don't rub off,
they grind them into our organs;

Those happy ones,
they've been busy scribbling;
by the end of one day
one has been by their words overscribbled:
Two Ways to Strip—
scrub their words away with
words of my own or with

silence

some words carry

silence,

winding, alive,
the hush of them

carries

like spoken evening

The chorten is a compromise between a traditional structure and a modern sculpture depicting a burned out lightbulb with a skirt of dead insects.

Thafeefa is sending me mental images of playing cards; that tells me she's all right. I'm alone. The air is fresh and light. For a moment I slough my sleeve of fear. Spectres of Earth, trying to catch me in their focal points, and transient specials going about their business, refracted through the weird temporal echo chamber of the Koskon Kanona bureaucracy. Now sky patterns fracture the light into scintillant flakes schooling down over us in curls and cladding the skyscrapers in shimmering jackets of mail.

"So, animal money is like knowledge, or language, or art, or cultural artifacts of a durable, interpersonal kind."

"Or sex," the first Professor Long says.

"Right. We'll put that at the top of the list."

"And the bottom too," the second Professor Long says, holding up his **JOKE** card.

I feel his whisper at the back of my neck and spin— nothing there. A new nothing, adding to and intensifying the nothing that shines around this monument. Was that a woman, was that Tripi, I just saw, rounding the corner and disappearing, and were there two big bodyguards, or perhaps simply guards, flanking her? It isn't death, it isn't any thing at all. It is the realization in me of the fact that the wave hits the beach, the breath stops, that we are living in and through life. I'm going to have a child without being a parent. This child will have my DNA, grow up knowing me through an ever-widening gulf of interstellar space. "Your other mother," Thafeefa will say. I don't write poetry. I don't mumble over morbid feelings. I write my poems in physics experiments, in bent light, in the reduction of all motion to a perfect stillness without tension, without pressure, the absolute stillness of a feather balanced on its edge, the immaculate stillness of least resistance that is not defying movement, but on the contrary that invites all possible movements with a demureness that works like an irresistible summons. I don't write poetry but I will give my child a cosmos that he or she can stop on a dime, turn this way and that with a divinely offhanded haughteur.

—With a cold flash it suddenly dawns on me there is no reason that he, he of the **JOKE** card, might not be the posthumous sperm donor, and will I some day see that strange look, the downcast look that nevertheless took in everything, saw everything, translated everything into a completely private and personal inner language of primary colors in smooth nameless shapes, on the face of my child? I look at the bulging crystal base of the chorten. My face lies pancaked and stretched out there, the eyes bunched at the top. Is that the goblin face of my third parent I see? It smiles at me. That third parent is a zipper I can unzip. I can wriggle out from under any boot. I can slip any snare. I can move in any way.

That stain there on the ground isn't where I thought it was: I think I've had an episode, a slip in time, speak of the devil here they come, using time fuses to join moments out of order and nab me in an overclocked ambush. What can I do—here's a monument, a posthumous citation, and maybe this is my child's secret parent—an idea worth considering in due time, I can come back to it in my cell or my grave or anywhere I end up, as long as I remember to remember it—meanwhile I know without having to look that there are two, at least two, men in track suits stinking of earth and trick-tracking in, homing on the chorten and on me. I pause to consult a moment with my inner Rascal Committee and almost at once I have the black file in my hand. Black pages with letters of clotted moonlight, dotted lines and boxed off areas for official use only.

Track suits one and two come stomping loudly up the poem to the chorten platform, one heading in directly while the other dashes around to the far side both of them contemporary bohemian types and zoom in a pincer movement to meet in the middle and spin around the chorten and when one is at nine o'clock and the other at three they come face to face with a naked shadow, with staring eyeballs and two neat rows of white teeth all bare and fresh from the black file, the eyes farther and farther apart and the jaws farther and farther apart, blackness opaque and riotous as a howling well banging with ocean tides down below roiling churning rending tearing swallowing mouthing frothing—

As Assiyeh steps from a watch store on one corner of the square a decorated sanitation officer is pertly trundling her cart up the ramp to the chorten to perform the day's upkeep. Clucking her tongue in disapproval, she bins first one and then another of two empty track suits, holding them up for inspection a moment each.

*

I want the time to pass so I skip to the end of the song, thinking that will move the time up too. I was so lost in my thoughts just then that I almost failed to notice my train had come in, and then left, and I took this for a good sign, an indication that my powers of distraction are still strong.

I hear a voice saying, "I only get lonely for fantasies."

... but who are you, how do you talk?

The city has disappeared except for the advertising. I'm issuing you a citation for trespassing in my mind, advertisers. What's more "private property" than my own mind? Naked women who all look like Kodak Shirley somehow are sitting on chilly-looking folding chairs holding up advertising posters for things like "Ham on Air." I skip down a side street, which is nothing but the friable edges of where the buildings and curbs might be, like glass overlaid on glass, check for cops, give the password and duck into a secret loan salon.

"I want ten at two."

"I can give you seven at four."

"What the fuck four? ... That's shit, man."

"Take it or leave it."

"The banks are offering seven at four."

"Yeah, but the banks can dial you halfway up to five if the bond market issues a bull. With me, you take it four it stay four."

No two sharks look alike. One is an old Hispanic man with daily moisturizer complexion, hair plugs and coarse black dye, another is a gawky teenaged girl with legs up to her neck and braces. The only tell is a hooded, ecclesiastical look that comes over them when they produce the cash. They keep their money in "sky purses," tiny, portable pocket dimensions that follow them around like helium balloons, and when two or more meet in these floating salons they have to walk carefully in crescents around each other to avoid tangling their sky purse tethers.

Outside, the city is all used up and gone. The last few buildings are being sucked into the earth. The mayor hasn't been heard from in years. The highest level official anyone can still manage to locate is the postmaster, who holds up his hands impotently, an expression of innocent bafflement on his face. The leavings of a constipatiratorial constipiracy abate us to the subtle extravagances of life ... this is dedicated to the two women on the train, one black, the other white, talking together, nodding sagely, advising each other, these two wise solid goddesses conferring. I choose them, they can judge my fate.

Since everything is now recorded, everything has to be more and more like television; this makes television even more controlling, and television isn't just television anymore, now everything is already television—the point isn't that you have to have perfect hair or anything like that, the point is that your every fart is recorded and judged by others—to be recorded by others is to be judged by others. So when you drive down a freeway that's more pothole than freeway and pay twenty dollars to cross a bridge and your neighborhood has no schools or businesses except a few bad chain stores with a waiting list for job interviews, and you go bankrupt the minute you get sick, and there's nowhere to go and nothing to care about and nothing to do but sit in your postage stamp 80000 a month apartment and peck at the internet since everything is online only now so they don't have to hire people to talk to you, you know that wealth strikes again, flyover private helicopters that don't have to see you, slave doctors and slave police and slave schools and museums and orchestras. Aesop is my name and I only say obvious things.

I plan out a bureaucracy of explosions. Blow up all the information. You go into the DED, the Department of Exploding Documents, stand in line and fill out a form that goes poof! the moment you sign it. Your form has been received, sir/ma'am. Then, after the hermetically determined interval, your criminal record, your credit report, your pre-nuptial agreement, your student loan—BLAM!

*

Meanwhile, the hedge fund leaders and other executives bask in their heedless billions and fortify in bastions like Prince Prospero welding out the Red Death. A heavyweight fund called Probity and Wytt where dead silence prevails in the plush corridors and conference rooms. An awed, reverent hush billows out from the hems of suit jackets and descends like ribbons of freezing air from silver heads to squirm away across the floor in venomous serpents of icy mist that bite and paralyze everyone susceptible. No one dare say a word. It's as whispery as a monastery in there.

"We hold our silence," the boss says in a booming, yet muted voice, a voice that goes right through you, "so that the money itself may be heard."

There's that feeling, as if "the money" were pulsing in the fabric of the building, circulating through us all like the air we breathe, the great inhale-exhale of the market, the ineffable and cryptic wisdom of the diaphragm. We must be ready like the Delphic oracle to blank our minds and hearts and let that deathwisdom murmur through us. The Wasp King sits behind a desk like a black ice floe against a blank white marble wall in a windowless office, the cell of a billionaire monk. Like a living monument to himself, he sits majestically pondering the latest Sibylline enigma of money, and inwardly saluting again the Great Mystery of finance, the most profound and cosmic of all the mysteries he can know. His acolytes have a feverish, inspired air about them. They look like they don't get enough sleep. They look like they don't get enough to think. On joining the firm, each one of them was presented with a parchment contract written in their own blood—

"And sopersuant, blood to blood, I the undersigned bind unto thee ..." the contract ends.

Their yearly bonuses are hand distributed by the chief himself, the recipients stagger away with each bonus a scroll the size of a rolled-up carpet and closed with a massy seal of funereally crimson wax the size of a manhole cover.

Across the street at Smith and Smith the scene is fashionably pornographic and all the brokers there are lathered in ghoulish sleaze. The males have rancid moustaches and the females are friably bronzed and blonded. The place is run by Tinker and Hatter, the Smith Brothers, that's with a *capital* B yuk yuk. Their sister Fletcher sits on the Senate Banking Committee. They all have icy blue eyes that seem painted on, flat. Eyes that trickle white ink. Their wantonly expensive trinketry and decor reproduces at huge costs a kind of discount bacchanalia from an all-purpose zero-history fantasy ghetto. The millionaires call each other "my nigga." They revel in hideous jewelry, solid gold anchor chains looped around their necks and dragging on the floor between their legs, diamond cotton swabs, mink kleenex. Hatter drags into Tinker's office throwing himself down on a snow white raw silk sofa that will be burned at the end of the day and replaced with a new one before the office opens again tomorrow, reaches out a hand ensconced in a boxing glove of rings and bangles to pick up a fig, one of only twelve brought laboriously overland by yak caravan from Samarkand by way of Anchorage, takes one bite and chucks the rest over his shoulder onto a rug that once adorned the throne room of Rajablahblahblah, lights a joint and asks his "nigga" about this latest Monsanto account, but his brother, who sits below a lucite canopy that shields him from a waterfall of gold dust continuously showering his solid platinum combination desk-throne and toilet, can't hear him over the opulence of the torrent. The other richies try to avoid the Smiths, especially not to be photographed with them, but they are so rich they are inevitable, and everyone admits, however bitterly, that their orgies are the cream of the crop.

Spin—nothing there. A new nothing. It isn't new, it's the old nothing, this time. The plane is not coming in for a landing, but turning back again. I shove myself back into my seat, going rigid, suddenly unable to breathe, knowing that the knot of resistance inside me will be cut and I will accept this too, resign myself to going back across the country again, and again, never landing. I can feel the pressure, the blade of the shituation cutting into me and I know any moment I will slump submissively into myself, into a four-color two-dimensional dead image—

Suddenly my weight disappears. Things around me, cups and plastic flatware, napkins and magazines, are rising in the air, the hard line of the ocean horizon floats weirdly into the window, at an angle—at a steep angle. My weight, such as it is, has pooled somewhere above my left hip, as if I were half leaning out of this seat I sit straight in, and that, I see, is because we're going down.

There's a thump and sway and the bottom drops out. The toilets are backing up into the aisles, running down the carpet in brown runners and white furbelows of toilet paper and all the blood is gone from my empty pinata of a head, drained out through the hole in my skull, and pouring down onto the runners in a stream of brown old blood, my life—I don't hear the screams, but there are gaping mouths all around me, staring eyes, there's a shuddering sensation in my dead ears that tells me they are screaming, and jellyfish dangle and bounce in our faces.

Out the window I can see individual waves.

The plane bellyflops into the ocean.

PART TEN:
NONE OF THIS IS REAL

Thafeefa, her father's wild ghost, the glass man, no one. None of them were real people. Why aren't any of the people surrounding Assiyeh real?

Vincent Long was the last real human being I touched, she thinks.

Thafeefa was real, she tells herself, bitterly.

Was she?

Yes—she was an artificial intelligence but her body was real, she was all real. Do I have to go on saying that forever? Don't I believe it?

Thafeefa's smile is permanently in front of Assiyeh's eyes. Smile. Smile. Smile. Smile down at the page. Smile at the words. Smile into your own fucking face. Again and again that smile spreads before her, not fixed, but always just as it begins and spreads.

Thafeefa smiled at me.

But why no human beings?

They won't have me. Or won't I have them? Is it my fault they aren't good enough? What a give away that question is! That peevish "is it my fault." Ugh.

Nestled in Thafeefa's fragrant breasts. That's where I want to be.

But isn't that because you—I—have to have my having myself, have to be alone, have all of me to me—where is everybody—what happened—what planet is this—

None of the people around you are real because you aren't real, Assiyeh. They made you up, those economists, to cover their asses, to distract pushy interviewers, to escape the categorization that would kill their message and silence their voices. You're just a decoy. You're just science fiction.

*

It was 1997 ... the union decided it was time to get workers. All of a sudden there were cameras, lawyers. I can't remember whether it was Chicago or San Francisco. It might have been dishwashers. Or it might have been the cab drivers. Point is, the employer was stealing the wages, and the authorities had already stopped enforcing labor laws.

My friend Gloominous died in prison choking on his own vomit. Someone made a mistake when they doled out the prescription medications. These mistakes happen all the time. Gloominous is a number now. Mistake number whatever. Somewhere there's a form with a signature absolving everybody in advance for this anyway.

So we received a call from some human accessory from the National Carriage and Barrel Workers Union and next thing you know there are cameras and lawyers, a lawsuit, really short protests for the cameras and then back to work. They said they were there to help us organize and get better wages so naturally we listened, but in hindsight you can tell they were looking out for NCBWU. There was a poorly-attended poorly-presented workshop, once, about organizing on the job, but it was an afterthought.

"Well, that's up to you," the accessory said, meaning the organizing. "I mean, we can't tell you, we don't want to dictate to you, how you organize, right? You tell us, you set up a structure (hand gesture), and we give guidance."

She was a vague, billowy sort of person, very short, like a heap of cushions. She was so nebulous you could tell she would go far. I bet she runs the Fudge Machine now. That sort of person always ends up in charge; committedly noncommittal in the committees and placating and respecting everybody right out of this world. Behind a facade of dull whiteboard meeting rooms there are sacred vaults that contain the Fudge Machine, a pile of cushions interconnected with hoses, hanging bladders, surrounded by curing meat and cheese like a delicatessen, a blue mold crust on everything and in the middle there's a trench cut neat and narrow into the stone floor, and the fudge pours into this trench from a concatenation of translucent bladders that look like a sea anemone. The fudge is a creamy confection of tan rubber tepidity, made from the mucus residue left behind by the collision of human energies with the softly ablative baffles that are the basic substance of the organization. In an adjoining chamber, the fudge is sliced into marvellously uniform rectangular tiles and doled out, still sort of warm, neatly wrapped in wax paper pages to be gobbled up, paper and all, by the accessories. The vaults smell like a candy store and there are candy dishes full of sticky, bland grandma candies, jordan almonds, butterscotches, virtually flavorless peppermints in both barber pole and chalk hunk versions, drab pastel jellybeans with no black ones of course.

All the same, the NCBWU did get us talking more to each other and that did bring about non-trivial organizing. That was good. But when you wanted to take it to the next level, talk more seriously, especially talk to anyone with real clout, you ended up being fudged out to some accessory again. I wanted to leave, but I was seeing Gina back then and I couldn't push too hard since she was counting on me to bring in some money. I never did learn whether or not she really was pregnant. So it was an IV drip of wait and see, let's fight it out on TV instead of the street, let's take it to court and not the street, and I'm never knowing why we don't just stop making the fudge, keep the cars in the lot, or the dishes unwashed in the bushel bins or whatever it was we were doing, just put it on hold and zap them like the old days. I knew all kinds of heavy heavy people, big women who could backhand a manager right over the deep frier and surprise themselves, not just angry but indignant, by which I mean angry on behalf of other people you identify with and care about, who would have gone toe to toe with Godzilla and comported themselves creditably, people without a crumb of fudge left in them. The hungry eyes of their kids burned their fudge out and it's long gone, and now they're hot and mean. I watched with my own hungry eyes as the gates of the boredrooms swung wide and a lake of shuddering foam rolled out to quench the flames. The accessories were all redolent of the fumes of fudge that numb the nerves and dull the brain, dull the pain of the heart, of smarting pride, spreading a kind of calm rationality that is actually murky, not clear at all. You open your mouth to speak, to utter your grievance and make your claim and what comes out, instead of the laser, is:

"Weeellllllll ...."

Thin and quavering and sponging away the real writing. And from that welll-moment it's gee you got to compromise and you know let's check the weather and you know you can never do too much planning—yes you can—you can never spend too much time at the drawing board—yes you can—Jumping clarity sags, melts, dribbles away sheepishly down the drain. See we can all get along, right, get along back to the same neighborhoods.

"Yeah, but you can't go on strike against them," I said to Gina, explaining. "You have to stick together or everything's just wasted."

"Everything's wasted now," she said.

"It's a hard struggle," I said. "You can't do it by yourself, and those guys need to make money too."

"Well, how much money are you making? How much are they making off you?"

"It takes time to build up to where you can make a difference," I said.

"Yeah, but are you building up, or are you just reinventing the wheel every generation? Are you working, doing all this, just to hold on?"

Looking back on this conversation I am amazed to see those fudge patties dropping one by one out of my mouth.

Now I'm remembering being in Gloominous' room,

with his paltry belongings. I'm at the window, looking down at a shitty hatchback parked in the street. I'm out there, loading the boxes. Big heap of junk by the curb. Not too big for non-union garbage pick up. The air is stale. I came over to the window to open it, let in the jasminy night air. On the windowsill, there's a tiny brass incense burner overflowing with ashes. Twilight outside. Reflected behind me the two of us sit on the floor with splashes of light up the walls from lamps sitting on the floor, and there's the boom box, and we're leaning against the walls talking and breathing jasmine air from the open window, which slides from side to side. I know I should take something to remember him by and I know I'll leave empty-handed, and empty-hearted too. I can't seem to get mad. I'm punched out. Something important got punched out the center of me and now I can't make the inner connection.

Point is, I was alone before I heard the news, because I've been alone the whole time. And while I run run run and do do do, behind me there's a tragic absence of footprints. Jesus won't put me down. Carolina isn't real. I look back and all I see is creamy undisruption, like sand the color of whatever, smoothed out where I've tried to roughen, glib and silly where I tried to make smashes. Not a speck. I didn't connect. The wheels are still grinding away and my monkey wrench is pulverized in the grist along with the lives of the people I care about but can't manage to find or help. How, how, how, how, how, how, how, how do I help?

*

Professor Budshah stretches out his neck twenty feet and plunges his head in through the aperture in the dripping stone wall. The other economists stand by and wait. Minute flashes of bluish and violet-hued sparks flicker and die in the soft opacity of their shadowy bodies. Eyes that are nothing more than glistenings swivel and shift from face to face.

Where are we now? How did we get so far away from ...

From ... what? Who? Was there someone else?

Ar... Ariello? Was that it?

She doesn't seem to be accompanying us any more.

But that's not who we're thinking of. We're looking for colder ... colder with the cold of being forgotten.

A cold spot?

Marks where something has been forgotten.

Someplace else?

Some idea?

Animal money?

Yes, the project! *Our* project! We remember! We remember? But there was something else we used to think about, and that we have misplaced. Us? We have a strong feeling of being misplaced. That cold—the cold of being forgotten. That's our cold now. We've all got it.

*

Assiyeh sits at the foot of my bed, one leg doubled under her and the other on the floor, and we talk.

"Am I still on the *Izallu Imeph?*" she asks. "Or is this Koskon Kanona now?"

"Neither," I say. "You're still on earth."

"Oh really?" She sounds unconvinced.

"You never left," I tell her.

"You think so?"

When I reach out to touch her naked body, she isn't there. She was never there, never existed.

Searing, interstellar loneliness—

A silent, dreamless explosion in the empty bedroom.

PART ELEVEN:
DISCOUNT RICHES

Through trash-strewn open lots and among the crumbling walls and shattered storefront windows I go tripping through the rubble on feet death has made light, and the wind slips easily through my dry corn husk body. I see nothing, I hear nothing, I feel nothing, I know nothing, I smell.

We crashed into the sea on the way back from Achrizoguayla. The panic, the crowding, people dashing for the rafts, pushing them off from the plane only half full, wailing as the rafts swamped and sank. The plane bobs on the water, the doors are all open, sea air wafts through. I still sit with my seatbelt on. Or I did.

Now I'm here, trash strewn lots and all that.

I can see sometimes, after all. I can smell the ruin around me, I can smell the dry grey light, I can smell the radiant emptiness. The smell varies a great deal. It is never so strong that I can smell it without having to concentrate. I don't inhale. The odors form lines that can be followed. I can smell my motion along them. It's a dry, sour smell, like dust from a mummified lemon. It's like seeing. The dry sour smell of my movements. I think it must be the particles of my own body. I can't hear, and I can't feel myself. I don't feel my limbs move. They might not move. I think they move, but I don't *feel* them move.

They might move, but, in my dream I see myself floating along over the ground like a leaking helium balloon. I don't see *that*, I see myself walking, from the inside, not as an observer. I look like a scarecrow. Shadows on my face, no matter what. Rags of shredded cinderblock poke holes in my wasp-nest feet. My ribs have flattened in toward my spine, irregularly. I'm wearing the formal suit and necktie of death, a plain black neck tie like none I ever owned. It isn't plain. In the dream that reflects my present moment, I watch from my own left shoulder as I pick up the tie and examine it, working my head around a little to get a better look, my stiff, grave-touseled hair rattling like straw. The tie, clamped in a hand that looks like a twist of wire, is white, not black.

It *is* black, but it has been blackened with writing, having *originally* been white. Thinking, putting words together like this, is a chore. I wonder why I do it. I wonder why I care what's on my tie or where I am, when there is no one to talk to, no destination of any kind. I try to ask a question, but I can't. Being able to ask questions must be a power that only the living have. Dead men don't ask questions, the movie villain says. Without curiosity, I look at the writing that blackens my white necktie. It's occult formulae. No it isn't, it's economic formulae. The writing is microscopic, but all in neat lines very close together. It is an extract from a treatise in technocratic economics, with a different pseudo-mathematical equation in every sentence.

Pluto means rich. The lord of the underworld is rich not only because he lives within and rules the Earth, with its veins of gold and deposits of precious stones, but also because his is the kingdom of neverending growth. No end of death, no end of growth. No end to the impious sorrow of the Teeming. Looking directly down into the energy field I see it's full of floating rays, like rays of sunlight in water. In the underworld of economists, where dead souls mutter hollow equations after the end of time, this necktie is a talisman that is going to get me into a place I don't want to go, a colossal planned economy of little exchanges between me and the elements of decay. I don't want to dissolve that way. There are no elements of decay. Decay is the evaporation of elements. There's no exchange. It's the opposite of animal money. Instead of doubling both sides of the equation, decay money doubles something with nothing, like paying money in the mirror. The mirror money is only your own money again, at the same time. When I see myself in the mirror, I see myself as nothing and say that's me, so death is a mirror, the mirror of my dream. No it isn't, my dream isn't a mirror. I don't watch my dream; my dream does the watching. My dream tells me what I'm smelling is light, or motion, or the necktie I rip from around my neck with fingers like wires and toss way up into the air. Maybe it will sail cinematically away across an overcast sky filled with white seams. In fact, it does fly away in the air, black against a grey sky. It flies like a snake, curving side to side. It flies like a battered, arthritic snake, with a permanent kink in its spine. Now it's out of smelling range, hidden by what's left of the flat rooftops. A linoleum of garbage trampled perfectly flat covers the streets. Everything of use is long scavenged. Even the shards of glass have all been pulled out of the windows. The street lamps have all been pulled down, and the signs. The cables are all gone, ripped down. The buildings have been burned and weathered and half ripped apart.

This smells like a major intersection. There's a huge parking lot on each corner, a big box store over there, looking stomped. Scorched wreckage of a gas station. Blasted shops and withered steel skeletal remains. No weeds in the cracks. Nothing grows here, not even mildew. I can't smell a fly. It feels desolate here. It feels exactly the way this intersection always felt. Minus the fuss. And that's a relief.

I smell my way along lines of memory. My last day. I made coffee, was going to have pancakes. I wasn't going to have pancakes, toast is what I was going to have. I had set out the butter to soften on the stove top. I'm not dreaming, not at all. What I've been thinking of as my dream is really my memory. Somehow I mistook remembering for dreaming. If I somehow ever recover my ability to ask questions, I should remember to ask why I have always been liable to make mistakes like that one. I mean, the kind of mistakes no one but me makes. This is livelier smelling than I expected. I fly down the street playing hooky from life. Something happened to me, a dream that came into my head so hard it broke my skull, pulped my brains, all while the butter softened on the stove. Hours passed, bugs haltingly crossed the floorboards by my feet. The window widened to fill the horizon. The butter softened.

Now what I smell is linseed oil, the museum smell. The smell of my movement is changing. Maybe people have emerged from inside the Earth and they are putting me in their museum. Even dead I remain in education. What I smell, no, is not a museum, it's fire. I must be burning. Maybe I moved too fast, and the friction of my corpse against the air caused my dry remains to catch fire.

The fire lightens me. I get lighter and lighter, with alarming swiftness. It's like being hauled up high into the sky. Hang there a moment. Then another long pull drawing me further and further up. Lighter and lighter, elongating toward the ... the top. Elongating up. Flying up. Sprinkling down, in crumbs of ash. The fire divides off pieces that fall away. Those pieces, I know, drop to the ground, even though I don't. My hair is all spiralling flames now, my head is a torch. I'm a big, pale torch. I think.

Now I am all burned up. My few remaining bones fall out of the sky. Those leaping flames are shyly retiring into my few remaining sections. They will gnaw at me with tiny orange teeth as long as there is anything there for them. I am in the fragments of bone, here on the ground, and the ash tossing all around, and in the smoke the air carries away, and in some other residues I don't have a name for, spreading out in all directions, some of me moving and leaving while the other parts stand still and remain. I'm thinning out between them all.

*

Thafeefa sits there at the table smiling. She's arranging flowers in a white vase, the "sun" sets alight her unblemished skin. She won't start to show for another month, but the glow is there.

"You will need a third parent," the doctor told her,

smiling pleasantly. He was a imperturbable man with an avuncular grin and thicker glasses than a doctor should have to wear, and his black hair kept slipping in sidelong locks across his brow. Thafeefa is an artificial person and much of her DNA is human incompatible, making her sterile under normal circumstances; impregnating her will require a considerable amount of supplemental DNA from a second human donor to produce a viable baby.

"But this would be true for the first donor in any case," the doctor went on offhandedly, turning back toward his office.

"What do you mean?" Thafeefa asked innocently.

The thought of being pregnant made Assiyeh "want to howl," as she once put it, but the doctor's tone suggested a somatic reason.

The doctor turned and regarded Thafeefa pointedly.

"She never told you she had a third parent?"

He came over beside her and pointed to the results labelled A. MELACHALOS, where a number of genes were circled and underlined.

"There. There. There."

He waved his hand.

"All of them, from a third party."

The doctor shook his head.

"This code would give anybody trouble because, you see, those genes there ... I've never seen anything like that. Whoever donated them was very strange. I mean, I couldn't even tell you the species," he said.

"Perhaps some animal had exactly the genes they needed to complete her code."

"Animal or plant!"

When the doctor slipped into his inner sanctum, Thafeefa searched her memory for any physical anomalies in Assiyeh and drew a blank. She was a terrible swimmer. Did that mean anything? She also searched their conversations for any anecdotal indications. No good. Everything was a clue and nothing was. Her mother's aversion to cats could point one way or the opposite way. It is clear she never knowingly encountered her third parent, even when performing her necromantic titrations.

Now Thafeefa is pregnant and glowing like a happy vanilla flame there with her flowers. The doctor found a posthumous donor from the neighboring arcology, referred by the *Izallu Imeph* fertility and population committee (IFAP). As rational as a flower herself, Thafeefa supervises gestation, braiding her programming into developing neurons, so that, even as she plays and smiles, happy and apparently as thoughtless as a toddler, she is composing thousands of tissue fugues in an eerie, unsettling key, because perfection is impossible for what is sui generis, and this child is being formed for maximum independence.

*

Today in the stark black and white street I saw a woman still reeking of Earth, clumsily making her way through the psychic rapids of Buzzatian pedestrian traffic, an obvious newcomer and equally obviously an agent. I evaded her easily this morning. Come on, my enemy!

Calmly I survey my tossed apartment. Thafeefa's leg lies severed on the floor, a gear protruding form the joint, wires trailing. They put her torso upright on the kitchen table and tucked flowers into her open throat, set her head across the room where it could watch. All right, pretty scary. But Thafeefa, my dears, is light years away, on board the *Izallu Imeph*, made of flesh and blood, not the gears and wires of this crude replica. She is probably arranging flowers right now, humming the Goldberg Variations under the skylight.

Assiyeh books a trip to Qazkerl, a city on the far side of Koskon Kanona, boards the hovercraft, and disembarks at the last minute, engulfed in the lush hour rush. Assiyeh modifies her interferometer, trying to find a way to jam the spies. Today an agent travelled the length of her street, twice.

*

Why is it never more light here? The buildings are only black regularities specked with bright points. The streets are wan grey arteries that stream glowing bloodcells. My own arm, my own hand, are not my own, or not that I can tell. They are only shadows. We all loom over the city like witches over a cauldron. I watch as one of us looms in over the street, but the features absorb the street glare and remain invisibly dark. We recline on our sides like Roman patricians, the city a pit of embers. We reach out to adjust this or that part of the city every now and then. Our bodies lie among the mountains, and along the shores. We chirp information back and forth, monitoring and adjusting, and we take phone calls. We are constantly talking on the telephone to other economists, specialists, scientists, journalists ... people ... people we never see. We communicate with this city using a local radio call-in show. We chant in a steady dream monologue without inflection, and the words all turn into things and actions before our eyes. We monitor the city and yet it is never even partially under our control.

Is this still about animal money? How did we get here? Why do we go on and on without stopping, as if we were afraid to stop?

When I was in my teens, I used to read fantasy books and project myself into them with a feeling that rivalled anything to be found in poetry. That is, it was a feeling that I could not analyze or name, but only rhapsodize about, unintelligibly. There was an upsweeping feeling of wild freedom expressed in terms of the opening of landscapes and of untrammeled movement in space. It resembled the surging of a tide, plains of tall grass, wind, launching into the air, the sight of distant mountains, the feeling of the weather. It felt like nakedness, sexual desire, a sexual desire to fly without dissolving into an eternally expanding landscape, and it also had something to do with music, especially music with a jewelled sound, if that makes sense. The sounds had a gleam at the higher pitches and a luster in the lower ones, and they struck me like vivid primary colors, contrasting without clashing. And there were precious metals in the sound as well, and glass or crystal sounds, very clear and pure but often with an exquisitely intolerable quality that was not beauty exactly, more like slicing. I associated that music with magic, and a magical liberty to unfold in an infinite planet consisting of superlatively beautiful natural vistas and intriguingly varied and strange human enclaves, all strictly isolated from each other, so that there was no place in the whole world that felt hemmed in and hopeless, inescapable, not bordering sharply on a territory belonging to everything that could be imagined.

At the same time, there was a lacerating sadness that would well up in me around these fantasies, and that was no more comprehensible. Why did these fantasies all seem to spin into a terrible sense of loss even as they were at the apex of their existences? Why did they seem more real in the moment I first turned to them again, and seem to lose reality the further I went with them? How could I have such inchoate desires in the first place? It was not their unreality that depressed me, or that I ran from, but their reality rejected me. I was not real enough for them, or, even though I did manage, I can not explain how, to exist, I existed in some wrong way, not their way, not like them. The problem was, perhaps, that I had always to uphold that reality myself, and that not a single thing ever presented itself to me as objective in those fantasies. Like Atlas, I had to hold the whole thing up by my own unflagging effort, so nothing came to me except as a more or less disguised act of my own will. The world had none of the spontaneity, surprise, antipathy, that I consider the sine qua non of real experience. And yet, there are times when the imagination produces something without being asked, without being told, without any explanation, something so arbitrarily complete in itself and satisfying, so persuasive, that it can only be called objective.

I confided something like this to a college friend, who was very taken with Freud at the time and found it entirely too easy to account for my fantasies. I had, of course, not asked him to account for them, had no desire for an account. I wanted them, not an account of them. Certainly the book covers were all very sexual, and my fantasies did not much avoid the erotic element. The celibacy of the economist did not balk me significantly because, once I discovered that the desires of women take no necessary interest in adventurous accomplishment, sexual satisfaction lost a surprising amount of its appeal, and began to seem a very perfunctory and mundane thing. It was not that I could imagine a more beautiful woman than I could find; on the contrary, my imaginary women, for all their often even stark concreteness, still fell far short of the inexpressibly astonishing variety of the women I met. It was the intensity of the circumstances of my fantasies, and the fierce energy with which they mirrored my own emotions, that was lacking. Instead of the explosion, there was more usually the hydraulic compression of a situation, growing ever more dense and solid, implacably determined and directed.

Now this, this experience that is my existence now, is exactly the same. As we turn round and round the glittering carpet of the city, our dark arms reaching out to adjust this or that, we are not exploding, not swooping away into a yonder that grows wider and bluer. We are screwing ourselves deeper and deeper into a socket, and yet we have never been more hidden away or more worthy of the chaste mockery of the Teeming; we have never been farther away from from the city and its people than we are now.

"Why do we go on and on without stopping, as if we

were afraid to stop?" I ask aloud.

"Because we *are* afraid to stop, obviously," the voice belongs to the remaining Professor Long, I am sure.

"What is the fearsome thing we believe will happen if we stop?" I ask.

"That we will stop mattering," the remaining Professor Long says.

"We don't matter," Professor Budshah says sharply, and I hear his sudden resolution.

I stand up and flinch, afraid of hitting the top of my head against the sky. I raise my arm and encounter nothing. Not so low? I twist my waist and look around at the planet curving away from me, and I see the silhouetted heads of the other economists, also standing, also looking around, like sleepers rousing themselves.

*

In her dream, the sun jumps to its next station in the sky just as they emerge from the barqot, just as if the sun had been waiting to salute them on their arrival. Assiyeh turns a full circle in methodical, even surveillance of the scene before she nods and, smiling, gestures to Thafeefa to step out. Thafeefa wears a billowing, ankle-length garment of green gauze. Jagged mountains rise before them, piebald with snow under powdery azure sky swept by a freshening wind. The ocean fills the world to the right. They watch the end of the barqot retreat and vanish around the campus, which consists of a half dozen buildings huddled like witches in a hollow; all projecting points at the corners and Mansard roofs and uplifted spikes like alerted ears. Assiyeh and Thafeefa walk hand in hand along a gravel drive into the campus.

"Why are we here?" Assiyeh half-murmurs to herself. "Because Thafeefa was feeling cooped up. She wanted to come here."

Startled out of their daydreams, the buildings flash their windows indignantly as they enter the quad. Huge ancient trees with long corkscrewing arms grow from trembling grass skirts, sheltering the flagged paths. There's no one in sight.

"They must all be inside," Assiyeh think-says.

The air is cool and frisks around them, so that Thafeefa's gown bellies out like a sail. She laughs as a rising gust nearly lifts it off her body, holding it down with the weight of her arms. Her warmth reaches out through the bracing wind and almost touches Assiyeh. Thafeefa pauses by a tree, lays her palm on it, smiles up into the chaotic spread of the branches above her, then turns to look at Assiyeh.

"Wouldn't you like to kiss me here?" she asks.

Assiyeh kisses her. Thafeefa bends forward and embraces her tightly, keeping her stomach down out of the way, branch shadows wafting over the two of them. It's so much the fulfillment of her desires that Assiyeh nearly wakes.

Now they are out in the open again.

"I like feeling the light," Thafeefa says.

Assiyeh is looking around for a sign. There's a concert tonight, at the performing arts center. But the campus is deserted. Assiyeh steers Thafeefa up a short flight of stone steps and toward a spacious building with a mural on a plank wall.

"Why did they paint the mural on those boards?" she asks. "They didn't even take the irregularities into account. They could have incorporated it into the picture."

A deep archway opens on stunning view of the sea and the mountainous coast, a deep green lawn rolling down a slope to disappear in trees, then the shore.

Inside the ceilings are low with heavy beams, the hall is wide, and the ponderous wooden doors are shaped like inverted shields. The place is open and filled with moving air, but no people. Assiyeh goes to the reception desk— nobody there. Facing the desk, a flight of stairs leading up the tower. A sign on the wall points to the theater.

Thafeefa laughs. She is a bit down the hall already, pointing to a mosaic depicting a priapic faun lounging on the back of a jellyfish wearing eyeglasses. Thafeefa floats along a little further, like a green balloon receding in the half-light, looking back at Assiyeh, demurely laughing behind her fingers.

Assiyeh catches her up and the two of them turn the corner and down the length of the hall to the closed double doors leading to the stage. The concert poster is tacked to the door with the word "cancelled" striking through the day's listing. Thafeefa says she has to go to the bathroom.

"I'll come too," Assiyeh says.

Assiyeh opens the stall door in time to see the outer door to the women's room just finishing its slow closing swing. She pauses to look under and then in the other stalls—empty. Thafeefa's garment hangs from a hook inside one of the doors.

Thafeefa calls her name in the hall, and her voice is

terrifyingly remote. Sick with fear, Assiyeh snatches at the door handle, which keeps slipping out of her fingers, or is snatched away, her fingers pushing the handle away, so she flings the door open by its edge, hearing that ambiguous call repeated, dwindling, dying, coming from no particular place as if the building itself were calling to her—

Something—the corner—and someone coming hastily down the hall beyond there's someone

"How did you get over there?" Thafeefa's voice asks.

Assiyeh's voice is pushing into her chest instead of out her mouth, then the warning bursts from her, she reaches the corner and the terror in her voice rebounds back at her from the walls and ceiling as she confronts all that untenanted space.

Try every door.

Check outside and in.

"Why did I take her here? I should never have let her talk me into coming here!"

There never was a Thafeefa. You came here alone. You are insane.

The sun lunges for the horizon and the shadows lurch, the air reddens, the waves redden, red shines back from the black slopes of the mountains.

"Thafeefa!"

"Thafeefa!"

"Thafeefa!"

*

"You masters of earth's transactions, now I set this exchange rate for you: one innocent equals one thousand of your richest men, plus one thousand of your richest women. Two thousand is the price I set on an innocent life.

"I have no doubt you are familiar with the concept of interest. The present average annual rate is three percent, I believe. So, for every year it takes me to collect the lives you owe, lives which are community property once again, I will add another three lives for every hundred owed. Compounded annually, of course.

"Nothing personal, you understand. The demand for growth is no respecter of persons, as you're so fond of saying. I merely follow market forces, as you do."

That year, the G18 summit was meeting in Naples when Mount Vesuvius unexpectedly erupted in a cataclysmic explosion. The concussion alone shattered whole buildings and knocked aircraft out of the sky. An inverted tornado of lava spurted a full kilometer straight up from the rent summit and the mountain split like the House of Usher. The flanks of the mountain belched a cataract of red lava that tore across the landscape at nearly two hundred kilometers an hour; the the G18 summit was meeting in a villa situated directly in the path of what researchers would later call a historically enormous pyroclastic flow. World leaders and their rich friends scrambled for their helicopters, and yet they all perished, engulfed in a wave of lava that casually devoured them, their security guards, the wait staff and servants. Experts pored over every piece of surviving evidence they could find. By all accounts, there should have been ample time for the people who mattered to escape; they never go anywhere without an escape plan—that goes with the territory. It was as if some unaccountable force slowed them down, dragged their steps. Two video cameras that were livestreaming the event over scrambled frequencies, uploading it in real time to secret servers, caught footage of summit participants rushing for their helicopters in what seemed like slow motion, even as the clouds of smoke from the approaching lava wave went sailing by at normal speed in the sky above. As the heat from the lava hit them, before the lava itself was even visible on camera, their expensive clothes spontaneously burst into flame, and their distress, their battering at their flaming clothes, the horror of men and women who dress with understated elegance suddenly turned into fiery and conspicuous spectacles for vulgar people to gawk at, was all recorded, all in slow motion. You can actually watch as they realize, one by one, that they are going to die, in a moment that draws itself out relentlessly and yet almost seems to refuse to pass, drawing out the horrific confrontation with death, inhaling flame with every breath, before the people themselves burst alight and become flaming human caricatures dancing in slow motion, ensconced in regular-motion flames, like blazing monks doing Tai Chi.

Here comes the lava—see how it covers everything on screen in less than two seconds, a surreally red, luminous blanket piebald with black. A colossal hologram of Nemesis towers out of the smoke high into the sky above them, raising in one hand the bridle of adamant that restrains mortal insolence, a great wheel of inversions beneath her feet, an umbrella over her head, her other hand sprinkling their wounds with black salt. She has a banner draped from one shoulder with a motto in English (the language of business):

"When it rains it pours."

*

Ashes bespatter my skeletal steel remains, damned among the brittle legions of the Misled. The smarting sweet salt of death is scattered all around us. We, the tenebrous minions of a nameless cabal, torture language and poetry alongside the writhings of our human victims. We are the nameless thralls in uniforms. The dire tolling of the nemesis bell awakened our unseen and unknown Misleaders to the next in an eternal litany of murderous crises, and so we are conjured once more from our sepulchral barracks, our hideous training camps, our pestilential bunkers and grim fortresses, once again to charge the frail barricades, to batter down the emaciated arms uplifted in feeble and bootless resistance, to squelch the doleful catechising of nightmare-haunted protestors, to erupt like hell's mastiffs among the daring and rebellious few. We are the midwives who deliver them swaddled in chains to a new birth of horror and bondage in the underworld of bottomless prisons and torture chambers where mutilated figures wail and braid their forms in arabesques of torment and a subterranean hurricane of screams fans waves across a turgid ocean of putrescent cinders, drives abyssal turbines, and urges on the shapeless and incurable lasciviousness of the concupiscent. Thou shalt rise unrefreshed from slumber at five in the morning. Thou shallt be at thy slavedesk by nine. There the hour of nine in the night shall find thee yet in anguish toiling. And then the pit, and the stench of numberless corpses, the ravenous drone of swarming flies.

Spontaneous brawls where the legions of the Misled clash with Black Metal Marxists. Bands with names like EXPROPRIATED and DOOMLEDGERS and LUMPEN. Their hardcoreness is expressed in abominable dryness and technicality. A typical album cover depicts combinations of guitar and labor tabulations rendered in unintelligibly convoluted, thorny black letter script on discolored, old-fashioned grids, early 1980s-era luminous spreadsheets green on black. The lyrics are drawn from nineteenth century factory inspector records, efficiency profiles, the second volume of *Capital* and Kafka's insurance reports.

Across the globe, very judiciously selected locations where the rich and powerful hide themselves are blanketed with a selectively focussed and filtered slowing field that retards the action of the human immune system in individuals possessing the physical attributes of wealth, power, and worthlessness. Certain politicians are brought up short in mid-speech their faces bubble and sag and slough off their bones. A slurry of decay gushes from government offices pouring down stairwells and slopping from windows. A frenzied scan through television channels is a stroboscopic nightmare of accelerated decomposition as lobbyists and journalists melt from underneath glorious hairstyles and ooze from expensive clothes and jewelry. Waiters table bussers cooks call girls and rent boys stampede out into the street from toney restaurants, clawing their way out windows and up from the cellars to escape a reeking inundation of undifferentiated putrescence that bubbles icily up behind them, a glabrous slop of black and yellow and grey and brown and green and congealing with diamonds rolexes tie tacks platinum cufflinks star sapphire labial piercings green cigars chugging mechanical hearts and implants that convulse like landed fish. Seconds are enough to turn think tanks into septic tanks, university departments into charnel houses, news channels are plague pits swarming with flies like the static on a dead television, police military and security headquarters burst like leprous fistulas spraying a vile rain of bluish rot for miles, the ground beneath them subsides to form a sinkhole filled to the brim with reeking sludge, with here and there a prisoner, a maintenance man or window cleaner, a secretary struggling to reach the edge. Those who avoid the curse and clamber onto the brink are doubled over retching, but when they can manage it, they try to rescue the others who are still trapped in the slough, one even leaping back in to help.

Who done it? Accusations, arrests, torture, killings; the arresting officers vanish, sometimes in the very act of carrying out their orders. Others, unable to believe they are being instructed to bring in a daffy old lady or a sulky fourteen year old, check back in for confirmation and can find no one on the other end of the line any more. No more agency. No more bureau. No more directorate. Your badge has gone blank. Your identification has turned into a cuneiform clay shard.

Where the hell is Koskon Kanona anyway? You could

ask an astronomer to tell you, of course, if you could find one, but nobody studies anything but business anymore. The astronomy departments all closed down years ago, along with all the other sciences. Students can take business with an astro-business concentration, but their teachers don't know much more about space and stars than they do—they mainly study different brands of spacecraft and colonization equipment manufacturers. Amateur astronomers? Impoverished astronomers? No such thing. Who has time? Who can see anything through the haze and the junk-lights anyway? Everyone is too busy either working or trying to find work, trying to stay alive. And those weird effects, the "slow-down fields"? The physics-business concentrations in the business schools create nothing more than educated consumers of mass produced physics products. All the former physicists are broken down relics going slowly insane in unpensioned retirements, living in basements and ruined garages, their fine brains cracked by years of fighting tooth and nail kitchen knife and baseball bat with their neighbors over batteries, cans of expired cat food, pairs of torn sweat pants, a few capsules of random medication, a book of matches. The military R&D men are interested, of course, in figuring out how it was done, but the most important of them were likewise casualties of the same phenomena, and the survivors are suspicious of each other. An experiment gotten out of hand, perhaps? Was it you? Or you?

*

Rats wearing bright orange vests crawl down the sidewalk in small groups and gather at the mouths of ratholes. One slips a tiny cigarette between its front teeth and lights it with an electric coil lighter it carries in a vest pouch. Minute wisps of bad tobacco smoke rise from the rats, punctuating their terse squeaks and unemphatic gestures. Ever since the latest batch of deep budget cuts, the city has made up for lack of personnel by training and hiring rats to perform electrical maintenance, to inspect plumbing and make minor repairs. Rats with live internet feeds have been trained to identify and follow suspicious persons, and rats now handle all the city's garbage. Since another round of cuts is expected soon, cockroach recruitment and training has already started. Discussion of replacing the handful of remaining postal workers with pigeons was nixed: pigeon meat is too valuable—mail delivery would finally end altogether as people catch and eat their mail pigeons, and how are they supposed to get their summonses and huge internet bills without postal carriers?

—Squirrels?

Same problem, and besides, squirrels are still too independent. Like raccoons, they are better left to roam subject to stop and frisk; let them forage up the buried acorns and discarded food, then take it from them. It saves us having to budget food money for the police.

And now there are bombings and explosions and fires, poison being sent through the mail, and significant shouting in the press, and the moment the unsettled feeling the most recent bit of news gives you begins to seat itself again and the butt of the soul re-nests itself here comes the next incomprehensible eruption, and history leaps out again in all directions going everywhere and nowhere, with a pat explanation about reichstag this and that, falling flat every time. This isn't something all over again; we haven't reached the point where we can say that yet. At present there really is no explaining the explanations. I can't explain my blood back into my body again, I can only watch it leave, my brain more alive and awake than it has ever been, and totally, impossibly empty of thought. Although unavailable for analysis in the moment of its being inflicted, being violently struck over the head is a very interesting experience, but you aren't exactly interested just at that moment, and there's nothing in that future reflection that's going to, here and now, displace me from the trajectory of that club or rock oriented to my head, no matter whether or not that head will go on to entertain this analysis or this right-now-whatever-this-is, not a repudiation of analysis, but maybe I want to know what analysis is for if I can't use it to remove my head from the path of a violent blow. "Get me out of the goddamn way" is more the thought at hand, according to my analysis. Shit is blowing up.

This just blew up. That just caught fire. Somebody is shooting up this town you never heard of. The chief of the Political Police just received a flaming hay bale in the mail and it nearly burned down his pile of confiscated flash drives. Here the cops have superefficiently corralled and captured a group of fascists in the advanced stages of a plan to anthrax a city. There the same cops have bunglingly massacred twenty five people at a swap meet in Downey CA on obviously fake evidence. Everything is so hypertrophied and elephantine and wildly careening that a swerve intended to spare one group of bystanders precipitates a collision with another. A woman who complains about sexism on the news is arrested and vanishes without a trace, although someone claims to have recognized her in a batch of prisoners delivered in dead of night to a foreign air force base and prison. At the same time, openly berserk fundamentalists of every variety apoplectically declare one holy war after another barking quotations, their mouths bigger and more and more square their cheeks and brows crushing like fists around their eyes. Muzak, a flyby over some lettering as the camera gazes numbly at well groomed, tranquil, collegial men and women blandly discussing the shrieking blood hurricane gobbling up the world around them even as an explosion blows away the backdrop and reveals the heavyset stage managers with headsets and tool belts running for cover, hands up around their heads, the coffee guy tossing the urn aside and climbing into the bottom of the trolley, propelling it to safety with his hands.

It's not that I don't understand, and it's not that I don't even sympathize, and it shurashell isn't that I weep for the the the the you know Genghis Khans of late capitalism watching their chickens come back, but what then? There's a lot of bystanders getting wiped out. Who's going to be left to pick up what pieces in what ripped up hands? Let's say we do get our golden chance, however bloodily paid for, to remake the world, not from scratch, but from rip, from disembowel, from a scream of anguish so loud it actually stops most of it—what? Can you read and write using no punctuation but question marks?

Sooner or later you will say something with a period or even an exclamation mark, even if it's only NO! NO!

*

Well, so we're phantoms. We're great starry silhouettes, black as night and stippled with constellations that move behind our outlines. We're just holes cut through to the starry cosmos. We have become dark economists. We met at a hotel in South America. We were all suffering from coincidental head injuries. There was a duel, as yet unresolved. We invented animal money, made some, let it loose. We became targets, we fled, further and further. We escaped. Now we are sharp-edged shadows, towering over San Toribio. We squat or recline beside the city combing its golden traffic streams, reaching out our void arms to make adjustments to a city like a luminous sand painting mixing in dully glowing ash and tiny vibrant embers. We aren't controlling the city. We're adjusting it. I reach out my hand to a light on a stalk, maybe an antenna, or an aircraft warning beacon, sprouting from a tall building. The light is a little crooked. I straighten it. That's all. No control. I could lay may hand across the freeway and the cars would pass right through it. We act, and here I believe I can say I speak for us all, without thought of the future, without trying to realize any plan, but only like someone who reaches out to right a picture hanging askew on a wall. We're forgetting which of us is which. That is to say, our plan has become our behavior.

How are we doing?

The question appears haphazardly in one of our minds,

I guess mine. It would be easier to let the thought-current carry it off, but I hold it. With an effort I manage to open the thought. It's like walking underwater. How are we doing means where are we going. Where we are going is to sleep. We are shutting down through our thinking. Our thinking is putting us under.

There is general concurrence. We are agreed. As things are going for us at present, we will soon be asleep, with no one to wake us. We are resolved against becoming sleepers of Ephesus.

We have to struggle against that mental drag, what must be the inert momentum of our own thinking habits. That means thinking against habit. Struggling to wake up from a dream, even a true dream, struggling toward a different dream, a waking dream, to live as dark economists. A dream of waking up. How do we do that?

Trial and error, and then one of us comes up with an idea: try to visualize something at ground level.

Visualize what?

The image is of someone leaning way down until his nose is level with a rough wooden counter and he has placed one blue coin that isn't metal or glass or porcelain but having qualities like all these, like a translucent wafer of blue conch shell, on the counter and his finger is still pressed down on the coin as if he wanted to keep it from jumping off the counter in a single bound and rolling out the door into the street, free money. This is happening in an old wild-west wood and glass shop, grainy, dim, creak and jostle of floorboards.

The man, his tongue sticking out the corner of his mouth, all his concentration focussed, is sliding the coin away from himself across the counter. What is he buying? Is he buying something?

It's more like he's just spending, but it's also as though he were taking stock in a certain way, like accounting, but instead of adding up columns of figures he's moving this one coin across the counter. He's like a child counting his Halloween haul. There's an idea that the coin will begin to unfold winglike tabs and become several coins, one screwing out of the shallow tray of the last—is he trying to prevent this or cause it, or postpone it till the proper time?

Is it a counterfeit, and what would counterfeit animal money be? Not passing one animal off as another, chicken feathers glued all over a turtle with a strap on wattle, not ordinary money, but a nightmarish hybrid of animal and nothingness, malignantly ugly—it attacks by being seen, like Medusa (remember it wasn't her gaze that did it to you, it was your own gaze, the pollution travelled up your eyebeam, not down hers).

Wall Street would be the Grande Animal Brothel, but in addition to the animal money there would also be the buying and selling of the gods and goddesses of animal money culture, the very laws themselves are bought and sold, coming into and going out of effect, being revised then de-revised, porpoise money shimmers in the daylight, tossing with ringing metallic chimes before the bow of a scudding sailboat. A cacophony of grunts and bellows and chirps from pig money, cat money, ant money, moth money, owl money, cricket money.

The sound of crickets is an open door and I step through onto soft grass, trees overhead, the lights of the city in the distance, the sky fading overhead. What are my hands, my feet? It's me, Professor Budshah. In the sky above the city I can see the colossal transparencies of my associates—four of them. Four? Who is the fourth, now that I am down here again?

I close my eyes and I see the golden lights spread out below my invisible hands, feel the mountain tops digging into my knee as I kneel on them, and the clouds of the night sky passing through my body cool and soft, the starlight passing through my body cool and soft. I am in both places at once, towering over the city, and standing here, on this slope, overlooking the town. The others are still in only one place—"up there." I can barely see them, but there is a strange, tactile sense of them. They feel like heavy velvet dolls filled with fine, cool ash. One of them has a satellite, a little companion who also has a dark, smaller companion. And there is a fifth figure in there somewhere, like the zero after the decimal point. I think the fifth figure is conferring with the one with the satellite. Now that one, the one with the satellite, is pantomiming something for me. I can tell it is directed to me, somehow. The two eyes, like yoked stars, are constantly finding me in the dark. The figure is pointing to the way out, and making a gesture of reaching in and scooping up, pulling up. If I reach out my arm, I know I will be able to draw them out of that tall, taboo night, and back down here to the slope.

I try it. Dark economics. I conjure the other economists—here comes Professor Crest, with his high kneeing marionette's walk, his upraised pointing finger; here is the remaining Professor Long, ideas boiling like smoke, slithering and gliding and warping and shapeshifting as they float away to the hiding places they chose for themselves; farther away, I see Professor Aughbui with Smilebot and Smilebot with Boringbot, stepping from seam to seam between empty mirrors reflecting each other, and whose direction is impossible to guess; and in the farthest distance I can see a tall, lean silhouette, a wavering, flamelike, long-armed figure: the late Professor Long, standing out wasted against a darkness not quite as dark as he.

There are only three of us here.

Professor Aughbui remained behind, only the godlike shade.

Now we are in two places at once, here on the ground again, and also hovering over the city in a night that doesn't end, because, as I now understand, everything we do in that state happens faster than the eye of the day can follow. How long have we been away?

"Without day and night, without the test book and the separation of beads ..."

"You were not separating beads or completing your tests?" Professor Crest cries.

"How could I do my tests without my book?"

"We have all taken countless tests, and they are each more the same than different. Surely you could have made one up in your head. You could have separated the beads mentally. It is not necessary to have actual beads. I did it easily."

"But there was no morning or evening. We did not go to sleep or wake up. As I recall we never slept."

"Immaterial. It is only necessary to perform both acts

at regular intervals. I timed mine to coincide with the illumination of offices in one of the high rise buildings that stood out from the rest. I would mentally separate my beads when the lights were all turned on, and test myself silently when the lights were turned off again. How could you simply drop the tests and the separation of beads like that?"

"What's the difference?" the remaining Professor Long asks.

"It makes a tremendous difference! Taking the tests and separating the beads are essential aspects of being an economist, every bit as much as is reading Smith or following GDPs."

"We were in a different time-frame," the remaining Professor Long says. "It might have been all one night, and you might have been performing many days' worth of bead separation and testing without realizing ..."

"I hadn't thought of that."

"It does no harm, but ..."

"No, it does no harm."

The question now before us, which must be addressed without the slightest delay, here, on the dry, herbally fragrant hillside over looking the city in the valley below, with the sun below the horizon but still shining up into the sky and burning pink on the mountaintops, is what we are going to do with what we have learned. I am explaining that, with our new, 'double vision,' we have to move away from that dead end of godly oversight to find a worldly solution.

Professor Crest raises his index finger. He's so much the marionette it's hard to keep a straight face as he disputes passionately with me, and I can't say whether I want to give him an affectionate smile or laugh derisively at him. He says that the vision only appears double to us because our perspective is still too limited; we need to discover what he calls the singularity of the vision, and, as he puts it, incarnate that singularity.

"To go back is retreat," he says emphatically.

"It's just the opposite," I explain. "There's already quite of that 'darkness,' of that 'night' about us already. We have to come out of the dark into the no less hideous light."

Professor Crest is starting to color under his white economist's mark. I can see how he must be looking at it, thinking that I am demanding he submit to me, summoning what he believes is righteous indignation.

"I honestly fail to understand how you can be so blind," he snaps.

"I think I see well enough."

"Does that mean we must follow you?"

"What is all this rubbish about leading and following? Did I ever demand anybody follow me?"

"No, you—"

"—In anything?"

"No, you merely imply it every time you speak."

"Nonsense!"

"You have a Messianic idea of yourself."

"I have no such thing, and that's more than you can say."

"Turning it around now, are you?" He folds his arms. "I don't accept Jesus Crest as my personal savior."

"No, you believe in the great king without luxury—"

"—Oh, would you be referring to me, now, is that me?—"

"—who is all the more superior to us mere mortals because he of his secret greatness and the austere purity of elective poverty."

"Don't be an idiot, Professor Crest," I say.

"*Do not*," Professor Crest says, lifting his index finger.

The three of us are breaking up. There is more here now than this group of us can hold.

"Do not be a monophysite, Professor Crest," Professor Budshah says, unhappily.

"I have no choice," Professor Crest says. "What is right is right."

The remaining Professor Long is no longer beside us. I turn and see her dark head drifting away. I call to her. She turns back to look at us, and I realize that she isn't going to come back again. The distance between us now can only grow. This is her contribution to our argument, I can see at once, on her face, even from this far away, her face overlaid with a dimly glowing pink sunset mask. She waves her hand at us quickly.

"The Surfeit is One."

She lowers her head and turns, resumes walking away.

I turn to face Professor Crest again. He is watching her go. Then his eyes flick to me again.

"Well," he says.

I raise my eyebrows.

"Good luck, Ronald," I say. He doesn't seem inclined to shake my hand, so I don't offer it to him.

"I did not drive her away," he says.

"No," I say.

"I did not!" he says.

"I'm not making any accusations, Ronald."

My voice sounds tired to me.

"Good luck," I say again. "The Surfeit is One."

I turn and go. For a moment, I wonder if I should follow the second Professor Long, or try to catch up to her, but there wouldn't be any point.

"Professor Budshah!"

The distance that has opened up between all three of us can't be reduced that way. There is a tangle of dirt tracks up here, and she took one—I can see some of the cup-like indentations her heels left. I take a route that will curve around the other way. At my back, I can feel, like the embers of a doused campfire, the ebbing out of our smouldering fellowship, the fading of its warmth. Then I stop and think, looking up.

Professor Aughbui is still 'up there.' I try to throw a message to him, far up into the forbidden nocturnal dimension he preferred. It's not unlike throwing a rock down a well and listening for a splash or a clack. And I do seem to 'detect' something, although I can't say whether it is a sound or a feeling. It could be the brief echo of a hum. He is still there, I take it. Insofar as he was ever anywhere, it might not make that much of a difference to him, except perhaps that it might be easier for him to remain behind.

After a few minutes more, a movement catches my eye by its corner. It's Professor Crest, who has I see, chosen the steep way, of course, straight down the side of the hill. He will reach the valley floor first, probably congratulating himself on having come down by the most difficult way. And what then? He will do what each of us will do whenever we find our way, all the way, down; he will pick a street and follow it.

*

The titans of finance convene a gigantic black mass after the destruction of the G18 leaders. Silverbacks of the world in designer robes and cowls and glittering diamond-encrusted fetishes drone incantations and sprinkle blood over writhing whores and catamites. The mass is conducted in the basement of a decommissioned church and there are windows at street level lined with intrigued onlookers who point and nudge each other, hold up their phones to take pictures and video. These masses become regular affairs and the street vendors outside do a hot business on pagan holidays.

Their incantations don't seem to be doing them much good. Regular money is bottled up, governments are out of assets and nobody will lend to them, people are out in the streets raving, people are running for their useless survival bunkers and coming back two weeks later out of supplies and half dead from rebreathing their own air. Governments are shredding to pieces and wherever that happens the military steps in to "take command," whatever that means. Generals don't know economics any better than politicians know war and "regular people" are taking a double hit from exploding economies and martial law.

Here in Achrizoguayla the re-re-election is coming up in a few days and there are placards all over the television, people in the streets of Etsimen bellowing at each other. I know Urtruvel is still sniffing for my scent. That shapeless gobbling media-bloated face of his is going to float to the surface of just about every advertisement and magazine cover, his eyes gushing adhesive slime all over my feet, gluing me down for arrest. This is the kind of thing that happens to people who know too much, but what do I know that's so damn important? It's like they're going through the motions. They're supposed to be the THEM that everybody talks about, so they just go ahead and do what everybody expects them to do, which is bad impersonations of movie villains, apparently. The equipment is all there, so they use it, as if using it will create a rationale for using it. The equipment just happens. Nobody ordered it. There's no plan it fits into. It goes after me because I'm not on their side, that's all. I am an unknown animal. I don't happen to know any other animals of my own species, but I seem dimly to recollect others like me. I wish I could, but I can't, say how they were like me, or what I am like. There doesn't seem to be a name for me as an individual or as a species. That's the problem. What they know doesn't matter, even to them. Their "knowledge" of me is meaningless. But they have to know everything, just because they can't allow anything to be beyond their reach in any way, even if it's worthless, even if no one looks at it, even if having it is worse than not having it.

Are they after me because we actually do have the real Tripi here, bedded down with chattering teeth and fever in our overcrowded motel room? In the last five days, two more have turned up of their own accord on our doorstep. Taking care of them all is a full-time job. They all seem to be delirious, almost too feeble to move, with a boundless capacity for absorbing soup, which is why I'm back on bucket duty today, heading out to the corner for more.

Man on the street: "Kill them all! Kill them all!"

Me: But why stop there? Why not kill everybody? The button still works!

Man: "Fine by me! Great! I'll be in heaven and—"

Me:—It's win-win!

Man: "—I'll be in heaven while you burn in hell!"

Me: Right on man we can share the ticket communistically, your heaven *is* my hell!

... All right you're not going to impress anybody with your revelation pop song lyrics. "Thought-provoking." "Impassioned." "Bullshit."

The Earth is currently on fire, and somehow I can sit here just watching it, over the ocean, see the orange sky, the silver level, the shadow birds streaking right along the surface so fast and heavy, and breathe in the calm that is breathed over me. People used to wail over the cruel impassiveness of nature when selfs are ground into hamburger, and now we stare incredulously at the selfless impassiveness of nature as human selfs destroy it once and for all.

The world is on fire, and yet one glance over there shows me Homer's waves. The sight slackens me so that my thoughts run on and on like children playing rather than like the heavy footfalls of important ideas. Leave those to the economists for now, or no, hope that they pick up the pace. Too much whipslamming and blamming going on, the streets, the boulevards, the avenues, are all jammed like subway cars with wall to wall people stuffed together like heaps of laundry bags. I've just run into Carolina again and we're trying to fill each other in on the shituation with some of our colleagues—who is under arrest, who has to stay out of sight. Talking and the woman eating next to me mistakes my mouth for hers stuffs a big bread roll into my mouth by accident. The guy smoking next to Carolina turns his head suddenly to see where the noise is coming from and the lit end goes right into her ear. Carolina spraying sealant on her ear, and the blood hasn't even coagulated so the whole thing is turning into a white and gelatinous and bloody swirl like a molten peppermint there in his eye. "I hear that Urtruvel is coming back from Paraguay," she says, then pivots to drive her taser into the smoker's kidney with a solid chunk. The smoker groans and stiffens. There's a big fat man behind us masturbating. "Uh," he says. "Uh," he says more urgently. The big masturbating man turns his head and belches garlic. Bloated cops shove their way through the crowd casually macing and beating anyone in reach. I get a drizzle of mace that slams my eyes shut, burning them like hot coals, my lungs grabbed with rough wool fingers. I can hear the melony sound of the clubs hitting heads, the soft grunts and moans, the gradually diminishing wail of the smoker. An explosion goes off somewhere in the distance. The cops flinch and then go on chewing their gum. A kinetic surge billows through us lurching me off my feet and weightlessing the buildings which swim up and by as the crowd shifts, recoiling from the blast, from people pressed in too tight to get away and burning, the fire spreads to people eating bag snacks and twiddling their melting, dripping phones with stripped bone and tendon fingers.

*

I cross the lobby, messy after my long walk and yearning for relief from the crowds. The lobby is teeming with people.

A woman is coming from the other direction; with her head flung back, mouth open, she waddles forward like an advancing walrus. I raise my elbow to fend off a collision. She clips me as she passes, without a word; the concussion, evidently, could not penetrate her numbness. I imagine she gets around seat to seat. Despite her weak legs, she manages to keep her bulk in motion by tunnelling through space in a headlong rush, and evading obstacles must be a bit beyond her. This is one type.

Now I see I am about to be compelled to deviate around a thick column to avoid a tall, lean, man mincing forward with small steps, staring vacantly at something in his hand.

"Excuse me!" I bark, without slowing, and I brush by him. I feel the murmur of indignation at my back, but coma will close over him again, I think, and the anger in his mind will dim. As I mentally condescend to the people around me, an evil smile wreathes my lips.

*

A vision of Nemesis roams the sky all over the world,

half shrouded in trailing clouds, riding on a huge indigo wheel, calling Greek words in an earsplitting voice. If only ... if only ...

From time to time the figure reaches into the cloud, pulls out a bow, and shoots an arrow at the ground or ocean. The arrow vanishes before it can strike, and cities sprout from its shadow, burgeoning up instantly and spreading cities of fungus and fire, sprouting up like the plumes of nuclear explosions and freezing to form great canopies and radiant puffballs like molten orange candy shells, huge translucent horns made of chitin rising up all the way to the top of the atmosphere, with legions of slow Uhuyjhns whirling around it, entering and leaving it through its oval portals like vast needle eyes. Where these cities sprout, they roll aside all human contrivances with a cold, unhurried, hydraulic displacement; the city foundation on a massive elastic pad whose edges crimp in rounded fingers. The towers emanate a cascade of superiority waves that batter apart puny human minds, the pink and pastel colored fungus cities are lit day and night by multicolored fires, and spindles soaring high into the sky stream out dense spore plumes like smokestacks. So now, on top of purely domestic problems, the human race has to contend with an infestation of Uhuyjhns, whose burning mycelial cities are hiring, are paying better wages, offering better benefits. Positions are advertised on parchment-like membrane scraps that explode from puffballs. New hires will find themselves completely covered in thin, flexible sporotic integuement within a few days. The fungus sprouts and falls off, but the worker is unharmed and unparasitized. Humans are provided with netlike filtration material to fit into the mouth and nostrils, to prevent spores entering the lungs. Other orifices are safe enough.

The Nemesis vision is a conspiracy, it's a hologram, it's a bizarre psychological weapon of the Uhuyjhn invaders. Her voice shatters windows and blasts apart frailer structures, scatters clouds abruptly curtailing rainstorms, sets off all the car alarms in town. The mountains shout the words back again and avalanches hurtle down their sides. What is she saying? People want to know.

"For Christ's sake, give the bitch whatever she fucking wants!"

*

The time traveller's error, Assiyeh decides, is that they take the direct approach. That's the route to contradiction. If I go back to that day and try to prevent—

Click!

... See? It doesn't work.

Assiyeh is chain smoking, taking puffs between bites of her lunch. Thunder and lightning outside. Kanonan storms come from nowhere and snap into place, turning the day brown, but thunder and lightning are the same here as anywhere.

BAM!

Light another one, although the first one is still going across the room.

If any given section of causality will be necessarily cone shaped, for the same reason that a slight deflection early in the trajectory of a moving object will cause it to diverge in an ever-expanding arc, then it should be possible to affect a whole swath of present events by making a minor change in past events, provided they are sufficiently far back in time.

CRACK!

How far back is far enough? What should she change? To know that, she would have to reconstruct that entire epoch in as much detail as possible, tracing out the finest meanderings of the web of causality, calculating the variations that might be introduced by this or that minor alteration. Even with the desired outcome to lariat the possibilities, the whole thing is too finical and risky. So that approach would take too long, unless she used time travel again to shorten it. If she can't find a solution in ten years of cause-mapping the period in question, go back let's say ten years in time, then come back to now with the results of those ten years and tell her present self—here's the map so far, here's the dead ends. Then another ten years, or rather the same again, but following up the map differently, and repeat this until an answer is calculated. Then take that answer back to now and use it immediately. Obviously she will not choose to do this, because if she had she would already have the answer from the by now. Her past self would have already told her.

CRASH!

Lightning strikes the building. The whole place jumps. Assiyeh's cigarette bounces out of her fingers and lands on the tile. The ember is knocked out and lies there, dying quickly on the floor. Assiyeh produces another and lights it with her pistol lighter.

Maybe the endlessly supercopious causality map can

be dismissed in favor of something more approachable and hands-on. That's what Assiyeh likes; enough theory to keep it interesting, but in the end you want a piece of equipment that mysteriously starts working again when you whack the sweet spot. She remembers a Nigerian colleague who was waxing nostalgic over a few drinks, telling them all that Ireland was importing Guinness from Nigeria and regaling the party with anecdotes detailing the inventive wizardry of Nigerian auto mechanics. A man brings in his car and the brakes are completely gone. A mortal mechanic would send for new brakes, but the wily Nigerian simply pours some ball bearings in there somehow and good as new. In ball-bearing this problem, the answer is to stop pretending there's no such thing as chance.

RUMBLE.

You pick your odds. Somewhere in that stretch of time, go. Tinkering with the so-called web of cause and effect would be impossible, because that web is infinite in cross-section. That is, it sets up an infinite number of variables, and an infinite number is here really only the vitiation of any concept of number applied to this problem. The possible model, the only one that would work if any could, would be one that understands the task like this: you go back and insert a new cause into the scheme, like adding another car to the grand prix, or putting wings on the horses. So go back at random into that selected patch of time, no later than this, no sooner than that, and inaugurate a completely new project. Uhuyjhn cities, for example. They had an ad on Kanona's List lately.

Now the only difficulty is that she can't go herself. The process is too dangerous for biologics. Grudgingly she resigns herself to the necessity of building yet another minion.

BLAM!

*

There's nothing quite so restoring after a long day of organizing fast food workers than sitting down to a hearty bowl of hot water followed by a deeply relaxing sixteen minutes of jackhammer sleep and having to get up again. This sure is the life.

So as I sit here in my luxurious tumbleover towers taking stock, I find disjointed fragments of homeless wisdom ricocheting across my mind searching high and low for bullseyes they are not very likely ever to find. I can do do do but do I really intervene? Eventually they bring out the bag of weed and everyone goes limp, because you can't live life like piano wire. So you have this bunch who want legal weed and this bunch and so on, and if you ask anybody I ever meet, they pretty much will all tell you yes they want that and no to white supremacy (and they aren't just saying that in front of me, I can tell), and no to male supremacy and no to heterosex supremacy. They all do and they all mean it. It looks meaningful at first, then meaningless, but, if you don't quit, if you're a donkey like me and for some reason you don't wander away into less contested plots, then you notice that it does mean something to have that many people say these things.

Because why. I feel it's true but now I have to prove it to myself.

Because why. Because you get the idea that what everyone glibly calls the system is like an actual brick and mortar labyrinth standing out in the rain, defying the sun and frost, humans sluicing through it forever, wearing down the paving stones and tagging the walls with graffiti or sometimes desperately attacking them with improvised tools or explosives or their foreheads, but that brick jail is no stronger than the opinions that keep its doors closed and locked. Not that much stronger. No wall can keep you in if there's an unlocked door in it. Unless you can't see the wall. Without the social practices that put people in them, those jails would be just ugly buildings no different from shopping malls and motels. The walls are real and physical, and it's not like one person making one decision is global liberation, but then if everybody really wanted that prison?

I can't remember why I wanted to think about this. Figure out what to do. What if there's no door in the wall? You can try to dig your way through or under, but if you have enough people with the right tools, you can just set a door in there, or is my metaphor dictating to my idea now?

Back outside, rain on my hood, no ode to street romance happening in my mind yet, maybe never. Don't steal my problems. My problems are useful. That's how you neutralize someone—"help" him right out of his problems, put him in neutral. Don't let me disconnect from my problems. I want a better fucking apartment, but let me get it from my problems, not in exchange for my problems. My problem is my currency, I pay my problems out and keep them anyway. That works because we have our problem. We are our problems. The key to that one is to see, no to establish, a clear, a really astutely clear distinction between problems and trouble. End the trouble. The trouble keeps getting between me and my problems.

I stop. I need to think. I hop up and sit on the trunk of a parked car and set off the alarm, sit there in the rain and alarm and think about reversing. Turned around, don't steal the money—it'll just end up back in the same swim again—steal problems, make trouble. Am I saying anything really? There's a glimmer there that could either be hope or another milestone along another endless way, but my mind keeps going blank when I try to follow it.

Exchange problems, right, and steal the enemy's problems. Steal their problem. Their problem is ruling us, so steal that equals self rule. That seems too easy. That seems a) too easy and b) too much like what everyone has always been saying to be commensurate with the newness of the idea as it occurs to me. I tremble (with disgust) for any civilization that makes a liability out of having a mind of your own, aka all of them. I get off the car. You have to do everything yourself. Sometimes it seems like we're pale imitators. None of that matters. Ruling us is not really their problem so much as it is a part of their problem, or a symptom, somehow one step down from the top, the real problem. Because when I say problem, I mean—

Nearly bumped into someone, sorry.

—ruling us is possible because they have the means, and they have those means because they rule. It's a closed loop. Right, fine, so—

She had her umbrella down, almost didn't see me in

time. I sidestep into a puddle. Uh-huh. Squelch along now. The way to get through a crowd is to blunder along, that's what gets results, not all my tapdance. I know it but I don't do it.

Closed loop. Break the loop. Why doesn't that thought satisfy me? It isn't new enough for the feeling of having an insight that wants to convince me I'm a genius this disgusting morning. Those are some pastries. Anyway, my thesis statement is the private ownership class keeps uncoupling the rest of us from our own problems in a variety of ways, and we have to really stay on top of things to prevent that or to link back up again, which means we're always following them. If we're going to disconnect them from their own problems we have to take the lead and get them chasing after and reacting to us. That's a fine, purely abstract and general statement of nothing whatsoever, and just now it seems my whole mind has gone dirty out of my head. I feel like shit and now I'm fucking preaching. I can't be bothered to decide where the shit I'm swimming in ends and I begin. I feel like shit. I'm so angry it hurts. So much I wish I were dead. I want to drop my weary headaching stomachaching self down in the gutter and sluice away like a diarrhea pile. What happened to me? What happened to Carolina? What happened to Etsimen?

*

Kanonan cities invade the earth. Overnight the towers of Buzzati appear like the bowsprit of a colossal new island in the Pacific. An invisible time bubble surrounds the

Kanonan projections. Investigators explore the streets of these entirely cinematic cities projected in three dimensions onto the Earth from a remote point in space, passing unseen through intangible images of buildings and people light years away, their phantom gestures, their distorted voices wail and croon indecipherable languages. Waves of interference burn through the projection at random intervals, like huge roving blots of billowing nothingness that damp out the scene and all light and sound, negative projections of darkness and silence that snuff out the will.

Uhuyjhn metropoli appear in nuclear explosions that transform blasted wastelands into thriving cities. Sporestacks gush into the sky like black smokers, the sky above these cities wavers and undulates in a long plume of turbulent air. The Uhuyjhn bob from tower to tower, nodding benignantly down at teeming multitudes of humans and other terran species engaged in eager commerce.

Watch—

You'll see—

The world is filled with wise human beings who are being mentally destroyed because there's something fundamentally wrong, and they can see what's wrong, can articulate clearly to others what's wrong, agree about what's wrong, can fix what's wrong. Engulfed in thick shadows and buried under heavy slabs of noise, they know, and, if asked, will patiently explain, what to do. And they are jammed, jammed, jammed. The Replicate will go to any lengths to keep them from fixing anything. Again and again, idiocy stays the intervention of intelligence, and sages watch from another dimension in impotent despair, in an enforced ataraxia they never chose, wondering if it matters that they aren't to blame.

Watch—

The Prison Roads: to deal with the self-renewing problem of an ever growing number of American prisoners, an enterprising lawyer gets federal funding to create the first Prison Road in Texas. Instead of being crammed into cells, convicts are set to work building highways in the middle of nowhere. When they aren't working, they are confined to barbed-wire pens along the roads. The Prison Roads feature an enclosed concrete structure that divides the two directions of the highway. This structure contains the cells, so as you drive to work or to school, you pass along an endless cell block, knowing that the prisoners are watching you pass through the holes they make in the thin strip of window filter. The filtration windows are translucent webs designed to strain out exhaust fumes so the prisoners don't suffocate, but you can't see out through them, so the prisoners usually bore holes in the crumbly stuff somehow and peep out. It's a special treat when there's heavy traffic and the prisoners can get a long masturbatory look at the women creeping by.

The Prison Road program is a big hit and existing highways get the treatment, too; closing schools and VA hospitals to maintain the ranks of the workers. Soon every great American highway is lined with captives who will never move an inch. More highways are planned. In some cases, the convicts, having built the road, will be required to walk its length forever, up and down in a subterranean concrete chute, performing maintenance.

When one of them drops dead, a guard pulls up on the covered causeway, bags the body and hauls the corpse into the box on the back of his weird little guard buggy, put-puts away again dragging a tail of sour gas fumes.

*

The black cloister and the luminous archways and me, tumbling along the ground like a dried leaf.

Now there's something interesting.

Just here there are clouds, white clouds, inside, dimly luminous, cold, oozing along.

If I watch these semeny-looking clouds they stop. When I transfer my attention to something else, they start moving again. Now, if I rivet my attention on one frond there. Keep on. And indeed, something is happening to it. It's condensing, and as it condenses it drops toward the ground. It has condensed into a crook shape. Just detached now, from the cloud that extruded it. Still sinking. It's tilting upwards, and the thing is, I was imagining this happening as it happened. Either I imagined it simultaneously to its happening, or it happened as a further exhibition of the power of my—

I don't want to lay claim to anything like will.

Something to do with me, though.

Now, I'll try this. Let me try getting that crook under the edge of the wall.

No ...

No ...

Almost ...

No. It keeps bumping up against the wall and flattening against it.

Swing it way back like a kicking foot and then down and under, scoop up the wall's hem.

Got it ...

Now lift gingerly up. My arms are useless twigs tangled up in my ribs or something. But this surprise gift, a manipulatable floating hook of steam, can pull up the wall and tip ... iiiit ...

Splat!

The wall collapsed like a curtain of tar.

I pull up all the walls.

*

I pick out a can of cat food.

"How much?"

"Six rats."

"Six rats?!"

She shrugs.

Shaking my head, I pull out my squirming bag of rats and peer down into it. Hand it to her.

"That's eight."

She turns to one of the rat cages and upends the bag into it, kneading out the rats. They drop flailing into the cages and start trying to scamper up the sides almost before they touch down. She hands me back the now much deflated bag with my two rats change, and the cat food can.

There are guys who stalk people leaving food stores. It's safest to eat in the store, but the owners don't like that. Some provide a safety zone in a corner or in another room, but even then you get brawls sometimes in the store, or big intimidating guys hanging around in the zone, ready to pull your food right out of your hands. You have to plan ahead. I tuck the can into my waistband and the rats into my backpack and wait. There's a big guy vagranting across the street, a few steps up, a few steps back, glancing up at the building as if he's waiting for someone. Presently he leaves, rubbing the back of his head. I'd wait to see if he's only just gone off a little way, to lure me out, but the owner says she's closing up. My flightpath is clear anyway. Out, down the block, quick around a corner and run the side street to the plaza and get lost in the crowd, my jacket closed, the can right against my stomach where I can feel it all the time. Big rips in capitalism now, big opportunities. The left is a pile of barf and the right fringe is jumping the gap unopposed. You see them squaring off, the berserk Southern Father vs. the robot Northern Father. And me cool and sarcastic and impotent dangling off to one side pretending, hiding out in a men's room stall scarfing air and cat food. Nobody's around. I can't find a soul from the old days. God damn it now I am going to have make myself a minion.

*

A darkened bedroom. Daylight outside stops at the glass of the window, not coming in. I put myself in bed, a small doll, then stand back and regard my work with neither satisfaction nor displeasure, a smooth easy feeling of neutral neutral neutral. Economic slide show at the side show. It will cost you all you have. Each scene is a transaction.

What I experience now is like vision again, as if my faculty of sense were roving from one sense to another. It had been smell, now it's vision. It isn't vision. It's imagination. I'm imagining things as they are, and this seems close enough to vision. What is presenting itself to me in images is a dark passage. It's not a passageway, it's more like a deep arcade. There are arched openings to an outdoors pale sunlight is incessantly washing away. It reminds me of being under a freeway. An abandoned freeway. Through open country. I can't see any landscape. Now it's more like I'm passing down the length of one boxcar after another, with gaping open doors, but it's too broad for a boxcar, maybe it's a lot. All this describing is not only not getting me anywhere, it's sapping the meager reserves I've got left. It's what appears in the luminous openings to the outside that matters. I must be in the backstage area that ghosts use between appearances, to get around. I'm in a position to narrate events because I'm dead and unable to intervene. I can meander up and down all of time and space, sticking my head now into this scene, now that.

Like this one:

An apartment in a big city. Someone moving. The remaining Professor Long, my namesake. She passes a pair of thick drapes with a little gap in between and the warm, heavy light of the afternoon glows over her face for a moment. She's not the remaining Professor Long. She might be her daughter, if she had one. She is the remaining Professor Long, much younger, about twenty. So this must be the past. She's straightening things all around the apartment. She looks at herself in the mirror.

She notices a newspaper behind the sofa. Perhaps someone set it down on the sofa back and it fell down. Quickly, she pulls it out and, carrying it in both hands, hurries with it into the kitchen, throws it in the trash. Photo in the paper: two thousand pig carcasses hauled out of the river, no explanation. Now she draws a glass of water for herself and puts it down untouched. Back into the living room. Look at each piece of furniture. Go over to the window, look at the sky. Turn to face the room and scan it again, from this new angle.

She rushes to answer the door. The two of them look at each other for a moment, smiling, making and breaking eye contact, taking each other in a moment before she turns aside to admit him. He notices the pin on the lapel of her new pink sweater; he gave her that pin a year ago, before he went away to study in the U.S. He looks the same as he did when he left. Perhaps a bit meatier. His hair is a bit shorter than she remembers. Perhaps he's only just had it cut?

"Did you just come from the barber?" she asks him playfully, pointing to his hair.

He doesn't seem to understand. He rubs his hand over his short hair for a moment, smiling and shaking his head.

They sit down together in the main room of the apartment. The curtains are half open on a golden-brown afternoon, hazy, but with the wind picking up now, an unseasonable wind.

"What would you like?" she asks.

"Nothing for me," he says. "I've just eaten."

Perhaps her expression strikes him as a little

disappointed, because he apologizes right away.

"We were working all morning, and then everybody wanted to go eat together."

She sits down.

"That's all right," she says.

Construction noises blend in and out of the sounds of traffic and helicopters. The apartment is not that high up, but it's situated on a side street away from the main avenue, so that mutes the din a little.

"Have something yourself," he says.

"Ah ..."

They are both sitting down, rather heavily in their seats; he in a chair, and she on one end of the small, deflated-looking sofa, near to him. She notices that he did not choose to sit on the sofa.

"You haven't changed," she says, still glancing around the room for imperfections to fix.

He shrugs and shakes his head, smiling affably. His eyes flick from one thing to another, one thing to another. He doesn't seem to be that different at all. The time that had passed since she last saw him had passed for her, but for him it had been no time.

"Tell me about America!" she says, shoving his arm playfully.

He sputters a little, smiling.

"When did you get back?" she asks.

"Six days ago."

"Already six!"

He nods with a lot of motion in the neck, emphatically.

"How is your family?" she asks.

"My father's a little worse," he says. "Otherwise the same. Like I never left."

He is still looking around the room. She is now alternately watching him attentively or averting her gaze.

"How about your family?" he asks. He smiles as the words come out of his mouth, and she thinks he is relieved at having come up with something to say, a question that will enable him to be silent and listen.

"Fine, same as usual," she answers with a microvengeful impulse to be short, block his escape, put the onus to speak back on him.

"Has your sister started college yet?"

"Yes," she says. "She's working hard. I barely see her."

"You're looking well," he says.

She contracts expectantly.

"Where did you get that pin?" he asks.

She allows the witticism to register and smiles.

"I don't remember," she says.

"Ah," he says, with mock exasperation, but it's only a dim echo of the much louder sound he would have made before.

The wind is coming up outside, sweeping the clouds away. It's late enough in the day that this clearing up doesn't add much more light to the air, but only unveils an impossibly deep and infinitely layered blue sky. Unusual to see blue out the window, such deep blue. There's construction noise from several different locations nearby, and all seems to revive together in an impersonal sort of shout, as if they were straining to make themselves understood to each other through the racket. He seems to be listening to the noise as much as to her.

Actually, they can still hear each other fine, even at a conversational tone. He is telling her his plans; he's found a place he will be sharing with two other men, and they're all going to pool their resources and work like maniacs to get good enough connections to go into serious construction. As he discusses his ambitions he becomes handsomer and more appealing and animated, the old features that she found so attractive, but he's not really seeing her there. The image of his life that he is painting for her seems very complete in itself, and suddenly she feels entirely small and localized in the room. Complete, and without her. This room is off on the margins. He didn't miss her, he doesn't need her. A horrible feeling of futility sweeps away her will to speak, but then it returns.

She wants to ask him where she fits in his scheme.

"Then, in maybe five or six years, I can afford my own place ..." he says.

All right, maybe this is the spot. Maybe he thinks I need to be persuaded. Maybe he thinks I am skeptical.

"But what I really want is to live in a building I designed." The wind drops out of his sails here. The construction noise revives a little, or so it seems. He picks at a flower printed on the arm of the chair. She sits with her hands in her lap, feeling as if her bottom were sinking steadily lower and lower into the cushions, as if her knees were coming up level with her chest.

"Do you still want red tiles?"

Let's see how that goes, she thinks. She feels like she could go straight to sleep, maybe a little nap, it might clear away this shadowiness that is floating its tendrils around her. Just at the moment almost not caring, she listens indifferently for his answer.

Before, when they used to walk together in the

afternoon or early evening, there was a particular house they used to pass, with a red tile roof, and he was always remarking on this or that pleasing feature of the house and speculating about either living there or in a similar house. Back then, especially when dusk was falling and the light of the city and sky grew weird, life together seemed possible, when they were most in harmony. Now something momentous is killing the spirit of play that used to embrace and hold them together so easily. The sun drops in the sky and accents the deepening gloom with vague bitterness.

If I could be anywhere but here and now ... she thinks. She misses the moments before he arrived, when she was still hopeful, nervous, and active.

Little traces of emotion, uncertainty in pronunciations, small talk. It keeps seeming like it's about to become play again, the way it ought to be, but the impulse never lasts long enough to get going.

"What do you mean?" she hears herself ask, her voice sounding strange. She's misheard everything he's been saying, as if he were speaking another language.

A gloating shadow hovers somewhere, hissing softly to itself and watching with possessive satisfaction as the old link dissolves.

He just shakes his head, and that line drops lifelessly off.

Time races by as they sit there like preserved specimens—traffic noises, construction noise—banalities about the weather—a last chance, she mentions a seminar on urban planning she will be attending two days from now, and he goes off on building again as before.

She still loves him but for no reason all she can do is passively watch herself being disappointed. She is not exactly suffering; it's like numbly sensing pain through an anaesthetic she's afraid will suddenly stop working.

The lights are coming on outside, although the sky is not yet dark. They are more and more polite with each other, the formality of strangers reasserting itself—going to graduation day I'll see you there all right?

Now she is closing the door—his head turned away, a strip of black hair in the light outside, turning to go, shrinking in the closing gap until the door is shut—that gloating shadow is still there, and when she turns, she meets its gaze helplessly.

*

SuperAesop here, putting the **I** back in b-u-l-l-s-h-**I**-t. There are some words calling, with a sound like water flowing along a baseboard, looking for a mouth to drain out of. Their silent minion on the other side raises the curtain with his latch of vaginations and the clouds open, the word rain releases its glittering darts. The one the story is about doesn't want to tell it, but it has to be told because that ghost is looking in on it, and whatever that ghost looks in on has to be related thereunto, so it looks like I'm getting drafted to tell this thing myself.

So, goaded on by a kind of inner jostle, and spurred by my passion for service, I'm searching through offices in a building that's been closed for the night. I got in, if you're curious, through the service entrance. A collapsed man in brown coveralls, laden with a collection of collapsed brown cardboard boxes bound together with plastic tape, happened to come crabwalking out the door, and I poured myself in, ran up the stairs behind his back, up and up, found a bathroom and camped out in a stall until all the lights went out. Now I'm searching, and now I find the glass man from the future, Assiyeh's minion, wearing a suit and tie, asleep at his desk, gurgling quietly to himself.

I pull up a chair and gaze into the glass head, into the glowing, sleeping mercury vortex inside it, until the spiral lets loose its pictures to where I can see them and start to tell the story:

I see a castle at night, Professor Aughbui at a gigantic medieval table with candelabras and skulls and astrolabes and theodolites and heaps of fruit and a dead ferret artistically draped over a pile of grimoires and there's a dagger there and some pearls rolling around loose. Professor Aughbui is squinting through a jeweler's loupe at a tiny mechanism. He keeps reaching in and trying to pinch a couple of tiny metal vanes that cross each other through the center.

Enter sneering FLUNKY.

FLUNKY: Hey fuckup, the villain's about to marry the Princess—any reaction?

PROFESSOR AUGHBUI: (without taking his eyes off what he's doing) Huh? (Glance up, then back at his device.) Mm, yes, right. Congratulations.

Exit FLUNKY with sneer and shrug.

PROFESSOR AUGHBUI: (to himself) How the deuce does this thing work?!

I leave the scene, my head reeling with untenanted

images. Go into a diner for cat food hash and a disgusting glass of hot caff-lent. The waitress, who has up until now done nothing out of the ordinary, stands very close to Professor Aughbui as she clears his dishes; she picks up the fork he's been using and, looking him directly in the eye, she puts the tines into her mouth and licks them clean.

The melancholy of the piano music they're piping in here is abstract; it would be laughably grandiose of anyone to apply it to anything they might actually be experiencing. It's music for contracting.

OK now I'm seeing Professor Aughbui as a youth. Like an owl chick. Lots of fluffy hair around his head. He's with his old school pal Lewis, who is much more handsome, with a mouth that turns up at the edges, skinny, hair shaped like a saddle. They're in some kind of alienating, weird school building, all white, with black arches in rounded white walls. It's a lobby, or open ground floor, tapering up toward a white apex high overhead. The air smells like paper. Maybe it's a library lobby. Or perhaps I'm reading, in some other part of me. The floor is shiny. Air conditioning. A few potted plants and dark sofas or benches are the only things that aren't white.

They're here to meet these two girls they like to have lunch with. There they are, sitting on a bench against a white wall. Cathleen and I swear to God Brigrun is the other one's name. Cathleen is getting up to throw some balled up something in a trash can like a big enamel smokestack. She's tall and thin, with light brown hair trimmed short, bony, pale, good legs with oddly heavy thighs, ballet flats on. Brigrun is compact, with chaotic black hair and heart-shaped face hosting an expression of eerie cunning. The two of them notice Lewis and Aughbui, look each other in the face, share a giggle, look back.

That silly giggle of theirs won't quit dripping. As the boys approach diffidently, Cathleen swings around and plants herself back down next to Brigrun as tight as Inca masonry, and they begin a regular alternation between watching the swervy approach pattern of the boys and eagerly consulting each other's faces. I get the idea this is Professor Aughbui's "that day."

They walk out together, the girls still joined at the hip and giggling, darting looks over their shoulders at the boys, who follow gingerly along behind them, the various parts of their bodies all moving a different velocities. They pass a cemetery that rises above the level of the street, and the view opens out to a lake with thickly forested sides, viscous-looking water with big lozenge-shaped mirror daubs squirming on it, small islands covered in trees that look too tall for it, and here at the shore there's an anarchic tangle of rope and boards and posts, some boats moored there, a few people around. Old fishing man with a red shirt and a floppy hat, carrying a bucket of aquaslime or crawslush or whatever, and here, this guy is a slim older man, erect, in white yachto pants and a short sleeve pastel vacation shirt, calling them. The girls wave and make sounds, go over to him still giggling, the boys plod plod plod up. The man's face is close-shaved and puffy, with delicate wrinkles around his large, mobile eyes and mouth. His hairline has receded up his scalp to expose a shiny egg forehead, and the short hair that's left, neither sandy nor grey, stands straight up. He greets the girls familiarly and they each dart in like fish to give him a peck on the cheek. The boys get a handshake each as the girls introduce them; his hand is large, firm, soft, warm. Gold watch. Big ring. Aftershave.

"This is Mr. Slutarp."

He nods and smiles at them. It seems like he should say, "call me Denny," something less formal, to break the ice, to induce social relaxations and lubrications, but he doesn't. They know his name anyway. They were expecting this, to go boating with this family friend of one or other of the girls, or maybe he's friends with both their families, and his name is Mr. Slutarp.

"Come on aboard," he says, in a slightly throaty, TV voice.

With nameless misgivings they follow him along a gangplank and board his boat. It's got a motor, no sail, and seems kind of large, kind of ostentatious, for this small lake. He will stand in the rear and pilot it, and there's a wide canopied area in the middle where they can sit and watch the black water glide, the plumage of black pines on the shores changing angles, the dwindling shore. The girls stand next to Mr. Slutarp, giggling, speaking in little spasms. He says something modulated and droll to them, and they laugh. Then they come forward and sit right in the front, glued together. The boys have been going from one side of the boat to another, taking in the sights with listless enjoyment. When the girls reappear, they keep looking at them, expecting some cue.

Now the boat skirts one of the islands. The trees come right up to the rocks at the edge. The boat comes around a little point of land and turns into a notch in the island, where there's a dock.

"Well, here we are. Welcome to Elu Island," Mr. Slutarp says, proprietarily.

They get off the boat and walk up onto the island, a heap of dark dirt tightly clutched in tree roots, risen from the depths of the lake like the roots reached down and pulled the dirt up under them from the lake bottom. It's hard to think that those watery depths aren't directly beneath their feet, and that the island isn't just a large, organic raft.

Young Aughbui notices a cemetery climbing one side of the island, the graves among the trees, cordoned off by an iron railing. He figures it's an extension of the cemetery on the mainland. It's all one cemetery, he imagines, with most of the graves under the lake. There are probably more on its opposite shore. With all these old trees and now this graveyard, the singing makes it almost impossible to think. He's a little out of sorts, a little dizzy, the light of the day and the weird luster of the lake seems to flicker behind the trees. The motion of the water makes it seem as if the island were adrift, the shore floating past over there.

Ahead and above on the ash pathway, Mr. Slutarp's white butt floats and his hands swing loosely as he takes each step. The girls are walking separated, holding out their arms for balance. Brigrun stops to fix her shoe. As Young Aughbui comes up, she takes his arm to stabilize herself, and keeps hold of it as they walk on. The instant her hands touch his arm, a nervous electrification shoots through him, rattling his not unpleasant disorientation. She is walking close by his side, he can smell her brand of face soap. The path bends, and Mr. Slutarp disappears, then Cathleen and Lewis. For a moment, no one can see the two of them, and Brigrun stops and looks at him, eyes mysterious, lips parted. Excitement, so abrupt and violent, cracks through his chest and tries to climb out his throat, a kind of gravity pulls her into his arms and they kiss. Her mouth tastes like metal and her lips are cool. Then she's looking at him, then she's lowered her gaze and doesn't want to look at him. She has him by the hand and they hurry along up the path toward the house, which seems to spread itself out as they first catch sight of it, like a rehearsed gesture of welcome. Set right in among the trees, the house is stucco and red tiles pulled out at the corners like curling toes, and all overgrown with creepers that combine with the gloom of the trees to dim the whitewash and make it look blue. There are no lights on; the windows are like charcoal smudges.

As they draw nearer, the house straightens up out of its slouch. It looms taller than it looked at first. They don't go up onto the veranda that faces them, but around to the other side of the house, passing under narrow slitlike windows. There's a soil bed with some severely pruned roses between the lumpily-paved path and the house.

Around the front, there's a vibrant lawn of long green grass, truncated by an abrupt drop above the water and they can see across the lake to the far shore, and to the witch-hat mountains already fading in the blue beyond the tops of the trees.

"Hello there!"

A woman in a pastel mu-mu that flies all around her like a sail is coming down the crumbling front steps of the house. She comes up and takes Mr. Slutarp's hand

and they stand there meeting each other. She's young, a suntanned blonde in her twenties, dressed like an older woman on vacation, in flip flops, white sunglasses with thick round frames baretting back her hair, which is cut in a sort of Louise Brooks kind of way, emphasizing her round head and her long neck. She wears heavy bangles on her wrists and huge dangling earrings. Gigantic baubles and beads are draped around her neck and press down between her breasts. Her body wiggles and jiggles inside the mu-mu.

She and Mr. Slutarp stand together, both of them squinting although it isn't that bright, and receiving introductions.

"I'm Diane," she tells them.

Then, after getting the basics down, she turns to Mr. Slutarp.

"I'll go get things ready," she says.

Then she turns and wiggles back into the house.

"Well," Mr. Slutarp says, waving at the mountain view. "Satisfactory?"

"It's wonderful," Brigrun says.

The conversation is desultory and awkward, the boys just want to venture off alone into the privacy of the woods with a girl and see what happens.

"This house has been here since the war," Mr. Slutarp says, looking up at it with his hands on his hips. "The Duke of Blaccio was going to live in it, but he died. Never even came to the lake."

Finally Diane reappears high above on the terrace and waves them up to a table set outside. They sit down and she circles the table, doling out preloaded plates. As she puts his plate down in front of him, one of her breasts brushes his shoulder. It clearly wasn't done intentionally, but then again she made no effort to prevent it from happening, either. When she serves Lewis his plate, the same thing happens.

They eat their sandwiches, except for Diane, who eats a salad, planting each forkfull on her outstretched tongue. Mr. Slutarp asks the boys masculine questions about their studies. When Lewis says he's interested in medicine, Mr. Slutarp seems to take an interest for the first time.

"Really? Do you plan on becoming a doctor?"

"Yes."

"A surgeon?"

"Well, yes, right!"

Mr. Slutarp claps his hands once.

"Now that's exciting! Not ..."—and here he turns to uh young Aughbui with a quick gesture—"... to say anything about economics, but surgical medicine has always fascinated me."

"Did you study medicine?" Lewis carefully asks.

Mr. Slutarp's face creases in a melancholy smile and he shakes his head.

"No," he says. "When I was your age, I had to work, and I was changing places all the time. By the time I had a stable enough life for studies ..."

He tosses one hand in the air, as if to say, "poof."

"... I'm too old for them. But, you know, Diane here is a nurse."

"Was a nurse," she says.

"The hospital was closed."

"They closed a hospital?"

"It was a mental hospital," she says. "Now they just give the patients drugs, and don't admit them. So, when the last one died, we weren't needed any more."

"She never did get a chance to assist a surgeon," he says, not looking at her. "Only the sort of first aid they do when a patient hurts himself, slices his wrists open, you know. And they used to induce insulin shock, as a form of treatment. You need nurses for that. Someone with medical know-how, to manage the seizure."

Brigrun is sitting next to young Aughbui, and, as his hand has happened to stray onto his leg, he feels her hand, very warm, alight on top of his, and squeeze it discreetly. He is very careful to give no sign of surprise. He's wondering if there's anything else going on under the table.

As the meal ends, it's getting dark, and Mr. Slutarp waves them all inside. He is talking to Lewis about surgery, and Cathleen is doggedly sitting it out with him. Brigrun has gone to the bathroom, Diane is moving to and fro tidying things and lighting candles. He is sitting on a sofa, doing nothing, topped up to the brim with novelty. When are they going back? The darkness keeps getting deeper. They aren't going to stay there, are they?

"We don't have power in all the rooms yet," Diane says, lighting candles on the mantelpiece. "But I think this is cozier, don't you?"

The room is a white cube with a malachite fireplace, a sofa, an iron coffee table on a small, dark Persian rug, arched and open doorways in two walls, deep blue windows, striped with black tree trunks. Diane wafts by leaving a wake of perfume as she goes through one of the archways. He suspects she is naked under that mumu. The house is dim, filled with yellow light. He sits there alone for a long time. Then he gets up and starts looking around. Though he sees no one, he can hear murmuring voices, the giggling of the girls, and he gets the impression there are more people in the house than just the four of them. Glancing down a hallway, he sees a door partially open, and a shadow inside, a figure raising its arms maybe, like someone putting on or removing some article of clothing over the head.

He wanders outside and takes the path back down the way they came, down to the cemetery, and stands there, his hands on the fence, listening in silence to the trees and graves singing. Their singing drew him back down here. He knows he should be back up at the house, that whatever strange things were happening up there were the sort of strange things he came here to find, and that, if they notice he is missing, if they find him here, they will think he is crazy. They'll gloss it over, but not by being discreet, not as joke, but with doubts and even aversion. Because they can't hear the singing of trees and graves, the ghostly comings and goings in and out of the graves, the trees, and his skull, growing more and more intense without becoming even the littlest bit louder, more and more intense, and when they find him he's doubled up on the ground crying and hugging himself, and they can't uncurl him or get him to explain.

*

What more is this?

A canopied patio at the school. She sits opposite you.

"Do you know Alec?"

"I don't think so. He's observed my economics class, but we've never spoken socially."

"He and his friends are having a cooking party in their, you know," she waves her hand. "Their housing. They fire up all the ovens in all the apartments and make a feast."

"What's the occasion?"

She shrugs.

"I'll ask Alec when I see him next week. In the department."

"Aren't you going?"

"Nobody's asked me," she says, looks at me and shrugs. "I don't like to go alone."

"Ah," you nod.

Me? Who's me? Aughbui? No. This isn't him. Another one.

Then you say, "Please excuse me."

A wry smile, twisting painfully. You get up and head to the bathroom. You don't have any physical urge to go, but you need her to see you heading in that direction. Go in, just in case. Wash your hands. Look at your face in the mirror. Ronald Crest. Ugly. Defeated. Aging. Young, but somehow aging, like a time lapse. The lips twisted in a smiling grimace.

She wants something from you, or so she thinks.

She *has an idea* of you.

That idea is *a lethal trap*.

Never mind why.

The ideas come into your head like bulletins.

I know. That's all. I just know.

It is a lethal trap.

Avoid it, deny.

Suppress.

Denial is like a cold current threading through the blood, spreading, numbing, rinsing away feeling. But denial is not cold. It is hot. Like a bonfire in the chest. Hot in your outlines, in your inner forearm, the edges of your ears. Hot far back behind the eyes, way back in the brain, and rushing out to your outline, your ear edges.

I will vanquish this emotion. I will not lower myself to do what it wants, or what she wants. What she thinks she wants. I will not *obey* her. She will not look inside my suit. I will not conform to her *idea*.

A superb and contradictory strengthweakness flows in and out of you through that "will not."

I will never again abbreviate the word *not*. I visualize the word **NOT** in my mind and reach out and take the faucet in my hand and bend it, the metal tube, straight back in one smooth, unhurried motion, the metal tube folds back on itself without a sound and splatters water upwards.

There.

NOT made a fountain.

Praise **NOT**.

*

What makes it difficult? You can not fantasize about simply anyone, because the self is the true object of the fantasy, or, the self is no less important than the other one. One, I should say one, not you. One is in the fantasy what one wants to be, but the other one, the desideratum, must allow for it.

I can feel myself reading, my eyes adhere magnetically to the lines of text and scan them automatically, but I am not doing what I would call seeing, let alone reading, and I am not thinking, because there is no inner echo of the writing, not even this rather nice description of an inward state is what should be called actual thinking, even this is happening automatically. I am becoming pure mechanism, pure chaos. Why does that seem right?

*

Now there is smoke, something burning. Swiss landscape of Kashmir Valley. Heartbreaking blue sky, green meadow, yellow flowers, white mountains. Smoke rubbing itself on all that.

I am fifteen, she is nineteen. I have come out by myself looking for birds, although I am not a 'birdwatcher' in the usual sense. I know nothing about birds, I cannot identify them by species. But there are a few individual birds I know on sight, because I know where their nests are, and I like to make my rounds and see them. I usually do this with my old friend Khaayal, but he's mourning the loss of a friend himself, and unable to enjoy anything right now.

Smriti turns, then notices me for the first time, and now she's looking at me like I'm an exhibit in a museum. How rapidly, how hideously, my narrative flies away from me when I desire her. My whole 'blueprint' is gone.

Which is worse? No blueprint, or blueprint? A huge blueprint, printed on stiff, stale paper, overspreading my entire life, and everything finished before it begins.

But what is she telling me now?

Her voice is speaking to me, saying innocuous things, but through those words I hear her tell me that the blueprint has no power of its own. Look how easily, with a casual word, an everyday encounter—which is all this is or will ever be, my poor fellow—that blueprint is flicked aside, leaving me blinking, like someone who has just come out of gloom into the blaze of midday, right out onto the battlements to look down into a void of wind and desert and mountains, deep and empty and beautiful, a boundless horde of meaning heaped up out there, and racing to and fro, zipping out of sight behind a low eminence like wild horses, or swooping up into the cloudless blue sky like a flock of vultures to be lost in nothing but the pure lostness of immensity. Wherever I see it, all I want to do with my life is produce immensities, and never live a moment without immensity being made from me.

I have followed her away from the lake, into the village. She is turning to me, the sun lancing at me from behind her, when there is a sudden hue and cry and the whole place flies up in panic, every path fills with rushing figures, the indescribable howls of old women who have had more than they can bear.

It was a false alarm. One person, a boy, hurt his leg in the scramble, and there are no other casualties but the peace of the day and the town, and my day with Smriti, because we were instantly separated the moment the alarm went up, and I never saw her again. There she stays, the blinding sun sharp above her left shoulder, turned to look at me, her figure obscured by the shade of the light, the whites of her eyes like moonlit snow and her gaze baffled, not reaching me, because that sun shade is between us like a wafer of smoked glass, muting her colors. Never again Smriti. What happened to you? What was that look on your face? Did you assume that, as I hadn't heard anything about a woman being hurt, I wouldn't have had cause to worry? And yet, I never exactly worried about you, Smriti. Thought, one thought that seemed at the time like a whole course and career of thought and never took a single step past the threshold of that meager handful of quotidian things we did together in a few months in one year that ended without closing. The next year the panic was real, the army was there, and, while I never heard the shooting and never happened to be anywhere near the violence, I had to go through it in my own way. I fell back on birds, fresh air, mountain beauty, silence up there. I went walking every day while we were staying in the village until the day I found a dead man lying face down in a shallow, muddy depression hidden between a heap of large stones. His head was bare. What had been covering it was lying nearby. On the opposite side of him his rifle lay and his outflung hand lay beside it. In falling, as he plainly had, his brow had been driven down into the mud. His legs had closed as he fell and were stretched out together, soles up, like a diver. I froze the moment I saw him, although I knew as if by magic he was dead. And there was no doubt about it.

When the first flash of shock began to waver, I felt a fierce upswelling of rage at this corpse for ruining my beautiful day. All violence was an intolerable offense, my fury told me, violently. It should be punishable by violence. When my anger died down, I felt pity both for the dead man and for the nightmarishly fragile beauty of the world, and it was at that moment that the corpse lifted its blind face out of the mud and spoke inhuman words in an inhuman voice, a buzzing, chorded, inhuman voice, not looking at me nor speaking to me, and I didn't scream or run, but only stood there unable to look away from the face that was devouring my day, a shaggy face with a horrible, ragged, triangular mouth that was black inside and grinned, and eyes like two muddy pebbles, the sharp nose with a hole in it and smashed, and all bespattered with black slime. The voice spoke, and then the head sank. The body lay as if nothing had happened. I couldn't leave it. Leaving it would have meant it was following me.

Staying with it was the only way I could leave it. It had to leave me. I remember the sun setting, the chill of evening, settling down on my haunches to wait, until the idea that the corpse would stir again once night fell, the idea that I would be sitting here in darkness, under the stars, with this corpse, jumped up in me and I fled, it was right behind me, looking behind myself so often I must have fallen more than once, because I came home smeared with blood and dirt. As I ran home, I suddenly imagined telling adults about the corpse, and I saw men's faces lengthening grimly, their hands grasping lights, their faces gathered in a circle of orange light while the blue night sang behind them, and then tramping out, following me, or my directions. If they did that, and brought back the body slung in a sheet, then what?

They didn't ask me to come along. I spent the night lying awake looking up at the ceiling but with all my attention on the window, glowing with 'blue nocturnal antiradiance' and the sullen outlines of the mountains. They're out there, they're finding it, they aren't finding it and cursing me, they're putting it in a sheet, they're finding out he's actually still alive and trying to revive him and blaming me for not helping him. He's crouched just outside my window—not him, it. It is there. Unbreathing. Lying face down. Like Smriti, though, I never knew any more about it than that, and I went on hating life for being so easily violated and resenting the beautiful day, mountains, flowers.

Now I lie in bed, not looking at you.

"So, now I've broken the Third Oath," I think, and the thought fills me with indifference. Your presence fills me with neutrality.

It's a neutral night, with grey squares of light on the dim walls, the sounds of the street seven floors below, a sighing bus, it's a weeknight. A little movement of air, the smell from the potted flowers you lay out on the broad plain plaster sill. Your even breathing. The smell of those flowers is the only thing that interests me. It interests me because it conjures out of the uncaring me that is here today, a me that did care, and I get fascinated by the memory of caring. A few hours ago I waited for you on a park bench. We have to meet well away from campus of course, and make our way back to your apartment from the far side, to make sure no other students see us together. Why we don't meet at your place is something you've explained but never satisfactorally. I think you may secretly season your pleasures with the risk of being caught. I sat waiting on the bench, bored with my book, leaning forward with my elbows on my knees and gazing across the path to the fenced meadow on the other side, a busy playground off to my left somewhere, to my right the park wardens moving grey plastic trash bins around the brick bathrooms.

I realize I have only to take one step forward off this bench to shake off the trance of encroaching age. The magic of the day will make me a boy again. I just have to step out of this aging form; only a single step. The grey brown earth of my youth, the grey brown youth of my earth, soil that lies in flat clots together, the bright voices of children in the playground, streaking like skyrockets over the bare plain of my earthyouth, a plain that isn't green yet, still brown and grey, torn by strife, but also just rippled up by the ripples of youth and life, opening the soil to the wind and light. The birds. Their cries are the light's cries. Light and birds caught in the precious few branches of the trees war left standing haphazardly. A young boy in the bushes, hiding in play for a change, there looking out through the branches, alert, using hard skills softly, trapped close to earth and leashed to space. It's one step away. If I could take that step, I could undo the ruin and plunge into the day and the dry soil I was.

*

The giant bats set us down at a nameless village fifty miles west of Tehuch, and from there we have to proceed into

the mountains on foot. No flying in the mountains—
there's too much lightning. The peaks are permanently
blanketed by thick black clouds like huge petrified fever
dreamers their sides raked with sizzling electric scars.
The few villages up here huddle close against the slopes,
beneath huge iron chevrons that serve as combination
lightning shields and avalanche deflectors. Rockfalls are
frequent as lightning rampages among the summits. At
a distance, the mountains of Balkhmahez sputter and
dance, appearing to flicker back and forth in the ceaseless
lightning storm parked on top of them.

The air here at the base of the range is moist and
surprisingly warm, with skeins of colder, drier air boring
through it. The robe they've given me might as well be new;
certainly it has no residual odor, and that is a consideration
on their part. But it's as heavy as a rug, with ungaingly,
flapping cuffs. I sweat under it for a few minutes and then
throw it off. I don't wear robes and cowls.

We have reached the elevator. It's a circular metal
chamber that climbs an iron screw, powered by a team of
huge, shaggy, red-eyed oxen. They stand side by side just
within the outer wall of the chamber and turn a geared
treadwheel that screws the chamber up a pair of rails set
into a more or less natural groove in a sheer rock wall.
We passengers stand in the middle of the chamber, on a
platform above the great circular base and surrounding the
oily, evil-smelling screw. The rock face crawls by outside,
now and then opening in plunging views striated with
dim sunbeams and vast bands of shadow. The elevator
is moored at the top of the wall and, to my surprise, the
two oxen are led out with us.

The road to the monastery of Maug Zunghun forks off from the main. The main road is a wide, shallowly furrowed clay causeway. The road to the monastery is black. A dull, black glaze with glittering motes embedded in it, like a frozen stream. The road climbs abruptly in steep, curving switchbacks up the side of Ci-andan Mohe, whose peak is flexed so far backwards that no one has ever seen it. We lean along the grade, but the black road is entirely level. The oxen find their footing readily. I don't understand why we aren't riding them.

The lightning is still mostly on the far side of the mountains just now, and muffled. The daylight clicks through several different set intensities of brightness with remote flashes. The air is clear, the light is losing the brownish tinge it had down in the valley, becoming more actinic and lunar, vividly contrasting lights and darks, rich greys and indigo shadows, vibrantly black rocks and the road. A flash of lightning turns the rocks to transparent smoke with veins of neon green. We pass a signpost topped with a leopard's head elaborately moulded in steel. My skin feels clammy. I'm getting lightheaded, like I've had too much to smoke. This point marks the spot where we have to put on our masks of activated charcoal.

The road turns a corner and the monastery comes into view, high above us, lightning flashing in the sky beyond, the rumbling and blast of thunder suddenly distinct again as we are out from behind the acoustic baffle of the slope. The compound is set into the base of a naturally mandorla-shaped cliff, with several terraces descending. At this angle, only the upright walls of pale stone can be seen, and the black road snaking up among them.

We pass among crumbling enclosures. Above us, lightning cracks against colossal steel plates riveted to the mountain sides, making them slam and snap and hum. The oxen look up suddenly, not at the noise—following their eyes, I see the head of a leopard, looking at us over a wall. More leopards appear on the slope above us as we approach, eyeing us with haughtily casual interest. The oxen plod on, but their scarlet eyes note each leopard, one by one.

The fitful light makes it hard to put all the details of the scene together. I can't prevent myself from flinching at the strikes, even though my guides assured me that the black road is never struck. Now we pass between fields of ash-blue soil with blue and silver crops growing in them, plants I don't recognize. What I took for scarecrows are the ornamented mummies of dead mathetes. There's a fresh body lying in a narrow coffin, propped up beside the road. The slack, sunken face and flabby hands crossed on its breast have the wavering phosphorescence of embers. The black ribbons festooning the coffin look like they're struggling to escape into the air. The garlands of wilting flowers bristle as the wind combs through their petals. As we approach, I hear a voice starting to speak, a male voice, reverberating as if the word were being spoken in a small empty room. I remember a Professor I once had, who could recite the most scandalous things in just that unflappably reasonable voice.

"The volatile capital flows lasted forty days, in review of its mandate in word and deed. The demons used paper, and related patience and resignation; they were exorcised, and yet never said anything about the bodies of the persons. Obeying the order system based on rate stability facilitates balance manifested neither in words nor from the earth nor from the body."

It's as if the corpse were dispersing itself in words instead of flies and stink.

A wall sweeps up before us; I've barely had an opportunity to get a look at it, because the boulders lining the path block the view. I see it only once distinctly, up close and almost in the same moment I go through it. An arched passageway through the thick wall, almost a tunnel.

The monastery is suddenly there before us. It's a collection of two and three storey buildings topped with squat onion domes of mottled steel. The domes are like gargantuan versions of those bells they use at the front desks of hotels; they don't join directly to the fabric of the buildings, but lift up on top of them with an aperture underneath. The mottling, I realize, is all Lichtenberg figures caused by lightning strikes.

The huge hoary heads of the oxen float at the ends of their powerful necks, and they blink impassively at me. Their eyes really are red, a smouldering, deep crimson, burning there behind a fringe of matted brown locks. The guides peel off with almost demure gestures, leaving me to find my own way forward.

Now up to the doorway, or rather socket, leading into the monastery itself. As I climb the many shallow steps a huge figure, robed, muffled, and wearing an apron embroidered in silvers and greys that somehow manages to look garish, and fringed around three sides with a translucent mane of clear fibers. The front of the hood has a mane, too, and the hands are lost inside sleeves that sweep the ground. Recalling my instructions, I take hold of the hood and thrust my head up inside. The luminous face I see far away is tiny, the size of a tomato, like a severed head resting on a dish. It picks up where the roadside cadaver left off.

"The assaults were followed by others still more violent, so that the marks of the blows are clear signs that found that the being exorcised responded to the staff and Chairman with new challenges waiting for their exchange arrangement. Oil shocks stopped his voice, fixed exchange rates collapsed alerting them to risks of possession."

I was expecting this challenge, which is primarily a ritual, and the agent in Chayariliane told me how to respond. She expressed herself very melodramatically, if you ask me. I think she wanted me to be terribly impressed with what was expected of the visitor to the monastery, and perhaps to be intimidated by her experiences as well. Most of it is a matter of bullying demons, which is nothing to me. The only real challenge involves running a needle right through your tongue. To do it right, you have to thrust up through the meat. As I was told, there was almost no bleeding. Something in the air, they said. It's like the air is full of clotting factor. I pierce my tongue, withdraw the needle, and wait. The taste in my mouth is like steel, not the iron flavor of blood.

Something starting now. I feel lightheaded right in the front of my skull, just between my eyes, as if there's a mild magnetic upward pull on that one spot. A little smarting too, where my ears join my head. A buoyant feeling, like when you stand with a hard wind blowing in your face and breathing itself into you. I have to allow it all to happen.

"There are four principal demons. Demons also interact with think tanks, which is essential for divine service, and they tempt others to unabated accumulation of international reserves, the space of a second interior blow, borne to earth. Through its economic surveillance, the monetary system monitors by magic low-income countries to help an inward order charged with overseeing international boundries."

My face and mouth are in motion, answering the cowled figure, while my mind is blank. A mentholation in my throat reaches down into my lungs with a flaming tickle and I break off coughing. The figure floats back into obscurity. I remove my head from the cowl and the monk, if this is a monk, steps out of the way.

We all go in together.

"Smoking is not forbidden within," someone says. I see only a shape sinking back into the gloom. The interior of the monastery is pitch black, a cavernous, many-columned chamber filled with shadowy people illuminated only by flashes of lightning. I toss my mask aside with relief. It's almost like a forest in here, and the air, although it has the musty, slightly sour odor of an old stone building, is strangely invigorating. My smoke is not being absorbed into this air; it gathers itself together into threads and trickles up into space without breaking. I don't taste it, and it feels funny inside, like coiling syrup. There's a hum of low voices. The people I can make out are all wearing bulky robes and there are several varieties of hats, tall fezzes, pill shaped hats with two points sticking up like little horns above the ears, bullfighter hats more or less, some are topped with an elevated crescent from ear to ear either horns up or horns down. People rustle to and fro. There are a few who sit with their backs against columns, and now I see they are writing or reading by very dim lights on drooping stalks. It is like a forest in here, but a forest adjacent to a country palace all alive with a gala ball, the guests straying in their finery out onto the paths at the forest's edge just after sunset.

Something—a detonation—

—a brief flash and a rapidly-fading glow, and a musical note that starts with a rasping whine and gives way instantly to a great mellow resonation that touches off my whole nervous system at once so that I feel my body tremble and a jolt of excitement and a sourceless light pops right before my eyes.

It takes me a while to get back together again. Lightning struck the dome right above our heads. There is an angry red rip in the metal up there, now cooling and dimming. The dome is a bell clapped by lightning, translating the electricity to sound so that we can all be struck by the same lightning bolt, and feel the vibration set fire to our nerves. When it happens, a light comes out of your forehead just between the eyes—that's the pop I saw—leaving you feeling unstoppered, a sudden climax of the brain alone. It so dazes me I have to sit down by the base of a column myself.

The two colossal heads of the oxen hang over me. They watch me rest, watch me rise, then follow me, silently, turning their heads to look up at the livid scar fading into the dome. Armed with my guides' description, I make my way to the abbot, Sluch Temnuck, who sits on a big rock just a bit out from one corner of this enormous room. He looks awful. He is bunched in a stiff, voluminous white garment, and there's a wide red streak of blood down the front of this garment and onto the floor before him—a trail of blood, blood that shoots in occasional gouts from his mouth and runs down over his streaked jaw. He is shockingly pale, and his eyes are invisible behind perfectly circular lenses that reflect some light whose source I can't see. Whether he can see me or only senses me, he stirs at my approach and fumbles one hand out of his voluminous sleeve. He holds out a dead hand like a pickled specimen before the tunnel mouth set in the wall. I see the tunnel now myself, a gulf of intense inky black, big enough for a train. The abbot's upturned cadaver hand vanishes into the darkness inside the tunnel. Then his arm dips slightly, once, and he brings his hand back out with a slip of paper in it, as if someone behind that shadow drape had firmly placed it in his outstretched palm. The abbot turns his face to me and reads the slip aloud in a matter-of-fact way.

"It keeps track of three other Deputy Managers when

he had come to the person possessed; the revelation threatened him once, while he was paying for imports. All necessary conditions lead to an international debt to be struck with violence. There are 188 invisible persons, and that Demon repeated his commands aloud. These signs undoubtedly point around the corner, supporting institutions that facilitate international air for a few moments. The Devil, who provided them with financial policy advice to rebalance demand growth, extends surveillance to secret thoughts, during many years with prudence and perfect care. We have learned to despise these grinning impostors."

His voice is hoarse and half-clogged with blood, which keeps spurting up out of his mouth and slopping down his chin. Although he leans forward, he is wearing a stiff, tall paper collar and his neck is a straight as his back is bent. He reminds me of a civil servant, not energetic, not tired, an old hand. This is the man I've come to see. It was at this point that I was to present my petition ...

As if in acknowledgment of the moment there is a stir somewhere in the depths of the room, a rustling of movement and a series of voices calling softly—

"Ahh ..."

"Ahh ..."

"Ahh ..."

—relayed from voice to voice towards me in the dark, as something comes toward me, and a way is cleared for its approach, and the stench of decay flies out of the blackness at me, snatches me by the throat and chokes me—

—I see it now! I see it!

*

I hear Assiyeh turn her face away.

"Oh God," I hear her say.

The others are used to visitations and feign indifference.

My voice is horrible. I can't tell her anything. Through the link in our memories, since our bodies were once joined in intimate contact, I receive impressions. Smoke still trickles from my bullet hole.

He's dead! That's why—... Shot! ... Shot!

For her this is the annihilating pain of surprise. She's turned away. I can smell her nausea. It's not love that brutally holds her open to this agony. It is love, but not love for me, or only a little love for me. It's love for someone else leaping up again now, the way the blood jumps from a wound when the scab is torn away.

Without being able to feel it, I have touched her face with my hand, and she jerks away, crawling from me. She came here to deliver sentence on Urtruvel, without knowing that the sentence would have to go through me.

The man beside me is a vortex of pale ribbons around an oleaginous central body of dead, tarry stuff. He conjured me. I don't know him. I don't know where he came from. He has to appear dead to me as I appear dead to him, that's the nature of the bond and spell. He stands on one side of me. My left. No. I can't tell. There is a leopard with me, on one side, and he is on the other. I can't find the leopard any more. Perhaps this man was the leopard before.

The abbot is a silent, living man, looking up at us calmly.

"I'm counsel for the decedent," the man beside me says.

The abbot holds his hand out to the tunnel and gets a slip.

"Proceed," he reads from the slip, and looks up.

"We are here for a decision on Eugenio Urtruvel," the man beside me says.

The abbot reaches out and gets another slip.

"What are your charges?" he reads. He's not reading from the slips automatically. He reads the slips silently to himself first, then says what they say, aloud.

"We accuse Eugenio Urtruvel of *Selcrimeo Detinay*," the man beside me says, or that's what it sounds like to me.

The abbot calmly slips his palm in the dark tunnel again and another slip is given.

"What is the judgement?" he reads.

The man beside me is silent. This part is up to me. I have to strain to use my voice, and it comes out in a barely articulate croon.

"Death ... Urtruvel ..."

The abbot is given another slip and reads it.

"Death," he says simply. "Urtruvel."

A whispering spiral detaches itself invisibly from him and plunges into a time aperture, one of many that honeycomb the air around the abbot.

One of the oxen says, "Death."

The other ox says, "Urtruvel."

The hot bond connecting me to Assiyeh thaws me, reopening desire and pain. The memory. I tremble inwardly. She hasn't run, but she's sitting by a column with her head averted, refusing to look at the shivering, panting mummy I am now. She's kneading her hands—

no, she's got them over her ears, because the sound of my voice was too appalling. I will have mercy on her and none for myself, and go.

I fall away from the brighter darkness into infinite gulfs of nothing, where I can resume my circular wandering like heavy chaff twisting just above the bottom of the ocean.

*

Urtruvel at the conference. He's sitting onstage with lights in his face, riding out a dilatory introduction from the podium. Any moment now the encomium will taper off, applause will follow, and, spurred on by a bleakly familiar pain, he will hasten to get to the microphone and put an end to it; it reminds him too much how dependent he is on it.

"Eugenio Urtruvel is an iconoclast, a maverick, a man who is not afraid to unmask sacred cows or to change his mind ..."

And when he changed sides he thought of Alcibiades. Not so much of cows with masks on.

Except Alcibiades was beautiful, he reflected ruefully. Urtruvel knows what kind of figure he cuts. A big rangy man, always a bit too heavy, a little too pale and shiny-pated and damp and obviously a little too much at home on a bar stool—it seemed as though wherever you saw him all he had to do was heave back and a bar stool would rise up out of the crust beneath him. The drinking is a holdover from an old journalism fantasy that has since become all too real.

"... Eugenio Urtruvel."

There's the little showmanlike pause.

Later that night of course it's drinks and compliments, and Urtruvel is offhandedly imperial and cordial, but behind all the bonhomie there is still a weirdly unreachable biliousness. You can see there is something pushing him that isn't going to let up; he wants more when he wins, and only very rarely, in those moments when success has overtaken him abruptly, do you ever surprise on his face a natural, relaxed and easy look, and that, within a very short interval, becomes a look of vindicated haughteur. He has to matter in the world and school up with the lords of creation, the Replicate, the chiefs of the Misled.

Yet for all his dragonism in writing, when challenged in person he becomes standoffishly shy and superior; he slows down, begins to stammer a little at the edges of statements before bearing down on the middle, trying to drive you back with a steady, slow, purely gestural pressure, now and then with a uncanny little leer if he happens to come up with something good—but really working; if he could only compose his words carefully enough he could turn talking into writing, disappear, and become invincible again. Even if it seems he bested his opponent, he does it joylessly, in fact, nothing gives him joy except the prospect that someone somewhere is talking about him, and that perhaps one day he might possess the important position that for now is still basically a posture, proving himself again and again. Sometimes he would tell himself sternly: that is all there is, only endlessly proving yourself until you wear out and drop along the wayside like the unknown solider, but there is no antidote to the dream that swam in front of him most of the time, that one day the proof will stick, they'll add his bust to the gallery, and, while he knows he is not the man who could live that day, by some miracle he will become that man, saved, immortal, delivered in biographies. Urtruvel in the bathroom mirror, pop-eyed and bilious, skin shining like wax and a little waxy in color, and those pop eyes are queerly yellow ...

They all wanted to go to this horrid little tourist trap down by the sea called the Mortuary or something. I had to grin and bear it while a greasy bear of a massive Achrizoguaylan homosexual—all their queer seem to be enormous for some reason—swatted me on the shoulder and forced this disgusting drink on me and not a drop of whiskey in the place. Mateo, that was his name. Not my mate, old boy. I think the bugger poisoned me with that rubbish of his. I can't seem to get the taste out of my mouth, like bad cream. Come to think of it, I don't look so good either. I look—I look *green!*

*

Wiped out after a long day of conjuring minions deep in the bowels of the projects, that is to say the bowels' bowels, but it's a wholesome fatigue, the way I enjoy imagining cave man farm days would be. There's often an especially nerve-wracking thing that happens, when I'm all ready for the spell to engage, and it's there, it will, but it wants to tread water for another couple of seconds and when it does come I've peaked already. That leaves me with an unsatisfied uncertain feeling about the outcome. I wish I'd thought of making minions before the beginning of history instead of after the end, but then it might have had to be this way.

My minions are unemployment elementals, the grimy spirits that hover over poor neighborhoods, standing completely still in the noonday sun like transparent smog, reaching into children's lungs with long tendrils of asthma, and loading the staggering outlines of adults with a heavy silt that settles in the legs, forearms, abdomen, head, like the mush at the bottom of a polluted river. But this is no metaphor. These hazes are the exhaust that fumes off chronically frustrated and despairing brains, filling the apartments and corridors and the rumpled up stores and the tumbling streets and the sooty parks. You walk down the street and it's like a bus tailpiping in your face, the steady revving groan as it heaves itself another leap down the block to the next stop.

I conjure these fuckers from a number of non-secret lab locations in basements and vacant lots, and from the ground zero intersections of avenues chancred with potholes, using electric fans to collect the fumes and trapping them in squares defined by high tension wires and chalk outlines. I pathfind for them, by walking circuits, and if I do it right, then images of me split off at certain acute angles of the circuit and go streaking out into the city as I turn, detaching from me like an uncoupled sidecar and zooming away. Since I have to turn to give them shape, I don't see them distinctly. It's like seeing my reflection in a glass door as it opens and shuts in the corner of my eye, a flat image that moves by turning its angles. These minions don't hang around for me to insult and bop on the head when they goof up; they do their goofing at a distance and are gone, like shouts. Away away, my pretties.

Sending them forth does two things. First, it creates a little employment, and that lightens the air a fraction. Second, it creates polarized axons through the unemployment-plasm that can carry coded messages to the Teeming. That's not a circuit I can close; closing that circuit is up to them. When the circuit closes, the current flows, right? When the current flows, up comes the juice, up comes the work, understood as a term in physics, up comes the potential for work, the radiant gradient. When you stop something, it becomes universally connected. But then the next step is to move in and censor the right connections, because you want to ... wait, let me come back to that later. My fucking brain won't leave me alone long enough for me to get back my wind. I'm hot and tired and I smell bad and I haven't eaten. If I keep on this way I'll thin out to a smear on the glass and flicker apart into dimming video stills. Concentration will burst you apart too, and dissipation can be just what holds you together.

Gloominous, Tenure, those others—they were my own elementals ricocheting through time. I got out ahead of them and I was already there when they arrived. I need to get them to use my shortcuts. I need them to get out ahead of me and stay there. I need them to lead me, like scouts. I need them, because I'm always alone.

Now I'm back in my squat with a steam-powered computer and reading an online-headline:

"MR. URTRUVEL, HE DEAD."

Liver failed, it says. Disney was right, wishes really do come true. Recommended to the country's top liver specialist, but refused to see her because she's an Arab and considering all the shit he wrote about Arabs, he'd been afraid to trust one with his life. Here's her picture in the paper, calmly asserting that she treats her patients and leaves their politics outside the door. Vacillating about whether or not to see this Arab liver specialist, he'd let his transplant window go by. The next available donor was Salvadoran. After vomiting all over El Salvador for so long it would have taken a Salvadoran liver to finally sober him up. Anyway, there's no shortage of heartless assholes where he came from and the niches are what really exist and we only fill them and yeah but some of us jokers fill niches with more zest than others and it's one thing to find yourself in some niche or other and shrug and keep on as usual, and it's another thing to claw your way into a bad niche and crown yourself king of bastards. There's always just enough scrim sticking out of your fly to hang a disgrace on. Now they're uncrating your honored name even before they've got your insides out on the embalming table. They incinerate the organs and bury the brittle shell, once it's been pumped full of formaldehyde and shellacked. Or do they flush the stuff, right down the sewer? There's that fucked up liver of yours touching down on the fire now, burning with a bright blue alcohol flame. Or maybe that's it, slurping down the drain, inching its way back into a shitflow that no doubt strikes it as homey and oddly familiar.

I used to think that pain and reasons went together. That's logic. Pain means something is wrong. I must have fucked up somewhere without noticing it, or forgotten to do something. But I know the pain I feel right now isn't caused by anything outside itself; it's just there. As if the switch got frozen pointing to pain and everything feels like pain now. Or this is a pain that's caused by everything at once, including pleasure, including even knowing that that pain will leave me one day, the pain of knowing I will lose this pain.

*

I wake up already out of bed. The beat of the floor against my bare feet helped to shake me from my dream. The sheet, heavy with sweat, hasn't even had time to finish falling where I flung it off.

Like so many times before, I dreamed that an animal was attacking me, and that I was cutting at its face with a small knife, horrified at what I do. Then I was back there in the darkness over the city, with the others. We were reaching out our long shadow arms to adjust this and manipulate that. I reached out and traced a line with my finger from the end of a half-constructed freeway overpass to the street beyond, and the cement causeway appeared behind my finger like magic. It connected to the street with a palpable click, and a thrill ran up my shadow arm as the traffic began to flow. It felt like the restoration of circulating blood to a sleeping limb. The radio transmissions of the people, so tiny with distance, tickled inside my fillings and kicked a spark up into my sinuses now and then.

A stir of glarings out there, in the deeper night beyond the city's gold haze. Pink and blue sprays of lightning, a palely luminous carpet of clouds is creeping toward us, undulating over the landscape like a living cape, a sting ray, sluicing in through a gap in the mountains and moving in on the city. Suddenly, it has arrived, throwing its darting lights all over the valley bowl beneath us. Looking up, I see Professor Crest's face right across from me, and the others. The sight of the faces shocks me, rattles me badly. I see them steadily, not flashing with the lightning. Professor Crest, the remaining Professor Long, Professor Aughbui, naked bronze statue bodies, living, marked with their white economists' marks like little splatters of pigeon droppings, and covered in blood, blood dripping from my own hand and dangling in tarry ribbons, not my own blood, it's the blood of the city— we spill it every time we reach out our shadow hands to touch this or that. The city is a vivisected patient pinned open under our hands.

"Oh no! No! God, no!"

The sound still lingers in the room.

I taste blood. I rub my mouth and chin, getting blood on my hand. My tongue hurts—I bit it in my sleep. I go to the window, which is tall and narrow in a bare concrete wall. Dorm window. Dorm room. I look out at the night motionless quad lined with huge primordial trees, banks of foliage full of lizards and enormous dragonflies. The campus is going back in time to prehistory. This room, a dorm room, could be a pueblo with air conditioning. I sit down, looking outside. I see one other room is lit up. It might be Professor Olendskaia—she's been staying in one or another of the rooms over there lately. She looks as though she has trouble sleeping.

Needing to be reassured, and to escape the miasma of

the dream, I decide suddenly to throw on some clothes and go knock on her door. We will sit alone in the night, in a little globe of light from her desk lamp, and talk about the fate of the university.

The concrete hallway, open to damp night air, tumbling insects.

I knock.

No response, unless perhaps there is a very faint scrape on the floor.

"Professor Olendskaia? It's Professor Budshah."

There's a soft vocal sound, a woman's voice, on the other side of the motionless door.

"I saw your light from across the quad—I'm staying there, myself. Are you ill?"

"I'm fine thank you," the voice says. The voice is even and calm, as if it were the door that spoke.

"Ah. Sorry to have bothered you," I say, embarrassed. "The Surfeit is One."

The concrete hallway, open on one side, overlooking an atrium with tall tropical plants basking ominously in the warm, humid night air. Any moment now their eyes will open with a fibrous rending sound and there will be vegetable money to deal with.

My feet don't seem to be moving. Inside me, an impulse is rising, brushing away the gossamer impediments of my embarrassment.

"Eh ... Professor?" I say, my voice rebounding from her door sounds queer. "... This is a little embarrassing, but I've just had a terrible dream and, a little conversation ..."

I trail off. I learned that from the remaining Professor Long.

The door unlatches and swings open. Professor Olendskaia is a tall woman in her fifties. There's something elusively goose-like about her. She is wearing a rather crisp jumper and a floor-length skirt. Admitting me into the room with a quizzical smile, she offers me one of the two identical hard wooden chairs, and sits down herself. The air in her room is close, heavy with fragrance; she isn't running her air conditioner. The overhead light is off; only a small desk lamp burns.

I thank her with an assurance I won't stay long.

"Some tea?"

"No, thank you."

The room is Spartan. Her books are arranged, on their sides, in the small bookcase. There is a bowl of fresh flowers on top of the bookcase and another on the windowsill. A photograph, probably her parents, stands on the desk. An enormous alembic full of frog eggs is brewing there beside it, forming a tableau of generation. The eggs wriggle from time to time. She must be using them for money, or hatching them into money.

"What do you think is going to happen to the university?" I ask.

Without being able to say why, I feel certain that, when I awoke just now, across the quad, she had been sitting just this way, not behind the desk but beside it, elbow propped and her head on her hand, brow pinched up in worry, looking out into the quad, as if that were the college. I hear a plop in the bathroom, a cold ceramic tank with a silent, palpitating mass of placental frogs in it.

Before answering, she sighs deeply.

"They're going to close it," she says. "Professor Boundas

told me. Some time next month, they say."

"Do you want to start up a committee with me?" I ask.

A pained expression flits across her face.

"What good would it do? The decision's been made."

"I don't mean a committee to save the college, I mean a committee to run it."

"Run it ourselves?"

"Right."

The hand comes down. She crosses her arms and leans back.

"Wouldn't they cordon it off? The campus?"

"Who? The police?"

This, it goes without saying, is no longer a cause for concern. The police are not going to want to bother with something like this, let alone reduce their already dwindling numbers by posting guards around the campus. They might raid it, or pounce on someone as they drive by, but they are too short-staffed to keep the whole place clear.

The police are out in the night, standing in a rhombus of police lighting, defending their own headquarters and city hall. I glance around at the night, the lush green of the planters outside looking ready to up roots and start shuffling up the sides of the buildings, the concrete walls in here, like the inside of a parking garage, and very faintly crinkling with a moistening sound. We are already on our own.

I imagine the police commissioner looking the board of directors square in the eye, incredulous, weary, fresh out of patience—"You mean to tell me you want us to bust people for trying to go to school?" A barricaded, empty campus is a magnet for all kinds of mischief ... If the place continued to be occupied by students and run as a school, wouldn't that do a lot to ...?

"But if they chain up the gates ..." Professor Olendskaia says.

"A campus this size you can get onto any number of ways. And with buildings as big as these, it's not hard to find a way in. So many doors, windows."

She thinks it over.

"We would need students," she says. "Would they stay?"

"Well, I know there are some who don't really have any way to get home, but even the rest, why shouldn't they stay? We could make our own community here."

"The faculty might stay. They've stayed this long. But we have to have staff stay. If the staff doesn't stay ... I don't know."

"We should ask."

The lines of worry are fading from her face, which is growing more resolute, because there is work to be done.

"All right," she says. "I'll talk to Andrew tomorrow. What else?"

*

There was no end of what else, but we have our committee, our students, and our staff. Classes are running. The groundskeepers and maintenance department personnel all have keys and, now that the spell of the paycheck is broken, they can do as they please with them. A few administrators defect to our side and there are roughly the same number on the other side. Two groups centered around the most vehement members as the remainder drifts away, feebly asserting that they aren't really washing their hands of the whole thing when they very plainly are. No trouble with the police apart from a few official statements about order and demonstrations and drugs. The message is clear: don't embarrass us, and we'll leave you alone as long as we have bigger problems.

*

The world contracts in a thousand fascisms. Where possible, a wheezing, sclerotic nationalism is revived, but in most cases the fascism is more tribal than national, centered around ethnicities, anti-ethnicities, religious sects, anti-sects, schisms, anti-clades. Officially, the blame is universally transferred onto the Uhuyjhn cities, and the people who flocked to them are branded in unsurprising ways. Unable to send money back to their families as they once did, thanks to a blockade, the Uhuyjhn migrants entreat their relatives to come join them in Andanksis, in Eunjlis, in Nzulkum, in Chaglesis Chuseh. Since they don't root in place, these cities tend to move out from within any cordon, and might be able even to dodge nuclear attack; infiltrators fall silent within hours; spying from the air is made impossible by the undefinable turbulence given off by the Uhuyjhn cities, which induces air to shimmer, knocks aircraft out of the sky, and lights up with radiant, polychromatic splashes that interfere with all forms of radiation. This is attributed to deliberate anti-aircraft measures, but it is apparent to anyone who bothers to check that no air activity is possible above an Uhuyjhn city, meaning this is something more basic, an intrinsic attribute of the vicinity of Uhuyjhn construction or possibly even Uhuyjhn metabolism. The Uhuyjhn themselves are approachable only within their cities, and communicate with human beings by means of telepathic devices that cannot be deceived. Information about the biology and culture of the Uhuyjhn is almost totally lacking. The Uhuyjhn cities are evidently untouchable, unreachable, except by a ground invasion. American military commanders bluntly reject war talk—no intelligence worth mentioning, no information at all about the offensive and defensive capabilities of the Uhuyjhn. The more stridently the politicians demand military action, the more stolidly negative are the answers, and now the generals are beginning to intimate that pressure on them to act could backfire. High ranking officers are all over the media, voicing their disgust at the impotence and ineptitude of the politicians, who return fire by accusing the military of anti-democratic, proto-fascist leanings, and so it goes on.

A group of people create an international party called Planetary Science in coalition with other groups in Brazil, Turkey, Egypt, Japan, Australia, Argentina, Honduras, Venezuela, Mexico ... Planetary Science balloons wildly, threatening to come apart.

While Planetary Science is outlawed, it has a political sister organization, the Institute for Rational Economics, that keeps its hands scrupulously clean and acts as a public voice for the party. Turn on the television, and there is the head of the Institute at the podium on screen, uplifting the pointing finger of a punctilious martinet drunk on the sadomasochism of little rules. When he first sees Professor Crest rebutting accusations and insisting that Planetary Science is not so naive as to expect any real protection under the so-called rule of law, and that the Institute is a demonstrably independent organization which shares no revenues or administrative ties to Planetary Science of any kind, Professor Budshah groans and drops his face into his hands. His fingers taffy-pull his features, and then his hands plop into his lap, incredulous. There's an establishing shot of Professor Crest, crossing the campus of his Institute; no doubt about it—that's him, the same needlessly hasty, fussy, acute-kneeing walk.

A series of committees, rituals, and public comment sessions are convened, largely through the Institute. Professor Crest contacts Professor Aughbui through a medium. A new bureaucratic system is invented, and Planetary Science is completely restructured. Anyone interested in joining, in need of resources or with resources to make available, will now know exactly where to go and what to do. Planetary Science policies and agenda are clearly articulated and presented. There is a grievance process, an internal credit system and bank, an internal employment system, a necromantic process for consultation of reanimated experts, a health system, a matchmaking system, a self defense system, a legal representation system, an obloquies system, an obsequies system. Planetary Science mints its own money based on glass time chips, carefully gestated in life banks, where life and money are one.

Planetary Science is interdicted and outlawed everywhere. Police, soldiers, spies, and paramilitants attack Planetary Science headquarters wherever they can be found. For the first six months or so, the results of these attacks are always uncertain; often the raided sites turn out to be, or seem, deserted or never used. On other occasions, the headquarters turn out to be Catholic missions, madrasas, NGO offices, private schools, medical clinics, and before the mistake can be recognized a great many innocents are killed maimed or brutally arrested. Then there's a raid on a confirmed PS committee center in Winnipeg, during which every government agent participating was killed. Principled voices of anti-violence speak up and there is a great deal of back and forth about the deaths. News stories laying responsibility for atrocities on Planetary Science begin to pile up, but nobody believes reporters any more.

So here I am hustling as fast as I can, which I have to say is fast, trying to stay on the wave. Looking out through the cracks, the streets are still as thronged with the legions of the unalive as they ever were, and you'd never know the cracks were there. I'm sorry there's no virile sexual reportage lengthily appended to this gripping narrative but I have my modesty. A gentle man don't tell where the kiss lands. The problem with writing about the current situation is that marketing propaganda has subtly warped even the most basic words. The "natural style"— that's an oxymoron that a moron like me will go on using because it's natural that we would want to have some style—is to use everyday language and hide the styling as if you were ashamed of yourself, like the billionaire on TV in a t-shirt, never mind that it was woven from baby hair by sobbing thalidomide mutants and can only be purchased with human souls. The transparent everyday style, I'm trying to explain, is a fucking mess, and you're better off writing your plangent "who we are now" novel in death rock lyrics. So you use the "natural style" and everyday words because that is so obviously true on its lying ass face and no matter what you think you're saying it all comes out tm-ized. To write that sort of language correctly, you have to write about everyday life as if it were a science fiction novel with a glossary in the back. A comparative glossary that sets the trademark version alongside the meaning you mean. Let's look up the word "job," shall we?

JOB(tm)—[moral term]—Reason for being; the one and only possible justification of human existence.

versus

JOB—Form of living death; obstacle course between human being and necessities of life.

Carolina steps outside into the blazing sun and takes off her clothes again. We get in shitty hatchback and aim the nose dent for a plume of spores that twists into the sky on the far orange horizon, the punctuation mark advertising the presence of an Uhuyjhn city. We managed at last to convince the boy up front to keep an eye on our clinic for amnesiac quasi-presidents after our attempts to contact the electoral committee failed. There's no news about the election yet. How's Incienzoa doing? Oh wait, he bowed out, the new one is Varvariollo. National

Federation. Nothing on the radio, either. New York has elected a cat governor and nobody knows what to do. Did they have the election here yet though? Carolina's dosing herself and she passes me some and I take some for a change. No sign of cyclops cars. I don't recognize this road; it isn't the main highway, it's a desert road and we should be choking in the dust but there was a heavy dew last night and the ground is still wet. Turn on the music instead, crash in prismatic celestial cliffs like a crystal cheese grater against my brain shredding out noodles and slivers of thought, the reasoning takes off and stops being a burden now my business is tight, I'm solving problems and avoiding mistakes, putting it all together—Carolina's an agent from fairyland and the Uhuyjhns are illegal human aliens from another timeline and the dark economists are resurrectees coming back, and Assiyeh is real after all. We're going to go to the Uhuyjhn city of Buzzati to find Tripi's fugitive spirit and bring her back with us, put her in the body of her choice, and lead her to a triumphant return, and we're going to win.

PART TWELVE: PRISON ROADS

From the sound of it, I would say the investigators are outside.

I am sitting in my room.

The investigators are not outside, they are investigating some other part of the house, they have finally stopped poking around in here.

They've lifted the blinds in here.

A blind, one blind, partially, to open a window, the lower half. I must smell.

The air is very clean and active. It frisks around me like a barber brushing off. The daylight crosses from behind me, falls past me onto the bookcase and the wall in front of me, has a cool, clear, white transparency, it's refreshing. I wouldn't have thought of the light of the sun shining through space on my books, lighting each of the spines distinctly up.

And it isn't even direct light. It's late, the sun is over on the other side of the house, it's reflecting from the white back wall of the house block across the alley, behind me.

It's not a bookcase, it has no back or sides, it's a bookshelf, a cheap one made from steel rails and particle board to hold all my books and let me double stack them. The wall is plainly visible through the shelves.

There's a barred reflected square bisected by the crease

where the ceiling joins the wall up to my right, and almost transparent shadows of leaves of the untended and exuberant back rose bushes keep blowing silently into the square from the right, in a north wind. The wall is an abstract nougat slab.

There's a cinematic line where the shadow of the shelf stands just below the rail, projected on the wall. Someone who can't move also has a shadow on the wall, that looks like a smirch of dust or smoke half on the books and half on the wall. What's going to happen to the books?

Later, the shadow on the wall has grown.

It is thicker now. So it can move, with the planet.

The line of light on the reflector wall behind me is creeping up toward the roof as this part of the Earth turns away from the sun, starting on its turn back.

The walls of the room are greying.

More and more grey.

When night falls, I'll still be sitting here in the dark, just like this.

The dark will turn colors and begin to separate.

Everything will turn blue.

Then the sun will rise behind me, pouring in, unless it's cloudy, on the back of my broken head, or it won't because I'm too slumped down.

Sun is in the sky, sun is out of the sky, I'm still here,

sun in,

sun out,

me here.

*

The remaining Professor Long returns to Shanghai and begins contacting everyone on her list of academics, writers, or other headworker contacts, over a hundred names, with the idea of starting up a publishing company. They will release written and electronic materials in several different Chinese languages as well as in Arabic, English, Hindi, and Spanish, with more languages to be added. The company will be called Unrelated Books and the logo will consist of two arrows pointing away from each other. Their books will be published in China with a sister printing facility and editorial staff in Los Angeles. They will publish books presenting scholarly ideas about current events in poetic and fantastic forms and their first volume will be an expanded edition of *Animal Money*, with cover art and interior illustrations by a group of artists and eye and brain experts, designed to induce abstract hallucinations.

She finds the streets of Shanghai jammed with people pouring in from rural areas, their faces tense, seeking, anxious, angry. Violent protests increase, and there have been mass prison breaks. A curfew is imposed in Shanghai. A visit from the General Administration of Press and Publication, which works with the Central Propaganda Department, would seem to be in order, but weeks turn into months and neither the remaining Professor Long nor anyone working with her has received so much as a sour look from the direction of the government. The Los Angeles faction too is puzzled by the absence of any gnarliness from the authorities or the media. The remaining Professor Long has apprehensions—are they building up to something ...? Are they forgoing the ordinary procedure, the pressure to conform gradually applied in methodical steps, preparing instead to ...? Or are we really ...?

She was sitting on her sofa reviewing manuscripts when the invitation to Chaglesis Chuseh arrived. She became suddenly aware of a rose perfume, which seemed to flood into her matchbox Shanghai apartment from around the front door. She was looking at the door when a shadow interrupted the bar of light beneath, and a blank red envelope skidded across the floor and turned slightly as it stopped. Look up—shadow gone, odor faded. She sat just there, not thinking, not moving, doing nothing, for a long time. She stared at the envelope as night fell and very soon she could no longer see it. This roused her to turn on the light that hung over the sofa. Then she sat with the light coming down on top of her, still looking at that envelope. The shadow outside the door had not swung into the bar of light from the side as it should have, it had ballooned out from the middle of the bar and spread, then contracted again.

Finally, she approached the letter and squatted to look at it. A plain white—white? hadn't it been red?—envelope, still smelling like roses faintly, with her name neatly printed on it. She lifted it by one corner. Heavy paper. She stood up and held it in both hands. For no intelligible reason there was something in the contact and heft of the letter, its various features, that reassured her. If she hesitated to tear it open, it was not fear but decorum that restrained her. She opened the letter with a scissor blade, being very careful to cut only along the fold at the top. It was her invitation. She was being offered an opportunity, in her capacity as the Editor in Chief of Unrelated Books, to interview Unsu-se Illion, Grand Rachnan of Chaglesis Chuseh ...

The island had appeared in the Pacific overnight. Heavy cloud cover screened it from the satellites; no one saw it come, unheralded by earthquake or tidal wave. Without a sound, the island was there, waves lapping its tranquilly impossible lagoons as if this piece of an alien world were somehow more Earthlike than Earth, primordially ancient, fern covered, buzzing with condor-sized dragonflies. Investigators learn to their cost that the island is screened with a rest field. Aircraft, ships, and submersibles approaching the island will decelerate at a point a mile out from the coast and will, if they keep coming, freeze in place. At the half mile point, the island is girdled by motionless ships and aircraft, tentatively haloed in streaks of powdered-sugar light. Animals don't seem to be affected, but cameras attached to birds do however stop working when they cross the line. The turbulence that normally interferes with flights over Uhuyjhn cities also cloaks the island from above. Every now and then a swarm of apparently unmanned Uhuyjhn airships will sail out to the perimeter to retrieve what paralyzed vehicles have accumulated there and fly them to one of several different islands in the vicinity. These collectors carry their burdens inside relative rest fields and leave them carefully on the ground. Shortly after the collectors were discovered there were attempts to force one down or to shoot them. Whatever was fired at them stopped abruptly a few feet short of the skin of its target and stayed there, held in place by a rest field like a dart stuck in a dartboard. The collectors would complete their tasks without even seeming to notice the clumsy interference, dropping trapped missiles and bullets straight to the ground or sea below with a sort of aerial shrug.

What is known about the island comes to the world from the islanders themselves, and is confirmed by observations with ultra long range optics. The island has an area of about 29,000 square miles and one very large city, Chaglesis Chuseh. After a few weeks, it is clear that human beings have been migrating there, although as yet it is not known how, since nobody has ever been observed coming or going.

The remaining Professor Long is instructed by her invitation to expect to be away no less than ten days, although she may stay as long as she likes. Pack lightly, it says; most of what she needs or wants will be provided for her free of charge on the island. Her contact will approach her in the quarry at the Shanghai botanical garden, date and time provided.

Her contact turns out to be a sprightly teenaged girl, who greets her effusively, baring both rows of her braces. Singing out and extending her arms above her head, the girl sweeps in for a weightless hug.

"I am your contact. Treat me like a prized former student."

The voice in her ear is level and businesslike. The face that pulls back into view again is vapid and grinning. Together, they enter the steel box that leads to the deep observing pool. The box is empty when they arrive. Moments later, it is empty again, although they have not been seen leaving it.

*

Inhabitants call the island Dagashe Yuteh. The phrase has an elusive meaning like a phrase from a dream, inclining now this way and now that inside a ring of meanings. The remaining Professor Long arrives with no recollection of the journey there, her last memory being of the steel box at the quarry garden in Shanghai. Now she and her contact are at the top of a tower on the outskirts of Chaglesis Chuseh, waiting to be picked up. From these heights, she can see for miles out over the rolling green landscape of the island, misty in the brilliant sun. Here and there she can see vortices of white creatures climbing into the air on thermals. Gigantic Theems stride across the open spaces, looking like vast burning haystacks on Sequoyah legs. The "smoke" that streams from them is actually a long train of ribbons that trawls nutrients out of the air. Theems are colony animals made up of millions of tightly interwoven eels, and their winged young surround the Theem in an undulating cloak of shoaling forms. The whole island was brought here from outer space, another planet, and the air is redolent with a vegetable smell entirely new to her. Almost like the aroma of raw tobacco, and something else a little like rubber cement. Chaglesis Chuseh rises in the other direction, looking like a cotton candy citadel of transparent pink and chartreuse balloon buildings.

They are picked up by a Vietnamese woman in a trajectory capsule. It looks like a car inside, with seats and so on, but it's actually a rocket. They travel so rapidly that the remaining Professor Long has no chance to look at the city streaking by.

The capsule is brought in by a rest beam. The effect would be appalling if it were any less brief. It brings her immediately back to a time last year when she was running to catch a bus, tripped on a piece of broken New York and fell flat on her face at full speed. There's the jolt, and then the body outrage that leaves her flushed with indignation and sadness. A spasm of petulance makes her want to refuse to get out of the capsule, but then she thinks, since the driver is not getting out of her seat, perhaps the capsule is about to go off again. She frees herself from her restraints and climbs out. Her contact is there, waiting for her.

"Are you feeling all right?"

"Yes, fine."

She catches a glimpse of herself and her disconcerted expression in the polished golden wax of the wall in front of her, and then searches the face of her contact for any sign of pity or amusement. No sign.

They go through an acute archway that curves with the concavity of the wall, down a sort of chute; they emerge into a pink glass cathedral space humming with low voices. Her contact leads her along one side and through a series of narrow passages. Stepping over the high lintel of the door, the remaining Professor Long knows instantly that her voyage is over. This is the place.

The building is plainly round, and she is in a sort of intestinal ring that goes around the outside of the inner chamber. The ring is more than 15 meters tall at is rounded apex, and the room inside is much higher.

While it is plainly a thick slab of solid stone, the floor shudders with heavy beats beneath her. It smells like a zoo.

Her contact leads her to a long basin set in the inner wall of the intestine. Following her example, the remaining Professor Long washes her face and hands carefully. Now her contact leads her around the wall and into the main room.

The chamber must be over forty meters high at the top of the dome, and eighty across. Part of the ceiling is sectioned and seems able to fold back like an observatory roof. There are dozens of people in the chamber, keeping mostly around the edges like wallflowers.

Unsu-se Illion is a gargantuan white spider, veiled in strands of webbing like a ragged bride. Her enormous abdomen rises nearly to the top of the dome, which visually echoes her shape. For such a colossal animal, the spider is very active, whizzing this way and that, its legs hum through the air and land on the stone floor with a wooden thunk. Every day it must build the great trawl net that it will let out into the sky at night to capture aerial krill. The web is anchored to enormous bollards of blue jade and carefully unfurled at dusk, when she flings it aloft into the wind coming off the sea. Some time before dawn she hauls it back in again, running it through her sieving mouth parts to nibble off the krill. She spends the day refurbishing the web.

Staring in astonishment, the remaining Professor Long absently paws at her breast pocket and then, in an absent, sleep-talker's voice, asks her contact if she has a cigarette. She does. The remaining Professor Long backs onto a seat and her knees fold under her, cigarette dangling from the center of her lower lip and smokes it down to the filter, staring at the spider and dribbling ashes down the front of her sweater.

Presently, her contact taps her firmly on the shoulder.

"Let's go," she says, showing her first indications of impatience. She leads the remaining Professor Long to a white porcelain dock or podium and holds her hand as she climbs up into it. The spider, Unsu-se Illion, stops fussing with its nets and comes over to her. Watching this massive animal approach, with its many enormous legs moving, is wildly alarming, but she remains where she is, holding on to the smooth rim of the dock. The spider gives off a strong aroma of fresh milk and roses. There are eight deep green crystal eyes, a transparent shadow inside each one, like eight radiant green aquariums. Those eyes are gazing at her, and each of them is bigger than her head. Every monstrous disproportion of the encounter is focussed in the meeting of her small gaze with its vast gaze, like having a personal encounter with a sunset. The mouth parts are geometrically regular polyhedrons of translucent chitin; ceaseless in their motion, their distinct facets glisten with transparent slime. Her contact has climbed into the dock beside her and holds up a slender glass tube. Unsu-se Illion leans forward and for a panicked moment she thinks it's going to mouth her with its parts. Instead, a thin stream of saliva pours into the tube. The young woman collects it carefully. Then the spider steps back away from the dock, and, with a whirl of its tunic of fine web fragments, it wheels in place and strides off, to resume work on its web again.

The contact leads her down off the dock and a bit

away, toward the inner wall. The remaining Professor Long follows with dread pooling inside her.

Her contact hands her the glass tube, which is still warm. There are about two grams of saliva in it, quivering viscously, clear, with a few small bubbles trapped in it.

"Unsu-se Illion can't speak, but she can communicate with us through the effects of her saliva. Drink it."

The remaining Professor Long hears a rushing in her ears, feeling with loathing the warm thickness of the fluid through the glass. The saliva has a slightly meaty odor. Her contact is looking her collectedly in the face, comprehending everything, not in the least withdrawing. She will wait.

Something that might be pride keeps her from refusing. Time passes, and her contact has adopted a standing posture that indicates she is prepared to go on standing there, go on waiting. Even the idea of asking for something, a cigarette, a mint, makes her stomach flip. She imagines shouting: "Why did you let me see where it comes from?!"

A sudden impulse steels her and she thrusts the glass at her mouth, opening her jaws as if she were making some other gesture unconnected to what her hands were doing.

"I think I am going to faint," she says.

Then a kind of blanket rises up inside her nervous zone, and a moment later, with a long, soft "oooh," she does faint.

She comes to a moment later on the ground. Her contact helps her to her feet and, holding her shoulders, steers her toward a reclining white seat, all made of shining ceramic like a giant tooth. Her contact's face seems nevertheless to recede into a boundless distance, the hand on her shoulder and the shoulder itself whirling away into space as if she were turning into a growing empty glass figurine. In a convulsive flash of memory she sees herself drink the saliva and gags, shrinking. Chills sluice down her body rinsing away her strength. The girl gets her lying down on the seat and the moment she is relieved of the effort of getting somewhere the full horror of her weakness alights on her savagely. Her body is a brittle husk surrounding a boneless interior of clammy, pulsating mucus. A thin cry emerges from her tensed mouth, the sound of a sleeper trying to scream in a nightmare. She keeps rubbing her face, drawing up her knees and then flexing her back to get them away from her. The feeling of any part of her body touching any other part is intolerable.

Now she is calmer. The idea of her recovered calm comes over her only after an indefinite period of terrifying inner disruption of self and writhing weakness. Her body is going numb, and a light without temperature is breaking through into her, into her abdomen, from the direction of the spine, and pushing up and down along the backbone. It's a kind of energy that belongs in her body but which is being amplified from outside. A bowed string, a physical sensation of her own existence, independented from any other particulars.

She holds. She imagines filling with avid larvae but the image has no emotion for her, she can look on it calmly because it's only a picture of fear devoid of reality or reference to reality. She knows the image isn't going to come true. She knows almost nothing, but what few things she does know at the moment, things she can't enumerate or call to mind, she knows with oracular certainty. She holds. She contains. She asks. Ridgy brown flames tiger-striped with black shadows are standing up all over her, like butterfly wings or gills of fungus, motionless flames. Looking around without using her eyes, her head, any organ, she relates things together in a certain way. The sounds are unsettlings of a vapor veil. There is a pounding like her heartbeat were being projected into her from an external organ.

It is dark and the room is dim when she struggles to her feet again. She stares at the dream image of a giant white spider hurling huge crescents of web up into the sky, perched half in and half out of the roof aperture. The web's purlings and scrollings are slow and weightless. There are almost no people left in the room. She sees a man lying on another one of the porcelain couches and wonders if he drank, too. Without knowing what she's doing, she wanders out into the ring intestine. It occurs to her to rinse out her mouth at the faucet, but her mouth is so dry she simply sucks up the water madly, feeling the cold splash in her stomach. She is outside on the street before her contact manages to catch up with her, watching the people on the moving glass sidewalks, the Uhuyjhns, like huge dry jellyfish, floating in the air along the skin of the coral reef high rises. The planters along the pavements are filled with luminous plants like giant sea anemones, brilliantly red, yellow, purple, and what appear to be living things like stone posts that look like ginger roots sculpted out of pink chalcedony, like taffy candies with peppermint ribbons.

Like ...

Like ...

Like ...

Her contact takes the remaining Professor Long by the arm and steers her to a dark room with shag carpeting, a bed and a round window hidden behind thick cream colored drapes, and that's where the dreams really hit her, wringing and twisting her like a human washcloth.

She doesn't remember clearly afterwards what she dreamt. She lay on her back staring at the ceiling. At times it seemed to her that the inside of her head was in contact with the lower apex of a flat black diamond whose edges went through her eyes and met in her brain, and her mind, or at least her point of view, spilled out along that vertical surface, spreading out and upwards for light years, relentlessly telescoping. She was looking at enormous still images of human faces, sailing over them like landscapes. Updrafts of invisible force perturbed her as she passed over eyes, mouths, expressions. Interstellar space. There were people in it. No planet, no space station. She sees the leaves of interstellar space. Shaped like flame. There are human beings in among those leaves. There is rational motion. They are hunting. All of them. Young and old, children, the blind, stalking. They are all deliberate. They move skillfully. Negative people in a void forest of clear black tree trunks and leaves all limned in dubious light, growing out of no ground, as if something were being translated into the kind of sensory information that she would find intelligible. She feels angry.

"Let me *see!*" she cries.

Did she see, finally? She can't say. There was in that

hunting group of people a feeling like *this* was *it*, this was a clue or an answer, but that idea might only be a registration of the fact that hunting involves seeking, following clues.

When she finally came out of it, she was exhausted, parched, hungry. Someone she doesn't know, a middle aged African woman, noticed she was awake, and called in her contact. Her contact appears soon, and then an older man bringing in some soup. The remaining Professor Long eats it feebly and falls into normal sleep. When she wakes up again, completely out of step with the world's time, she feels better, very hungry, and she wants to wash up and change her clothes. Her contact appears some time later and tells her to be ready to return to China in a few hours.

"But what am I supposed to write?"

"Don't worry," her contact says. "You'll write it."

And she does write it. The words come like magic, surprising her as they take shape on the page. She reads them over with the same sense of discovery she would have had if they had been written by someone else. Who? The person she is going to be from now on, apparently.

She's noticed it ever since she got back. No one knows that she's been away; she has often retreated from sight to work on this or that project in isolation. But everyone she meets asks her if she's gotten some sun, or lost weight, or changed her hair. While as far as she can tell she looks the same as ever, she's nevertheless now invested with a new intellectual glamour; people hang on her words, and now everybody turns when she comes into the room with the same smile and slightly ducking head, the same uplifted hand, the same rapid step, as ever.

*

Storms rip through the ethereal plane. With shadow Smilebot at his side, and shadow Boringbot at its side, the shadow of Professor Aughbui works frantically, adjusting the city, throwing off black wind waves to hold back the lightning, but the chaos proliferates in a thousand tiny fractures in all directions faster than he can respond and he is being overwhelmed like the sorcerer's apprentice— except he was the good apprentice, he never strayed out of line, he barely even existed, and now he has to clean up and contain the rampant consequences of other people's sloppiness and irresponsibility. He gnashes his shadow teeth with an irritation on its way to becoming madness. The silhouettes of the other economists are still with him, but, since their decision to bilocate, they have been preoccupied with their business on the Earth plane while their ethereal shades have become listless and sluggish. In a rage of activity, Professor Aughbui tries to buy himself time to create minions he can put to work propping up what small order remains. It is beginning to seem as if the economists on earth are vying with him, working against him. Lightning dances all around, each flash threatening to disorient him, and he struggles to concentrate despite the incessant thunder blasts. He has to resist a wild impulse to plunge his hands into the city before him, plunge them in up to his elbows and rear back, ripping it in fragments, then shredding these larger pieces into smaller and smaller ones in a frenzy of overstimulation.

More time is needed, silhouette Professor Aughbui

thinks. It's a precious gleam of rational thought in a blur of activity. If he could bundle all the gestures and interventions he's been making together by species, then a single movement would then radiate off all the ancillary gearing movements needed. He is trapped in a reactive state with no future, only dearly bought time. He needs to throw the other into the reactive position, force it to scurry after him. Time bought with animal money is doubled. With one movement he opens the zoos while at the same time enclosing the city. He opens the landscape and the sky, and closes himself. His darkness gets deeper, and more solid, while his outline grows less distinct. He no longer resembles his human silhouette; now he looks more like a featureless mannikin. He gathers up handfuls of animals of all kinds and holds them out to the storm to zap with lightning, then returns these charged individuals to the enclosure. There, they whizz around above, on, and below the ground, lighting up the whole city with a feverish bio-glow. The silhouette looks like an animal. All of them do. There are figures down on those city streets who move in eccentric, maze-like paths, and every now and then tacking abruptly away, sending an image or a second self gliding rapidly on down the original line. Professor Aughbui touches one of these figures and switches places with it, driving on down the street against a pelting rain in waterlogged clothes and squelching shoes, then tack and send another Professor Aughbui shadow creature sailing into another department. SuperAesop looms over the city reaching out to adjust this little luminous point and that bright segment and knocking down barriers with a fingertip to allow the animals to come out. He looks at the shadow faculty around him, and the storm becoming part of the city. He runs his feelers out and makes the city part of the storm. He waves his hand over one or another neighborhood and sucks up the lights. He upends a cupped hand and the activity over in this part of the city speeds up. Professor Aughbui reaches up through his own back and grabs the looming hand, the two of them swing around again. SuperAesop drives on down the street. Professor Aughbui looms over the city. SuperAesop reaches out and takes Assiyeh by the hand. They swing. Assiyeh drives down the street, tacking, throwing off images when she tacks, vanishing without a trace her empty clothes still warm flutter down into a pothole and there in her place—an alien artifact: the left quarter raggedly broken off a hexagon suspended in total darkness, all the leftmost and nearly all of the upper and lower left facets—this thing is made of small bright yellow blocks of varying size, some cubes and some rectangular boxes, so that it resembles a cramped adobe city—there are three of these hexagon fragments hovering in space stacked one on top of the other, parallel and evenly spaced, the same color and composition but with minor differences—they move exactly in unison, rushing further to the "left" and then stopping abruptly, and with that abrupt stop, a heavy, invisible fluid seethes among the blocks across the fragments and collects in a slosh against the hard hexagon edge.

Sharp contrasts of muted colors ... the limpid black night tear shadow—the desert has autumn and winter too ...

The Uhuyjhn city rises up suddenly all around us as

cyclops cars lunge out too late, careering in impotent rage around behind us but unable to follow this escape route. Shitty hatchback gives out—there's a pop and a rattle and white smoke and oh shit and get out and what now, and who cares because we're here and that's all that matters, we made it. The Uhuyjhn floating above a tobacco kiosk turns to greet us, abrupt steps of its boneless legs the magnetic way the tiny feet in black shoes seem to cling to the floor, the way its diaphanous bulk rolls and settles on itself, billowing and nodding like a benign monarch.

PART THIRTEEN:
LIVING SKELETONS,
ELDERLY DRONES

Summer time for flesh and skin;
In Autumn—skeleton time begin.

The annual festival of the dead. At midnight the dead arise and fuck the living. Shadows creep from the cemeteries, the unmarked graves in out-of-the-way places. Shadows grope into houses. Warm bodies pressed by cool purple cadavers, foul kisses, crumbling paws. Sepulchral croons of release in the silence of a still and breathless night, a new moon.

Achrizoguayla is rocked by the news of Tripi's return. She is already in session with the electoral committee, who are trying to explain to her that she cannot simply pick up where she left off.

"I am still the elected President," she insists.

"Madame President," Dr. Besik, committee chair, replies patiently, "We cannot overlook the fact that new elections have already taken place. There is no constitutional precedent or procedure to guide us; if we void the results of the elections, even though they are inconclusive, I guarantee you there will be outrage, there will be violence, very likely widespread violence, necessitating a serious crackdown. If the army gets involved, as you must realize, our democracy will not last."

"And what about the people?" Tripi asks. "Should the votes they cast for me, in exercise of their already hard-won democratic right to vote, be voided? What sort of precedent does that set? Do they not have the right to vote for the candidate they want, now that I have come back? At the least, if you are not prepared to honor their original intentions, you should at least make allowances for their current intentions."

"This has been an extremely long and emotional campaign, Madame President. We have already had several extensions, and now the committee has had to appoint a new member to replace Professor Muoitisorpio, which made yet another delay necessary. The interim government is withered to a skeleton and has barely enough means to keep going."

"The people know me," Tripi says. "All I ask is a few days to make my case to them."

At this point the party representatives rear up in protest.

"We can't postpone the election again!"

"Our campaign funds are nearly all gone! How can we go on?"

A visibly aging Dr. Besik lifts her hands and sighs.

"If I may ..." she keeps repeating softly, into her microphone. "If I may ..."

Presently, when it is possible to be heard speaking in a normal tone of voice, she goes on.

"We must consider the public in both cases. If President Pina is given time to run, this will stretch the already depleted resources of the other two parties and cause their supporters to become frustrated and angry—"

Here she pauses to give both party representatives a lingering look.

"—if the party leadership does not make a serious effort to address and to dissipate that anger. However, President Pina still enjoys considerable support and popularity with the people, who have not forgotten the great strides Achrizoguayla has made with her leadership. If she is *denied* the opportunity to run, those people will—and, I remind you, they are not a few—we have to foresee that they will not be likely to accept as democratic and fair the outcome of such an election."

In the end, the committee votes to postpone the election yet again. Tripi has a narrow opening—four days. Many of her advisors are surprised at her uncharacteristic insistence. Why not sit out the election for the good of the country? After all, there would probably be another election some time, right? Now that elections seem to be the order of the day. Why not wait?

"Something must have happened to her out there," they say. "There's something hard in her look that wasn't there before."

"Or that was buried. Something her ordeal tested and brought out."

The official story was an amnesiac episode induced by a blow to the head, almost certainly as a consequence of a fall down the slope. She had seen a child in some distress, as nearly as she can recall, and, in trying to find and help this child, she must have strayed too near the edge. Her mind is a blank from the time she finished her cigarillo, standing a little way off from the gas station, to the time when she recovered her memory in a hotel room in Etsimen, where some good Samaritans had given her shelter. How she got all the way to Etsimen is not known—perhaps some unsuspecting truck driver gave her a lift. The hotel manager and his young son received the public credit for sheltering her during her recuperation.

News of the postponement is met with loud, precarious protests and there are minor eruptions of violence in the crowd. Will they remain minor? People dressed for the festival of the dead, all in black, with black rings painted around their eyes and white gloves, shout political slogans. A fight breaks out in a cemetery as members of two factions clash while visiting the graves of their loved ones.

*

She's increasingly worried about the owls—police in China are owls because they say who? Who invited you to the conference? Who did you meet there? Who does Dr. Sulekh Budshah work for? Who do your Los Angeles associates associate with? Who is the brother of the woman who cuts your hair? What's his wife's name? His daughter's name? His best friend's barber's name?

The remaining Professor Long lies awake in the dark playing out the interrogation, anticipating questions and testing herself instead of sleeping. Why did you call it Unrelated Books? What aren't they related to—Marxism? Isn't that a rather weird name for a publishing company? Are the books unrelated or is it the company? What do the two arrows mean? Did you design the logo yourself? On and on, all over tea, with every outward appearance of a social call, and suppression spraying out in an invisible haze from the bodies of the two plainclothes officers.

Given the bizarre inaction of the police in her case she is beginning to get really worried. Why would they let her go for so long without a scare chat unless they were planning something worse? They could be giving her enough rope. They could be monitoring her contacts, using her to ferret out other nonconformists, but she's never published anything by anyone in China who wasn't already openly critical, at least by the narrow standard prevailing. Anything stiff was coming from exiles and from random people around the world. The worst suspicion of all was that they were using the press for their own purposes, that someone in the company was a plant or had been recruited or manipulated into working with the authorities. Actually, the worst suspicion was that the whole press had been body-snatched and she was the only real person left in it, deludedly going about her business inside a prison that looks just like everyday life. Then again, there's a reason it's so easy to make a prison look like everyday life, once you take away the more extreme manifestations. Take away the rape, the inmate violence, the guards beating you—maybe that's why the prison reforms are happening now; not to make the prisons nicer, but to make it harder to tell the difference between being in or out of prison.

Within a few months of its publication, the Unrelated Books expanded edition of *Animal Money* was everywhere. The remaining Professor Long pounded out a seventy page afterword over a single weekend and emerged exhausted and shaky. It was that afterword which prompted those states which had not already done so to ban the book, on the ground that it was "cult literature" or "religious propaganda" or some form of ultra-subtle indoctrination into Chinese ideology. The remaining Professor Long, who had had enough brains not to sign the afterword, is bombarded by demands to reveal the author's name, but something about those demands smells wrong to her.

Still no scare chat, or any of the other tell-tale signs of official interest. The demands all come from the wrong places, government agencies she's never heard of, non-governmental agencies, newspaper editors. Of course she refuses with what some take to be a heroically stalwart stand against censorship, but she also uses a business trip to Los Angeles as a pretext to abandon Shanghai. Why did they let her go? She stays with friends in San Gabriel, applies for jobs, ends up back in her weird gazebo-office in San Toribio a few months later, gazing absently out the narrow door into the indistinct greenery of the garden as if it had all been a daydream. There is in the world the same feeling she gets in dreams, of everything being different and yet nothing having changed.

She wrote that afterword in a frenzy. It fastened on her almost the very instant she got back from Chayar'iliane. Anyone who knows anything about the subject can tell at once that the material in that afterword is of Uhuyjhn origin; much of it details a mystical kind of procedure, ostensibly included in the text as an example drawn from an anthropologist's description of the practices of an anonymous tribe in an unspecified place and time. The celebrants sit on the ground close together in two rows facing each other, hands joined across the gap, softly chanting certain formulas and invocations, rocking to and fro faster and faster drawing closer together in contracting circles their heads going up and down like pistons. If this can be sustained long enough a haze of luminous golden particles will precipitate itself around the actors nodding in cantilever unison, rippling with their movements, tracing their exhalations and the plumes of heat given off by their bodies in branching, swirling arabesques of glittering motes. Make one mistake, lose concentration for one instant, and they will find you later, petrified, a gilded statue, nodding awfully. Do it correctly, and the mist will form a runway between the two rows. Something is coming down that runway, something that flashes, twists, luminous. A hand is raised to snatch it as it goes darting past, closing it in black fingers firm and dry as wood. A coin of thick, heavy gold, purer than pure, with a deep amber glow, blank, weirdly absent any temperature, and inexplicably easily mistaken for a butterfly. The coin never stays, but those who summon it will never be without again. They become impoverishedly wealthy; as Camus noted, the poor have the sun, the beach, the sky, the weather. Those who have conjured the coin acquire the ability to transmute their circumstances, to turn dead debts and obligations into something living and changeable, to make sleepwalking institutions wake up and dream another dream. What they owe becomes elastic and subtly variable, so that owing elicits more, and repaying elicits more, and buying and selling are a kind of respiration, and their wealth does not materialize in objects but in time. The late Professor Long was right: the exchange of animal money creates suspensions of continuity, which she terms "disengagements," that allow for the direct application of alternative systems. The mystery of the missing value is solved, as far as she and Professor Budshah are concerned—Professor Crest being unconvinced, Professor Aughbui abstaining—by seeking it in an escape back into exchange, which is to say the mystery of its disappearance is put into circulation. Professor Crest complains that this makes animal money nothing more than a currency with a mystery standard in place of a gold standard. Nevertheless, this was the Uhuyjhn message the remaining Professor Long was selected to relay.

*

I am buying wine for Carolina and me when a meaty paw alights gently on my left shoulder and pulls me around with soft irresistibility to confront myself—I'd know that almost too-narrow skull anywhere, adorned with a Hapsburg lip, and a pair of eyes popped out of horror cartoons. I hear a heavy laugh bubbling heavily up.

"Me, not him! Over here!"

The other hand points me to a glistening jovial face, a meaty man in a tropical shirt, stubble on his cheek, a mop of black curls showing some grey to top it off.

He asks me if I'm me and I say yes, and he says he's Mateo and digs a folded note out of his tropical pocket to give me between two fingers. It's from Tripi.

"Don't say anything," he says quietly.

I know Mateo. He's death. Everybody knows it. He is what they call a "Bronson." That means he kills people, but he doesn't take sides.

I read the note. She's asking me to come see her right away in her room at Hotel Jose Blounga. It looks like her handwriting—all the Tripis.

"Which one?"

"Which one do you think?" he chuckles. "Come on."

I let that light but heavy hand float me out the door. There's a cab waiting outside. I think I might bolt, but somehow I get in and we are whirring through the glittering streets of San Toribio. It's a warm dusky time of day. Mateo sits in front talking Achrizoguaylan whatever to the driver, an older man in a white cap and a crisp red shirt, with a gold chain around one wrist.

I should be scared to death, but Tripi's handwriting somehow consoles me. The idea of dying at all, but particularly now, when the night air comes in soft off the transvestites through the window, it just isn't real. It isn't my time. I know that the way I know I am sitting upright, that this is my hand.

This part of town plotted out its traffic light scheme based on what must have been some very optimistic appraisals. Waiting at one light after another I watch the people. I could jump out and join them. Everywhere the same pleasing, even browns. The dry air, the dusk. My mother told me that she had taken me to Africa when I was a boy, a very small boy, but that was a dream, come to think of it. I dreamt, when I was a small boy, about lying in a bed in an African house, and I told my mother. At rest in the dream, the sun going down like a glob of hot glass, setting over Africa, all so vivid, and the feeling too. The dryness. The nameless smell I would recognize if I ever smelt it again, wouldn't it be weird to go and smell that smell there? Something else in the air too, as the night came down, a rustle, like dust rustling against itself, mixing with voices, with insect noises. I was lying in a cot or something, a crib, on the floor, looking at a plaster wall with a rough line about a foot up from the bottom, and above the line the wall was a very pale green, maybe with a bit of festive, tentative red piping around the window, which had no sill, no sash, just a slot in the wall perfectly framing a setting sun that shone on me at an impossible angle, as if I were hovering over it and yet as if the horizon were a wall higher than the sill. It was so real because the primary sensation there was the absence of any pressure, as if the air had lost weight, as if I controlled all aspects of weight concerning myself, so that I would feel it in and from my body only. I felt safe in a dangerous place, an eerie place. I could look out the window and see unreal things, but they couldn't come through to get me. I woke up and told my mother, who slept on the sofa across the room from me.

"I've never gone there," she said, when I asked her, thinking somehow her memory had given me my dream. She was a vague shape made of blankets over there against the far wall, with a comb of streetlight raking the wall over her through the blinds. The wind was blowing outside. I looked toward the window and saw stars in the blinds. The wind rushed and wind chimes jingled. I could only imperfectly distinguish between the chimes, the wind, the night sky, the stars; I thought the chimes were a sound the stars made; and since the wind made the stars easier to see by sweeping the dirt out of the sky, the wind affected the stars from my point of view, that logically the wind was among the stars, a star wind. I knew these ideas were beautiful and maybe more beautiful than true, although I couldn't have explained that or even understood it then.

I see my mother now, coming toward me through the kitchen door. I see her from my man's height, although I never saw her that way in reality. She is all one lump, all at once and slopeshouldered like a popsicle or should I say a momsickle. She carried her head low, like her neck had retracted, and shuffled on skinny ankles. She's in the shadow, in the kitchen. The kitchen is orange with early morning light behind her but she's shadowed in the doorway, and now she steps out to look at me. She turns up her sagging, smiling face at me, like she never had the chance to do since I was never this tall when she was able to do any looking. My mother.

She was a real philosopher. Everything upset her and nothing fazed her. I'd cut my body in half slowly if that meant I could see her come out of the kitchen now and smile at me one more time. She was a real philosopher. She knew the only thing that mattered. I don't have a collection of her wise sayings, or I guess I do, but they don't sound like anything repeated. Some of my mother's aphorisms include: "Well, all right," or "Then, you just have to do it, that's it," or "I know it's tough," or "You should go," (with reference to some trip). or "That's it." There's the moral, use it wisely.

My mother was never married. She had me because she met a Mexican and they moved in together in his little shack-house in Eagle Rock. Evidently they lived together for a while before she got pregnant with me; he went out one day and never came back, but she would always underline the fact that he was in the US illegally and that he could have gotten picked up. I would always mentally underline the fact that they have telephones in Mexico too. I think my mother was less concerned about defending herself against the idea she'd been abandoned and more concerned about defending herself against the idea that US immigration might have killed my father somehow. She did believe immigrants were summarily killed by immigration officers, and she also thought a lot of immigrants died during deportation, getting stuck in overcrowded cells with no water and no air conditioning and no medical facilities and no toilet for days. "Would he just leave the house?" she would ask rhetorically.

The cab stops in front of a low building painted dark red with black shutters, nearly engulfed from behind by palm trees that grope over the roof like a head of hair. There's a single golden point of light, like a shining coin, I can see through the slats of one shutter. The wind comes up as we walk to the door, tousselling the trees, whooshing and gushing like waves, and the sound and the light through the slat makes me think again of the room after my dream, the blinds, stars, wind, chimes, my mother on the sofa, and I wonder if this is a warning, if I'm going to die here looping back.

Mateo throws open the black door with its brass knob and in we go; red tile floors, ghostly white walls in the gloom, and a smell like corn bread gone cold.

"Hey Tripi!" he bellows.

I get a whiff of tobacco smoke as we pass through into the room with the one lamp. Tripi sits at a table there, looking the same as ever, tweedy and professorial, and tired. Carolina is sitting across the round table from her, same side as me, back lit, naked as usual. That's probably her dress tossed over the back of the sofa, her sandals there where she kicked them deftly off. Even without getting a clear look at her I can already tell her eyes are all pupil.

"Here he is!" Mateo roars, gesturing at me.

I sit down.

"What you want? Coffee? Mate? You want whiskey?"

What I want is a time machine.

"I don't know man, I'll have whatever you have."

Mateo goes crashing off into the back of mystery zone saying something loud enough to come rebounding off the walls and yet I can't make it out.

Tripi gets up and I get up again and we shake hands and sit again.

"I didn't want to be too obvious about all this," she says for openers. She straightens her skirt nervously.

"You see, someone might want to kill me, to keep me out of the election."

"OK," I say vaguely, looking at Carolina.

"It seems that, during my time away, people I trusted have changed in ways that make trusting them more difficult. I have my doubts about who I can rely on now. At the moment, the country is at a watershed in its history, an opportunity to join in the greater economic community of Latin American states. You must know that integrating into that community was something I really struggled to achieve, and I think—and hopefully this is not mere pride talking—that I am genuinely the best one to lead the country during this time."

"You have my vote," I say.

"I want your help," she says. "I want you to run my campaign."

"That's crazy," I say without thinking, the words flat facts.

"Show me something sane in all this by way of comparison," she says without batting an eye.

I am sitting next to a stark naked woman who is, at the moment, calmly snapping off tabs of acid and forming them into a little cake to put beneath her tongue, next to the two or three she already has in there, and I am conversing with the quasi-president of the country. Mateo comes back with mate on a tray for me and for Tripi. He does not even glance at Carolina.

"You're not having anything?" I ask her.

"No," she says.

Mateo throws a look at me.

"No, I'm OK," he says.

"I would have thought I'm the last person you'd want," I say. "I'm the one who sheltered all your counterfeits and people wouldn't be questioning whether or not you're really you if I hadn't or is that why you want me, right? Because I will—"

She's nodding.

"Right," she says.

"Getting me on your side means taking that weapon away from the opposition."

Still nodding, she says, "There's another reason as well, which is why you bothered sheltering all those false versions of me. Although naturally I am glad that you seem to accept me for who I am without any fuss. The other reason is however the most important, and that is your devotion to the image. I feel I must not fail to tell you, that I am not under any illusion—I think—about any loyalty you may personally feel for me. While I would welcome and esteem loyalty as it is worthy to be welcomed and esteemed, what matters more, most of all, is fidelity to what I have come to stand for. An untold amount of hard work was necessary to get me into the running, to make our voices heard in quarters of influence, some even lost their lives doing it, and perhaps, provided you take for granted my boundless gratitude and admiration for all that work, a very huge element of good fortune also. To maintain a clear appraisal of my own contribution, that it is a contribution I make, and not an exalted foreordained consummation or a solitary and heroic labor entirely of my own, is something I struggle with every day. So, when I speak of what I stand for, I don't want you to think I am really speaking about myself. I am speaking about the people of this country, everyone still languishing in slums, the Basques, and I am speaking, too, about Latin America, our role in it, and the world, even if all we stand for here is the insistence that our country, small and poor as it is, should likewise have a voice in a global chorus, and that this should be true for all small and poor countries.

"You've noticed," she says with a mirthless little smile, "that I am campaigning at the moment. If you'll forgive the high rhetoric, I hope you won't overlook the sincere sentiment and values that hold the rhetoric up. Those are the only things that should influence your decision on my side; certainly I can't offer you much else. I have very little campaign money, and at present I can't begin to think how the election will turn out or if we will even be able to hold one. The grumbling of the generals has been sub-sonic up to now, but I'm sure you've started to hear it. They are chafing to restore what they consider 'order.' And I know that some of them believe this election will lead to violence no matter what happens."

"You keep telling people they have to accept the results of the election," I say.

"Yes, but there may be riots anyway, because not everyone will be angry on my behalf, but simply because they will assume the elections are illegitimate. While I have my criticisms of the way the electoral committee has handled itself, I don't believe it is corrupt. However, it is an irony of the time that the more adjustments they make, in their attempts to defend democratic processes, the more they seem to be tampering with them."

"Have you thought about coalition?"

"Of course! Matild can't make up her mind whether she wants me as a partner, junior partner, senior partner, advisor, this, that, the other thing—I get different messages every time I talk to her about it and the emails go round and round. And the NFP won't even talk to me. They have decided to treat me as a pretender."

"Is that what I owe this invitiation—invitation to?"

"I make this *invitation* to you," she declares, "because I think you are an idealist."

"OK," I say. "Where do we start?"

*

"Did you notice," I ask Carolina later. "Mateo didn't see you."

"Who's Mateo?" she asks.

"The one who brought me to Tripi's."

"Oh," she says absently. "But you came in alone."

"He came in with me."

"You came in alone, my dear."

*

"Your *Animal Money* has caused a bit of trouble," she says, coolly adopting the superior position. She sits on a bare stage, legs crossed, fashionable, as her mouth moves in speech I see flashes of the writhing sea louse inside. She is the next Urtruvel, trained in an Ursuline convent.

The publication of *Animal Money* was a non-event having no effect at all, or it changed the world. It did both. Like a laser whose points of emission and of contact can be seen, but not the transit in between. Two lights or one in two ledgers. What really changed? What can a book do? Don't fantasize the people. They do it. The book is like a person in certain respects, when it can become part of some kind of trouble. The book that is making trouble for me right now fell into my lap in the library the other day, handed to me by one of my more troublesome because inquisitive students. *Hermetic Instruction among Leafcutter Ants*, by a Palestinian entomologist named Assiyah Malahasoud. In this book, she describes her chance discovery of intricate pheromonal tracings, laboriously constructed by leafcutter ants in forms closely resembling the seals, circles, and composite symbolic images of hermetic magic. There are certain typical icons, repeated in variant forms from hive to hive even across enormous distances and over long periods of time, featuring in particular typical representations of very old drones. Ant drones are typically short lived, she observes, surviving maturation only for a few weeks, while queens can live for decades and even ordinary worker ants can live for over a year. Hence, an old drone would be a genuine anomaly, and something the ants would not likely know from experience. Uniquely among insects, ants have been observed teaching each other various skills—could they have some kind of folklore as well, including a story of a drone who lived a very long time?

There were also special images representing pathfinder ants, those who venture out into the unknown in order to find a way around an obstacle. These are represented with modified versions of pheromones associated with queens, as if to dignify them. Sometimes they are depicted as surrounded by ants of other species, particularly those with cruder social structures; these "savage" ants are marked with odors associated with the unfamiliar and the dangerous, leading Dr. Malahasoud to conclude that these images show stylized encounters between leafcutter pathfinders and "wild ants," the myrmecological equivalent of cave men. Again and again, these images stress an ambivalence about the hindquarters of the ant, specifically the way the ovipositor is modified to become a death-dealing stinger among the sterile workers. Dr. Malahasoud speculates that this means the ants may have their own version of ambivalence, postulating that, while ants lack sophisticated neural organs, the collective mass of ants may develop intelligence socially. She points to a symbol that she claims to have found in every leafcutter diagram, and which she names the "air-eater" symbol. It shows an ant's head, depicted by a minute representation of odor variations over the surface, with streaks of earth meticulously scrubbed bare of any smell at all near the mouth area. These streaks of earth actually have faint traces of smell at the end farthest from the mouth, deliberately attenuated as they draw closer to the mouth. Ancillary clues show that this "air-eater" symbol has extraordinary significance, causing ordinarily very active pathfinder ants to pause whenever they encounter one. Even when alarmed, leafcutter ants will not step on or disrupt the "air-eater" symbol. What's more, Dr. Malahasoud has found that, shortly after the death of a queen, a new "air-eater" symbol will appear in or near the hive.

All this is very interesting, but what struck me in particular was the far less esoteric observation that ant hives are considered "social stomachs." That is, all the food is shared even in the process of digestion. How much, I wonder, of the concept of "yours" and "mine" arises from the fact that a given morsel of food, once consumed, will not be retrieved by another? It is sealed inside a body that will either have to be cut open or compelled to disgorge the food: an unappetizing prospect. Is this an example of animal money, too?

I am refreshed by this speculative turn to my thoughts. It's like stepping out of a stuffy house into the cool evening air, and it brings home to me how little use I've made lately of my faculties of speculation. Now I am trying to run this grey market free university, the remaining Professor Long is publishing controversial books, and

Professor Crest is an upper echelon in cosmic science. We came back down to earth. We took up our tools and set to work on concrete things, practical goals, and I suppose we all think of Professor Aughbui, who stayed behind, in a certain way, a critical way—but perhaps we are still wandering, too. In another way, an everyday way. A ticking of tasks off an endless list. We can see the shape, or the points, but why not both?

Every man and woman is a star—you can see them out there in the dark, burning. Writhing, screaming stars. The blackened, cindered star flesh is blasted off the living skeleton in flakes, disbursed in tranches to the four winds, consumed, the bones charring and boiling brains foam from the apertures of the skull to be carried off like sea froth percolating on star wind. A bit lands on a flayed cheek or a burning leg, touching the bared nerve and for an instant there is an oasis of baffling, disjointed memory or fantasy in the death agony as the nerve contact transfers the memory. That was it. Pearl of great price fizzled out forever.

Waves of desperate, frenzied animals ravage human cities and settlements, shattering the night with bellows and cries of all possible kinds, smashing glass, shrieking sirens and alarms, popping of guns and thudding of bombs. The capital is undergoing an imbalance correction. In twelve hours, San Toribio has deflated by as many percent, billowing into the sky. Coyotes erupt out of laundry hampers, refrigerators, jaws snapping shut on human throats. Songbirds swarm anyone who ventures outside in Avenida Nigelato, and the fires are coming this way—but San Toribio's troubles are mild compared with the brutal spectacles unfolding elsewhere. Ravenous bacteria are liquefying the assets of citizens all across the northern hemisphere. In the wake of each devastating onslaught come opportunistic mercantile infections, people trying to make a buck selling bottled water to drowning victims and vaccines to people dead of the plague, fire extinguishers to human-shaped smudges of ash, bullet-proof armor to perforated corpses, sucked into threshing machines and wood chippers, sucked into the vacuum of a deficit belt that rings the globe.

Uhuyjhn cities sprout in the midst of existing cities, bursting out like expanding foam from the cracks in the pavements, casually shoving aside the ugly scrim of glass boxes and gas stations.

"Wait! Wait! We're all still here, trapped in despair!"

It's not waiting for you or anyone and it brushes you aside as well, leaving you trapped forever and you're the ones who wait and will go on waiting forever for something that is not only not coming but that you know is not coming. There's nothing profound in your dead end, or not anymore anyway, and did you ever ask yourself if you would be feeling this hopelessness if your petty little country were "winning" instead of "losing" or "lost"? Who lost it? What was lost? Defeated—who by? Time? As opposed to what timelessness? What shit! The Uhuyjhn cities don't care. The foam expands hydraulically and sprouts needle-like spires, big bubbly mushroom cap domes, coral reef angularities budding off little floating trams. There's a bizarre music—can you hear it?—coming from somewhere in the middle of all that yeasty flocculation, and parchment scrolls elegantly inscribed sail past unfurling in the wind, diplomas, stocks and bonds, maps, title deeds, certificates of appreciation and acknowledgment and gratitude for coming up with more synonyms to apply to a hundred flavors of thank you notes. Military might is as impotent to stop this inhuman urbanism as it is against the march of time or against death. The development is visible from space, as pale puddings coagulate into cities and push the straw houses of humanity out into evacuated suburbs, peat bogs, into the sea, the desert, or crushes them against the feet of the mountains.

*

The music whips around and around with a thousand and one different things that go bang in the percussion kit sounding like a thousand kitchens turned upside down and brass brass brass, sweat pouring down their faces as they blow those notes faster and faster—Tripi is going to address the crowd. People can't wait. I'm stepping out to the podium now, going to say a few words, slip a few casual asides to the Teeming like it was nothing, wearing my cool cerulean blue jacket and a shirt as white as snow, and went back and forth about it but finally opted to put the fluorescent orange silk neckerchief around my neck kind of halfway proletarian. I slip through a covey of unbelievably flamboyant transvestites thinking I'm going to need a machete to hack my way through all the fucking feathers. Suddenly there's a grand cheer and surge as the crowd washes toward me and I look back in time to see Tripi bringing up the rear, shaking hands and more alive than I've ever seen her. Love is the name for what I see in her face; love of these people.

"It really is her!" I think.

Turning to avoid colliding with someone I notice a flat black something in a rising hand pop pop pop pop—

*

I'm on the ground.

I'm on the ground.

"What hit me?"

Faces, noise, but no band.

"The band stopped. Why did the band stop?"

Carolina is standing over me, looking impassively down at me as if to say, "Get up."

She's naked in this huge crowd how the fuck does she get away with it.

I see an economist too, the dead one from *Animal Money*, between some faces up there, and Tripi's face. She looks frightened. Upset.

This is pain like no pain, like the first real pain—

"I get run over?"

Tripi keeps saying "They got him" and "I'm OK," moving her mouth really emphatically to make sure I understand. I can't feel my arm and I'm dizzy.

"They got ...?"

Black at the edges, smoking.

I can't feel my hand. It appears there, lifted, somehow, and it's bloody. That's all my blood.

This is me.

This is me.

This is it for me.

A voice says: "A billion years in the future Earth will lose all its water into space and all life will end."

I hold my blood out to her in my fingers like a coin.

A voice says: "Let this be recouped against it. Money based on time recouped against the end."

I can't make out what Tripi is saying but I'm pretty sure she's calling for ...

... for help. Light head.

It takes a huge effort for me to talk, like rolling a bowling ball off my chest.

"Die like Hamlet. At play. Not understanding."

This is important. I have to get this out. One last joke. I don't know if anybody's listening, the light disappears around Carolina's face. One last joke ...

"But he ... he only *dressed* in black. I *am* black."

*

"It's disgusting, horrible," the remaining Professor Long says, rubbing her forehead.

"Senseless," Professor Budshah says.

"A *tragedy*," Professor Crest corrects him. "*Not* a senseless death."

Emaciated, so bloodless it hurts just to look at him, glassy-eyed, Professor Crest sits in his chair like a dummy, his eyes glaring with alarming luster. He has lived long enough to raise his index finger one more time, in that marionette-like gesture that amused us once, but which now has an appalling effect since he really does look like a mannikin now.

"He wasn't her bodyguard," Professor Budshah says, a little nettled.

"Even if he was," the remaining Professor Long says, "he was just in the way, it wasn't a voluntary act. He wasn't shot protecting her."

"His altruism was his reason for being there in the first place," Professor Crest insists. "He could not have been ignorant of the threats against the life of Ms. Pina. His work for her was pro bono. As a foreign national, he could not serve in the government."

*

You tell me if I died. You tell me if I'm another black martyr or not. I'd rather be a living black martyr if possible. How much longer can I go on talking? Since I don't know, let's make it count. Let's make this time worth its money. No, let's make this money worth its time.

End money, OK?

End money.

What is money? Social human power made numb and separate. Amputated under anaesthesia. You'll feel all that pain later, though. Without knowing what it is.

End money. Why let others decide how your social power, your time, your work will be unitized and stored up? Why not make your own money? Why not make your own society? What choice do you really have? A bank is a symbol of fear. End money. End it by making it. It's all counterfeit, that stuff you use. End money. It didn't come from you. It is you taken away from you by somebody else. Fed back to you in dribs and drabs and drabber every day. Money is not a means of exchange. Money is a means of preventing exchange. Look at the countries where there is the greatest volume of money circulating: those societies are frozen. There is relentless change but there is no difference. Everyone is bound by the enchantment of the money spell, cast by the most pedestrian magicians the world has ever seen. Exchange of what? Exchange is change ex'd out; ex-change. A real exchange: this for that. What you see if you will wake the fuck up and look: something for nothing. The endless augmentation of the nothing you have, which is the opening for an endless expansion of the everything on the other side. Everything is not fixed; it grows. So does nothing. The more everything, the more nothing. The more censorship, the clearer the censored message becomes. The spell is cast and the clarity itself magically becomes an impediment to realization; the sweeping wand of the minute hand is turning keys into locks. The buying and selling machines perform transactions by the nanosecond—even in the time it takes to reach over and shut the machine off, thousands of further transactions have taken place. And wouldn't there be considerable advantage to the one who leaves the machine on? And aren't there machines that are only pretending to be off? And are you still calling this indiscernible blur of microfrenzy among the processors "exchange"?

Animal money culture grows to form a mycelial currency bed that fruits out counter money, types of money that are totally irreconcilable with primitive, simplistic international currency coordination rubrics. Irreducible money, like animals. Living and growing in the cracks of an international money system, deranging and polluting it, opening temporary escape chutes people can use to shift levels, dash around to the other end of the line, double dip, triple dip. Complicate, confuse, baffle, stun. Stun and stun again. End money. There is no intelligence that can deal with this. Intelligence gatherers gather only wool where animal money is concerned. Corpses rip free of their graves with thick coins in their fists, gloved in scales of nitre, the coins oxidized, iridescent from the earth like discs of oil, and oil wells up in empty graves, overflowing like pus from an infected wound. The bull market encounters matadors.

Soil is alive. It billows like the ocean. It has currents, undertows, surf. A body in a shallow forest grave can feel, not with its nerves but with its quick bones, body filaments that scintillate faintly as they knit to the bone, flickering blue and red mycelial fibres overspreading it like long hair, the shifting thin coverlet of earth and leaf mold, the odor of smoke from the trees and rotting logs. The seasons change, Autumn comes, the sweat dries and hazy sights sharply snap into Autumn focus. The divinity of Autumn, whom we refer to as Barren October, his formal title, stands in waist-high wheat surrounded by trees who confetti him with orange and red leaves. He wears eighteenth century small trousers with knee stockings and buckled shoes, his torso covered in soot, by his dense mantle of dreadlocks and a beard streaked with white, with fringed deerskin on his forearms and a hood on his head, adorned with a pair of antlers. His wealth is the leaf rain falling around him, the space he swings through, the refreshed transparency overhead deepening in blue, and above all the escape system of the forest, rising up out of a heaving ocean of soil, peeling back to the bare but living bones of its skeleton by gusts of cheese-grater wind. Write the future in earthquake money.

Me dying. Him maybe. A bullet rips through the wrong ribcage. Now I am dead.

So now it's just you and me. I am the animal you hold in your hands. I am here and there.

*

A jostle in the street—look up—a sinister figure with upturned collar and hat pulled down low hands you a crisp snow-white envelope and vanishes, eyes glittering, back into the fracas, people battering each other with purses and umbrellas over the last can of cat food—the luminous rune of the International Economics Institute seals the envelope.

Your presence is requested at a hearing to be held in four days time at the location encyphered in the black square below. The duelling committee is going to announce its verdict. Look up from the paper at the narrow slot of sky and see an end coming, visible between the buildings, buildings strung with laundry, windows broken, smoke pouring from improvised fires, primitive traps for catching pigeons dangling from balconies. Somewhere SuperAesop is staring, riveted, at the outcome of his absolute halt experiment. Assiyeh Melachalos rises to deliver a boring economics paper at a conference of academic economists. Professor Aughbui weaves expertly down a desert highway strewn with wrecks, cyclops cars bearing down on him, the remaining Professor Long naked in the passenger seat tripping in cosmic grandeur under the effects of a Rabelaisian dose of hallucinogenic drugs. The silversaliva voice is the monastic tunnel howl. You have to wear a space suit to live on Earth now.

*

I am an animal. I don't know what kind. Alllll that's left. Of the left.

I am an animal lying in a bed. I drink through my arm. I ...

Sometimes I am on land, although I can't exactly call it walking. Sometimes I am in the air, although I can't exactly call it flying. Sometimes I am in the water, although I can't exactly call it water. Just kidding. I can't exactly call it swimming, what I do. I move through and over and around and under. I eat, I sleep.

I eat through my arm. I can't stand this metal thing.

I sleep a lot. I sleep with my eyes open, looking up at the dim white sky and the rectangular white sun which is very faint and very near, like I could touch its corrugated surface if I could only stand up, if I could only feel my legs.

I seek out others of my kind, but I am normally solitary. I am a riddle to myself.

Oh hi Professor Long. You look like shit. You paying me a house visit?

What do you mean I'm not at home?

You always take back what you say. Maybe you could take me back, too. Back ... which way is back for me? I want to go with Carolina.

Carolina! How long have you been there?!

They've started arresting corpses, reviving the dead for interrogation in secret police bunkers.

"You cannot take refuge in God," Urtruvel wrote once. "We can and we will drag you back from God's protecting embrace and put you to the question. Death will not save you from interrogations any more."

Screams of the dead, faint in the night. They have your dead mother, your dead friend, in there. You'll talk.

Now then ...

Why did you leave your last job?

*

I have to escape toward everyone else. Don't ask me how I know because I don't; I can't know anything now. If I live, we can start to talk about what I supposedly knew now, what it turns out I knew. What you want, if you want to be a wizard, is to know that you know, especially if you know you're wrong. I have found it's safe to assume the uncanny dude who fixes you with eyes suddenly sprouted out incandescent and says "I *know!*" is tripping. I mean, that voice he's hearing is not the voice of experience. So he's got to escape the massive breakdown of everything, but his brainstorm is to escape toward the catastrophe, and gather up the flames in bouquets by the armfull, build the water buildings so that the advancing tidal wave's wall has illuminated windows in it. Volcanoes gush molten gold and crazed mobs burn trying to collect it.

The voices of countless ghosts sing to him from blue white hellparadise clouds or in the woods written in sunshine on every leaf—their words are impossible to understand, but the emotions in the voices are impossible to mistake—imploring, indignant, sorrowfully urgent, throbbing with hope and burning tears as they beg you to see, see, to act, act. You look at that leaf and turn it this way and that, watching the sunblaze slide back and forth. There's nothing there, and it has something to say to you. There are arms outstretched to receive us there, like the arms reaching out to the drowning man, clutching at the air, straining.

THE END*

MYRTLE

The neighborhood called Myrtle is a place of incessant economic activity, all of it nearly too small and too quick to see. None of the shops are open. The shelves are bare, the floor unswept, the windows opaque with dirt and soap. The place is a battered, beat-up chunk of town where you have to pay for every lick of recycled paint, every fragment of glass you fit together rubbing down the edges taping them into a sheet you can stick into a frame. You can buy fish from this Mexican guy sitting on a rock by the fire hydrant. He has a crate full of gelatinous grey fish from somewhere and for pocket change he'll snatch one out put it on top of the crate and slice you off some crescent-shaped pieces with his pocket knife. As I watch the footage or digitage, here's a black guy in a white t-shirt and baseball cap, in his thirties, gold chain around his neck, and another guy I can't see comes up to him and sticks him up with a knife. The first guy passively hands him a leather wallet that looks worn smooth and flattened out like half-sucked ice cream. Then he just embraces the other man, who returns his quick embrace while unlacing the gold chain from his neck all in one gesture. Then the thief is gone. The victim just stands there, his face impassive, nothing on his face.

Here are some children, haggling.

"How much for this dollar?"

"One cent."

"No this dollar's special you got to pay more for this dollar."

"One dollar one cent."

"One dollar two cent."

One of the bargainers is explaining.

"You gotta be good with your money, invest it, check prices, or you lose all the time. You have to keep ahead of everybody—" and here his voice takes on an especially knowing tone he must have picked up, along with the idea itself, from a parent or some other adult, "—or then they'll just hand you over to the Latins."

You can see the adult he's going to turn into; big, cautious, cagey, with a long coffin chin and legal tender vice-gripped in thick fingers, keeping his savings in the fat of his body and the gold around his neck. If you got fat, you last longer when there's no food. If you got gold, you can trade when the bank breaks and the credit card machines are offline. The skinny girl is bidding up her dollar.

"This a special dollar," she says smiling. They all giggle because it's still mostly a game. I don't like to think what they may be giggling about as grown ups. What kind of kids know this much about haggling? Shouldn't they know more about kickball or some other ancient children's rite? The girl is actually pretty funny, her jokes are making me smile and I never smile. Maybe it's just affection from a passing ghost dad; maybe being obsessed with money makes you funny. Something about the substitutions, the symbolism, the absurdity of price tags on everything. They have a pay to piss proto-scam in the works where they stake out a likely piece of wall near a bar or something and they charge you a penny a second to piss against it. You can piss on the ground for free, but if you want to hit the wall, if you want the sound-blur that pissing against an upright surface gives you, you pay by the second, and they watch you do it, too, counting off the seconds at the top of their piping voices, which might seem to defeat the purpose, but the urinators they target are fucked up enough to regard the shrieked out numbers as cover noise.

The enterprising coffin-jawed kid says: "Get them to pay first. Then they have to guess how long it's gonna take, and if they don't take that long you say 'no refund'."

THE END*

PAGES OF NO NARRATION

The pages can't be left blank. They must be complete pages of text, in order to keep the right pace.

The reader begins by picking a point in time to begin. This choice will have been made already when the reader reads these words, because this piece begins as the reader reads the title, "Pages of No Narration."

The reader must not at any point during this reading go back and reread anything. The text must be read thoroughly, slowly, all the way through, one way, without rereading, as if the reader were performing from a musical score with no repeat figures and in front of an audience.

There will be no elaboration of alternate possibilities. Readers may come and go, stop and start, as they please. It is only necessary to state that the intention of this composition is that the reader will begin it with the reading of the title and continue through all of the pages, without rereading. Interruptions are allowed for at designated times. The reader may reread the piece only after the reader has already read it. The reader picks the time to begin insofar as the reader has chosen to read this now, rather than at some other time.

The reader begins by noting that they are reading.

The reader fantasizes the reader reading.

The reader notes that there are traces of the reader's personal past in the fantasizing.

By increasing attention, the reader notes that these traces show how the reader came to be reading at the moment picked.

The reader also notes memories of incidents which are somehow elicited by the reading.

The reader may recall other experiences of reading.

The reader notes the trace of the most recent event prior to beginning to read, and, so to speak, sights down its length in the direction of the immediate past.

At this point, there is an intervention by the writing, which instructs the reader to think back to the last experience of waking up. The reader is to go back to the last time the reader woke up and then recount in order the events leading from that moment up to the reading.

Having first reviewed these events in a single, rapid sweep, the reader must then go back over them again, until the reader is satisfied that nothing significant has been overlooked.

The reader should also not overlook nagging feelings that something significant has been overlooked.

Once the reader is satisfied that nothing that can be recovered has been neglected, the reader should fantasize the entire sequence of incidents, using an indistinctly visualized string of beads as an assisting metaphor. The beads are the incidents, and the unadorned string between beads is the vague sense of empty or insignificant time which has already lost its salience in the memory. The reader, fantasizing the entire sequence, will have a chance to take empty time into account as well as full time.

Now the reader must go over these incidents again. This time, these incidents must be recounted as if they were being described to someone else, a stranger who has no familiarity at all with the reader or the reader's circumstances.

Descriptions will now have to be added by the reader. The reader should make the effort to describe the circumstances of waking up, with the particulars of time and place. Likewise all subsequent actions. The descriptions should not be too copious.

The reader should be sparing in explanation. It is taken for granted that the stranger is familiar with common objects and practices. Only what is more or less idiosyncratic to the reader should be explained, and that briefly.

Emphasis must remain on the incidents leading up to or directly connected with the present moment of reading.

As the incidents are presented, one after another and in order, omitting nothing without dwelling on trivial things, the reader should proceed all the way up to the reading of this page, and include that reading among the incidents recounted.

The reader is now recounting the experience of

reading these words, as the foremost end of a sequence of incidents extending back to the reader's last experience of waking. The entire period of that past sequence should be more and more distinct and present to the reader now.

The reader should note any effect that this is having on the reader.

The reader should fantasize the reader reading and fantasizing. The fantasizing should be effortless. The effect should be a doubling and redoubling of the reader's action.

The reader should describe, again without being too copious, the current circumstances of reading, not over-looking sounds, odors, tastes, textures, or other sensations.

The reader should include as much as possible of the reader's current circumstances in the reading.

This inclusion should be effortless. It isn't necessary to make any laborious inventory of details. The circumstances should fill the reader's fantasizing, without exhausting it or being exhausted by the fantasizing. There should be no exhaustion. The reader should pause at this point and fix the fantasizing in the reader's mind.

At this point, the reader is to set this reading aside and do something else.

*

The reader has now done something else and has returned to the reading.

The reader should now recover the fantasizing, without retreating or rereading.

The reader should now model the reader fantasizing the old reading.

The reader will not incorporate any of the intervening incidents between having been instructed to set the reading aside and resuming the reading after the break.

The reader will be lingeringly aware of those recent incidents, and will note whether or not they impinge at all on the fantasizing.

The reader will note whether or not those recent incidents are seeming to demand that they be included in the fantasizing.

If the effort of preventing inclusion of these incidents into the fantasizing is becoming a distraction, then the reader should include them. The reader will note what is the sensation when the reader stops making the effort to prevent inclusion.

If the effort of preventing inclusion is not distracting, then the reader will continue to prevent inclusion. If there is no effort, then the reader will continue.

The reader will now have a sense of the fantasizing of incidents experienced by the reader, which will include both the prior experience of reading, and the current one.

The reader will note that, just as there are traces of past incidents in the present fantasizing, there are also future possibilities.

These future possibilities are wishes.

The reader will note that some of these wishes are frightful.

In noting these wishes, the reader will not begin thinking of all the things the reader wants, or wants to avoid.

The reader will only note the presence of these wishes.

The reader should not imagine future incidents.

The attention of the reader must be fixed entirely on the present.

The reader should not be thinking about finishing this reading.

The reader should be fantasizing the reading, and seeing it as the latest in a series of incidents.

The reader should see the reader in the fantasizing. This means seeing what the reader wishes.

Now:

Does the reader want the incidents the reader fantasized?

Does the reader want to escape from the incidents the reader fantasized?

Does the reader want to have not lived those incidents?

Does the reader want to live incidents of an entirely different kind, without going into the details of the difference?

Does the reader want things to change or things to freeze?

Does the reader want to escape from these questions?

ABOUT THE AUTHOR

Michael Cisco is the author of novels *The Narrator* (Lazy Fascist Press, 2015, Civil Coping Mechanisms, 2010), *The Divinity Student* (Buzzcity Press, 1999, winner of the International Horror Writers Guild award for best first novel of 1999), *The Tyrant* (Prime, 2004), *The San Veneficio Canon* (Prime, 2005), *The Traitor* (Prime, 2007), *The Great Lover* (Chomu Press, 2011), *Celebrant* (Chomu Press, 2012), and *MEMBER* (Chomu Press, 2013). His short story collection, *Secret Hours*, was published by Mythos Press in 2007.

His fiction has appeared in *Leviathan III* (Wildside, 2004) and *Leviathan IV* (Night Shade, 2005), *The Thackery T. Lambshead Pocket Guide to Eccentric and Discredited Diseases* (Bantam, 2005), *Cinnabar's Gnosis: A Tribute to Gustav Meyrink* (Ex Occidente, 2009), *Last Drink Bird Head* (Ministry of Whimsy, 2009), *Lovecraft Unbound* (Dark Horse, 2009), *Phantom* (Prime, 2009), *Black Wings I* (PS Press, 2011), *Blood and Other Cravings* (Tor, 2011), *The Master in the Cafe Morphine: A Homage to Mikhail Bulgakov* (Ex Occidente Press, 2011), *The Thackery T. Lambshead Cabinet of Curiosities* (Harper Voyager, 2011), *The Weird* (Tor, 2012), and elsewhere. His scholarly work has appeared in *Lovecraft Studies*, *The Weird Fiction Review*, *Iranian Studies* and *Lovecraft and Influence*.

Michael Cisco lives and teaches in New York City.

Lightning Source UK Ltd.
Milton Keynes UK
UKHW011830090619
344072UK00002B/693/P

9 781621 052128